"A major work, a glittering combination of brilliant craftsmanship, psychological perception and objective reporting. Rarely in modern fiction have so many interesting and even bizarre characters been brought to more intense life. Rarely has a time and a place and a political and social crisis been more brilliantly and more dispassionately described. Rarely have the sounds and smells and total atmosphere of India been so evocatively suggested. So comprehensive is Mr. Scott's scope, so detailed his knowledge, that reading his novel becomes a major experience and a prolonged one."
Orville Prescott, *New York Times*

Also by Paul Scott and available in Mayflower

THE CORRIDA AT SAN FELIU
THE ALIEN SKY
THE MARK OF THE WARRIOR

THE JEWEL IN THE CROWN

Paul Scott

A Mayflower Paperback

in association with
William Heinemann

THE JEWEL IN THE CROWN
Paul Scott

Originally published by William Heinemann 1966

Published as a Mayflower Paperback 1968

Mayflower Paperbacks are published by
Mayflower Books Ltd.,
3 Upper James Street, London, W.1
Made and printed in Great Britain by
C. Nicholls & Company Ltd.,
The Philips Park Press, Manchester 11

---

to Dorothy Ganapathy
with love

Contents

This is a work of fiction
All the characters are imaginary

PART ONE

Miss Crane

IMAGINE, then, a flat landscape, dark for the moment, but even so conveying to a girl running in the still deeper shadow cast by the wall of the Bibighar Gardens an idea of immensity, of distance, such as years before Miss Crane had been conscious of standing where a lane ended and cultivation began: a different landscape but also in the alluvial plain between the mountains of the north and the plateau of the south.

It is a landscape which a few hours ago, between the rainfall and the short twilight, extracted colour from the spectrum of the setting sun and dyed every one of its own surfaces that could absorb light: the ochre walls of the houses in the old town (which are stained too with their bloody past and uneasy present); the moving water of the river and the still water of the tanks; the shiny stubble, the ploughed earth, of distant fields; the metal of the grand trunk road. In this landscape trees are sparse, except among the white bungalows of the civil lines. On the horizon there is a violet smudge of hill country.

This is the story of a rape, of the events that led up to it and followed it and of the place in which it happened. There are the action, the people, and the place; all of which are interrelated but in their totality incommunicable in isolation from the moral continuum of human affairs.

In the Bibighar Gardens case there were several arrests and an investigation. There was no trial in the judicial sense. Since then people have said there was a trial of sorts going on. In fact, such people say, the affair that began on the evening of August 9th, 1942, in Mayapore, ended with the spectacle of two nations in violent opposition, not for the first time nor as yet for the last because they were then still locked in an imperial embrace of such long standing and subtlety it was no longer possible for them to know whether they hated or loved one another, or what it was that held them together and seemed to have confused the image of their separate destinies.

*

In 1942, which was the year the Japanese defeated the British army in Burma and Mr. Gandhi began preaching sedition in India, the English then living in the civil and military cantonment of Mayapore had to admit that the future did not look propitious. They had faced bad times before, though, and felt that they could face them again, that now they knew where they stood and there could be no more heart-searching for quite a while yet about the rights and wrongs of their colonial-imperialist policy and administration.

As they were fond of putting it at the club, it was a question of first things first, and when they heard that Miss Crane, the supervisor of the district's Protestant mission schools, had taken Mr. Gandhi's picture down from the walls of her study and no longer entertained Indian ladies to tea but young English soldiers instead, they were grateful to her as well as amused. In peace time opinions could be as diverse and cranky as you wished. In war you had to close the ranks; and if it was to be a question of sides Miss Crane seemed to have shown at last which she was really on.

What few people knew was that the Indian ladies themselves had taken the initiative over the question of tea on Tuesdays at Edwina Crane's bungalow. Miss Crane suspected that it was the ladies' husbands who had dissuaded them from making the weekly appearance, not only because Mr. Gandhi's picture had gone but in case such visits could have been thought of, in this explosive year, as a buttering-up of the *raj*. What hurt her most was that none of the ladies had bothered to discuss their reasons with her. They had one by one or two by two just stopped coming and made feeble excuses when she met any of them in the bazaar or on her way to the mission school-rooms.

She was sorry about the ladies whom she had always encouraged to be frank with her, but not at all sorry about Mr. Gandhi's portrait. The ladies had an excuse. Mr. Gandhi did not. She believed he was behaving abominably. She felt, in fact, let down. For years she had laughed at Europeans who said that he was not to be trusted, but now Mr. Gandhi had extended what looked like an open invitation to the Japanese to come and help him rid India of the British – and if he thought that they would be the better masters then she could only assume he was out of his senses or, which was worse, revealing that his philosophy of non-violence had a dark side that added up to total invalidation of its every aspect. The

Japanese, apparently, were to do his violence for him.

Reacting from her newly found distrust of the Mahatma and her disappointment in the behaviour of the ladies (the kind of disappointment she had actually become no stranger to) she wondered whether her life might not have been spent better among her own people, persuading them to appreciate the qualities of Indians, instead of among Indians, attempting to prove that at least one Englishwoman admired and respected them. She had to admit that a searching analysis of her work would show that in the main the people she had got on with best of all were those of mixed blood; which seemed, perhaps, to emphasise the fact that she was neither one thing nor the other herself – a teacher without real qualifications, a missionary worker who did not believe in God. She had never been wholly accepted by Indians and had tended to reject the generality of the English. In this there was a certain irony. The Indians, she thought, might have taken her more seriously if she had not been a representative of the kind of organisation they were glad enough to make use of but of which old suspicions died hard. By the same token, if she had not worked for the mission she would, she believed, never have acquired an admiration for the Indians through love and respect for their children, nor been led to such sharp criticism of her own race, in whose apparently neglectful and indifferent care the future of those children and the present well-being of their parents were held. She had never been slow to voice her criticism. And this, possibly, had been a mistake. The English always took such criticism so personally.

However, Miss Crane was of a generation that abided by (even if it did not wholly believe in) certain simple rules for positive action. It was, she told herself, never too late to mend, or try to mend. Thinking of the young British soldiers who were in Mayapore in ever-increasing numbers, and remembering that most of them looked fresh out from home, she wrote to the Station Staff Officer, had an interview with him, and arranged to entertain a party of up to a dozen at a time at tea every Wednesday afternoon from five o'clock until six-thirty. The SSO thanked her for her generosity and said he wished more people realised what it meant to an English lad to be in a home again, if only for an hour or two. For all their flag-wagging the ladies of the cantonment tended to have a prejudice against the British Other Rank. The SSO did not say this but the implication was there. Miss Crane guessed from his speech and manner that he had risen from the ranks himself. He said he hoped she would not have cause to regret her invitation. Young soldiers, although mostly maligned, were indeed apt to be clumsy and noisy. She had only to ring him up if things proved too much for her or if she had anything to complain about. She smiled and reminded him that the life she led had never been sheltered and she had often heard herself referred to in Mayapore as a tough old bird.

The soldiers who came to Miss Crane's bungalow for tea spoke with cockney accents but they were not clumsy. With one exception, a boy called Barrett, they handled the bone china with big-fisted dexterity. They were not too shy and not over noisy. The parties always ended on a gratifyingly free and easy note. Afterwards, she stood on the front verandah and waved them down the path that led through her pretty, well-kept garden. Outside the gate they lit cigarettes and went back to barracks in a comradely bunch making some clatter with their boots on the hard surface of the road. Having helped her old Indian servant Joseph to clear away, Miss Crane then retired to her room to read reports and deal with letters from the headquarters of the mission, and – since the soldiers' tea was on a Wednesday and Thursday was her day to visit and stay overnight at the school in Dibrapur, seventy-five miles away – prepare her gladstone bag for the journey and look out a tin of boiled sweets as a gift for the Dibrapur children. While she did these things she also found time to think about the soldiers.

There was one particular boy who came regularly of whom she was very fond. His name was Clancy. He was what middle-class people of her own generation would have called one of nature's gentlemen. It was Clancy who sat down last and stood up first, Clancy who saw to it that she had a piece of her own fruit cake and that she did not go sugarless for want of the passing back up the table of the bowl. He always asked how she was, and gave the most lucid answers to her inquiries about their training and sports and communal life in the barracks. And whereas the others called her Mum, or Ma'am, Clancy called her Miss Crane. She was herself meticulous in the business of getting to know their names and dignifying them with the prefix Mister. She knew that private soldiers hated to be called by their surnames alone if the person talking to them was a woman. But although she never omitted to say Mister Clancy when addressing him, it was as Clancy that she thought of him. It was a nice name, and his friends called him that, or Clance.

Clancy, she was glad to notice, was liked by his comrades. His attentiveness to her wasn't resented, or laughed at. He seemed to be a natural leader. He commanded respect. He was good-looking and fitted his uniform of khaki shirt and shorts better than the other boys. Only his accent, and his hands – with torn finger-nails, never quite clean of vestiges of oil and grease from handling rifles and guns – marked him as an ordinary member of the herd.

Sometimes, when they had gone and she worked on her files and thought about them, she was sad. Some of those boys, Clancy more easily than the others because he was bound to get a position of responsibility, might be killed. She was also sad, but in a different way, when the thought passed through her head, as it couldn't help doing, that probably they all laughed at her on the quiet and talked about her when she wasn't there to hear as the old maid who served up char and wads.

She was, as mission headquarters knew, an intelligent and perceptive woman whose understanding, common sense and organising ability, more than made up for what in a woman connected with a Christian mission were of doubtful value: her agnosticism, for instance, and her fundamentally anti-British, because pro-Indian, sympathies.

*

Edwina Crane had lived in India for thirty-five of her fifty-seven years. She was born in London in 1885 of moderately well-to-do middle-class parents; her mother died early and she spent her youth and young womanhood looking after her lost lonely father, a schoolmaster who became fond of the bottle and his own company so that gradually the few friends they had drifted away along with the pupils who attended his private school. He died in an Edwardian summer when she was twenty-one leaving her penniless and fit for nothing, she felt, except the job of paid companion or housekeeper. The scent of lime trees in fading flower stayed with her afterwards as the smell of death. She thought she was lucky when the first job she got was as governess to a spoiled little boy who called her Storky and tried to shock her once with a precocious show of sexuality in the night-nursery.

She was not shocked. In the later stages of her father's illness she had had to deal with his incontinence, and before that with his drunken outbursts in which he had not been above telling her those facts of life she had not already learned or ridiculing her for her long nose and plain looks and slender hopes of marriage. Sober, he was always ashamed, but too uncourageous to tell her so. She understood this, and because of it learned to value courage in others and try hard, not always successfully, to show it herself. In some ways her father was like a child to her. When he was dead she wept, then dried her eyes and sold most of the few remaining possessions to pay for a decent funeral, having refused financial help from the rich uncle who had kept away during her father's lifetime and moral support from the poor cousins who reappeared at his death.

So the little boy did not shock her. Neither did he enchant her. Living alone with her father she had tended to believe that he and she were of a kind apart, singled out to support a special cross compounded of genteel poverty and drunkenness, but the wealthy and temperate household in which she had now come to live seemed unhappy too, and this had the effect of making the world she knew look tragically small just at the moment when it might have been opening up. It was the desire she had to find a place in an unknown world that would come at her as new and fresh and, if not joyful, then at least adventurous and worth-while, that made her apply for a post as travelling nurse-companion to a lady making the passage back to India with two young children. The lady, who had a pale face and looked delicate, but turned out resilient, explained that if proved satisfactory the person who obtained the post could stay on in India after they arrived, with a view to acting as governess. If unsatisfactory, such a person would easily find a similar job with a family taking the passage home, failing which her passage home would be paid. The lady seemed to take a fancy to her and so Miss Crane was employed.

The voyage was pleasant because Mrs. Nesbitt-Smith treated her like a member of the family, and the children, a blue-eyed girl and a blue-eyed boy, both said they loved her and wanted her to live with them for ever. When they reached Bombay Major Nesbitt-Smith met them and treated her like one of the family too; but Miss Crane could not help noticing from then on that the major's wife gradually withdrew, and by the time they reached the husband's station in the Punjab was treating her not exactly like a servant but like a poor relation with whom the family had somehow got saddled and so for the present made use of. It was Miss Crane's first experience of social snobbery abroad, which was never the same as snobbery at home because it was complicated by the demands, sometimes conflicting, of white solidarity and white supremacy. Her employers felt a duty to accord her a recognition they would have withheld from the highest-born Indian, at the same time a compulsion to place her on one of the lowest rungs of the ladder of their own self-contained society – lower outside the household than in, where, of course, she stood in a position far superior to that of any native servant. Miss Crane disapproved of this preoccupation with the question of who was who and why. It went against the increasingly liberal grain of her strengthening conscience. It also seemed to make life very difficult. She thought that Mrs. Nesbitt-Smith was sometimes hard put to it to know what expression to wear when talking to her and decided that the confusion she must often have been in accounted for the frequent look of concern, almost of pain, at having to speak at all.

She was with the Nesbitt-Smiths for three years. She had a strong constitution which meant she was seldom ill even in that difficult climate. She was fond of the children and reacted to the politeness of the servants by overcoming the shyness she had been used to feel at home. There was, as well, India, which at first had seemed strange, even frightening, but presently full of compensations that she found difficult to name but felt in her heart. She had few friends and still felt isolated from people as individuals, but she was aware now of a sense of community. That sense sprang, she knew, from the seldom-voiced but always insistent, even when mute, clan-gathering call to solidarity that was part of the social pattern she had noted early on and disapproved of. She still disapproved of it but was honest enough to recognise it as having always been a bleak but real enough source of comfort and protection. There was a lot of fear in India, and it was good to feel safe, to know that indifferently as Mrs. Nesbitt-Smith might sometimes treat her, Mrs. Nesbitt-Smith and her like would always rally round if she found herself in any kind of danger from outside the charmed circle of privilege on whose periphery she spent her days. She knew that the India she found full of compensations was only the white man's India. But it was an India of a kind, and that at least was a beginning.

At this stage she fell in love, not with the young assistant chaplain to the station who sometimes conducted the services at the local Protestant church (which would have been a possible match, indeed was one that in her good moods Mrs. Nesbitt-Smith chaffed her about and smilingly pushed her towards) but hopelessly and secretly with a Lieutenant Orme who was as handsome as Apollo, as kind, gentle and gay with her as any hero in a romantic novel, as ignorant or unheeding of her regard as his good looks so well enabled him to be in a station remarkable that year for the number of pretty well-placed girls of whom he could have his pick: hopelessly in love, because she had no chance; secretly, because she found she did not blush or act awkwardly in his presence, and Mrs. Nesbitt-Smith, even had she bothered to observe the reactions of her children's governess to a man so splendidly equipped, in every sense, as Lieutenant Orme, would not have been able to tell that Miss Crane had longings in directions which were, by tradition, totally closed to her. That she neither blushed nor acted awkwardly puzzled Miss Crane. Her heart beat when he stood close by and perhaps there came a slight dryness into her mouth, but her feelings, she decided, must have been too intense, too adult, for her to act like the fluttering stupid girls who knew nothing of the world's reality.

When Lieutenant Orme was posted away, still uncommitted and with his usual glittering luck, as ADC to a general, to the frenzied disappointment of up to twenty pretty girls, as many plain ones and all their mothers, no one, Miss Crane believed, could have suspected the extent to which his departure darkened her own life. Only the children, her two most intimate human contacts, noticed that her manner changed. They gazed at her through those still remarkably blue but now older and calculating upper middle-class eyes and said, "What's wrong, Miss Crane? Have you got a pain, Miss Crane?" and danced round her singing, "Old Crane's got a pain," so that she lost her temper, slapped them and sent them away screaming through shadow and sunlight to be comforted by the old ayah of whom, she knew, they had become fonder.

Before the next hot weather began Major Nesbitt-Smith's regiment was ordered home. "I and the children will be going on ahead," she overheard Mrs. Nesbitt-Smith say to a friend, "and of course Crane will be coming with us." Speaking of her to others Mrs. Nesbitt-Smith usually referred to her as Crane, but as Miss Crane to her face and the children, and, in rare moments of warmth and gratitude, as Edwina, as when for instance she lay in her darkened punkah-cooled room with Miss Crane kneeling by her bedside soothing with cologne one of her raging headaches.

For many days after the news of the regiment's impending return to England, Miss Crane went about her duties with no particular thoughts in her head because she had firmly put Lieutenant Orme out of them some time ago and nothing had come to take his place. "And he," she said to herself presently, "was a fancy, a mere illusion that never stood a chance of becoming real for me. Now that I've banished the illusion from my thoughts I can see them for what they are, what they have always been, empty, starved, waiting to be filled. How will they be filled at home, in England? By care of the children as they grow, and become old, beyond me? By substituting different children for these and a different Mrs. Nesbitt-Smith for this one? Households that are not the same household and yet the same? And so on, year after year, as Crane, Miss Crane, and sometimes, increasingly rarely, until no more, Edwina?"

In the evenings between five o'clock – when the children had had their tea and became the temporary sole charge of the ayah for play and bath – and seven o'clock when she supervised their supper before going in to dine alone or, if circumstances permitted, with the family, Miss Crane was free. Mostly she spent those two short hours in her room, having her own bath, resting, reading, writing an occasional letter to another of her kind who had exchanged this station for another or gone back to England. But now she began to feel restless and took to putting on her boots and – parasol opened and protectively raised – walking down the lane of the civil lines in which the Nesbitt-Smiths' bungalow stood. The lane was shaded by trees that thinned out gradually as the bungalows gave way to open cultivated fields. Sometimes she walked in the opposite direction, towards the cantonment bazaar beyond which lay the railway station and the native town which she had entered only on one occasion – with a group of laughing ladies and timid companions in carriages, stoutly accompanied by gentlemen – to inspect a Hindu temple which had frightened her, as the native town had frightened her with its narrow dirty streets, its disgusting poverty, its raucous dissonant music, its verminous dogs, its starving, mutilated beggars, its fat white sacred Brahmini bulls and its ragged population of men and women who looked so resentful in comparison with the servants and other officiating natives of the cantonment.

On the day that she found herself questioning the prospect of a future that was, as it were, an image seen in a series of mirrors that reflected it until it became too small for the eye to see – a diminishing row of children and Nesbitt-Smiths and Edwina Cranes – the walk she went on at five was the one that brought her out to the open spaces where the road led on into the far distance. Reaching this point she stopped, afraid to go farther. The sun was still hot, still high enough to make her narrow her eyes as she gazed from under the brim of her hat and the cotton canopy of the parasol, towards the horizon of the flat, wide, immense Punjabi plain. It seemed impossible, she thought, that the world continued beyond that far-away boundary, that somewhere it changed its nature, erupted into hills and forests and ranges of mountains whose crests were white with eternal snows where rivers had their source. It seemed impossible too that beyond the plains there could be an ocean where those rivers had their end. She felt dwarfed, famished in the spirit, pressed down by a tremendous weight of land, and of air and incomprehensible space that even the flapping, wheeling crows had difficulty keeping up in. And she thought for a moment that she was being touched by the heavy finger of a god; not the familiar uplifting all-forgiving God she went through the motions of praying to, but one neither benign nor malign, neither creating nor destroying, sleeping nor waking, but existing, and leaning his weight upon the world.

Acknowledging that women such as herself tended to turn to if not actually to seek sanctuary in religion, she walked on the following evening in the other direction and when she came to the Protestant church she turned into the compound and went up the broad gravel path, past the hummocky graves marked by the headstones of those who had died far from home, but who in their resting place, had they woken, might have been comforted by the English look of the church and its yard and the green trees planted there. The side door of the church was on the latch. She went in and sat in a pew at the back, stared at the altar and gazed at the darkening east window of stained glass which she saw every Sunday in the company of the Nesbitt-Smiths.

The god of this church was a kind, familiar, comfortable god. She had him in her heart but not in her soul. She believed in him as a comforter but not as a redeemer. He was very much the god of a community, not of the dark-skinned community that struggled for life under the weight of the Punjabi sky but of the privileged pale-faced community of which she was a marginal member. She wondered whether she would be Crane to Him, or Miss Crane, or Edwina. If she thought of Him as the Son she would, she presumed, be Edwina, but to God in His wrath, undoubtedly Crane.

"Miss Crane?"

Startled by the voice she looked over her shoulder. It was the senior chaplain, an elderly man with a sharp pink nose and a fringe of distinguishing white hair surrounding his gnomic head. His name was Grant, which caused restrained smiles during services when he intoned prayers that began Grant, O Lord, we beseech Thee. She smiled now, although she was embarrassed being found by him there, betraying herself as a woman in need almost certainly not of rest but of reassurance. A plain somewhat horse-faced woman in her middle twenties, alone in an empty Protestant church, on a day when no service was due, was somehow already labelled. In later years, Miss Crane came to look upon that moment as the one that produced in her the certainty of her own spinsterhood.

"You are resting from your labours," Mr. Grant said in his melodious congregational voice, and added, more directly, when she had nodded and looked down at her lap, "Can I be of any help, child?" so that without warning she wanted to weep because child was what her father had often called her in his sober, loving moments. However, she did not weep. She had not wept since her father's death and although there would come a time when she did once more it had not arrived yet. Speaking in a voice whose steadiness encouraged her, she said, "I'm thinking of staying on," and, seeing the chaplain's perplexity, the way he glanced round the church as if something had begun to go on there which nobody had bothered to forewarn him of but which Miss Crane knew about and thought worth staying for, she explained, "I mean in India, when the Nesbitt-Smiths go home."

The chaplain said, "I see," and frowned, perhaps because she had called them the Nesbitt-Smiths. "It should not be difficult, Miss Crane. Colonel and Mrs. Ingleby, for instance, strike me as worth approaching. I know you are well thought of. Major and Mrs. Nesbitt-Smith have always spoken highly."

The future looked dark, a blank featureless territory with, in its centre, a pinprick of light that seemed to be all that was left of Edwina Crane.

"I think I should like," she said, giving expression to a thought that had never properly been a thought until now, "to train for the Mission."

He sat down next to her and together they watched the east window.

"Not," she went on, "no, not to carry the Word. I am not a truly religious woman." She glanced at him. He was still watching the window. He did not seem to be particularly upset by her confession. "But there are schools, aren't there?" she said. "I meant train to teach at the mission schools."

"Ah yes, I see, to teach not our own children but those of our dark brethren in Christ?"

She nodded. She found herself short of breath. He turned to look at her fully, and asked her, "Have you seen the school here?"

Yes, she had seen the school, close to the railway station, but – "Only from the outside," she told him.

"Have you ever talked to Miss Williams?"

"Who is Miss Williams?"

"The teacher. But then you would be unlikely to know her. She is a lady of mixed blood. Would you like to visit the school?"

"Very much."

The chaplain nodded and presently after the appearance of having thought more deeply, said, "Then I will arrange it, and if you are of the same mind I will write to the superintendent in Lahore, not that there is anything much for you to judge by in Miss Williams's little school." He shook his head. "No, Miss Crane. This isn't an area where we've had much success, although more than the Catholics and the Baptists. There are of course a great number of schools throughout the country, of various denominations, all committed to educating what I suppose we must call the heathen. In this matter the Church and the missions have always led the way. The government has been, shall we say, slow to see the advantages. So, perhaps, have the Indians. The school here, for instance. A handful of children at the best of times. At the times of the festivals none. I mean, of course, the Hindu and Moslem festivals. The children come, you see, mainly for the chappattis, and in the last riots the school was set fire to, but that was before your time."

*

The mission school was not the one she had had in mind which was close to the railway, the Joseph Wainwright Christian School, a substantial building, a privately endowed school for Eurasian children, the sons and daughters of soldiers, railway officials and junior civil servants whose blood had been mixed with that of the native population. The mission school was on the outskirts of the native town itself, a poor, small, rectangular building with a roof of corrugated iron in a walled compound bare of grass, with nothing to identify it apart from the cross roughly painted on the yellow stucco above the door. She was too ashamed to admit her mistake to Mr. Grant, who had brought her in a tonga, and now handed her down and led her through the opening in the wall where once, before the last riots, there might have been a gate.

To come with him at midday she had had to obtain permission from Mrs. Nesbitt-Smith and explain her reason for wanting leave of absence from the task of teaching the young Nesbitt-Smiths. Mrs. Nesbitt-Smith had stared at her as if she were mad and exclaimed, "Good heavens, Crane! What on earth has possessed you?" And then added, with what looked like genuine concern, which was touching and therefore far more upsetting than the outburst, "You'd be with blacks and half-castes, cut off from your own kind. And besides, Edwina, we're all very fond of you."

She was undoubtedly acting like a fool, far from sure even that she was acting on an impulse she had interpreted correctly. To begin with, to have confused the Eurasian school with the mission school proved how ignorant she was of what was there under her own nose, proved how little was really known by people such as herself about the life of the town they were supposed to have a duty to, a duty whose proper execution earned them the privileges they enjoyed. If she had not even known where this particular mission school was, what, she wondered, could she hope to contribute to other mission schools or deserve to gain from them?

The door of the school was open. There was a sound of children singing. When they reached the door the singing stopped. Mr. Grant said that Miss Williams was expecting them and then stood aside. She crossed the threshold directly into the schoolroom. The woman on the dais said, "Stand up, children," and motioned with her arms at the pupils who were seated on several rows of benches, facing her. They stood up. A phrase written in block capitals on the blackboard drew Miss Crane's attention. Welcome Miss Crane Mem. At another sign from the teacher the children chanted it slowly. "Welcome, Miss Crane Mem." Trying to say, "Thank you", she found her tongue and the roof of her mouth dry. The visit on which she had set out in the role of a suppliant for employment was looked upon here as the visit of an inquisitive memsahib. She was terrified of the obligation this put her under and of the stuffy whitewashed room, the rows of children and the smell of burning cowpats that was coming through the open door and windows from the back of the compound where no doubt the God-sent chappattis were being cooked. And she was afraid of Miss Williams, who wore a grey cotton blouse, long brown skirt and black button boots, and was younger than she and sallow-complexioned in the way that some of the most insufferable of the European women were who had spent a lifetime in the country; only in Miss Williams's case the sallowness denoted a half-Indian origin, the kind of origin for which Miss Crane had been taught to feel a certain horror.

Miss Williams left the dais on which there were the teacher's desk and only one chair. Invited, Miss Crane sat, and the chaplain stood next to her. He had said, "Miss Crane, this is Miss Williams," but had not said, "Miss Williams, this is Miss Crane," and as Miss Crane sat down she attempted to smile at the girl to apologise for an omission not her own, but her lips were as parched as her mouth, and she was conscious, then, of an expression growing on her face similar to that which she had seen so often on Mrs. Nesbitt-Smith's. It became etched more deeply when at last she submitted to the duty to look at the children, found herself the lone, inarticulate object of their curiosity and awe, perhaps their fear. The simple dress she had put on, her best in order to look her best – white muslin with a frilled hem but no other decoration beyond the mother-of-pearl buttons down the pleated choker; and the hat, a straw boater perched squarely upon her piled up hair; the folded parasol of white cotton with a pink lining, a gift from Mrs. Nesbitt-Smith last Christmas – now seemed to envelop her, to encumber her with all the pompous frippery of a class to which she did not belong.

At Miss Williams's command a little girl, barefoot and dressed in a shapeless covering that looked like sacking, but whose pigtail was decked with flowers for the occasion, came forward with a nosegay, curtsied and held the nosegay up. Miss Crane took it. Again she tried to say "Thank You", but her words must have been unintelligible because the little girl had to look at Miss Williams for confirmation that the ritual of presentation was over. Neither seeing nor smelling the flowers, Miss Crane held them to her nose, and when she looked up again the little girl was back in her place, standing with the other little girls in the front row.

"I think," Mr. Grant said, "that the children may sit down again, don't you, Miss Crane? Then presently they can either sing the song or say the poem I'm sure Miss Williams here has been rehearsing hard all morning."

For a moment Miss Crane stared helplessly at the flowers in her lap, aware that Miss Williams and Mr. Grant were both watching her, both waiting for her. She nodded her head, ashamed because in the first public duty of her life she was failing.

Sitting down when Miss Williams told them to, the children were silent. Miss Crane thought that they had sensed her discomfort and had interpreted it as displeasure or boredom. She forced herself to look at Miss Williams and say, "I should love to hear the song," then remembered Mr. Grant had said poem or song, and added, "or the poem. Or both. Please let them do what they have rehearsed."

Miss Williams turned to the class and said in her slow, curiously accented English, "Now children, what shall we sing? Shall we sing the song about There is a Friend?" and then, "Achchha," a word Miss Crane knew well enough, but which was followed by rapid words in Hindustani she could not catch because they sped by too quickly. I can't, she thought, even speak the language properly, so how can I hope to teach?

Once more the children got to their feet. Miss Williams beat time in the air, slowly, and sang the first line of the hymn which otherwise Miss Crane might not easily have recognised; and then paused, beat again and set them all singing, unevenly, shyly, and in voices still unused to the odd, flat, foreign scale.

"There's a Friend for little children
  Above the bright blue sky,
A Friend Who never changes,
  Whose love will never die;
Our earthly friends may fail us,
  And change with changing years,
This Friend is always worthy,
  Of that dear Name He bears.

There's a rest for little children,
  Above the bright blue sky,
Who love the Blessèd Saviour
  And to the Father cry;
A rest from every turmoil,
  From sin and sorrow free,
Where every little pilgrim
  Shall rest eternally."

As they sang Miss Crane looked at them. They were a ragged little band. As a child the hymn had been one of her favourites and if it had been sung as English children sang it, with a piano or organ accompaniment, as it used to be sung in her father's shabby school, she might have been borne down by an intensity of feeling, or regret and sadness for a lost world, a lost comfort, a lost magic. But she was not borne down, nor uplifted. She felt an incongruity, a curious resistance to the idea of subverting these children from worship of their own gods to worship of one she herself had sung to when young but now had no strong faith in. But she had, too, a sudden passionate regard for them. Hungry, poor, deprived, hopelessly at a disadvantage, they yet conveyed to her an overwhelming impression of somewhere – and it could only be there, in the Black Town – being loved. But love, as their parents knew, was not enough. Hunger and poverty could never be reduced by love alone. There were, to begin with, free chappattis.

And it came to Miss Crane then that the only excuse she or anyone of her kind had to be there, alone, sitting on a chair, holding a nosegay, being sung to, the object of the awe of uninstructed children, was if they sat there conscious of a duty to promote the cause of human dignity and happiness. And then she was no longer really ashamed of her dress, or deeply afraid of the schoolhouse or of the smell of burning cowpats.

The cowpats were all that there was for fuel, the schoolhouse was small and stuffy because there was not enough money spent, not enough available, to make it large and airy, and her dress was only a symbol of the status she enjoyed and the obligations she had not to look afraid, not to be afraid, to acquire a personal grace, a personal dignity, as much as she could of either, as much as was in her power, so that she could be a living proof of there being, somewhere in the world, hope of betterment.

When the singing was sung and she had said, in halting Hindustani, "Thank you. It was very good," she asked Miss Williams whether she could stay while they had their chappattis and perhaps watch some of their games, and then, if Miss Williams had time to answer, ask one or two questions about the kind of work a teacher was required to do.

And so Miss Crane set out on the long and lonely, difficult and sometimes dangerous road that led her, many years later, to Mayapore, where she was superintendent of the district's Protestant mission schools.

*

Although she had taken Mr. Gandhi's portrait down, there was one picture, much longer in her possession, which she kept hanging on the wall above the desk in her combined bedroom and study. She had had it since 1914, the fifth year of her service in the mission, the year in which she left the school in Muzzafirabad, where she had assisted a Mr. Cleghorn, to take over on her own account the school in Ranpur.

The picture had been a gift, a parting token of esteem. The head of the mission himself had presided over the gathering at which the presentation was made, although it was Mr. Cleghorn who handed the gift over while the children clapped and cheered. In the drawer of her desk she still had the inscribed plate that had been fixed to the frame. The plate was of gilt, now discoloured, and the lettering of the inscription was black, faded, but still legible. It said: "Presented to Edwina Lavinia Crane, in recognition of her courage, by the staff and pupils of the School of the Church of England Mission, Muzzafirabad, NWFP."

Before she reached Ranpur she removed the plate because she was embarrassed by the word courage. All she had done was to stand on the threshold of the schoolhouse, into which she had already herded the children, and deny entry – in fluent Urdu, using expressions she could hardly have repeated to her superiors – to a detachment of half-hearted rioters. At least, she had assumed they were half-hearted, although later, only an hour later, they or more determined colleagues sacked and burned the Catholic mission house down the road, attacked the police station and set off for the civil lines where the military dispersed them by shooting one of the ringleaders and firing the rest of their volleys into the air. For four days the town lived under martial law and when peace was restored Miss Crane found herself disagreeably in the public eye. The District Magistrate called on her, accompanied by the District Superintendent of Police, and thanked her. She felt it imperative to say that she was by no means certain she had done the right thing, that she wondered, in fact, whether it wouldn't have been better to have let the rioters in to burn whatever it was they wanted to get rid of, the prayer books or the crucifix. She had refused to let them and so they had gone away angrier than ever, and burned the Catholics to the ground and caused a great deal of trouble.

When Mr. Cleghorn returned from leave, anxious for news of what he had only heard as rumour, she decided to apply for a transfer so that she could get on with her job without constant reminders of what she thought of as her false position. She told Mr. Cleghorn that it was quite impossible to teach children who, facing her, saw her as a cardboard heroine and no doubt had, each of them, only one eye on the blackboard because the other was fixed on the doorway, expectant of some further disturbance they wanted her to quell. Mr. Cleghorn said that he would be sorry to see her go, but that he quite understood and that if she really meant what she said he would write personally to mission headquarters to explain matters.

When the instructions for her transfer came she discovered that she had been promoted by being put in sole charge of the school at Ranpur. Before she left there was a tea, and then the presentation of the picture – a larger, more handsomely framed copy of the picture on the wall behind her desk in the Muzzafirabad schoolroom, a semi-historical, semi-allegorical picture entitled *The Jewel in Her Crown,* which showed the old Queen (whose image the children now no doubt confused with the person of Miss Crane) surrounded by representative figures of her Indian Empire: Princes, landowners, merchants, money-lenders, sepoys, farmers, servants, children, mothers, and remarkably clean and tidy beggars. The Queen was sitting on a golden throne, under a crimson canopy, attended by her temporal and spiritual aides: soldiers, statesmen and clergy. The canopied throne was apparently in the open air because there were palm trees and a sky showing a radiant sun bursting out of bulgy clouds such as, in India, heralded the wet monsoon. Above the clouds flew the prayerful figures of the angels who were the benevolent spectators of the scene below. Among the statesmen who stood behind the throne one was painted in the likeness of Mr. Disraeli holding up a parchment map of India to which he pointed with obvious pride but tactful humility. An Indian prince, attended by native servants, was approaching the throne bearing a velvet cushion on which he offered a large and sparkling gem. The children in the school thought that this gem was the jewel referred to in the title. Miss Crane had been bound to explain that the gem was simply representative of tribute, and that the jewel of the title was India herself, which had been transferred from the rule of the British East India Company to the rule of the British crown in 1858, the year after the Mutiny when the sepoys in the service of the Company (that first set foot in India in the seventeenth century) had risen in rebellion, and attempts had been made to declare an old moghul prince king in Delhi, and that the picture had been painted after 1877, the year in which Victoria was persuaded by Mr. Disraeli to adopt the title Empress of India.

The Jewel in Her Crown was a picture about which Miss Crane had very mixed feelings. The copy that already hung on the classroom wall in Muzzafirabad when she first went there as assistant to Mr. Cleghorn she found useful when teaching the English language to a class of Muslim and Hindu children. This is the Queen. That is her crown. The sky there is blue. Here there are clouds in the sky. The uniform of the sahib is scarlet. Mr. Cleghorn, an ordained member of the Church and an enthusiastic amateur scholar of archaeology and anthropology, and much concerned with the impending, never-got-down-to composition of a monograph on local topography and social customs, had devoted most of his time to work for the Church and for the older boys in the middle school. He did this at the expense of the junior school, as he was aware. When Miss Crane was sent to him from Lahore in response to his requests for more permanent help in that field of his responsibility he had been fascinated to notice the practical use she made of a picture which, to him, had never been more than something hanging on the wall to brighten things up.

He was fond of remarking on it, whenever he found her in class with half a dozen wide-eyed children gathered round her, looking from her to the picture as she took them through its various aspects, step by step. "Ah, the picture again, Miss Crane," he would say, "admirable, admirable. I should never have thought of it. To teach English and at the same time love of the English."

She knew what he meant by love of the English. He meant love of their justice, love of their benevolence, love – anyway – of their good intentions. As often as she was irritated by his simplicity, she was touched by it. He was a good man: tireless, inquisitive, charitable. Mohammedanism and Hinduism, which still frightened her in their outward manifestations, merely amused him: as a grown man might be amused by the grim, colourful but harmless games of children. If there were times when she thought him heedless of the misery of men, she could not help knowing that in his own way he never forgot the glory of God. Mr. Cleghorn's view was that God was best served, best glorified, by the training and exercise of the intellect. Physically timid – as she knew him to be from his fear of dogs, his mortal terror, once, of a snake which the watchman had to be sent for to despatch, his twitching cheeks and trembling hands when they were met on one or two occasions on the outskirts of villages by delegations of men who looked fierce but were actually friendly – he was morally courageous, and for this she admired him.

He fought long and hard for any money he thought the mission could afford and he could spend well. He had an ear and an eye for injustice and had been known to plead successfully with the District Magistrate for suspension of sentences or quashing of convictions in cases he believed deserved it. Mr. Cleghorn – the District Magistrate used to say – was wasted in the Church and should have gone into the Civil.

He showed most determination, however, in promoting the education of boys of the middle-class – Anglo-Indians, Hindus, Muslims, Sikhs. If they had above average intelligence they were all one to him, all "children whom the Lord has blessed with brains and sensibilities". His work here was chiefly that of detecting just where a youth's talents lay and in persuading him and his parents to set a course in that direction. "Look at young Shankar Ram," he might say to Miss Crane, who had but the vaguest notion which Shankar Ram he referred to, "he says he wants to be a civil servant. They all want to be civil servants. What chance has he got, though, beyond the post office and telegraphs? He should be an engineer. It may not be in his blood, but it is in his heart and mind." And so he would set about depressingly often without success looking for ways, for means, for opportunities to send young Shankar Ram out into the great world beyond Muzzafirabad to build bridges. In this, Miss Crane used to think, Mr. Cleghorn looked remarkably unlike any ordinary man of God, for the Shankar Ram in question, ninety-nine times out of a hundred, turned out to be as far away from conversion to Christianity as the women of India were from social emancipation. And over the question of women, British or Indian, Mr. Cleghorn was infuriatingly conservative. Women's interests were his blind spot. "Your sex is made, alas," he said once, "and yet not alas, no, Heaven be praised, your sex is made, Miss Crane, for marriage or for God," and in the one intimate moment there ever was between them, took her hand and patted it, as if to comfort her for the fact that the first, the temporal of these blessings, was certainly denied her.

Sometimes Miss Crane wanted to point to the picture on the wall which showed the old Queen resplendent on her throne and say to him, "Well there, anyway, was a woman of affairs," but never did, and was touched when she unwrapped the presentation parcel and saw an even gaudier copy of the enigmatic picture; touched because she knew that Mr. Cleghorn, deeply considering the parting gift she might most value, had characteristically hit upon the one she could have done without.

But a couple of days later, as he saw her into the Ladies' First-Class compartment of a train, while young Joseph, a poor boy who had worked in the mission kitchens but had asked to serve and was coming with her, was seeing to the luggage, Mr. Cleghorn handed her his own personal gift which, unwrapped as the train moved out into the bleak frontier landscape, turned out to be a copy of a book called *Fabian Essays in Socialism*, edited by Mr. George Bernard Shaw. It was inscribed to "My friend and colleague, Edwina Crane," signed, "Arthur St. John Cleghorn", and dated July 12th, 1914.

This book she still had, in the bookcase in her room in Mayapore.

*

When she paused in the work she was doing at her desk, as she felt entitled to do at her age, which was one for contemplation as well as action, she would sometimes glance at the picture and find her attention fixed on it. After all these years it had acquired a faint power to move her with the sense of time past, of glory departed, even although she knew there had never been glory there to begin with. The India of the picture had never existed outside its gilt frame, and the emotions the picture was meant to conjure up were not much more than smugly pious. And yet now, as always, there was a feeling somewhere in it of shadowy dignity.

It still stirred thoughts in her that she found difficult to analyse. She had devoted her life, in a practical and unimportant way, trying to prove that fear was evil because it promoted prejudice, that courage was good because it was a sign of selflessness, that ignorance was bad because fear sprang from it, that knowledge was good because the more you knew of the world's complexity the more clearly you saw the insignificance of the part you played. It was, possibly, Miss Crane felt, this concept of personal insignificance which, lying like the dark shadows of the rain clouds behind the gaudy colours of the picture of the Queen and her subjects, informed them with a graver splendour. There was, for Miss Crane, in the attitude of the old Queen on her throne, something ironically reminiscent of the way she herself had sat years ago on a dais, dressed in white muslin; and the message that she was always trying to read into this stylised representation of tribute and matriarchal care was one that conveyed the spirit of dignity without pomp, such as a mother, her own mother, had conveyed to her as a child, and the importance of courageously accepting duties and obligations, not for self-aggrandizement, but in self-denial, in order to promote a wider happiness and well-being, in order to rid the world of the very evils the picture took no account of: poverty, disease, misery, ignorance and injustice.

And it was because (turning late, but perhaps not too late, to her own countrymen) she saw in a young man called Private Clancy, beneath the youthful brash male urge to thrust himself into prominence (and she was not blind to that aspect of his behaviour) a spark of tenderness, an instinct for self-denial that made him see to it that she had a slice of cake and sweetened tea, and, perhaps (she admitted it) because he reminded her physically in his plebian way of the privileged and handsome Lieutenant Orme (who was killed in the First World War and won a posthumous VC) that she thought of Clancy more often than she thought of his more plodding comrades. The tenderness, she guessed, was wafer-thin, but it was there, she believed; there, for instance, in his cheery attitude to Joseph with whom he cracked good-natured jokes in soldier's Urdu that set the old servant grinning and looking forward to the soldiers' visits; there in his friendship with the boy called Barrett who was clumsy, dull, ugly and unintelligent. In fact it was his friendship with Barrett, as much as his special politeness to her and attitude to Joseph, and the way he and Barrett never missed coming to tea, that caused her to consider what she really meant, in Clancy's case, by tenderness; caused her, indeed, consciously to use that word in her thoughts about him. She knew that boys like Clancy often made friends of those whose physical and mental attributes would show their own superior ones to the best advantage. She knew that in choosing Barrett as what she understood was called a mucker, Clancy was simply conforming to an elementary rule of psychological behaviour. But whereas in the normal way Barrett would have been used by a boy like Clancy as a butt, frequently mocked, defended only if others tried to mock him, she felt that Clancy never used Barrett to such a purpose. While Clancy was present the others never mocked him. Poor Barrett was a primitive. In that spry company he could have stood out like a scarecrow in a field of cocky young green wheat. For Miss Crane, for a while, he did, but then she noticed that for the others he did not, or no longer did, and she thought that this was because over a period, through Clancy's influence, Barrett had been accepted as one of them, that with Clancy's help Barrett had developed facets of his personality that they recognised as those of the norm, and, through Clancy's insistence, no longer noticed facets they must at first have thought foreign.

It was Barrett who – when the rains came and tea had to be indoors, and she gave the soldiers the run of the bungalow and even remembered to provide ashtrays and cigarettes and invite them to smoke rather than spend an hour and a half in an agony of deprivation whose relief she had originally noticed but not easily understood in the way they all lighted up directly they got to the gate on the first leg of the journey home – Barrett who first commented on the picture of the old Queen on her canopied throne; commented on in his dull-ox way, simply by going up to and staring at it, Clancy who spoke for both of them by joining Barrett and then saying, "It's what they call an allegorical picture, isn't it, Miss Crane?" using the word with a kind of pride in his hard-won education that she found endearing and a bit shattering, because, watching Barrett looking at the picture, she had been on the point of saying, "It's really an allegory, Mr. Barrett," but had not, remembering that Barrett would not begin to know what an allegory was.

"Yes, it is an allegory," she said.

"It's a nice old picture," Clancy said. "A very nice old picture. Things were different those days, weren't they, Miss Crane?"

She asked him what he meant. He said, "Well, I mean, sort of simpler, sort of cut and dried."

For a while Miss Crane considered this, then said, "More people thought they were. But they weren't really. You could almost say things are simpler now. After all these years there can't be any doubt. India *must* be independent. When the war's over, we've *got* to give her up."

"Oh," Clancy said, looking at the picture still, and not at her. "I really meant about God and that, and people believing. I don't know much about the other thing, except a bit what Congress is and old Gandhi says, and if you ask me, Miss Crane, he's barmy."

"Barmy's right," Barrett said dutifully.

Miss Crane smiled.

"I used to have his picture up too. Over there. You can see where it was."

They turned to look where she pointed: the upright oblong patch of paler distemper, all that was left to Miss Crane of the Mahatma's spectacled, smiling image, the image of a man she had put her faith in which she had now transferred to Mr. Nehru and Mr. Rajagopalachari who obviously understood the different degrees of tyranny men could exercise and, if there had to be a preference, probably preferred to live a while longer with the imperial degree in order not only to avoid submitting to but to resist the totalitarian. Looking at Clancy and Barrett and imagining in their place a couple of indoctrinated storm-troopers or ancestor-worshippers whose hope of heaven lay in death in battle, she knew which she herself preferred. There was in this choice, she realised, a residual grain of that old instinct to stay within the harbour of the charmed circle, an understanding of the magic of kind safeguarding kind and of the reliance she could place in a boy, for instance, such as Clancy, should poor old Joseph suddenly go berserk and come into the room armed and mad and dangerous to pay her back for imaginary wrongs, or real wrongs she had not personally done him but had done representatively because she was of her race and of her colour, and he could not in his simple rage any longer distinguish between individual and crowd.

But there was as well in her choice, she believed, an intellectual as well as emotional weight tipping the scales in favour of lads like Clancy who, ignorant as they might be of the source and direction of its flow, were borne nevertheless on the surface of waters native to them, waters she had come to think of as constituting the moral drift of history; waters of a river that had to toss aside logs thrown into it by prejudice or carry them with it towards the still invisible because still far-distant sea of perfect harmony where the debris would become water-logged and rotten, finally disintegrate, or be lost, like matchsticks in a majestic ocean. Clancy, after all, was not simply Clancy or Clance, but the son of his father and of his father's fathers, and so long as they stayed at home the English – for all their hypocrisy, or even because of it – had always done as much as any other European race to undam the flow; as much, perhaps a fraction more, because of their isolation, their unique position in the European land-mass, a position that hampered their physical invasion but not the subtler invasion of their minds by the humane concepts of classical and Renaissance Europe that rose into the air and flew like migratory birds to wherever they were perennially welcome.

It was, Miss Crane believed, this ability of Clancy's to hear the faint rumble, which was all that was audible to him of the combined thunder of centuries of flight, that enabled him to say, partly in sorrow, partly in pride – life patently being better for his own kind now than then – "Things were different those days, sort of simpler, sort of cut and dried." He felt, however unconsciously, the burden of the freedom to think, to act, worship or not worship, according to his beliefs; the *weight* left on the world by each act of liberation; and if in his relative innocence he read a religious instead of a social message into the picture that provoked his comment, well, Miss Crane told herself, it came to the same thing in the end. God, after all, was no more than a symbol, the supreme symbol of authority here on earth; and Clancy was beginning to understand that the exercise of authority was not an easy business, especially if those who exercised it no longer felt they had heaven on their side.

*

That year the rains were late. They reached Mayapore towards the end of June. The young soldiers suffered from the extreme heat that preceded them, welcomed the first downpours, but by the end of the second week of July were complaining about the damp and the humidity.

Miss Crane had become used to ignoring the weather. In the dry she wore wide-brimmed hats, cotton or woollen dresses and sensible shoes; in the wet, blouses and gaberdine skirts, gumboots when necessary, with a lightweight burberry cape and an oilskin-covered sola topee. For transport in and around Mayapore she rode a ramshackle-looking but sturdy Raleigh bicycle; the car – a ten-year-old Ford – was kept for longer runs. In the past the Ford had taken her as far as Calcutta, but she no longer trusted it for that. On the few occasions – once or twice a year – that she needed to go to Calcutta she now went by train, and she went alone because Joseph, aged fifty in a land whose native expectation of life was still less than forty years, felt too old to accompany her. He fretted if away from Mayapore, and pretended that he did not trust the chaukidar to guard the bungalow from thieves. Joseph shopped, did the cooking, looked after the stores and supervised the sweeper, a twelve-year-old girl from the bazaar. In the hot weather he slept on the verandah; in the cold and in the wet, on a camp-bed in the storeroom. He still went regularly to church, on Sunday evenings, and borrowed her bicycle for that purpose. The church – that of the mission, not the church of St. Mary in the civil lines – was situated not far from Miss Crane's bungalow, close to the Mandir Gate bridge, one of the two bridges that spanned the river-bed that divided the civil lines from the native town.

On the native town side of the Mandir Gate bridge was to be found the Tirupati temple within whose precincts was a shrine that sheltered the recumbent figure of the sleeping

Vishnu. Between the Mandir Gate bridge, on the civil lines side, and the second bridge, the Bibighar bridge, lived the Eurasian community, close at hand to the depots, godowns and offices of the railway station. The railway followed the course of the river-bed. The tracks crossed the roads that led to the bridges. At the bridgeheads on the civil lines side, consequently, there were level-crossings whose gates, when closed to let railway traffic through, sealed both bridges off, making a barrier between the European and the native populations. When the gates of the level-crossings were shut, road traffic coming from the town to the civil lines became congested on the bridges. Miss Crane, returning on her bicycle from the native town, was sometimes held up in such congestions, hemmed in by other cyclists and by pedestrians, clerks going back to work at District Headquarters after lunch in their homes, servants returning to the civil bungalows after shopping in the bazaar for vegetables; tailors on their way to measure a sahib or a sahib's lady who preferred the work and the prices of a bazaar tailor's to those of the cantonment tailor, Darwaza Chand; pedlars with boxes on their heads, farmers driving their buffalo carts back to villages in the plains north of the cantonment, women and children going begging or scavenging; and, occasionally, car-borne Europeans, a bank official or businessman, the District Superintendent of Police, the Station Commander, English and Indian Army Officers in yellow-painted fifteen-hundredweight trucks. Sometimes on these journeys she would see and nod to, but never speak to, the white woman – said to be mad – who dressed like a nun, kept a refuge for the sick and the dying and was called Sister Ludmila by the Indians.

Miss Crane used the Mandir Gate bridge into the native town in order to go from her bungalow to the Chillianwallah Bazaar school, a journey that took her past the church of the mission and the principal mission school, over the bridge, past the Tirupati temple, through narrow dirty streets of open shop fronts, past the gateway of the Chillianwallah bazaar itself where fish, meat and vegetables were sold, and into an even narrower street, a dark alleyway between old, crumbling houses, down whose centre ran an open water-duct. The alley was a cul-de-sac. At its closed-in head were the high wall and arched gateway of the bazaar school. The gateway opened into a narrow mud compound where the children played. Stunted banana trees gave a little shade in the early mornings and late afternoons. The mud was reddish brown, baked hard by the sun and pressed flat by the pupils' bare feet. Even in the wet monsoon an afternoon's sunshine would dry and harden it to its old concrete consistency.

The Chillianwallah Bazaar schoolhouse was a two-storey building with steps up to a verandah with shuttered balconied windows above the verandah roof. At least seventy years old, the house had been the property of Mr. Chillianwallah, a Parsee who left Bombay and made a fortune in Mayapore out of government building contracts in the 1890s. Mr. Chillianwallah had built the barracks in the civil lines, the church of St. Mary, the bungalow presently lived in by the Deputy Commissioner, and – in a philanthropic fit – the bazaar in the native town. Still in the throes of that fit he presented the house in the alley to the church of St. Mary, and until the mission built a more substantial schoolhouse in the civil lines, opposite the mission church, the house in the alley had been its only foothold on the shaky ladder of conversion. For several years after the building of the larger mission school in the civil lines in 1906, the Chillianwallah house and compound had been used by the mission as a place of refuge for the old and sick and dying but as the civil lines school became filled to overflowing with the children of Eurasians, and the numbers of Indian children attending fell away, the mission reopened the house in the alley for lessons in the hope of regaining the foothold they had virtually lost, and the old and sick and dying had some thirty years to wait for the coming of Sister Ludmila.

The Chillianwallah Bazaar school was now the second of Miss Crane's responsibilities in Mayapore District. Her third was in Dibrapur, near the coalmines; her first the larger school in the civil lines, opposite the mission church, where in co-operation with a succession of English teachers whose qualifications to teach were more apparent than her own and whose religious convictions put hers to shame, she supervised the work of the Anglo-Indian class mistresses and taught mathematics and English to the older Eurasian and Indian Christian girls. From this school most of the pupils passed into the Government Higher School whose foundation in 1920 had done much to undermine the mission's influence.

The teacher at the Chillianwallah Bazaar school, whose pupils were all Indian, was a middle-aged, tall, thin, dark-skinned Madrassi Christian, Mr. F. Narayan: the F for

Francis, after St. Francis of Assisi. In his spare time, of which he had a great deal, and to augment his income, of which he had little, Mr. Narayan wrote what he called Topics for the local English language weekly newspaper, *The Mayapore Gazette*. In addition, his services were available as a letter-writer, and these were services used by both his Hindu and Muslim neighbours. He could converse fluently in Urdu and Hindi and the local vernacular, and wrote an excellent Urdu and Hindi script, as well as his native Tamil and acquired Roman–English. In Europe, Miss Crane thought, a man of his accomplishments might have gone a long way – in the commercial rather than the pedagogic field. She suspected him, because Joseph had hinted at it, of selling contraceptives to Christian and progressive Hindu families. She did not disapprove, but was amused because Mr. Narayan himself had an ever-pregnant wife, and a large, noisy, undisciplined family of boys and girls.

His wife Mary Narayan, as dark-skinned as himself, was a girl he brought back one year from leave in Madras. He said she was a Christian too, but Miss Crane doubted it, never having seen her go to church but instead, on more than one occasion, entering and leaving the Tirupati temple. He said she was now twenty-five, which Miss Crane doubted as well. She wouldn't have been surprised if Mrs. Narayan had only been thirteen or fourteen at the time Francis Narayan married her.

Mr. and Mrs. Narayan lived in the upstairs rooms of the Chillianwallah Bazaar school. Their children, three girls and two boys to date (apart from the one still suckling whose sex she had somehow never made a note of) sat on the front benches in the schoolroom and were, Miss Crane had begun to notice, virtually the only regular attendants. On Sunday mornings, Mr. Narayan and his two eldest children – one boy, John Krishna, and a girl, Kamala Magdalene – left the house in the Chillianwallah Bazaar in a cycle-tonga driven by a convert called Peter Paul Akbar Hossain, precariously negotiated the water-duct down the cul-de-sac, crossed the Mandir Gate bridge, and attended the service at the mission church where Mr. Narayan also assisted with the collection. His wife, he said, had to stay at home to look after the younger children. Miss Crane took this information, too, with a pinch of salt. She wondered whether it might be interesting to stand outside the Tirupati temple on a Sunday morning to see whether Mrs. Narayan's absence from the mission church was due to the stronger call of Lord Venkataswara, the god of the temple whose image was taken from the sanctuary once a year and carried down to the banks of the river to bless all those from whom he received the prescribed sacrifice.

But on Sunday mornings Miss Crane was otherwise engaged. She went to the service at St. Mary's, cycling there rain or shine along the tidy, tree-lined, geometrically laid out roads of the cantonment, holding an umbrella up if the weather was inclement. Miss Crane's umbrella was a cantonment joke. In the rains, reaching the side door, parking the Raleigh, she worked the canopy vigorously up and down to shake the drops from it. This flapping bat-wing noise was audible to those in the pews closest to the door, the pews on the lectern side of the church, whose English occupants smiled at the unmistakable sounds of Miss Crane's arrival, much as years before other people in another church had smiled when Mr. Grant offered up his prayers.

The other congregational joke about Miss Crane was over her tendency to fall asleep during the sermon, which she did with great discretion, maintaining a ramrod back and squared shoulders, so that only her closed eyes gave the game away, and even her closed eyes seemed, initially, no more than a likely sign of her preoccupation with images conjured by the chaplain's words which, for a moment, she thought of having a closer personal look at. Her eyes closed, then opened; presently closed again, only to open again. The third time that the lids snapped shut – abruptly, never slowly or heavily – they usually stayed shut; and Miss Crane was then away; and only a slight backward jerk of her head when the chaplain said Now God the Father God the Son and the congregation exhaled a corporate sigh of relief, proved that she hadn't heard a word and that the eyes she now just as abruptly opened had been closed in sleep.

Her violent shaking of the umbrella – not unlike the sound of alighting angry angels – and her firm fast sleep during the service, her reputation for outspokenness, her seeming imperviousness to the little drops of condescension falling from those who, in the way these things were reckoned, were above her in social station – all these had contributed to the idea the Mayapore English had of her as a woman whose work for the missionaries had broadened rather than narrowed her. There was certainly nothing sanctimonious about Edwina Crane. The somewhat grudging personal regard she was held in was increased by her refusal to be browbeaten on the women's committees she sat on. Since the war began the English ladies of Mayapore had not been slow to recognise the need and answer the call for committees: knitting-bee committees, troops entertainment committees, social welfare committees, Guides recruitment committees, War Week committees, committees to direct the voluntary work done in the hospital and the Greenlawns nursing home and by the ladies who had in mind the welfare of the children of Indian mothers working on the road extension and proposed airstrip out at Banyaganj and in the British-Indian Electrical factory. Called in originally to help with the Guides recruitment by Mrs. White, the wife of the Deputy Commissioner, she was now a member of the social welfare, the voluntary hospital workers and the Indian mothers committees and if among themselves the ladies spoke of her in tones that would have suggested to a stranger that Miss Crane was only a mission school teacher and as many rungs below them as it was socially possible to be and still be recognised, they themselves collectively understood that actual denigration was not intended, and individually respected her even if they thought her "cranky about the natives".

It was the wife of the Deputy Commissioner who was responsible for creating an image of Miss Crane which the ladies of Mayapore had now come to regard as definitive of her. "Edwina Crane," Mrs. White said, "has obviously missed her vocation. Instead of wasting her time in the missions and thumping the old tub about the iniquities of the British Raj and the intolerable burdens borne by what her church calls our dark brethren, she should have been headmistress of a good school for girls, back in the old home counties."

Until the war Miss Crane had not gone out much in European society. Occasional dinners with the chaplain and his wife (it was the chaplain who was responsible for calling the station's attention to Miss Crane's tendency to sleep during his sermons), an annual invitation to the Deputy Commissioner's garden party and once a year to his bungalow during the cold months when his wife "dined the station" – these had been the main events on her white social calendar, indeed still were, but her work on the committees had widened the circle of English women who were ready to stop and talk to her in the cantonment bazaar or invite her to coffee or tea, and the particular dinner at the Deputy Commissioner's to which Miss

Crane now went was the one to which higher ranking English were invited, and eminent Indians such as Lady Chatterjee, widow of Sir Nello Chatterjee who had founded the Mayapore Technical College.

For these full-dress occasions, Miss Crane wore her brown silk: a dinner gown that revealed the sallow-skinned cushion of flesh below her now prominent collar-bones. She decorated the dress with a posy of artificial flowers, cut and shaped out of purple and crimson velvet. The dress had half sleeves. She wore elbow-length gloves of brown lisle silk so cut at the wrists that the hands of the gloves could be removed to reveal her own bony brown hands. Her greying hair, for these occasions, would be combed more loosely above her forehead and gathered into a coil that hung a fraction lower than usual at the back of her neck. Her fingers, unadorned, were short-nailed, thin but supple. From her, as her table companions knew, came a scent of geranium and mothballs, the former of which grew fainter as the evening progressed, and the latter stronger, until both were lost for them in the euphoria of wine and brandy.

On her wrist before and after dinner, and on her lap during it, she carried a home-made sachet handbag of brown satin lined with crimson silk. The brown satin did not quite match, nor did it complement, the brown of her dress. In the bag which could be drawn open and shut on brown silk cords was a silver powder compact – which was the source of the geranium smell – a plain lawn handkerchief, the ignition key of the Ford, a few soiled rupee notes, her diary of engagements, a silver pencil with a red silk tassel, and a green bottle of smelling salts. At the DC's dinners Miss Crane drank everything she was offered: sherry, white burgundy, claret and brandy, and always smelled the salts before setting off home in the car, to clear her head, which Mrs. White had been relieved to find was a strong enough one for her not to fear the possibility of Miss Crane being overcome and letting the side down.

Reaching home, driving the Ford into the corrugated iron garage beside the bungalow, she would be met by old Joseph and scolded for being late. In the house she drank the milk that he had warmed and re-warmed, ate the biscuits he had put out on a doily-covered plate, took the aspirin he said she needed, and retired, answering his "God bless you, madam" with her own "Good night", entered her room and slowly, tiredly, got rid of the long skirted encumbrance which in the morning Joseph would air and put back in the chest where she kept her few bits of finery and spare linen; put it there proudly because his mistress was a Mem in spite of the bicycle, the topee and the gum-boots and her work which took her into the stinking alleys of the heathen, native town.

*

By this summer of 1942 Miss Crane had been in Mayapore for seven years, and during them she had seen many Europeans come and go. The Deputy Commissioner and his wife, Mr. and Mrs. White, had been there only four years, since 1938, the year that the previous DC, an irritable widower called Stead, had retired, nursing a grievance that he had never been promoted Divisional Commissioner or sent to the Secretariat. The Assistant Commissioner and his wife, Mr. and Mrs. Poulson, had come to Mayapore shortly afterwards. The Poulsons were friends of the Whites; in fact White had especially asked for Poulson to be sent to Mayapore. Ronald Merrick, the District Superintendent of Police, was a bachelor, a young man sometimes over-anxious, it was said, to excel in his duties, quarrelsome at the club, but sought after by the unmarried girls. He had been in the town only two years. Only the District and Sessions Judge, who together with the DC and the Superintendent of Police formed the triumvirate of civil authority in the District, had been in Mayapore as long as Miss Crane, but he was an Indian. His name was Menen and Miss Crane had never met him to talk to. Menen was a friend of Lady Chatterjee who lived on the Bibighar bridge side of the civil lines in the old MacGregor House, so called because rebuilt by a Scotsman of that name on the foundations of the house built by a prince in the days when Mayapore was a Native State. The raja had been deposed in 1814 and the state annexed by the East India Company, absorbed into the province of whose score of districts it now ranked as second in size and importance.

Although Lady Chatterjee was the leader of Indian society in Mayapore, Miss Crane scarcely knew her. She met her at the Deputy Commissioner's but had never been to the MacGregor House which, it was said, was the one place where English and Indians came together as equals, or at least without too much caution on the part of the Indians or too much embarrassment on the part of the English. Miss Crane did not actually regret never going to the MacGregor House. She thought Lady Chatterjee over-westernised, a bit of a snob, socially and intellectually; amusing enough to listen to at the DC's dinner-table but not in the drawing-room afterwards, when the women were alone for a while and Lady Chatterjee asked questions of them which Miss Crane thought were calculated to expose them as lacking in social background at home or cosmopolitan experience abroad, finally lapsing into dignified silence and letting the English small-talk get under way without attempting to contribute to it, content to wait for the men to rejoin them when she would again have the opportunity of sparkling and making everybody laugh. The English women found Lady Chatterjee easier-going if they had the men with them. They were all, Miss Crane concluded, rather afraid of her. And Lady Chatterjee, Miss Crane thought, was – although not afraid of them – certainly on her guard, as stuffy in her own way as the English women. For Miss Crane she seemed to have no feelings whatsoever; a disinterest that might have been due to her discovery by direct questioning at the first dinner they attended together that Miss Crane had no degree, in fact no qualifications to teach other than the rough and ready training she had received years ago in Lahore after leaving the service of the Nesbitt-Smiths. On the other hand, Lady Chatterjee's indifference was equally probably due to a disapproval of missions and missionaries and of anyone connected with them. Westernised though she was, Lady Chatterjee was of Rajput stock, a Hindu of the old ruling-warrior caste. Short, thin, with greying hair cut in European style, seated upright on the edge of a sofa, with the free end of her saree tight-wound round her shoulders, and her remarkably dark eyes glittering at you, her beaky Rajput nose and pale skin proclaiming both authority and breeding, she looked every inch a woman whom only the course of history had denied the opportunity of fully exercising the power she was born to.

Widowed some years earlier by the death of a husband who had been older than she and by whom she had had no children, an Indian who was knighted for his services to the Crown and his philanthropy to his own countrymen, Lady Chatterjee, so far as Miss Crane was concerned, now seemed to be continuing what must have been Sir Nello's policy of getting the best out of both worlds. She thought this in rather bad taste. Friends in the old days of Sir Henry Manners and his wife who, for a time, had been Governor and Governor's lady of the province, Lady Chatterjee still went annually to Rawalpindi or Kashmir to stay with Lady Manners, now a widow like herself; and a Manners girl, Daphne, a niece of Sir Henry, rather plain, big-boned and as yet unmarried, was working in the hospital at Mayapore for the war effort and living in the MacGregor House as Lady Chatterjee's guest. It was, no doubt, Lady Chatterjee's standing with distinguished English people like old Lady Manners as much as the position she enjoyed in Mayapore as Sir Nello's widow and as member of the board of Governors of the Technical College, member of the committee of the purdah hospital in the native town, that caused her to be treated with such outward consideration by the leaders of the English colony. With the DC and his wife she was on Christian name terms. (She had not been with Stead, their predecessor in office.) She was always welcome at the DC's bungalow. She played bridge there and Mrs. White played bridge at the MacGregor House. But whatever from the Whites' point of view in this cordiality ranked as part of their duty to be seen as well as felt to be the representatives of a government that had at heart the well-being of all the people living in the district, Indian or British, there certainly seemed to be from all accounts a genuine sympathy and understanding between them and Sir Nello's widow.

But – and this was what interested Miss Crane – at the MacGregor House, said to be equally welcome were Indians: barristers, teachers, doctors, lawyers, municipal officers, higher civil servants, among whom were men of the local Congress Party sub-committee, and men not of that committee but known for the possibly even greater vehemence of their anti-British views.

How often such men found themselves at the MacGregor House face to face with the liberal English, Miss Crane did not know; neither did she know whether Lady Chatterjee would hope by such confrontations to dampen their anti-British ardour or inspire even more radical feelings in the hearts of the liberal English. All she knew was that from her own point of view Lady Chatterjee appeared to lack the true liberal instinct herself. She admitted, though, that behind her lack of empathy for Lady Chatterjee there were probably the particular kinds of blindness and deafness that followed social rebuff. Admitting this, she also admitted a more fundamental truth.

And that truth was that after virtually a lifetime of service in the mission schools she was lonely. Since the death of old Miss de Silva who had been the teacher in Dibrapur, there was not a man or a woman in Mayapore, in India, anywhere, British or Indian, she could point to as a friend of the sort to whom she could have talked long and intimately. When, in the May of 1942, Mr. Gandhi demanded that the British should leave India – leave her, he said, "to God, or to anarchy," which meant leaving her to the Japanese – and she took down his portrait and her Indian ladies stopped coming to tea, she saw that the bungalow would not be particularly empty without them because they had not looked on her as a person, but only as a woman who represented something they felt ought to be represented. She also saw that she herself had looked on the teas not as friendly but as meaningful gatherings. There was no one else in Mayapore to drop by, nowhere in Mayapore she could casually drop by at herself. Such acts of dropping by as were undertaken by herself or others were for reasons other than human intimacy. Now the soldiers came in place of the ladies, on a different day, Wednesday and not Tuesday (as though to keep Tuesdays free in case the ladies underwent a change of heart). And in the case of the soldiers there had probably been a notice put up in the Regimental Institute: "Personnel wishing to avail themselves of an invitation to tea on Wednesday afternoons at the home of Miss E. Crane, superintendent of the Church of England Mission Schools (Mayapore District) should give their names to their Unit Welfare Officer."

Sometimes she wondered to what extent her decision to entertain the soldiers had been due to an instinct finally to find refuge in that old privileged circle that surrounded and protected the white community. Her social and political beliefs were, she could not help realising, by the standards of the present day, somehow old-fashioned, over-simplified. Lacking a real education she had matured slowly and had, she supposed, grasped hold of the ideas of a generation previous to her own as if they were mint-new. Events had gone ahead of her, taking with them younger people who were, in their opinions, in advance of her. She understood, it seemed, little of practical present-day politics. This comparative ignorance defined the gulf that separated her not only from the younger liberal English people such as she met at the Deputy Commissioner's and whom she found it difficult to talk to, but from Lady Chatterjee who, lending half an ear to what she might have to say about Indian independence and the sacred duty of the British to grant it, conveyed at once an impression of having heard it all too long ago for it to be worth hearing again.

"I am," Miss Crane told herself, "a relic of the past," mentally crossed out "of the past" as a redundant clause, and looked up at the picture of the old Queen, stared at it waiting for it to reveal something simple but irrefutable that perhaps the MacGregor House set had lost sight of. What seemed to her so extraordinary was that although her own ladies had stopped coming to tea the parties at the MacGregor House continued. The English community apparently saw nothing wrong in this even though they knew they now had their backs to a wall that the Indians seemed set on removing, brick by brick. It was, they said, the duty of people like the DC and his wife to keep their ears to the ground, and where better to do that than at the MacGregor House? It was rumoured, for instance, that on instructions from Government the DC had already prepared a list of Congress party members in the Mayapore district who would have to be arrested under the Defence of India Rules if Congress voted in favour of Mr. Gandhi's civil disobedience resolution, a resolution under which the British would be called upon to leave India on pain of finding the realm impossible to defend, their armies on the Assam-Burma frontier impossible to feed, clothe, arm or support; impossible, for the simple reason that there would be no one who was willing to operate the railways, the posts and telegraphs, the docks, the depots, the factories, the mines, the banks, the offices, or any of the administrative and productive services of a nation they had exploited for over two hundred years and, by failing to defend Burma, brought to the point of having to succumb to yet another set of imperialistic warmongers.

Miss Crane feared such an uprising. For her the only hope for the country she loved lay in the coming together at last of its population and its rulers as equal partners in a war to the death against totalitarianism. If Congress had not resigned from the provincial ministries in 1939 in a fit of pique because the Viceroy without going through the motions of consulting them had declared war in the name of the King-Emperor on India's behalf, and if Mr. Gandhi had not had a brainstorm and seized the moment of Britain's greatest misfortune to press home his demands for political freedom, if things had been left to Mr. Nehru who obviously found Gandhi an embarrassment and to Mr. Rajagopalachari (who had headed the provincial ministry in Madras and had wanted to arm and train the entire nation to fight the Japanese) then at this moment, Miss Crane believed, an Indian cabinet would have been in control in Delhi, Lord Linlithgow would have been Governor-General of a virtually independent dominion and all the things that she had hoped and prayed for to happen in India would have happened, and the war would be under process of firm and thoughtful prosecution.

Sometimes Miss Crane woke up in the night and lay sleepless, listening to the rain, and was alarmed, conscious of dangers that were growing and which people were preparing to face but not to understand, so that virtually they were not facing them at all. We only understand, she said, the way to meet them, or, sometimes, the way to avert them.

But on this occasion they were not averted.

*

In the first week of August Miss Crane caught one of her rare colds. She had never believed in running risks with her health. She telephoned to the school in Dibrapur to say that she would not be coming on the Thursday but would come on the following Saturday. Then she went home and put herself to bed and sweated the chill out. By the weekend she felt perfectly fit again. And so on the morning of the 8th of August – on the day on which Congress were to vote on Mr. Gandhi's resolution – Miss Crane set off in her Ford the seventy-odd miles to Dibrapur.

The school in Dibrapur, the third of Miss Crane's responsibilities in Mayapore District, was situated in comparative isolation, on the road midway between the village of Kotali and the town of Dibrapur itself. Dibrapur lay on the southern border of the Mayapore District. There was no church, no European population. The Dibrapur mines, so-called, were now administered from Aligarh in the adjoining district of the province.

Most of the children who attended the school came from Kotali. They had only three miles to walk. If they went to the school run by the District Board in a neighbouring village the distance was four miles. The mission schoolhouse had been built in its isolated position years ago so that it could serve the surrounding villages as well as Dibrapur. Since the expansion of the Government's own educational programme and the setting up of primary schools by District Boards the mission school had not lost many pupils for the simple reason that it had never attracted many. The Kotali children came because it was nearer and a few children still came from Dibrapur because at the mission school the English language was taught. The Dibrapur children were usually the sons – very occasionally the daughters – of shopkeepers, men who fancied their male offspring's chances as government contractors or petty civil servants and who knew that the gift of conversing fluently in English was therefore invaluable. And so, from Dibrapur, up to half a dozen boys and two or three girls would tramp the three miles every day to the school of the mission, carrying with them, like the children from Kotali, their food tins and their canvas bags. In the school of the mission there were no chappattis; only instruction, good intentions and medicine for upset stomachs.

Having stood now for nearly thirty years the Dibrapur schoolhouse was in constant need of some kind of repair, and, in the summer of 1942, certainly a coat of whitewash that it would have to wait for until the end of the rains. What it most urgently needed was attention to the roof and during this summer Miss Crane's thoughts in connexion with the school had been almost exclusively concerned with the estimates periodically obtained by Mr. Chaudhuri, the teacher, and the Allocation, which in crude terms meant the money available. So far Mr. Chaudhuri had failed to obtain an estimate from any local builder that came within sight of balancing what had to be spent with what there was to spend. He did not seem to have much of a head for business or talent for bargaining. "We need," Miss Crane had been thinking, "another five hundred rupees. We need, in fact, more; not only a repair to the roof, but a new roof, in fact practically a new school." Sometimes she could not help wondering whether they also needed a new teacher-in-charge, but always put the thought out of her head as uncharitable, as one sparked off by personal prejudice. The fact that for one reason or another she and Mr. Chaudhuri had never hit it off should not, she realised, blind her to his remarkable qualities as a teacher.

Mr. Chaudhuri had held the Dibrapur appointment for not quite a year. His predecessor, old Miss de Silva, a Eurasian woman from Goa, had been dead for just a bit longer. With

Mary de Silva's death Miss Crane had lost the last person in the world who called her Edwina. On her first visit to Dibrapur as superintendent, seven years ago, the older woman – fat, white-haired, ponderous, and with a voice as dark and forthcoming as her extraordinary popping black eyes – had said, "You got the job *I* wanted. My name's Mary de Silva. My mother was as black as your hat."

"Mine's Edwina Crane," Miss Crane said, shaking the pudgy, man-strong hand, "I didn't *know* you wanted the job, and my mother's been dead for longer than I care to remember."

"Well in that case I'll call you Edwina, if you don't mind. I'm too old to bow and scrape to a *new* superintendent. And also if you don't mind we'll start by talking about the bloody roof."

So they had talked about the roof, and the walls, and the tube-well that wanted re-sinking in another place, and then about the children, and Mary de Silva's intention to send, by hook or crook, a boy called Balarachama Rao to the Government Higher School in Mayapore. "His parents won't hear of it. But *I'll* hear of it. Where do *you* stand, Edwina Crane?"

"In matters of this sort, Mary de Silva," she replied, "I stand to do what the teachers on the spot advise me should be done."

"Then find a decent lodging in Mayapore for Master Balarachama. That's the snag. He's got no place to live if he's admitted. The parents say they've no relatives there. Which is nonsense. Indians have relatives *every*where. I ought to know." Her skin was no sallower than little Miss Williams's had been.

Miss Crane found lodgings in Mayapore for Balarachama and spent a month, which is to say most of her time in four weekly visits to Dibrapur, persuading his parents to let him go. When she had at last succeeded Mary de Silva said, "I'm not going to thank you. It was your duty. And it was mine. But come back now and help me break into the bottle of rum I've been saving since Christmas." So she went back with Mary de Silva to the bungalow the Chaudhuris now lived in, half a mile down the road from the school, and drank rum, heard the story of Mary de Silva's life and told her own. There had been many other occasions of drinking rum and lime in Mary de Silva's living-room, discreetly, but in enough quantity for tongues to be loosened and for Miss Crane to feel that here, in Dibrapur, with Mary de Silva, she had come home again after a lifetime travelling. For six years she went weekly to Dibrapur, and stayed the night with Mary de Silva. "It's not necessary you know," Miss de Silva said, "but it's nice. The last superintendent only came once a month and never stayed the night. That was nice too."

At the end of the six years, when the roof of the school had been repaired once and needed repairing again, and the new tube-well had been sunk, the walls patched and painted twice, there came the day she reached the schoolhouse and found it closed, and, driving on to Mary de Silva's bungalow, found the old teacher in bed, lying quietly, temporarily deserted by the servant who had gone down to Dibrapur to fetch the doctor. Miss de Silva was mumbling to herself. When she had finished what she had to say, and nodded, her eyes focused on Miss Crane. She smiled and said, "Well, Edwina. I'm for it. You might see to the roof again," then closed her eyes and died as if someone had simply disconnected a battery.

After seeing Mary de Silva's body safely and quickly transported to Mayapore and buried in the churchyard of St. Mary, Miss Crane put the task of finding a temporary teacher into the hands of Mr. Narayan to give him something to do, and went back to Dibrapur to reopen the school and keep it going until the temporary arrived. She also wrote to the headquarters of the mission to report Miss de Silva's death and the steps she had taken to keep the school going until a permanent appointment was made. She recommended a Miss Smithers, with whom she had worked in Bihar. She did not get Miss Smithers. She got first of all a cousin of Mr. Narayan who drank, and then, from Calcutta, Mr. D. R. Chaudhuri, BA, BSc – qualifications which not only astonished her but made her suspicious. Mission headquarters had been rather astounded too, so she gathered from their letter, but not suspicious. Mr. Chaudhuri did not profess to be a Christian, they told her, on the other hand he did not profess any other religion. He had resigned from an appointment in a Government training college and had asked the mission to employ him in the humblest teaching capacity. They had offered him several posts, all of which he declined until, suddenly, the post in Dibrapur fell vacant, and this, from their description, had appealed to him as "the right kind of beginning". "He will be wasted in Dibrapur, of course, and is unlikely to be with you for long," they wrote, in confidence. "He will be accompanied by his wife, so perhaps you would arrange to see that the late Miss de Silva's bungalow is made ready for them. We understand he has private but limited means. You will find Mr. Chaudhuri a reserved young man and, by and large, unwilling to discuss the reasons for his decision to abandon a more distinguished academic career. We have, however, satisfied ourselves from interviews with Mr. Chaudhuri and inquiries outside, that his wish to teach young children in the villages arises from a genuine sympathy for the depressed classes of his own race and a genuine belief that educated men like himself should more often be prepared to sacrifice their private interests in the interest of the country as a whole. It appears, too, that he feels his work in this direction should be with schools such as our own, not because of the religious basis of our teaching but because he has a low opinion of the local government primary schools and thinks of them as staffed by teachers to whom politics are more important than any educational consideration."

In spite of this promising situation there had been between herself and Mr. Chaudhuri right from the beginning what Miss Crane thought of as an almost classical reserve – classical in the sense that she felt they each suspected the other of hypocrisy, of unrevealed motives, of hiding under the thinnest of liberal skins deeply conservative natures, so that all conversations they had that were not strictly to do with the affairs of the school seemed to be either double-edged or meaningless.

For weeks Miss Crane fought against her own reserve. She did not minimise her grief for and memories of Miss de Silva when it came to analysing the possible causes of it. Knowing that Mr. Chaudhuri had been told she visited Miss de Silva once a week, she visited him once a week too and stayed overnight in old Miss de Silva's bungalow, now unrecognisable as the same place, furnished as it was by Mr. and Mrs. Chaudhuri in the westernised-Indian style. She did this in case he should misunderstand her not doing it; at the same time she was aware that he might have taken her visits as a sign of her not trusting in his competence. She continued the visits in the hope that eventually she would feel at home there once more.

Tall, wiry, and square-shouldered, Mr. Chaudhuri had the fine-boned face of a Bengali, was handsome in a way Miss Crane recognised but did not personally consider handsome. With every feature and plane of his face sharp and prominent and in itself indicative of strength, the whole face, for her.

still suggested weakness – and yet not weakness, because even weakness required to be conveyed as a special expression, and Mr. Chaudhuri's face was capable of conveying only two: blank indifference or petulant annoyance. His smile, she saw, would have been pleasant if it had ever got up into his eyes as well.

His English was excellent, typically Indian in its inflexions and rhythms, but fluent as spoken and crisply correct when written. He also taught it very well. He made Mr. Narayan, by comparison, look and sound like a bazaar comedian. And yet, with Mr. Narayan, Miss Crane found conversation easy and direct. Not so with Mr. Chaudhuri. There had been a period in her career when, highly sensitive herself to the sensitivity of Indians who knew the English language, even some of its subtlest nuances, but seldom if ever the rough and tumble of its everyday idiom, she had inured herself to the temptation to say things like, Don't be silly; or, Nonsense. For some years now, though, she had not bothered to put a curb on her tongue, and wished she never had. When you chose your words the spontaneity went out of the things you wanted to say. She had learned to hate the feeling it gave her of unnaturalness. If she had always been as outspoken as she was now, she thought, then even if she had made enemies she might also have made friends. By developing self-confidence in the manner of her speech earlier in her career she believed she might have developed an inner confidence as well, the kind that communicated itself to people of another race as evidence of sincerity, trustworthiness. Too late for that, the outspokenness, she knew, often looked to Indians like the workaday thoughtless rudeness of any Englishwoman. Only Englishwomen themselves admired it, although with men like Mr. Narayan she could conduct a slanging match and feel no bones were broken. With Mr. Chaudhuri she found herself reverting to the soft phrase, the cautious sentiment, and then spoiling whatever effect this had had by letting slip words that came more easily to her. She had said Nonsense! to him early on in their association and had seen at once that her tenuous hold on his willingness to co-operate was temporarily lost. From this unfortunate set-back they had never made much advance. If Mrs. Chaudhuri had been a more sophisticated woman Miss Crane felt she might have made progress with Mr. Chaudhuri through intimate contact with his wife, but apart from a High School education and her years spent at the feet of a music teacher, Mrs. Chaudhuri was uninstructed in the ways of the sophisticated world and had a remarkably old-fashioned notion of the role of a wife.

*

Before Miss Crane set out in the Ford for Dibrapur on the morning of the 8th of August Joseph tried to dissuade her from going. He said there would be trouble. He had heard rumours.

She said, "We are always hearing rumours. Does that stop you from doing your work? Of course not. I have work in Dibrapur. So to Dibrapur I must go."

He offered to come with her.

"And who will look after the house, then?" she asked. "No, Joseph, for both of us it is business as usual."

It was business as usual all the way to Dibrapur, which she reached at four o'clock in the afternoon, having stopped on the way to eat her sandwiches and drink coffee from the flask. In the villages there were people who shouted Quit India! and others who asked for baksheesh. Driving slowly to avoid hitting cows and buffalo, dogs, hens and children, she smiled and waved at the people whatever they shouted.

In Kotali, the last village before the schoolhouse, she stopped the car and spoke to some of the mothers whose children went to Mr. Chaudhuri for lessons. The mothers said nothing about trouble. She did not mention it herself. They would know better than she what was to be expected. Kotali looked very peaceful. Leaving the village behind she met the children making their way home, carrying their food tins and canvas bags. Their average age was eight. She stopped the car again and distributed some of the boiled sweets.

Reaching the schoolhouse she drove into the compound. Here there were trees and shade. She found Mr. Chaudhuri tidying up the schoolroom. "Is there any news?" she asked, rather hoping that if trouble were coming and this were to be an eleventh hour it would be made productive of something more than politeness.

"News?" he replied. "What sort of news, Miss Crane?"

"Of the Congress vote."

"Oh, that," he said. "No, I have not listened."

In the room of the schoolhouse that served as an office

there was a radio. Sometimes Mr. Chaudhuri used the radio as a medium of instruction. She turned it on now. There was music. She switched off. It was European music. The only music she ever listened to when with the Chaudhuris was Indian classical music.

"Perhaps, however," he said, "there is news of the roof?"

"No, there isn't. I've checked through all the estimates again and there's not one that's low enough. Can't you find someone to do it cheaper?"

"I have tried all who are willing to do it at all. If we wait much longer even the low estimates will go up. And these people cannot work for nothing."

She was about to say, Well, that's not what I'm asking, I'm not asking them to do it for nothing. She would have said that to Mr. Narayan. She held back from saying it to Mr. Chaudhuri. Instead she said, "No. Well, come on. I'd like a cup of tea." And even that sounded brusque.

Mr. Chaudhuri closed the school, padlocked the door, and joined her in the Ford. At his bungalow tea was not ready. He did not apologise; but while she was resting on her bed, waiting to be called, she heard him taking his wife to task for not ordering things better. When tea was ready it was served on the verandah. Mrs. Chaudhuri did not join them. She moved between kitchen and verandah, carrying things with her own hands, smiling but saying little, and when there seemed to be nothing more that they wanted stood in the shadow of the doorway, pretending not to be there, but watching her husband for the slightest indication from him that something had been forgotten, or was wrong, or needed to be replenished.

"It is *this*," Miss Crane often told herself, "this awful feudal attitude to his wife that makes it difficult for me to like him."

But it was not that. In the evenings Mrs. Chaudhuri sometimes sang to them. Directly she was seated cross-legged on the rush mat, gently supporting the onion-shaped tamboura, she became a different woman; self-assured, holding her bony body gracefully erect, not unlike the way Lady Chatterjee held hers when sitting on a sofa at the DC's. After Mrs. Chaudhuri had sung a couple of songs Mr. Chaudhuri would say, almost under his breath, "It is enough," and then Mrs. Chaudhuri would rise, take up the tamboura and disappear into an inner room. And Miss Crane knew that Mr. and Mrs. Chaudhuri loved one another, that Mr. Chaudhuri was not a tyrant, that the woman herself preferred the old ways to the new because for her the old ways were a discipline and a tradition, a means of acquiring and maintaining peace of mind and inner stillness.

On this night, the night of August the 8th, which Miss Crane felt in her bones was a special night, one of crisis, she longed to make Mr. Chaudhuri talk, to find the key to his reticence, a way of breaking down his reserve. It would have been easier for her if he had been as old-fashioned in his manners as his wife, because then their association would have been of an altogether different kind. But he was not, He was westernised. He wore European clothes at the school and, at least when she was staying with them, at home. They ate at a table, seated on hardwood chairs and talked about art and music and the affairs of the school, but never politics. There was a cloth on the table, there were knives and forks to eat with, and ordinary china plates. At dinner Mrs. Chaudhuri sat with them, although she took almost no part in the conversation and ate practically nothing. A woman servant waited on them, the same woman who did the cooking. Miss Crane would have felt more comfortable if the woman had been an untouchable because that would have proved, in the Chaudhuris, emancipation from the rigidity of caste. But the woman was a Brahmin.

They had coffee in the room that overlooked the verandah, in which she and Miss de Silva had sat on old cane chairs, but where they now sat on low divans with their feet on Kashmiri rugs. Miss de Silva had been content with an oil lamp; Mr. Chaudhuri had rigged up an electric light that ran from a generator in the compound. They sat in the unflattering light of one naked electric bulb around which moths and insects danced their nightly ritual of primitive desire for what might burn their wings. At this point, between the eating and the singing, Mrs. Chaudhuri always left them, presumably to help or supervise the woman in the kitchen.

Tonight Miss Crane drank the bitter coffee, more conscious than ever of the unsympathetic silence that always fell directly she and Mr. Chaudhuri were alone. She longed to know the news but accepted in its place as proof that in one respect at least the night was normal: the croaking – beyond the verandah – of the frogs who had come out in their invisible battalions after the evening rains.

She wanted to say: Mr. Chaudhuri, what honestly is the school to you? but did not. To say that to a man was to question a course which, to judge by his actions, he had set his mind, even his heart on.

"You are a fool, Edwina Crane," she told herself later as she undressed, preparing for bed. "You have lost another opportunity, because hearts are no longer set on anything and minds function as the bowels decide, and Mr. Chaudhuri would talk if you knew the questions to ask and the way to ask them. But he is of that younger generation of men and women who have seen what I have seen, understood what I understand, but see and understand other things as well."

*

And so she slept, and woke at four, as if aware that at such an hour people of her colour might have cause to be wakeful, on their guard. For at this hour the old man in spectacles was also woken and taken, and the Deputy Commissioner in Mayapore was woken, and warned, and told to set in motion those plans whose object was to prevent, to deter. And in the morning, having slept again only fitfully, Miss Crane was also woken and told by Mr. Chaudhuri that on the day before in Bombay the Congress had voted in favour of the working committee's resolution, that the Mahatma was arrested, that the entire working committee were arrested, that this no doubt was the signal for arrests all over the country. At nine she walked to the school with Chaudhuri to take the Sunday morning Bible class and found that only the children from Kotali had arrived. So she sent him on his bicycle into Dibrapur. He returned shortly before eleven and told her that the shops were closing in the town, that the police were out in force, that the rumour was that three of the municipal officers had been arrested by order of the District Superintendent of Police in Mayapore and taken to Aligarh, that crowds were collecting and threatening to attack the post office and the police station.

*

"Then I'll ring Mayapore and find out what is happening there," Miss Crane said.

She put down the reports she had been co-ordinating. There was a telephone in Mr. Chaudhuri's bungalow.

"You can't," he told her. "I have already tried. The lines have probably been cut."

"I see. Well then. One of us must take the children back to Kotali, rather than risk anything happening to them here. So I'd better do that and be getting on my way. You had better go back to look after Mrs. Chaudhuri, and perhaps keep an eye on the school if you can manage it."

Mr. Chaudhuri looked round the shabby little room and then at Miss Crane.

"There is nothing to safeguard here," he said, "except the children. Take them in the car and I will come with you on my bicycle. If there are bad people on the road you will be safer if I am also seen."

"Oh, I shall be safe enough. What about your wife?"

"You are the only English person here," he said. "My wife will be all right. They may well come here after they have finished with the post office and the police station, or whatever it is they have in mind. They may come from either direction. So we will both go with the children to Kotali."

Miss Crane looked round the room too. The schoolhouse had always reminded her of the one she visited years ago with Mr. Grant. Mr. Chaudhuri was right. There wasn't much in the building worth saving, except the building itself, and even the worth of that was doubtful. She doubted, too, that either of them, in present circumstances, could stand in the doorway and successfully deny entry to an angry crowd. She glanced at Chaudhuri, remembering Muzzafirabad where she had been alone.

"You seem pessimistic," she said.

"I have seen the people and heard the talk."

"You're sure about the telephone?"

"Yes, I am sure."

For a moment they looked at each other straight, and Miss Crane thought: This is the way it happens when there is real trouble – the little seed of doubt, of faint distrust, of suspicion that the truth is not actually being told. If the phone is cut, then it is cut. If it is not cut perhaps Mr. Chaudhuri has picked it up, got no immediate answer and jumped to conclusions. Or it may not be cut and Mr. Chaudhuri may know that it is not but tells me it is because he wants me to set off on the road to Kotali.

"Very well, Mr. Chaudhuri," she said. "I think you are right. We'll cram the kids into the Ford somehow and you can come along on your bike."

He said, "One thing I hope you understand. I am not afraid

to stay here. If you wish the building to be protected I will stay and chance my arm."

"If they find it empty they may leave it alone," she said.

"It is as I was thinking."

She nodded, and stood up, collecting the reports, putting them tidily together, edge to edge. Chaudhuri waited. She said, "Tell me your honest opinion. Is it serious this time?"

"It is serious."

They always know, she thought, and then: This is how it happens too, to call them "they" as though they are different.

"All right then, Mr. Chaudhuri. Perhaps you'd collect the children together."

He nodded, went to the door and out to the courtyard at the back where the children were playing.

She put the reports into her brief-case and then remembered that her gladstone bag, although already packed for the journey home, was still at Mr. Chaudhuri's bungalow. She went out, called to him above the yelling of the children to whom he had just broken the news that school was over.

"My bag," she shouted. "It's at the bungalow. I'll pop down and get it and say goodbye to your wife."

"I have sent my wife to the house of a friend," Mr. Chaudhuri shouted back. "And your bag is in the car. I brought it with me."

"Thanks," she said, and went back into the office for the brief-case. She switched on the radio. Again there was only music, from All-India Radio, English music for the forces. She left the radio on while she closed the straps of the brief-case. The radio was a lifeline of sorts. I am calm, she thought, automatically calm, as in 1914, and 1919, and 1930, other times. Over thirty-five years I have become used to sudden alarms. But I am also afraid. In such circumstances I am always a bit afraid. And I am ashamed, and am always ashamed, because of my suspicions – this time first over the telephone, and now over the gladstone bag.

"Mr. Chaudhuri," she called, going to the doorway. "When they're ready bring them round to the front and I'll get the car started."

And in my voice, she said to herself, there – always there – the note of authority, the special note of *us* talking to *them*, which perhaps passes unnoticed when what we talk about is the small change of everyday routine but at times of stress always sounds like taking charge. But then, she thought, we are, we are in charge. Because we have an obligation and a responsibility. In this present instance her main responsibility lay seventy miles away in Mayapore. Things were always worse in the towns.

When she brought the car from its shelter at the side of the schoolhouse, Mr. D. R. Chaudhuri, BA, BSc, was standing waiting, with the children of the poor and the sometimes hungry gathered round him, playing their games.

*

In times of civil disturbance news or rumours of riots in the towns attracted from the villages men whose main preoccupation was the prospect of loot. This is what Mr. Chaudhuri had in mind when he spoke of bad people on the road between Dibrapur and Kotali, and Miss Crane knew that in leaving Dibrapur behind they were probably running into trouble as well as away from it.

There was also the question, for her, of continuing on from Kotali the seventy-odd miles through village after village to Mayapore. In this southern part of the district the land was slightly undulating, but still open, with cultivation on both sides of a good metalled road, and few trees. At least on most parts of the road you would be able to see trouble coming from a distance. From experience Miss Crane knew what to look out for: in the dry weather, when the dirt strips on either side of the metal were powdered to the consistency of ground chalk, the cloud of dust which as it got nearer revealed men strung out across the road; in the wet, the same men, but more suddenly, without the earlier warning of the dust they raised, so that at first glimpse you could already make out that some were carrying staves. Starting from one village, three or four men in the course of several miles could become a score. A car, coming at speed, showing no signs of stopping, could scatter them at the last moment, but still be vulnerable to the stones they might pick up at the car's approach. Miss Crane had, once in her life, in the troubles of 1919, run such a gauntlet, but the car she was in that time was driven by a determined young European policeman who had come to rescue her from an outlying schoolhouse where, as her superintendent back at headquarters had suspected, she was virtually a prisoner.

"Whether I could do the same as the young policeman," she thought, "blowing the horn and driving like mad, will depend on the size of the crowd." Mr. Chaudhuri could not drive. She did not know whether to be glad or sorry.

The size of the crowd depended on three things: the nature of the disturbance in the town which dictated the likely quantity of loot to be expected; the general temper of the surrounding villages and the number of men in each of them who had time and inclination to take the opportunity of filling their pockets; and finally the degree of control that the village headmen and rural police were able to exercise.

Each village had its watchman or chaukidar, a paid servant of the Government, and the villages were organised in groups under police detachments. A gang reaching a village where the police post was effectively manned, might then be dispersed. At a post where the police decided to look the other way or judged from the temper of the crowd that it was wiser to lock themselves in, the crowd passed by; and grew.

Reaching the village of Kotali with the cargo of laughing children, Mr. Chaudhuri still pedalling some distance behind, Miss Crane was met by the chaukidar and the headman and several men and women who had been on the point of setting out to bring the children back from school. The chief constable in charge of the police post in Garhwar, the next village along the road, had sent a message to say that he could no longer get through on the telephone to sub-divisional police headquarters in Dibrapur, that he assumed trouble had broken out following the news of Mr. Gandhi's arrest, and that the people of Kotali should therefore be on their guard to protect their property and their lives from dacoits and rioters.

The people of Kotali were, the headman said, very angry with the chief constable in Garhwar. They said he must have been warned at least the day before to expect trouble, and had not bothered to tell them. If they had been told they would not have let the children go to school that morning. The mothers thanked Miss Crane for returning them safely and offered her some tea, which she drank by the roadside, sitting on the chair they brought out and put under a tree. They gave Mr. Chaudhuri tea as well.

"I shall pray for rain," she told him, smiling. "There's nothing like a good downpour to cool people off. If it's wet they'll stay at home."

Mr. Chaudhuri said nothing. He finished his tea and walked

away and spoke for some time to the chaukidar and the headman. When he came back Miss Crane was finishing her second cup. She was hungry but had refused the offer of food.

"You must stay here, Miss Crane," Mr. Chaudhuri told her. "In this village everyone is your friend because of the children. It is dangerous to drive to Mayapore."

She shook her head, put the cup down on the tray a young girl stood holding in readiness. "No," she said, "I have to be getting on."

"They will look after you. The headman invites you to stay in his home."

"It's very kind of him and I truly appreciate it, but I must try to get back."

"Then stay for just an hour or two only. I will go back to Dibrapur. Who knows but that it is all a storm in a teapot? If it is then you can stay one more night in the bungalow and go to Mayapore tomorrow. The telephone will probably be working again by then."

"And if it isn't all a storm in a teapot?"

"Then you shouldn't go to Mayapore at all. You should stay here where everyone is your friend."

"I've got friends in Mayapore too. And Mr. Chaudhuri, I also have responsibilities. I know you mean it kindly but I do really have to be getting on."

"You have had nothing to eat."

"I'm not hungry."

"I will get you something to eat."

"I don't think I *could* eat. You see this sort of thing always makes me feel a bit sick." It wasn't true. This sort of thing always made her ravenously hungry. But if she stayed for the food, she thought, her determination to be on her way might weaken.

Mr. Chaudhuri raised his arms slightly, a gesture of surrender. "Then I am coming with you," he said, "we had better go now," and turned away, ignoring her reply of, "Don't be silly, it's quite unnecessary," went to speak again to the chaukidar and the headman. Two or three of the children gathered round her. To please her they recited "One, Two, Buckle my Shoe". She laughed and said that it was well done. Mr. Chaudhuri was walking up the road to the headman's house. He glanced back and indicated he would not be very long. A mother came with a plate covered by a napkin. Beneath it there were piping hot chappattis. More tea was offered.

Another woman brought a bowl of dal, and a spoon. She waved the spoon aside and began to eat, breaking off bits of chappatti and scooping the dal up with them. The sweat was forming on her forehead. It was so hot and humid. While she ate the people stood watching. I hate it, she thought, I have always hated it, this being watched, like something in a zoo, seated on a chair, under a tree, by the roadside.

"You see," she said to Mr. Chaudhuri when he came back, "they've forced it on me."

"It is for kindness," he said, as if giving her a lesson she had never learned properly, "and for hospitality."

"Well, I know that," she couldn't help replying. "But help me out with the chappattis. There are far more here than I can cope with."

"No," he said, "they are for you. Try to finish them. Do not give offence. I also will eat. They are preparing. Then we will go to Mayapore."

"What about Mrs. Chaudhuri?" she asked.

"She is safe with her friend. They will send someone from here to tell her where I have gone."

After a moment, looking up, catching his watchful eye, she said, "Thank you, Mr. Chaudhuri," and then, after a bit of difficulty, "I should have been afraid alone."

*

In the next village, Garhwar, the police were waiting, squatting by the roadside in the shade of a banyan tree. Near the tree there was a whitewashed Hindu shrine. The priest in charge of the shrine sat half-naked on the hard-mud verandah of his hut, watching them. The police were armed with sticks. Seeing the car approach, the head constable got up from his haunches and flagged them to a stop. It was his duty to warn her, he told Miss Crane in Urdu, having saluted her and glanced at Mr. Chaudhuri, that it was dangerous to proceed. He had been instructed to stand by and to expect trouble.

"When were you so instructed?" Miss Crane asked, also in Urdu.

He had been instructed early that morning to stand by, and yesterday to be prepared for trouble.

"You should have sent a message at once to Kotali," she said.

He had sent a message to Kotali. He had done so on his

own initiative. He had not been instructed to send any message but only to stand by and be prepared for trouble.

"You should have sent a message yesterday, but it's no matter," Miss Crane said. Perhaps he would be good enough to tell her if he had any information about what was happening in Mayapore and between Garhwar and Mayapore.

"I have no information," he said. "The telephone line to Dibrapur is now out of order."

"You mean cut?"

It was possible that it was cut. Also possible that it was just out of order. It was because he had been warned to stand by and to expect trouble and because immediately afterwards he found the telephone out of order that he had sent messages to Kotali and to the other villages in his jurisdiction. He had sent the messages by ordinary men and women from Garhwar as he could not afford to send any of his men in case trouble came suddenly. He had done everything possible. There was not much he could do with a handful of men if real trouble came. There were many bad people in the villages. His life and the lives of his men were in danger. Perhaps the memsahib would tell the sub-inspector sahib in Tanpur that Head Constable Akbar Ali in Garhwar was standing by as instructed but was without means of communication.

"Shall we reach Tanpur safely then, do you think?" Miss Crane asked.

He did not know, but the police in the Tanpur division of the district, under whose jurisdiction the Dibrapur subdivision came, were all men of character and determination. He thought it possible that she would reach Tanpur, but it was his duty to warn her that it was dangerous to proceed, and of course he could not answer for the division beyond Tanpur, where there were many villages full of bad people who might be converging on Tanpur, and perhaps on Mayapore, if Mayapore was in a state of civil disturbance. But Sub-Inspector Govindas Lal Sahib in Tanpur would no doubt be in a better position to advise her about that.

They reached Tanpur at two o'clock. Tanpur was a small town, dirty, poor, and smelling of ordure. The police who were out in force, patrolling the main street, consisted of six men and the assistant sub-inspector. But there was no sign of Sub-Inspector Govindas Lal who, his assistant said, had been trying to make contact with the District Superintendent Sahib's headquarters in Mayapore and had gone out an hour ago in a truck with one constable and three linesmen from the posts and telegraphs to find out where the wires were cut between Tanpur and Mayapore. The lines were also cut between Tanpur and Dibrapur, but the line to Mayapore was the most vital. Mr. Chaudhuri told the assistant sub-inspector that the police post in Garhwar was also cut off, but that they had seen no lines down between there and Tanpur itself, or indeed any lines down all the way from the schoolhouse in Dibrapur. The assistant sub-inspector explained that to telephone from Garhwar to Tanpur or from Tanpur to Garhwar the call had to go through the Dibrapur exchange, and that it looked as though the lines must have been cut close to the Dibrapur exchange or even that the Dibrapur posts and telegraphs had been destroyed.

"Is it safe to proceed?" Mr. Chaudhuri asked.

"Who can say?" the man replied. "If no harm has come to the sub-inspector sahib, then you will find him on the road ahead." In Tanpur itself there had been crowds collecting in the morning but the sub-inspector sahib had persuaded them to disperse. He had put it about that the military were on their way from Mayapore to maintain order. The shops were still closed, which was contrary to regulations, but the people were staying in their homes and the last instructions from Mayapore, early that morning, were to the effect that crowds should be persuaded to disperse if possible, but not provoked. The shopkeepers could have been forced to open their shops, but if people were not to be provoked it was better to let them stay shut. So far, then, all was quiet, but if the sub-inspector sahib did not return soon he did not know how long this state of affairs would continue. "But we are pulling on all right," he said to Miss Crane, suddenly, in English.

"We'll see the sub-inspector and tell him."

But they did not see the sub-inspector. Five miles beyond Tanpur they found what looked like his truck, upside down on the roadside where it had been overturned in the place where it must have been parked, next to a telegraph pole. If the truck belonged to the sub-inspector then he had found where the wires were cut, but not been given time to repair them. They lay tangled and coiled in the ditch at the side of the road.

"We must go back," Mr. Chaudhuri said. "They have abducted Sub-Inspector Govindas Lal."

"And the linesmen," Miss Crane pointed out.

"Perhaps it was the linesmen who abducted him. The posts and telegraphs people are sometimes very bolshie."

"But there were only three linesmen. And the sub-inspector had a man with him and was probably armed. There must have been other men."

"Which is why we should turn back, Miss Crane."

The sky was clouded over, but there was still no rain. "It's ridiculous," she said. "Yesterday I drove along this road and everything was as quiet as the grave and safe as houses. Now suddenly there are cut telegraph wires, upturned trucks and vanished sub-inspectors of police. It is really very *silly*." She laughed. "No, Mr. Chaudhuri, if you like I'll take you back to Tanpur, but I shall press on afterwards to Mayapore because I've just seen the *funny* side. But if I take you back to Tanpur the people will know we've gone back for a good reason, and then it will come out about the sub-inspector. And the assistant sub-inspector will probably panic and the funny side might stop being funny."

Mr. Chaudhuri was silent for a while. Presently he sighed and said, "I don't follow your reasoning, Miss Crane. It is an example no doubt of British phlegm. You are mad. And I am mad to let you go, let alone go with you. All I ask is that if we see a crowd of people on the road, you put your foot hard on the accelerator."

She turned her head and again they looked at each other straight. She had stopped smiling, not because she was annoyed with him for calling her mad or had already stopped seeing the funny side, but because she felt there was between them an unexpected mutual confidence, confidence of the kind that could spring up between two strangers who found themselves thrown together quite fortuitously in difficult circumstances that might turn out to be either frightening or amusing.

And for Miss Crane there was something else besides, a feeling she had often had before, a feeling in the bones of her shoulders and in the base of her skull that she was about to go over the hump thirty-five years of effort and willingness had never really got her over; the hump, however high or low it was, which, however hard you tried, still lay in the path of thoughts you sent flowing out to a man or woman whose skin was a different colour from your own. Were it only the size of a pebble, the hump was always there, disrupting the purity of that flow, the purity of the thoughts.

"Yes, I will try," she said, "try to put my foot down and keep it there," and then wished that there were words she could use that would convey to him the regard she held him in at that moment, a regard deeper, harder than that she had felt for the ragged singing children years ago; deeper, harder, because her regard for the children had sprung partly from her pity for them – and for Mr. Chaudhuri she had no pity; only respect and the kind of affection that came from the confidence one human being could feel in another, however little had been felt before.

"Then," Mr. Chaudhuri said, "let us proceed." His lips looked very dry. He was afraid, and so was she, but now perhaps they both saw the comic side, and she did not have to say anything special to him just because his skin was brown or because she had never understood him. After all, he had never fully understood her either. She set the car in motion again and after a while she began to sing. Presently to her surprise and pleasure he joined in. It was the song she always liked the children to learn. All over India, she thought, there were brown and off-white children and adults who could sing the song or, at least, remember it if they ever heard it again and, perhaps, remember it in connexion with Miss Crane Mem. She sang it now, not sentimentally, but with joy, not piously, but boldly, almost as though it were a jolly march. When they had sung it right through once, they began again.

"There's a *Friend* for little *chil*dren
  Ab*ove* the bright blue *sky*,
A *Friend* Who never *changes*,
  Whose *love* will never *die*;
De *da*, de da, de *da*, *dum*
  And *change* with changing *years*,
This *Friend* is always *worthy* –"

Ahead of them the rioters were spread out across the road.

*

"I can't," she said, as the car got nearer.

"You must," he said. "Blow the horn, keep blowing it and press the accelerator, *press*."

He leaned out of the window to show his dark Bengali face, and waved his arm in a motion demanding right of way. "Faster," he shouted at her. "Faster, you're slowing down, keep pressing and blowing."

"I shall kill someone," she shouted back. "I can't. I can't. Why don't they move away?"

"Let them be killed. Faster. And blow!"

For a moment, closing on the crowd, she thought she and Mr. Chaudhuri had won, that the men were moving to give way, but then they cohered again into a solid mass. They must have seen her white face. A man in front began to wave his arms, commanding them to stop.

"Keep going!" Mr. Chaudhuri shouted. "Close your eyes if you must but keep going!"

She tightened her mouth preparing to obey, but failed. She couldn't drive into a mass of living creatures. "I'm sorry," she cried, and began to press on the brake pedal. She stopped the car some twenty yards from the man who was waving his arms, but kept the engine running. "They weren't going to move, they'd have died. I'm sorry."

"Don't speak," Mr. Chaudhuri said. "Now leave it to me. Don't speak." He put a hand on her wrist. "Trust me," he said. "I know you never have, but trust me now. Do whatever I say. *Whatever* I say."

She nodded. "I trust you. I'll do what you say." In her physical panic there was a kind of exhilaration as though she were drunk on the Deputy Commissioner's brandy. "But don't run risks. I'm not worth risks. I'm old and it's all gone and I've failed." She laughed. The men were approaching, swaggering. "After all, it's me they want," she said. "Not you. So that's it. If this is where it ends for me, let it end."

"Please, Miss Crane," he said, "don't be ridiculous."

The car was surrounded now. She found it difficult to distinguish face from face. They all looked the same, they all smelt the same: of liquor and garlic and sweat-soaked cotton cloth. Most were dressed in white homespun shirts and dhotis. Some wore the white Congress cap. They were chanting the words that the whole of India, it seemed to her, had been chanting since early in the spring. *Quit India! Quit India!* Mr. Chaudhuri was talking to the leader. The leader was asking what he was doing riding in a car with an Englishwoman. Mr. Chaudhuri was not answering his questions but trying to shout him down, trying to tell him that Miss Crane was an old friend of India, that only that morning she had saved the lives of many Indian children from drunken power-mad policemen and was on her way to a secret meeting of the

Congress Committee in Mayapore whose confidence she enjoyed and whose efforts to overthrow the English she wholeheartedly endorsed.

The leader said he did not believe Mr. Chaudhuri. Mr. Chaudhuri was a traitor. No self-respecting Indian male would ride with a dried-up virgin memsahib who needed to feel the strength of a man inside her before she could even look like a woman, and what would Mr. Chaudhuri do if they decided to take the memsahib out of the car and show her what women were for and what men could do? Not, the leader said, spitting on to the bonnet of the Ford, that he would waste his strength and manhood on such a dried-up old bag of bones. "She speaks Hindi," Mr. Chaudhuri said, "and hears these insults. Are you not ashamed to speak so of a *guru*, a teacher, as great a *guru* as Mrs. Annie Besant, and a follower of the Mahatma? Great evil will come to you and your seed if you so much as lay a finger on her."

"Then we will lay one on you, brother," the leader said, and dragged open the door, whose lock Miss Crane had failed, month after month, to have repaired. "Go," Mr. Chaudhuri said, as he was taken out. "Go now. It's all right. No harm will come to me."

"Pigs!" she cried in Urdu, trying to hold on to Mr. Chaudhuri's arm, using the words she had used years ago, in Muzzafirabad. "Sons of pigs, cow-eaters, impotent idolaters, fornicators, abhorred of the Lord Shiva . . ."

"Go!" shrieked Mr. Chaudhuri, from outside the car, kicking the door shut, his arms held by four men, "or do you only take orders from white men? Do you only keep promises you make to your own kind?"

"No!" she shouted back. "No, no! I don't!" and, pressing the accelerator, released the brake, nearly stalling the engine so that the car jerked, paused, and jerked again, throwing the laughing men away from the bonnet, and then it leapt away so that they had to jump out of its path. A couple of hundred yards further on she stopped and looked back. Three of the men were chasing after the car. Behind them Mr. Chaudhuri was being pushed from one man to the other. A stick was brought down heavily on his shoulders. She shouted, "No! No! Mr. Chaudhuri!" and opened the door, climbed out. The three men held their arms out, laughing, and called, "Ah, memsahib, memsahib," and came towards her. Remembering, she reached into the car and found the starting handle, stood in the road, threatening them with it. They laughed louder and struck postures of mock defence and defiance, jumped about grinning, like performing monkeys. Mr. Chaudhuri had his head covered by his hands. The sticks were coming down, thwack, thwack. Then he was on his knees, and then out of sight, surrounded by the men who were beating him. Miss Crane cried out, "Devils! Devils!" and began to move towards the three men, still waving the starting handle. They moved back, pretending to be alarmed. The youngest of them reached into his dhoti as if about to expose himself, shouted something at her. Suddenly they turned and ran back to their leader who had called out to them. The other rioters were standing over Mr. Chaudhuri who lay unmoving in the middle of the road. A couple of them were going through his pockets. The leader was now pointing at the car. Five or six men left the group surrounding Mr. Chaudhuri and came towards Miss Crane. Instinctively she backed, but held her ground next to the car. Reaching her they pushed her aside, roughly, angrily, as if ashamed they had not yet summoned up the courage to disobey their leader and attack her. Bending to the task they got their weight under the running-board and the mudguards and began to heave rhythmically, until of a sudden the car turned over. From this display of strength one of them, anyway, got courage. Turning from the car he came at Miss Crane, raised his hand and hit her across the face, once, twice, then pushed her back towards the ditch and, using both arms, tumbled her down the three-foot embankment. Falling, she lost consciousness. When she came to and had collected her senses and strength she scrambled up the bank on her hands and knees and found the Ford burning and the rioters in the distance.

Limping, she walked to where Mr. Chaudhuri still lay. Reaching him she knelt and said, "Mr. Chaudhuri," but could not touch him because of his bloody face and open eyes and the awful thing that had happened to the side of his head. "No," she said, "no, it isn't true. Oh God. Oh God, forgive me. Oh God, forgive us all," and then covered her face and wept, which she had not done for years, and continued weeping for some time.

She dried her eyes by wiping them on the sleeve of her blouse, once, twice, three times. She felt the first heavy drops of rain. Her raincape had been in the back of the car. She said, in anguish, "But there's nothing to cover him with, nothing, nothing," and stood up, crouched, got hold of his feet and dragged him to the side of the road.

"I can't help it," she said, as if to him, when he lay bloody and limp and inhuman in the place she had dragged him to. "There's nothing I can do, nothing, nothing," and turned away and began to walk with long unsteady strides through the rain, past the blazing car, towards Mayapore. As she walked she kept saying, "Nothing I can do. Nothing. Nothing."

A hundred yards past the car she stopped. "But there is," she said, and turned and walked back until she reached Mr. Chaudhuri's body. She sat down in the mud at the side of the road, close to him, reached out and took his hand.

"It's taken me a long time," she said, meaning not only Mr. Chaudhuri, "I'm sorry it was too late."

*

As Mr. Poulson said afterwards, the troubles in Mayapore began for him with the sight of old Miss Crane sitting in the pouring rain by the roadside holding the hand of a dead Indian. On that day, the day of the arrests of members of the Congress sub-committees in the district, Mayapore itself had been quiet. The uprising got off to a slow start. Only Dibrapur and the outlying districts appeared to have jumped the gun. Mr. Poulson set off from Mayapore in the afternoon, in a car, accompanied by one of Mr. Merrick's inspectors of police, and a truck-load of constables, to investigate rumours of trouble in the sub-divisions that couldn't be contacted by telephone, and although when he reached the village of Candgarh he found the sub-inspector of police from Tanpur, one constable and three linesmen from posts and telegraphs, locked in the police post, it was not until he proceeded along the road to Tanpur and found first of all Miss Crane's burnt-out car and then Miss Crane herself that he really began to take the troubles seriously.

The troubles which Mr. Poulson and several others began by not taking seriously took until the end of August to put down. Everyone in Mayapore at that time would have a different story to tell, although there were stories of which each individual had common knowledge. There was, to begin with, the story of Miss Crane, although that was almost immediately lost sight of following the rape of the English girl in the Bibighar Gardens on the night of August the 9th, at an hour when Miss Crane was lying in the first delirium of pneumonia in a bed in the Mayapore General Hospital. Later, when Miss Crane found it impossible to identify any of the men arrested that day in Tanpur, for a short while she came again into prominence. People wondered whether she was genuinely at a loss to recognise her own attackers and Mr. Chaudhuri's murderers, or whether she was being obstinate, over-zealous in the business of being fair at all costs to the bloody blacks.

But the Bibighar Gardens affair was not lost sight of. It seemed to the European population to be the key to the whole situation they presently found themselves in, the sharpest warning of the most obvious danger to all of them, but most especially to the women. Afterwards it was never clear whether the steps taken by the authorities following the rape of the English girl in the Bibighar Gardens sparked off worse riots than had been planned or whether the riots would have taken place in any case. There were some who said one thing and some the other. Those who held that there would have been little or no rioting if it hadn't been for the rape and the steps taken to avenge it believed that the men the Deputy Commissioner had ordered to be arrested on the morning of the 9th August were the right ones to have arrested, and that the action taken in regard to the Bibighar Gardens affair had caused worse disorders than the civil disobedience that was stopped by the arrests. Those who held that there would have been disorders in any event and that the Bibighar Gardens affair was purely symptomatic of general treachery said that the members of the local Congress committees whom Mr. White had no alternative but to arrest were simply figureheads, and that the real ringleaders of the intended rebellion had been under cover in places like Tanpur and Dibrapur. But at the time, there was no distinguishing cause from effect and the events of the following three weeks were of the kind that could only be dealt with as and when they arose.

It was not until the first week of September, the first week of quiet, that Miss Crane returned from hospital to her bungalow, and another fortnight was to pass before she felt strong enough to attempt to take up the reins again. It was therefore some six or seven weeks after the beginning of the uprisings in Mayapore district and some three or four weeks after their end, that on a Tuesday afternoon Miss Crane once more opened her home to soldiers from the barracks.

They would be, she knew, changed in some respects from the boys they were before the riots began. In hospital, and since, she had closed her mind to stories of the troubles, but she knew that the military had been called out in aid of the civil power, that for three or four days Mr. White was said to have lost his head and handed Mayapore over to the control of the local Brigade Commander. She had heard Indians say, although she had tried not to listen, that in those few days of Brigadier Reid, things had been almost as bad as in the days of General Dyer in Amritsar in 1919. There had not been any indiscriminate shooting of unarmed civilians, but there had been, apart from controlled shootings and consequent deaths, the forcible feeding with beef – if the story were to be believed – of six Hindu youths who were suspected or guilty of the rape in the Bibighar Gardens. There had been no public whippings, as in General Dyer's day, when youths were clapped to a triangle in the open street and flogged simply as suspects in an attack on an Englishwoman, but there were rumours that the youths who had been forcibly fed with beef had also been whipped and had now disappeared into the anonymous mass of those imprisoned with or without trial.

In the native town itself, as Mr. Francis Narayan repeatedly told her, there had been many charges by mounted police, and firing by the military to disperse crowds and punish looters and fire-raisers. In the district as a whole, as in many other provinces of India, there had been widespread disruption of railways, posts, telegraphs, looting of warehouses, shops, houses and Government grain and seed stores (which the people would be sorry for next year, Mr. Narayan pointed out, if the crops failed). Police posts had been attacked, policemen murdered. In one sub-division of the district, so it was rumoured, the Indian magistrate had run the Congress flag up over his courthouse, released prisoners from custody, fined liberals and moderates, illicitly collected revenues and hidden away money that should have been paid into the treasury. Miss Crane suspected that the story was apocryphal, but there did seem to be evidence that one of Mr. White's Indian subordinates was in disgrace and, since order was restored, had spent an hour weeping at the Deputy Commissioner's bungalow.

She was, in fact, too old a hand to believe everything told

her as incontrovertible truth, and too old a hand not to know that her simple soldiers who had found themselves fresh out from England, suddenly acting in aid of the civil power to reduce rebellion in a colonial empire they knew little about but must now think badly of (remembering home and the blitz and their comrades dead on the plains around Mandalay), would find it difficult to make sense of what had happened, and why it had happened, and why, now that it was over, the English and the Indians had apparently patched their quarrel and come together once more in a compulsive harmony.

There was in that word compulsive, she knew, the idea of a key to the situation, the idea of there being somewhere in this curious centuries-long association a kind of love with hate on the obverse side, as on a coin. But Miss Crane found herself now too tired, too easily weighed down by the sheer pressure of the climate and the land and the hordes of brown faces and the sprinkling of stiff-lipped white ones, to channel any of her remaining pneumonia-sapped energy into solving moral and dialectical problems. But she wished that in the days when she had had the energy, days which had ended abruptly on the road from Tanpur, she had taken one of the soldiers aside – and she was thinking of Clancy – and said:

"For years, since the eighteenth century, and in each century since, we have said at home, in England, in Whitehall, that the day would come when our rule in India will end, not bloodily, but in peace, in – so we made it seem – a perfect gesture of equality and friendship and love. For years, for nearly a century, the books that Indians have read have been the books of our English radicals, our English liberals. There has been, you see, a seed. A seed planted in the Indian imagination and in the English imagination. Out of it was to come something sane and grave, full of dignity, full of thoughtfulness and kindness and peace and wisdom. For all these qualities are in us, in you, and in me, in old Joseph and Mr. Narayan and Mr. White and I suppose in Brigadier Reid. And they were there, too, in Mr. Chaudhuri. For years we have been promising and for years finding means of putting the fulfilment of the promise off until the promise stopped looking like a promise and started looking only like a sinister prevarication, even to me, let alone to Indians who think and feel and know the same as me. And the tragedy is that between us there is this little matter of the colour of the skin, which gets in the way of our seeing through each other's failings and seeing into each other's hearts. Because if we saw through *them*, into *them*, then we should know. And what we should know is that the promise is a promise and will be fulfilled."

But she had never said this to anyone, even to Clancy. And the day came when Clancy reappeared, coming in force with his mates who had heard that the old maid had had a bad time and been brave and nearly died, and they were anxious to make her laugh and feel happy, so that she would forget her troubles and know that she was among friends, stout lads who had been through it a bit themselves, and who were grateful to her for the small thing she did for them that reminded them of home and safety.

But throughout that tea-time, not one of them, not even Clancy, so much as looked at old Joseph, so when they had gone and she had helped Joseph clear away but found no words to heal the wound to the old man's pride and self-respect, she left him to finish and, going into her room, took down the picture of the old Queen and locked it away, in the chest, against the time when there might, remotely, be an occasion to put it back up again.

PART TWO

The MacGregor House

Dooliya le aō
re morē babul ke kaharwa.
Chali hoon sajan ba ke des.

(O my father's servants, bring my
palanquin.
I am going to the land of my husband)

(A morning raga.)
Translation by Dipali Nag

NEXT, there is the image of a garden: not the Bibighar garden but the garden of the MacGregor House: intense sunlight, deep and complex shadows. The range of green is extraordinary, palest lime, bitter emerald, mid-tones, neutral tints. The textures of the leaves are many and varied, they communicate themselves through sight to imaginary touch, exciting the finger-tips: leaves coming into the tenderest flesh, superbly in their prime, crisping to old age; all this at the same season because here there is no autumn. In the shadows there are dark blue veils, the indigo dreams of plants fallen asleep, and odours of sweet and necessary decay, numerous places layered with the cast-off fruit of other years softened into compost, feeding the living roots that lie under the garden massively, in hungry immobility.

From the house there is the sound of a young girl singing. She sings a raga, the song of the young bride saying goodbye to her parents, before setting out on the journey to her new home far away. There are ragas for morning and evening. This one is for morning. The dew is not yet off the ground. The garden is still cool. A blue-black crow with a red-yellow beak swoops from the roof of the house looking for its breakfast. Where the sunlight strikes the lawn the dew is a scattering of crystals.

Surrounding the lawn there are bushes of bougainvillaea; white and red. Some of the bushes are hybrids and have branches that bear sprays of both colours. Elsewhere there are jasmine and beds of dark-red canna lilies. The house stands in the middle of the garden, protected from the outside world by close-formed battalions of trees; neem, pipul, gol mohur, tamarind, casuarina and banyan; it goes back to the late eighteenth century and was built by a prince who conceived a passion for a singer of classical music. To build a house and install a woman in it is an expensive way to beg her favours. It was said that he came to visit her morning and evening, and that she sang to him, the same songs perhaps that the girl is singing now, and that he became enamoured finally only of her voice and was content to listen while she instructed the pupils he permitted her to receive. Scheherazade told stories to postpone the hour of her execution. The singer sang to guard her honour. When the singer died the prince grieved. People said he died of a broken heart. The house was deserted, closed. Like the state it decayed, fell into ruin. The prince's son succeeded to the *gaddi*. He despised his father for his futile attachment to the singer. He would let no one live there. He built another house nearby, the Bibighar, where he kept his courtesans. He was a voluptuary. He emptied the treasury. His people starved. An Englishman at his court was poisoned and so the new prince was deposed, imprisoned, his state annexed, and his people were glad of it until time lay over the memory of the old bad but not the badness of the present. The decayed house of the singer was rebuilt by a red-faced Scottish nabob called MacGregor who feared God and favoured Muslims, and was afraid of temples. The story goes that he burnt the Bibighar to the ground because he said it had been an abomination. He died at the hands of mutinous sepoys.

His young wife is the first ghost. She comes dressed in the fashion of the times and stands on the verandah, swaying to and fro, as if nursing her dead baby, but her arms are empty. There is blood on her torn bodice. Her name is Janet MacGregor. A Muslim servant called Akbar Hossain died defending her.

MacGregor rebuilt the singer's house more than a hundred years ago on the decayed princely foundations, with money got, it was rumoured, from bribes. Foursquare, there is a flagged inner courtyard; on the outer aspect, verandahs with rounded arches shading the upper as well as the ground floor rooms. The brickwork is stuccoed and painted cream that always dries yellow. Stone steps lead from the gravel driveway to the front entrance. In the arches of the verandahs green chicks can be lowered or rolled up according to the season and the time of day. On the upper verandah there is a balustrade, but not on the lower whose level is three feet from the ground. Ranged along the ground, in front of it, there are clay pots filled with shrubs and flowers, and climbing plants that have embraced the pillars of the arches. An old man with a grizzled head, dressed in a white vest and khaki shorts that expose the knobs and sinews of his rheumatic legs, tends the plants and the flowers. This is Bhalu. His black skin is burnt purple. His bare toes cling to the gravel and are as horny as the shell of a tortoise.

It was on the stone steps leading to the verandah that the girl stumbled at the end of her headlong flight in the dark from the Bibighar Gardens; stumbled, fell, and crawled on her hands and knees the rest of the way to safety and into the history of a troubled period.

*

Yes, I remember Miss Crane, old Lady Chatterjee says. Long ago as it is, I still regret having thought of her at the time as a mediocre person but I only ever met her at Connie and Robin White's, and only at those awful dull dinners poor Connie had to give as Mrs. Deputy C when she needed Miss Crane as an extra woman to make up her table and balance the bachelors. Miss Crane wasn't my cup of tea. With one or two exceptions such as Connie White and Ethel Manners the European women never were and those who come out to India now don't seem to be anybody's except their husbands' and not always then. They're mostly lumps. In those days they were nearly all harpies. I used to think Miss Crane would have been a harpy if she'd got married and had a position to keep up. As it was, she was a lump with a harpy exterior, the kind of person who had nothing much to say but gave the impression of thinking a lot, which is all right in a man but distasteful in a woman. There aren't many women in positions of real authority and so it seems to me the rest of us have a duty to speak our minds. It's the only way the world can judge us unless we are among the fortunate few who are allowed to express themselves through action. Otherwise we have to rely on our tongues. I'm thinking of talk in mixed company. Woman-chatter has never greatly appealed to me because the minds that are spoken between the withdrawal from the dining-room and the return of the gents usually prove to be empty and you might as well give yourself a rest and think of something bleak and cool like snow.

I wrote Miss Crane off as mediocre because although she chatted quite pleasantly and intelligently over coffee she was mostly mumchance at the dinner table. Oh, not mumchance *tout court*. No. She never struck me as shy, although she was probably afraid of me. Her silence was of the ominous kind, which is where the idea of harpy came in because nothing was more ominous than the silence of a European harpy. But true harpy silence is always accompanied by a sly look or a vulgar little grimace from one harpy to another. There was nothing of that kind of harpy about Miss Crane. And then, over coffee, which is the time real harpies bare their talons, she showed herself, as I have said, surprisingly capable of *chat,* chat of an ingenuous nature, and this suggested lumpishness and made me think of her as another woolly liberal, a poor woman who had struggled hard against odds, even injustice, or plain bad luck, and had had to latch on to something both soothing to the mind and enlivening to the physique, like struggling through the monsoon on that dotty bicycle of hers to check that all the children were learning to be unselfish and public-spirited and keeping clean and reasonably well-fed in the process.

There was that typical silliness of a picture of Mr. Gandhi that she took down or was said to have taken down because she decided the old boy was being naughty whereas of course he was simply being astute. The English have always revered saints but hated them to be shrewd. English people who thought Gandhi a saint were identifying themselves with the thousands or millions of Indians who said he *was,* but saintliness to an Indian means quite a different thing than it means to an Englishman. An English person automatically thinks of a saint as someone who is going to be martyred, a man whose logic isn't going to work in a final show-down with the severely practical world, a man in fact who is a saint *per se*. Apart from occasional temptations (for which they prescribe hair-shirts) they expect these saints of theirs to be so *un*-earthbound that they have one foot in heaven already. And of course by heaven they mean the opposite of earth. They divide the material from the spiritual with their usual passion for tidiness and for people being orderly and knowing their place. On the other hand, to the Hindu there can't be this distinction. For him the material world is illusory and Heaven a name for personal oblivion. Personally I have always found the material world far from illusory and have never welcomed as pleasurable the idea of mindless embodiment in a dull corporate state of total peace, which is how you could describe the Hindu concept of God. The point is, though, that on this difficult journey from illusion to oblivion *anything* counts as practical, because everything is speculative. Well, but to come back to Mr. Gandhi, the Hindus called him a saint because for thirty years he was the most *active* Hindu on the scene, which may sound like a paradox to European ears but after all, given our bodies, to travel from illusion to oblivion requires tremendous mental and physical stamina – and, if you are anxious to shorten the journey for others, a notable degree of leadership and a high content of hypnotic persuasion in oratory. But as for Western religious *mores,* well, to get from the practical world of affairs to an impractical heaven requires nothing but an act we're all capable of, dying I mean, although disappointment in the event undoubtedly follows. Irreligious as I am I can't help being contemptuous of the laziness of western religions, and I can't help criticising myself for not being even a bad Hindu. But at least I don't make the kind of mistake Miss Crane made. If Mr. Gandhi thought of his material acts as largely illusory, as private steps taken in public towards his own desirable personal merging with the absolute, I really do as a practical woman have to admire his shrewdness, his perfect timing in putting the cat among the pigeons.

But for Miss Crane, poor woman, pigeons were vulnerable creatures and cats soft little beasts, and both had lessons to learn. I found out a lot about her when all that awful business was over, in fact I tried to make up for my previous bad judgment, but by then she was difficult to get to know, and in the event there wasn't much time. Rather late in the day I invited her here, but she never came. So I called on her once or twice. Her virtues were still less obvious to me than her failings. She still gave me the impression she thought pigeons were to be taught the benefits of giving themselves up and cats the advantages of restraint. Both benefits and advantages were spiritual and therefore for her divisible from the material kind – which to me, passionately committed to what goes on around me, is a nullification of nature. I am not a Hindu but I *am* an Indian. I don't *like* violence but I believe in its inevitability. It is so *positive*. I hate negation. I sit here in the MacGregor House in a positive state of old age, bashing off here and there and everywhere whenever the mingy old government gives me a P form, and it doesn't worry me in the least that in the new India I seem already to be an anachronism, a woman who remembers everything too well quite to make her mark as a person worth listening to today. You could say that the same thing has happened to Mr. Nehru for whom I have always had a fondness because he has omitted to be a saint. I still have a fondness for him because the only thing about him currently discussed with any sort of lively passion is the question of who is to succeed him. I suppose we are still waiting for the Mahatma because the previous one disappointed and surprised us by becoming a saint and martyr in the western sense when that silly boy shot him. I'm sure there's a lesson in that for us. If the old man were alive today I believe he'd dot us all one on the head with his spinning-wheel and point out that if we go on as we are we shall end up believing in saints the way you English do and so lose the chance of ever having one again in our public life. I have a feeling that when it was written into our constitution that we should be a secular state we finally put the lid on our Indian-ness, and admitted the *legality* of our long years of living in sin with the English. Our so-called independence *was* rather like a shot-gun wedding. The only Indians who don't realise that we are now really westerners are our peasants. I suppose they'll cotton on to it one day, and then they'll want to be westerners too, like practically everyone else in the East and Far East.

*

She sits, then, an old Rajput lady, wound in a dark silk saree whose glittering threads catch the light, with her white hair cut short, waved, tinted with the blue of dust from an enamelled Rajputana sky, much as years before she sat erect on the edge of a sofa and frightened Edwina Crane into the realisation that to work to, and put her trust in, the formula of a few simple charitable ideas was not enough.

*

But Miss Crane (the old lady goes on), if you are really interested in her, well let me explain why in the end I changed my opinion of her. She was not mediocre. She showed courage and that's the most difficult thing in the world for any human being to show and the one I respect most, especially physical courage. I usually suspect cant in all the chat that goes on about moral courage. Moral courage smells of refusal. The physical sort is like an invitation, and I find that open. I find it appealing. And in any case, you know, physical courage is not without morality. We speak of moral courage as if it's on a higher human plane, but physical courage is usually informed by moral courage too, and often couldn't be expressed without it. Perhaps you could say the same the other way round. Perhaps these notions of courage are western notions, divisible in the usual western way that says black is black, and white is white, and right is the opposite of wrong.

What an old mess I'm in with my Rajput blood, my off-white skin, my oriental curiosity, my liking for the ways of your occidental civilisation, and my funny old tongue that is only properly at home in English. At my age I smoke too many cigarettes and drink too much black-market whisky. I adore the Gothic monstrosities of the old public buildings of Bombay and the temple by the sea at Mahabalipuram. I think Corbusier did an interesting job at Chandigarh and the Taj Mahal brings a stupid lump into my throat. Did you ever see what they call the floating palace at Udaipur? Or the long vista from the Arc du Carrousel through the Place de la Concorde the whole length of the Champs Elysées at night with the traffic clustered at the Etoile? Or the city of London deserted on a Sunday morning when the sun is shining in October? The Malayan archipelago from the air? The toe of Italy from 40,000 feet up in a Comet? New York by night from the Beekman Tower, the first sight of Manhattan from the deck of a liner coming up the Hudson late in the afternoon? An old woman drawing water from a well in a village in Andhra Pradesh, or my great-niece Parvati playing the tamboura and singing a morning or evening raga? Well, of course you've seen *her*. But have you understood yet who she is?

These are not divisible, are they, these sights and people I've listed except, I suppose, in the minds of the people who encounter them and decide their meaning. Oh dear, I'm as bad as you, as any of us. Even when I'm not looking for a meaning one springs naturally to my mind. Do you think it is a disease?

Have the other half and then we'll bash off in and have dinner.

*

In the MacGregor House there is a room where the late Sir Nello Chatterjee deposited souvenirs of a life-time's magpie habit of picking up whatever caught his eye that might be reckoned a curiosity. He obviously engaged in a love affair with cuckoo clocks and cheap brightly coloured leatherwork, mostly orange, of the kind bought from bumboats at the Red Sea side of the Suez Canal. Perhaps the leatherwork celebrated a boyish delight not so much in the pouffes, purses and handbags, as in the lucky dip of baskets and ropes by which they were raised for inspection from the bobbing coracle-bazaars to the austere rock-firm height of the deck of an ironclad ocean-going steamer. He can seldom have resisted the temptation to possess the risen prize, or the obverse temptation to feel the feathery weight of the basket going down empty, weighted only by the coins or notes which were his response to and interpretation of the bargaining gestures of the fezzed nightgowned figure precariously astride below.

The pouffes and purses are scattered round this room in the MacGregor House, curiously dry and lifeless, like seaweed taken from its element, but also capable of bringing to the nose of a knowledgeable traveller the recollected smell of oil and water, of the faint stagnation that seems to surround a big ship directly it stops moving. India also seems to be at anchor. The cuckoo clocks are silent, ornate artificial bowers gathering dust, harbouring behind their shutters a score or more of startled birds who are probably hysterical from long incarceration and imminent expectation of winding and release. In Sir Nello's day the visitor to the room was entertained by the simultaneous cacophonous display of each bird's jack-in-a-box emergence, a sight Lady Chatterjee says she remembers as putting her in mind of a fantasy she suffered after visiting the morgue in Paris with an amorous medical student. Normally kept embalmed in their own disuse by her orders even when Sir Nello was alive, they have remained so, permanently, since his death. The visitor is discouraged from asking a command performance; instead, invited to admire the stuffed tiger prowling in a nightmare of immobility on a wooden plinth, the glassed ivory replica of the Albert Memorial that plays "Home Sweet Home" on a mechanical dulcimer, shells and stones from the Connecticut shore, a bronze miniature of the Eiffel Tower, little medallions from the kiosks in the Notre Dame Cathedral that are cold with the blessing of the commercial piety they evoke. There are paper lanterns that were carried away from a restaurant in Singapore in exchange for the payment of Sir Nello's grasping admiration and substantial appetite, the mangy boots of some Mongolian merchant encountered in Darjeeling after a journey over the Himalaya and engaged in Sir Nello's brand of thrusting acquisitive conversation. There are no weapons, no illuminated Moghul manuscripts or ancient jewellery, no Brobdingnagian trappings purloined from a flattered and impecunious prince's elephant stables: nothing of value except in the terms one eccentric might use of another eccentric's relics. There is, for instance, under glass, the old briar pipe that long ago was filled and tamped by the broad but increasingly shaky finger of Sir Henry Manners, one-time Governor of the province in which the town of Maypore played, in 1942, its peculiar historic role, but Manners was gone ten years before that, carried temporarily away by retirement to Kashmir and then off permanently by the claret and the sunshine which he loved, and a disease which even now is curable only in Paris, Athens and Mexico and of which he knew nothing until it ate through the walls of his intestines and attacked his liver, which the doctors described as a cancerous invasion. And Sir Nello has been dead almost as many years, of a simple heart failure. They had been friends and their wives had been friends and, as widows, remained so right up until Lady Manners's death in 1948.

Of an admirable quartet – admirable because they overcame that little obstacle of the colour of the skin – only Lili Chatterjee survives to recall directly the placid as well as the desperate occasions. Of the other actors Reid has gone, and the girl, and young Kumar into oblivion, probably changing his name once more. The Whites and the Poulsons and young Ronald Merrick seem to be lost, temporarily at least, in the anonymity of time or other occupations. Miss Crane set fire to herself. They are the chance victims of the hazards of a colonial ambition. Museums, though, arrest history in its turbulent progress. So – the MacGregor House.

*

"When I first saw Daphne," Lady Chatterjee said, referring to the girl, old Lady Manners's niece, "she struck me as, well, good-natured but inept. She was big and rather clumsy. She was always dropping things."

The MacGregor House still echoes faintly to the tinkling of shattered glass that can't be traced to present accident or blamed on any servant. Both Lili Chatterjee and her great-niece Parvati tread lightly and the servants go barefoot: so how account for the occasional sound of stoutly shod feet mounting the stairs or crossing the tiled floor of the main hall except by admitting Miss Manners's continuing presence? Through the insistent weeping of the summer rains there would be, one imagines, a singing of songs other than the ragas, in a voice not Parvati's, and the songs would be too recent to be attributable to Janet MacGregor. In any case Janet was a girl who can be imagined as given more to silence than sound, even at the end with the blood on her bodice and death approaching. Was the blood that of her baby or her husband? Perhaps it was her own. History doesn't record the answer or even pose the question. Janet MacGregor is a private ghost, an invisible marginal note on the title deeds of the MacGregor House that passed from European to Indian ownership when Sir Nello bought it in the early nineteen-thirties to mark the occasion of his return to the province and district of his birth. Lili Chatterjee was his second wife, fifteen years his junior. He had no children from either, which accounted possibly for the cuckoo clocks. And Nello was Lili's second husband. Her first was a Rajput prince who broke his neck at polo. She had no children by this athletic heir to a sedentary throne. And this, perhaps, followed by her similarly unproductive life with Nello accounts for her air of unencumbered wisdom, her capacity for free comment and advice. Widow first of a prince she was also the daughter of one. Her education began in Geneva and ended in Paris. For her second husband, reduced as she had been by academic training and worldly experience from a state of privilege to one of common-sense, she chose a man who had a talent for making money as well as for spending it. There were – perhaps still are although she does not mention them – blood relations who never spoke to her again for marrying out of the Rajput into the Vaisya caste. Sir Nello's father had only been a pleader in the courts of law.

And Nello's grandfather (she says) and his grandfather's fathers were only prosperous merchants and small landowners. Nello used to have some old family property still, out near

Tanpur, but it all went a long time ago. I think Nello gave some away to the peasants. He told me he had, but it may just have been a yarn, he may have got the idea from Tolstoy. He adored *Resurrection*. And he was very impressionable and eager to act out what he was impressed by. We Indians often are. Nello was a terrific mimic. He did Henry Manners at a party once and the Governor heard about it. So next time they met – Nello used to be called in quite often in an advisory capacity over questions of industrialisation in the province – next time they met Henry said, Well come on, Chatterjee, let's see it. And the point about Nello is that he couldn't resist doing the man right in front of him. He liked an audience that could judge him by the highest standards. That's how they became friends and why Henry gave him that old briar pipe you've seen in the glass case. Henry said he thought Nello's imitation would be even better if he had a real pipe in his mouth and not just an imaginary one. Of course, it wasn't better, but Nello pretended it was, and that's very Indian too, to pretend rather than give offence. Nello didn't even like the feel of the pipe in his mouth. He never smoked. Or drank. In fact on the quiet he was a bit of a glutton for self-denial, which is probably why he made a lot of money. And he was half-serious about religion. He said to me once, "Lili, what would you say if I became *sannyasi*?" You know what that means? It means when a man chucks everything up, leaves his home and family and bashes off with a staff and a begging-bowl. So I said, "Well, Nello, I'd bash off with you." So that put paid to that.

It's the fourth stage, you know, *sannyasa,* the fourth and last, on earth anyway. I mean in the Hindu code of how you should live your life. The first stage is training and discipline and celibacy, the next is raising a family and establishing a household. In the third stage – I suppose you'd call it middle-age, what you English call a man's prime, but really a time when your children are beginning to find you a bit of a bore and think their ideas best – in the third stage you prepare to loosen the bonds. You make sure your children are married off and provided for, and you bless your grandchildren and try not to stand in anybody's way. Then you reach the fourth. You bash off into the forest before you become a doddering old burden, and try to make up for lost time in the business of earning religious merit, which of course you can earn all your life but earn best near the end when you give up your worldly possessions, reject the world's claims and try to forget Self. Of course, the English are always aghast at the idea of *sannyasa*. They think it's awful, opting out of your responsibilities like that and then expecting to live off the charity of strangers. I always point out to them that they have their *sannyasis* too: all those poor old people nobody wants who get sent to Twilight Homes. You must admit the Hindus are practical. You needn't bother your head about the religious side. It's like the cow in that respect. The cow became holy and beef unclean to stop the peasants eating it when they were hungry. If they ate their cows there'd be no milk, no bullocks to pull the carts to take stuff to the market or to help plough the fields or draw the water or turn the grindstone. Well, everybody knows that. But it's the same with *sannyasa*. We persuade old people to bash off and make one less mouth to feed by making them think it's a way of acquiring merit. And we make sure they're fed and not left to starve by persuading people who can afford it to believe they acquire merit too every time they give a wandering *sannyasi* a copper or a few grains of rice. We do have our own special brand of social security, you see. And we've had it far longer than anyone else. And nobody pays taxes for it.

Women can also become *sannyasi*. Shall *I*, do you think? Is the MacGregor House becoming my ashram? These days I'm much alone as you can guess from my talking your head off like this. But I was really thinking of Miss Crane. You say her name was Edwina. That's something I didn't know. I find it rather difficult to get used to. I should have thought of her more as Mildred. Anyway, to me she has always been Crane, Miss Crane. A bird with long legs and elongated neck trying to flap its way out of danger, too slowly, you know, like in slow motion at the movies. On one of those three or four occasions I went to see her after the trouble, when people were saying she was already round the bend, I tried to get her to tell me why she'd resigned from the mission. There weren't any pictures on the walls. But there were these two blank spaces where you could see pictures had been. Well, I knew about one blank space, but not the other. I said, "I see you're beginning to pack." Mr. Gandhi had gone, as I knew, but I was curious to know what the other picture had been. A picture of Mr. Nehru? The founder of the mission? The Light of the World?

But all she said was, "No, I shan't need to pack." so I

guessed the mission johnnies had given her permission to stay on in the bungalow. You must visit it. It's still there. I went past it the other day on my way to the Purdah Hospital. I'm still on the committee, still making a nuisance of myself. Look out! they say, here comes old Chatters. I bash off there the second Tuesday of every month and usually go the Bibighar bridge way but they're resurfacing the road and you get stuck for ages in the traffic, so this time we went by the Mandir Gate bridge, and Shafi took the wrong turning, stupid fellow. So there we were, not going past the old mission church but Miss Crane's bungalow. I haven't been down that road for years. It seems to be full of banias who've moved in from the bazaar. There was this big gross fellow on Miss Crane's little verandah picking his toes and listening to his transistor, and I think there were a couple of goats eating what there was of the grass and half a dozen children playing tag. She had such a pretty garden, too. Horticulture was the only subject we seemed to have in common. I told her she must come and see the garden here when she felt up to it, but she never did. The garden here at the MacGregor House is the same as it was then, so you can imagine it in those days. Bhalu grows the same flowers in the same beds year after year. He's always been an orderly type of man. Daphne used to pick the marigolds for the table, but she did tend to trample the edges of the beds and she'd only been with me a few days before Bhalu came and begged me to stop young memsahib trying to help him. Because he *grew* the flowers he thought he should be allowed to cut them. I told him the young memsahib liked flowers and wanted to help and although she was always smiling had had a lot of unhappiness and had lost all her family except her Auntie Ethel, so we had to be patient, but perhaps try to get her interested in ferns and evergreens which always grow wild in the shrubbery and made much *chic*-er decorations than marigolds. Now it's Parvati who picks the marigolds. But she's as light as a feather and old Bhalu's only too glad to have extra time to snooze and dream he's back in the army, looking after Colonel James Sahib's garden. I haven't the faintest idea who Colonel James was, but as Bhalu gets older the colonel gets more and more VIP in his imagination, and now it seems the colonel can't have been anything less than personal aide to the Viceroy. It used to be a status symbol for an Indian family to hire a servant who'd worked for the old-style British. It still is, but that kind of servant is getting so old now, and useless, that it's better to get someone from the bazaar and train them up. Bhalu used to refer to Nello as the Chota Sahib. Indians were always called that by servants who'd worked for *your* people, to distinguish them from British burra Sahibs. Burra means big, and chota means small. But you must know that too. Nello always laughed, but I think it hurt him a bit, knowing his head gardener called him a chota sahib.

I wish Daphne had known Nello, but of course he died several years before she came to stay with me. They had the same sense of fun. In a big girl that kind of thing is more noticeable, isn't it? Or do I mean that big girls are jollier than ordinary size ones? But tiny girls are often jolly too, aren't they? I mean tiny English girls. Indian girls are mostly tiny. Look at Parvati now. If they're big they're awfully earnest and sometimes violent. They seem to act as if they have a special position to keep up. If they're taller than their husbands the situation becomes fraught. I was an inch shorter than Nello and five inches shorter than my first husband Ranji.

I'm trying to remember how tall Miss Crane was. Taller than I of course, but medium English height probably. The neck and the legs and the nose are all I vividly remember. I mostly saw her sitting down or sitting up. Dinner at Connie White's, and then when I visited her at the British General Hospital and at her bungalow after she'd been discharged but still wasn't well enough to get up. She received me the first time I went to her bungalow lying on a charpoy on the verandah. It was difficult seeing her in the British hospital. The English friends I had who were ill usually went to the Greenlawns nursing home and had private rooms they couldn't afford. If I wanted to visit there I could always fix it with Doctor Mayhew. And if anyone was in the general hospital they always seemed to have a room in the private wing and all I had to do then was ring Ian Macintosh who was the Civil Surgeon and ask him to tell someone to warn the sister-in-charge. But Miss Crane was in the public wing in a ward with three or four other beds and Ian was out of station the day I decided to go. I'd never been in at the main reception before. The girl there – she was Anglo-Indian, but as white as a European – said I couldn't see Miss Crane, and when I insisted she kept me waiting in the hall and only pretended to have sent a message to the ward sister. What she had done was send a warning up to her. It was rather silly because Daphne had been doing voluntary work at the hospital and she *lived* with me, but because I was an Indian I wasn't really allowed in, anyway, not welcome. There wasn't actually a rule about it, just an unwritten one. I could have gone to the military wing because there were Indian King's commissioned officers on the station. That meant I could have visited say Lieutenant Shashardri or his wife, but the civil wing was sacrosanct. When Mrs. Menen who was the wife of the District and Sessions Judge was ill she had a room in the nursing home, which Ian Macintosh always insisted should be multi-racial, provided people could pay for a room there. Although even then there was an unwritten rule that an Indian patient had to be of a certain type to get a bed. It didn't matter much and never caused any trouble because if an Indian was rich enough to afford it but not the right type his wife anyway was almost bound to be the kind of woman who wouldn't dream of going anywhere but the Purdah Hospital.

Anyway, there I was, the day I went to visit Miss Crane, sat down in the hall, hoping I looked as if I hadn't the slightest idea that anything was wrong, and after a bit all these lumpy QAs and harpy VADs started popping into reception on some excuse or other but actually to see if the rumour were true, that an Indian woman had had the brass to present herself at the desk and expect to be allowed up into the wards. I felt like something in a zoo, but then we often did in those days. I would probably have been sitting there still if Bruce Mayhew who had a consultant appointment there hadn't come whirling in and stopped dead and said, "Hello, Lili, what on earth are you doing sitting *there*?" I told him I'd come to visit Miss Crane and that the girl at reception was trying to get hold of the ward-sister for me. I didn't want to get the receptionist into trouble, but of course Bruce knew what was happening. He said there was no need to bother the ward-sister and that he was going up there himself and would take me. When we got into the room where Miss Crane was he stayed with us long enough to make it clear to the other English women in the ward that I was *somebody*. Not that it made any difference. When Bruce went out one of them rang the bell. Ordinarily a nurse would have answered it, but the ward-sister came in herself. I know Bruce spoke to her on his way out because he told me so afterwards. He went specially to her cubby hole and apologised for taking a visitor in to see Miss Crane without her permission. He didn't say who I was because he knew it wasn't necessary. I mean he knew she had been told an Indian woman had been trying to get in, and that she had intentionally locked herself in her cubby-hole so that she couldn't be "found". Anyway, in she stalked a few minutes after Bruce had gone and only a few seconds after this woman had rung the bell. She stopped in her tracks as if amazed to see anyone there. She said, "What are you doing here, don't you know visitors aren't allowed at this time of day?" I told her Doctor Mayhew had given me permission because no one had been able to find her. Oh, *I* am in charge of this ward, not Doctor Mayhew, she said, please leave at once. Was it you who rang the bell, Miss Crane? As if Miss Crane had rung to get me thrown out. And before Miss Crane could say anything, this woman who'd actually rung piped up, No, it was me who rang, my rest is being disturbed. She sounded like the wife of a foreman from the British-Indian Electrical. Cockney, overlaid with a year or two of listening to how the wives of the directors spoke. I'm sorry. That's awfully snob of me, isn't it, but I was upset and angry not only because of what was happening, but also because I saw I'd probably put myself in the wrong over the question of official visiting hours. But Daphne had always said nobody took any notice of them and just wandered about at almost any old time. And there *were* other people going in to visit patients. It was my bad luck that there was nobody visiting any of these other women in Miss Crane's ward just then. And what was so awfully unfair was the fact that poor old Miss Crane had only had two visitors the whole time she'd been there – the chaplain and Mr. Poulson who really only saw her officially. The poor man didn't have time for more than that. It was he who rescued her, you remember. After she'd come through the pneumonia he had to ask her a lot of questions about the men who had killed Mr. Chaudhuri. He didn't *have* to do that, it was really Ronald Merrick's job, but Mr. Poulson and Mr. White knew Miss Crane had to be treated gently and they knew Merrick wasn't a gentle sort of man. And Miss Crane hadn't been helpful with her answers. She wasn't popular any longer in the hospital. People thought she was holding something back so that an Indian killer would go free. When I visited her she'd been in the hospital three weeks and had only just been taken out of a side ward into this room with the lumps and harpies. Bruce Mayhew had told me on the way up that he appreciated my coming to see her. She had almost no white friends. For a day or two at the beginning she'd been thought a lot of in the hospital because she'd come through a bad time in the first riots. They would have liked her to be a heroine of the kind that breathed fire and got a few rioters swinging on the end of a rope. But she didn't breathe fire, and although in the end they got some of the men who'd led the mob and killed Mr. Chaudhuri, that was due to the tenacity of the sub-inspector in Tanpur, and people thought justice would have been done quicker if Miss Crane had helped with proper descriptions. I suppose it didn't help her, my going to see her, and certainly didn't help me, my going to see *her*, although there was nothing much that would have helped *me* in the circumstances. The few white friends she had were the kind who hadn't the time to go and see her, and her Indian friends weren't the kind who'd have dared even to try. Some of the soldiers from the barracks clubbed together and sent her flowers and there were a few gifts from poor Indians like Mr. Narayan who taught at the Chillianwallah school. Probably more gifts of that kind than ever reached her. The hospital staff wouldn't even have to look at the card to tell whether flowers came from an Indian or a European. I expect a lot were thrown away, so that she never had the chance of knowing how much the Indians liked her, not just for not giving evidence that wasn't absolutely in line with what she remembered, but for herself. I know Connie White and Mavis Poulson always *meant* to go and see her in hospital, but things were in such a frightful state, almost a state of siege, they never had the proper opportunity. It must have made her feel loved by no one. And about my own visit, you must bear in mind that Indians were hardly popular among the whites just then, and then of course, there was the other business, too. They all knew I was the woman in whose house Daphne was staying. It's what I told myself when I'd got over the anger and annoyance of being thrown out by that harpy sister.

What made being thrown out more or less bearable was the fact that Miss Crane didn't seem to care whether I stayed or went, so the situation resolved itself. The sister stood over the bed and I got up and Miss Crane said, "Thank you for visiting me, Lady Chatterjee." But the way she said it made it sound as if I were too late, or she were too late, or as if nothing that happened now could alter the way she saw things. A couple of days later Bruce rang me and said any time I wanted to visit Miss Crane I only had to appear at the reception desk. He'd kicked up an awful fuss apparently. He said the hospital staff simply hadn't realised who I was. I said, Oh Bruce, of course they realised. If I'd been just Mrs. Chatterjee the whole thing would have been a joke to them, something they could score over and then forget. But being Lady Chatterjee, the widow of a man knighted by their own King, that made it awfully serious, something they really had to take a stand over, quite apart from the personal jealousy they might feel not being Knights' ladies themselves. After all, practically every Indian who had them gave up his title and honours about this time and returned his decorations to the Viceroy for forwarding to King George or whatever, and that was thought frightful. If it wasn't thought frightful it was thought only right, because the Europeans always looked on Indian titles as a bit of a joke. If Nello had been alive I expect he'd have reverted to plain Mister along with the rest of them. These days a lot of people still use their titles even though they're not recognised by Government but in *those* days people used to say to me, Why don't you drop the Lady? Nello would have dropped the Sir. So I said I can't choose a course of action for a husband who's dead. If I drop the Lady I'm really dishonouring *him*, just for my own peace of mind. Anyway, he *deserved* his title.

There were people in Mayapore who said I only kept up with Lady Manners for snob reasons, *Indian* snob reasons, like calling an English person by his Christian name. They said the same when I had Daphne come to live here at the MacGregor House. She was Henry Manners's brother's daughter. Connie White told me people tried to snub Daphne in places like the Gymkhana, snub her by pretending not to know where Daphne was staying so that they could smirk or look shocked when she said the MacGregor House. She didn't go to the club much – at least not at first – because I wasn't allowed in there, even as a guest. The Deputy Commissioner himself couldn't have got me past the door. Even the Viceroy couldn't. She only went to show friendly to the girls she worked with at the hospital, but then Ronald Merrick tried to set his cap at her and began to take her out and around and she was at the club with him several times. That was another bad mark against her. Mr. Merrick was just about the most eligible bachelor on the station. He was quite good-looking, if a man with a permanent sneer in his eyes can ever be called that, but the main thing about him was his position as District Superintendent of Police. All the unmarried girls who didn't mind too much that he had no "family" to speak of had hopes of hooking him. He'd never taken much notice of them so they didn't take very kindly to Daphne for apparently getting hold of him without so much as a finger raised. Neither Robin White nor Jack Poulson liked him much, but they said he was good at his job. Judge Menen couldn't stand him, but never said so in so many words. I had him round at the MacGregor House because I'd been on good terms with his predecessor, a rather older man called Angus MacGilvray. I thought Mr. Merrick would be annoyed if he didn't even get an invitation, but I was surprised when he accepted it. He only came, though, because it was here he had the opportunity to meet Indians socially. You could see his mind working away, storing up little things that were said, so that he could go home and make a note on the confidential files that were kept so that whenever there was any civil trouble the most influential Congress wallahs and anyone who ranked as dangerous could be locked up right away. I guessed he cottoned on to Daphne because he saw it as a duty to be on terms with someone who might let slip things that were going on here that were kept from him when he visited. He saw the MacGregor House as a sort of Cliveden, a hot-bed of Indian intrigue, a forcing-house for English reds – which of course would be the opposite of Cliveden-ish, but you know what I mean. But I was wrong, I think. His reasons for cottoning on to Daphne were much more complicated than that. By the time I realised how complicated, it was too late.

I often wish I could have that time all over again, but knowing what I know now. Not just for Daphne's sake, but for Miss Crane's sake. I think I could have stopped Miss Crane from becoming *sannyasi* in that especially horrible way. It's all right to give everything up as long as you realise just what it is you've *had*. Poor Miss Crane didn't. That last time I saw her at the bungalow, when she was sitting in her room and I noticed the two blank spaces on the walls, she said, "Lady Chatterjee, why do you come to see me?" And all I could think of to say was, "To see if you want anything." Well, I ask you, what was the good of that? Can you imagine a woman of Miss Crane's temperament admitting that she needed help? What should I have said, do you think? Said instead of what I did say? Well, if she were there now, and not that fat fellow picking his toes and listening to film music on his little radio, I think I'd say, "Because neither of us must give up, and I can see you're about to."

I must get my times sorted out. I work it out that I paid her *three* visits, not four. The first time in the hospital, and then on the occasion when she was still laid up but at home and I found her resting on the verandah with that old servant of hers hovering about, watching from the doorway to make sure she wasn't upset, and then a few weeks later when I'd heard about her resignation which came as a surprise to everybody. After my first visit to the bungalow I thought I should keep away for a while, but then people told me she'd had her soldiers to tea again. So I thought, Now's the time. Now we can get to know each other. But I didn't go right then. I had so much to do. I didn't go until I heard about her resignation and that people were saying she must have gone a bit bats. I called one afternoon. The servant was on the verandah, which of course was perfectly normal, but I realised he was on guard. He said Miss Crane was very busy and couldn't see anyone and I was about to go when she called out, Who is it? and he went inside, then came out again and said I could go in. She was in her bedroom, sitting in an armchair. She didn't get up and didn't ask me to sit down, but I sat all the same and it was then she said, Lady Chatterjee, why do you come to see me? I thought for a moment, and then came out with this silly remark, To see if you want anything. It's kind of you, she said, but there's nothing I want. I said, I hear you've resigned from the mission. She simply nodded her head. I looked round the room, as you do, don't you, when you're with someone in a room you've just heard they're going away from. And I saw those two blank spaces on the walls, one of which must have been made by Gandhi and the other by someone else. So I made this remark about packing already. Oh, I shan't need to pack, she said, and then after a bit, while I was trying to work out why, she *smiled*, but to herself, not to me, so I thought, Well, it's true. She's nuts. It was because I thought, Oh, she's nuts, that I didn't ask what she meant, didn't say, The mission johnnies are going to *give* you the bungalow then? I didn't ask because it seemed so unlikely and I thought her answer would only add to the feeling I had that she was off her head, and I didn't feel up to coping with the embarrassment of having it proved. So I left it at that, she wouldn't need to pack. Poor Miss Crane. I ought to have followed up, I ought to have said, Why? Not that she'd have come right out with the real answer. The awful thing is it was in my mind afterwards that it may have been only then, when we were sitting there talking about not needing to pack, that she really understood why she wasn't going to pack, saw why there wouldn't be any need. That smile, you see, coming some while after she'd said, Oh I shan't pack, I shan't be packing, I shan't need to. Then she changed the subject. She asked how Daphne was. How is Miss Manners? Like that, in that tone of voice, of someone asking about a *colleague,* as if between them they represented something, which I suppose they did. She didn't know young Kumar. If she'd known about Hari Kumar I expect she'd have said, How is Miss Manners? in the same tone as before but added, Is it true what I hear, what I hear about what they've done to young Mr. Kumar?

*

Dinner is the only meal Parvati has with the family, such as the family is: that is to say, Lili Chatterjee and young Parvati, the two of them. When there are no guests there is this picture to be had of them sharing one end of the long polished dining-room table, with two places laid close together, the old woman and the young girl, talking in English because even now that is the language of Indian society, in the way that half a century ago French was the language of polite Russians.

The man who serves them is quite young, too young to have been more than a small lad about the house at the time Miss Manners lived there, and actually he was not even that. He is a recent acquisition. He is from the south, a cousin of some kind of Bhalu, the old gardener. It amuses Lady Chatterjee that although it was on Bhalu's recommendation that Ram Dass, whom she calls Ramu, got the job of houseboy he has since had little to do with the gardener because Bhalu's position is so inferior to his own. He will not even admit a family connexion. Sometimes from the servants' quarters behind the house you can hear them quarrelling. The cook despises them both. He has cooked for a maharanee in his time. There is a girl sweeper called Sushila. Lady Chatterjee turns a blind eye to evidence that the Muslim driver, the handsome grinning Shafi, sleeps with Sushila. It is difficult to get enough servants and their wage demands get higher every year. Some of the rooms in the MacGregor House are shut up.

With all the chicks lowered the house is dark and cool even at midday. The ceilings are very high. In such rooms human thought is in the same danger as an escaped canary would be, wheeling up and up, round and round, fluttering in areas of shadow and in crevices you can imagine untouched by any human hand since the house was rebuilt by MacGregor. In these rooms, at night, even the artificial illumination of lamps and brackets fails to reach the remoter angles and areas that would lie far beyond the reach of a man standing on the shoulders of another. It is best to depend upon a humdrum eye-level for impressions; the strain on the neck otherwise is no less acute than the strain on the senses then of other years impinging on the present. There is in any case always a lulling feeling of immediacy in these ground-floor rooms, the present lying as it does in the lower levels, like the mist of a young day in ancient hollows. It is in going upstairs that the feeling of mounting into the past first comes and ever afterwards persists, no matter how many times the routine journey is undertaken. Bedrooms, after all, are more specifically the repositories of their old occupants' intimate sensations than the public rooms below.

Collecting a key from some arcane source or other – a guest never penetrates the barrier from behind which the control and ordering of the household is directed – Lady Chatterjee goes up the broad uncarpeted polished wood staircase that curves from the black and white tiled hall to the complex of landings and corridors and opens the mahogany, brass-knobbed door of the room where Miss Manners slept and which she still calls Daphne's room. It smells musty, as unused as the late Sir Nello's museum of schoolboy curios which suitably enough lies directly below it, with a view to the garden when the chicks are raised and a continuing view through the gaps between the bushiness of the shorter trees to the plains that surround Mayapore and the smudge of hills on the horizon. There is the spire of St. Mary's church, a mile or two distant, still standing, still as irrelevant to its background as any architecture, Anglo or Indian, seems to be in this strangely unfinished landscape that makes the monotonous chanting of the crows which are never at rest sound like the cries of creatures only partially evolved, not yet born, but sharpened already by desires the world will eventually recognise as hunger.

In the desk there are two of the letters Miss Manners wrote

to her aunt which Lady Manners afterwards gave to Lili Chatterjee, perhaps not wanting them herself, or the recollections they stirred; and these, possibly, reveal similar hungers and contrasting desires: unco-ordinated, irrelevant. She must have written them – unless she wrote them at night when the crows fitfully slept, impatient of morning – to the same accompaniment they are read to all this time after. The letters, read to the accompaniment of this continuing unchanging sound, are curiously dead, strangely inarticulate. Why pretend otherwise? They do not resurrect the writer. They are merely themselves; like the photograph of Miss Manners which is signed with a calligraphic flourish by one Subhas Chand who used to take portraits of those people on the station who wanted a record for friends and relatives of what Mayapore had done to them. Subhas Chand, Lady Chatterjee says, had a booth in the shop of the chemist, Dr. Gulab Singh Sahib. And Clancy was pictured there, in full-face, as his handsome pushing self in spotless khaki drill, and in matey combination with the rustic Barrett, staring out at the world from a background (again irrelevant) of draped velvet and gothic fern (maidenhair in a brass bowl on a romantic revival monumental column around which graveyard ivy is invisible but naggingly present to the impressionable eye).

The pictures of Clancy lie irrelevant too, like gifts kept from a Christmas cracker, among the rest of Miss Crane's unclaimed personal effects which have somehow been preserved at Mission Headquarters in Calcutta; mouldering relics not of Miss Crane alone but also of sustained Christian honesty, and of the disinterested shrugs of distant Crane cousins, offspring of those poor ones who on her father's death turned up for the funeral in the mild hope of benefit and then departed, putting her out of mind and of temptation's reach of their own slender pockets in case the brave funeral face and declarations of self-sufficiency turned out to be untrustworthy. Having already seen in Calcutta pictures of Clancy, the Subhas Chand technique and signature, the quality of the matt-surfaced sepia paper he used for his prints (small cabinet size), all strike harmonious echoes of recognition when the picture of Miss Manners, memorially enclosed in a silver-plated frame, is first lifted from its place on the dressing-table which she sat at combing her apparently curly short-cut sepia hair.

You can't from this (Lady Chatterjee says, rubbing at a

speck of tarnish on the frame) get a real idea of her personality. I think looking at pictures of people you don't or didn't know but only know about is intensely unsatisfactory. Of course, it's fascinating to see for the first time a portrait of someone like that, someone whose name was at one time on a lot of people's lips, as they say. You're probably feeling that now, but once the initial curiosity has been satisfied there's a sense of anti-climax, isn't there? Or perhaps even of no climax at all because you can't be absolutely sure the picture is anything like a good likeness or even that it's a picture of the right person? Do you know, I sometimes take a second look at pictures of myself and Nello – that one downstairs taken at the garden party in Simla for instance, where we're sandwiched between Lord Willingdon and the Aga Khan, and I think: Is that really Nello? Did I really look like that? Did I ever smile in quite such a smug way? Almost coy-smug, glancing at something that has caught my eye but isn't in the picture. Since I can't even guess what it could have been that caught my eye, let alone remember what it was, I begin to wonder whether the woman in the picture (who anyway doesn't *feel* like me) isn't an impersonator, and the plump chap with her a man who isn't Nello but is taking Nello off almost as successfully as Nello used to take off Henry Manners. Willingdon and the Aga Khan look all right, but then when you meet and chat to blokes as high up as that you tend to look at them in only two dimensions, which is the way the camera looks at them too, so the photographic result is bound to seem authentic.

Daphne had this picture taken by Subhas Chand two or three months after she came to stay here. It wasn't her idea. Lady Manners wrote me and said: Tell Daphne I'd like a picture of her for my birthday but not to bother to frame it because I've got trunks full of frames from Henry's old Rogues' Gallery. It's what she and Henry called their collection of photographs. The Rogues' Gallery. Everything from old daguerreotypes of Henry's pa with his foot on a dead buffalo to groups taken at some beano with all the princes except one scowling at the camera because Henry's handsome aide had got the protocol wrong and stood a chap with a nine-gun salute closer to the Governor than a chap with eleven guns. And then there were all the snaps given to Henry and Henry's pa by servants – timid old boys pretending to look like tribesmen, all white whiskers and lopsided turbans. Henry never threw a single snap away. They all got framed and went with him wherever they were posted. When he died, Ethel had them packed up and put into trunks. I often wonder who this old silver frame originally had in it. I inherited it complete with Daphne's picture along with the two letters. I think if Daphne had given me a copy too, at the time she bashed off to Subhas Chand to have her picture taken for her Aunt Ethel's birthday, I think if I'd always had it, I'd see it as far more like Daphne than I do. But it came afterwards. It came here into this house, into this bedroom, when Daphne wasn't alive to come back in herself. I expect I resented it. It's always struck me as not quite belonging. It's Daphne all right – she had that kind of hopeful smile – perhaps she'd nearly knocked over one of old Subhas Chand's spotlights just before she sat down, and was still thinking: There I go again, just like me, catch me in a china shop, Auntie. It's a sweet smile though, isn't it? And that's come through. But photographers like Subhas Chand always make people's skin look like wax. There's not the tiniest crack in it anywhere, and around the eyes where there ought to be cracks, lines anyway, it's all been smoothed out by touching up and the real Daphne simply isn't looking out of them.

She had a habit of blinking whenever she began to speak, as if she couldn't get out the first word or two with her eyes open. And often she shut her eyes at the end of what she was saying. When she shut her eyes this little smile you see in the photograph used to come on automatically, as if her eyelids and lips were working off the same set of nerves. And it *was* nervousness that made her do it. I used to think of it as affectation. I met her for the first time when I went up to Pindi to spend Christmas with Ethel Manners. It was Daphne's first Christmas in India and Ethel wanted to cheer her up. I'd expected to find someone mopey, instead there she was, blinking at me and chatting at me. I sensed the affectation before I pinpointed the mannerism, before I *noticed* the blinking, but once I'd separated the cause from the effect I realised that what I called affectation was nothing more complicated than straightforward shyness. The eye-shutting and the smiling were to give herself confidence in company. Once she got used to you the mannerism disappeared. But it came back at once if a stranger came into the room. People instinctively liked her, though, and she never gave in to her shyness, she never seemed at a loss for a word.

What old Subhas Chand hasn't been able to disguise, at least from me, is that this is the portrait of a girl who was more comfortable in specs. She had to wear them to read or to write letters. According to the oculists, she really needed them all the time but her aunt discouraged her and said specs were a lot of nonsense for young people. What she meant was that specs just weren't attractive, especially on a girl. I discouraged her too, not because I thought specs could be unattractive, but because I knew you could cure bad sight by exercises, splashing the eyes with cold water, looking alternately from short to long distances, looking up from concentrated work like writing a letter or reading a book and focusing on some fixed object in the room several feet away. But Auntie, she used to say, she got into the habit of calling me Auntie, I can't *see* into long distances, I can't even see short distances properly. She used to stand at the window there, putting her specs on and taking them off. Eventually she made out where the hills are. She wanted so much to see everything there was to see. India was what we used to call a thing with her. She'd always wanted to come out. She was born in the Punjab but didn't remember any of it because her mother couldn't stand the climate and her father resigned from his service and went home into private practice when Daphne was still almost a baby. He was IMS. Years younger than his brother Henry. I don't think he minded leaving India at the time. He obviously chose to be a doctor instead of an administrator so that he wouldn't have to compete with clever brother Henry all his life. By all accounts his wife, Daphne's mother, was a tartar. She had to have everything her own way and she was a frightful snob. India obviously didn't suit her as the wife of a junior man in the IMS. Law and medicine are the two things we Indians have always shone at so I expect George – Daphne's dad – had too many Indian colleagues for Mrs. George's liking. She wanted him to be what today you people call a Top Person, with rooms in Harley Street and masses of top hospital appointments. But when he was in a fair way to getting what she wanted she changed her tack and saw herself as a leader of county society, so then there was the flat in town and the house in Wiltshire and poor George working himself to death bashing off from one place to the other. You can tell the effect it had on him from something Daphne said to me. She said, "Poor daddy always regretted leaving India, didn't he? I wish he were here with me now to see it all again." There were times when I thought she worked doubly hard at knowing India simply to make up to her father for what he had missed and probably admitted regretting having given up just to please her mother. And like all those apparently frail women who can't stand the Indian climate Daphne's ma turned out as strong as an ox. At least until she got cancer. And in my opinion that is a disease of the strong rather than of the weak.

*

Picture her then: Daphne Manners, a big girl (to borrow a none too definite image from Lady Chatterjee) leaning on the balcony outside her bedroom window, gazing with concentration (as one might gaze for two people, one being absent, once deprived, since dead, and now regretted) at a landscape calculated to inspire in the most sympathetic western heart a degree of cultural shock. There is (even from this vantage point above a garden whose blooms will pleasurably convey scent if you bend close enough to them) a pervading redolence, wafting in from the silent, heat-stricken trembling plains; from the vast panorama of fields, from the river, from the complex of human dwellings (with here and there, spiky or bulbous, a church, a mosque, a temple), from the streets and lanes and the sequestered white bungalows, the private houses, the public buildings, the station, from the rear quarters of the MacGregor House. A smell. Could it be of ordure?

After a few months the newcomer will cease to notice it. Ubiquitous, it translates itself from repellent through almost attractive because familiar stages into an essence distilled by an empirically committed mind, so that an old hand, temporarily bereft of it, nostalgically remembering it in some less malodorous place, will describe it to himself as the sub-continental equivalent of acrid wood-smoke at the end of a burnished copper autumn. But let the old hand's bereavement be of comparatively short duration: European leave, a rarified, muscular effort above the Himalayan snow lines. Let it not be, for instance, an eighteen-year absence ended by chance and luck and the lepidopteristic intention to pin down the truth about Miss Crane, Miss Manners and young Kumar, and the events that seemed first to flutter and then to shatter Mayapore but actually seem to have left it untouched, massively in continuing brick-and-mortar possession of itself (if not of the landscape feebly invaded by its architectural, artisan formation). No, let it not be long, let it be short so that on renewed association the returning traveller will cry, possessively, even gratefully: Ah, India! Otherwise, after eighteen years and a too swift transition by Comet through the increasingly disturbing ambience of Beirut and Bahrein (the warmth correspondingly mounting, bringing the smell out like the warmth of a woman's skin releasing the hidden but astonishing formula of an unusual perfume) the nose – unused, but imagining itself prepared – will flex its nostrils against the grave revelation of the car or taxi drive from Bombay's Santa Cruz airport, along a road that leads through fields where the source of the wafting smell may be tracked to the squatting early morning figures of male labourers casting their pellets upon the earth, there to lie, and harden, and encrust, and disintegrate, and lift in the currents of air into the generality of the prevailing winds.

Taking possession of the room to help, as Lady Chatterjee says, in the business of getting to know the surroundings that were Daphne's, left alone there, moving across the broad acres of uncarpeted floor, between the mosquito-net-shrouded bed and the door that leads into the private bathroom, one might – by attempting the journey from one island of Kashmir rug to another, not wetting one's feet in the striated sea of dark stained boards – play a variation of that old childhood game of not stepping on the cracks between paving stones and wonder if Daphne had time for similar absurdities. The bathroom is long and narrow. Green glazed tiles act on the walls from floor to shoulder height as shadowy mirrors of the room's contents and of its headless occupant. Perhaps Daphne, with her uncertain sight, was unaware of this and strode oblivious of truncated duplication by reflection from the door to the porcelain pedestal whose cistern, high up, is activated by one's pulling like a bell ringer on a long chain whose pot handgrip, moulded to the shape of the palm, emphasises the luxuriousness of a comparatively rare machine. The porcelain tub is as big as an artificial lake, empty at this moment as if drained for an annual scraping. Its webbed claw feet are those of some dead, amphibious monster sentenced to support it like Atlas supporting the world. The immense brass taps suggest twin flows of piped-out water of ship's pump velocity, but only the cold tap works; the hot – when the stiff faucet is finally budged – produces a hollow rasping echo and a skitter of rust flakes. But the cold is warm enough. The bathroom is airless. There is no fan and only one window high up above the lavatory pedestal. At the opposite end of the bathroom – fifteen paces on bare feet across lukewarm mosaic that is slightly uneven and impresses the soles with the not unpleasant sensation of walking over the atrophied honeycomb of some long forgotten species of giant bee – there is an old-fashioned marble-topped washstand with an ormolu mirror on the wall above it, plain white china soap-dishes and a white jug on the slab; beneath the stand a slop-bowl with a lid and a wicker-bound handle. Here too is the towel-rack, a miniature gymnastic contraption of parallel mahogany bars and upright poles, hung with immense fluffy towels and huckabacks in a diminishing range of sizes, each embroidered in blue with the initials LC.

Returning to the other end, literally ascending the throne which is mounted on a broad dais anciently carpeted in the deep blue red of mouldy cherries, the splendour of the paper-holder fixes the attention. Here are lions, gilt-maned, gilt-faced, each holding in its gilt jaws an end of the bracket which supports the roll of buff, wood-chip austerity paper. The jaw of the nearer lion (and presumably that of its mate on the other side) adequately receives the ball of the little finger. Its head is as large as a clenched fist, so large that its cheek rests almost upon the cheek of its gilded counterpart. The effect is of two big cats grinning over the simple duty they have to hold, in readiness, something that is required for a cat-like but, because of the paper, ridiculous human function.

Lying in the bath, the eyes engage the single 75-watt bulb in a shade the shape of a pantomime Aladdin's hat, and attempt to see, above, the distant shadowy ceiling. A brass jug, dented from falls on to the mosaic floor, rests on the wooden rack that lies athwart the tub. The scoop. One remembers and, having soaped, stands and scoops and pours and scoops again and so, closing the eyes against the contrary evidence of the sex, attempts a re-enactment of Miss Manners refreshing herself after a hard day on the wards of the Mayapore hospital.

*

(To Lady Manners)

The MacGregor House,
MacGregor Road,
Mayapore, 1.
26th February, 1942

Dear Auntie Ethel,

Please forgive me for not having written sooner. I hope you got Lili's telegram saying we'd arrived here safely. I'm sure you did. I can hardly believe it's a week since we said good-bye to you in Rawalpindi. It was sweet of you to let me come. The days have flown and looking back on them there scarcely seem to have been enough of them for us to have packed in everything we've done. I've just come back from my *second* day on the wards in the hospital which will show you no time has been wasted!

After Lahore the journey down was very interesting, much nicer than the one I did alone last year from Bombay to Pindi, which rather scared me because it was all so new and strange. I suppose I enjoyed this one because I've learned some of the ropes and anyway had Lili with me. She really *is* extraordinary, isn't she? Those awful English women in the carriage got out the next morning in Lahore. They were utterly beastly and never said a civil word to either of us. And those mounds of luggage they had that took up more than half the space! They hogged the little wc cubicle for over an hour after the train pulled out, and then sat up for ages drinking and smoking and talking as if neither of us was there while Lili and I were trying to get to sleep. (We had the upper and lower berth on one side of the carriage and they had the upper and lower on the other side.) I was so fagged I didn't wake up until the train had stopped at Lahore and there was all the fuss of them getting out. There was a chap to meet them, the husband of the one with her brains tied up in a scarf, I think. He came into the carriage at one point to look for something the one with the scarf was complaining had either been lost or *stolen*. They'd been out on the platform for some time while the coolies collected the luggage and he came in prepared to be rude. The poor chap looked awfully embarrassed when he saw *me*. They'd only complained to him about Lili, I expect. I was sitting up on the top bunk keeping an eye on *our* bags, with my hair all over the place. Lili had been up and dressed since five (so she told me afterwards) and was sitting there below me looking marvellous and cool as a cucumber, reading a book and pretending to be quite unaware of what was going on. Anyway he begged our pardon and thrashed about for a time, and the coolies thrashed about, searching under the seat and everywhere that didn't make it look too pointed that these women had suggested *we* might have pinched whatever it was one of them had lost. Then one of them called through the doorway, "It's all right, Reggie, luckily it's been found." I liked that "luckily"! Reggie was as red as a beetroot by now and went out with his tail between his legs, and I think there was a row when he got back on the platform. The last thing we heard was the harpy saying very loudly, "I don't care. The whole thing is a disgrace. I don't know what the country's coming to. After all first class *is* first class." That word of Lili's is awfully apt, isn't it? Harpy.

It was marvellous from then on though. We had the whole compartment to ourselves and a lovely breakfast brought in. You know, until now I never did quite believe that story you told me about the time Sir Nello was turned out of a first class compartment by a couple of box-wallah Englishmen. It seemed to me that if the railways allow an Indian to make a first class booking then no one should be able to stop them using what they've paid for. I think if you hadn't been at Pindi station to see us off, though, there'd have been trouble with these two women about Lili and me actually getting in. Me only because I was with Lili. Was that why you got into the carriage first and condescended to them in that marvellous nineteenth-century way, before they had a chance of seeing her and realising they were going to have to travel with an Indian woman?

When I remember how awful it is travelling at home in the blackout, with no heating in the trains, just a dim blue light, and the stations in darkness, people jam-packed in the corridors as well as in the compartments, but on the whole everyone helping everyone else and trying to be cheerful, I get really angry about the kind of thing that happens over here. Honestly, Auntie, a lot of the white people in India don't know they're born. Of course I never travelled first class at home, and there was sometimes bad feeling among the non-commissioned boys in the services when they were packed like sardines and the pinkest young subaltern fresh out of Octu travelled in comparative comfort, but that's service life. *This* is to do with civilians. Well, I mustn't go on about it.

It's much warmer here in Mayapore than Pindi. I only need a sheet at night and it won't be long before I have to have a fan going all the time. Lili's given me a marvellous room all to myself, and a super bathroom (although the seat's a bit wonky on the wc! and there's an inhibiting paper-holder guarded by lions). The MacGregor House is fascinating. I have to keep reminding myself that you never actually visited it because Uncle Henry had retired and left the province before Nello bought the place. But of course you remember

Mayapore itself, although Lili says there have been lots of changes since then. The Technical College, for instance, the one Nello built and endowed and got his knighthood for, and the new buildings put up by the British-Indian Electrical. They're building an aerodrome out at Banyaganj which the English people say has ruined the duckshooting! How Hitler would laugh! (There are some lakes out there which Lili says were a favourite European picnic spot.) A couple of evenings ago we went to dinner with the Deputy Commissioner and his wife, Robin and Constance White, who said they met you and Uncle Henry years ago, but didn't think you'd remember them because they were very junior. Mr. White was under a Mr. Cranston at the time, and they said you'd remember *him* all right if only because of the occasion when he was in camp, touring his district, and you and Uncle Henry, who were also touring, called in unexpectedly and found him bathing in a pool. Apparently you both stood on the bank talking for ages and he stood there doing his best to answer sensibly and be polite, standing very straight as if at attention, up to his waist in rather muddy water, and not daring to move because he had no bathing-drawers on. He thought afterwards that you and Uncle Henry *knew*, and were just keeping him in that awkward situation for the fun of it. I promised Mr. White I'd mention this when I wrote to you, and ask if you really did know, because he's always wondered. It seems Mr. Cranston never was certain. But it is one of the funny stories about the Governor and his Lady that went around for years and years – as you can judge, since it came up only the other night here in Mayapore, after all that time.

I liked Mr. White, and his wife, although like all pukka mems *she* is a bit frightening at first. (I used to be frightened of *you*.) But they both seem to admire and respect Lili. It was a very private and friendly sort of party, with just two other men to balance Lili and myself at the table – Mr. Macintosh the Civil Surgeon, who is a widower and another old friend of Lili's, and Judge Menen. He's married, but his wife is in the local nursing home at the moment. I liked the judge. He has a wonderful sense of humour, or so I realised later in the evening. At first I thought him a bit snooty and critical, and put it down to an inferiority complex about being the only male Indian present. He's much older than Mr. White, but then of course it takes an Indian longer to rise to a position of authority, doesn't it? Anyway, after a bit I saw that he was pulling my leg in a way I'd have cottoned on to at once if he'd been English. It reminded me of when I first met Lili. Those dry amusing things she sometimes comes out with. If she were English, you'd laugh at once, but because she's not, then until you get to know her you think (as I used to think) What is she getting at? What's behind that remark? How am I supposed to reply or react without giving offence or appearing to have taken offence?

From what Lili tells me a lot of the English here are rather critical of the DC. They think of him as a man who does more than is absolutely necessary to show friendly to the Indians. They say he'll find himself taken advantage of, eventually. They talk about the 'good old days' of his predecessor, a Mr. Stead, who kept 'a firm hand' and made it quite clear in the district 'who was boss'. This kind of attitude has been brought home to me in the two days I've worked at the hospital and I realise how lucky I've been so far, living with you, and not getting mixed up with average English people. Matron, a marvellous woman who's been out here for years and knows the score, said one particularly interesting thing when she interviewed me. The interview was fixed up by Lili through the Civil Surgeon who is medical overlord of everything that goes on in the district – but you know that! Matron said, "You have three sponsors, Mr. Macintosh, myself, and your own surname which is one people in this area remember as distinguished even if at the time there were a lot who disagreed with your uncle's progressive policies. If you're wise you'll trade on all three but avoid too obvious an association with the fourth." Well, I knew what she meant by "the fourth" and I must say I got my hackles up, and said, "My *real* sponsor is Lady Chatterjee." She said, "I know. It's mainly why I'm taking you on. Even voluntary workers have to pass my personal test of worthiness. But this is a *British* general hospital, and I am its matron, and have long ago learned the lesson I had to learn if I were ever to do my job properly, and that lesson was to understand the necessity of excluding as extraneous any considerations other than those of the patients' well-being and the staff's efficiency" (she talks like that, rather officially, as if she has learned a speech). "There's a lot" (she went on) "that you may instinctively dislike about the atmosphere in which you'll be working. I don't ask you to learn to like it. I only ask, indeed demand, that your work won't be affected *by* the atmosphere." "Perhaps the atmosphere should be changed," I said. At that moment, you know, I couldn't have cared less whether I was allowed to work at the hospital or not. After all, I wasn't going to be *paid*. She said, quick as a flash, "I'm sure it should. I hope one day it will. If you'd prefer to delay working here until it does, and let someone else do the rewarding job of making sick people as comfortable as you can you only have to tell me. I shall quite understand. Although I'm sure that when you were driving an ambulance at home in the Blitz you never stopped to worry about what the wounded people you were taking to hospital felt about life or what their prejudices were. I imagine you were more concerned to try and stop them dying." Well of course it was true, what she said. I stared at her through these awful glasses I have to wear if I'm to feel absolutely confident and I wished I was driving an ambulance still. I did get a kind of kick out of it, even if I was terrified a lot of the time. 1940. How long ago it seems! Only eighteen months, but an age and a world away, as they say. Here the war has only just begun – and sometimes I'm not sure a lot of people realise that it has. Back home it seemed in a curious way to be already over, or to be settled down to go on for centuries. In Mayapore I think more than ever of poor Daddy and poor David. The war that killed them has only just caught up with Mayapore. At times it's like waiting for them to be killed all over again, at other times like thinking of people who lived and died on another planet. I'm glad Mummy went before it all started. I can't, as most of the English here do, blame the Indians for resisting the idea of war, a war they have no proper say in. After all I've seen the real thing, in a minor civilian way, but most of the people who lay down the law here about beating the Jap and the Hun (those *awful* old-fashioned expressions that seem to give *them* heart but always depress *me*) haven't even heard a rifle fired in anger. British India is still living in the nineteenth century. To them Hitler is only a *joke*, because "he was a house-painter and still looks like one even in uniform". Three cheers for the Cavalry. Up the Navy! Sorry! I guess I've had one too many of Auntie Lili's gimlets. I've got to get the old glad rags on soon, because we're having a party to which no less a person than the District Superintendent of Police is coming. Lili says he's a bachelor. I hope a dedicated one! I can't bear the type of man who tries not to look as if he's noticed I'm not really attractive. Remember Mr. Swinson?!! Auntie dear,

I love you and think often of you and of us together in Pindi. I long really to be going up to Srinagar with you in May, but Auntie Lili seems determined to keep me here, and of course I'm now committed to the hospital. And I am seeing more of India this way. There are a couple of other local voluntary bodies like me in the civilian wing, but the rulers of the roost are the official VADs and the QAs. You should see the airs some of the QAs give themselves. At home they'd simply be ordinary ward nurses, or staff nurses at most. Here they rank as sisters. Neither they nor the voluntary bods are supposed to do anything menial. That's all left to the poor little Anglo-Indian girls. Today, for the war effort, I rolled miles of bandages – I mean rolling bandages is *clean*. But I stood on my feet to do it, and they're killing me! Well, the boy has just come in to draw my bath. More presently. I'm loving it but finding it strange all over again, as I did when I came out last year. Mayapore is a bit off-putting in a way dear old Pindi isn't. Is it something to do with the fact that that part of the world is predominantly Muslim, and here it is Hindu? Please look after yourself and think often of your loving niece.

Daphne.

*

The MacGregor House,
MacGregor Road,
Mayapore, 1.
Friday, 17th July, 1942.

Dear Auntie Ethel,

Many thanks for your letter and news of the goings on in Srinagar. Glad you got the photograph safely and in time for your birthday, but gladder still that you like the dress length. The photograph seemed to me so awful that I had to send something else as well to make up for it, and then wondered choosing that colour whether I hadn't made everything worse! Not much clothes sense, I'm afraid, although I did feel that particular piece would suit you. Relieved you think so too! Hope old Hussein doesn't make a mess of it. Actually he's a better tailor than the man we have here. Lili and I had an iced cake in honour of your birthday, and a few people in to share it who stayed on afterwards for drinks (which I felt you would approve of!).

The rains have really set in now down here after a late start that set everyone in Mayapore hoarding foodstuffs in case of famine. I mean everyone in Mayapore who could afford it. Jack Poulson says it's the curse of India, the way the middle-class and well-to-do Indians swoop into the stores the moment a crisis even threatens. But that's apparently nothing to the corruption that goes on in higher circles where bulk food-stuffs are handled.

The grass at the front of the house is unbelievably green. I adore the rains. But how damp everything gets. The boy cleans *all* my shoes, every day, just to stop them from going mouldy. I've bought myself a huge cape and a sort of sou'wester, not that I've had much need of either because I mostly get a lift to and from the hospital in Mr. Merrick's car which he sends round with a police driver (a very militant Muslim who tells us all the Hindus have concealed weapons in their houses to chop off the heads of English and Mohammedans alike). If it's a petrol-less day (how we all complain about *that*) Mr. Merrick sends his official truck, ostensibly on urgent duty (transferring prisoners from the jail to the courthouse). I find it a bit embarrassing and have told him several times that I can quite easily go on my bicycle on *any* day, or anyway get a tonga, but he insists that with all this Congress-inspired anti-British feeling boiling up again, and the MacGregor House being isolated on the outskirts of the cantonment, it's really his duty to see I don't come to any harm.

I like him better than I used to. I can't close my eyes to the fact that he's been kind and considerate. It's his manner that's against him (and something behind his manner, naturally). And of course a District Superintendent of Police *is* a bit off-putting. But now that I've got used to him – and got over something that I think I must tell you – I quite enjoy the times he takes me out. Except when he adopts an official tone, as on a night or so ago when he warned me against what he called my association with Mr. Kumar, which he said had set people talking, not English people only but Indians as well. I'm afraid I laughed and thoughtlessly said, Oh stop acting like a policeman all the time. Which I realised at once was the last thing one ought ever to say to him because he takes his job very seriously and is proud of having got where he is and is determined to shine at the job and not to care who dislikes him for doing it properly.

I feel I must tell you, *but please keep it to yourself,* I've told nobody, not even Aunt Lili. About a month ago he invited me to his bungalow for dinner. He'd gone to a lot of trouble. It was the best English-style meal I've had in India (except that time when you had the Swinsons and they made such a fuss beforehand about hating Indian food). Another point in his favour from my point of view was that his house-boy is obviously devoted to him, and took pleasure in arranging everything properly for his sahib's candle-lit dinner for two. The excuse for the dinner, if there had to be an excuse, was for me to hear some of his records afterwards. You remember I told you at the time about the show put on by the military at the end of April, complete with band and parade? And about meeting Brigadier Reid who said he met us in Pindi? And how I went to the show with a couple of the girls from the hospital and on to the club afterwards with some young army officers? Ronald Merrick looked in at the club later that evening (he had had a lot to do, controlling the crowds, etc.). Well we were all saying complimentary things about the music and the marching – it *was* rather striking – and I must have been more full of it than the others. Anyway Ronald turned to me and said, "Oh, you like military bands? So do I." Apparently he had piles of records. He said I must hear them some time.

So this was the occasion. I don't like them all that much! Not well enough to want to listen to records, so whenever he raised the subject afterwards I sort of put it off. Actually I'd almost forgotten about the records when he finally asked me to dinner. I said yes before I knew what I was doing, and when he said: "Good, and afterwards you can hear some of those records I've been promising to play," I thought Oh Lord! What have I let myself in for! In the event it wasn't too bad (the music I mean). We'd been around quite a bit together and there was tons to talk about. By now the music was just a part of a pleasant evening. I'd been to his bungalow before, but only with other people for a Sunday morning beer party, but seeing it empty I realised how comfortable and pleasant it was. He doesn't smoke, or drink much, so I suppose his money goes further than that of men in similar positions who do. The bungalow is mainly PWD furnished, of course, but he has several rather glamorous things of his own. To begin with there was this super radiogram (on which he played a couple of Sousa marches.) Then he had very nice tableware, and a marvellous Persian rug that he said he'd bought in an auction in Calcutta. His taste in pictures though was what really struck me. He's so very conventional in his behaviour you'd expect something nondescript on his walls. It's true there were pig-sticking and polo pictures in the dining-room and a David Wright cutie in his bedroom (he showed me round the whole bungalow but in such a sweet way that there wasn't anything awkward about the bedroom, as there might have been with another man) but in the living-room there was nothing on the walls except these two rather good reproductions of those Henry Moore drawings of people huddled in the underground during the Blitz, which I find difficult to look at, but do admire. He seemed touchingly pleased when I said, "Oh, Henry Moore! What a surprising man you are!" One other thing that struck me – in the closet (the one used by guests just off the hall) he'd had the boy put out scented soap (Coty Chypre) and a little pink hand towel which was obviously brand new. I had the feeling it had been bought especially for the occasion. (The soap in his own bathroom was Lifebuoy, so don't jump to the wrong conclusion!)

There was another surprise too. After he'd played a couple of these Sousa marches he put on another record and said, "I like this kind of thing, too," and what do you think it was? The *Clair de Lune* movement from Debussy's *Suite Bergamasque*, played by Walter Gieseking. It was one of my brother David's favourites. When it began I thought: Whenever did I tell Ronald that David loved this? Then knew I never had. It was extraordinary. All that awful blaring (but sometimes stirring) Sousa and then this tender moonlit music that actually I could hardly bear to listen to, but loved all the same, although it seemed such an unusual thing for a policeman to like as well.

While it was playing the boy brought in the coffee – *Turkish*. There was a choice of brandy or liqueurs (curaçao or *crème de menthe*, very dull). All the bottles were unopened – fresh from the store, just for me. I expect if I ever dine there again the brandy will be at the same level we left it. While we were drinking it he asked me a lot of questions about my family, about how David was killed, and about daddy, and then about me, and what I thought about life and all that sort of thing, but in a chatty, sympathetic way that made me open up. (He must be a wizard at interrogation! That's not fair. But you know what I mean.) Gradually I realised he had begun to talk about himself. And I was thinking: People don't like you much, but you're fundamentally *kind,* and that's why you and I have always got on surprisingly well. He said he came of "a very ordinary family" and that although his father had done well enough, he was still only a grammar school boy and his grandparents had been "pretty humble sort of people". He had worked hard and done all right so far in the Indian Police which he thought of as an essential if not especially attractive service, and his main regret was that being in it he wasn't allowed to join up. His other regret was that he'd never really had any "youth" or met "the right sort of girl" for him. He was often "pretty lonely". He knew he hadn't much to offer. He realised his background and mine were "rather different". Our friendship meant a lot to him.

Then he dried up. I just didn't know what to say, because I didn't know if I'd understood or misunderstood what he was driving at. We sort of stared at each other for a while. Then he said, "I'm only asking whether after you've had time to think about it you'd consider the possibility of becoming engaged to me."

Do you know, Auntie, that's the only proposal I've ever had? I'm sure by the time you were my age you'd had dozens. Does every girl find the first one oddly moving? I suppose it depends on the man. But if he's, you know, all right, decent enough, you can't *not* be touched, can you, whatever you *feel* about him as a person? I don't think my feelings for Ronald Merrick could ever be described as more than passingly affectionate. He's fair-haired and youngish and has blue eyes and is really awfully good-looking but there was and still is (perhaps more so than ever) a distinct reservation (from my point of view) that must be something to do with what I feel as the lack of *real* candour between him and whoever he's dealing with. I never feel quite *natural* when I'm with him, but can never be sure whether that is my fault or his. But when he came out with this request (you can hardly call it a proposal, can you?) I wanted very much to have been able to make things *all right* for him and say "Yes". Do men know how vulnerable they look when they slough off that tough, not-caring skin they mostly seem to wear when there are more than two people in a room? Far more vulnerable than women, when *they* let their hair down.

What made it so extraordinary was that he never so much as touched my hand. At the time, this *not* touching added to my wish not to hurt him. Later, thinking about it, it added to the sense I had of the coldness surrounding the occasion.

We were sitting at opposite ends of the sofa. Perhaps I ought to have taken my specs out and put them on! Looking back on it I can't really recall whether I felt that what had been said was a shock or not. It seemed to be a shock, anyway a surprise, but in retrospect the whole evening was *obviously* leading up to it, so I can't think why I should have been surprised, or even believe that I was. There must have been lots of things said before he came out with it that I inwardly took notice of. At some stage or other I decided that physically, in spite of his looks, he repelled me, but I think that came later, and was only momentary, when I'd established for both of us the fact that although I didn't want to hurt him I had never thought and never would think of him in the way he seemed to want me to. The feeling of faint repulsion probably came through because of the sense I had of relief, of having got out of a difficult situation and retreated *into myself* in a way that left no room for others whoever they might be. I was now more concerned about the possible effect of my "refusal". Honestly, I'm sure that all I said was "Thank you, Ronald – but –" but that was enough. You know how people talk about faces "closing up"? I think "close-down" is nearer to it, because close up suggests a sort of *constriction,* a *change*, whereas what actually happens is that the face remains exactly the same but all the lights go out. Like a house where the people have gone away. If you knock at the door now there won't be any answer.

We had some more Sousa and presently he drove me home and we talked quite easily about nothing. When we got to the MacGregor House I asked him whether he'd like to come in for a nightcap. He said no, but escorted me up the steps to the verandah. When we shook hands he hung on to mine for a moment and said, "Some ideas take some getting used to," from which I gathered he hadn't yet given up, but it was a different man who said it. The District Superintendent of Police, the Ronald Merrick I don't care for. The same one who later – only a few days ago – annoyed me by warning me about my "association with young Kumar".

One of the servants was waiting on the verandah. I thanked Ronald for the evening, and then said goodnight to them both. I heard the car drive away and the servant beginning to lock up as I went upstairs. I knew Aunt Lili had planned an early night for once, so I didn't go to her room. The house was very quiet. It's the first time I've ever been conscious of the fact that it's supposed to be haunted. It didn't feel haunted in the eerie sense. Just big and empty and somehow desolate and occupied in the wrong way. What am I trying to tell you? Not that I felt frightened. But that I suddenly wanted to be with *you*.

I never told you, but there was a time – my second month in India last year – when if someone had offered me a passage home I'd have accepted like a shot. Goodness knows I loved being with you. But during that second month, perhaps not the whole month but two or three weeks of it, I had what I can only describe now as a permanent sinking heart. I hated everything, hated it because I was afraid of it. It was all so alien. I could hardly bear to leave the bungalow. I started to have awful dreams, not *about* anything, just dreams of faces. They used to come up out of nowhere, normal looking at first but then distorting and exploding, leaving a blank space for others to come up and take their place. They weren't the faces of people I knew. They were people I invented in alarming detail – alarming because it didn't seem possible to imagine faces so exactly. I suppose I was obsessed by the idea of being surrounded by strangers and had to have them even in my dreams. I never told you but I think that day on the verandah with the durzi you guessed what I was going through. I remember the way you looked at me when I lost my temper and snatched away that blouse he was doing his best to copy. You know, if I'd been living with the Swinsons that would probably have been the point of no return for me. I'd have been assimilated from then on into that inbred little cultural circle of English women – men, too, but particularly women – abroad in a colony.

I suppose it's only natural that wherever we go we should need the presence of someone known and dependable and proven. If there's no someone there has to be some*thing*. In Pindi during those particular weeks I became ridiculously attached to my luggage, my clothes, as if they were the only things I could trust. Even you, you see, seemed to have failed me. You knew everybody, everything, and I felt cut off from you because *I* didn't, however much you took me out and about. And you took the dirt and poverty and squalor in your stride, as if it didn't exist, although I knew that's not what you actually felt about it. But this is why I snatched the blouse from Hussein. I couldn't bear to see him holding it up, examining it, *touch it with his black fingers*. I *hated* myself for feeling that, but couldn't stop feeling it, so I shouted at him. When I went to my room I sat down and wanted to burst into tears and be rescued and taken home. I've never felt so badly the fact that I no longer have a home in England, with Mummy gone, and Daddy, and David.

Much the same thing happened to me the second week I was here at the MacGregor House, and my initial curiosity in my surroundings had been satisfied. But in Mayapore "home" had become the bungalow in Pindi, and you. I hope none of this showed in my letters and worried you. I'm over it now. I love it all. But for a while I hated Mayapore. I asked myself what on earth had I done, coming to this awful place? I even suspected Aunt Lili of having me here only because I was English and it was a feather in her cap to have a white person staying in her house. (Isn't that disgraceful?) And I even thought back on that train journey and found myself less critical of those two beastly women. After all, I thought, how were they to have known that Lili wouldn't do something that *revolted* them? And in the hospital I realised how much easier it was to talk to another English woman, even if you disagreed with everything she said. People of the same nationality use a kind of shorthand in conversation, don't they? You spend less effort to express more, and you've got so used to the effortlessness that anything that needs effort is physically and mentally tiring, and you get short-tempered, and then tireder and more short-tempered from trying not to let the temper show.

I think this is why *I failed to keep my resolution never to go to the club. I made that resolution originally because it was impossible for Lili Chatterjee ever to go with me*. I have never liked the club, but it amuses me – it is so self-conscious about its exclusiveness and yet so vulgar. Someone is always drunk, the talk is mostly scurrilous, and yet its members somehow preserve, goodness knows how, an outward air of rectitude, almost as though there were inviolable *rules* for heartless gossip and insufferable behaviour. It was a week or two before I realised that because I lived at the MacGregor House most of the women I met at the club disliked me and a lot of the men were embarrassed by me. Not to have noticed the dislike straight away shows the extent of the relief I must have felt at first *simply to be there among my own kind*.

Mummy once said to me, "You seem to like *everybody*. It's unnatural. It's also unfortunate. You're going to waste so much time before you've worked out who the people are *it's worth your while to know*." I used to think she meant worth while in the ambitious sense. Now I wonder whether she meant worth my while in the sense of the interests of *my privacy and peace of mind and sense of security*. But either way she would be wrong, wouldn't she? I'm sure this longing for security and peace is wrong and that we should extend our patience time and time again almost right up to its breaking point, put ourselves out on a limb, dare other people to saw the limb off, whoever they are, black or white.

But it isn't easy, is it? The night I came home from my evening with Ronald Merrick I thought, as I was climbing the stairs, that at the top I was in for something unpleasant and I wanted to turn and run and get back to *him* of all people. I actually stood still, halfway up, and looked down into the hall and there was this servant, a boy called Raju, staring up at me. Oh heavens, he was only making sure he didn't turn out the light before I got up on to the landing, only doing his job, but I said to myself: What are *you* staring at? I was in my long green dress, the one you like that shows my awful shoulders. I felt – well, you know what I felt. He was too far away for me to see his expression. He was just a brown blob in white shirt and trousers, and then in the place where his face was one of my imaginary faces came, that of someone I'd never seen before. I called out, "Goodnight, Raju," and heard him say, "Goodnight, madam" (he's a South Indian Christian so he says "madam"), and then I continued up the stairs and when I got on to the landing I think I expected to see our resident ghost, Janet MacGregor. But there wasn't anything. I've not seen her *yet*. I felt relieved, but also cheated.

One day I must tell you about Hari Kumar. So far in my letters to you he's really just a name, isn't he? And I must tell you about a curious woman called Sister Ludmila who wears nun's clothing and collects dead bodies. I wish you were here so that I could talk to you any old time. The gong's just gone for dinner. It's raining frogs and the lizards are playing hide and seek on the wall and making that peculiar chopping noise. Tonight Lili and I are dining alone and afterwards I expect we'll play mahjong. Tomorrow I hope to visit the local Hindu temple with Mr. Kumar.

Love, Daphne.

*

I wish you could have been here in the rains (Lady Chatterjee says) and then you would have seen it how Daphne loved it best. But I understand. You have to travel about and the wet season wouldn't have been the best time to do so. The garden is already beginning to look dry and tired and brown. I love every season, though. And I especially love it at night like this. I always sit on the front verandah because you don't get the smell of the river – which I never notice, but know that English guests do – and anyway you can see down the drive, which is nice, remembering the people who used to come up it, and anticipating those who might come up it now, and you can just make out the beds of canna lilies when we have the verandah light on like this. When there's a moon it's best with the light off, but when I give my party for you we'll have all the lights on, including those in the garden itself. I'd put them on for you now, for you to see the effect, but we're asked to conserve things as much as possible because of the war with China, and I suppose that includes conserving electricity.

Let me go on, then, about Miss Crane. She was an old school English liberal in the sense I grew to understand the term, someone who as likely as not had no gift for broad friendships. In Miss Crane's case I think it went further than this. I think she had no gift for friendship of any kind. She loved India and all Indians but no particular Indian. She hated British policies, and so she disliked all Britons unless they turned out to be adherents to the same rules she abided by. I suppose what I'm saying is that she made friendships in her head most of the time and seldom in her heart. To punish someone whose conduct didn't coincide with her preconceived notions of what he stood for she took his picture down. How ineffectual a gesture that was. But how revealing, how symptomatic of her weakness. As a gesture it lacked even the pathetic absurdity of turning the portrait of the black sheep of the family to the wall. At least in that gesture there was – and would be still if anyone ever did it nowadays – a flesh and blood anger, something positive. But she had courage. The Miss Cranes of the world often do, and I think at the end the reason for her madness was that she also had the courage to see the truth if not to live with it, see how all her good works and noble thoughts had been going on in a vacuum. I have a theory that she saw clearly but too late how she had never dirtied her hands, never got grubby for the sake of the cause she'd always believed she held dear, and that this explains why Mr. Poulson found her like that, sitting in the rain by the roadside, holding the hand of that dead schoolteacher, Mr. Chaudhuri.

Daphne, though, Daphne was different. Wouldn't you say? You've read those two letters now? Don't bother to make copies. Take them with you. Let me have them back one day when you've finished with them. I know them almost by heart. I only wish I'd known about them at the time. Yes, I wish it, but ask myself, Well how would it have helped if I had known, what could I have done if I'd seen them? She had to make her own marvellous mistakes. I say marvellous. *She* didn't ever shrink from getting grubby. She flung herself into everything with zest. The more afraid she was of something the more determined she was not to shrink from experiencing it. She had us all by the ears finally. We were all afraid for her, even *of* her, but more of what she seemed to have unlocked, like Pandora who bashed off to the attic and prised the lid of the box open.

Is this why I always sit here, on the front verandah? Those are the steps, you know. Well of course you do. You keep on looking at them, and looking down the drive, almost expecting to see someone who has run all the way in darkness from the Bibighar. On that night I was in the hall with Mr. Merrick, just there by the entrance to the living-room. We couldn't see the steps from there. His car was parked away from the steps, in shadow. Afterwards, thinking about that, I wondered if he had left it so that it wasn't at once obvious to the outside world that he was here, actually at the MacGregor House when the whole of British Mayapore was seething with rumours about the riots in the sub-divisions, and rumours about Miss Crane who was already in hospital.

He said as soon as he came in, "Are you all right, Lady Chatterjee?" which amused me really, because for the first time since we'd known each other he seemed to be treating me as one of you, as if I were Lady Green or Brown or Smith, living alone in a house only just on the fringe of safety. I gave him a drink, he said he hadn't much time, but drank it willingly enough, which I thought unusual, because he was an abstemious sort of man. I remember thinking: When you are worried, when you are concerned, when your face is alive, you're really quite good-looking. I said, "I expect you've come to see Daphne, but she's at the club," and he said, "Yes, they said at the hospital she'd gone straight on to the club, but she isn't there." "Oh, isn't she?" I said, and I got worried too, but tried not to show it, so I said, "But I'm sure she's all right."

And then he asked outright, "Is she with Hari Kumar?" I said, "No, I don't think so." I hadn't thought she was with Kumar. I'd even had the impression the association Mr. Merrick warned her against had ended. I didn't know he'd warned her against it. I didn't know Mr. Merrick had proposed to her. She'd kept all that from me. But she hadn't been able to keep from me the feelings she'd had for Kumar, nor the fact that she hadn't seen him for at least a week, in fact more like three weeks. So when Mr. Merrick said, "Is she with Kumar?" I replied, quite truthfully, "No, I don't think so." And then I wondered. But I said nothing. One did not voluntarily mention Kumar's name to Mr. Merrick. He said, "Well, at this time of night where can she be?" I said, "Oh probably with friends," and I went to the phone and rang several places where she might have been. It took ages. The telephone lines in Mayapore were blocked with official calls. Mr. Merrick kept going to the verandah and coming back again each time I'd finished a call. "She'll be in soon," I said, "come and have another drink," and again, to my surprise, he said he would. He was in uniform still. He looked awfully tired.

"Is it serious?" I asked him. "It seems to be," he said, and then blurted out, "What a damned mess," and looked as if he was about to beg my pardon for swearing. "Some of the people you know," he said, "are locked up." I nodded. I knew which ones. I didn't want to talk about them. "But here I am," he said, "having a drink with you. Do you mind?" I laughed and told him not a bit, unless when he'd finished his peg he was going to haul me off to jail in a black maria as a suspected secret revolutionary. He smiled but said nothing, and I thought: Oh, am I in for it? Then he came out with this special thing, "I asked her to marry me. Did she tell you?" It was a shock. I told him, no, and realised for the first time how awfully dangerous the whole situation was. "Is Miss Crane all right?" I asked. I didn't want to talk to him about Daphne, or Hari Kumar. Or about where they might be. Mr. Merrick had always disliked young Kumar and I have to confess that my own feelings towards him were mixed. It always seemed to me that he had too big a chip on his shoulder. And he was in some trouble once. Mr. Merrick had had him in for questioning. At that time I didn't know the boy from Adam, but a friend – Anna Klaus of the purdah hospital – once rang me and said the police had arrested this boy for apparently no good reason. So, well, you know me. I asked Judge Menen about it. So far as I could see it all turned out to be a storm in a teacup and he hadn't really been arrested at all but only taken in for questioning. It turned out that my old friend Vassi knew him. That's Mr. Srinivasan, who still lives here, and whom you must meet. Anyhow I asked young Kumar round one evening because my curiosity had been aroused and that's how he came into my life, or rather into Daphne's life. He was brought up in England. His father had had tremendous plans for him, but the plans collapsed when the father died a bankrupt and poor Hari was sent home here to Mayapore, only of course it wasn't home to him. He was two years old when his father took him to England, and eighteen when he came back. He spoke like an English boy. Acted like one. Thought like one. They say that when he first reached India he was spelling his name the way his father had spelled it. Coomer. Harry Coomer. But probably his aunt stopped that. She was the closest relative he had and I think in her own rather orthodox Hindu way she was very good to him, but that meant not disciplining him enough, letting him waste his time which also meant letting him have time to brood about his bad luck. It worried me a bit, the way Daphne seemed to take to him, worried me because I couldn't be sure whether he felt quite the same way about her. She knew I had these reservations. So did young Kumar. Perhaps I should have come right out with it. But I didn't. And I think I must blame myself for any note of furtiveness that crept into what Mr. Merrick called the association between Kumar and Daphne. And when Mr. Merrick was here that night and said that he had asked Daphne to marry him and I realised how dangerous things could be, I remembered that in the morning she had seemed especially happy – not especially happy for the Daphne I knew, but especially happy for the Daphne who had been mooning about for days and hardly going out anywhere except to the club and pretending in her typical way that nothing was wrong, and there suddenly seemed to be no doubt at all that she *was* with Kumar, that she had been happy because they'd agreed to meet again. No doubt in my mind, nor I think in Mr. Merrick's. And believing I knew for sure that she was with Kumar I also believed I knew where and made the mistake of thinking that if *I* knew Mr. Merrick might also guess, and go there and find them together, which I did not want. In fact it struck me that the less said the better, because the place where I guessed they were was also the place where Mr. Merrick had first met young Kumar and taken him in for questioning, and so the whole situation had come full-circle and I felt that some kind of disaster was inevitable. So I made us both stop talking about Daphne and asked about poor old Miss Crane who had been taken to hospital. I said, "Is she all right?" and he said yes, so far as he knew, and then looked at his watch and got up and asked if he might use the phone to talk to his headquarters. Before he got to it the phone rang. It was the Deputy Commissioner. Mr. Merrick had told his people where he'd be. I remember Mr. Merrick answering it and telling Robin White he'd personally checked all his patrols, that the town itself was quiet for the moment because nearly all the shops in the bazaar had closed and the people seemed to be staying indoors, almost as if there was an official curfew. Then he said, "No, I'm here because Miss Manners is missing." He made it sound as if I'd *reported* her missing, and it seemed to be such a ridiculous word to use, but at the same time true. He spoke a bit longer then handed the phone to me and said Robin would like a word with me and would I forgive him if he didn't wait but got off straight away. Robin said, "Lili, what's this about Daphne?" I said I didn't really know, that I thought she had gone straight to the club from the hospital, but Mr. Merrick said she wasn't there, so now I supposed I was worried too. I said, "Are things bad, Robin?" and he said, "Well, Lili, we don't know. Would you like to come and stay the night with us?" I laughed and asked, "Why? Are people moving into the funk holes?"

There was a plan as you probably know to move English women and children into places like the club, Smith's hotel and the DC's bungalow if the threatened uprising really got going, and finally into the old barracks if things got as bad as in the Mutiny which some of the Jonahs said they would. Robin had had to work the plan out with Brigadier Reid, but this was the first time I'd ever heard him talk seriously about it. He said, "No, not yet, but one or two of the women whose husbands are out of station have gone into the club." "Well," I said, "that's one place I can't go, isn't it, Robin?" He told me afterwards he hadn't quite known how to take that, he'd never heard me say anything bitter. But I didn't mean it to sound bitter. It just slipped out. It was just a case of my automatically stating my position. He said, "Well, give me a ring, when Daphne gets back. Perhaps you'd ring in half an hour in any event?" I said I would. When I came away from the phone Mr. Merrick's car was gone. It was nearly nine o'clock. Daphne had always rung if anything came up at the last moment that meant she couldn't get back at her usual time. I thought, well perhaps she's tried to ring, but simply hasn't been able to get through. But I didn't really believe it. I had only one clear picture in my mind and that was of Daphne and young Kumar, and of the place they used to call the Sanctuary. It was a place I had personally never been to, which was absurd of me. I had a horror of it, I suppose, in spite of what Anna Klaus used to say, and a horror of the woman who ran it, who called herself Sister Ludmila and collected people she found dying in the streets. Daphne was awfully impressed with Sister Ludmila. Anyway, I went round the back to see what the servants were up to, because I suddenly noticed none of them was about. They'd been very glum all day. There was no one in the kitchen, nobody attending to the dinner. I went to the kitchen door and shouted across the compound and after a bit Raju appeared. He said cook wasn't feeling well. I said, "You mean he's drunk. Tell him dinner at nine-thirty or you'll all be looking for a job, including you. *Your* business is at the front of the house, Raju."

I went back to the living-room and poured myself a peg, and then I heard Raju at the front. I thought: He's drunk too *and* incapable, the stupid boy's fallen flat on his face by the sound of it. So I went out to scold him. It wasn't Raju. I couldn't take it in at first. She was on her hands and knees. She'd fallen and hurt herself on the steps, but only fallen because she was already hurt and exhausted from running. She looked up and said, "Oh, Auntie." She was still in her khaki hospital uniform. It was torn and muddy and she had blood on her face. Even when she said, "Oh, Auntie," I couldn't take it in that it was Daphne.

*

The lights are on in the garden of the MacGregor House, in honour of the stranger. The shrubs, artificially illuminated by the manipulation of a battery of switches on the wall of the verandah, looking strikingly theatrical. There is no breeze but the stillness of the leaves and branches is unnatural. As well as these areas of radiance the switches have turned on great inky pools of darkness. Sometimes the men and women you talk to, moving from group to group on the lawn, present themselves in silhouette; although the turn of a head may reveal a glint in a liquidly transparent eye and the movement of an arm the skeletal structure of a hand holding a glass that contains light and liquid in equal measure. In the darkness too, strangely static and as strangely suddenly galvanised, are the fireflies of the ends of cigarettes.

The people in the garden are the inheritors. Somewhere, farther away in time than in distance, the fire that consumed Edwina Crane spurts unnoticed, licks and catches hold. In this illuminated darkness one might notice this extra brilliance and hear, against the chat and buzz of casual night-party conversation, the ominous crackle of wood.

There was a shed in the compound behind Miss Crane's bungalow. In true English fashion she kept gardening instruments there. How typical of her to choose (on a windless day when the first post-monsoon heats had dried the wood out and prepared it for a creaking season of contraction and pre-cool-weather warmth) a site where a conflagration would not threaten the bungalow itself. She locked herself in and soaked the walls with paraffin and set them alight and died, one hopes, in the few seconds it took for the violently heated air to scorch the breath out of her lungs.

The story goes that for this act of becoming *suttee* (which Lady Chatterjee describes as *sannyasa* without the travelling) she dressed for the first time in her life in a white saree, the saree for her adopted country, the whiteness for widowhood and mourning. And there is a tale that Joseph, returning empty-handed from some wild-goose errand she had sent him on, fell on his knees in the compound and cried to the smouldering pyre, "Oh, Madam, Madam," just as, several weeks before, Miss Manners, falling on her knees, had looked up and said, "Oh, Auntie."

In such a fashion human beings call for explanations of the things that happen to them and in such a way scenes and characters are set for exploration, like toys set out by kneeling children intent on pursuing their grim but necessary games.

PART THREE

Sister Ludmila

HER origins were obscure. Some said she was related to the Romanovs; others that she had been a Hungarian peasant, a Russian spy, a German adventuress, a run-away French novice. But all this was conjecture. What was clear, at least to the Mayapore Europeans, was that saintly as she might now appear she had no business calling herself Sister. The Catholic and Protestant churches withheld their recognition, but accepted her existence because she had long ago won the battle of the Habit by declaring to the irate Roman priest who turned up to cast out this particular abomination that the clothes she wore were of her own design, that although a genuine religious had superior status and a larger stake in life eternal, she could not possibly have any exclusive claim to modesty or special vulnerability to heat-stroke: hence the long light gown of thin grey cotton (unadorned either by cross or penitential cord, and tied at the waist by an ordinary leather belt obtainable in any bazaar) and the wide winged cap of white starched linen that sheltered her neck and shoulders from the sun and could be seen on the darkest night.

"But you call yourself Sister Ludmila," the priest said.

"No. It is the Indians who call me that. If you object take your objections to them. There is anyway a saying, God is not mocked."

In those days (in 1942), on every Wednesday morning, Sister Ludmila set out on foot from the cluster of old buildings where she fed the hungry, ministered to the sick, and cleansed and comforted those who for want of her nightly scavenging would have died in the street.

She carried a locked leather bag that was attached to her belt by a chain. Behind her walked a stalwart Indian youth armed with a stick. It was seldom the same boy for more than a month or two. Mr. Govindas, the manager of the Mayapore branch of the Imperial Bank of India in the cantonment, which was the place she was bound for on these Wednesday outings, said to her once, "Sister Ludmila, where does that boy come from?" "From heaven, I suppose." "And the boy who accompanied you last month? From heaven also?" "No," Sister Ludmila said, "he came from jail and has recently gone back in." "It is what I am warning you of," Mr. Govindas pointed out, "the danger of trusting a boy simply because he looks strong enough to protect you."

Sister Ludmila merely smiled and handed over her cheque made out to cash.

Week by week she came to Mr. Govindas for two hundred rupees. The cheques were drawn upon the Imperial Bank of India in Bombay. The Imperial Bank has long since become the State Bank and Mr. Govindas long since retired. His memory remains sharp, though. Since she never paid money in and was known by Mr. Govindas to pay all her trade accounts by cheque as well, he could only assume that either her fortune was large or her account credited regularly from elsewhere. The long-standing instruction from the Bombay branch authorising the cashing facilities at Mayapore described her as Mrs. Ludmila Smith and the cheques were signed accordingly. By pumping a friend in Bombay, Mr. Govindas eventually discovered that the money came from the treasury of a small princely state and might be reckoned as some sort of pension because Mrs. Ludmila Smith's husband, said to be an engineer, had died while on the ruler's pay-roll. She took the two hundred rupees as follows: fifty rupees in notes of Rs. 5 denomination, one hundred rupees in notes of Rs. 1, and fifty rupees in small change. Mr. Govindas estimated that most of the small change and a fair proportion of the one-rupee notes were distributed to the poor and that the rest went on wages for her assistants and casual purchases in the market. He knew that her meat, grain and vegetables were supplied on monthly account by local contractors, and that medicines were bought from Dr. Gulab Singh Sahib's pharmacy at a trade discount of 12% plus 5% for monthly settlement. He knew that Sister Ludmila drank only one glass of orange juice a day and ate one meal of rice or pulses in the evening, with curds to follow, except on Fridays when she had a modest curry of vegetables and, on Christian festivals, fish. The rest of the food was consumed by her assistants and in meals for the hungry. He knew many such things about her. He sometimes thought that if he were to write down all the things he knew or heard about her he would fill up several pages of the bank's foolscap. But knowing all this he still believed that he knew nothing of importance. In this belief, in Mayapore, in 1942, Mr. Govindas was not alone.

Her age, for instance. Well – how old was she? Under the nunnish pleats and folds and fly-away wings of starched linen her face described by some as inscrutable lived perpetually in an aseptic, reverent light. Her hands were those of a woman who had always directed the work of others. Time had barely touched them. A single ring, a gold band, adorned her wedding finger. Her throat was protected by a high-necked starched white linen bib that also covered her breast and shoulders. Her eyes were dark and deep-set, and there was an impression of prominent cheekbones – proof perhaps of Magyar blood. Her voice, also dark and deep, matched the eyes. She spoke fluent but rather staccato English and a vile bazaar Hindi. Mr. Govindas had heard English people say that her English accent was Germanic. It was also said that she possessed a French as well as a British passport. At a guess, it was assumed she was about fifty years old, give or take five years.

Having collected the two hundred rupees and deposited them in the leather bag that was chained to her waist, Sister Ludmila bade Mr. Govindas good-day, thanked him for escorting her personally from his inner sanctum to the door, and set out on the journey home, attended by her young man of the moment who had spent the ten minutes or so that it took her to cash her cheque sitting on his hunkers in the street outside, gossiping with anyone who also happened to be waiting or idling his time away. Such talk as went on between the bodyguard and his chance companions was usually vulgar. The other men would want to know whether the crazy white woman had yet invited him to share her bed or when exactly it was that he planned to run off with the cash she hired him to protect. The ribaldry was good-natured, but behind it there might always have been detected a note of black uncertainty. To a man in health, her business seemed too closely connected with death for comfort.

*

From the Mayapore branch of the Imperial Bank which was situated in the arcaded Victoria road, the main shopping centre of the European cantonment, Sister Ludmila's journey back to the Sanctuary took her through the Eurasian-quarter, past the church of the mission, over the level crossing for which, like Miss Crane – to whom she had nodded but never spoken – she sometimes had to wait to be opened before she could continue across the crowded Mandir Gate bridge. Once over the river, outside the Tirupati temple, she paused and distributed money to the beggars and to the leper who sat cross-legged, displaying the pink patches of a diseased trunk and holding up lopped tree-branch arms. On this side of the river the sun seemed to strike more fiercely and indiscriminately as though the smells of poverty and dirt would be wasted in shade. Colour was robbed of the advantage of its singularity, its surprise. At ground level, the spectrum contracted into ranges of exhausted greys and yellows. Even the scarlet flower in a woman's braided hair, lacking its temperate complementary green, was scorched to an insipid brown. Here, the white starched cap of Sister Ludmila looked like some prehistoric bird miraculously risen, floating, bobbing and bucking, visible from afar.

Beyond the temple the road forks into two narrower roads. At the apex a holy tree shelters a shrine, ruminant cows, old men, and women with their fingers held to their nostrils. At the head of the road that forks to the right towards the jail the Majestic Cinema announces an epic from the Ramayana (now, as then). The left-hand fork is narrower, darker, and leads past open-fronted shops to the Chillianwallah Bazaar. Down this road Sister Ludmila, all that time ago, proceeded with the boy behind her and a dozen children running by her side and to her front, each hopeful of an anna. She walked upright, the locked bag in her folded arms, and ignored the cries of the shopkeepers inviting her to buy pān, cloth, soda-water, melons or jasmine. At the end of the lane she turned left and entered the Chillianwallah Bazaar through the open archway in the high concrete wall that surrounds it.

In the middle of the walled area there are fish and meat markets – large open-sided godowns floored in concrete and roofed with sloping sheets of corrugated iron supported by concrete pillars. In the open, ranged along the enclosing walls, women have set out their rainbow vegetables and spices on mats, and sit among them holding their idle scales like so many huddled figures of unblindfolded and so sharp-eyed mercantile justice. From one of them Sister Ludmila bought green chillis and then marched on until she reached the exit on the other side of the walled square. Here, before passing through the exit, she turned aside and mounted a flight of rickety wooden steps to an open doorway on the upper floor of a building – a warehouse, obviously – whose side, at this point, forms part of the bazaar wall. Across the face of the building a sign in blue characters on a faded white background announces "Romesh Chand Gupa sen, Contractors". Her bodyguard waited at the foot of the steps and smoked a bidi, squatting on his hunkers again, impatient of this unaccustomed interruption in the journey home. After ten minutes Sister Ludmila came out of the doorway and down the steps and led the way out of the bazaar, through another complex of lanes and alleys of old Muslim houses with shuttered windows above and closed doors at street level; until, abruptly, the houses gave way to open ground that was (still is) scattered with the huts and shacks of the untouchables. Beyond the huts there is a stagnant water-tank on whose farther bank are laid out to dry the long coloured sarees and murky rags belonging to the black-skinned, braceleted, barelegged women who stand thigh-high in the water, washing themselves and their clothes. There are three trees but otherwise the land looks waste and desolate. Crows screech, flap and wheel aloft making for the river which is not visible from where Sister Ludmila walked, but can be smelt, and sensed – for behind a rise in the ground the land seems to fall away, then reappear more distantly. On the opposite bank are the godowns and installations belonging to the railway. The lane Sister Ludmila took lies roughly parallel to the winding course of the river and leads to a gateless opening in a broken-down wall that surrounds a compound. Within the compound there are three squat single-storey buildings, relics of the early nineteenth century, once derelict but patched up, distempered white, calm, silent, stark, functional, and accompanied (these days) by a fourth building of modern design. This was the Sanctuary, since re-named.

*

Sister Ludmila? Sister? (A pause.) I have forgotten. No, I remember. Put on the garments of modesty, He said. So I obeyed. The priest who came was very angry. I turned him away. When the priest had gone I asked God whether I had done wisely. Wisely and well, He said. And laughed. He likes a good joke. If God is never happy what chance of happiness is there for us? Such long dolorous faces that we pull. Never a smile when we say our prayers. How can one bear the thought of Eternity if in Heaven it is not permitted to laugh? Or come to that, permitted to weep? Is not our capacity to laugh and cry the measure of our humanity? No matter. It is not for this you have come. I have not thanked you. So I do so now. These days there are few visitors, and those that there are I cannot see. After they have gone He describes them to me. I'm sorry about your eyes, He said, but there's nothing I can do unless you want a miracle. No, I said, no miracle, thank You. I shall get used to it and I expect You will help me. Anyway, when you've lived a long time and can hardly hobble about on sticks but spend most of the day in bed your eyes aren't much use. It would need three miracles, one for the eyes, one for the legs and one to take twenty years off my age. Three miracles for one old woman! What a waste! Besides, I said, miracles are to convince the unconvinced. What do You take me for? An unbeliever?

It will be interesting, after you have gone, to find out who you are and what you look like. I mean from His point of view. It is almost a relief no longer to have sight of my own. I feel closer now to God. These days it is amusing to have the day described to me first by one of the helpers here and afterwards by Him. It is raining, they say; Sister, can you not hear the rain on the roof? Today has been hot and dry, He tells me after they have gone and I have said my prayers to summon Him. My prayers always bring Him. However busy He is, He finds time to drop by before I go to sleep. He talks mostly of the old times. Today in the heat and dryness you went to the bank, He says, surely you remember? Surely you remember your relief when Mr. Govindas accepted your cheque and gave it to the clerk and the clerk came back with the two hundred rupees? And remember thanking Me? Thank God! you said in a voice only I could hear, the money has not been stopped; and remembered the old days in Europe and your mother saying, The money has been stopped, am I a woman to starve, am I not destined for splendour? I loved my mother. I thought her beautiful. When she was in luck she gave money to the Sisters. They are clothed like that, she said, in answer to my question, because those are the garments of modesty which God has bid them put on.

One day the Sisters passed by. Sister, my mother said to one of them, here is something for your box. But they continued. My mother called after them. She had recently had a special stroke of luck. I remember her telling me, This week I had a special stroke of luck. She bought gloves and good red meat. She would have given money to the Sisters, but they passed by. She cried out after them: Are we not all creatures of chance? Is one coin more tainted than another?

You understand . . .? Yes, you understand. This I am telling you about was in Brussels. I remember there was a fine apartment and then a poor one. We shall go back soon to St. Petersburg, my mother used to say, but at other times she said we would go back to Berlin, and at others to Paris. Where then, I wondered, did we really live, where did we belong? There was about our lives a temporary feeling. Even a child of six could sense it. Since then I have always felt it. I am six years older than the century. It was 1900. I remember my mother saying, Today is the first day of the new century. It was an exciting moment. We had gloves and warm coats and stout shoes. The magic of Christmas was still in the streets. On everyone's face I could see a look of satisfaction at the thought of the new century beginning. My mother said: This will be our lucky year. Oh, the warmth of our gloved hands together! Our cosy reflection in the windows of the shops, my mother leaning down to whisper a promise or a fancy to me, her gloved finger on the pane, pointing out a box of crystallised fruits lying in a nest of lace-edged paper. A gentleman with a fur collar to his coat raised his hat to us. My mother bowed. We walked on through the crowded street. There was a park, and a frozen lake, and roast chestnuts sold at a stall. Perhaps that was another winter, another place. All the lovely things that happened to me as a child I seem to gather up and press together and remember as occurring on that first day of our lucky new century; our lucky new year after a warm, well-fed Christmas when a gentleman who smoked a cigar gave me a doll with flaxen hair and bright blue eyes. The things that happened that were not lovely I remember as happening on the day the Sisters refused to take my mother's charity. I was a bit older then, I think. Surely it was the time of the poor apartment? With the money that the Sisters had refused my mother bought me barley sugar and sugared almonds. I watched her give the tainted coins to the shop assistant and take the bags in exchange. She held the bags for me in one of her gloved hands. I was afraid of the sweets because they were bought with money the Sisters had refused and this was the same as with money refused by God because I thought the Sisters were in direct communication with Him. Why are they dressed like that? That is the question I had asked. And my mother said they were dressed like that because God had bid them put on the garments of modesty. Whatever the Sisters did had the stamp of God's special authority on it. I did not fully know the meaning of tainted, but if the money given for the sweets was tainted then the sweets had become tainted and my mother's gloves had become tainted. The glove on my own hand held in hers would also be tainted, and the taintedness would seep through the soft leather into my palm. But the worst thing was the feeling that God did not want anything to do with us. The Sisters were His special instruments. He had used them to turn His back on us.

Ah, but then suddenly I saw the truth! How could I have been so blind? How angry He would be with them for refusing the money my mother had offered! I was not sure what modesty was, but if there had been a time when He had been forced to bid the Sisters wear its garments, had not this been a mark more of their punishment than their grace? Were they not also the garments of penance? What had they done to be made to wear those special clothes? What more dreadful clothes would He bid them put on now, as further punishment? They had refused money. The money was to help people God said should be helped, the poor, the hungry. And how poor, how hungry such people must be if they were poorer than us, and hungry all the time! And the Sisters, walking the streets in garments that betrayed some earlier shame, had condemned those poor to even greater poverty and sharper hunger. Would He now put some red ugly mark on their foreheads, so that the poor could get out of their way when they saw them coming? Or make them dress in the kind of clothes they'd not dare show themselves in for fear of being laughed at or having stones thrown at them? I clung to my mother's hand. I said, "Mother, what will He do to them?" She stared at me, not understanding, so I repeated, "What will He do? What will God do to the Sisters this time?" She said nothing, but started walking again, holding my hand tightly. We went past a beggar woman. I hung back. We must give her some of the barley sugar, I said. My mother laughed. She gave me a coin instead. I put it in the old woman's dirty hand. She said God bless you. I was afraid, but we had good shoes and gloves and warm coats and God's blessing, and had made up to Him for what the Sisters had done wrong. The fire would be burning in the grate at home and there were the barley sugars and sugared almonds still to be eaten. I said to my mother, "Is *this* our lucky year?" For the first time I felt that I knew what she meant by luck. It was a warmth in the heart. Without realising it you found that you were smiling and could not remember what had made you smile. Often on my mother's lips I had seen this kind of smile.

*

The Sanctuary? Yes, it has changed. Now it is for orphan children. There is a new building and a governing body of charitable Indians. There are few who remember that old name, The Sanctuary. By God's grace I am permitted to stay, to live out my life in this room. Sometimes the children come to the window and stare through it, half-afraid of me, half-amused by the old woman they see here confined to her bed. I hear their whispers, and can picture the way their hands come up suddenly to cover their mouths to stifle a laugh. I hear when one of the helpers calls them, and then the scampering of their little bare feet and then farther away their shouts which tell me they have already forgotten the sight they have just found so enthralling, so funny. There is one of them, a little girl who brings me the sweet-sour smelling marigolds whose stalks and leaves are slightly sticky to the touch. Her parents died of hunger in Tanpur. She does not remember them. I tell her stories from the Ramayana and from Hans Andersen and feel the way her eyes stay fixed and full of wonder, seeing beyond me into the world of legend and fantasy, the reality behind the illusion. What a blessing to the old is blindness. I thank God for it now. There was a time when I wept, for I have always loved to look upon the world, although I dried my eyes and would not bother Him with it, but smiled at Him and said Good Luck! when He came into the room to say He was sorry. Good luck, I said, the world You made is a wonderful place. Whatever is Heaven like? Why, Sister Ludmila, He said, the same as here. He has got into the habit of calling me that for old time's sake and perhaps for His own. Am I forgiven? I asked. For what? He wanted to know. For calling myself Sister, for allowing them to call me Sister, for putting on the garments of modesty? What is this nonsense? He asked. Look, imagine that today is Wednesday. It has been hot and dry and Mr. Govindas has honoured your cheque. Why should you think Mr. Govindas would honour it and I refer it to drawer? He is, you know, a considerable Man of the world.

But you have not come to talk about this. Forgive me. Allow, though, a blind old woman an observation. Your voice is that of a man to whom the word Bibighar is not an end in itself or descriptive of a case that can be opened as at such and such an hour and closed on such and such a day. Permit me, too, a further observation? That given the material evidence there is also in you an understanding that a specific historical event has no definite beginning, no satisfactory end? It is as if time were telescoped? Is that the right word? As if time were telescoped and space dovetailed? As if Bibighar almost had not happened yet, and yet has happened, so that at once past, present and future are contained in your cupped palm. The route you came, the gateway you entered, the buildings you saw here in the Sanctuary – they are to me in spite of the new fourth building, the same route I took, the same buildings I returned to when I brought the limp body of young Mr. Coomer back to the Sanctuary. Coomer. Harry Coomer. Sometimes it was spelled Kumar. And Harry was spelled Hari. He was a black-haired deep brown boy, a creature of the dark. Handsome. Such sinews. I saw him without his shirt, washing at the pump. The old pump. It is gone. Can you picture it where it was, under the foundations of the new building that I know from people's descriptions of it looks like a fantasy of Corbusier?

– but in the old days, before Corbusier, only the pump – and young Kumar washing there, the morning after we had found him lying as if dead in the waste ground near the river and carried him home on the stretcher. We always took the stretcher with us on those nightly missions. When we got him back Mr. de Souza examined him. And laughed. "This one is drunk, Sister," he said. "All the years I have worked for you I have said to myself: one night we shall lay upon the stretcher and carry home the useless carcase of a drunken man." De Souza. He is a new name to you? He came from Goa. There was Portuguese blood in him somewhere, but a long way back. In Goa every other family is called de Souza. He was darker, darker by a shade or two than young Kumar. You prefer me to pronounce it Kumar. And why not? To hear him speak you might think him Coomer. But to see him, well, Coomer was impossible. And the name of course was rightly Kumar. He told me once that he had become invisible to white people. But I saw white women, how they watched him on the sly. He was handsome in the western way, in spite of his dark skin.

It was so with the policeman. The policeman saw him too. I always suspected the policeman. Blond, also good-looking, also he had sinews, his arms were red and covered with fine blond hairs, and his eyes were blue, the pale blue of a child's doll; he looked right but he did not smell right. To me, who had been about in the world, he smelt all wrong. "And who is that" he said. "Also one of your helpers? The boy there? The boy washing at the pump?" This was the morning the policeman came to the Sanctuary; six months before the affair in the Bibighar. They were looking for a man they wanted. Do not ask me to remember who the man was or what he was supposed to have done. Published a seditious libel, incited workers to strike or riot, resisted arrest, escaped from confinement. I don't know. The British Raj could do anything. The province was back under the rule of the British Governor because the Congress ministry had resigned. The Viceroy had declared war. So the Congress said, No, we do not declare war, and had gone from the ministry. Anything that offended was an offence. A man could be imprisoned without trial. It was even punishable for shopkeepers to close their shops at an unappointed time. To hear of these things, to read of them, to consider them now, an element of disbelief enters. At the time this was not so. Never it is so.

And so there he was, Merrick, the policeman, with his hairy red arms and china blue eyes, watching young Kumar at the pump in the way later I saw Kumar watched on other occasions. I did not fully appreciate. Even if I had fully appreciated what could I have done? Foreseen? Intervened? So ordained things that the affair in the Bibighar six months later would not have occurred?

For me Bibighar began on the night we found young Kumar on the waste ground near the river, lying as if dead. Some distance off were the huts and hovels of the outcastes, but it was late and no lights were showing. It was by chance that we found him as we came back from the nightly scouring of the bazaar by way of the Tiruptai temple and the river bank, a journey that brought us by the other side of the tank where the untouchable women wash their clothes, as you will have seen on your way here. You can picture us as we always went, Mr. de Souza in front with the torch, then myself and the boy behind with a folded stretcher over his shoulder and a stout stick in his free hand. Only once ever were we attacked, but they ran off when the boy threw the stick down and made for them, whirling the rolled stretcher over his head as if it weighed nothing. But that was a good boy. After a month the kind of boy I needed to take most of the weight of the stretcher would become bored, and when such a boy became bored his mind would usually turn to mischief. I never promised these boys more than four or five weeks' work. Towards the end of them I would begin to keep my eyes open for another lad wandering in the bazaar, sturdy and fresh from his village or some outlying district, a lad looking for work in a place where he believed fortunes were going for the asking. Sometimes such a boy would come to me, being told that there was easy money to be made with the mad white woman who prowled the streets at night looking for the dead and dying. Sometimes the previous boy would be jealous of the new boy and make up bad things about him, but usually the old one was glad enough to be off, with a bonus in his pocket and a chit addressed to whom it might concern extolling his honesty and willingness. Seeing the soldiers in the barracks some of the boys enlisted, others became officers' servants, one went to jail, and another to the provincial capital to become a police constable. The police were often at the Sanctuary. The boy who joined them had seen and admired the uniform and the air of authority. In the villages the police are local men. They do not have the same glamour for a boy as the police here in town. Some of these boys sent letters to tell me how they were getting on. Always I was touched by such letters because the boys were all illiterate and had paid good money to a scribe to send me a few lines. Only once did such a boy come back to the Sanctuary to beg.

We walked in darkness. "Over there," I called to Mr. de Souza, "flash your torch, there, in the ditch." My eyes were sharper than anyone's in those days. I knew every inch of the way, where a hump should be, or a shadow, and where there should be neither. There are images that stay vividly in your mind, even after many years; images coupled with the feeling that at the same time came to you. Sometimes you can know that such an image has been selected to stay with you for ever out of the hundreds you every day encounter. Ah, you think, I shall remember this. But no. That is not quite correct. You do not think that. It is a sensation, not a thought, a sensation like a change in temperature for which there is no accounting and only some time afterwards, forgetting the sensation, do you think, I expect I shall always remember that. So it was, you see, that first night of young Kumar. In the light of the torch, his face; the two of us down in the ditch, kneeling. Above us, the stretcher boy with the rolled stretcher aslant his shoulder, a young giant, dark against the stars. I must have glanced up and asked him to get the stretcher ready. The smell of the river was very strong. On a still night, when the earth has cooled, the water continues warm and the smell near the banks is powerful. When there is a wind the smell reaches the Sanctuary. The river flows downstream from the temple past the place appointed for the outcastes. In entering the river for any reason at this point the outcastes will not pollute the water the caste Hindus bathe in, but this is to reckon without the pollution from other towns upstream of Mayapore. In the waste ground where we knelt, in the ditch, the smell of the river mixes with the smell of night-soil. At dawn, here, the untouchables empty their bowels. Without the blessing of God upon you it is a terrible place to be. Poor Kumar. Lying there. Such a place of human degradation. India is a place where men died, still die, in the open, for want of succour, for want of shelter, for want of respect for the dignity of death.

Who is it, Mr. de Souza? I asked. It was the standard question. He knew many people. It was the first step in the drill of identification. Sometimes he knew. Sometimes I knew. Sometimes the stretcher-boy knew. For instance, a man known to be starving or dying of a disease, a man who would not go to hospital or come voluntarily to the Sanctuary, a man whose family were dead or lost or scattered, who had no hope of the world but only of a happier reincarnation or of an eternity of oblivion. But we usually knew where such men were to be found – such women too – and there would come the night when they could be lifted on to the stretcher, beyond protest, beyond defeat, and carried to the Sanctuary. For a fee the Brahmin priests would see to it that after they were dead they were suitably disposed of. The Hindus took their dead from us, the Mohammedans theirs, the State theirs. The State's dead were those we found dying, who were not identified. Such dead were taken to the morgue and if unclaimed after three days delivered to the students in the hospitals.

Every morning at the Sanctuary there would be women whose husbands, sons, and sometimes I suppose lovers, had not come home the night before. And often, too, the police. But all this was none of my business. I left that side of things to Mr. de Souza. My business was with the dying, not the dead. For the dead I could do nothing. For the dying, the little neither I nor the Sisters had been able to do for my mother: a clean bed, a hand to hold, a word through layers of unconsciousness to reach and warm the cold diminishing centre of the departing soul.

"Who is it?" I asked Mr. de Souza. He was a man of heart and a man of talent, a lapsed Catholic, who took nothing from the Sanctuary except his bed and board and clothing. "I don't know," he said. He turned young Kumar over then, to see if there were wounds on his back. We had found him lying partly on his side, which is not usually the position of a drunken man. Someone, you see, had been ahead of us, and had been through the pockets, whoever it was from the huts who must have seen him staggering along the river bank and had now returned home, possessing the wallet, turned out the lamps and feigned sleep. From the huts there was wakefulness, unnatural silence.

And we turned young Kumar back again, shining the torch on to his face again. And this is what I remember. This is the image. The face unchanged even after the body had been turned once, twice. The eyes shut, the black hair curling over the forehead which even in that state of his insensibility seemed to be furrowed by anger. Oh, such determination to reject! It was an expression you often saw on the faces of young Indians in those days. But in Kumar the expression had unusual strength. We got him on to the stretcher. I led the way back here to the Sanctuary. It was into this room where I lie and you sit that we brought him. It used to be Mr. de Souza's office. I had a room in the next building where the clinic used to be, which is now the children's sick bay. And here in this room Mr. de Souza, bending over young Kumar, suddenly laughed. "This one is drunk, Sister!" he said. "It is what I have been waiting for all the time I have worked for you. To find that only we have carried home a useless carcase of a drunken man."

"This one," I said, "is only a boy. To be so drunk he must also be unhappy. Let him lie."

And so he lay. Before I went to sleep I prayed for him.

Each night into sleep I took with me the memory of the face of one of the rescued and it almost pleased me that for once it was the face of a young man who was neither dying nor suffering from injury. We went, you know, into places where the police did not care to because they were afraid of being attacked, which is why sometimes we brought home hurt and wounded. When we did this we sent the police a message. Sometimes they came here on their own initiative, as they did on the morning after we brought young Kumar back. But never before had the District Superintendent come himself. If he had come the day before, the day after, there might never have been Bibighar. You might then have been able to say Bibighar to me now and I would have nothing stronger than an impression of ruins and a garden. But he came that day, Merrick, in short sleeves showing his red arms and with a clarity in his blue eyes, a determination to miss nothing, a madness, an intention to find evidence. Ah, but of what? "I want to see," he said, "the woman who calls herself Sister Ludmila."

And Mr. de Souza replied, "It is we who call her that." Mr. de Souza was afraid of nobody. I was through there, in the little room next door where now they hoard the clothing for the children, the books and stationery and games and rubber balls and cricket bats, but where in those days we kept special medicines from Dr. Gulab Singh Sahib's, under lock and key, and the safe for the money I collect each week from the Mayapore branch of the Imperial Bank, a safe for which Mr. de Souza also had a key. He slept here, where I am lying, with his desk there, where you are sitting, and the table there by the window the children stand at, under the light-bulb that at night no longer glares at me. That was where we put the stretcher when we came in. Sometimes we made more than one journey. He was standing there, Merrick, early on this Wednesday morning. I was opening the safe to get out the bag and the cheque book, and through the open doorway I heard him say this: "I want to see the woman who calls herself Sister Ludmila."

"It is we who call her that," Mr. de Souza said. "Right now she is busy. Can I be of help?" And Merrick said, "Who are *you*?" And de Souza smiled, I could hear the smile in his voice. "I am nobody. Hardly worthy of your consideration." In what they call a police transcript those words might look servile. To me they sounded defiant. So I came out and said,

"It is all right, Mr. de Souza," and saw Merrick there, carrying a little cane, dressed in shorts and a short-sleeved shirt, and a Sam Browne belt with a holster and a pistol in the holster, and his china blue eyes taking us all in. "Mrs. Ludmila Smith?" he said. I bowed. He said, "My name is Merrick. I am the District Superintendent of Police." Which already I knew, having seen him on horseback commanding the police who were controlling the crowds at the times of festivals, and driving in his truck over the Mandir Gate bridge. He had with him Rajendra Singh, the local sub-inspector who took bribes and stole watches from the men he arrested. Rajendra Singh had such a wrist-watch on. It was a finer watch than the one on Mr. Merrick's wrist, but less serviceable perhaps. The Indians always had a tendency towards the tawdry, the English towards the apparently straightforward, the workable. But there was nothing straightforward about Mr. Merrick. He worked the wrong way, like a watch that wound up backwards, so that at midday, for those who knew, he showed midnight. Perhaps no one could have cheated destiny by so arranging things that Kumar and Merrick never met. But I am sorry that it was here, although that was probably destined too, written on the walls when I first came here and saw the tumbledown buildings and recognised that they would serve my purpose.

"In what way can I assist you?" I asked him, and with a gesture I dismissed Mr. de Souza, because I knew this would please Merrick. But also it confirmed that it was I who was in command. In my white cap, my garments of modesty. To match Merrick's uniform. One does not live in the world of affairs for nothing. One learns the rules, the unwritten laws, the little by-ways of the labyrinth of protocol. I offered Mr. Merrick Mr. de Souza's chair, but he preferred to remain standing. He said he wished to conduct a search. Again, with a gesture, I gave assent or at least indicated awareness that to resist such a thing was not worth the trouble, indeed that the search itself was the only troublesome thing, that it was he, Merrick, who was putting himself out, using up his time. I did not even ask him what or whom the search was for. There are so many things that one could say in such circumstances. With less experience of official interference I might have said all of them. And he was sharp. He looked at me and showed me with his eyes alone that he had instinctively divined the reasons for my unprotesting acquiescence. He guessed that I had nothing to hide that I knew of, but also guessed that I was a woman whose luck had often been better than her judgment but might not always be.

"Then where shall we begin?" he said. I told him wherever he wished. When we got outside I saw his truck at the gate of the compound and a constable posted there, and then, after he had been through the first two buildings and we were walking towards the third building, I remember the sight of young Kumar, without his shirt, bending his head under the pump. He straightened up. We were a hundred yards away from him. He looked round. And Merrick stood still. And gazed at him. "And who is that?" he asked, "also one of your helpers?" Over this distance he stared at Kumar. I called Mr. de Souza who was following us. "He spent the night with us," I told Mr. Merrick. "Mr. de Souza perhaps knows his name." You understand, at this point I had not yet spoken to Kumar, but that morning had been told by de Souza only that the boy was all right but suffering from hangover and uncommunicative and not especially grateful for being brought to the Sanctuary, and had so far withheld his name. I thought that perhaps while Mr. Merrick was conducting his search de Souza might have gone to the boy and said, Look, the police are here, who are you? and been told.

"Mr. de Souza," I said, "the boy who spent the night with us –?" And de Souza said casually, "As you see he is all right now and making ready to go." "I'm afraid no one can go until I say so," Merrick said, not to me but to the sub-inspector, avoiding cleverly, you see, a direct engagement. "Are we then all under arrest?" I asked, but laughed, and indicated that arrested or not I wished to conduct him to the third building. He smiled and said that they were looking for someone, as no doubt I had guessed, and then walked on with me and Mr. de Souza, leaving the sub-inspector behind. Some sign from Merrick had made the sub-inspector stay put, to keep an eye on Kumar. When we reached the third building Merrick stopped on the verandah steps and turned round. I did so too. The boy had resumed his washing under the pump. The sub-inspector stood where we had left him, his legs apart and hands behind his back. I looked at Merrick. He also was watching the boy. They formed a triangle, Merrick, Kumar, Rajendra Singh – each equidistant apart. There was this kind of pattern, this kind of dangerous geometrical arrangement of personalities. "This building where we are now," he said, but not looking at me, still looking at Kumar, "is what is known as the death house?" I laughed. I said I believed that sometimes people who had never been to the Sanctuary called it that. "Are there any dead this morning?" he asked. "No, not this morning. Not for several days." "Homeless?" "No, I do not house the homeless." "The hungry?" "Those who are hungry know the days when there is rice. Today is not such a day." "The sick?" "The clinic receives only in the evening. Only people who cannot afford to lose a morning or a day's work come to our clinic." "And your medical qualifications?" "Mr. de Souza is in charge of the clinic. He gave up paid work as a lay practitioner to work with me for nothing. The health authorities of the municipal board sometimes come to see us. They approve of what they find. As District Superintendent of Police you must know most of these things." "And the dying?" "We have the voluntary services of Dr. Krishnamurti, and also of Dr. Anna Klaus of the purdah hospital. You can of course also inspect my title to the land and buildings."

"It is a curious arrangement," Mr. Merrick said.

"It is a curious country."

We went on into the third building. We had six beds in one room and four in another. In the year of the famine they were always occupied. Similarly in the year of the cholera. Now there was no widespread famine, no present outbreak of cholera. But scarcely a week went by that two or three of the beds were not in use. On this morning, however, they were all empty. The white sheets gleamed. He said nothing but seemed astonished. Such cleanliness. Such comfort. What? For the dying? The starved unwashed dying? Such a waste! Go into the bazaar and look around and in a few hours you would find occupants for each of the beds – occupants who would benefit, get well. The world has a vested interest in those capable of being made well. At one moment he turned as if to say something, but thought better. The Sanctuary was outside his comprehension. He had not yet worked it out that in this so efficiently organised civilisation there was only one service left that was open to me to give, the service that in a country like India there was no official time or energy left over for. The service that a woman such as myself could supply out of unwanted, unearned, undeserved rupees. For in this life, living, there is no dignity except perhaps in laughter. At least when the world has done its worst for a man, and a man his worst for the world, let him savour dignity then. Let him go out in cleanliness and such peace as cleanliness and comfort can give him. Which is little enough.

Perhaps in his bones, in his soul, Merrick was conscious of the meaning of the room he stood in, in his shorts and short-sleeved shirt and belt and holster. He looked at the polished floor and then with a sort of childish rudeness at my hands. Yes, they have always been soft and white. "Who does the work?" he asked. "Anyone," I said, "who needs to earn a few rupees." Why should I do the work myself when I had unearned undeserved rupees that would help fill the cooking pot of one of the untouchable women you saw on your way here, washing in the stagnant tank? "Where are these helpers today?" he said. I led him out into the compound behind the building where the helpers' quarters were. Perhaps there he saw it too, the distinction between the place of the living and the place of the dead: the smoky cookhouse, the mud and thatch and the men and women who earned rupees and lived in what among the living passed as cleanliness but in comparison with the rooms for the dying was dirt. He made them come out of their quarters, and stand in the compound, and then entered those hovels, going alone and coming out empty-handed, having found no one in hiding.

He pointed at the people with his cane. "These are your regular helpers?" he asked, and I told him that in the Sanctuary nobody was regular, that I hired and fired without compunction, wishing to spread whatever benefit it was in my power to give. "Is Mr. de Souza also irregular?" he asked. "No," I replied, "because the Sanctuary is as much his as mine. He sees the point of it. These people are only interested in the rupees."

"In life," he said, "rupees are a great consideration," and continued to smile. But the smile of a man wearing a belt and holster is always a special smile. It was in the great war when I first noticed that an armed man smiles in a way that keeps you out of his thoughts. And this is how it was with Merrick. When he had satisfied himself that the death house had no secrets he said, "Then there is just your night visitor," and went back to the front verandah, to that dangerous geometrical situation, pausing at the head of the steps, glancing to where the sub-inspector still stood, and then at Kumar who was still standing by the pump, buttoning up his shirt. Smiling, Mr. Merrick I mean, smiling and standing there. He said, "Thank you, Sister Ludmila. I need take up no more of your time," and saluted me by bringing the tip of his cane into touch with the peak of his cap, and ignored Mr. de Souza who was waiting behind us, and walked down the steps. And when he began to walk the sub-inspector was also set in motion. And they converged, in this way, on young Kumar who also continued, standing, buttoning his shirt, doing up the cuffs. Waiting. Having seen, but making no attempt to avoid. Without moving I spoke quietly to Mr. de Souza. "Who is the boy?" "His name is Coomer." "Coomer?" "In fact, Kumar. A nephew by marriage, I believe, of Romesh Chand Gupta Sen." "Oh," I said, and remembered having heard something. But where? When? "Why Coomer?" I asked. "Ah, why?" Mr. de Souza said. "It would be interesting, if not best, to go down." So we went down, following a few yards behind Mr. Merrick, so that we heard the first words, the first words in the affair that led to Bibighar. As we approached. Merrick. A clear voice. As if speaking to a servant. That tone. That language. The Englishman's Urdu. *Tumara nām kya hai?* What's your name? Using the familiar *tum* instead of the polite form. And Kumar. Looking surprised. Pretending a surprise not felt but giving himself up to its demands. Because it was a public place.

"What?" he said. And spoke for the first time in my hearing. *In perfect English. Better accented than Merrick's.* "I'm afraid I don't speak Indian." That face. Dark. And handsome. Even in the western way, handsome, far handsomer than Merrick. And then Sub-Inspector Rajendra Singh began to shout in Hindi, telling him not to be insolent, that the Sahib asking him questions was the District Superintendent of Police and he had better jump to it and answer properly when spoken to. When he had finished Kumar looked back at Merrick and asked, "Didn't this man understand? It's no use talking Indian at me." "Sister Ludmila," Merrick said, but still staring at young Kumar, "is there a room where we can question this man?" "Question? Why question?" Kumar asked. "Mr. Kumar," I said, "these are the police. They are looking for someone. It is their duty to question anyone they find here for whom I cannot vouch. We brought you here last night because we found you lying in a ditch and thought you were ill or hurt, but only you were drunk. Now, what is so terrible in that? Except hangover." I was trying to smooth over, you see, to make laughter or at least smiling of a different kind than Mr. Merrick's. "Come," I said, "come to the office," and made to lead the way but already the Bibighar affair had gone too far. In those few seconds it had begun and could not be stopped because of what Mr. Merrick was and what young Kumar was. Oh, if they had never met! If young Kumar had never been drunk, or been brought back; if there had never been that night-procession – the four of us, myself leading with the torch, Mr. de Souza and the boy bearing the stretcher, and Kumar on it, but now recovered, standing there by the pump in the compound, facing Merrick.

"Is that your name: Ku*mar*?" Merrick asked, and Kumar replied "No, but it will do." And Merrick, smiling again, said, "I see. And your address?"

And Kumar stared from Merrick to me, still pretending surprise, and said, "What is all this? Can anyone just barge in, then?"

"Come," I said. "To the office. And don't be silly."

"I think," Mr. Merrick said to me, "we won't waste any more of your time. Thank you for your co-operation." And signed to Rajendra Singh who stepped forward and made to take the boy by the arm but was brushed aside. Not with a violent motion, more with a shrug away to avoid distasteful contact. At this moment perhaps Merrick could have stopped it. But did not. Rajendra Singh was not a man to be shrugged off if Mr. Merrick was there to back him up. And he was bigger than Kumar. He hit him across the cheek with the back of his hand. A soft, glancing blow, done to insult as much as to sting. I was angry. I shouted, "That will be enough of that." It stopped them. It saved Kumar from the fatal act of retaliation. I said, "This is my property. In it I will not tolerate such behaviour." That sub-inspector – he was a coward. Now he was afraid that he had gone too far. When he struck Kumar he had also taken hold of his arm, but let it go. "And you," I said to Kumar, "stop being silly. They are the police. Answer their questions. If you have nothing to hide you have nothing to fear. Come," and again I made as if to lead them to the office. But Merrick, no, he was not going to take the smooth way out. He had already chosen the twisted, tragic way. He said, "We seem to have got beyond the stage when a talk in your office would have been a satisfactory preliminary. I am taking him into custody."

"On what charge?" Kumar said.

"On no charge. My truck's waiting. Now, collect your baggage."

"But I have a charge," Kumar said.

"Then make it at the *kotwali*."

"A charge of assault by this fellow with the beard."

"Obstructing or resisting the police is also an offence," Mr. Merrick said and turned to me. "Sister Ludmila. Has this man any possessions to be returned to him?" I looked at Kumar. His hand went to his hip pocket. Only now had he thought to look for his wallet. I said to him, "We found nothing. We turn out pockets, you understand, for the purpose of identification." Kumar stayed silent. Perhaps, I thought, he thinks it is we who have robbed him. Not until his hand went like that to his hip pocket was I certain that he had been robbed as he lay drunk the night before, out there in the fields, near the river bank. But in any case a lesser man would have cried out, "My wallet!" or "It's gone! My money! Everything!" drawing, attempting to draw a red herring. Ah, a lesser man would have cried out like that, if not to create a diversion, then in the little agony of sudden loss that always, to an Indian, in those days anyway, looked like the end of his constricted little world. And Kumar was an Indian. But had not cried out. Instead, let his hand fall away, and said to Merrick, "No, I have nothing. Except one thing."

"And that?" Merrick inquired, still smiling as if already knowing.

"A statement. I come with you under protest."

And all the time in those accents so much more English even than Merrick's. And in Merrick's book, this counted against him. For in Merrick's voice there was a different tone, a tone regulated by care and ambition rather than by upbringing. It was an enigma! Fascinating! Especially to me, a foreigner who had known an Englishman more of Merrick's type than Kumar's, and had heard this Englishman often rail against the sharp clipped-spoken accents of privilege and power. And here, in spite of the reversal implied by the colours of the skin, the old resentments were still at work, still further complicating the conflict. Kumar walked of his own accord towards the gateway and the waiting truck. But Merrick showed no sign of concern because he had the sub-inspector to trot after the prisoner. Another Indian. In this way mating black with black, and, again, touching his cap with the tip of his cane and thanking me for my services, keeping me talking, while I watched, at increasing distance, the affair between Kumar and the sub-inspector which was one of catching up, then push, and pull, and finally of what looked from where I stood like a violent meeting between Rajendra Singh, Kumar, a constable and the back of the truck with Kumar pushed, shoved, perhaps punched into the back of it, so that he fell inside rather than climbed. And the constable going in after him. And then the sub-inspector waiting, for Merrick. "Why do you let them treat him like that?" I asked. I was not surprised. Only pained. For these were violent, difficult times. But Merrick had already turned and was on his way to the truck and pretended not to hear. When he reached the truck he talked to the sub-inspector and then the sub-inspector got into the back too. Well, so it went. Such things happened every day. And at this time, you understand, I had no way of telling what Kumar was suspected of, let alone of judging what he might have been guilty of. Only I had seen the darkness in him, and the darkness in the white man, in Merrick. Two such darknesses in opposition can create a blinding light. Against such a light ordinary mortals must hide their eyes.

*

It is good of you to come again so soon. Have you yet seen Bibighar? The ruins of the house, and the garden gone wild in the way most Indians like gardens to be? They tell me it has not changed, that sometimes even now Indian families have picnics there, and children play. The Europeans seldom went, except to look and sneer and be reminded of that other Bibighar in Cawnpore. And at night it was always deserted. People said it was haunted and not a good place then, even for lovers. It was built by a prince and destroyed by an Englishman. I'm sorry. You are right to correct me. A Scotsman. Forgive me for momentarily forgetting. Such nice distinctions.

Bibighar. It means the house of women. There he kept his courtesans. The prince I mean. You have seen the purdah hospital here in the town, in the old black town as it used to be called? Beyond Chillianwallah? Surrounded now by houses? And changed. But it was a palace in the days when Mayapore was the seat of a native ruler and the only foothold the English had was one cut out by trade, need, avarice, a concern to open the world God had given them, like an oyster suspected of a pearl. Here all the pearls were black. Rare. Oh infinitely desirable. But it must have taken courage as well as greed to harvest them. Go into the old palace now, the purdah hospital, and look at what remains of the old building, the narrow gallery of tiny airless rooms, the kind of room these English merchants had to enter to strike bargains, and there is an impression – from the size of the rooms – of cruelty, of something pitiless. And it must have been like this in the Bibighar. We cannot know for sure because only the foundations are left and there never was an artist's impression of the place as it was before the Scotsman destroyed it. The Bibighar bridge was a later construction, and so to visit his women the prince must have gone either by the Mandir Gate bridge or by palanquin and boat, and so must his father in order to visit the singer in the house that he also had built on that side of the river, the house the Scotsman rebuilt and renamed after himself. Indeed yes, the house where you are staying. Before the Scotsman rebuilt and renamed it, was the MacGregor House also a warren of tiny rooms and low, dark galleries? Or was the singer given unaccustomed space, room for her voice to spread, her soul to expand?

Go to the Purdah Hospital. Lady Chatterjee will take you. Ask to go to the room at the top of the old tower. From there you can see over the roofs of the black town across the river and make out the roof of the MacGregor House. I wonder how often the prince who loved the singer climbed the steps of the tower to look at it? And I wonder whether his son also climbed the tower to look across the river at the Bibighar? From the Bibighar also it must have been possible in those days to see the house of the singer. They are only one mile distant. Not far, but far enough for a girl running at night.

In those days, when Mayapore was a kingdom, on that side of the river there were no other buildings, and so those two houses were marks on the landscape, monuments to love, the love of the father for the singer and the love of the son for the courtesans, the son who despised his father for an attachment which, so the story goes, was never consummated. Day by day I think the son climbed the tower of the palace or to the highest room in the Bibighar to survey that other house, the singer's house, to glory in its decay, and said to himself, *Such is the fate of love never made manifest*. And night after night caroused in the Bibighar, his private brothel, aware of the ruin that grew stone by mouldering stone one mile distant. Now it is the Bibighar that is nothing and the singer's house that still stands, the one destroyed and the other re-built, in each case by this man, this MacGregor.

Let me explain something. In 1942, the year of Bibighar, I am in Mayapore more than seven years and knew little of Bibighar, little of MacGregor. This was the case with most people. Bibighar. MacGregor. These were just names to us. Take the road, we might say, over the Bibighar bridge, past the Bibighar gardens, and then turn into the MacGregor road and follow it along until you reach the MacGregor House which stands at the junction of MacGregor and Curzon roads, and Curzon road will lead you straight to the Victoria road and the cantonment bazaar.

This would have been the quickest way to the bank – it is only a short distance from here to the Bibighar bridge. But usually I went the other way, through the Chillianwallah Bazaar and past the Tirupati temple. The real life of Mayapore is on the Mandir Gate bridge side. I would go over the bridge and past the church of the mission and the girls' school, through the Eurasian quarter, Station road, Railway cuttings, Hastings avenue, and into Victoria road from that side.

But then, after that day in August nineteen forty-two, the names Bibighar and MacGregor became special ones. They passed into our language with new meanings. What is this Bibighar? we asked. Who was MacGregor? we wanted to know. And then there seemed to be no scarcity of people able to tell us. Take MacGregor. It was said of him that he feared God, favoured mosques and Muslims and was afraid of temples, and burnt the Bibighar because it was an abomination, burnt it and then knocked down what was left, leaving only the foundations, the gardens and the surrounding wall. It was also said that he did this following the poisoning of an Englishman at the prince's court, an event which was used as an excuse for the annexation of the state by the British government, the old East India Company. But MacGregor did not burn the Bibighar so soon. The first record of MacGregor in Mayapore was in 1853, just four years before the Mutiny, but nearly thirty years after the annexation. In 1853 Mayapore was not the headquarters of the district. MacGregor was not an official. He was a private merchant, of the kind who began to flourish after the old East India Company ceased to trade but continued to govern. He made his money out of spices, grain, cloth and bribes. His old factory and warehouse stood where the railway depot now stands and there is still a siding there that bears his name, the MacGregor siding. The railway did not come to Mayapore until ten years after he died, so obviously his influence was still felt, his memory fresh. You can picture his laden wagons setting off along the road that became the Grand Trunk road, and picture Mayapore at that time, before the railway. Still on that side of the river there were not many buildings, no barracks, no civil lines. There was, I think, a chapel where St. Mary's is, and a Circuit house where the Court house stands. The District Officer lived in Dibrapur then. He would have stayed in the Circuit house when he came to Mayapore to hear petitions, settle cases, collect revenues. I wonder how many times he had to listen to subtle complaints which when he boiled them down he was able to see as complaints about MacGregor? I think of MacGregor as red-faced, his cheeks devastated by ruptured veins, virtual ruler of Mayapore, snapping his fingers at authority, terrorising clerks, merchants, landowners, district officers and junior civilians alike; corrupt, violent – and yet in a few years lifting Mayapore out of the apathy it sank into after the annexation that should have transformed it from an old feudal backwater into a flourishing modern community, safe and happy under the rule of the Raj. I think he was the kind of man the merchants and landowners he dealt with would understand. It is said that he spoke the language of the greased palm, and this language is international. I think they would always know where they stood with MacGregor. But not with the austere, incorruptible, so perfect, so English District Officer.

You see how these facts about MacGregor do not fit the story that he burned the Bibighar because it was an abomination? But then this was the European version of the tale. Perhaps, also, it is the story he told his wife, whom he married and brought to Mayapore only after he had established his fortune and rebuilt the singer's house and called it by his own name. By that time he had already burned Bibighar, not, according to the Indian version, because it was an abomination in his eye and the eye of the Lord, an abomination even twenty or thirty years after its last occupation, but because he fell in love with an Indian girl and lost her to a boy whose skin was the same colour as her own. There are two versions of the Indian account of the burning of Bibighar. The first is that he discovered the girl and her lover met in the Bibighar, and that he then destroyed it in a fit of jealous rage. The second is that he told the girl she would have to leave the MacGregor House and live in the Bibighar. He took her there and showed her the repairs he had made to it and the furnishings and clothes he had bought for her comfort and enjoyment. When she asked him why she must leave the MacGregor House he said: Because I am going to Calcutta to bring back an English wife. So that night she stole away with her true lover. When he found that she had gone he ordered the Bibighar to be burned to the ground, and then utterly obliterated.

And these stories ring truer, don't they? Truer than the tale that he burned Bibighar because it was an abomination. Poor MacGregor! I think of him only as a man of violent passions, and of emotions lacking any subtlety. If he had not burned the Bibighar like a child destroying a toy it had been told it mustn't play with, I wonder – would he have survived the Mutiny? The rebellious sepoys murdered their officers in Dibrapur and then roamed the countryside, eventually setting out for Mayapore with some idea of reaching Delhi, or of joining up with larger detachments of mutineers. It doesn't seem to be known where MacGregor was killed, perhaps on the steps of his house or with the Muslim servant Akbar Hossain whose body was found at the gate. History was left the impression that nothing could have saved MacGregor because the sepoys knew he had burned the Bibighar and it was rumoured that his Indian mistress and her lover died in the fire. One wonders – did Janet know these tales? Was she happy with MacGregor or was her life in Mayapore a constant torment? Is it only for her dead child that her ghost comes looking? Or to warn people with white skins that the MacGregor House is not a good place for them to be?

It is curious. But there has always been this special connexion between the house of the singer and the house of the courtesans. Between the MacGregor House and the Bibighar. It is as though across the mile that separates them there have flowed the dark currents of a human conflict, even after Bibighar was destroyed, a current whose direction might be traced by following the route taken by the girl running in darkness from one to the other. A current. The flow of an invisible river. No bridge was ever thrown across it and stood. You understand what I am telling you? That MacGregor and Bibighar are the place of the white and the place of the black?

To get from one to the other you could not cross by a bridge but had to take your courage in your hands and enter the flood and let yourself be taken with it, lead where it may. This is a courage Miss Manners had.

I think at first she was not in love with Kumar. Physically attracted, yes, and that is always a powerful compulsion. But I saw other white women, the way they looked at him. Well, they found it easy enough to resist temptation because they saw him as if he stood on the wrong side of water in which even to dabble their fingers would have filled them with horror. Perhaps there were times when the girl felt the horror of it too, but resisted such a feeling because she knew it to be contradictory of what she first felt when she saw him. And then she rejected the notion of horror entirely, realising that it was no good waiting for a bridge to be built, but a question of entering the flood, and meeting *there*, letting the current take them both. It is as if she said to herself: Well, life is not just a business of standing on dry land and occasionally getting your feet wet. It is merely an illusion that some of us stand on one bank and some on the opposite. So long as we stand like that we are not living at all, but dreaming. So jump, jump in, and let the shock wake us up. Even if we drown, at least for a moment or two before we die we shall be awake and alive.

She came several times to the Sanctuary. With him. With Kumar. She had said to him one day (at least I suppose she had said to him): Do you know anything about this woman, this woman who calls herself Sister Ludmila? Echoing something Mr. Merrick had said to her. Or Lady Chatterjee. And young Kumar probably smiled and told her that he did; even that once I had found him and taken him for dead and carried him back drunk on a stretcher to the Sanctuary. Unless he kept that quiet. I think he did. But they came. And looked at everything. Walking hand in hand. Which had become natural for her but not I think for him. I mean he seemed to be aware of the effect such a gesture might have on those who observed it. But she seemed unaware. She came also several times by herself. She brought fruit and her willing hands. She had it in mind to help. Once she offered money. Her mother had died the year before the war and her father and brother had both been killed in it. She had a small inheritance, but all her aunt's money, Lady Manners's money, was to come to her when the old lady died. I said, No, I have no need of money, unless it is stopped. If it is ever stopped, I said, then I will ask you. She said, Then how else can I help? And I asked her why she wanted to. Surely, I said, there are countless other good causes you could support? I remember how she looked at me then. When she was alone with me she often wore spectacles. I do not think *he* ever saw her wearing them. Not wearing them for him was a vanity. She said, "I have not been thinking in terms of good causes." I acknowledged with a smile, but did not fully understand. Later I understood. I think, yes later I understood. She did not divide conduct into parts. She was attempting always a wholeness. When there is wholeness there are no causes. Only there is living. The contribution of the whole of one's life, the whole of one's resources, to the world at large. This, like the courage to leap, is a wholeness I never had.

You know of course the image of the dancing Siva? He of the two legs and four arms, dancing, leaping within a circle of cosmic fire, with one foot raised and the other planted on the body of ignorance and evil to keep it in its place? You can see it there, behind you on my wall, carved in wood, my Siva dancing. The dance of creation, preservation and destruction. A complete cycle. A wholeness. It is a difficult concept. One must respond to it in the heart, not the intellect. She also looked at my little wooden Siva. Peering at it. Putting on her glasses. She was a big girl. Taller than I. With that northern bigness of bone. I would not call her pretty. But there was grace in her. And joy. In spite of a certain clumsiness. She was prone to minor accidents. She smashed once a box containing bottles of medicine. On several occasions they met here. She and young Kumar. She came from her work at the hospital and while she waited helped with the evening clinic. Once he was late. We left the clinic and waited in my room until he came. I felt that he had intended not to come but changed his mind. So I left them together. And on that other evening, the night of Bibighar, he did not come at all. When it was dusk she went away alone. I saw her to the gate. She took the road to the Bibighar bridge, going on her bicycle. I begged her to be careful. The town was still quiet, but the surrounding countryside was not. It was the day, you remember, the day of the first outbreaks in Dibrapur and Tanpur. In the hospital that day she had seen the woman from the mission who had been found holding the hand of the dead man. She came direct from seeing her, from the hospital to the Sanctuary, to meet young Kumar surely. But he never came. We sat in my room and she told me about the woman from the mission who was ill with pneumonia because she had sat out like that, in the roadway, in the rain, holding the dead man's hand. Crane. Her name was Crane. Miss Crane. It was raining also while we sat and talked, waiting for Kumar who never arrived, but at sunset the rain stopped and the sun came out. I remember the light of it on Miss Manners's face. She looked very tired. As the light began to go she said she must be getting home. And went on her bicycle. By way of Bibighar. The same bicycle. I mean the same that was found in the ditch in the Chillianwallah Bagh near the house of Mrs. Gupta Sen, where Hari Kumar lived. By Merrick. Found by Merrick. So it was said. But if Hari was one of the men who raped her why would he steal her bicycle and leave it like that, close to his home, as evidence?

And you see, when she left, wheeling her bicycle from the gate, turning to wave and then mounting and going into the twilight, I felt that she was going beyond my help, and remembered young Kumar driven only a few months before in the back of Merrick's truck, going alone to a place where he also would be beyond reach of help. On that day when Merrick had driven away, taking young Kumar to be questioned, I said to Mr. de Souza, Kumar? Kumar? The nephew of Romesh Chand Gupta Sen? This is what you think? And then went with him back to the office to finish the business Mr. Merrick had interrupted me in, getting ready, it being a Wednesday, to go to the bank, saying a prayer to God that on my arrival Mr. Govindas would not look embarrassed and take me on one side and say: "Sister Ludmila, this week there is no money, we have heard from Bombay cancelling your facilities."

But when I got to the bank, leaving the boy to wait outside, Mr. Govindas came out of his inner room and smiled as usual and took me in, to sit and talk, while they cashed my cheque for two hundred rupees. "Sister Ludmila," he said, "that boy outside. Where did he come from?" It was a joke between us. So I said, "Why, from heaven I suppose." "And the previous boy? Also he came from heaven?" "Well no," I said, "he came from jail and has recently gone back in." "It is what I am warning you against. Not to trust a boy simply because he looks strong enough to protect you."

But of course I knew this. I knew that after a week or two

such a boy would become bored and that when this happened his mind would turn to mischief. The boy on that particular day, already he was bored. When I got back outside with the two hundred rupees and the locked bag chained to my waist he was gossiping with people who had nothing better to do and was reluctant to leave them. But. He followed. He knew his duty. And so back we went, through the Eurasian quarter, past the church of the mission, and over the Mandir Gate bridge to the Tirupati temple. I have never been into the temple. The god of the temple is Lord Venkataswara who is a manifestation of Vishnu. And in the courtyard of the temple there is a shrine and an image of Vishnu asleep. It was of the image of the sleeping Vishnu that we talked, Miss Manners and I, that evening of Bibighar. Kumar had taken her there about two or three weeks before. Although he believed in nothing like that. But she wished to see the temple. His uncle had arranged it with the Brahmin priest. And so they had gone together and now she talked of it, to me who had never been. The rain stopped and the sun came out. It lighted her face, her tiredness, her own wish to sleep. I was able to visualise what she told me because of her tired face and because I had seen an image of the sleeping Vishnu in the temple at a place called Mahabalipuram, a temple by the sea, in the south, not far from Madras. Also there is in the south, you know, a very famous temple called Tirupati. High on a hill. The temple here in Mayapore takes its name from it. It is said that originally the people of Mayapore came from the south, that a Maharajah of Mayapore married a South Indian girl and built the temple to honour her and to honour the god she worshipped. Since then there has been so much assimilation it is impossible to divide and detect.

But in Mayapore there is the Tirupati temple. Mandir means temple. It is a word from the north. And so you have the meeting of south and north. The Tirupati temple, the Mandir Gate. In ancient days the town was walled. At night the gates were closed. The Mandir Gate then opened on the Mandir Gate steps. Coming from the north you would have had to cross the river by boat and climb the steps to the Mandir Gate. Later they built the Mandir Gate bridge. The steps remained but became simply the steps you see that lead up to the Tirupati temple. There were other gates to the south. There was never a Bibighar gate. The wall had gone, I think, before the Bibighar was built. The Bibighar bridge was built after

MacGregor's day. What a mixture! MacGregor, Bibighar, Mandir and Tirupati.

Leaving the bank that day with the boy following, armed with his stick, I passed through the Eurasian quarters, and went past the church of the mission where the Eurasians worshipped. A little Church of England in miniature. And waited at the level crossing because it was closed to allow a train to pass. And eventually moved, going with the crowd over the Mandir Gate bridge, and paused on the other side, to distribute some money to the beggars and to the leper who always sat there, with his limbs cut back like those of a bush that had to be pruned in order to ensure the bloom. And then, taking the left fork from the holy tree, past the open shop-fronts, turning a deaf ear to the offers of pān, cloth, soda-water, melons and jasmine, and through by the open archway in the wall surrounding the Chillianwallah Bazaar, stopping to buy chillis which Mr. de Souza had a liking for, and going then to the other side of the market square, past the loud meat and the stinking fish and the hunched figures of the market women with their scales lying idle like sleeping metal reptiles and up the stairway to the offices of Romesh Chand Gupta Sen, whose dead brother's widow, Mrs. Gupta Sen, lived in one of those concrete houses built on the Chillianwallah reclamation, in the Chillianwallah Bagh.

"Arrested!" he said. The uncle-by-marriage. Romesh Chand. "That boy," he said, "that boy will be the death of me. Who does he think he is? Why cannot he learn the ways of honour and obedience, the ways befitting a young Indian?" And called, ringing a little brass bell as though the office were a temple, so that I understood better young Kumar's disobedience, remembering from that morning the voice, the Englishness, and those northern sinews, that handsomeness. Do you understand? How it was alien, this background, this warren of little dirty rooms above the warehouses of the contractor? To him. Alien to him, to Kumar? Who spoke English with what you call a public school accent? Who had been taken to England by his father when he was too young to remember the place he was born in, and lived there, lived in England, until he was eighteen years old? But whose uncle back in India was a bania, sitting at a desk wearing the achkan, the highnecked coat, and with clerks under him, squatting in little partitioned cells, among grubby papers, one even holding paper money in his toes? For a time, after his father's death and his return to India, young Kumar was made to work there. But had rebelled and now did some work for the *Mayapore Gazette*. So much I gathered. I did not ask questions. Simply I went there to tell the uncle of Mr. Merrick's action. So that steps could be taken. What steps I did not know. But he rang the little bell for his head clerk and sent him away with a chit, a note to a lawyer to come at once. There was no telephone in that place. One could tell that Romesh Chand was a man who did not believe in telephones, in the necessity for telephones, or in acting in any way that could be counted "modern" or foreign. But who believed in his own power, his own importance. He asked how it was that his nephew came to be at the Sanctuary. I did not tell the whole truth. I said only that he had stayed the night there, that in the morning the police had come looking for a man they wanted and had taken Kumar away for questioning because he was the only stranger there. "It is kind of you to take trouble to inform me," he said. I said it was no trouble and came away. But all day I did not get young Kumar out of my mind. That afternoon I sent Mr. de Souza into the bazaar to find out what he could and went myself to the purdah hospital to speak to Anna Klaus, the doctor from Berlin who came to India to escape from Hitler and who was my good friend. After she had heard my opinion of the kind of boy young Kumar was, she telephoned Lady Chatterjee who was on the hospital committee. And said after she had telephoned, "Well, that is all I can do. Lady Chatterjee will speak to Judge Menen or the Deputy Commissioner. Perhaps. And your Mr. Merrick will find himself asked questions. Which is all right as far as it goes. But it depends, doesn't it, depends on your young Mr. Kumar, on what he has done? Or on what he is suspected of having done? If it is anything remotely subversive they can lock him up without a by-your-leave." Which I knew. And came back here, and found Mr. de Souza ahead of me. "It is all right," he said, "the police only kept him a couple of hours. When the lawyer sent by Romesh Chand arrived at the police station they had already let him go." I asked de Souza how he knew this. He said he had spoken to Romesh Chand's head clerk who was not supposed to have known what was going on but had found out by gossipping to the lawyer's clerk. So, Mr. de Souza said, it is all right, and we can forget Mr. Kumar. Yes, I said. It is all right. Dr. Klaus, also she came that evening. And I told her.

She said, "Well, that's all right then. That's all over." And again I said yes. But did not think so. When we went out that night with the stretcher I could not get it out of my mind that it was not all right and not all over. I asked myself, Did I then do wrong? To warn Romesh Chand? To get Dr. Klaus to arrange it that important people would ask questions? Young Kumar was questioned and then allowed to go. And after he had gone his uncle's lawyer arrived. Merrick probably knew this but took no notice. An Indian lawyer was nothing. But later that day, when perhaps so far as Merrick was concerned the case of young Kumar had been settled and forgotten, he would have been rung by the Judge or Deputy Commissioner, or by someone ringing on the Deputy Commissioner's or the Judge's instructions and asked: Who is this boy Kumar you've got at one of the kotwalis for questioning? And Merrick would have said, He's not there any longer, why do you ask? And whoever it was who was ringing would say, Well, that's probably a good thing. We have been asked what's happening. Your young suspect seems to have a lot of influential friends.

To be asked after by people in authority could undo all the good Kumar might have done for himself by answering questions properly once he got to the police station, would count against him in Merrick's book – in Merrick's book, where Kumar had already gone down as a boy who spoke better English than he, and would now go down as a boy who had friends who were able to speak to Judge Menen or the Deputy Commissioner, just as if he were a white boy, and not a black boy. And had stared arrogantly and said, Didn't this fellow understand it's no good talking Indian to me?

And later, yes, later, walked in public, here in the Sanctuary in view of anyone who cared to watch, hand in hand with the white girl, Miss Manners. And perhaps walked like that elsewhere, where Merrick would hear about it, or see it. I did not know until too late that Merrick also knew Miss Manners. All Europeans all knew each other, but theirs, Merrick's and Miss Manners's, was a special way of knowing, it seemed. And that night of Bibighar I understood that it was this special way. Merrick came when it was dark. In his truck. Alone. He said, "I believe you know a girl called Daphne Manners? I have just come from the MacGregor House. She isn't home yet. Have you seen her?" "Yes," I said. "She was here. But left just before it got dark." I did not think there was any personal interest in his inquiry. There was trouble in the district. And he was a policeman. I thought only of the girl. Of what could have happened to her. I assumed, you see, that Lady Chatterjee had rung the police because Miss Manners had not reached home.

He said, "Why was she here?" I told him she sometimes came to help at the clinic. He seemed surprised and said, "I didn't know that. I knew she came here once because she talked about it. How often does she come?" "Very rarely," I said. For suddenly I was cautious. And then he asked, did she come alone, had she been alone tonight, did I know where she had planned to go when she left at dusk? Yes, alone, I said, alone tonight, and home so far as I knew, back to the MacGregor House. By which route? "Well, from here," I said, "it's quicker by the Bibighar. Didn't you come that way from the MacGregor House?" It seemed that he hadn't, that from the MacGregor House he had driven first to the kotwali on the Mandir Gate bridge side, and then remembered she had once talked to him of a visit to the Sanctuary and drove here from that direction. "So you probably missed her," I said, and Merrick replied, "But you say she left at dusk. I was at the MacGregor House more than an hour after dusk and until nearly nine o'clock and she hadn't got back."

And then because I was worried for her and momentarily forgot about Merrick and Kumar, I said what I had not intended to say, said what could not help putting the name Kumar into his mind. I said, "Perhaps she called at Mrs. Gupta Sen's." Seeing his face I wished that I had not said it. It was as if in mentioning Mrs. Gupta Sen I had actually pronounced the name Kumar. He said, "I see." Behind his eyes there was a smile. And everything fitted into place, fitted back into that dangerous geometrical position I had had warning of, with Merrick and Kumar as two points of a triangle, with the third point made this time not by Rajendra Singh but by Miss Manners. I had that sensation which sometimes comes to us all, of returning to a situation that had already been resolved on some previous occasion, of being again committed to a tragic course of action, having learned nothing from the other time or those other times when Merrick and I may have stood like this, here in this room where I am bedridden and you ask your questions, with the name Kumar in our minds and the name of a girl who was missing and who had to be found. The revelation that Merrick was concerned as more than a policeman and my own betrayal of the boy, of Kumar, through talking of the house in Chillianwallah Bagh, talking of Mrs. Gupta Sen's – these were the springs that had to be touched each time our lives completed one revolution and again reached the point where Merrick and I stood in the room. And each time the springs *were* touched, touched as surely as night follows day, touched before they could be recognised for what they were. I should have known that Merrick knew the girl. It was stupid of me. It was the price I paid for devoting myself to the interests of the dying instead of the living. I should not have assumed that just because she was a friend of Hari Kumar she could not also be a friend of Mr. Merrick. If I had not been stupid then we might have escaped from the cycle of inevitability and Merrick would not have left, as he did, already convinced that Kumar alone could solve the mystery of the girl's disappearance.

But I had not known that Merrick knew the girl or that in his own curious way he was fond of her. But I guessed it then, after I had said, "Perhaps she called in at Mrs. Gupta Sen's," and saw the excitement behind his otherwise blank but revealing china blue eyes. For he had long ago chosen Hari Kumar, chosen him as a victim, having stood and watched him washing at the pump, and afterwards taken him away for questioning, to observe more closely the darkness that attracted the darkness in himself. A different darkness, but still a darkness. On Kumar's part a darkness of the soul. On Merrick's a darkness of the mind and heart and flesh. And again, but in an unnatural context, the attraction of white to black, the attraction of an opposite, of someone this time who had perhaps never even leapt into the depths of his own private compulsion, let alone into those of life or of the world at large, but had stood high and dry on the sterile banks, thicketed around with his own secrecy and also with the prejudice he had learned because he was one of the white men in control of a black man's country.

Merrick had known for a long time about Miss Manners and Kumar. I realise that therefore Kumar was already in his mind as someone who might know where she was. But there is something that perhaps you do not know yet. Something I partly gathered when she came that night of Bibighar, the night when Kumar did not arrive, something I learned more fully of on a later occasion, when she came to say goodbye because she was going up north to stay with her aunt, Lady Manners, until it was all over. She was pregnant. She made no secret of it. For a time we spoke of ordinary unimportant things. I was greatly struck by her calmness. I remember thinking, It is the calmness of a beautiful woman. And yet she was not beautiful, as you know, as everyone you have spoken to will have told you, as you have seen for yourself from her photograph. At one point we both fell silent. It was not the silence of people who have run out of things to say. It was the silence of people who felt understanding and affection, who were only uncertain just how much at that moment the friendship should be presumed upon. It was I who made the decision. To speak of Kumar. I said, "Do you know where he is?" meaning where he was imprisoned. I did not need actually to pronounce his name. She looked at me and the expression on her face told me two things, that she did not know but hoped, just for a second or two before the hope faded, that I did. She shook her head. She had asked. But nobody in authority would tell her. She had also called at the house in Chillianwallah Bagh, hoping that his aunt might know. But Mrs. Gupta Sen would not so much as come out of her room to speak to her. More than this, I think, for the moment she had not dared to do in case she did him harm. He had been arrested, that night of Bibighar, with some other boys. Earlier that day, you remember, several people had been taken into custody for political reasons. It was said they had been put into closed railway carriages and taken away, no one knew where. It was also said that the arrests of five or six boys on the night of the Bibighar affair had caused the riots in the town. But the riots no doubt were already planned. Perhaps the riots were worse because of the rumours of the terrible things that were happening to the boys arrested after Bibighar. Or perhaps they seemed to be worse because among the English there was this belief that after Bibighar none of their women was safe. They said that it was because of Bibighar that the Deputy Commissioner was persuaded to see the situation as one that was out of hand and called in the military before it was actually necessary. Perhaps the truth of these things will never be known. Before Miss Manners came to say goodbye to me it had occurred to me that perhaps it weighed on her mind that unwittingly she had been at the very centre of all those troubles. But when she came she had this look of calmness, of concentration, the look, I think, of all women who for the first time are with child and find that the world around them has become relatively unimportant. I put my hand on hers and said, "You *will* go through? Go through to the end?" She said, "Why do you ask?" and smiled, so that I knew she would go through. I said, "Have they tried to dissuade you?" She nodded. Yes, they have tried. She said, "They make it sound awfully simple. Like a duty."

But of course it was not simple at all. For them, perhaps, yes it would be simple. An obligation even. To get rid. To abort. To tear the disgusting embryo out of the womb and throw it to the pi-dogs. That's what I heard a woman say. A white woman. Is it true, she asked another – "Is it true that that Manners girl is pregnant and has gone to Kashmir to *have* the baby?" They were in Gulab Singh's pharmacy buying cosmetics. Things were back to normal by then. And being told that it seemed to be true, she said, "Well, what are we to make of that? That she *enjoyed* it?" Poor Miss Manners. How short a time it took for her to become "that Manners girl". Perhaps before Bibighar she had also sometimes been called this. But immediately after Bibighar her name was spoken by Europeans with the reverence they might have used to speak of saints and martyrs. But now. That Manners girl. And that ugly comment – "Perhaps she enjoyed it." And then the woman smiled and said in a loud voice, "Personally, if it had happened to me, I would have had a public abortion outside their bloody temple and thrown the filthy muck to the pi-dogs. Or made them stuff it down their priests' throats". And continued selecting powders and lotions for her white skin and succeeded, as that kind of woman always did, still does, in talking to the man who was serving her without once looking at him or letting her hands come within touching distance of his. One of the women, perhaps, that I had seen months before watching young Kumar when he accompanied me to the pharmacy, having met me on the way and stopped and talked for a while and offered to carry back to the Sanctuary the medicines I was going to buy, offered because that day I had no boy with me. Young Kumar and I had become friends. At least I felt that he was mine and I was his in spite of the fact that there was still an idea in his head that he had no friends at all. When he came out of the pharmacy he said, "As you saw, I've become invisible to white people." Perhaps he had not noticed the way the white women eyed him. Perhaps only he had noticed the way they pushed past him, or turned their backs, or called to the assistant he was already speaking to. He hated going into the cantonment shops for this reason. And yet I know for him there must have been a terrible longing to go into them, to become again part of them, because of their Englishness, because England was the only world he knew, and he hated the black town on this side of the river as much as any white man fresh out from England would hate it. Hated it more, because for him the black town was the place where he had to live, not the place he occasionally had to pass through with his handkerchief held to his nose on the way back across the bridge to the civil lines and the world of the club where white people gathered.

But Kumar is another story, isn't he? One that you must come to. I will tell you a name that might help you, that possibly no one heard of but myself, or has long ago forgotten. Colin. Colin Lindsey. Kumar told me about Colin when I saw him drunk on a second occasion. It was because of Colin Lindsey that he was drunk that first time, that night we found him and brought him back to the Sanctuary. In England Colin Lindsey was Hari Kumar's closest friend. They went to the same school. Colin tried to get his parents to look after Hari when Hari's father died and Hari was forced to come back to India. When he was not quite eighteen. With that Englishness. That English voice, that English manner, and English name, Harry Coomer. Speaking no Indian language. An Englishman with a black skin who in Mayapore became what he called invisible to white people.

But not invisible to the women in the pharmacy. Or to Miss Manners. Or to Merrick. And I was telling you something. About Merrick and what he already knew of the association between the girl and Kumar. I said to her, this day that she came to say goodbye, "Miss Manners, I have a confession. It has been a lot on my conscience." And told her how Merrick had come to the Sanctuary on the night of the Bibighar. How at this time I did not know that she and Merrick knew each other more than in the way one white person might know another on a civil and military station. But realised now that his interest was not only that of a policeman who had been told a white girl was missing. And then forgot, in my concern for what might have happened to her, that it was dangerous to mention the name Kumar to him, realised too late that it was especially dangerous to mention Kumar even obliquely in any connexion with herself. And had said, "Perhaps she called in at Mrs. Gupta Sen's."

"Why does it worry you," she wanted to know, "why is it on your conscience? I know Mr. Merrick came here and that when he left he went to Hari's house." I said: But later he went back. He left here and went to the house in Chillianwallah Bagh and asked for Hari and was told he was not at home. And then drove back to the MacGregor House. And found you had returned. In that state. And at once gathered patrols and surrounded the whole Bibighar area, and arrested the first five boys he found in that vicinity. *And went back to the house in Chillianwallah Bagh*. And went upstairs with constables and found Hari. With marks on his face, they say, bathing them, attempting to reduce evidence. And outside in the ditch, your bicycle.

Yes, she said. This is true. How did you know?

From Mr. de Souza, I said. He has many friends and finds out a lot of things. Some are true, some are just rumours. This obviously is true. And it is on my conscience. That if I had not mentioned the house in Chillianwallah Bagh Mr. Merrick would not have gone looking for Hari Kumar. Because *you* said nothing. We all of us know that *you* said nothing. That you said you did not see who it was who attacked you. We know that you have never implicated anyone. We know this from what Lady Chatterjee has said. I know it from Anna Klaus. We know that you even refused to attempt to identify the other boys who were arrested because you insisted you had never seen them properly in the dark. There is indeed one question in my mind. If Mr. Merrick had not gone back to the MacGregor House and found you, like that, would you have let it be known, at all, what had happened?

After a moment or two she said: "Why should I keep it secret? A crime has been committed. There were five or six men. Four of them assaulted me. What are you trying to say to me? That you too think Hari was involved?"

No, I said. No, not that. Only I am trying to unburden. To ask you to help me to unburden. There is, you see, this other thing I remember. On that evening of Bibighar, when you came to the Sanctuary to wait for Kumar. While you waited you told me about the visit to the temple. As you talked I had an impression. An impression that you had not seen him since then. Had not seen him for two weeks or more. That on the day of the visit to the temple there had been some disagreement between you. A quarrel. That it disappointed but did not surprise you that by dusk he still had not come to the Sanctuary to meet you and you had to leave on your own. As you left, I had the idea that you would call at his house before going home. To see him. To put right between you whatever had gone wrong. Which was why when Merrick was questioning me I said that you might have gone to the house in Chillianwallah Bagh. And this made him think at once of Kumar, because he knew where Kumar lived. He would have remembered it clearly from the day he took him away to the police station for questioning. I was not able to put all this into words to myself at the time, at the time Merrick was standing here in this room on the night of Bibighar. But the words were there, waiting to come. And came later, when I heard that Kumar was among the boys arrested, Kumar among those who had been taken away, and then I remembered how Merrick's expression changed because I said that you might have gone to Mrs. Gupta Sen's. And he looked round the room. As if he could tell that you and Kumar had been in the room on other occasions, had waited for each other here, that on this evening you had also been waiting for Kumar. As if at last he had discovered one of the places where you and Kumar met. I saw how important the discovery was to him, and that he was not just a policeman making inquiries about a missing girl. I had sensed this a moment or two before, when he seemed surprised to hear that you sometimes came to help at the clinic. It was the surprise of a man who felt he had a right to know all about your movements. Am I right?

Yes, she said. He seemed to think he had a right.

And he knew about you and Kumar?

Everybody on that side of the river knew, she said. Mr. Merrick warned me against the association.

And after this warning, I said, perhaps it was that you and Kumar had the quarrel, when you visited the temple? And did not see each other again? So that Mr. Merrick thought you had taken his warning to heart?

Yes, she said. I suppose that is the way it happened. The way it might have looked to him.

So then, you see, she could not unburden me. Of blame, of guilt, of treacherously saying to Merrick: Perhaps she has called in at Mrs. Gupta Sen's? Of being instrumental in reviving in him the exciting suspicion that Miss Manners and young Kumar still met in secret, here in the Sanctuary. Of opening up for him a way of *punishing* Kumar whom he had already chosen, chosen as a victim. For Merrick was a man unable to love. Only he was able to punish. In my heart I feel this is true. It was Kumar whom Merrick wanted. Not Miss Manners. And it was probably her association with Kumar that first caused Merrick to look in her direction. This is the way I see it. And there is another thing I see.

This.

That young Kumar was in the Bibighar that night. Or on some other night. Because the child she bore was surely Kumar's child? Why else should she look, carrying it, like a woman in a state of grace? Why else should she refuse to get rid, refuse to abort, to throw the disgusting embryo to the mongrels? Why else? Unless having leapt she accepted the logic of her action, and all its consequences? Including the assault in darkness by a gang of ruffians. And believed that from such an assault she carried India in her belly? But would this fit the picture I had of her as she sat here, calm, concentrated, already nursing the child in her imagination, feeling that so long as she had the child she had not entirely lost her lover?

There was one question I longed to put to her. Partly I did not because I felt I knew the truth and partly I did not because I believed it was a question she would refuse to answer. For Kumar's sake. There are ways, aren't there, in which one person can enjoin another to her own silence? And she had surrounded herself, and Kumar's memory, with this kind of silence. They hated her for it. The Europeans. Just as they criticised that woman from the mission – Miss Crane – criticised her for being unable to describe the men who murdered the teacher. But in the case of Daphne Manners the situation was worse, because for a time, after the rape, she was for them an innocent white girl savaged and outraged by black barbarians and it was only gradually that they realised they were going to be denied public revenge. Because she would not identify either. Because at one point she was reported as saying that for all she knew they could have been British soldiers with their faces blacked like commandoes. Because she asked if the boys arrested were all Hindus and on being told they were said that something must be wrong because at least one of the men who raped her was circumcised which meant he was probably a Muslim. She said she knew he was circumsised and would tell them why she knew if they really wanted her to. She said this in front of witnesses at the private hearing they held at the MacGregor House. The hearing was held because the whites were lusting for a trial. But what kind of trial could they have when it looked as if the victim herself would stand up in court and cast suspicion even on their own soldiers? And openly discuss such immodest details as a man's circumcision? So they got no trial. But what need did they have of a trial? The boys they arrested did not have to be found guilty of anything, but simply locked up and sent away, God knew where, with countless others. And with them, Kumar.

And then of course they turned on her. Oh, not publicly. Not to her face. Among each other. It would not have done for the Indians to know what they were thinking. But for the first time you would hear the English asking each other the questions Indians had been asking all the time. What was she doing at night in the Bibighar Gardens anyway? Obviously she had gone into the gardens voluntarily because nothing had ever been said about her being dragged off her bicycle as she rode past. And if she had been dragged off the bicycle wouldn't she have seen at least one of the boys who dragged her off? Wasn't there a street lamp on the roadside opposite the Bibighar? And wasn't there, not a hundred yards away, at the head of the Bibighar bridge, the level crossing and the hut where the gatekeeper lived with his family, all of whom are said to have sworn they had seen and heard nothing until Mr. Merrick's patrols stormed in and lined them all up for questioning?

I will tell you the story that was finally told, that was finally accepted by all the gossips of British Mayapore as the unpalatable truth. You do not have to look far for its source of origin. No farther I think than to Mr. Merrick. She had gone, they said, to Bibighar because Kumar had asked her to. Anyone could see the kind of boy Kumar was. The worst type of educated black. Vain, arrogant, puffed-up. Only by consorting with a white woman could his vanity be satisfied. And only a plain girl like Daphne Manners could ever have been inveigled into such an association. So confident did he become she would do anything he asked that he sometimes had the nerve to keep away from her for days, even weeks, at a time, the nerve to arrange a meeting and not turn up, to quarrel publicly with her, to humiliate her. And would then allow her the pleasure of being with him again for an hour or two. And all the time planning the biggest humiliation of all, which coincided, in all likelihood not by chance, with the time chosen by those Indians who thought to show the English who was master. For days before the planned uprising he kept away from her, working her to a fever pitch of desire for him, then sent her a message to meet him in the Bibighar. She flew to the rendezvous and found not only Kumar but a gang of toughs who then one by one systematically raped her. It was her shame and humiliation that made her keep silent. What English girl would want to admit the truth of a thing like that? But young Kumar was not as clever as he thought. That kind of so-called educated Indian never was. So arrogant and stupid had he become that he stole her bicycle and hadn't the common sense to leave it even a short distance from his own house. Perhaps he thought it didn't matter because by morning he expected the British would all be fighting for their lives. For one other thing was certain. A vain boy like that, for all his so-called English ways, was almost certainly playing a treacherous part in the uprising. Ah no, waste no pity on young Kumar. Whatever he got while in the hands of the police he deserved. And waste no pity on her either. She also got what she deserved.

This is what the English said. I spoke of it to Anna Klaus. Anna was fond of Miss Manners. It was Anna Klaus who treated her after the assault. I did not ask her the truth of the other rumour that went round. That Anna Klaus had told the Deputy Commissioner that in her opinion Miss Manners, before the assault, had not been *intacta*. For what could this prove either way about the affair of Bibighar? No doubt the Deputy Commissioner had his reasons for feeling he had to ask Dr. Klaus the question. If he asked it. There was, you see, after everything was over, and the English had re-established their control, there was for a while, before other subjects of gossip took it out of their minds, a desire in Mayapore to destroy Miss Manners, her reputation and her memory.

And perhaps they would have succeeded. Except for this one fact. That Mayapore is an Indian town. And after a while when tempers had cooled and the English had forgotten the twenty-one-day wonder of the affair in the Bibighar, the Indians still remembered it. They did not understand it. Perhaps because of the punishments people said had been exacted they would have preferred to forget it too. But out of it, out of all its mysteries, to them there seemed to be at least one thing that emerged, perhaps not clearly, but insistently, like an ache in an old wound that had healed itself. That Daphne Manners had loved them. And had not betrayed them, even when it seemed that they had betrayed her. Few Indians doubted that she had indeed been raped by men of their own race. Only they did not believe that among the boys arrested there was even one of those responsible. And this, they felt, was a belief they held with her. A cross, if you like, that they shared with her. And so, after the event, honoured her for the things she was reported to have said which shocked them at the time as much as they shocked the English. And particularly they remembered how she had said: For all I know they could have been British soldiers with their faces blacked.

Well! What courage it took to say that! In those days! When the cantonment was full of white soldiers and the Japanese were hammering at the gates down there in Burma, and the British were prone to describe as treachery anything that could not be called patriotic. And you must remember that. That these were special days. That tempers were very short because consciences were shorn. What sort of white Imperial power was it that could be chased out of Malaya and up through Burma by an army of yellow men? It was a question the Indians asked openly. The British only asked it in the unaccustomed stillness of their own hearts. And prayed for time, stability and loyalty, which are not things usually to be reaped without first being sown.

Perhaps, though, your prayers were granted. Because you are a curious people. In the main very conscious, as you walk in the sun, of the length or shortness of the shadows that you cast.

PART FOUR

An Evening at the Club

THE Mayapore district of the province is still administered in five sub-divisions as it was in the days of the British. It covers an area of 2,346 square miles. In 1942 the population was one and a quarter million. It stands now, in 1964, at one and a half million, 160,000 of whom live in the town of Mayapore and some 20,000 in the suburb of Banyaganj where the airport is. From the airport there is a daily Viscount service to Calcutta and a twice weekly Fokker Friendship service to Agra for the Delhi connexion. The area in the vicinity of the airport has become the centre of a light industrial factory development. Between Banyaganj and Mayapore there are to be found the modern labour-saving, whitewashed, concrete homes of the new British colony, and then, closer to town still, the old British-Indian Electrical factory, newly extended but still controlled by British capital. From the British-Indian Electrical the traveller who knew Mayapore in the old days and came in by air would find himself on more familiar ground as he passed, in succession, the red-brick Mayapore Technical College which was founded and endowed by Sir Nello Chatterjee, and the cream-stucco Government Higher School. Just beyond the school the railway comes in on the left with the bend of the river and from here the road – the Grand Trunk road – leads directly into the old cantonment and civil lines.

*

Going from the cantonment bazaar which is still the fashionable shopping centre of Mayapore, along the Mahatma Gandhi road, once styled Victoria road, the traveller will pass the main police barracks on his left and then, on his right, the Court house and the adjacent cluster of buildings, well shaded by trees, that comprised, still comprise, the headquarters of the district administration. Close by, but only to be glimpsed through the gateway in a high stucco wall, similarly shaded, is the bungalow once known as the chummery where three or four of Mr. White's unmarried sub-divisional officers – usually Indians of the uncovenanted provincial civil service – used to live when not on tour in their own allotted areas of the district. Beyond the chummery, on both sides of the road, there are other bungalows whose style and look of spaciousness mark them also as relics of the British days, the biggest being that in which Mr. Poulson, assistant commissioner and joint magistrate, lived with Mrs. Poulson. Almost opposite the Poulsons' old place is the bungalow of the District Superintendent of Police. A quarter of a mile farther on, the Mahatma Gandhi road meets the south-eastern angle of the large square open space known as the *maidan*, whose velvety short-cropped grass is green during and after the rains but brown at this season. If you continue in a northerly direction, along Hospital road, you come eventually to the Mayapore General Hospital and the Greenlawns nursing home. If you turn left, that is to say west, and travel along Club road you arrive eventually at the Gymkhana. Both the club and hospital buildings can be seen distantly from the T-junction of the old Victoria, Hospital and Club roads. And it is along Club road, facing the *maidan* that the bungalow of the Deputy Commissioner is still to be found, in walled, arboreal seclusion.

At half-past six in the evening the sun has set behind and starkly silhouetted the trees that shelter the club buildings on the western side of the *maidan*. The sky above the *maidan*, colourless during the day, as if the heat had burnt out its pigment, now undergoes a remarkable transformation. The blue is revealed at last but in tones already invaded by the yellowing refraction of the sun so that it is awash with an astonishing, luminous green that darkens to violet in the east where night has already fallen and reddens in the west where it is yet to come. There are some scattered trees on the edge of the *maidan*, the homes of the wheeling sore-throated crows which Lady Chatterjee says were once referred to by an American woman as "those durn birds". Certainly, in India, they are ubiquitous. Driving slowly down Club road with Lady Chatterjee, in a grey Ambassador that belongs to a lawyer called Srinivasan whom one has not met but is about to, one might indulge in the fancy of a projection from the provable now to the hallowed then, between which the one sure animated connexion is provided by the crows, the familiar spirits of dead white sahibs and living black inheritors alike. At this hour the *maidan* is well populated by an Indian middle class that enjoys the comparative cool of the evening. There are even women and young girls. They stroll or squat and talk, and children play games. But the overall impression is of the whiteness of men's clothes and caps and of boys' shirts, a whiteness which, like the brown of the grass, has been touched by the evening light to a pink as subtle as that of that extraordinary bird, the flamingo. There is a hush, a sense emanating from those taking the air of their – well, yes, a sense of their what? Of their self-consciousness at having overstepped some ancient, invisible mark? Or is this a sense conveyed only to an Englishman, as a result of his residual awareness of a racial privilege now officially extinct, so that, borne clubwards at the invitation of a Brahmin lawyer, on a Saturday evening, driven by a Muslim chauffeur in the company of a Rajput lady, through the quickly fading light that holds lovely old Mayapore suspended between the day and the dark, bereft of responsibility and therefore of any sense of dignity other than that which he may be able to muster in himself, as himself, he may feel himself similarly suspended, caught up by his own people's history and the thrust of a current that simply would not wait for them wholly to comprehend its force, and he may then sentimentally recall, in passing, that the *maidan* was once sacrosanct to the Civil and Military, and respond, fleetingly, to the tug of a vague generalised regret that the *maidan* no longer looks as it did once, when at this time of day it was empty of all but a few late riders cantering homeward.

Not that the *maidan* did not find itself in those days – on certain occasions – even more densely populated than it is this evening. The British held their annual gymkhana here, and their Flower Show, and it was the scene of displays such as that put on by the military complete with band in aid of War Week, which Daphne Manners attended with other girls from the Mayapore General Hospital and several young officers from the military lines, which, like St. Mary's Church, are to be seen on the far side of the *maidan*. The flower show is still held, Lady Chatterjee says; indeed until five years ago she exhibited in it herself; but the roses that used to be grown by English women who felt far from home and had infrequent hopes of European leave are no longer what they were and most of the space in the marquees is taken up with flowering shrubs and giant vegetables. The gymkhana, too, is still an annual event because Mayapore is still a military station, one – that is to say – with a certain formal respect for tradition.

Cricket week draws the biggest crowds, bigger even than in the old days, but then any event on the *maidan* now is bound to be more crowded, because although the British gymkhanas, flower shows and cricket weeks were also attended by Indians, that attendance was regulated by invitation or by the cost of the ticket, and the *maidan* was then enclosed by an outer picket of stakes and rope and an inner picket of poles and hessian (except in the case of the cricket when the hessian had to be dispensed with in the practical as well as aesthetic interests of the game) – pickets which effectively conveyed to the casual passer-by the fact that something private was going on. Nowadays there are no pickets other than those – as at the gymkhana, for instance – whose purpose is to separate the spectators from the participants, and there are influential Indians in Mayapore, the heirs to civic pride, who feel that it is a mistake to leave the *maidan* thus open to invasion by any Tom, Dick and Harry. Last year's gymkhana [Lady Chatterjee explains] was ruined by the people who wandered about on those parts of the *maidan* where the gymkhana was not being held but got mixed up with the people who had paid for seats and even invaded the refreshment tents in the belief that they were open to all. So great was the confusion that the club secretary, a Mr. Mitra, offered to resign, but was dissuaded from such a drastic course of action when his committee voted by a narrow margin to reinstate the old system of double enclosure in future. As for the cricket, well, on two occasions in the past five years, the players walked off in protest at the rowdyism going on among the free-for-all spectators, and the last time this happened the spectators invaded the field in retaliation to protest against the players' highhandedness. There followed a piched battle which the police had to break up with *lathi* charges just as they had in the days when the battle going on was of a more serious nature.

From problems such as these the British living in Mayapore today naturally remain aloof – so far as one can gather from Lady Chatterjee (who, when questioned on such delicate matters, has a habit of sitting still and upright, answering briefly and then changing the subject). It is rare (or so one deduces from her reluctance to swear that it is not) to see any member of the English colony at a public event on the *maidan*. They do not exhibit at the flower show. They do not compete at the gymkhana. They do not play cricket there.

There would seem to be an unwritten law among them that the *maidan* is no longer any concern of theirs, no longer even to be spoken of except as a short cut to describing something mutually recognisable as alien. Indeed, you might ask one of them (for instance the English woman who sits with another in the lounge-bar of the Gymkhana club, turning over the pages of a none-too-recent issue of the *Sunday Times* Magazine – today's fashionable equivalent of *The Tatler* or *The Onlooker*) whether she went to the flower show last month and be met with a look of total incomprehension, have the question patted back like a grubby little ball that has lost its bounce, be asked, in return, as if one had spoken in a foreign language she has been trained in but shown and felt no special aptitude or liking for: "Flower show?" and to explain, to say then, "Why yes – the flower show on the *maidan*," will call nothing forth other than an upward twitch of the eyebrows and a downward twitch of the mouth, which, after all, is voluble enough as an indication that one has suggested something ridiculous.

Apart from this Englishwoman and her companion there are several other English people in the lounge. But Lady Chatterjee is the only Indian and she has only sat where she is sitting (bringing her guest with her) because the first person met, as the club was entered and found not yet to house Mr. Srinivasan, was an Englishman called Terry who had been playing tennis and greeted her gaily, with a reproach that she came to the club too seldom and must have a drink while she waited for her official host and so had led her and her house-guest to the table where the two English ladies already sat and then gone off to shower and change, leaving Lady Chatterjee wrapped in her saree, the stranger in his ignorance, and the table in awkward silence punctuated only by Lady Chatterjee's attempts at explanations to the guest of his surroundings and his attempts to engage Terry's waiting ladies in a small talk that grows large and pregnant with *lacunae*, for want of simple politeness.

A question arises in one's mind about the extent to which the club has changed since Daphne Manners's day. The servants still wear white turbans beribboned to match the wide sashes that nip in the waists of their knee-length white coats. White trousers flap baggily above their bare brown feet, and stir old memories of padding docile service. Perhaps in the decor of this particular lounge-bar, change of an ephemeral nature may be seen: the formica-topped counter instead of the old wood that needed polishing, glazed chintz curtains decorated with spiral abstractions instead of cabbage roses, and chairs whose severe Scandinavian welcome brings the old cushioned-wicker comfort gratefully back to the mind.

But it would be foolish to suppose that such contemporaneity is a manifestation of anything especially significant, or to jump to the conclusion that the obvious preference shown for this room by the handful of English members present proves, in itself, their subconscious determination to identify themselves only with what is progressive and therefore superior. This lounge-bar, giving on to a verandah from which the tennis can be watched, was always the favourite of the Mayapore ladies, and for the moment at any rate the only ladies in the club, apart from Lady Chatterjee, are English. If Indian ladies on the whole are still happier at home, who but they are to blame for the look the room has of being reserved for Europeans?

But then, why are there no Indian men in the room either? And why are some of the Englishmen not sitting with their own women in the lounge-bar but standing in the other room where drinks are served, talking to Indian men? And why do they manage to convey (even at a distance, in the glimpse you have of them between square pillars across the passage and through wide open doors to the old smoking-room) a sense of almost old-maidish decorum, of physical fastidiousness unnatural to men when in the company of their own sex? Why, whenever one of them breaks away, crosses the passage and enters the lounge-bar to rejoin his lady, is there presently a rather too noisy laugh from him and a shrug and secret little smile from her? Why does he now exude the aggressive, conscious masculinity that seemed to be held in abeyance in the smoking-room?

The arrival in the lounge-bar of a grey-haired, pale-brown man of some sixty-odd years puts only a temporary stop to such private speculations. Mr. Srinivasan is of medium height, thin, punctilious in manner. His skin has a high polish. He is immaculately turned out. The light-weight suit, the collar and tie, point another interesting difference. The inheritors come properly dressed but the Englishmen expose thick bare necks and beefy arms. Mr. Srinivasan makes a formal old-fashioned apology for being late, for having failed to arrive first and greet his guests. He also makes a joke (once current among the English) about Mayapore time which it seems is still generally reckoned to be half-an-hour in arrear of Indian Standard. One gets up to shake his hand, and meets the mild but penetrating gaze that reveals a readiness to withstand the subtlest insult that an experience-sharpened sensibility is capable of detecting. Lady Chatterjee who addresses him as Vassi, says, "You know Terry Grigson's wife, of course?" and Srinivasan bows in the direction of the English woman who, still protectively immersed in the shallow enchantment of the *Sunday Times* Magazine achieves a token emergence by a slight lift of the head (which would be a look at Mr. Srinivasan if the eyelids did not simultaneously lower) and by a movement of the lips (that might be "Good Evening" if they actually opened more than a gummy fraction). Her companion, also introduced, nods, and being younger and less inhibited perhaps by ancient distinctions looks as if she might be drawn into the general conversation, but Mrs. Grigson, with a perfect sense of timing, turns the *Sunday Times* Magazine towards her and points out some extraordinary detail of Coventry Cathedral so that they are then both lost in the illustrated complexities of modern Anglo-Saxon art; and the uncharitable thought occurs that, for the English, art has anyway always had its timely, occupational value.

And it could occur to you, too, that Mr. Srinivasan is not at ease in the lounge-bar, that if he had only managed to conduct his affairs in accordance with Indian Standard instead of Mayapore time he would have been waiting at the entrance when his second best car, the Ambassador, drove up and deposited its passengers, and would then have taken them into the old smoking-room, not had to leave them to the jovial Terry Grigson whose wife finds nothing to laugh about but with whom Mr. Srinivasan and his guests are momentarily stuck, for politeness' sake, at least until Terry comes back from the showers and changing-room –

– as he does, beaming and raw-faced, in a creased bush shirt and floppy creased grey trousers, but not before Mr. Srinivasan with a thin, almost tubercular finger, has summoned a bearer and asked everybody what they are drinking and sent the bearer off to collect it, having been answered even by Mrs. Grigson, and by her companion who taking her cue from Mrs. Grigson also said, "Nothing for me, thank you." Terry comes back between the sending away of the bearer with the curtailed order and his return with a tray of three lonely gins and tonics, by which time Terry has also been asked by Mr. Srinivasan what he will drink, thanked him, and said, "I'll go a beer." When the gins and tonics arrive and Srinivasan says to the bearer, "And a beer for Mr. Grigson," Mrs. Grigson pushes her empty glass at Terry and says, "Order me another of these, Terry, will you?" which he does, with a brief, almost private gesture at the bearer. The other woman, lacking Mrs. Grigson's nerve for studied insult, would go drinkless did Terry not say, while Srinivasan talks to Lili Chatterjee, "What about you, Betty?" which enables her to shrug, grimace, and say, "Well, I suppose I might as well." Since no money passes and no bills are yet presented for signing, one wonders who in fact will pay for them, but trusts – because Grigson looks almost self-consciously trustworthy – that he will see to it afterwards that Mr. Srinivasan's bar account is not debited with a charge it seems his wife and her friend would rather die than have an Indian settle.

And now, perhaps abiding by yet another unwritten rule, perhaps having even received some secret, clan-gathering sign, a dumpy Englishwoman at an adjacent table leans across and asks Mrs. Grigson a question which causes Mrs. Grigson to incline her angular body by a degree or two and with this inclination fractionally shift the position of her chair, so that by a narrow but perceptible margin she succeeds in dissociating herself from those with whom she actually shares a table. It is difficult to hear what it is that so arouses her interest, because Lili Chatterjee, Mr. Srinivasan and (to his lone, team-captain's credit) Mr. Grigson are also talking with animation, and the stranger can only observe and make possibly erroneous deductions: possibly erroneous but not probably. There is nothing so inwardly clear as social rebuff – a rebuff which in this case is also directed at the stranger because he has arrived with one Indian as the guest of another.

And in the momentary hiatus of not knowing exactly what it is that anyone is talking about, one may observe Terry Grigson's off-handsome face and see that old familiar expression of strain, of deep-seated reservation that qualifies the smile and points up the diplomatic purpose; a purpose which, given a bit more time, may not prevail against the persistence of his sulky segregationist wife. And this, perhaps, is a pity, considering all the chat that goes on at home about the importance of trade and exports and of making a good impression abroad.

"Well no," Terry Grigson says, in answer to Mr. Srinivasan's for-form's-sake inquiry whether he and his wife will join the trio of Srinivasan, Lili Chatterjee and her house-guest for dinner at the club, "It's very kind of you, but we're going on to Roger's farewell and have to get back and change."

The Roger referred to is, one gathers, the retiring managing director of British-Indian Electrical. Almost every month one more member of this transient European population ups stakes, retires, returns to England or moves on to another station. For each farewell, however, there is a housewarming, or a party to mark the occasion of a wife's arrival to join her husband in the place where for the next year or two he will earn his living. Whatever that living actually is – with the British-Indian Electrical, with one of the other industrial developments, or teaching something abstruse at the Mayapore Technical College, it will be earned by someone considered superiorly equipped to manage, guide, execute or instruct. He will be a member of that new race of Sahibs. He will be, in whatsoever field, an Expert.

"There is actually a most interesting but undoubtedly apocryphal story about the status of English experts in India nowadays," Mr. Srinivasan says in his rather high-pitched but melodious lawyer's voice when the party in the lounge-bar has been broken up by the quick-downing by Terry Grigson of his beer and by the ladies of their gin-fizzes, and their departure to change into clothes that will be more suitable for the purpose of bidding Roger God-speed. Upon that departure Mr. Srinivasan has led Lady Chatterjee and the stranger across the lounge, through the pillared passage and the open doors into the comfortable old smoking-room that has club chairs, potted palms, fly-blown hunting prints and – in spite of the spicy curry-smells wafted in from the adjacent dining-room by the action of the leisurely turning ceiling fans – an air somehow evocative of warmed-up gravy and cold mutton. In here, only one Englishman now remains. He glances at Mr. Srinivasan's party – but retains the pale mask of his anonymity, a mask that he seems to wear as a defence against the young, presumably inexpert Indians who form the group of which he is the restrained, withheld, interrogated, talked-at centre. It is because one asks Mr. Srinivasan who this white man is, and because Mr. Srinivasan says he does not know but supposes he is a "visiting expert" that the interesting but perhaps apocryphal story is told.

"There was," Mr. Srinivasan says, "this Englishman who was due to go home. An ordinary tourist actually. He fell into conversation with a Hindu businessman who for months had been trying to get a loan from Government in order to expand his factory. A friend had told the businessman, 'But it is impossible for you to get a loan from Government because you are not employing any English technical adviser.' So the businessman asked himself: 'Where can I get such an adviser and how much will it cost me seeing that he would expect two or three years' guarantee contract at minimum?' Then he met this English tourist who had no rupees left. And the Hindu gentleman said, 'Sir, I think you are interested in earning rupees five thousand?' The English tourist agreed straight away. 'Then all you will do, sir,' the Hindu gentleman said, 'is to postpone departure for two weeks while I write to certain people in New Delhi.' Then he telegraphed Government saying, 'What about loan? Here already I am at the expense of employing technical expert from England and there is no answer coming from you.' To which at once he received a telegraph reply to the effect that his factory would be inspected by representatives of Government on such and such a day. So he went back to the English tourist and gave him five thousand rupees and said, 'Please be at my factory on Monday, are you by any chance knowing anything about radio components?' To which the English tourist replied, 'No, unfortunately, only I am knowing about ancient monuments.' 'No matter,' the Hindu gentleman said, 'on Monday whenever I jog your elbow simply be saying – "This is how it is done in Birmingham."' So on Monday there was this most impressive meeting in the executive suite of the factory between the Hindu businessman who knew all about radio component manufacture, the English tourist who knew nothing and the representatives of Government who also knew nothing. Before lunch they went round the premises and sometimes one of the officials of Government asked the Englishman, 'What is happening here?' and the Hindu gentleman jogged the Englishman's elbow, and the Englishman who was a man of honour, a man to be depended upon to keep his word said, 'This is how we do it in Birmingham.' And after a convivial lunch the Government representatives flew back to Delhi and the English tourist booked his flight home first class by BOAC and within a week the Hindu businessman was in receipt of a substantial Government loan with a message of goodwill from Prime Minister Nehru himself."

And one notes, marginally, that the new wave of satire has also broken on the Indian shore and sent minor flood-streams into the interior, as far as Mayapore.

*

Mr. Srinivasan is the oldest man in the smoking-room.

"Yes, of course," he says, speaking of the younger men – the Indians, "they are all businessmen. No sensible young man in India today goes into civil administration or into politics. These fellows are all budding executives."

Several of the budding executives wear bush shirts, but the shirts are beautifully laundered. Their watch-straps are of gold-plated expanding metal. One of them comes over and asks Lady Chatterjee how she is. He declines Srinivasan's invitation to have a drink and says he must be dashing off to keep a date. He is a bold, vigorous-looking boy. His name is Surendranath. When he has gone Mr. Srinivasan says, "There is a case in point. His father is old ICS on the judicial side. But young Surendranath is an electrical engineer, or rather a boy with a degree in electrical engineering who is working as personal assistant to the Indian assistant sales director of British-Indian Electrical. He took his degree in Calcutta and studied sales techniques in England, which is a reversal of the old order when the degree would have been taken in London and the sales technique either ignored or left to be picked up as one went blundering along from one shaky stage of prestige and influence to another. He is commercially astute and a very advanced young man in everything except his private life, that is to say his forthcoming marriage, which he has been quite happy to leave his parents to arrange, because he trusts to their judgment in such relatively minor matters.

"The thin, studious-looking boy is also a case in point. His name is Desai. His father was interned with me in 1942 because we were both leading members of the local Congress party sub-committee. His father told me last year when we chanced to meet in New Delhi that young Desai said to him once, 'Just because you were in jail you think this entitles you to believe you know everything?' They were quarrelling about Mr. Nehru whom this mild-looking young man had called a megalomaniac who had already outlived his usefulness by 1948 but gone on living disastrously in the past and dragging India back to conditions worse than in the days of the British because he knew nothing of world economic structure and pressures. My old friend Desai was secretary to the minister for education and social services in the provincial Congress Ministry that took office in 1937, and resigned in 1939. Before becoming secretary to the Minister he was in the uncovenanted provincial civil service and a lawyer like myself. But his son, this young man over there, is a potential expert on centrifugal pumps and says that people like us are to blame for India's industrial and agricultural backwardness because instead of learning everything we could about really important things we spent our time playing at politics with an imperial power any fool could have told us would beat us at that particular game with both hands tied. Such accusations are a salutary experience to old men like me who at the time thought they were doing rather well.

"Also you will have noticed, I think, that there are no old men in this room except for myself. Where are my old companions in political crime? Lili, please do not put on your inscrutable Rajput princess face. You know the answer. Dead, gone, retired, or hidden in our burrows grinding the mills of the administration exceeding slow but not always exceeding fine. You might find one or two of us at the other club. Didn't you know about the other club? Oh well, that is an interesting story. We sit with the lady whose husband was one of the founder members."

"Nello put up money but rarely went," Lady Chatterjee says.

"Also he chose the name, isn't it?"

Sometimes one could suspect Mr. Srinivasan of deliberate self-parody.

Lady Chatterjee explains, "They wanted to call it the MHC. All Nello did was get them to drop the H."

"So MHC became MC, which stands simply for Mayapore Club. The H would have made it the Mayapore Hindu Club. No matter. An English wag anyway dubbed it the Indian Club which I believe is an instrument for body-building. Also it was known among Indian wits as the Mayapore Chatterjee Club, or MCC for short. But whatever you called it it was always the *wrong* club. Of course it was originally meant to be an English-type club for Indians who were clubbable, but it was not for nothing that the H for Hindu was suggested. It became a place where the word Hindu was actually more important than the word Club. And Hindu did not mean Congress. No, no. Please be aware of the distinction. In this case Hindu meant Hindu Mahasabha. Hindu nationalism. Hindu narrowness. It meant rich banias with little education, landowners who spoke worse English than the youngest English sub-divisional officer his eager but halting Hindi. It meant sitting without shoes and with your feet curled up on the chair, eating only horrible vegetarian dishes and drinking disgusting fruit juice. Mayapore, you understand, is not Bombay, and consequently the Mayapore club was not like the Willingdon club which was founded by your viceroy Lord Willingdon in a fit of rage because the Indian guests he invited – in ignorance – to a private banquet at the Royal Yacht Club were turned away from the doors in their Rolls-Royces before he cottoned on to what was happening. Ah well, perhaps dear old Nello imagined in Mayapore a little Willingdon? But what happened? One by one the type of Indian who would have loved the club because it was the nearest he was then able to get to enjoying the fruits of what he had been educated up by your people to see as just one but an important aspect of civilised life – one by one this type of Indian stopped going to the Mayapore and with each abstention the feet of the bania were more firmly established under the table –or rather, upon the seat of his chair –

"I think they are ready in the dining-room."

*

"The point is, you see," Mr. Srinivasan says, having apologised for the absence of beef, the omnipresence of mutton, "that these old men, my peers, my old companions in crime and adversity, those who aren't dead, those who are still living in Mayapore, now find themselves somehow less conspicuous at the Mayapore club than at the Gymkhana. Just look at the young faces that surround us. So many of these boys are telling us that we cannot expect to dine out for ever on stories of how we fought and got rid of the British, that some of us never dine out at all, except with each other, like old soldiers mulling over their long ago battles. And when it comes to spending a few hours at a club, most of us – although not I – choose the company of men who rest on laurels of a different kind, men with whom it is easier to identify than it is with the members here because here everyone is go-ahead and critical of our past. I mean, for instance, that it is easier for us to identify with men like Mr. Romesh Chand Gupta Sen, now a venerable gentleman of nearly eighty years and still going every morning to his office above his warehouse in the Chillianwallah Bazaar. To the chagrin of his sons and grandsons, I should add. And on one evening a week to the Mayapore club to discuss business prospects with men who were not interested in politics then, and now are interested neither in technical experts nor in theories of industrial expansion, but instead interested as they always were simply in making money and being good Hindus."

*

There have been prawn cocktails. Now the curried mutton arrives. The chief steward comes to oversee its serving, but breaks off from this duty to walk over and greet a party of English, two of the men and two of the women who were in the lounge-bar. The steward indicates the table he has reserved for them, but they ignore him and select another more to their liking. Both the men are still wearing shorts. Their legs are bare to the ankles. The women have plump, mottled arms, and wear sleeveless cotton shifts. Without the knitted cardigans you feel they would put on at home of an evening over these summer dresses they have a peeled, boiled look. They are young. They sit together – opposite their husbands – an act of involuntary segregation that by now is probably becoming familiar to the Indians as they get used to a new race of sahibs and memsahibs from Stevenage and Luton but may still puzzle them when they recollect how critical the old-style British were of the Indian habit of keeping men and women so well separated that a mixed party was almost more than an English host and hostess could bear to contemplate.

The dining-room, like the smoking-room, has probably changed little since Daphne Manners's time. It is a square room, with a black and white tiled floor, and walls panelled in oak to shoulder height, and whitewashed above. Three square pillars, similarly panelled to the same height, support the ceiling at apparently random but presumably strategic points. There are something like a score of tables, some round, some rectangular, each with its white starched cloth, its electro-plated cutlery and condiment tray, its mitred napkins, its slim chromium flower vase holding a couple of asters, its glass jug filled with water and protected by a weighted muslin cover. There is a large Tudor-style fireplace whose black cavity is partly hidden by a framed tapestry screen. Above the fireplace there is a portrait of Mr. Nehru looking serene in a perplexed sort of way. One can assume that when Daphne Manners dined here the frame contained a coloured likeness of George VI wearing a similar expression. Four fans are suspended from the ceiling on slender tubes that whip unsteadily with the movement of the turning blades. There are two arched exits, one leading into the smoking-room and the other into the main hall. There is also a third exit but that only leads into the kitchens. Against the wall, close to the kitchen exit, stands a monumental oak sideboard or dumb-waiter. On its top tier there are spare napkins, knives, forks and spoons, water-jugs, and on the lower tier, baskets of bread, bowls of fruit, bottles of sauce and spare cruets. Light is provided by stubby candle-style wall-brackets and a couple of wooden chandeliers with parchment shades, and during daytime by the windows that look on to the porticoed verandah at the front of the club, windows whose curtains are now pulled back and are open to let in the night air.

Well: it can be pictured all those years ago, especially on a Saturday evening, with a band thumping in the lounge-bar from which the old wicker tables and chairs have been cleared, and the dining-room rearranged to provide for a cold buffet supper. In the flagged yard at the back that fringes the tennis courts there are coloured lights slung in the trees, and couples used to sit out there to cool off between dances, waiting for the next foxtrot or quickstep. Some swam in the little flood-lit pool that lies behind the changing- and shower-rooms, the pool which, tonight, is in darkness, in need of scraping (Mr. Srinivasan says as he conducts his guests on a tour of inspection after the ice-cream that followed the curried mutton), and is seldom used because it is open to all and neither race seems particularly to fancy the idea of using it when it can't be guaranteed that the person last using it was clean. There is a story that two or three years ago an Englishman emptied all the chamber pots from the ablution cubicles into it.

*

"But I was telling you earlier on," Mr. Srinivasan says,

leading the way back through the now deserted lounge-bar to the smoking-room – which has filled up and even sports a few ladies in sarees who are, one gathers, military wives – "I was telling you about the kind of man whom old fellows like myself who were reared on briefs and files and nurtured on politics now find it easier to fit in with than we find it here at the Gymkhana."

Mr. Srinivasan raises his finger and a bearer appears and takes an order for coffee and brandy.

"And I mentioned Romesh Chand Gupta Sen," he continues. "He is a case in point. With Romesh Chand it has always been a question of business first and politics last. Well, not even last. Nowhere. He has made three fortunes, the first during the old peace-time days, the second during the war and the third since independence. None of his sons was allowed to continue education beyond Government Higher School. I asked him why this was. He said, 'To succeed in life it is necessary to read a little, to write less, to be able to calculate a simple multiplication and to develop a sharp eye for the main chance." He married a girl who could not even write her name. She could not run a household either, but his mother trained her up to that, which is what Hindu mothers are for. When his younger brother married a girl called Shalini Kumar, Romesh prophesied no good coming of the union, because she came of a family who allowed education even if they did not wholly believe in it, and as a result Shalini's brother went to live in England and Shalini herself could write beautifully in English. She was widowed at an early age. You may find this difficult to believe, but on her husband's death the women of Romesh Chand's family did their best to persuade her to defy the law and become *suttee*. Of course she refused. What woman in her right mind wants to burn alive on her husband's funeral pyre? Also she refused to leave her dead husband's house in Chillianwallah Bagh. I tell you this because it is perhaps relevant to your interest?

"It was Romesh Chand who insisted that that Anglicised nephew of hers, Hari Kumar, should be brought back from England when her brother, Hari's father, died and left him homeless and penniless. Actually we suspected Hari's father of committing suicide when he realised he'd come to the end of a series of foolish speculations. Be that as it may, when Mrs. Gupta Sen heard the news of her brother's death she went to Romesh and asked him for money that would enable Hari to stay in Berkshire to finish at his public school and go on to a university. This would be, what? 1938. She had almost no means of her own. She lived as a widow, alone in the house in Chillianwallah Bagh, mainly on her brother-in-law Romesh's charity. It was because she had always wanted a son, a child of her own, that she fell in with Romesh's counter-proposal that Hari should be brought home to live with her and learn how to be a good Hindu. To bring about this satisfactory state of affairs Romesh said he would even be willing to pay Hari's passage and increase Mrs. Gupta Sen's monthly allowance. She had lived a long time alone, you know, seldom leaving the house. Almost she had become a good Hindu herself.

"She lived with great simplicity. Young Hari must have had a shock. From the outside the house in Chillianwallah Bagh looked modern. I suppose it still does. What I believe you used to call suntrap. All the houses on the Chillianwallah Bagh reclamation and development were put up in the late 'twenties. It was waste ground before then, and was called Chillianwallah Bagh because the land belonged to the estate of a Parsee called Chillianwallah. The Parsees have also always concentrated on business but they are much more westernised, hardly Indians at all. The land was bought from the Chillianwallah heirs by a syndicate of Mayapore businessmen headed by old Romesh Chand, who would never have lived in the sort of modern European-style house that was to be put up there, but saw nothing new-fangled in the anticipated profits. In fact it was to make sure of the amenities for development, such as lighting and water and drainage, and a Government grant-in-aid, that he saw to it his otherwise unsatisfactory younger brother – the one who married Shalini Kumar – got a seat on the Municipal Board. So, in time, up went these concrete suntrap-style monstrosities – suntrap only in the style because with so much sun about it's necessary to keep it out, not trap it, to have very small windows, you see, unless you have wide old-fashioned verandahs. And into one of them, into number twelve, Romesh's brother moved with his wife Shalini, the same house young Hari came to live in nearly ten years later and must have been shocked by, because inside they are dark and airless, with small rooms and steep stairs and no interior plan and Indian-style bathrooms. And in number twelve there was almost no furniture because although Mrs. Gupta Sen's husband had bought a lot to go with the house, Romesh paid for it with a loan, and had since sold most of it to pay himself back. The house itself also belonged to him on mortgage. I know these things because I was what in England you would call the family lawyer.

"Yes, you are right. Lili bet me you'd cotton on. Indeed yes. It was I. I was the lawyer Romesh Chand sent for that morning Sister Ludmila went to his office and told him Hari Kumar had been taken away by the police. They thought he was arrested. This, of course, was about six months before my own arrest. It never bothered Romesh that I was politically committed. He understood the uses of politics in the same way that he understood the law of diminishing returns. After I had gone to the police station and found that Hari was already released I went back to my office, sent my clerk with a message to Romesh, and then went on to the house in Chillianwallah Bagh, to find out what it had all been about.

"Hari would not come down from his room to see me. But Mrs. Gupta Sen and I were good friends. We always spoke in English. With Romesh I had to talk in Hindi. She said, 'Tell Romesh everything was a mistake. There is nothing for him to go to botheration over.' I asked her whether it was true, what the police had told me, that Hari had been drunk and taken by that mad woman to what she called her sanctuary. I had not known him ever to drink heavily. He was a great worry to his family but he had always seemed to be sober in his habits. She did not know whether he had been drunk. She said, 'But I know that his life here, and therefore mine, is becoming unbearable.'

"Young Hari Kumar, you know, was typical of the kind of boy Nello had in mind when he financed and founded the Mayapore club. But by Hari's time it was already choc-a-bloc with the banias looking like squatting Buddhas contemplating the mysteries of profit and loss. And of course there were no women. It wasn't intended to be a club for men only but that is what it had become and has remained. Which is one of the reasons why I am the exception to the rule, a staunch Gymkhana supporter! The lady over there is the wife of Colonel Varma. She is delightful. You must meet her. General and Mrs. Mukerji aren't here tonight, but that is because no doubt they are invited to Roger's number one farewell. Next Saturday will be number two farewell and even I am invited to that."

"So am I," Lady Chatterjee says. "I was supposed to go to number one with the other governors of the Technical Coll but said I couldn't, so I'm at number two as well."

"Then we will go together? Good. Meanwhile you, my dear fellow, have noticed, I expect, that all the English have now left the club?"

"To go to Roger's?"

"Oh, no. Of your fellow-countrymen who were here this evening only Mr. and Mrs. Grigson and the lady who was with Mrs. Grigson will be at number one party. The Grigsons are senior. The other English you saw were junior. They will go to number two. Roger refers to them as foremen. In fact Roger has been known to call the Gymkhana the Foreman's Club. It was one of the gentlemen of the type Roger refers to as foremen who emptied the chamber pots into the swimming pool. After he had emptied them one of his friends had the idea of making a little Diwali, a parody of our festival of lights. So they got hold of some candles and stuck them into the pots and lighted them and set them afloat. A few of our Indian members who were present complained to the secretary, and one of our youngest and strongest members even complained directly to the gentlemen who were having such an enjoyable time at our expense. But they threatened to throw him into the pool, and used language that I cannot repeat. As an innocent bystander I found the whole situation most interesting. It was an example of the kind of club horseplay we had heard of at second or third hand and a person like myself couldn't help but remember student rags from his college days. This particular demonstration was hardly a student rag, however. Of course they were drunk, but *in vino vertias*. They were acting without inhibition. Forgive me, Lili, you find the subject disagreeable. Let us have Colonel Varma and his wife to join us."

The colonel is a tall wiry man and his wife a neat wiry woman who seems to wear traditional Indian costume more for its theatrical effect than for comfort or from conviction. The tough little shell of skin-thin masculinity that used to harden the outward appearance of the British military wives also encloses Mrs. Varma. What terror she must strike in the tender heart of every newly commissioned subaltern! Her wit is sharp, probably as capable of wounding as her husband's ceremonial sword. Tonight he is in mufti. They are going to the pictures, the ten o'clock performance; the

English pictures at the Eros, not the Indian pictures at the Majestic. For a while the talk is of Paris, because the film is about Paris – the film itself is said to be rotten but the photography interesting – and then the Varmas say good-bye; Mr. Srinivasan's party breaks up and Lili goes to powder her nose.

"While we wait for Lili," he says, "let me show you something –" and leads the way into the black and white tiled hall where between two mounted buffalo heads there is a closed mahogany door with brass finger-plates and a brass knob. The mounted heads and the door all bear inscriptions: the latter on enamel and the former on ivory. The first buffalo was presented by Major W. A. Tyrrell-Smith in 1915, and the second by Mr. Brian Lloyd in 1925. The enamel plate on the door bears the single word: Secretary.

Mr. Srinivasan knocks and getting no answer opens the door and switches on the light and so reveals a small office with an old roll-top desk and an air of desuetude. "As the first Indian secretary of the Gymkhana, from 1947 to 1950 actually, I have a certain right of entry," he says and goes to a bookcase in which a few musty volumes mark the stages of the club's administrative history. Among them are books bound like ledgers and blocked on the spine in gilt with the words "Members' Book", and in black with the numerals denoting the years covered.

"You would be interested in this," he says, and takes down the book imprinted "1939-1945".

The pages are feint-ruled horizontally in blue and vertically in red to provide columns for the date, the member's name and the name of his guest.

"If you look through the pages you will see the signatures of one or two Indian members. But they were of course all officers who held the King-Emperor's commission. By and large such gentlemen found it only comfortable to play tennis here and then go back to their quarters. The committee were in rather a quandary when King's commissioned Indian officers first began to turn up in Mayapore. It was always accepted that any officer on the station should automatically become a member. Indeed it was compulsory for him to pay his subscription whether he ever entered the place or not. And you could not keep him out if he was an Indian because that would have been to insult the King's uniform. There was talk in the 'thirties of founding another club and reserving the Gymkhana for senior officers, which would have made it unlikely that any Indian officer on station would have been eligible. But the money simply wasn't available. In any case the Indian officers more or less solved the problem themselves by limiting their visits to appearances on the tennis courts. One was never known to swim in the pool, seldom to enter the bar, never to dine. There were plenty of face-saving excuses that both sides could make. The Indian could pretend to be teetotal and to be reluctant to come to the club and not share fully in its real life. The English would accept this as a polite, really very gentlemanly way of not directly referring to the fact that his pay was lower than that of his white fellow-officer and that therefore he could not afford to stand what I believe is still called his whack. If he was married the situation was easier still. The English always assumed that Indian women found it distasteful to be publicly in mixed company and so there was a tacit understanding that a married Indian officer would appear even less frequently than his bachelor colleagues, because he preferred to stay in quarters with his wife.

"And really there was remarkably little bad feeling about all this kind of thing on either side. An Indian who sought and obtained a commission knew what problems he was likely to encounter. Usually it was enough for him to know that he couldn't actually be blackballed at the Gymkhana merely because he was Indian, and enough for the English members to know that he was unlikely to put in any prolonged or embarrassing appearance. And of course British commanding officers could always be relied upon to iron out any difficulties that arose in individual cases. It wasn't until the war began and the station began to fill up not only with a larger number of Indian King's commissioned officers but also with English officers holding emergency commissions that the committee actually had to meet and pass a *rule*. But then happily, you see, a realistic analysis of the situation provided its own solution. In the first place the influx of officers into the station obviously meant a severe strain on the club's facilities. In the second place the new officers were not only holders of temporary commissions but tended to be temporary in themselves, I mean liable to posting at almost any time. And of course among them there were likely to be men called up from all walks of civilian life, men of the type who, well, wouldn't be at home in the atmosphere of the club. And so for once the committee found themselves thinking of ways of keeping out some of their own countrymen as well as Indians. We, who were not eligible, watched all this from the sidelines with great interest. The rule the committee passed was a splendid English compromise. It was to the effect that for the duration of the war special arrangements would need to be made to extend club hospitality to as many officers on station as possible. To do this the compulsory subscription was waived in the case of all but regular officers and two new types of membership were introduced. Officers with temporary or emergency commissions could enjoy either what was called special Membership, which involved paying the subscription and was meant of course to attract well-brought-up officers who could be assumed to know how to behave, or Privileged Temporary Membership which entitled the privileged temporary member to use the club's facilities on certain specific days of the week but which could be withdrawn without notice. Outwardly the no notice provision was meant to advertise the committee's thoughtful recognition of the temporary nature of war-time postings to the station. What it really meant was that an emergency officer who misbehaved once could be barred from entry thenceforth. The privileged temporary member had to pay his bills on the spot. He also had to pay a cover charge if he used the dining-room and what was called a Club Maintenance Subscription if he used the pool or the tennis courts. He was allowed to bring only one 'approved' guest at any one time, for whom he paid an extra cover charge. Approved was officially held to mean approved by the committee but it also meant approved by the man's commanding officer who no doubt made it clear to these young innocents who were in uniform for a specific and limited purpose what kind of guest would be admitted. Officially it was said to be an insurance against a young man bringing the wrong sort of *woman*. Unofficially it meant bringing no Anglo-India or Indian woman, and no Anglo-India or Indian man unless that man was himself a King's commissioned officer. In any case, the expense of an evening at the club was usually reckoned to have been raised to the level that no war-time temporary officer would be able to afford more than once a month unless he was well-off. This was the period during which Smith's Hotel really flourished. So did the station restaurant, and of course the Mayapore Indian club enjoyed unaccustomed affluence. The Chinese restaurant in the cantonment bazaar made a fortune and you had to book a seat at the Eros Cinema two or three days in advance. As for the old Gymkhana club, well, it had its unhappy experiences, but by and large managed to maintain its air of all-white social superiority.

"The curious anomaly was, though, that even in those expansive days which the die-hards used to refer to as the thin end of the wedge, Indian officers of the civil service, even of the covenanted civil service, were not admitted as guests let alone as members. Which meant that the District and Sessions Judge, dear old Menen, such a distinguished fellow, couldn't enter, even if brought by the Deputy Commissioner. There was no written rule about it. It was simply an unwritten rule rigorously applied by the committee and if you take Menen as a leading example, never challenged by those who were excluded.

"Here in this book, though, you will see that as far back as May the twenty-second, 1939, the Deputy Commissioner, Mr. Robin White, had the temerity to bring *to* and the luck to succeed in bringing *in* no less than three Indians who did not hold the King-Emperor's commission – the provincial Minister for Education and Social Services, the Minister's secretary – my old friend Desai – and myself. That is Mr. White's own handwriting, of course. Perhaps you can judge character from handwriting? Well, but all this is a long story. We must leave it for tonight. Lili will be looking for us."

Before the book is closed, though, a flick through the pages relating to 1942 reveals familiar names. The rule of the club has always been that a member signs his name on his first visit and then again on those occasions when he brings a guest. Brigadier Reid's almost illegible signature appears on a date in April; Robin White's on one or two occasions as host to men Mr. Srinivasan identifies variously as members of the Secretariat, Revenue Settlement Officers, the Divisional Commissioner, and – once – the Governor and his lady. And there too on several occasions is a curiously rounded and childlike signature easily read as that of Mr. Ronald Merrick, the District Superintendent of Police, and, in the same hand, the name of his guest, Miss Daphne Manners.

And on a date in February 1942 a Captain Colin Lindsey signed in, presumably on his first appearance as a temporary privileged member of the Gymkhana Club of Mayapore. Captain Lindsey's signature is steady and sober, unlike the signature that does not actually accompany it, but which one can see, by its side, in the imagination: the signature of his old friend Harry Coomer who round about this time was found drunk by Sister Ludmila in the waste ground where the city's untouchables lived in poverty and squalor.

*

At night the old cantonment area, the area north of the river, still conveys an idea of space that has only just begun to succumb to the invasion of brick and mortar, the civilising theories of necessary but discreet colonial urbanisation. From the now dark and deserted *maidan*, across which the uninterrupted currents of warm – even voluptuous – air build up an impetus that comes upon the cheek as a faintly perceptible breath of enervating rather than refreshing wind, there issues a darkness of the soul, a certain heaviness that enters the heart and brings to life a sadness such as might grow in, weigh down (year by year until the burden becomes at once intolerable and dear) the body of someone who has become accustomed to but has never quite accepted the purpose or conditions of his exile, and who sees, in the existence of this otherwise meaningless space so curiously and yet so poetically named *maidan*, the evidence of the care and thought of those who preceded him, of their concern for what they remembered as somehow typical of home; the silence and darkness that blessed an enduring acre of unenclosed common which, if nothing else, at least illustrated of its own accord the changing temper of the seasons. With here a house. And there a steeple. And everywhere the sky. Bland blue. Or on the march with armoured clouds. Or grey, to match the grey stone of a Norman church. Or dark: an upturned black steel receptacle for scattered magnetic sparks of light or, depending on the extroverted or introverted mood, an amazing cyclorama lit only by the twinkling nocturnal points of a precise but incalculable geometry.

And there is, at night, a strengthening of that special smell: a dry, nostril-smarting mixture of dust from the ground and of smoke from dung-fires: a smell that takes some getting used to but which, given time, will become inseparably part of whatever notion the traveller, the exile, the old hand, may have of India as a land of primitive, perhaps even tragic beauty. It is a smell which seems to have no visible source. It is not only the smell of habitation. It is the smell, perhaps, of centuries of the land's experience of its people. It is to be smelt out there on the broad plains as well as here in the town. And because it is also the smell of the plains, to smell it – perhaps a degree or two stronger – as the car turns a corner and passes a roadside stall lighted by a naphtha lamp, only deepens the sense of pervasiveness, of ubiquity, of vastness, of immensity, of endless, endless acre of earth and stone lying beyond the area of the lamp's light.

This is the bigger car, the Studebaker. This is the long way home: northwards along the western boundary of the *maidan*, with the old Smith's Hotel on the left, built in the Swiss Chalet style and dimly lit as befits an institution that has years behind it but isn't finished yet. This is Church road. It leads to St. Mary's and to the military lines. It is the road that old Miss Crane cycled along, every Sunday, rain or shine, and it cannot have changed much, although the banyan trees that shade it during the day and clasp branches overhead to make a theatrically lit green tunnel at night, must have sunk a few more roots during the last twenty years. Church road is an extension of the Mandir Gate Bridge road and at this hour the car is slowed by the plodding processions of carts drawn by white humped oxen lumbering homeward, back to the villages on the plains to the north of Mayapore. The bells on their necks can be heard through the open windows of the Studebaker – dulled by but insistent on the hot wind created by mechanical movement. The carts return empty of produce. The produce has been sold in the Chillianwallah bazaar. Now they are more lightly loaded with private purchases and the farmers' children, most of whom lie huddled, asleep, although a few sit upright staring with the fixity of waking dreams into the headlights.

For a moment, as the Studebaker half-circles the roundabout and takes the right-hand road along the northern edge of the *maidan*, the spire of St. Mary's may carry the stranger into a waking dream of his own; so English it is. So perfect. It must, surely, be very like the church in a district of the Punjab which Miss Crane entered all those years ago, looking for an image of herself that would not diminish her. The same grey stone. The same safe comfortable look of housing the spirit of England's personal protector. But few English now attend the services. This has become the church of the Anglo-Indian community. The minister is the Reverend A. M. Ghosh. Is there, perhaps, a congregational joke about his holiness?

Close by St. Mary's and its churchyard is the Minister's house. Like the church it is, tonight, in darkness. A few bungalows lie back on the left, continuing the line of building from St. Mary's corner to the beginning of the military lines opposite the *maidan*. From the air, by day, these are revealed as a geometrical complex of roads and clusters of old and new buildings: the red, tree-shaded Victorian barracks lying closest to the road the Studebaker travels on; the newer low concrete blocks farther back. But from the road, at night, the impression is of space, infrequent habitation marked by lonely points of light. It is not until farther on that the large palladian-style mansion of the old artillery mess comes into view, and the first jawans are seen: two soldiers on guard duty at a white pole barrier that denies free entry by a left-hand turn into the dark. The old artillery mess is now the area headquarters. In 1942 it was the headquarters of the brigade commanded by Brigadier Reid. Once past it, the sense of space diminishes. Tree-backed stucco walls, and side-roads lit by infrequent street-lamps, mark the neat suburban area of the senior officers' bungalows. And then, ahead, is the main block of the ocean-liner-lit Mayapore General Hospital. The Studebaker turns right, into Hospital road, the road that runs along the eastern edge of the *maidan* and leads back to the T-junction of Hospital road, Club road and Mahatma Gandhi road – once Victoria road – the principal highway of the civil lines.

"Let us," Mr. Srinivasan says, "extend the tour a little more. It is not very late," and directs the driver to go down past the chummery, the Court house, and the police barracks, into the cantonment bazaar and then to turn right again following the route that Sister Ludmila used to take, to and from the Imperial (now the State) Bank of India, through the narrower roads where the Eurasians lived in small bungalows backing on to the installations of the railway and out again, with a left turn, into the Mandir Gate Bridge road, past the main mission school and the church of the mission (both of which still flourish) to the level crossing where the car is halted to wait for the mail train that comes from the west and is due at any moment.

Beyond the level crossing lies the bridge and beyond the bridge the black town, still well-lit and lively. The steps leading up from the river to the Tirupati temple are floodlit by a neon standard. There are men walking up and down them, coming from, going into the temple precincts by the river gate. From here the river smell lying upon the warm air enters the open windows of the stationary car.

"They always close the level crossing gates," Mr. Srinivasan complains, "at the precise moment the train is officially scheduled, even if they know jolly well it is half an hour late. Let me fill in the time by telling you the story of how Robin White took the Minister for Education and me and my old friend Desai to the club in May 1939.

*

"We were all at the DC's bungalow and at six in the evening after three hard hours of conference, Robbie said to us, 'How about a drink at the club?' Naturally we thought he meant the Mayapore, but then he said, 'The Gymkhana.' We were astonished. The Minister begged to be excused. Perhaps he thought it was a joke. But Mr. White would not hear of it. He said, 'It is all arranged, the car is outside. Just come for an hour.' So off we went. It was the first time I had entered, the first time any Indian civilian had entered. Also it was the last because Mr. White was stopped by the committee from repeating his social indiscretion. But on the night when we arrived, you should have seen the porter's face when he opened the car door and saw us! Robbie said to the porter, 'Hossain, tell the secretary I am here with the Minister for Education, and his party.' It was quite a moment! We walked, Desai and I, slowly in the wake of Mr. White and the Minister, slowly because Robbie was obviously giving the porter time to run in and find the secretary. On the verandah we all stopped and although it was nearly dark Robbie made great play of standing there and pointing out the amenities of the club's grounds, in fact he kept us there until he judged that the secretary had been found and warned. By now, you understand, it was clear to me that the visit had not been arranged at all, only considered as a possibility. The Deputy Commissioner had waited with typical British restraint to see what kind of a man the Minister for Education was before committing himself to the risky enterprise of taking him to the club. But it was all right. The minister had turned out to be Wellington and Balliol, and to share with Mr. Deputy Commissioner a love of Shakespeare, Mr. Dryden and the novelist Henry James, as well as a concern for the

Government Higher School and the schools run by the District Boards. Also they enjoyed a disagreement about Mr. Rudyard Kipling whom Mr. White thought poorly of but the Minister, anticipating Mr. T. S. Eliot, thought well of. It is always necessary to have a mutual irritant, it's the best way of testing the toughness of individual fibre.

"And so the secretary came out. A man called Taylor, an ex-ranker of the Cavalry who had achieved gentleman's status by being commissioned Lieutenant Quartermaster and official club status because what he didn't know about organising the annual gymkhana could have been written on the face of a threepenny bit. I saw him coming from his office into the hall. Robbie White had a great talent for seeing through the back of his head. He turned round and called out, "Oh, hello, Taylor, we have the honour of entertaining representatives of our provincial government. Allow me, Minister, to introduce you to our most important member, the Secretary, Lieutenant Taylor." Which left poor Taylor in an impossible position, because although he hated Indians he adored Deputy Commissioners and being thought important. Which Robbie knew. Robbie was a senior member of the committee but he had been clever enough to hold his fire for months, until the proper opportunity arose. I mean the opportunity to bring as guests men whom it was not socially inadmissible to describe as honourable. Even a provincial minister of state, after all, is a minister of state, and however much the run-of-the-mill English colonial might object to his colour, it couldn't be denied that the Minister had been appointed as the result of a democratic election, an election held with the full approval and authority of the King-Emperor's Governor-General. And all in accordance with the *official* English policy to promote their Indian Empire by easy stages to self-governing dominion status.

"All the same, Robbie White was sticking his neck out. A club was a club, a private institution no outsider could enter, even as a guest of the Deputy Commissioner unless a club official allowed it. Remember Lord Willingdon and the Royal Yacht Club fiasco in Bombay! But Robin knew his man. The secretary looked sick, but he was afraid to make a scene. He tried to lead us into the little ante-room along the corridor from here, but Robbie knew he had got us in now, so he stalked straight into the smoking-room and totally ignored the silence that fell like a stone.

"My dear fellow, shall I ever forget my embarrassment? The more acute, you know, because it was an embarrassment aggravated by a pride I cannot properly describe. There was I, a just-on-middle-aged man who had thought never to enter this sacred edifice. Do you know what struck me most about it? Its old-fashioned shabbiness. I can't think what I had expected. But it was a shock. Let me qualify that. By shock I mean the sort of shock you describe as one of recognition. I suppose that by keeping us out the English had led us too easily to imagine the club as a place where their worst side would be reflected in some awful insidious way. But the opposite was the case. And the opposite was what one recognised and what one saw at once one should have really expected. Perhaps you will understand this better if I describe Robin White to you as I remember him. He was quite a young man, still in his thirties, very tall, and with one of those narrow English faces which used to appal us when we saw them for the first time because they seemed to be incapable of expressing any emotion. And we wondered: Is it that this man is very clever and potentially well-disposed, or is it that he is a fool? If he is a fool is he a useful fool or a dangerous fool? How much does he know? What on earth is he thinking? When he smiles is he smiling at one of our jokes or at a joke of his own? Is it distaste for us that makes him put up his chilly little barrier, or is it shyness? Almost it was more comfortable to deal with the other type of English face, the extrovert face, even though we knew that the chances of it remaining open and friendly for more than six months were remote. At least in that sort of face there was no mystery to solve. The stages of its transformation were not only clear to see but also predictable. But with this narrow, introverted face, it took a long time to feel at ease. Often a man with a face like this would appear and disappear without our ever knowing the truth about him. Sometimes we heard no more of him. At other times we heard he had succeeded to some important position, and then at least we realised that he had been no fool, although his subsequent reputation might also prove that he had been no friend either.

"For instance, with Stead, Robin White's predecessor, we all knew what we were up against. There were members of the local Congress sub-committee who preferred Stead's regime because Stead was almost a caricature of the traditional choleric Collector. We always said that he punished the district to avenge himself for what he considered unfair treatment by his own superiors in the service. If he had not been approaching retiring age in 1937 our first provincial minister for internal affairs would have tried to get him promoted to the relatively harmless position of Divisional Commissioner and pressed the claims of an Indian to succeed him. In which case we should not have had Robin White. We could have done worse, but not, I think, any better. This was my personal view. It was not shared by us all. Some of us, as I said, preferred Stead because he gave our committee so many reasons to complain to Congress in Delhi where questions would be asked in the so-called central legislative assembly, and so many reasons for the District and Municipal Boards to complain to the provincial ministry. There were too many of us who preferred gnawing at the bone of short-term contention to pursuing a long-term policy that could lead from co-operation to autonomy.

"Stead, you know, was a Muslim lover, if lover is the right word to describe a man who basically thought all Indians inferior. He made no secret of his preference, and this only added fuel to that ridiculous communal fire. Two of his sub-divisional officers were Muslims. When the Congress Ministry came into power he transferred one of these Muslims from an outside area to Mayapore itself, which meant that this man was really acting as assistant commissioner and joint magistrate in the town. Unfortunately this Muslim Syed Ahmed was of the militant kind. All Muslim offenders either got off lightly in his court or were acquitted. Hindus were dealt with very severely. In retaliation the Hindu-dominated District Board decided that in the village schools all the Muslim children had to sing Congress songs and salute the Congress flag. Communal differences have always tended to snowball. There were riots in Tanpur, which was in the jurisdiction of the second of Stead's Muslim sub-divisional officers, a man called Mohammed Khan. Our committee complained to the ministry that Mohammed Khan and Syed Ahmed were both inciting the Muslim community to create disorders. The ministries had no jurisdiction over the civil service but in certain circumstances pressure could be brought to bear, especially if you could make out a good case. Stead was eventually directed by the Divisional Commissioner to transfer Syed Ahmed to Tanpur. Mohammed Khan was posted to another district and Stead found himself with a young English assistant commissioner called Tupton, who was posted here from another district. It didn't make much difference because this fellow Tupton also thought Muslims manlier than Hindus, so Stead was laughing up his sleeve – until he was retired and we got Robin White. And it didn't take Robin long to cross swords with Tupton and arrange for him to be replaced by a man of his own choice, young John Poulson.

"In fact, I can tell you, it was the way he got rid of Tupton and brought in Poulson that first made us see that behind that not unfriendly but curiously expressionless face there was more than met the eye. To begin with, his getting rid of Tupton made it clear that there was an understanding of what constituted an unnecessary irritant. When it became clear also that he was not moving in a reverse direction, away from the Muslims towards the Hindus, but making a point of showing friendliness to both, we saw that he was strictly the fair-minded type. There was also a statesmanlike air about him. He requested, in the most diplomatic terms, that the District and Municipal Boards should reconsider the rule they had laid down about the compulsory salutation of the Congress flag in the primary schools. I recall the words in one part of his letter. 'The Congress, I appreciate, inspires the allegiance not only of a majority of Hindus but of quite a large number of Muslims. I submit however that although Congress is fundamentally an Indian national party and that it is correct to lead Indian children towards a patriotic sense of national duty by ritual observances, it is perhaps unwise to leave an impression on their minds of the kind of exclusion the Congress itself is rightly at pains to eradicate.'

"Well, you see, he had us by the hip, or at least had by the hip those of us who appreciated the subtlety of the English language. As a member of the sub-committee – and he had had the foresight to send us a copy of his letter to the District and Municipal Boards – as a member of the sub-committee who considered his submission I argued for an hour over the significance of the words 'impression' and 'exclusion'.

"Perhaps to you Congress is synonymous with Hindu. To us – originally – it was always the All-India Congress – founded, incidentally, by an Englishman. But since there have always been more Hindus than Muslims in India, it has also always gone without saying that its membership is and was predominantly Hindu. This did not in itself make it a party of Hindu policy. Unfortunately, there is always an unmapped area of dangerous fallibility between a policy and its pursuit. Do you not agree? Well, surely as an Englishman, a member of a race that once ruled us, you must agree? Was there not an unmapped area of dangerous fallibility between your liberal Whitehall policies for India and their pursuit here on the spot? What had Mr. Stead to do with official English policy without irrevocably violating it by his personal passions and prejudices? Do you not agree that the Mr. Steads of your world kicked and swore against every directive from Parliament and Whitehall that seemed to them to be reprehensible? As reprehensible as it would be for the garrison of a beleaguered fort to wave the white flat when plenty of ammunition was still to hand? Did not such people always feel themselves to be the quantity left out of the official equation, the unofficial but very active repository of the old sterling qualities they thought the politicians had lost sight of or never had? Don't you agree, my dear fellow, that those of your compatriots whom you have observed this evening, by and large, are still in the grip of some traumatic process that persuades them to ignore the directives of your government at home to export or die? Don't you think that we should get on better with the Russians and the Americans?

"Well, so it was, you understand, with members of the Congress. Perhaps even in a great degree because the official Congress policy wavered between the extremes of that curious unworldly man and our sophisticated Kashmiri Pandit who realised always and perhaps still realises that half a cake is better than no cake at all.

"So why should you expect the Congress to abide by rules no one else ever abided by? In countless places like Mayapore it became narrowly exclusive. In the same way that Stead became narrowly impenetrable, and your compatriots in the lounge-bar have become narrowly insular, needing the money they earn, the money we are quite prepared to pay them, but affecting to despise the people they earn it from.

"Forgive me. Lili is signalling me to shut up. But I am an old man. I am entitled, am I not, to say what I think? – and of course to stray from the point. I was telling of the Deputy Commissioner's letter and the perfect English flexibility of that sentence: 'It is perhaps unwise to leave an impression on their minds of the kind of exclusion Congress itself is rightly at pains to eradicate.'

"He was not only calling us to reaffirm the official party

line which held Congress to be a body representative of all India, but pointing out very subtly what in our hearts we knew, that many of our local activities were contrary to the party line, if you judged the party line on its highest originating level, especially when those activities were directed at children. 'It is perhaps unwise to leave an impression on their minds.' This made us think of the kind of minds we left an impression on. The minds of children. Once we had to face the fact that we were acting as adults who knew the rough and tumble of everyday party politics, but acting in a world of children who didn't, also we had to face the fact that these children for a long time now had equated Congress with Hinduism and the singing of Congress songs and the salutation of the Congress flag as an act of defiance not only of the British Raj but of Muslim national aspirations. Because it was we, their elders, who had simplified the issues in this convenient way.

"Unfortunately my arguments in favour of supporting the Deputy Commissioner's submission, my arguments in favour of dropping the morning ritual in our district schools, were defeated by a five to two majority. And I was deputed, as a disciplinary exercise, to draft the committee's reply to Mr. White. I remember only one sentence because the rest of my draft was torn to shreds, and this sentence alone remained as mine. Let me repeat it. It makes almost no sense out of context, but the interesting thing is that the Deputy Commissioner recognised its authorship. When he next met me he quoted it: 'The salutation of the Indian National Congress flag should not be susceptible of any narrow, communal interpretation.' He said: 'I quite agree, Mr. Srinivasan. At least, on one point your committee answered my letter.' From that moment we were friends, which is why when he heard that I was lunching with Mr. Desai and the Minister for Education he invited me to accompany them when they went to his bungalow to discuss the extension of primary education in his district. By then, as you probably realise, our provincial ministries had got over their teething troubles. But of course it was already 1939, although none of us could have guessed on that evening he took us to the club that by the end of the year the Ministry would have resigned over the ridiculous point of order raised on the Viceroy's declaration of war on Germany. Or guessed that we should then get thrown back on to the old personal autocratic rule of British Governors with a nominated council. That evening when we went to the Gymkhana it seemed as if the whole world was opening up to us.

"But this is the point I am tortuously trying to make. It was not until I came into the club with Desai and the Minister and Mr. White that I really understood what it was that men like Robin White stood for, stood for against all narrow opposition. I do not mean opposition in Whitehall. But opposition here. On the spot. In Mayapore. I saw then how well he *fitted* the club. How well the club fitted him. Like him, it had no expression that you could easily analyse. It was shabby and comfortable. But rather awe-inspiring – I suppose because the English as a ruling class attached so much importance to it. And yet the majority of the people who were there – well, you felt that no matter how well they thought they were made for the club the club wasn't really made for them. In the club, in the smoking-room to be exact, for the first time I saw the face behind the face of Robin White. It seemed to go awfully well with the shabby leather chairs that looked forbidding but turned out to be amazingly comfortable to sit on. And Robin, you know, *looked* at the servants when he spoke to them. You could see him receiving a brief but clear impression of them as men. He did not feel superior to them, only more responsible for them. It was his sense of responsibility that enabled him to accept his privileged position with dignity. That is always the kind of attitude that makes for confidence. In one dazzling moment – forgive the dramatic adjective – in one dazzling moment I really felt I understood what it was the English always imagined lay but only rarely succeeded in showing *did* lie behind all the flummery of their power and influence. And that is why I have always loved the club since then –"

"Even now –?"

"Oh well – I love it for what it was and even now it is really no different if you know what you are looking for. One always saw and sees through pretence. It is only that now that their responsibility has gone there is no longer any need for the average English person to pretend. And you have as well this very interesting situation in which emptying chamber pots into the pool can also be interpreted as a gesture of *your* own one-time under-privileged people against the kind of social forces that no longer work but used to keep them in their place. I mean, well, please forgive me, so many of your present-day experts are not what members of the club of twenty years ago would have called gentlemen, are they? They are what the English ladies of Mayapore would have called BOR types? British Other Rank? Well, you know, you send a chap like that to Mayapore today to teach us how to run one of those complicated bits of machinery and of course he is treated as a member of a superior race but I do not feel that he generally has much of a feeling of *responsibility* to teach, merely a need to earn a living in relatively pleasant surroundings and a feeling that what he finds so simple other people also should find simple, so that he is likely to become impatient. We cotton on very quickly to the superficial aspects of machinery, but not to its inner logic. This is what young men like Surendranath and Desai mean when they say we wasted time playing at politics. Anyway our shortcomings give the expert a feeling of considerable superiority and he also gets a bit of a kick, of which perhaps he is also slightly ashamed, to be automatically entitled to be a member of the Gymkhana. He laughs at what the Gymkhana used to represent – that old-fashioned upper-class English stuffiness and pretence – which is why I suppose he comes dressed in shorts and short-sleeved shirts and uses vulgar expressions. He knows almost nothing about British-Indian history, so writes off everything that seems to be connected with it as an example of old type British snobbery. Which means also that in a way he writes *us* off too. And of course underneath all this there is this other thing, his natural distrust of us, his natural dislike of black people, the dislike he may think he hasn't got but soon finds he has when he's been out here a while, the distrust and dislike he shares with those old predecessors of his, but has the rude courage to express in physical action, like emptying chamber pots into the swimming pool. There is as well a more subtle complication. In his heart he also shares with that old ruling-class of English he affects to despise a desire to be looked-up to abroad, and shares with them also the sense of deprivation because he has not been able to inherit the Empire he always saw as a purely ruling-class institution. If you said any of this to him openly he genuinely would not understand, and would deny what of it he did understand. But we understand it. To us it is very clear. But clearest of all now that there is no official policy of foreign government or mystique of foreign leadership that calls for pretence in public and private life, is the fact that behind all that pretence there was a fear and dislike between us that was rooted in the question of the colour of the skin. Even when we most loved, there was the fear, and when there was only the fear and no love there was the dislike. In this odd love-hate affair we always came off worst because you see – the world being what it was, what it is – *we* recognised and still recognise only too clearly that you were, that you are, far ahead of us in the practical uses of practical knowledge and we still equate fair skin with superior intelligence. Even equate it with beauty. The sun is too strong here. It darkens us and saps us. Paleness is synonymous with worldly success, because paleness is the mark of intellectual, not physical endeavour, and worldly success is seldom achieved with the muscles. Well – here already is the train."

And presently, with a mechanical precision recognisable as one not wrought by local invention but by foreign instruction, the gates of the level crossing swing back and leave the road open to the bridge and the temple and the black town. The Studebaker (also a foreign importation, sold by its American owner for a handsome profit to a Brahmin friend of Mr. Srinivasan's in Calcutta) glides forward and there below is the sweep of the river, glittering with the artificial jewels of the night's illumination. Obstructing the traffic that has been waiting to move in the opposite direction, from the black town to the civil lines (the old descriptive usages die hard), is another but shorter procession of carts drawn by white, hump-backed oxen. Their round eyes glint red in the headlights.

"Stop!" Mr. Srinivasan cries suddenly. "Would you like to see the temple? It is not too late? Oh no, come, Lili – let us show at least one thing tonight that is truly *Indian,*" and directs the Muslim driver to park wherever he can find a place.

At the bridgehead on the black-town side, with the Tirupati temple on the left, the road broadens into a square whose other end is marked by the holy tree and wayside shrine. On the right, almost opposite the temple, is the Majestic Cinema where the epic from the Ramayana is showing to packed houses. Beyond the square – it may be remembered – the road forks to the right in the direction of the jail and to the left to the Chillianwallah Bazaar. The square is lighted by a single standard close to the holy tree, but it is not dark because the shops are open-fronted and not yet shuttered, still open for custom, and lit by unshaded electric bulbs or glaring pressure lamps that hurt the eye to look at. Somewhere nearby – yes, from the coffee-house – there is the amplified sound of recorded music, a popular song of a celluloid civilisation – a girl's voice, nasal, thin, accompanied by strings, brass and percussion. There are a cow or two, parked cycle-rickshas, many people, and several beggar women who converge upon the Studebaker, carrying sleeping children aslant their bangled arms. Their eyes and the rings in their nostrils capture, lose, and recapture, shards of splintered light.

They reached the car and surround it, accompanying it, half-running, half-walking. When it stops their hands come through the open windows. It is necessary, in the end, for Mr. Srinivasan to threaten them with the police. They retreat, but only far enough to allow the passengers to alight. The driver stays with the car and he is left in peace, but the party that now makes its way back towards the temple is followed by the most persistent of the women. Sometimes, making a way through the crowd, you think they have given up. A hand lightly touching your sleeve and then tugging it proves otherwise. To look straight into her eyes would be fatal. In India the head too often has to be turned away. "You must not give them anything," Mr. Srinivasan says. An observer of the scene would notice that since leaving the car the beggar women have concentrated on the more vulnerable flank of the trio walking towards the temple: the white man. The observer would perhaps notice too that the woman who makes her dumb appeal through that gesture, that brief contact with the white man's sleeve, and who now keeps her voice down to a whisper and limits her vocabulary of begging to one urgently repeated word, "Sahib, Sahib," is the last to admit defeat, walking with the visitors almost to the entrance of the temple.

"I'm afraid," Mr. Srinivasan says, "that you will have to take off your shoes. If you like you could keep your socks on."

Socks? Ah, well, risk all!

The open gateway is fairly narrow, but it is deep because the gate is at the base of the tall stone tower that mounts in diminishing tiers of sculpted figures, the details of which cannot be seen at night. Inside the passage through the tower a temple servant squats by an oil-lamp, surrounded by chappals and shoes. With chalk he makes a mark on the soles and gives Mr. Srinivasan a slip of paper. The stone floor of the passage is warm to the bare feet and rather gritty. The descent into the main courtyard of the temple is by a shallow flight of four steps. The feet come into contact with sand. There are people walking, people praying and people sitting on the ground who seem to be gossiping. The illumination is dim. In the centre of the courtyard is the square building of the inner sanctuary, with steps leading up, and carved pillars supporting an ornamental roof. Around the walls of the courtyard there are other sanctuaries. Some are in darkness; others are lit to show that the god or goddess is awake. The figures, often no bigger than dolls, are painted and garlanded. A bell is rung in the main sanctuary: by a devotee of Lord Venkataswara warning the god that he seeks admittance. Slowly the trio of visitors walks round the courtyard until the entrance into Lord Venkataswara's sanctuary is revealed. A man with a shaved head, bare chest, and the string of the sacred thread looped over his light brown shoulder stands near a pillar. He is one of the priests of the temple. The black-skinned, loin-clothed devotee stands at the open doors of the sanctuary in an attitude of prayer – both arms raised above his head, the palms together. The short length of rope attached to the tongue of the iron bell that is suspended from the roof still moves. It is possible to get only a glimpse of the inner sanctum: a gleam of gold, silver and ebony, in the heart of the stone. There is a bitter-sweet smell in the air. The sand beneath the feet varies from grit to velvet softness. Through the river entrance comes the smell of the water.

There are trees in the courtyard. In the day they afford some shade. Behind the main sanctuary is the sanctuary of the sleeping Vishnu. The stone of the sanctuary floor is rubbed black and shiny. Inside, in the dim light of the oil-lamps set in the walls the carved recumbent god sleeps through an eternity of what look like pleasant dreams. He is longer than a lying man would be. He is part of his own stone pallet, carved into it, out of it, inseparable from it. He is smooth and naked, with square shoulders and full lips that curve at the corners into a smile. The eyelids are shut but seem always to be on the point of fluttering voluptuously open. Once this imminent awakening has made its impression, the stiff limbs begin to suggest a hidden flexibility as though, at least, the god may be expected to ease the cramp of long sleep out of them. The delicately carved but powerful hand would then drop from the stone pillow and fall aslant the breast. And then perhaps the full lips would part and he would speak one word, speaking it softly, as in a dream, but revealing a secret that would enable whatever mortal man or woman happened to be there to learn the secret of power on earth and peace beyond it.

"I am sorry we cannot take you into the holy of holies," Mr. Srinivasan says, "although I might swing it if I can convince the priest that you are a Buddhist. But perhaps some other time. Lili is looking tired."

Not only tired but, oddly, out of place.

"These days," Srinivasan explains, as shoes are found, socks retrieved from pockets and a coin given to the shoe-minder, "the temples are all controlled by Government. In fact you could really say the priests have become civil servants. They are paid salaries, and collect fees according to official scales. It cuts down a lot on all that extortion that used to go on. This is one of the things we old congressmen insisted on ... that India should be a secular democratic state, not a priest-ridden autocracy."

Before the car is reached, the same beggar-women encroach. Settled and safe in the Studebaker, Srinivasan says, "Well, we are holy now, I suppose. It is in order to be charitable," and throws some coins out of the window. The women scrabble for them in the dust, and the car, free of them, moves forward, taking the left fork from the square, where Sister Ludmila walked with her leather handbag chained to her waist. The lane is narrow, and harshly lit, and crowded. The bonnet of the Studebaker is like the prow of a boat, ploughing through a busy waterway. The chauffeur drives on the clutch and the horn. At the end of the lane, where it opens on to the walled square of the Chillianwallah Bazaar market the town is suddenly dark and dead. The market is closed. The houses are shuttered. Only a few lights show. The headlamps create dense angular shadows. The smell off the river comes through the narrow openings between deserted buildings.

Turning a corner there is a glimpse of the old palace, the Purdah Hospital: a high wall, an iron gateway in it, foliage inside the grounds, a light showing behind the leaves. A dog with white and yellow markings crosses the road in front of the car. The sky ahead expands, displaying its stars in counter-attraction to the goods that were for sale in the shops. Somewhere, to the left, is the place once known as the Sanctuary and to the right the Chillianwallah Bagh reclamation.

"She died years ago, they say," Mr. Srinivasan explains, speaking of Mrs. Gupta Sen who had been Shalini Kumar before her marriage. The car enters an area of well laid out but unmetalled badly lit roads, along which the suntrap houses of the rich merchants cluster in walled compounds, a few showing lights behind barred windows. Here there are the black, feathery silhouettes of coconut palms, leaning tall and drunken between the gaps in the houses. The car turns twice. But each road, each collection of dwellings, looks the same. Number twelve is an anonymous dark bulk. A grandson of Romesh Chand lives there for a few months in the year in the cold weather. The car, on Srinivasan's order, stops outside the iron, padlocked gate. There is nothing to feel except the night warmth and nothing to see except the shadows in the compound, and the culvert that leads from the road to the gate across the monsoon ditch in the bordering grass where the bicycle was found.

And young Kumar? Where is he now? Srinivasan shrugs. Dead perhaps. Upon Kumar's arrest after the rape in the Bibighar Romesh Chand disowned him. Perhaps, also, young Kumar disowned his family. Well, it is a vast country. Easy to get lost in. And again the sense of immensity (of weight and flatness, and absence of orientating features) blankets the mind with an idea of scope so limitless that it is deadening. Here, on the ground, nothing is likely, everything possible. Only from the air can one trace what looks like a pattern, a design, an abortive, human intention. The Studebaker noses forward, lost, at bay, but committed to automatic progression, out on to the Chillianwallah Bagh Extension road, which to the south leads to the now non-existent southern gate of the old walled town, and to the north of the Bibighar bridge.

The bridge has a low, stone parapet and is arched, as if perpetually tensed against the ache of rheumatism from having its supports so long in water. And so, down, to its northerly head, having led the traveller back across the invisible water (which in these less well-lit reaches does not glitter) to the second level-crossing: having led across the eternal back to the transitory, from the waters that have their source in the snows of far-off mountain ranges to the parallel lines of steel that carry the trains eastward to the unimaginable coast.

And here is the hut of the level-crossing keeper lit these days by a neon standard. The well-sprung car bounces luxuriously over the uneven surface of the wooden boards that have been set between the rails. It is not difficult to imagine the sensation of cycling over the crossing, with the light system showing green and, coming from the left, the smoky metallic railway smell that is the same anywhere in the world, and was certainly no different twenty-two years ago, so that it is possible to breathe in sharply and think: This is what she smelt as she cycled back from Sister Ludmila's Sanctuary.

But ahead, there is a change. The road is being re-surfaced. One remembers Lili Chatterjee having mentioned it. There are now warning lamps and mounds of chipped stone and x-shaped trestle ends that support long barricading poles: a familiar manifestation of public works-in-progress. The work in progress sends the car over to the right-hand side of the road, a few feet closer to the wall of the Bibighar Gardens.

An ordinary wall, such as you would find anywhere in India, a little higher than a man, stuccoed, greying, peeling. Old. With trees behind it screening an interior. As the car goes by nothing is said, but the silence is commentary enough.

Bibighar.

After a time even the most tragic name acquires a kind of beauty.

From here the car follows the route taken by the girl who ran in the darkness. Yes. This is what she must have felt: beyond the darkness of the buildings and the habitation, the space, the limitless territory. Through such ordinary ways, such unspectacular, unlit avenues. And all the time the curious smell – not of the railway now, but of the land – which perhaps she had learned to accept or not to notice, if not to love, to need.

PART FIVE

Young Kumar

WHEN Hari Kumar's father died of an overdose of sleeping pills in Edinburgh and the lawyers told him that there wasn't even enough money to pay in full what was owed to Mr. and Mrs. Carter who ran the house in Berkshire he rang the Lindseys and asked them what they thought he should do. Although the lawyers insisted that he could put the notion right out of his head he had an old-fashioned idea that he was responsible for his father's debts, if in fact there were debts. The Lindseys found it as difficult to believe the lawyers' tale of bankruptcy as he did himself. They said he must come over to Didbury right away and stay with them. He was not to worry, because Mr. Lindsey would see the lawyers and get proper sense out of them.

His father's death occurred in the middle of the Easter holidays of 1938, a few weeks before Hari's eighteenth birthday. The Lindseys were in Paris when it happened. If they had been at home Hari would probably have been with them and certainly have had their support at the funeral. He spent most of his vacations with the Lindseys. Their son Colin was his oldest friend. He had been with them up until the day before they were due to entrain for Paris. If his father had not written from Edinburgh and warned him that he was coming down to Sidcot and wanted to discuss plans for the future, he would have gone to Paris too, relying as usual on his father's agreement *in absentia*. Instead the letter had come and he had gone home and found his father not arrived and the housekeeper and her husband, Mr. and Mrs. Carter, in a disagreeable mood. He hadn't been expected and the Carters said they knew nothing of his father's plans to leave Edinburgh. He did not care very much for the Carters. In Sidcot the staff seldom stayed long. The Carters had been in residence for a couple of years, which was something of a record. He could not remember how many different housekeepers and handyman-gardeners his father had employed. In the old days, before he went to prep school and then on to Chillingborough, there had been a succession of disagreeable governesses and tutors as well as of domestic servants, some of whom made it plain that they preferred to work for white gentlemen. The house had never been to him what, since he had got to know the Lindseys, he had learned to think of us as a home. He saw his father three or four times a year and seldom for longer than a week at a time. He did not remember his mother. He understood that she had died in India when he was born. He did not remember India either.

The reason he found it difficult to believe what the lawyers told him was that there had always seemed to be plenty of money. When he was old enough to appreciate the difference in degrees of affluence he realised that the house in Sidcot was substantial, bigger and more expensively furnished than the Lindseys'; and as well as the house in Sidcot there was a succession of flats in London which his father moved into and out of, in accordance with some principle Hari did not understand and took no interest in beyond what was necessary to record accurately the change of address and telephone number, so that his letters should not go astray and he could be sure of going to the right place if his father rang the school and suggested lunch in town on Hari's way home at the end of term. On such occasions he usually took Colin with him. And Colin once said, looking round the sumptuous but unwelcoming flat. "Your father must be stinking rich." And Hari shrugged and replied, "I suppose he is."

This was probably the moment when he began consciously to be critical of his father who spoke English with that appalling sing-song accent, spelled the family name Coomer, and told people to call him David because Duleep was such a mouthful. Duleep had chosen the name Hari for his only surviving child and only son (the son for whom he had prayed and longed and whose life had now been planned down to the last detail) because Hari was so easily pronounced and was really only distinguishable in the spelling from the diminutive of Saxon Harold, who had been King of the English before the Normans came.

*

The story is that Duleep Kumar, against the wishes and with only the reluctant permission of his parents, went to England to study for the law, just about the time that Miss Crane left the service of the Nesbitt-Smiths and entered the fuller service of the mission, about the time, too, that there died, in a penury as great if not as spectacular as Duleep's, the mother of a young girl who then entered an orphanage and in later years called herself Sister Ludmila.

The Kumars were landowners in a district of the United Provinces. They were rich by Indian standards and loyal to a foreign crown that seemed ready to respect the laws of property. There were many Kumars, but as a youth Duleep began to notice that no matter how much they were looked up to by people whose skin was the same colour as their own, the callowest white-skinned boy doing his first year in the covenanted civil service could snub them by keeping them waiting on the verandah of the sacred little bungalow from whose punkah-cooled rooms was wafted an air of effortless superiority. Power, Duleep felt, lay not in money but in this magical combination of knowledge, manner, and race. His father – one of those frequently kept waiting – disagreed. "In the end," he said, "it is money that counts. What is a snub? What is an insult? Nothing. It costs nothing to give and nothing to receive. Hurt pride is quickly nursed back to health in the warmth of a well-lined pocket. That young man who keeps me waiting is a fool. He refuses gifts because he has been taught that any gift from an Indian is a bribe. At home he would not be so careful. But in forty years he will be poor, living on his pension in his own cold climate."

"But in those forty years," Duleep pointed out, "he will have wielded power."

"What is this power?" his father asked. "He will have settled a few land disputes, seen to the maintenance of public works, extended a road, built a drain, collected revenues on behalf of Government, fined a few thousand men, whipped a score and sent a couple of hundred to jail. But you will be a comparatively rich man. Your power will be material, visible to your eyes when you look at the land you own. Your trouble will be a single one – the slight inconvenience of being kept waiting by one of this young man's successors who will also refuse gifts and in his turn wield what you call power and die rich in nothing except his colonial recollections."

Duleep laughed. He laughed at his father's wry humour. But mostly he laughed because he knew otherwise. When his father died the land so proudly possessed would be divided by his children, and later by his children's children, and then by his children's children's children, and in the end there would be nothing and the power would have dwindled away field by field, village by village. And a young man would still sit in the sacred bungalow, making himself ready to listen with an agreeable but non-committal expression to tales of distress and poverty and injustice; thinking all the time of his own career, planning to follow his predecessors one step at a time up the ladder to a desk in the Secretariat, or a seat on the Governor-General's Council, or to a place on the bench of the High Court of Justice.

Duleep Kumar was the youngest of a family of four boys and three girls. Perhaps a family of seven children was counted auspicious, for after his birth (in 1888) it seemed for several years that his parents were satisfied and intended no further addition. He was the baby, the last-born son. It could have been that his brothers and sisters grew up to be jealous of the attention and affection lavished on him. Certainly in later years, in the matter of his own son Hari's welfare, no interest was shown by and no help forthcoming from those of Duleep's elders who survived him. In the long run, things might have worked out better if there had been no surviving Kumar at all to take an interest; but there was Shalini, the little girl Duleep's mother bore when he was in his eleventh year. The evidence points to a special bond between the last-born son and the last-born daughter, one that in all likelihood originated in Duleep's sense of isolation from his older brothers and sisters, when the first flush of his parents' spoiling had worn thin, and caused him even at that early age to cast a critical eye upon the world around him and a restless one towards the world beyond. Of the four brothers only Duleep completed the course at the Government Higher School and went on to the Government College. His family thought that to study at the college was a waste of time, so they opposed the plan, but finally gave in. In later years he was fond of quoting figures from the provincial census taken round about this time, that showed a male population of twenty-four and a half million and a female population of twenty-three million. Of the males one and a half million were literate; of the females less than fifty-six thousand, a figure which did not include his three elder sisters. His father and brothers were literate in the vernacular, semi-literate in English. It was because as a youth Duleep had acquired a good knowledge of the language of the administrators that he began to accompany his father on visits to petition the sub-divisional officer, and had the first intimations of the secrets hidden behind the bland face of the white authority. There grew in him a triple determination – to break away from a landlocked family tradition, to become a man who instead of requesting favours, granted them, and to save Shalini from the ignorance and domestic tyranny not only his other sisters but his two elder brothers' wives seemed to accept uncomplainingly as all that women could hope for from the human experience. When Shalini was three years old he began to teach her her letters in Hindi. When she was five she could read in English.

Duleep was now sixteen years old. The Government College to which he had gained admittance was at the other end of the earth: a hundred miles away. His mother wept at his going. His brothers scoffed. His elder sisters and sisters-in-law looked at him as if he were setting out on some shameful errand. His father did not understand, but gave him his blessing the night before his departure and in the morning accompanied him to the railway station in a doolie drawn by bullocks.

And perhaps that is when what could be called the tragedy of Duleep Kumar began. He was a boy whose passion for achievement was always just that much greater than his ability to achieve. And it was a passion that had become used to the constant irritants of home. Far removed from there, in the company of boys of diverse backgrounds but similar ambitions, the original sense of frustration upon which these passions had thrived began to diminish. Here, everyone was in the same boat, but as the BA course progressed he became uncomfortably aware of the process that separated the quick-witted from the plodders. For the first time in his life he found himself having to admit that other boys, if not actually cleverer, could certainly be quicker. Analysing this he came readily to an explanation. The quick boys, surely, all came from progressive homes where English was spoken all the time. On the college teaching staff there was a preponderance of Englishmen. At the Government Higher School, most of the instruction, although in English, had been in the hands of Indians. He had always understood exactly what the Indian teachers were saying, and he had often felt that what they were saying he could have said better. But now he sat through lectures increasingly at a loss to follow not the words so much as the thinking behind the words. And he did not dare to ask questions. Nobody asked questions. They listened attentively. They filled exercise books with meticulous notes of what they thought had been said. To ask questions was to admit ignorance. In a competitive world like this such an admission would probably have been fatal.

He was, however, discovering a new irritant: the frustrations not of a hidebound orthodox Indian family, but of the English language itself. Listening to his fellow students he was amazed that they seemed unable to comprehend the difference between the way they spoke and the way the Englishmen spoke. It was not only a question of pronunciation or idiom. He was too young to be able to formulate the problem. But he was aware of having come close to the heart of another important secret. To uncover it might lead to an understanding of what in the sub-divisional officer looked like simple arrogance and in the English teachers intellectual contempt.

There came a time when he was able to say to his son Hari: "It is not only that if *you* answer the phone a stranger on the other end would think he was speaking to an English boy of the upper classes. It is that you *are* that boy in your mind and behaviour. Conversely when I was your age, it was not only that I spoke English with an even stronger *babu* accent than I speak it now, but that everything I said, because everything I thought, was in conscious mimicry of the people who rule us. We did not necessarily admit this, but that is what was always in their minds when they listened to us. It amused them mostly. Sometimes it irritated them. It still does. Never they could listen to us and forget that we were a subject, inferior people. The more idiomatic we tried to be the more naïve our thinking seemed, because we were thinking in a foreign language that we had never properly considered in relation to our own. Hindi, you see, is spare and beautiful. In it we can think thoughts that have the merit of simplicity and truth. And between each other convey these thoughts in correspondingly spare, simple, truthful images. English is not spare. But it is beautiful. It cannot be called truthful because its subtleties are infinite. It is the language of a people who have probably earned their reputation for perfidy and hypocrisy because their language itself is so flexible, so often light-headed with statements which appear to mean one thing one year and quite a different thing the next. At least, this is so when it is written, and the English have usually confided their noblest aspirations and intentions to paper. Written, it looks like a way of gaining time and winning confidence. But when it is spoken, English is rarely beautiful. Like Hindi it is spare then, but crueller. We learned our English from books, and the

English, knowing that books are one thing and life another, simply laughed at us. Still laugh at us. They laughed at me, you know, in that Indian college I went to before I came over here that first disastrous time to study law. At the college I learned the importance of obtaining a deep understanding of the language, a real familiarity with it, spoken and written. But of course I got it mostly all from books. A chapter of Macaulay was so much easier to understand, and certainly more exciting, than a sentence spoken by Mr. Croft who taught us history. In the end I was even trying to speak Macaulay-esque prose. Later I found out that any tortuous path to a simple hypothesis was known among the English staff as a Kumarism. And it was later still before I really understood that a Kumarism was not something admirable but something rather silly. But I think this notoriety helped me to scrape through. I was a long way down the list. But it was a triumph by my standards."

And it was in the glow of this triumph that, aged nineteen, he returned home, not for the first time since going to the station in the doolie – naturally enough there had been the vacations – but for the first time as a young man of proven worth, and of ambitions that now pointed to the necessity of making the passage across the black water, to England, to sit for the examinations of the Indian Civil Service, which in those days was the only place where the examinations could be taken: a rule which effectively restricted the number of Indians able to compete.

He found his parents less jubilant over his academic success than they were concerned about his failure to fulfil a primary function: to be married, to increase, to ensure at least one son who could officiate eventually in his funeral rites and see him on the way, with honour, to another world.

The girl they had in mind, whose name was Kamala and whose horoscope, according to the astrologers, was in an auspicious confluence with his own, was already fifteen; in fact, they said, nearly sixteen.

"Kamala!" he shouted. "Who, what, is Kamala?" and would not even listen to the answer.

The Kumar home was a rambling rural agglomeration of low buildings built around a central courtyard, walled within a large compound, on the outskirts of the principal village within their holding, a distance of five miles from the town where the English sub-divisional officer had his headquarters.

Five miles by buffalo cart to the nearest outpost of civilisation, Duleep thought. Ah! What a prison! He played with Shalini and in intervals of playing retaught her the lessons he was pleased to find she had not forgotten in the three months that had gone since he last saw her. Between them now there was an adoration; she, in his eyes, such a sweet-tempered pretty and intelligent child, and he, in hers, a handsome, godlike but miraculously earthbound and playful brother whose wisdom knew no end, and kindness no inexplicable boundaries of sudden silence or bad temper; no temper anyway when they were together. But she heard him shouting at her brothers, quarrelling with her father. Once too, when he thought he was alone, she heard him weeping; and gathered flowers to charm away his unhappiness so that he should smile again, and tell her tales of Rama, the god-king.

In the end he decided to strike a bargain with his parents. He would agree in principle to the marriage with the girl Kamala. But there could be no question of actual marriage until he had completed his studies in England and sat for the examinations. He would submit only to a formal betrothal.

And how long, his father wanted to know, would he be away in England?

Two or three years, perhaps. His father shook his head. By then Kamala would be eighteen or nineteen and still living with her parents. Did Duleep want his wife to be a laughing-stock before ever she came to his bed? And had he thought of the cost of going to England to study? Where did he think so much money was coming from? Duleep was prepared for this objection. He would sign away to his elder brothers whatever proportion of his inheritance might be reckoned to equal the cost of his studies abroad.

"There are only so many maunds to a sack, and you cannot give up what has not yet come to you," his father pointed out. "Besides which your inheritance is what makes you an attractive proposition to your future parents-in-law."

"My education, my career, mean nothing to them?" Duleep asked.

His father shook his head. "What you call your career has not yet begun. Perhaps you have overlooked the advantage of the dowry your wife would bring to this household? With such advantage money might be found to send you to England. But you would have to marry first. You are nineteen already. And all your brothers were married before their nineteenth year. Your future wife will soon be sixteen. By that age all your elder sisters were already married. I have had to find three dowries already. I am not a man with a bottomless pocket. And in a few years there will be yet another dowry to find for Shalini."

Family affairs were the one thing there was always time for. The negotiations with his father extended over many days. Towards the end of them Duleep went to him and said, "Very well. I will marry Kamala. But then immediately I will go to England."

For these interviews they met in the room his father had, these past few years, set aside for meditation – an act which might have warned them all of what was to come later. In this room there was no furniture. They sat on rush mats on the tiled floor. On the whitewashed walls there was no decoration other than a highly coloured lithograph of the God of Fortune, Ganesha, in a little rosewood frame, and, in the sill of the small unglazed barred window, a pewter jug that usually held a handful of marigolds or frangipani.

"I do not wish you," his father said now, raising a new objection, "to enter the administration. If you are not content to look after your property then I suggest that you become a lawyer. For this you can study, I believe, in Calcutta."

"What have you got against the administration?" Duleep asked.

"It is the administration of a foreign government. I should feel shame for my son to serve it. Better he should oppose the administration in the courts to help his own people."

"Shame?" Duleep said. "But you do not feel shame to be kept waiting on the verandah of the little burra-sahib. You have said yourself: What is an insult? What is hurt pride?"

"I should feel shame," old Kumar said, "if the little burra-sahib were my own son."

It was a subtle point. It took a day or two for Duleep to swallow it, to judge the actuality of his father's sudden antipathy towards the Raj which, if it was not sudden, had always been kept well concealed.

"All right," Duleep told him a few days later. "I have thought about it. I will become a lawyer. Perhaps a barrister. But for this I must study in England."

"And first you will marry the girl Kamala?"

"Yes, Father. First I will marry Kamala."

*

Of his close family only his mother and an aunt had seen Kamala Prasad, his future wife. To do so they had paid a visit to the Prasads' home. Pleased with what they saw and with what was known about her upbringing, they reported back to Duleep's father. Reassured by the astrologers and satisfied with the proposed dowry, all that remained from the Kumars' point of view – granted Duleep's obedient submission to their wishes – was to seal the arrangement with a formal betrothal and then to fix the date of the wedding.

Kamala Prasad lived some twenty miles away. For the betrothal ceremony only male Prasads made the journey to the Kumars' house: the prospective bride's father and uncles, and two of her married brothers. They brought sweets and small gifts of money, but came in the main to satisfy themselves that the house Kamala would live in was up to the standard they had been led to expect. Duleep, who had watched his brothers perform the same duties, bowed to his future father-in-law and then knelt to touch his feet in a gesture of humility. The father-in-law marked Duleep's forehead with the tilak – the sign of auspiciousness. For a while the guests sat in formal conversation, took some refreshment and then went back to the station on the first stage of their journey home. The ceremony left little impression on him; it had seemed rather pointless, but for Shalini, with Duleep as the centre of attraction, it had been magical. "On your wedding day, will you wear a sword and ride a horse, just like a king?" she asked.

"Well, I suppose so," he said, and laughed, and privately thought: What a farce! His main interest lay in the arrangements he had begun to make with the advice and help of the principal of the Government College to go to England in September for the opening of what, fascinatingly, was called the Michaelmas term.

The betrothal ceremony took place in January, and then almost immediately there was difficulty over fixing the date of the wedding. The astrologers said that the ideal time fell in the second week of March. Kumar suggested the first week in September. The boat on which he had booked his passage through an agent in Bombay left in the second week. The astrologers shook their heads. If the wedding could not be managed in the second week of March it would need to be postponed until the fourth week of October.

"It is all nonsense," Duleep insisted. "All they mean is that by April the weather will be too hot and from June until October likely to be too wet." He had no intention of spending nearly six months as a married man before setting out for England. In fact he had no intention of sleeping with a barely sixteen-year-old girl, however pretty, however nubile. He would go through the ceremony. He would even spend one night or two with her so that she would not be disgraced. But he would not make love to her. He would kiss her and be kind to her, and tell her that when he returned from England as a young man qualified in an honourable profession it would be time enough for her to take on the duties of a wife and the burdens of motherhood. He almost hoped that she would turn out to be unattractive.

Sometimes he woke in the middle of the night and thought that every step he had taken since leaving the college had been the wrong one. He had given up his plan to enter the administration. He had submitted to the demands of his parents to marry. He had undertaken to study for a profession his heart had not been set on. All he had succeeded in hanging on to was his determination to go to England. When he woke in the mornings the prospect of England was enough to enable him to enter the new day bright and cheerful, and he could not help responding to the warmth of parental approbation that had settled about him. He heard his father say once to an old friend, "After his marriage, of course, Duleepji is to continue his studies in England," as if that had been his father's wish, not his own, and he judged that paternal pride could grow like good seed in the most unlikely ground so long as that ground were first soaked with the sweat of filial duty. But, in the darkness of half-sleep and half-waking, he would search without success for a practical interpretation of that single, challenging word, England; for an interpretation that would ease him, bring comfort that extended beyond his general desire to his particular purpose. Power – in the sense he understood it – seemed to have been potentially lessened by his all too easy, equivocal agreement to enter the services of the law where power was interpreted, perhaps challenged, but never directly exercised. In myself, he thought, there is possibly a fatal flaw, the dark root of the plan of compromise that never bears any blossom that isn't rank-smelling; and turned over, to sleep again, his hand upon the firm breast of the submissive, loving girl who now always followed him into his dreams.

He had his way. The astrologers discovered an unexpected conjunction of fortunate stars. The marriage was arranged to take place in the first week of September. "You see, Shalini," he told his little sister, "it was all nonsense, as I said," but stopped himself from adding, "Like the Kumars, the Prasads carry the burden of too many daughters and are only too anxious to have Kamala off their hands, even at the tail-end of the wet monsoon." Looking at Shalini he found himself assessing the burden that she, in her ninth year, already represented in terms of the complicated sum of her necessary dowry and her parents' desire that she should be happy, and suitably matched, transferred to a household that would bring honour to them and good fortune to her, be given to a husband who would bless her with kindness and whom she would find it possible to feel affection for and be dutiful to, and so give satisfaction to him and to his family, and to herself and to hers.

"I hope," he told himself, thinking of his own future wife, "that I can find it in my heart not to hate her."

The first list of guests on the groom's side which his father prepared ran to nearly three hundred names. After negotiations with the Prasad family the list was cut to just below two hundred. There would be twice that number on the bride's side. To the bride's family the cost would be crippling. In the middle of August the Prasads began to gather. The Kumars also gathered. They came from the Punjab, from Madras, from Bengal, from Lucknow and the home province, and from Bombay, from as far off as Rawalpindi. Duleep was the last of old Kumar's sons. There would only be one other marriage in this particular generation: Shalini's. The house was full. The guest house that had been erected outside the compound for the weddings of Duleep's sisters was also full.

The journey to Delali was made early in the morning of the day of the wedding. Miraculously the rains had ended early, which was counted a good omen. In Kamala's home the first ceremonies had been going on for two days. Three coaches of the train to Delali were reserved for the groom's party. A delegation of Prasads was at Delali station to meet them. Duleep and his family were taken to the house of a brother of the bride's father. And there Duleep was dressed in the style of a warrior king, in tight white trousers, embroidered coat, sword, cloak and sequined turban upon which was placed a tinsel crown from which garlands of roses and jasmine hung, half shadowing his face, filling his nostrils with their sweet narcotic scent. As evening came he was led out to the caparisoned horse on which he mounted, with his best man, a young cousin, behind him in the saddle. The procession to the bride's house began at half-past six. It was accompanied by men with lanterns, drums, trumpets and fireworks. The evening was loud with the noise and explosion of their progression. It gave him a headache. The procession was followed by the people of Delali who wanted to see for themselves what kind of a husband old Prasad's youngest daughter had managed to get hold of. They shouted good-natured insults and Duleep's champions replied in kind.

Dismounting at the entrance to the bride's house, he was led through the compound to the married women's courtyard, sat down, and put through the first of his ordeals.

"So next week you are going to England," one of the women said. "Do you tire so quickly that you need to run away?"

"Oh no," Duleep replied, entering into the spirit of the testing, "but a young husband is wiser to accept the truth of the saying: Moderation in all things."

"Perhaps the bride will have different ideas," another woman said.

"The pot of honey," Duleep said, "tastes better after a long abstinence."

"What if the honey should go sour?" an even bolder woman asked.

"To a faithful tooth even the sourest honey tastes sweet."

The women laughed and hid their faces. Duleep was a man. The news was quickly carried to the bride who had sat for hours in her inner chamber, after her ritual purifying bathe, attended by the women whose job it was to clothe her in her red robes and heavy jewellery, put henna on her hands and feet and kohl on her eyes.

"As handsome as a prince," they said, "and bold with it. Ah, what eyes! But also gentle. Assuredly yes, you are fortunate. Such husbands do not grow on trees. He will be worth the waiting for, after the initial taste."

The second ordeal was the ceremony itself which was due to begin at the auspicious hour of half an hour before midnight, in the main courtyard, and would go on for hours, in accordance with the Vedic rites. He sat next to his bride, facing the sacred fire on the other side of which the pandit sat. She was heavily veiled and kept her head bowed. Duleep dared not look at her. But he had the impression of her scent and smallness and temporary magnificence. The veil over her head was tied to the pommel of his sword – which, in the olden days, he would have had to use to cut off the branch of a tree to show his vigour. Already they were united, indissolubly, throughout life and perhaps beyond it. And he had not yet seen her face. She had not yet looked at his. If she saw anything of him at all it could be no more than his gold, embroidered slippers and tight-trousered legs. Unless she had peeped. He did not think she had. The pandit was intoning mantras. Incense was thrown on the flames of the fire. Duleep and Kamala walked round the fire with Duleep leading, and then again, reversing the order, with Kamala ahead. She received rice into her cupped hands, and poured it into his, and he threw it into the flames. Together they walked the seven auspicious steps, and then the pandit recited their names and the names of their forebears, and Kamala was led away and he would not be close to her again until the night after the next when she would be led by his own mother into his room at home. But already it was morning. Tomorrow, then, Kamala would travel to Duleep's house, in clothes brought to her as gifts from the Kumars.

Duleep slept late, got up and broke his fast and inspected the dowry that was on show on trestle tables under awnings, in case a miserable, unexpected rain ruined the proceedings. There were clothes for himself and the bride, jewellery, small coffers of silver coins and one hundred rupee notes, family ceremonial costume, plate, household utensils, and, in a box, title deeds to land. He went to bed early, astonished by so much personal wealth, the cost to a girl's father of a husband for her, and in the morning was dressed again in his king's raiment, encumbered by his velvet sheathed sword and mounted on the caparisoned horse to lead the coolie procession to the railway station. The small figure of his still-veiled wife, dressed in scarlet, heavily jewelled, was supported by her father and mother out to the palanquin. He fancied that the moment before she entered she faltered and wept and was only persuaded to enter by some comforting, courage-giving words of her mother.

When the doolie curtains were closed the bearers took up the weight, and the women who followed the palanquin began to sing the song of the bride, the morning raga, the song of the young girl who leaves her childhood home for the home of her husband.

Dooliya la aō
re morē babul ke kaharwa.
Chali hoon sajan ba ke des.

*

On the outskirts of their own village which they reached in procession from the railway station towards evening, they were met by what looked like the whole population. The married women approached the doolie (a doolie provided by the Kumars to replace the doolie left behind with the Prasads at Delali) opened the curtains and inspected the bride. From the way they looked at him afterwards he assumed that they had found no major fault. Of the family only Shalini had been left behind. She ran from the compound and clung to the bridle of his horse which, like the new doolie, had been waiting at the station.

"Duleep, Duleep," she cried, "oh, how beautiful you are. Why did you marry her? Why didn't you wait for me?" And walked proudly, possessively, leading the horse into the compound. But came later, long after she should have been in bed, to the room in which he prepared himself and said, "I am sorry, Duleep."

"Why sorry?" he asked, taking her on to his knee. She encircled her arms around his neck.

"Because," she said, "because I have seen her."

"Then why should you be sorry?" he asked, his heart beating so loudly he could hardly bear the pain and uncertainty of it.

"Because she is like a princess," Shalini told him. "Did you fight for her? Did you slay evil spirits and rescue her? Did you, Duleepji? Did you? Did you?"

"I suppose I did," he said, and kissed her, and sent her away, and then waited in the room into which Kamala would presently be led by his mother and given into his care.

*

The trouble was, he told Hari years later, that when he unveiled Kamala, and saw her, he fell in love with her. Perhaps this was true and accounted for the fact that his career in England reading for the law was a failure from the start. His final return, defeated, was hard to bear because no word of reproach was spoken by his father for the wasted years, the wasted money. Returning to India, he laboured under the weight of many burdens: the burden of knowing that his mind was incapable of adjusting itself to the pace set by better men, and the burden of knowing that time and again, in England, allowances had been made for him because he was an Indian who had travelled a long way, at considerable cost, and had so obviously set his heart on lifting himself by his bootstraps from the state of underprivilege into which he had been born. And then there was the burden of knowing that he could not blame his parents for the fact that in England he had often been cold, miserable and shy, and not infrequently dismayed by the dirt, squalor and poverty, the sight of barefoot children, ragged beggars, drunken women, and evidence of cruelty to animals and humans: sins which in India only Indians were supposed to be capable of committing or guilty of allowing. He could blame his parents for forcing him into a premature marriage that disrupted the involved pattern of his scholarly pretensions, but he could not blame them for this dismay, nor could he blame them for the constant proof he had that among the English, at home with them, he was a foreigner. He was invariably treated with kindness, even with respect, but always with reserve; the kind of reserve that went hand in hand with best – and therefore uneasy – behaviour. He found himself longing for the rough and tumble of life at home. To learn the secret of the Englishness of the English he realised that you had to grow up among them. For him, it was too late. But it was not too late for his son. He never anticipated successors in the plural. One son was enough. One son would succeed where he had failed, so long as he had advantages Duleep himself had never enjoyed.

The trouble was, Duleep thought, that India had made its mark on him and no subsequent experience would ever erase it. Beneath the thin layers of anglicisation was a thickness of Indianness that the arranged marriage had only confirmed and strengthened. "And for an *Indian* Indian," he told Hari, "there simply isn't any future in an *Anglo*-Indian world." Of one thing Duleep was certain: the English, for all their protestations to the contrary, were going to hold on to their Empire well beyond his own lifetime and far into if not beyond Hari's as well. If he had a theory at all about the eventual departure of the English it was that they were waiting for Indian boys who would be as English, if not more English, than they were themselves, so that handing over the reins of power they would feel no wrench greater than a man might feel when giving into the care of an adopted son a business built up from nothing over a period of alternating fortune and disaster.

To Duleep, Indian independence was as simple as that, a question of evolution rather than of politics, of which he knew nothing. He believed in the intellectual superiority of the English. Manifestly it was not with physical strength that they ruled an empire. They ruled it because they were armed with weapons of civil intelligence that made the comparable Indian armoury look primitive by comparison. As witness to that was the example of the pale-skinned boy who sat on the verandah of the sub-divisional officer's bungalow. And no one had ever made *him* marry a sixteen-year-old girl. It did not matter to this boy, fundamentally, whether he went to the grave with male or female issue or without. He had never been distracted from his duty or ambition by the overwhelming physical sensation of finding, in front of him, a girl who had been thrust into the room by his own mother, a girl who when unveiled had filled him with the simple impulse to possess, to forget, to cast out the spirits of discipline and learning and celibacy, and enter, in full vigour, into the second stage of life which was attended by spirits of an altogether different nature.

"The fact that I fell in love with your mother," he told Hari, "proved one thing, which in itself proved many others. It proved my Indianness. It wasn't just a case of there being here opportunity for a young man to satisfy his sexuality in the terms you would understand it. What young man anyway could resist that excitement, of removing the veil and not being disappointed in what he saw, and of knowing that the girl who stood so meekly in front of him was his to do as he liked with? No, it wasn't as simple as that. At that moment, you see, I automatically entered the second stage of life according to the Hindu code. I became husband and householder. In my heart, then, my ambitions were all for my family, my as yet non-existent family of sons and daughters. Do you see that? Do you understand this strong psychological undertow? Oh, well, yes, naturally I would have pleasure, physical pleasure. But where else should this pleasure lead except to happiness and fulfilment for my own flesh and blood? Certainly it should not have been followed by another long period of celibacy, of learning and education. I was now, in an instant, already past that stage. In the Hindu code

I was no longer a student but a man, with a man's responsibilities, a man's sources of delight, which are not the same as a boy's and not the same as a student's. And yet, in the eyes of the western world, which I took message to, I was still a boy, still a student. In that old lower middle-class English saying: I was living a lie. Isn't it?"

In such a way Duleep Kumar excused his failure, if failure it was in fact, but tortured himself with it because he was not reproached by his father or mother. Perhaps he was reproached by his wife, Kamala, who had also entered the second stage, having herself been entered, torn open, and then abandoned and left with recollections of her extraordinary and painful translation from child to woman, living at some seasons of the year with her own parents, at other seasons with Duleep's; and greeting him on his return with a humility that had gone a bit sour, so that Duleep felt it, and decided that if you looked at the situation squarely he had managed to get for himself the worst of both worlds. After all, he brought back no crock of gold, no princely raiment, no means to free her from the tyranny of a matriarchal household which his absence in England had probably given her expectations of. If she had no proper notion of the ambition that attended his departure she had, certainly, an understanding of the failure that attended his return.

"I went away," Duleep said, "a feared but adored Hindu husband. I returned as a half-man – unclean by traditional Hindu standards and custom because I had crossed the black water. But I had crossed it to no obvious advantage. To purify myself I was persuaded to consume the five products of the cow. Which includes the cow's dung and urine. Although not, of course, its flesh."

In England he had never admitted to people that he was married. He was ashamed to. For a month or so he had anticipated and feared news of Kamala's pregnancy. His relief was relative to his disappointment. He could not have borne the distraction of knowing he was to be a father, but only with a sense of the reflection on his virility was he able to enjoy the freedom of finding he was not. He longed to receive letters, but their arrival filled him with frustration, even despair. His father wrote in Hindi, and addressed the envelopes in English in block capitals such as you would find figured by children in a kindergarten. Each letter was a sermon, a formal communication from father to son. The few letters he received from Kamala were as naïve as those of a child, the result of hours of labour and instruction. He knew that his own letters had to be read aloud to her. Only his letters to and from Shalini were pleasurable.

Restored to his wife, still unqualified even for the career he had not set his heart on, he set about the business of instructing her in lettering. She submitted ungraciously. She did not want to learn more than she already knew. She thought it a waste of time, an affront to her status as a married woman. Her sisters-in-law poked fun at her if they saw her with books. "It is only because Shalini is cleverer than you that you act in this stupid way," he said, when she pretended to have forgotten the lesson he had taught her the day before.

The old rambling house was a hive of inactivity. The women quarrelled among themselves. His mother's voice, raised above all in pitch and authority, brought only a brooding truce. His father spent hours alone in meditation. His brothers idled the days away, gambling and cock-fighting. For a time Duleep himself fell into a similar state of inertia. He need never lift a finger. He need do no work. He played with Shalini, now aged nearly twelve. We are waiting, he told himself, for our father to die. And then we shall have the pleasure of squabbling among ourselves over the inheritance. We shall squabble for three or four years and by then my brother's children will be old enough to marry and the money so carefully hoarded will begin to be squandered, land will be sold and divided and my prophecy will come true.

He had toyed with the idea of continuing his studies in India, and then with the notion that he could apply for a post in the uncovenanted provincial civil service. He had also thought to take his wife away and set up house on his own, but he did not want to leave Shalini behind. Her parents would not let her go to school. He tried to get hold of a teacher from the Zenana Mission, an organisation that sent teachers into orthodox Indian homes to instruct the women privately, but the Mission lost interest when it was learned that only one young girl would attend the lessons. For a couple of years or more, he realised, Shalini's education would be his own responsibility. And by now Kamala was pregnant and he began to make plans for his son's future: a future which at times seemed very unlikely to take the shape he wanted it to. He could not imagine Kamala being persuaded to cross the black water. He could not imagine her living in England. In any case, he knew he would be ashamed of her. In England she would be a laughing-stock. Here it was he who was the laughing-stock. The problem looked insoluble. His son would grow up with precisely the same disadvantages he suffered from himself. He could have blamed himself for marrying such a girl. Or he could have blamed his parents for forcing him to marry her. He could have blamed India, and the Hindu tradition. It was easier to blame Kamala. Already she had become shrill and demanding. They quarrelled frequently. He was no longer in love with her. Occasionally he felt sorry for her.

Their first child, a daughter, survived two days. A year later, in 1914, in the first year of England's war with Germany, there was a second daughter; and she survived for a year. A third child, another daughter, was stillborn in 1916. Poor Kamala seemed to be incapable of bearing a healthy baby, let alone a son. Deprived in this way too, their quarrels became bitter. He discovered that she blamed him for her failure. To bear a strong son was her duty. She was determined to do it. "But how can I do my duty alone?" she asked. "It is *you*. All your years studying books have sapped your manhood." Furious, he left the house, taking some money, intending never to return. He had a vague idea that he would join the army; but remembered Shalini and went home when the last of his money had been spent. He returned penniless and disgraced. In the month that he had been away Shalini had become betrothed to one Prakash Gupta Sen. The Gupta Sens were previously connected by marriage with the Lucknow branch of the Kumar family.

Shalini complained to him – not about her betrothal but about his absence during the ceremonial formalities. "Why did you stay away, Duleepji?" she wanted to know. "If you had been here you could have gone with my father and my brothers to Mayapore. And if you had gone you could have told me truly what kind of boy this Prakash is. *They* say he is intelligent and good-looking. Why cannot I know what *you* think? I could have believed you."

"Is that all you can say? Is that all it means to you? What he looks like?"

But already she had become a woman.

"What else can it mean, Duleepji? Besides, I am fifteen. One cannot stay a child for ever."

Shalini's marriage took place almost a year later – in 1917.

Again the house was full. Duleep was astonished at the calm way she accepted the situation and even blossomed in the warmth of the formal flattery always accorded to a bride. When he saw young Prakash Gupta Sen he was horrified. Fat, vain, pompous, lecherous. In a few years this would be proved. Duleep avoided Shalini. "My nerve has gone," he told himself. "Why don't I make a scene? Why do I let this terrible thing go forward?" And knew the answer. "Because already I am defeated. The future holds nothing for me. I am only half Anglicised. The stronger half is still Indian. It pleases me to think the future holds nothing for anyone else either."

On the night of Shalini's wedding he slept with his wife again. She wept. They both wept. And exchanged undertakings that in future they would be kind, forgiving and understanding. On the morning of Shalini's ritual departure he watched from the gateway. She entered the palanquin without hesitation.

And Duleep saw one thing at last: that in helping her to open her mind and broaden her horizons he had taught her the lesson he himself had never learned: the value of moral as well as physical courage. He only saw her on two subsequent occasions: the first during the week she spent after her marriage in her parental home, with Prakash, and the second five years later when on the eve of his departure for England with his two-year-old son Hari, he visited her in Mayapore during the festival of *Rakhi-Bandan*, bringing her gifts of clothing and receiving from her a bracelet made of elephant hair: the festival during which brothers and sisters reaffirm the bond between them and exchange vows of duty and affection. By this time his wife Kamala had been dead for two years and poor Shalini was still childless. Her husband, Duleep knew, spent most of his time with prostitutes. He died some years later of a seizure in the house of his favourite.

"Imagine," Shalini wrote to her brother at that time, "Prakash's sisters actually suggested I should become suttee to honour such a man and acquire merit for myself!"

And Duleep replied from Sidcot, "Leave Mayapore, and come to us in England."

"No," she wrote back. "My duty – such as it is – is here. I feel, Duleepji, that we shall never see each other again. Don't you feel the same? We Indians are very fatalistic! Thank you for sending me books. They are my greatest pleasure. Also for the photograph of Hari. What a handsome boy he is! I think of him as my English nephew. Perhaps one day, if ever he comes to India, I shall meet him if he can bear to visit his old Indian aunt. Think of it – I shan't see thirty again! Duleepji – I am so pleased for you. In the picture of Hari I see again my kind brother on whose knee I used to sit. Well. Enough of this nonsense."

*

These were all stories that Duleep eventually told to Hari. In turn, when Hari's father was dead, in the few weeks of English boyhood that were left to him, Hari told them to Colin Lindsey. He thought of them as stories which had no bearing on his own life – even then, with his passage to India booked, and paid for by the aunt with the peculiar name, Shalini.

There was one other story. This too he told Colin. It seemed incredible to both of them; not because they couldn't imagine it happening, but because neither of them could think of it as happening in Harry Coomer's family.

It went like this: that two weeks after Shalini's ritual return to her parents' home, and one week after her final departure to Mayapore with her husband, her father announced his intention to divest himself of all his worldly goods, to depart from his family and his responsibilities, and wander the countryside: become, eventually, *sannyasi*.

"I have done my duty," he said. "It is necessary to recognise that it is finished. It is necessary not to become a burden. Now my duty is to God."

His family were shocked. Duleep pleaded with him but his resolve was unshaken. "When are you leaving us, then?" Duleep asked.

"I shall go in six months' time. It will take until then to order my affairs. The inheritance will be divided equally among the four of you. The house will belong to your elder brother. Your mother must be allowed to live here for as long as she wishes, but your elder brother and his wife will become heads of the household. All will be done as it would be done if I were dead."

Duleep shouted, "You call this good? You call it holy? To leave our mother? To bury yourself alive in *nothing*? To beg your bread when you are rich enough to feed a hundred starving beggars?"

"Rich?" his father asked. "What is rich? Today I have

riches. With one stroke of a pen on a document I can rid myself of what you call my riches. But what stroke of a pen on what kind of document will ensure my release from the burden of another lifespan after this? Such a release can only be hoped for, only earned by renouncing all earthly bonds."

Duleep said, "Ah well, yes! How fine! In what way could you be ashamed now to find your son a little burra sahib? What difference could it make to you now, what I was or where I was? Is it for this that I gave in to you? Is it to see you shrug me off and walk away from me and my brothers and our mother that I obeyed you?"

"While there is duty there must be obedience. My duty to you is over. Your obedience to me is no longer necessary. You have different obligations now. And I have a duty of still another kind."

"It is monstrous!" Duleep shouted. "Monstrous and cruel and selfish! You have ruined my life. I have sacrificed myself for nothing."

As he had found earlier it was easier to blame anyone than to blame himself, but he regretted the attack. He suffered greatly at the recollection of it. He tried to speak about it to his mother, but these days she went about her daily tasks dumb and unapproachable. When the time drew near for his father to go he went to him and begged his forgiveness.

"You were always my favourite son," old Kumar admitted. "That was a sin, to feel more warmly towards one than to the others. Better you should have had no ambition. Better you should have been like your brothers. I could not help but exert authority more strongly over the only son who ever seemed ready to defy it. And I was ashamed of my preference. My exertion of authority perhaps went beyond the bounds of reason. A father does not ask his son to forgive him. It is only open to him to bless him and to commit to this son's care that good woman, your mother."

"No," Duleep said, weeping. "That duty is not for me. That is for your eldest son. Don't burden me with that."

"A burden will fall upon the heart most ready to accept it," old Kumar said, and then knelt and touched his youngest son's feet, to humble himself.

Even in the business of becoming *sannyasi* old Kumar seemed determined upon the severest shock to his pride. He underwent no rituals. He did not put on the long gown. On the morning of his departure he appeared in the compound dressed only in a loin cloth, carrying a staff and a begging-bowl. Into the bowl his stony-faced wife placed a handful of rice. And then he walked through the gateway and into the road, away from the village.

For a while they followed him, some distance behind. He did not look back. When Duleep and his brothers gave up following him their mother continued. They watched but said nothing to each other, waiting for their mother who, after a while, sat down on the roadside and stayed there until Duleep joined her, urged her to her feet and supported her back to the house.

"You must not give in to sorrow," she told him later, lying on her bed in a darkened room from which she had ordered the servants to remove every article of comfort and luxury. "It is the will of God."

*

Thereafter his mother lived the life of a widow. She gave her household keys into the care of her eldest daughter-in-law and moved into a room at the back of the house that overlooked the servants' quarters. She cooked her own food and ate it in solitude. She never left the compound. After a while her sons and daughters-in-law accepted the situation as inevitable. By such behaviour, they said, she was acquiring merit. They seemed content, then, to forget her. Alone, Duleep went every day to her room and sat with her for a while and watched while she spun khadi. To communicate at all he had to say things that needed no answer or ask simple questions which she could respond to with a nod or shake of the head.

In this way he brought her news: of the end of England's war with Germany, of business affairs he had begun to take an interest in, of his wife Kamala's latest pregnancy, of the birth of yet another stillborn child, a girl. Once he brought news, a rumour, that his father had been recognised but not spoken to by one of the Lucknow Kumars who had been travelling in Bihar and had seen him on the platform of a railway station with his begging-bowl. His mother did not even pause in her spinning. In 1919 he told her something of the troubles in the Punjab, but did not mention the massacre of unarmed Indian civilians by British-commanded Gurkha troops in Amritsaw. In this same year he brought the news that Kamala was again with child, and in 1920, a few weeks after the festival of Holi, the news that he had a son. By now the old lady had taken to muttering while she spun. He could not be sure that she ever heard what he said. She did not look at him when he told her about Hari, nor two days later when he told her that Kamala was dead; that now he had a strong healthy son but no wife. She did not look at him either when he began to laugh. He laughed because he could not weep; for Kamala, or for his son, or his father or old mad mother. "She made it you see, Mother," he shouted at her hysterically in English. "She knew her duty all right. My God, yes! She knew her duty and did it in the end. It didn't matter that it cost her her life. We all know our duty, don't we? Just like I know mine. At last I've got a son and I have a duty to him, but I've also got you, and Father charged me with a duty to you as well."

It was a duty that took another eighteen months to discharge. One morning he went to his mother's room and found the spinning-wheel abandoned and the old woman on her bed. When he spoke to her she opened her eyes and looked at him and said:

"Your father is dead, Duleepji." Her voice was hoarse and cracked through long disuse. "I saw it in a dream. Is the fire kindled yet?"

"The fire, Mother?"

"Yes, son. The fire must be kindled."

She slept.

In the evening she woke and asked him again, "Son, is the fire kindled?"

"They are making it ready."

"Wake me when they have finished."

She slept again, until morning, and then opened her eyes and asked him, "Do the flames leap high, Duleepji?"

"Yes, Mother," he said. "The fire is kindling."

"Then it is time," she said. And smiled, and closed her eyes, and told him: "I am not afraid," and did not wake again.

*

It was in the October of 1921 that his mother died. A year later, when he had sold his property to his brothers and paid a visit to his sister Shalini, in Mayapore, he took his son to Bombay and there embarked for England. When he sailed he was comparatively well-off and during the course of the next sixteen years he managed from time to time to increase his capital and income with fortunate investments and lucky enterprises. Perhaps it was true that he had in him what he once referred to as a fatal flaw, although if there was a flaw like this it was not one that led to compromise, as he had thought. He had compromised, certainly, in his youth, but had stood by his duty in early manhood. The flaw was perhaps more likely to be found in the quality of his passion. There may have been impurities in it from the beginning, or the impurities may have entered with the frustrations that, in another man, could so easily have diluted the passion but in him roused and strengthened it to the point where the passion alone guided his thoughts and actions, and centred them all on Hari.

A stranger could look at the life, times and character of Duleep Kumar – or Coomer as he became – and see a man and a career and a background which in themselves, separately or in combination, made no sense. The only sense they made lay in Hari: Hari's health, Hari's happiness, Hari's prospects, power for Hari in a world where boys like Hari normally expected none; these were the notches on the rule Duleep used to measure his own success or failure: and these were what he looked for as the end results of any enterprise he embarked upon.

When Colin Lindsey's father kept his promise to see the lawyers, to try and make some sense out of the apparently absurd report that Duleep Kumar had died a bankrupt, the senior partner of that firm said to him:

"In his own country, Coomer would probably have made a fortune and kept it. He told me once that as a boy he'd only wanted to be a civil servant or a lawyer, and had never once thought of becoming a businessman. The curious thing is that he really had a flair for financial manipulation. I mean a flair in the European sense. It was the most English thing about him when you boiled it down. In his own country he might have knocked spots off the average businessman out there. He saw things in a broad light, not a narrow one. At least, I should say he always began every enterprise seeing it that way, but then narrowed it all down to a question of making money as fast as possible for that son of his so that he could become something he isn't. What a pity! In the last year or two when his affairs began to go down hill, I was always warning him, trying to head him off from foolish speculation. And I suppose this is where – well, blood, background, that sort of thing, finally begin to tell. He got frightened. In the end he went right off his head, to judge from the mess he's left behind. And of course couldn't face it. I don't think he committed suicide because he couldn't face the consequences but because he couldn't face what he knew those consequences would mean for that boy of his. Back home to India, in other words, with his tail between his legs. Coomer, you know, might have found himself in pretty serious trouble. I've said nothing to the son on that score. It's probably best that he shouldn't get to know. But there's one aspect of the business that the bank says looks like a clear case of forgery."

Mr. Lindsey was shocked.

The lawyer, seeing his expression, said, "you can be thankful you haven't invested in any of Coomer's businesses."

"I never had that sort of money," Lindsey replied. "And actually I scarcely knew him. We were sorry for the boy, that's all. As the matter of fact, it's a surprise to me to hear you say his father was so devoted to him. So far as we could see the opposite was true. I suppose we're a pretty soft-hearted family. My own son included. He asked Harry to spend a summer holiday with us some years ago when he found out that he was going to be on his own. It's been like that ever since."

The lawyer said, "But you see, Mr. Lindsey, keeping himself out of Harry's light was Coomer's way of devoting himself to his son's best interests. I don't mean that he deliberately tried to give people the impression his son was neglected so that they'd invite him to their homes and he'd grow up knowing what English people were really like. He kept out of Harry's way because he knew that if Harry grew up as he wanted him to there'd come a time when Harry would be ashamed of him. For instance, there was the question of Coomer's accent. It seemed pretty good to me, but of course it *was* an Indian accent. He certainly didn't want Harry to learn anything from it. He didn't want Harry to learn anything from him at all. He told me so. He said he looked forward to the day when he'd see Harry didn't care much for his company. He didn't want the boy to be ashamed of him but too dutiful to show it. All he wanted for Harry was the best English education and background that money could buy."

And not only money, Lindsey thought. The bitter seed had been sown. It was probably this as much as anything that finally dispelled whatever doubts he may have felt about the reasonableness of his rejection of his son Colin's impossible story-book proposal that Harry should come to live with them permanently if it could possibly be arranged – this – even more than the shock to his well-bred system of learning that young Coomer's father had put someone else's name to a document – this: that young Coomer's lonely situation had not been the result of neglect but of a deliberate policy that had a special and not particularly upright end in view – entrance into a society that stood beyond his father's natural reach to gain for him wholly on his own resources.

Now Lindsey remembered – or rather allowed to make the journey from the back of his mind to the front of it – the comments passed by friends whose judgments he trusted except when they clashed with his liberal beliefs (which were perched, somewhat shakily, on the sturdy shoulders of his natural clannish instincts). He could not actually recall the words of these comments, but he certainly recalled the ideas which lay behind them: that in India, so long as you kept them occupied, the natives could be counted on very often to act in the common interest; that the real Indian, the man most to be trusted, was likely to be your servant, the man who earned the salt he ate under your roof, and next to him the simple peasant who hated the bloodsuckers of his own race, cared nothing for politics, but cared instead, like a sensible fellow, about the weather, the state of the crops, and fair play; respected impartiality, and represented the majority of this simple nation that was otherwise being spoiled by too close a contact with the sophisticated ideas of modern western society. The last man you could trust, these people said (and damn it all, they knew, because they had been there or were related to people who had been there) was the westernised Indian, because he was not really an Indian at all. The only exceptions to this rule were to be found among the maharajahs, people like that, who had been born into the cosmopolitan ranks of those whose job was to exercise authority and were interested in preserving the old social *status quo*.

There had been a time when his son Colin had thought Harry's father was a maharajah, or rajah; or anyway, a rich landowner of the kind who stood next to maharajahs in importance. Over the years the impression had gradually been adjusted (sometimes by these same friends who said that Hari's father was probably the son of a petty zamindar, whatever a zamindar was). But had the initial impression ever been adjusted to anything like the truth? Had the whole thing been a sham? Lindsey hated to think so. But thought so now, and returned home from his altruistic visit to the lawyers feeling that by and large he and his own son had been put upon, led by the nose into an unsavoury affair because they had been too willing to believe the best about people and discount the worst, ignored the warnings of those who had watched the Lindsey adoption of Harry Coomer with expressions sometimes too clearly indicative of their belief that no good could be expected to come of it.

At dinner that night, listening to his fair and good-looking son talking to black-haired, brown-faced Harry, he was surprised to find himself thinking: "But how extraordinary! If you close your eyes and listen, you can't tell the difference. And they seem to talk on exactly the same wave-length as well."

But his eyes were no longer to be closed. He took Harry on one side and said to him, "I'm sorry, old chap. There's nothing I can do. The lawyers have convinced me of that."

Harry nodded. He looked disappointed. But he said, "Well, thanks anyway. I mean for trying," and smiled and then waited as if for the arm Lindsey was normally in the habit of laying fondly on the boy's shoulders.

Tonight Lindsey found himself unable to make that affectionate gesture.

*

His sharpest memories were of piles of leaves, wet and chill to the touch, as if in early morning after a late October frost. To Hari, England was sweet cold and crisp clean pungent scent; air that moved, crowding hollows and sweeping hilltops; not stagnant, heavy, a conducting medium for stench. And England was the park and pasture-land behind the house in Sidcot, the gables of the house, the leaded diamond-pane windows, and the benevolent wistaria.

Waking in the middle of the night on the narrow string-bed in his room at Number 12 Chillianwallah Bagh he beat at the mosquitoes, fisted his ears against the sawing of the frogs and the chopping squawk of the lizards in heat on the walls and ceiling. He entered the mornings from tossing dreams of home and slipped at once into the waking nightmare, his repugnance for everything the alien country offered: the screeching crows outside and the fat amber-coloured cockroaches that lumbered heavy-backed but light-headed with waving feathery antennae from the bedroom to an adjoining bathroom where there was no bath – instead, a tap, a bucket, a copper scoop, a cemented floor to stand on and a slimy runnel for taking the dirty water out through a hole in the wall from which it fell and spattered the caked mud of the compound; draining him layer by layer of his Englishness, draining him too of his hope of discovering that he had imagined everything from the day when the letter came from his father asking him to meet him in Sidcot to talk about the future. This future? There had never been such a meeting so perhaps there wasn't this future. His father had never arrived, never left Edinburgh, but died in his hotel bedroom.

Sometimes when a letter reached him from Colin Lindsey he looked at the writing on the envelope as if to confirm to some inner, more foolishly expectant and hopeful spirit than his own that the letter was not one from his father telling him that everything was a mistake. He longed for letters from England, but when they arrived and he tore them open and read them through, first quickly and then a second time slowly, he found that the day had darkened in a way that set him brooding upon some act of violence that was motiveless; aimless, except to the extent that it was calculated to transport him miraculously back to his native air, his native heath, and people whose behaviour did not revolt him. In such moods he never replied to a letter. He waited until the acutest pain of receiving it was over, and, in a day or two, made a first attempt at an answer that would not expose him as a coward; for that would never do; it would be foreign to the scale of values he knew he must hang on to if he were to see the nightmare through to its unimaginable, unforseeable, but presumably logical end.

In this way Colin Lindsey never had the opportunity of guessing the weight of the burden of exile his friend struggled under. In one letter, he wrote to Harry: "I'm glad you seem to be settling down. I'm reading quite a lot about India to try and get a clearer picture of you in it. Sounds terrific. Wish I could come out. Have you stuck any good pig lately? If you do, don't leave the carcase in front of a mosque, or the devotees of the Prophet will have you by the knackers. Advice from an old hand! We drew the match with Wardens last Saturday. We miss that Coomer touch – those elegant sweeps to his noble leg and those slow snazzy off-breaks.

Funny to think that your cricket will be starting just about the time the school here begins its football season. Not that I shall be seeing the football this year. Has it been decided yet what you are going to do? I'm definitely leaving at the end of this summer term. Dad says he'll stump up for a crammer if I want to matriculate (some hopes) but I've decided to accept my uncle's offer to go into the London office of that petroleum company he's something to do with."

To this, after several days, Hari replied, "The idea always was, you remember, that I'd swot for the ICS exams after leaving Chillingborough and sit for them in London, then come out here and learn the ropes. These days you can sit for the exams over here as well, but I don't think I'll be doing that. My aunt's old brother-in-law runs some kind of business in Mayapore and I gather the idea is that I should go into it. But first I'm supposed to learn the language. Although my uncle-in-law thinks my own language could be useful he says it's not much good to him if I can't understand a word of what 90 per cent of the people I'd be dealing with were talking about. It's raining cats and dogs here these days. Sometimes it gives over and the sun comes out and the whole place steams. But the rain goes on, I'm told, until September, and then it begins to cool down, but only for a few weeks. It starts getting hot again pretty soon in the new year, and by April and May I gather you can't even sweat. I'm down with gippy-tum, and can only face eating fruit, although I wake up thinking of bacon and eggs. Please give my love to your mother and father, and remember me to Connolly and Jarvis, and of course to old Toad-in-the-hole."

Sealing such a letter once he was tempted to tear it up and write another that would give Colin some idea of what it had meant to find himself living on the wrong side of the river in a town like Mayapore. Then he would have said: "There is nothing that isn't ugly. Houses, town, river, landscape. All of them are reduced to sordid uniform squalor by the people who live in them. If there's an exception to this, you'd no doubt find it on the other side of the river, in what are called the civil lines. And perhaps you'd eventually get used to it, even enjoy it, because the civil lines are where *you*'d be; that would be *your* retreat. But I am here in the Chillianwallah Bagh. It's what they call modern. You're somebody by their standards if you live in one of these stifling concrete monstrosities. The whole place stinks of drains, though. In my room – if you can call it a room: with unglazed barred windows it looks more like a cell – there's a bed (a wooden frame with a string mesh), a chair, a table which Aunt Shalini has covered with a ghastly piece of purple cloth embroidered in silver thread, a wardrobe called an almirah with a door that doesn't work. My trunk and suitcases are mildewed. There's a fan in the middle of the ceiling. More often than not it stops working during the night and you wake up suffocating. My aunt and I live alone. We have four servants. They live in the compound at the back. They speak no English. When I'm in a room downstairs they watch me from doorways and through windows because I'm the nephew from 'Bilaiti'. My aunt, I suppose, is a good woman. She's not forty yet but looks more than fifty. We don't understand each other. She tries to understand me harder than I can bother to try to understand her. But at least she is bearable. I detest the others. From their point of view I'm unclean. They want me to drink cow-piss to purify myself of the stain of living abroad, crossing the forbidden water. Purify! I have seen men and women defaecate in the open, in some wasteland near the river. At night the smell of the river comes into my bedroom. In my bathroom, in one corner, there is a hole in the floor and two sole-shaped ledges to put your feet on before you squat. There are always flies in the bathroom. And cockroaches. You get used to them, but only by debasing your own civilised instincts. At first they fill you with horror. Even terror. It is purgatory, at first, to empty the bowels.

"But the house is a haven of peace and cleanliness compared with what's outside and what goes on out there. We get our milk straight from a cow. Aunt Shalini boils it, thank God. The milkman comes in the morning and milks his cow outside the house, near a telegraph pole. To this pole he ties a dead, stuffed calf which the cow nuzzles. This keeps her in milk. The calf was starved to death because the cow's milk was taken by the milkman to sell to good Hindus. Since I knew that, I take only lemon or lime in my tea when Aunt Shalini can get them from the bazaar. I've only been to the bazaar once. That was during the first week I was here, towards the end of May. The temperature was 110 degrees. I hadn't yet taken in what was happening to me. I went to the bazaar with Aunt Shalini because I wanted to be decent to her and she seemed keen for me to go. What was it? Some kind of nightmare? The leper, for instance, who hung about at the entrance to the bazaar and whom nobody seemed to take any special notice of. Was he real? Yes, he was real enough. What was left of his hand came close to my sleeve. Aunt Shalini put a coin into his bowl. She knows about lepers. They are part of her daily experience. And when she put the coin into his bowl I remembered that story my father told me, which I told you, and neither of us quite believed – about the way my grandfather was said to have left his home and gone begging to acquire merit and become part of the Absolute. Well – did he end up as a leper too? Or did he just find himself communing with God?

"All those stories that my father told me; at the time they seemed to be simply stories. A bit romantic even. To get the full flavour of them you have to imagine them taking place here, or somewhere like it, somewhere even more primitive. I look at Aunt Shalini and try to see her as that young kid who was married off at all that cost to the fellow who died of syphilis or something. Died in a brothel, anyway. I wish Father hadn't told me about that. I find myself watching her at table, hoping she won't touch anything but the outer rim of the plate. Poor Aunt Shalini! She asks me questions about England, the kind of question you can't answer because at home it never gets asked.

"Home. It still slips out. But this is home, isn't it, Colin? I mean I shan't wake up tomorrow at Chillingborough or Sidcot, or in what we always called 'my' room at Didbury? I shall wake up here, and the first thing I'll be conscious of will be the sound of the crows. I shall wake up at seven and the household will have been up and about for at least an hour. There'll be a smell from the compound of something being cooked in ghi. My stomach will turn over at the thought of breakfast. I'll hear the servants shouting at each other. In India everybody shouts. There'll be a pedlar or beggar at the gate out front. And he'll be shouting. Or there may be the man who screams. When I first heard him I thought he was a madman who'd got loose. But he is a madman who has never been locked up. His madness is thought of as a sign that God has personally noticed him. He is therefore holier than any of the so-called sane people. Perhaps underneath this idea that he's holy is the other idea that insane is the only sensible thing for an Indian to be, and what they all wish they were.

"The sun will probably be out in the morning. It hurts the eyes to look out of the window. There's no gradation of light.

Just flat hard glare and sudden shadow as a cloud passes. Later it will rain. If the rain falls heavily enough you won't be able to hear the people shouting. But after a bit the sound of the rain sends you barmy too. Since coming here I've started smoking. The cigarettes are always damp though. About eleven o'clock an old man called Pandit Babu Sahib arrives, ostensibly to teach me Hindi. My aunt pays for the lessons. The pandit has a dirty turban and a grey beard. He smells of garlic. It sickens me to catch his breath. The lessons are a farce because he speaks no English I recognise. Sometimes he doesn't turn up at all, or turns up an hour late. They have no conception of time. To me they are still 'they'.

"You ask me what I'm going to do. I don't know. I'm at the mercy of my aunt's in-laws for the moment. There are some Kumars still in Lucknow, apparently, and a brother of Aunt Shalini's and his wife in the old Kumar house in the United Provinces. But they want nothing to do with me. Aunt Shalini wrote to them when she got the news of Father's death. They weren't interested. Father cut himself off from everyone but Aunt Shalini. He sold his land to his brothers before emigrating to England. This brother of his who's still alive is afraid – so Aunt Shalini thinks – that I plan to claim back part of the property. She suggests going to a lawyer to see if the original sale was in order. In this she's like every other Indian. If they can get involved in a long and crippling lawsuit they seem to be happy. But I want nothing to do with that sort of thing. So I'm dependent on her and her brother-in-law, Romesh Chand Gupta Sen, until I can earn a living. But what decent living can I earn without some kind of recognised qualification? Aunt Shalini would let me go to one of the Indian colleges, but it's not for her to say, because Romesh Chand controls the purse-strings. (After all, the Gupta Sens *own* her.) There's a Technical College here that was founded by a rich Indian called Chatterjee. Sometimes I think I might try and get in there and work for an engineering degree or diploma or whatever it is a place like that hands out.

"Do you know the worst thing? Well, not the worst, but the thing that makes me feel really up against it? Neither Aunt Shalini nor Romesh Chand, nor any of their friends and relatives, know any English people, at least not socially, or any who matter. Aunt Shalini doesn't know any because she doesn't have any social life. The others make it a point of principle not even to try to mix. This is a tight, closed, pseudo-orthodox Hindu society. I'm beginning to see just what it was that my father rebelled against. If they knew a few English I don't think it would be long before some kind of special interest was taken in my future. My five years at Chillingborough can't mean nothing, and there must be all kinds of scholarships and grants I could be put on to. But Aunt Shalini knows nothing about them, and seems afraid to raise the subject with anyone, and the Gupta Sens clearly don't want to know. Romesh Chand says I'll be useful to him in his business. I've seen his offices. I think I'd go mad if I had to work there. The main office is over a warehouse that overlooks the Chillianwallah Bazaar, and there's a sub-office at the railway sidings. He's a grain and fresh vegetable contractor to the military station on the other side of the river. He's also a grain dealer on his own account. And Aunt Shalini says he's got his fingers in a lot of other enterprises. He owns most of the Chillianwallah Bagh property. This is the India you won't read about in your pig-sticking books. This is the acquisitive middle-class merchant India of money under the floorboards, and wheat and rice hoarded up until there is a famine somewhere and you can off-load it at a handsome profit, even if most of it has gone bad. Then you sell it to the Government and bribe the government agent not to notice that it's full of weevils. Or you can sell it to the Government while it's still in good condition and there's no famine and the Government can let it go bad – unless of course it's stolen from their warehouses and bought up cheap and stored until the government official can be bribed to buy it all over again. Aunt Shalini tells me about such things. She is very naïve. She tells me things like this to make me laugh. She does not realise that she is talking about the people I'm supposed to feel kindred affection for, men like her husband, for instance, the late Prakash Gupta Sen. Somehow I must fight my way out of this impossible situation. But fight my way to where?"

*

Indeed, to where? It was not a question Colin could have helped him to answer because Hari never asked it of anyone but himself, and it was several months before he put it even to himself so directly, in such unequivocal terms. He had not asked himself the question before because he could not accept the situation as a real one. In that situation there was a powerful element of fantasy, sometimes laughable, mostly not; but a fantasy that was always inimical to the idea of a future stemming directly from it. In terms of a future, first the fantasy had to be destroyed. Something projected from the real world outside had to hit and shatter it. During this period he hung on to his Englishness as if it were some kind of protective armour, hung on to it with a passionate conviction the equal of that which his father had once had that to live in England was probably enough in itself to transform life. And because he now felt that his Englishness was the one and only precious gift his father had given him he liked to forget that he had once been critical of him and year by year more ashamed of him. He fell into the habit of saying to himself whenever a new horror was revealed to him: "This is what my father hated and drove himself mad trying to ensure I'd never be touched by." Madness was the only way he could explain his father's "suicide". And he was old enough, too, to guess that loneliness had heightened the degree of insanity. If Duleep Kumar had not been lonely perhaps he might have found the courage to face up to the financial disaster which the lawyers had succeeded in convincing his son of but never in explaining to that son's satisfaction. In Mayapore, Hari saw that disaster as the work of the same malign spirit that now made his own life miserable.

Through most of his first experience of the rains he was chronically and depressingly off-colour. Whatever he ate turned his bowels to water. In such circumstances a human being goes short on courage. His indisposition and his distaste for what lay outside Number 12 Chillianwallah Bagh kept him confined to the house for days at a time. He slept through the humid afternoons as if drugged and grew to fear the moment when his Aunt Shalini would want his company, or suggest a walk because the rains had let up and the evening was what she called cool. They would go, then, towards the stinking river, along the Chillianwallah Bagh Extension road to the Bibighar bridge, but turn back there as if what lay on the other side was prohibited, or, if not actually prohibited, undesirable. In all that time from May until the middle of September he did not cross over into the Civil Lines. At first he did not cross because there was no call to; but later he did not cross because the other side of the river became synonymous with freedom and the time did not strike him as ripe to test it. He did not want to tempt the malign spirit.

He crossed the river in the third week of September, in 1938, when the rains had gone and his illness was over and he could no longer find any excuse not to go through the motions of pleasing his uncle, Romesh Chand Gupta Sen; when, in fact, he had decided to please his uncle as much as was in his power, because he had talked to his uncle's lawyer, a man called Srinivasan, and now had hopes of persuading the uncle to send him to the Mayapore Technical College, or to the college in the provincial capital.

"I will become," he told himself, "exactly what my father wanted me to become, and like this pay the malign spirit out. I'll become an Indian the English will welcome and recognise."

His father's death had raised the question of moral indebtedness.

*

He went with some documents Romesh Chand told him were needed by a Mr. Nair, the chief clerk at the warehouse near the railway sidings. He travelled by cycle-ricksha. Few of the clothes he had brought from England were of any use to him. His aunt had helped to fit him out with shirts and trousers run up by the bazaar tailor. The trousers he wore today were white and wide-bottomed. With them he wore a white short-sleeved shirt, and carried a buff-coloured sola topee. Only his shoes were English; and those were hand-made and very expensive. One of Aunt Shalini's servants had polished them by now to a brilliance he himself had never achieved.

The traffic was held up on the Mandir Gate bridge. Immediately in front of the ricksha, obstructing the view, was an open lorry loaded with sacks of grain. A sweating, half-naked coolie sat on top of the sacks smoking a bidi. Abreast of the ricksha was another; behind, a bus. The ricksha had come to a halt opposite the temple. There were beggars squatting in the roadway near the temple gate. He looked away in case he should recognize the leper. He heard the clanking of the train on the opposite bank but could not see it because of the lorry. Five minutes after he heard the train the traffic began to move. The bridge had a parapet of whitened stone. He had a brief impression of water and openness, and banks curving away in muddy inlets and promontories, and then the three wheels of the ricksha were juddering over the wooden planks of the level crossing and he was translated into this other half of the world.

His disappointment was as keen as his anticipation had been. The road from the Mandir Gate bridge to the railway station was lined with buildings that reminded him of those on the Chillianwallah Bagh Extension road: but before the ricksha boy took a turn to the right, ringing his bell and shouting a warning to an old man who was chasing a berserk water-buffalo, he saw a vista of trees and a hint, beyond the trees, of space and air. When the ricksha boy drew up in the fore-court of the station goods-yard, which looked like all goods-yards, graceless and functional, he told him to wait. The boy seemed to object, but young Kumar could not understand what he said, and walked away without paying, the one sure way he knew of keeping him there. He entered the godown that bore across its front the sign *Romesh Chand Gupta Sen and Co., Contractors*. Inside there was the nutty fibrous smell of all such places. It was dark and comparatively cool. Labourers were carrying sacks of grain from a stack out into the sunlit siding on the other side of the warehouse and loading them into a goods wagon. The air was full of floating dust and chaff. Set into the wall closest to him was an open door and a bank of windows that overlooked the vast cavern of the godown. This was the office. It was lit by naked electric light-bulbs. He entered. The head clerk was not there. Two or three young men in dhotis and shirts of home-spun cotton sat at trestle tables writing in ledgers. They remained seated. In his uncle's office over the warehouse in the Chillianwallah Bazaar the young clerks stood up whenever he went into their musty ill-lit rooms. That embarrassed him. All the same, suspecting that these clerks at the railway godown knew who he was, he could not help noticing the difference in their behaviour and momentarily feeling diminished by it. He asked where the chief clerk was. The man he spoke to replied fluently enough, answering English for English, but in a manner that was obviously intended to be offensive.

"Then I'll leave these papers with you," Kumar said, and put them on the desk. The young man picked them up and threw them into a wire basket.

"They are marked urgent, by the way," Kumar pointed out.

"Then why do you leave them with me? Why don't you take them with you and look for Mr. Nair in the station master's office?"

"Because that's your job, not mine," Kumar said, and turned as if to walk out.

"These documents are entrusted to you, not to me."

They stared at each other.

Kumar said, "If you're not competent to deal with them by all means let them lie in your little wire basket. I'm only a delivery boy."

When he was at the door the other man called, "I say, Coomer."

He turned, annoyed to have it proved that the other man did know who he was.

"If your uncle wants to know whom you gave these papers to, tell him – Moti Lal."

It was a name he expected to forget but in fact had cause to remember.

When he got outside the warehouse the ricksha boy had turned nasty. He wanted to be paid off. Kumar climbed in and told him to go to the cantonment bazaar. He had worked out how to say it in Hindi. When the boy shook his head Kumar repeated the order but raised his voice. The boy took hold of the handlebars and wheeled the ricksha around, ran with it for a few paces and jumped on to the saddle. Kumar had to shout at him again when he began to turn back along the way they had come. They had another argument. Kumar guessed the reason for the boy's objections. He did not want to take an Indian passenger so far. An Indian passenger seldom paid more than the minimum fare.

Eventually the boy submitted to his bad luck and turned towards the cantonment, and then Kumar found himself travelling along wide avenues of well-spaced bungalows. Here there was shade and a sense of mid-morning hush such as fell at home, between breakfast and lunch during the holidays at Didbury. The road was metalled but the pathways were kutcha. In the sudden quietness he could hear the rhythmic click of the pedals. He lit a cigarette because the odour of the leather cushions and the smell of the boy's stale sweat were now more noticeable.

The boy made a series of left and right hand turns and Kumar wondered whether he was being taken out of his way deliberately, but then – where the road they were now travelling on met another at a T-junction – he could see a section of arcaded shops, and one with a sign over it: Dr. Gulab Singh Sahib (P) Ltd: Pharmacy. They had reached the Victoria road. He told the boy to turn left and indicated with a curt flick of the hand, whenever the boy looked over his shoulder to suggest that now was the time to stop, that the journey should continue. He wanted to see beyond the cantonment bazaar. He wanted to go as far as the place he knew was called the *maidan*.

There were English women in the arcades of the Victoria road. How pale they looked. Their cars were parked in the shade along one side of the bazaar. There was this shade to be had because at ten-thirty in the morning the sun was casting shadows. There were also horse tongas. The tonga-carts were painted in gay colours, and the horses' bridles were decorated with silver medallions and red and yellow plumes. Some of the English women were wearing slacks. Briefly he had an impression that these made them look ugly, but this was an impression that did not survive the warmth of the feeling he had that here at last he was again in the company of people he understood. He looked from one side of the road to the other: here was a shop called Darwaza Chand, Civil and Military Tailor; here the Imperial Bank of India; there the offices of the *Mayapore Gazette* which it interested him to see because Aunt Shalini had made a point of ordering the *Gazette* especially for him so that he could read the local news in English. The shops in the cantonment all advertised in the *Gazette*. The names were familiar to him. He wished that he had a lot of money so that he could tell the ricksha boy to stop at the Imperial Bank, go in and cash a cheque, and then stroll across the road to Darwaza Chand and order some decent suits and shirts. He wished, as well, that he had the courage to go into the English Coffee House, drink a cup or two and smoke a cigarette and chat to the two pretty young white girls who were just now entering. And he would have liked to tap the ricksha boy on his bony back, get out at the Mayapore Sports Emporium and test the weight and spring of the English willow cricket bats that were for sale there, at a price. The sight of the bats in the window made him long to open his shoulders and punish a loose ball. After he had selected a bat he would go across the road to the Yellow Dragon Chinese Restaurant and eat some decent food; and, in the evening, pay a visit to the Eros Cinema where at 7.30 and 10.30 that evening they were showing a film he had seen months ago with the Lindseys at the Carlton in the Haymarket. He would have liked the Lindseys to be here in

Mayapore to see it with him again. Going past the cinema – a building with a white stuccoed façade and a steel mesh concertina gate closing the dark cavern of the open foyer, and set well back in a sanded forecourt – he felt the pain of his exile more sharply than ever.

He told the boy to go in the direction of the *maidan*. The cinema was the last building in the cantonment bazaar – or the first, depending which way you came. Beyond it there was a section of tree-shaded road with low walls on either side and, on the other side of the walls, the huts and godowns of the Public Works Department. The ricksha boy got up some speed on this stretch, negotiated the crossroads formed by the Victoria and Grand Trunk roads and rode on past the Court house, the Police barracks, the District Headquarters, the chummery, the District Superintendent's bungalow and the bungalow which the Poulsons were to take over in 1939.

In this way Hari Kumar reached the *maidan*. He told the ricksha boy to stop. The vast space was almost empty. There were two riders – white children mounted on ponies. Their syces ran behind. The crows were wheeling and croaking, but to Hari they no longer looked predatory. There was peace. And Hari thought: Yes, it is beautiful. In the distance, on the other side of the *maidan*, he could see the spire of St. Mary's. He got down from the ricksha and stood in the shade of the trees and watched and listened. Half-closing his eyes he could almost imagine himself on the common near Didbury. The rains had left their green mark on the turf, but he did not know this because he had never seen the *maidan* before; he had never seen it in May when the grass was burnt to ochre.

He wanted to mount and ride and feel the air moving against his face. Could one hire a pony from somewhere? He turned to the ricksha boy. It was impossible to ask. He did not know the right words. Perhaps he did not need to know, or need to ask because he could guess the answer. The *maidan* was the preserve of the *sahib-log*. But he felt, all the same, that he would only have to speak to one of them to be recognised, to be admitted. He got back into the ricksha and told the boy to go back to the cantonment bazaar. He would buy a few things at Dr. Galub Singh's pharmacy; some Odol toothpaste and some Pears' soap. Surreptitiously, he felt in his wallet. He had a five-rupee note and four one-rupee notes. About fifteen shillings. The ricksha boy would ask for three but really be content with two.

On the return journey he became aware that there were very few cycle rickshas on the road. There were cars, cycles and horse-tongas. In the cycle-rickshas the passengers were always Indians. In one ricksha the passenger had his sandalled feet up on a wooden crate of live chickens. He felt the shame that rubbed off on to him because he travelled by ricksha, so marking himself as out of his own black-town element because the cycle-rickshas all came from the other side of the river.

When they reached Gulab Singh's he told the boy to stop, and got down, mounted the double kerb and entered the shadowy arcade. In Gulab Singh's window there were brand goods so familiar, so Anglo-Saxon, he felt like shouting for joy. Or in despair. He could not tell which. He entered. The shop was dark and cool, set out with long rectangular glass cases on table-legs, as in a museum. It smelt faintly of pepper and richly of unguents. At one end there was a counter. There were several English women walking round, each attended by an Indian assistant. There was a man as well, who looked a bit like Mr. Lindsey. The Englishman's clothes showed his own up for what they were. Babu clothes. Bazaar stuff. The English were talking to each other. He could hear every word they said if he paid attention. The man who looked like Mr. Lindsey was saying: "Why hasn't it come? You said Tuesday and today is Tuesday. I might just as well have ordered it myself. Well, give me the other thing and send the rest up jolly sharp."

Kumar stood at the counter and waited for the assistant to finish serving the Englishman. The Englishman glanced at him and then turned his attention back to what the assistant was doing: wrapping an unidentifiable cardboard carton.

"Right," the Englishman said, taking the package. "I'll expect the other things by six this evening."

When the Englishman had gone Kumar said, "Have you got some Pears' soap?"

The assistant, a man several years older than himself, waggled his head from side to side, and went away. Kumar could not be sure that he had understood. Another assistant came through the doorway marked *Dispensary,* but he was carrying a package which he took over to a woman who was studying the articles for sale in one of the glass cases. At the other side of the shop there was a photographic booth. Kumar waited. When he next saw his own assistant the man was opening another of the glass cases for a group of white women.

Kumar moved away from the unattended counter and took up a position from which he judged he would be able to catch the assistant's eye. He was right. He did. But the assistant's expression was that of someone who did not remember ever having been spoken to about Pears' soap. Kumar wished that the assistant's new customers had been men. He could have interrupted their conversation, then, without putting himself in the wrong. Instead, he found himself in the ignominious role of watcher on the sidelines, in a situation another man was taking advantage of: hiding, as Kumar put it to himself, behind the skirts of a group of women. He looked around and saw the man who had come from the dispensary going back there. He said to him, "I asked someone if you had any Pears' soap."

The man stopped: perhaps because Kumar's voice automatically arrested him with its sahib-inflexions. Momentarily he seemed to be at a loss, assessing the evidence of his eyes and the evidence of his ears. "Pears'?" he said at last. "Oh yes, we have Pears'. Who is it for?"

It was a question Kumar had not expected, and one he did not immediately understand. But then did. Who did this fellow think he was? Some *babu* shopping for his master?

"Well, it's for me, naturally," he said.

"One dozen or two dozen?"

Kumar's mouth was dry.

"One bar," he said, trying to be dignified about it.

"We only sell it by the dozen," the man explained, "but you could get it in the bazaar, I expect," and then added something in Hindi, which Kumar did not understand.

He said, "I'm sorry. I don't speak Hindi. What are you trying to say?"

And was conscious, now, that because he was annoyed he had raised his voice, and other people in the shop were watching and listening. He caught the eye of one of the Englishwomen. Slowly she turned away with a smile he could only attach two words to: bitter, contemptuous.

"I was saying," the man replied, "that if you are only wanting one bar of Pears' soap you will find it cheaper in the Chillianwallah Bazaar because there they are taking no notice of regulated retail prices."

"Thank you," Kumar said, "you have been most helpful," and walked out.

*

The room in the Chillianwallah Bazaar office where Kumar worked was larger than the rest. He shared it with other English-speaking clerks. They were afraid of him because of his manner and his family connexion with their employer. Proud of their own fluency in what passed among them for English – a language not generally in use at Romesh Chand's warehouse – they resented his intrusion but in a perverse way were flattered by the sense of further elevation his presence gave them. They were boys who, if they could help it, never spoke their mother tongue, and so looked down on the men in the small, airless partitioned cells, old clerks who conducted their business and correspondence in the vernacular. By arriving in their own midst Kumar had confirmed their superiority but threatened their security. In front of him they no longer dared to criticise Romesh Chand, or the head clerks, in case one of Kumar's jobs was to act as a family spy. And even when they felt reassured that it was not they could not help wondering which of them might lose his job to the Anglicised boy who knew nothing about the business but had the manner of a burra sahib. Their conduct towards him was a compound of suspicion, awe, envy and servility.

They sickened him. He thought them spineless, worse than a bunch of girls, giggling one day and sulking the next. He found it difficult to follow what they were saying. They ran all their words one into the other. They sang their sentences. Their pronunciation was peculiar. At first he tried to understand them, but then saw the danger of trying too hard. He wondered how long a man could work among them and not fall into the same habits of speech, not acquire the alien habits of thought that controlled the speech. At night, alone in his bedroom, he sometimes talked aloud to himself, trying to detect changes of tone, accent and resonance in order to correct them. To maintain the Englishness of his voice and habits became increasingly important to him. Even after the disastrous visit to Gulab Singh's pharmacy it remained important. He remembered what his father had said: "If you answer the telephone people think it is an Englishman speaking." There were no telephones at his uncle's office. There was no telephone at Number 12 Chillianwallah Bagh. Even if there had been telephones there would have been no Englishman to ring or to be rung by. But this absence of Englishness in his exterior public life he saw as a logical projection of the fantasy that informed his private inner one.

It was at this period, after the visit to the pharmacy, that the notion of having become invisible to white people first entered his head, although it took some time for the notion to be formulated quite in this way. When he had become used to crossing the river from the bazaar to the railway warehouse and used to the way English people seemed to look right through him if their eyes chanced to meet his own, the concept of invisibility fell readily enough into its place, but still more time was needed for that concept to produce its natural corollary in his mind: that his father had succeeded in making him nothing, nothing in the black town, nothing in the cantonment, nothing even in England because in England he was now no more than a memory, a familiar but possibly unreal signature at the end of meaningless letters to Colin Lindsey; meaningless because, as the months went by, the letters deviated further and further from the truth. The letters became, in fact, exercises by young Kumar to keep his Englishness in trim. He knew this. He knew his letters were unsatisfactory. He recognised the signs of growing-away that could be read in Colin's replies. But the association with Colin continued to be precious to him. Colin's signature at the bottom of a letter was the proof he needed that his English experience had not been imagined.

*

Where does one draw the line under the story of Hari Kumar, Harry Coomer: the story of him prior to Bibighar?

Sister Ludmila said that for her Bibighar began on the morning Merrick took Kumar away in his police truck; so at least Kumar has to be brought to that point, brought anyway to the moment when, in the dark, his body was turned over by Mr. de Souza and his face lit by the torch. Such darkness, Sister Ludmila said; the kind of expression which was familiar to her on the faces of young Indians, but was, in Hari's case, especially significant.

And where does one go for the evidence of the story of Kumar prior to Bibighar? Well, there is the lawyer Srinivasan. There is Sister Ludmila. There is no longer Shalini Gupta Sen; no Gupta Sen who knows, or will admit to knowing. There are other witnesses: and, specifically, there is that certain signature in the Members' Book of the Mayapore Gymkhana Club. There is also the signature of Harry Coomer in the Members' Book for 1939 of the Mayapore Indian Club. The Mayapore Chatterjee Club. The MCC. The other club. The wrong one. And this is to be found in a ledger somewhat similar to those used at the right club, under a date in May 1939, which oddly enough roughly coincides with the day the Deputy Commissioner challenged a tradition and made a forced entry at the Gymkhana.

"I put young Kumar up for the Indian Club" (Srinivasan said) "because it has something I felt he needed. We only met a few times. I'm afraid he didn't like me. He distrusted me because I was his uncle Romesh's lawyer. Apart from that English manner of his which I found overbearing I quite liked him as a person, if not as a type. If we'd got on better, if he'd trusted me, perhaps I should have been able to do something for him, taken him to Lili Chatterjee's for instance and got him into a few mixed English and Indian parties. But by the time he got into what used to be called the MacGregor House set it was too late. He'd already got on the wrong side of the policeman, Merrick, and been taken in for questioning. The evening in 1939 I took him to the Indian Club wasn't a success. The banias were there, with their feet on the chairs. He hated it. I don't think he ever went again, and a few weeks later he left his uncle's office. He'd got wind of the marriage the Gupta Sens were thinking of arranging for him, and he'd given up hope of getting his uncle to agree to his going to the Technical College. I can tell you this, that if it hadn't been for his Aunt Shalini he'd have been in a bad way when he walked out of Romesh Chand's office. The old man was ready to wash his hands of him. I remember how she begged and pleaded with Romesh to continue the allowance he paid her. Well, he kept it going but cut it down. She pinched and scraped and went without things herself to give Hari something for his pocket; and of course she fed and housed and clothed him. I told her that as long as she did that she was stopping him from standing on his own feet. He was already nineteen. A man by our standards. But she wouldn't hear any criticism of him. And don't get the wrong impression. He didn't just sit back. I remember for instance that he applied for a job at the British-Indian Electrical. He had two or three interviews and for a time it looked as if he'd got in. Naturally they were interested. His English public school education didn't count for nothing. It didn't matter to them that he had no qualifications. They could have taught him what he needed to know, and trained him up on the administrative side. But he fell foul of one of the Englishmen there, so Shalini Gupta Sen told me. It wasn't difficult to guess why. In those days, you know, the commercial people were always looked down upon as the lowest form of Anglo-Indian life. Even schoolmasters ranked higher in the colonial social scale. The man Hari fell foul of probably spoke English with a Midlands accent, and resented the fact that an Indian spoke it like a managing director.

"After the British-Indian Electrical debacle I tried to get Romesh to understand that the boy's talents were being wasted. But let me confess. It wasn't a problem I spent any sleepless nights over. You want me to be frank. And frankly I did not much care for the kind of Indian Duleep Kumar had turned his son into. Please remember that in those days I was only in my forties, also that my main interest was in politics. And I did not respond to Hari Kumar as a political animal. His father had taught him no doubt that Indian politics were all a nonsense, all window-dressing. Hari did not take them seriously. He had no real knowledge of them, no conception for instance of the step forward that provincial power had meant to the Congress. He scarcely realised that the province he lived in had once been ruled directly by a British Governor and a nominated council. He took democracy for granted. He had no experience of autocracy. Politically he was an innocent. Most Englishmen were. In those days I had no time for such people. Today, of course, I am a political innocent myself. It is the fate that awaits us all, all of us anyway who ever had strong views about political affairs when we were younger. Particularly it awaits those of us who paid for our views with imprisonment. Prison left its disagreeable mark. It made us attach too much importance to the things that led us to it."

*

When Hari left his uncle's employment he also told Pandit Baba Sahib he no longer wanted Hindi lessons. He did this to save his aunt from spending money uselessly. He had picked up enough Hindi to give orders, picked up in fact what the average Englishman in India thought worth while bothering with. His series of interviews with the British-Indian Electrical Company took place in the early part of the rainy season of 1939. His rejection was a blow, even though he had expected it after his final interview. For the first time he wrote a letter to Colin that gave young Lindsey – or should have given him – a clearer idea of what Hari Kumar was up against.

"There was a strong likelihood of being sent back home to learn the technical ropes," he told his friend in Didbury. "First in Birmingham and then in the London office of the parent company. Things went swimmingly at the first interview with a pleasant chap called Knight who was at Wardens from 1925 to 1930. He played in the Chillingborough-Wardens match of 1929, when apparently they beat us by twenty-two runs. We didn't talk about the job at all, really, although it was Knight who mentioned London and Birmingham and got my hopes up. It sounded like the answer to a prayer, one that had been here on my doorstep all these months. I told him the whole thing, about father, etc. He seemed pretty sympathetic. The next interview was with the managing director, and that was stickier – probably because, as Knight had let slip, he was grammar-school with a university veneer. But even so, I still thought it was going well, even when he poured a bit of cold water on the idea of sending me home for training. He said there was a sort of understanding with the Technical College here to look primarily among their graduates for young Indians who had executive prospects, but that they were also working on a scheme with the college for extramural courses for their own 'promising men', something to do with part-time training in the firm and part-time education at the college. If I got some kind of diploma from the college then it might be possible to send me home for more intensive instruction. He made rather heavy weather of my not having matriculated and said, 'Of course, Coomer, at your age most young Indians have a BA or a BSc.' I felt like saying, 'Well, of a sort,' but didn't, because I guessed anyway that he appreciated the difference between a BSc Mayapore and a man who'd been at Chillingborough on the classical side. Anyway, the second interview ended on an optimistic note. I saw Knight again for a few minutes afterwards and he said that in the month since he and I had had a chat he'd written to someone at the London office who'd been in touch with old Toad-in-the-hole, and that I'd been given a good reference.

"I had to wait another two weeks for interview number

three which both Knight and the managing director had warned me about, but given me the impression was not much more than a formality, an interview with a fellow they called the Technical Training Manager, a fellow called Stubbs, who is best described as a loud-mouthed —. He began right away by shoving a little cylinder at me, across his enormous desk, and asking me to tell him what it was and what it was used for. When I said I didn't know but that it looked like a sort of valve he smirked and said, 'Where are you from, laddie? Straight down from the tree?' Then he picked up a printed sheet and read out a list of questions. Long before he got to the end I said, 'I've already told Mr. Knight I know nothing about electricity.' He took no notice. Probably I shouldn't have mentioned Mr. Knight. He went on until he'd asked me the last question and I'd said, 'I don't know,' for the last time. Then he glared and said, 'You some sort of comedian or something? Are you deliberately wasting my time?' I told him that was for him to decide. He leaned back in his swivel chair, and we stared at each other for what seemed ages. Then he said, 'There's only you and me in this room, Coomer or whatever your name is. Let me tell you this. I don't like bolshie black laddies on my side of the business.' I got up and walked out. Which is what he wanted me to do and what I couldn't avoid doing unless I wanted to crawl.

"So now you know what I am, Colin, a bolshie black laddie. (Remember that bastard Parrott, in our first year at Chillingborough?) I'm a bolshie black laddie because I know how to construe Tacitus but haven't any idea what that fellow Stubbs was talking about. And that wasn't the end of it. I had a letter from Knight about three days later asking me to go and see him. He told me that for the moment there weren't any vacancies. He was quite a different fellow. Puzzled and embarrassed, doing the right thing by an old Chillingburian, but underneath it all bloody unfriendly. Stubbs must have spun them all a yarn. And because Stubbs was a white man they felt they had to believe him. After all, for the job I was applying for, there were probably a score of BAs and BScs, failed or otherwise, who would be willing to jump when Stubbs said jump.

"The one thing that puzzled me was why it was Stubbs who was allowed to call the tune? Why him? Surely Knight knew what kind of a man he was? But he never so much as hinted he'd like to hear my side of what happened. He never referred to my interview with Stubbs at all. In fact when I came away I wondered why he'd bothered to call me in. He could have given me the brush-off by letter. Later I realised he probably wanted to have another look at me – sort of through Stubbs's eyes, bearing in mind whatever it was Stubbs had told them. And then I guessed that at this second interview with Knight I couldn't have made much of an impression, although it was hardly my fault because as soon as I sat down in front of him I could tell it was no go, and I was damned disappointed. Trying not to show it probably made me look as if I didn't care a damn. But I cared like hell, Colin. After a while the conversation just dried up because he had nothing more to tell me and I had nothing I could say except something like Please, sir, give me a chance. Perhaps he was waiting for me to say 'sir'. I don't think I ever said 'sir' at the first interview, but if I didn't he hadn't noticed. But since he'd talked to Stubbs he was probably on the look-out for that sort of thing. Anyway, he suddenly stopped looking at me, so I got to my feet and said thank you. He said he'd keep a note about me in case something turned up, and stood up too, but stayed behind his desk, and didn't offer to shake hands. I think he had it in mind to give me some kind of tip about remembering that this wasn't Chillingborough and that I should start learning how to behave in front of white men. Anyway that was the feeling in the room. There was that desk between us. For me to be in his office at all had suddenly become a privilege. A privilege I ought to know how to respect. I don't remember coming away – only finding myself outside the main gate of the factory, and getting on my bike and riding back along the Grand Trunk road, over the Bibighar bridge, back to my side of the river."

*

For a while after what Srinivasan called the British-Indian Electrical debacle, Hari did nothing. He regretted writing that letter to Lindsey, regretted it more and more as week after week went by and he got no reply. Other things fell into place in his mind: Mr. Lindsey's attitude to him towards the end of his last few weeks in England, which he had always attributed to the man's embarrassment at having been unable to do anything constructive for him financially; the experience on the boat, in which, once past Suez, the English people who had spoken to him freely enough from Southampton onwards began to congregate in exclusive little groups so that for the last few days of the voyage the only Englishmen he managed to talk to were those making the passage for the first time. He had shared a cabin with two other boys, Indian students returning home. He had not got on very well with them because he discovered that he had nothing in common with them. They asked his opinion on subjects he had never given a thought to. They were students of political economy and intended to become university teachers. He had thought them incredibly dull and rather old-maidish. It seemed that he shocked them by sleeping in the nude and dressing and undressing in the cabin instead of in the lavatory cubicle.

And so Hari came, one painful step at a time, to the realisation that his father's plans for him had been based upon an illusion. In India an Indian and an Englishman could never meet on equal terms. It was not how a man thought, spoke and behaved that counted. Perhaps this had been true in England as well and the Lindseys had been exceptions to the general rule. He did not blame his father. His anger was directed against the English for fostering the illusion his father had laboured under. If he had felt more liking for his fellow-countrymen he might at this stage have sided with them, sought an occasion for paying the English out. But he did not care for any Indian he had met and what he knew or read of their methods of resisting English domination struck him as childish and inept. In any case *they* did not trust him. Neither, it seemed, did the English. He recognised that to the outside world he had become nothing. But he did not feel in himself that he was nothing. Even if he were quite alone in the world he could not be nothing. And he was not quite alone. There was still Colin, at home, and Aunt Shalini in Mayapore. The affection he had for her, grudging at first, when he first recognised it as affection, had become genuine enough. In her self-effacement he saw evidence of a concern for his welfare which was just as acute – perhaps more acute than Mrs. Lindsey's which had been so effusively, openly and warmly expressed. He could not help knowing that in her odd, retiring way his Aunt Shalini was fond of him. The trouble was that her fondness could not reach him or encourage him outside the ingrown little world which was the only one she knew, one that stifled him and often horrified him. It was difficult for him to enter it even briefly to show her that he returned fondness for fondness. To enter it he had to protect himself from it by nursing his contempt and showing his dislike. He could not help it if often she believed the contempt and dislike were meant for her. When she gave him money he could not thank her properly. It was Gupta Sen money. Perhaps she understood his dislike of such money and the way his dislike grew in proportion to his increasing need; or perhaps he had hurt her by the curt words with which he acknowledged it. She took to putting the money in an envelope and leaving it on his bedroom table. It touched him that in writing his name on the envelope she always spelled it Harry.

It touched him too that she seemed to consider him as head of the household, head in the Hindu family sense because he was a man; potentially a breadwinner, husband and father; procreator. He could not imagine himself becoming a married man. Indian girls did not attract him. The English girls he saw in the cantonment seemed to move inside the folds of some invisible purdah that made their bodies look unreal, asexual. His lusts centred upon an anthropomorphous being whose sex was obvious from the formation of the thighs and swollen breasts but whose colour was ambivalent; dumb, sightless and unmoving beneath his own body which at night, under waking or sleeping stress, sometimes penetrated the emptiness and drained itself of the dead weight of its fierce but undirected impulse.

*

Four weeks after the final meeting with Knight, Hari applied for another job. He had spent the intervening time trying to work out the logic of a situation which he now accepted as real and not illusory. That precious gift from his father, his Englishness, was clearly, in many respects, a liability, but he still regarded it fundamentally as an asset. It was the only thing that gave him distinction. He was strong, healthy, and not bad-looking, but so were countless other young men. Where he scored over them was in his command of the English language. Logic pointed to a deliberate exploitation of this advantage. It occurred to him that he might well earn money by setting up as a private tutor and coaching boys who wanted to improve their speech; but such a life did not appeal to him. He doubted that it would be active enough or that he would have the patience it needed, let alone the skill.

The other possibility, perhaps the only other one, was much more interesting.

Having read the *Mayapore Gazette* now for over a year he saw where his qualifications might gain him a natural foothold. Owned by an Indian, edited by an Indian, it was also obviously written and sub-edited by Indians. Its leaders and general articles were of a fairly high standard, but its reports of local events were often unintentionally funny. Hari imagined that the paper's reputed popularity among the Mayapore English was due to the fact that it gave them something to laugh at, as well as an opportunity to see their names in print on the social and sporting pages. For an Indian-owned newspaper it was shrewdly non-committal. It left political alignment to the local vernacular newspapers, of which there were several, and to an English language paper called *The Mayapore Hindu,* which some of the official English read as a duty and others bought in order to compare its reports with the Calcutta *Statesman* and *The Times of India,* but which most of them ignored. It had been suppressed on more than one occasion.

Once Hari had decided to apply for a job with the *Mayapore Gazette* he spent several days copying out particularly bad examples of syntax and idiom from old issues, and then rewriting them. When he was satisfied that he could do the work he had in mind to persuade the editor to give him, he wrote and asked for an interview. He drafted the letter several times until he was satisfied that he had stripped it to its essentials. According to the headings at the top of the leader column on the middle page of the *Gazette* the editor's name was B. V. Laxminarayan. He told Mr. Laxminarayan that he was looking for a job. He told him his age, and gave brief details of his education. He said that to save him the trouble of replying he would ring Mr. Laxminarayan in two or three days to find out whether he could see him. He hesitated, but in the end decided, to add that Mr. Knight of the British-Indian Electrical Company would probably be prepared to pass on the references that had been obtained from the headmaster of Chillingborough. He signed the letter "Hari Kumar" and marked the envelope "Personal" to reduce the odds on its being opened and destroyed by some employee who was concerned for the safety of his own position. He had not worked in the office of his uncle for nothing. He doubted that Mr. Laxminarayan would know Knight, or know him well enough to ring him, or – if he was wrong in either of these two suppositions – that Knight would have the nerve to tell an Indian any story other than that there had been several interviews but no vacancy. Also he relied on Knight's conception of what it was gentlemanly to say as one prospective employer to another about a young man who had played cricket against his old school.

Hari was right in the second of his suppositions. Laxminarayan knew Knight, but not well enough to ring him unless he wanted confirmation of a story about the British-Indian Electrical Company's activities. In any case he would not have rung him about Kumar's letter. Laxminarayan did not like Mr. Knight, whom he described to himself as a two-faced professional charmer whose liberal inclinations had long ago been suffocated by his moral fear of the social consequences of sticking his neck out. "Knight," he told Hari later, "can now only be thought of as a pawn." He had these harsh things to say about Knight in order not to have to think them about himself.

Laxminarayan was interested in the letter signed by Hari Kumar, but when he replied, "By all means ring, although I have no immediate vacancy," he had no intention of employing him. In fact he had been told by the absentee proprietor, Madhu Lal, who lived in Calcutta, to reduce the overheads and produce a more rational percentage of net profit to total investment. His own private view was that the *Gazette*'s circulation would be increased if the paper could be seen to commit itself to the cause of Indian nationalism. He knew that the *Gazette* was anathema to the members of the local Congress sub-committee, and that it was a bit of a joke to the English. He believed that he could sell it even more widely among the English if he could get up their blood pressure. The bulk of its present readership – self-consciously westernised Indians and snob English – would not be lost, because they were sheep by definition. But he reckoned that over a twelve-month period he could add five or ten thousand copies to the weekly circulation if Madhu Lal ever allowed him to make the paper a repository of informed and controversial local and national opinion – non-Hindu, non-Muslim, non-British, but Indian in the best sense.

Laximinarayan conscientiously believed in his paper. Believing in it was a way of continuing to believe in himself and frank criticism of its shortcomings was a more rewarding occupation than criticism of his own. He had found a way of substituting positive thought for negative action; which perhaps was just as well. He was too deeply committed to the compromise of early middle age to be able to rekindle – in a practical, sensible way – the rebellious spark of his youth. Certainly it was just as well from Hari's point of view. When Laxminarayan first met him it took no more than a few minutes of conversation for the smothered demon in the older man to kick out, to attempt – impotently – to take control of his judgment. The demon disliked Kumar: the manner, the voice, the way the fellow sat, with his head up, his legs crossed, one black hand resting on the other side of the desk – an embryo black sahib, talking with a sahib's assurance, the kind of assurance that conveyed itself as superiority subtly restrained in the interests of the immediate protocol. The demon only stopped kicking because Laxminarayan's internal flanks were inured to the pain of the demon's spurs and because he saw, in Kumar, a potential asset, an asset in terms of the type of periodical Mr. Madhu Lal wanted the *Gazette* to be. And when Kumar handed him some papers, written proof of his talents as a sub-editor – paragraphs and columns that he recognised as extracts from old issues now transformed into the simple, clear, standard English that in times of stress even eluded the overworked editor, he knew that he would offer Kumar a job and probably get rid of one of the boys who worried him but for whom he cared most, one of the boys who had little talent but a lot of heart and would in all likelihood turn out eventually to be an embarrassment.

*

Laxminarayan. These days he lives in a bungalow that once belonged to a Eurasian family who left Mayapore in 1947 – a bungalow in the Curzon road. He is now an old man. He is writing a history of the origins of Indian nationalism that will probably never be finished, let alone published: his apologia for many years of personal compromise. He recognises that the policy of Madhu Lal paid off because the *Mayapore Gazette* has enjoyed an uninterrupted existence. Left to him, to Laxminarayan, it might have been done to death in 1942, in which year *The Mayapore Hindu* was suppressed for the third or fourth time. But he is amused, now, at the *Gazette*'s Hindu-National basis – its air of having always supported the causes it has become locally popular to promote. Its new owner is a Brahmin refugee from Pakistan. Its new editor is the owner's cousin. With regard to politics at the centre it gives most space to the speeches and activities of Mr. Morarji Desai. It plans, next year, to publish itself in a simultaneous Hindi edition, as a first step towards dispensing entirely with English. This, more than anything, saddens Mr. Laxminarayan who throughout his life has had what he calls a love-hate relationship with the English language. It is the language in which he learned to think his revolutionary thoughts, and the language which so readily lent itself to the business of making the cautious middle-way he took look and sound like common sense instead of like a case of cold feet.

"What am I now?" (he would ask you, if you went to see him at his home where he is surrounded by grandchildren whose high-pitched voices seem to come from every room and from the sunlit garden which – as the English would say – has been let go). "Well, I will tell you. I am an old man who has lived through one of the greatest upheavals of modern history – the first, and I think the most passionate, of a whole series of upheavals, rebellions against the rule of the white man which have now become so commonplace they are almost boring. And I came through it without a scratch. A veritable Vicar of Bray, you understand. Retired now on pension. Honorary life member of the Mayapore Club where good Hindus forgather. Young journalists come to see me when they hear that I steered the *Gazette* through those stormy pre-independence waters and say, 'Sir, please tell us what it was really like in the days of the British.' Just like your own young people may occasionally say, What was it really like during Hitler and Mussolini? The old colonial British have become a myth, you see. Our young men meet the new Englishmen and say to themselves, 'What was all the fuss about? These fellows don't look like monsters and they seem only to be interested in the things we are interested in. They are not interested in the past and neither are we except to the extent that we wonder what the fuss was about and aren't sure that our own government is doing any better, or even that it is a government that represents us. It seems more to be the government of an uneasy marriage between old orthodoxy and old revolutionaries, and such people have nothing to say to us that we want to hear.'

"I gave Kumar a job and later got rid of a fellow called

Vidyasagar who was arrested in 1942 with several other members of the staff of *The Mayapore Hindu,* and was then put in prison. I was asked to take some steps in that disagreeable business young Kumar was involved in at the time of Bibighar. I'm afraid I refused. No one asked me to use my good offices in the cause of poor Vidyasagar who was given fifteen strokes for an infringement of prison regulations. Not that there was anything I could have done for either of them. But it stuck in my throat that when both of these boys were arrested, for different reasons, only Kumar had people to speak for him, people to ring me up and say, 'Can't you get Hari out of jail? You were his employer. Can't you do something for him? Can't *you* prove he was nowhere in the vicinity of the Bibighar?' People like Lady Chatterjee. And that fellow Knight at the British-Indian Electrical whose conscience probably bothered him. Even the assistant commissioner, Mr. Poulson, sent for me and asked me questions about what Hari Kumar's political affiliations really were. I said, 'Mr. Poulson, he is like myself. He has none. He is a lickspittle of the Raj.' I was angry. I did not see why I should raise a finger to help him. If the British couldn't see for themselves that he was innocent, who was I to intervene? He was more British than they were."

*

A week after Hari got his job on the *Mayapore Gazette* he received a letter from Colin Lindsey. It was dated towards the end of July 1939. Colin apologised for not having written for so long. "A few months ago I joined the Territorial Army and your own last letter reached me in training camp," he explained. "We were pretty busy. If there's a war – and the odds are there will be – I shall put in for a commission; otherwise I get a kick out of just being an acting unpaid lance-corporal. (They made me up in camp, this summer.) I expect you'll be thinking of the army too, won't you, Harry? I mean if anything happens. I'm told the Indian army is quite an outfit, and no longer officered only by the British. Maybe we'll meet up in some dugout or other, like Journey's End! Sorry you had such an unpleasant experience at that factory or whatever it was. I can't understand why your aunt's in-laws wouldn't stump up to see you through the ICS. Dad tells me a friend of his says Indians can become High Court judges even, so the ICS seems to be the thing. That or the army. I recommend the latter. It's a great life. And honestly, Harry, you'd make a first-rate platoon commander – which is what I want to be if the war ever gets going. Then you could waggle a couple of fingers at that fellow Stubbs who was obviously other rank material only. Like me, at the moment! I've got a feeling that by the time you get this I shall be in France. Why the hell does it always have to be France? The feeling in my own unit is that the Jerrys ought to come straight over here. Then we could really show them a thing or two. Major Crowe, our CO, reckons that with all that guns-and-butter stuff the poor blighters are half-starved anyway and haven't got the strength to shoulder a rifle, let alone manhandle their artillery. Dear old Harry! Wish you were here. Then we could be in it together. For my money it's the only thing to be in, these days. The fond parents send their love."

*

"One time he spoke to me of a letter from that boy Lindsey" (Sister Ludmila said). "Why did he treat me as a mother-confessor? This I never earned. He spoke in that way he had, of believing in nothing, which was not natural to him, but was what he had acquired. 'Sister,' he said, 'what would you have done if you had received a letter from an old friend that showed you suddenly you were speaking different languages?' I do not remember what I replied. Unless I said, 'There is only God's language.' Meaning, you understand, the truth – that this language matters and no other. He did not hold himself entirely free of blame for what happened because when he wrote he did not tell Lindsey what was in his heart. Perhaps he did not tell him because he could not. Did not tell him because he did not know himself."

*

From the *Mayapore Gazette* Hari received sixty rupees a month, the equivalent of just over four pounds. He gave half to his Aunt Shalini because Uncle Romesh Chand reduced her allowance on the day Hari began work for Mr. Laxminarayan. The sixty rupees were paid to Hari as a sub-editor. If Laxminarayan published any of Hari's original reports he was to pay him at the rate of one anna a line. For sixteen lines, then, Hari would earn a rupee.

All this he told Colin when he replied to young Lindsey's letter. He was looking, perhaps, for a way of showing Lindsey that in Mayapore the threat of German ambitions seemed very far away, and Lindsey's curiously pre-1914 heroics strikingly out of tune with what Hari felt about his own immediate obligations and clearly recollected as the contempt for war which he and Colin had shared, or at least professed to share. Something had happened to Colin. It puzzled Hari to know what. There had been a time when they agreed that it might be necessary to pursue a line of conscientious objection to what they called compulsory physical violence in the interests of a nation's political and economic aims. Now, here was Colin talking nostalgically about Journey's End. Did the wearing of a uniform so corrupt a man? And what, anyway, in Colin's case had led him voluntarily to put one on? Colin had once said that patriotism, like religious fervour, was a perversion of the human instinct for survival. Chillingborough was a forcing house of administrators, not of soldiers. To an administrator a soldier represented the last ditch defence of a policy: one to which, on the whole, it was shameful to retreat.

"I'm glad," Hari wrote, "that you're finding life in the TA not too wearing –"

That English subtlety! It struck him even as he wrote the words that they could be read either as manly understatement or bitchy criticism.

"– and I suppose if things come to a head India will be in the war too. Which will mean me."

He sat and thought for a moment. He did not feel that it would mean him at all.

"It's difficult to apply a theory when faced with a situation that calls for some kind of positive reaction," he continued. "I suppose you've been faced with one in much the way that I have."

He remembered the time when Mr. Lindsey had described Adolf Hitler as a bloody housepainter, and later as a man who, "anyway, got things done". He also remembered that during Munich, which had coincided with his own act of appeasement of Uncle Romesh Chand, Colin had written him a letter which expressed relief that Mr. Chamberlain's common sense had averted hostilities. To Hari in Mayapore, Munich had meant nothing. He judged retrospectively that to the Mayapore English, blanketed as they were in the colonial warmth of their racial indestructibility, it had meant nothing either. He did not doubt, though, that the tone of Colin's latest letter was an accurate reflection of a mood now shared by the English as a whole, at home and abroad. He tried to enter it himself, but could not. The inspiration for it was not to be found in the Chillianwallah Bagh, nor was it to be found in the cantonment, in the magistrates' courts, in the sessions and appeal court of the District Judge, or even on the *maidan*, places with which Hari had become increasingly familiar as a result of his job on the *Gazette*. It was not to be found in them because he entered such places as an Indian. He entered by permission, not by right. He did not care for what he saw. He did not care for what he felt – the envy of the English and their institutions that came to fill the vacuum left by the loss of his own English identity. He found it depressingly easy to imagine Colin in the place of the young Englishman who sat as a magistrate – not precisely with the power of life or death (because his judicial powers were restricted) – but with the power to send a man who was old enough to be his father to jail for a year; depressingly easy because in this young man Colin himself could be seen, if only symbolically, in an unpleasant light. On the other hand, he could not imagine himself presiding in the place of the Indian magistrate who appeared one day in the place of the Englishman, and conducted his court with no less acidity or assurance. For the first time Hari found himself asking: What is an Indian doing sitting there, fining that man, jailing this woman, sending this case up to the court of sessions? He felt an unexpected resistance to the idea of an Indian doing an Englishman's work. When he paused to consider this resistance he realised that he had responded as a member of a subject race. The thought alarmed him.

"Such a fuss," he wrote to Colin two months later (when, far away in Europe, the war had already begun) about the resignation of those provincial ministries which had been dominated by the Congress. "Of course you can see both points of view. The Viceroy had to declare war on India's behalf because he's the King-Emperor's representative, and the Germans now rank as the King's enemies. But since for some time now the British policy towards India has been to treat her as an embryo Dominion that only needs time to become self-governing, the Viceroy might at least have gone through the motions of consulting Indian leaders. Some people say that under the 1935 Act he was actually committed to consultation, but even if he wasn't how much more effective it would have been if the declaration could have been made with a simultaneous Indian statement of intention to co-operate freely. And one can understand why with all this talk going on about British War Aims the Indians feel one of them should be independence for India immediately the war is over. Failure to state that as a definite aim, with a definite date, has led a lot of Indians to believe that independence should be insisted on *now*. They say that only a free country fights with a will. And they fear a repetition after the war of all the prevarication that's been going on these last ten years or more. But I think they're a lot to blame for the delay themselves. The Congress says it represents all-India, but it doesn't. All this disagreement among themselves about who represents what just plays into the hands of the kind of English who don't want to give India up – the kind of people my father always assumed would get their way. On the whole I think he was probably right. For instance, now that the Congress ministries have all resigned most of the provinces are back under old-style rule of a Governor and a council, which seems to me the very sort of thing a sensible party would have wanted to avoid because it puts them back years politically. But then I have never been and probably never will be able to make sense of Indian politics. As for the effect of the war on the English here, so far as I can see there hasn't been any. Frankly, it's something that seems to be taking place in almost another world – if you can say that it's taking place anywhere. To judge from the news nothing much is happening, is it? The English here say that Hitler now realises he's bitten off more than he can chew and will end up by being a sensible chap and coming to some arrangement with France and Britain. Some Indians say that their own leaders, Nehru especially, have been warning the West for years about the threat Hitler has always represented."

Apart from a short letter from Colin which was written over the Christmas of 1939, a Christmas which Colin had spent at home, after completing a course of training as an officer cadet, Hari heard nothing for nearly a year. A note from Mr. Lindsey in the spring of 1940 informed him that Colin was "somewhere in France" and that Hari's last letter had been forwarded to him. He said that the best thing for Hari to do in future would be to write to Colin at Didbury so that the letters could be sent on to wherever he happened to be.

Hari could not help remembering the attitude Colin's father had taken in 1938, an attitude he had begun to see during the past two years as proof that the man had stopped trusting him. "What will he do with my letters?" he asked himself. "Read them? Censor them? Not forward them if I say anything he thinks might upset Colin, or if I say something he doesn't personally like?" The shadow of Mr. Lindsey fell across the notepaper whenever he wrote. Here was a further disruption to the even flow of thoughts going out to his old friend. The belief that he and Colin were growing further and further apart as a result not only of circumstances but also of the intervention of the powerful force of the malign spirit that had driven his father to death and himself into exile, now took hold of him, but the letter he eventually received from Colin in the August of 1940 seemed to show that between them nothing had fundamentally changed. The structure of a friendship is seldom submitted to analysis until it comes under pressure; and when Hari attempted an analysis of his friendship with Colin he found it healthily straightforward. It was an attraction of like for like that had long ago outgrown whatever initial morbid or childish curiosity there had been in the colours of the skin and the magic of the genes. Colin's letter turned back the years. Here was the authentic voice of his friend Lindsey. Reading between the lines Hari understood that Colin had not had an easy passage. This pegged them level again. The letter gave him little general information. Young Lindsey had been at Dunkirk, and since then "in hospital for a bit, not because I was badly hurt but because it took rather a long time to get the proper treatment and dressings, and things went bad on me, but are all right now." The letter was written from home on a spell of leave between leaving hospital and returning to his unit.

"It was a bloody shambles if you ask me. It amuses me when I hear Dad say to people his son was at Dunkirk, as if that was something to be proud of. My lasting reaction is one of anger, but undirected anger because no one person or even group of persons could be held responsible more than any other person or any other group. I suppose it was our old friend Nemesis catching up with us at last. I lost one good friend. I went to see his sister the other day. Ridiculous how one gets involved in these trite melodramatic situations. We both hated it. When I got back from hospital Dad gave me a couple of letters from you that he'd saved up. We had a bit of a row about that. I was worried what you'd have been thinking, not getting any answers. At first he said he hadn't wanted to bother me, and that you'd understand anyway that I was otherwise engaged. Then he admitted he'd read them and thought them full of a lot of 'hot-headed' political stuff. Hari, I only tell you this so that if you ever write letters to me care of home again you can bear in mind that they might be read. He's promised not to do that ever again, and sees that it was wrong, but he's got some funny notions in his head nowadays. I don't want to hurt the old boy but in lots of ways he seems like a stranger to me. And that's a cliché situation too, isn't it? So cliché that I almost distrust my reactions to it. But there are so many things he says and does that get on my nerves. He keeps a *Times* wall map, and sticks pins in it like a general. The pin that's stuck in Dunkirk has a little paper union jack on it. I have an idea it represents me. Write and tell me some sensible things."

Sensible things? On the day Hari received this letter he had been in the District Court listening to the appeal against conviction of a man accused and found guilty in the magistrates' court at Tanpur of stealing another man's cow and selling it to a man who had given it away as part of his daughter's dowry. The accused men said that the cow had become his property because its owner refused to stop it wandering on to his land and it had fed constantly free of cost and consumed fodder in excess of its market value. The appeal was based on the grounds that the Tanpur magistrate had not admitted the evidence of two witnesses who would swear to the fact that the convicted man had given the original owner repeated warnings of his intention to sell. Judge Menen dismissed the appeal and Hari then left the court because the next and last case was an appeal against imprisonment under section 188 of the Indian Penal Code, and Hari's editor never published reports of such controversial matters.

"Sensible things?" Hari wrote back to Colin. "I suppose that in wartime especially you can reckon it sensible if not actually fair to imprison a man for speaking his mind. But this is not a purely wartime measure. It is a long-standing one provided for in a section of the criminal procedure code. Section 144 enables the civil authority to decide for itself that such and such a man is a potential local threat to public peace, and thus to *order* him to stay quiet on pain of arrest and imprisonment. If he disobeys the order he gets prosecuted and punished under section 188. I believe he can appeal as far as the provincial High Court if he has a mind to. I was at the District and Sessions Court on the day your letter came. I left the court just before the Judge (an Indian) heard such an appeal, so I know nothing of the actual proceedings. But I saw the prisoner on my way out, waiting with two constables, and recognised him as a fellow called Moti Lal. He recognised me too and said, 'Hello, Coomer,' and was then hustled in through the door prisoners enter the court by. The last time I saw this man he was working as a clerk at my uncle's depot at the railway sidings. I made inquiries when I got back to the office. It seems my uncle sacked him a few months ago, ostensibly for inefficiency. But I guess from what my editor told me that the real reason was that my uncle heard from someone that Moti Lal was mixed up with what you could call the underground side of the Congress Party. I asked my uncle's lawyer, a Brahmin called Srinivasan, what Moti Lal had actually been arrested for. It seems he was always 'inciting' workers and students to strike or to riot and had disobeyed an order prohibiting him from giving a speech at a meeting of senior students at the Technical College. He was also suspected of being the leader of a group of young men who were printing and distributing seditious literature, but no evidence was found. Anyway, he got six months. And his appeal was dismissed. An ex-colleague on the *Gazette* – a fellow called Vidyasagar who now works for a radical newspaper called *The Mayapore Hindu* – told me about it when I met him in court yesterday.

"Vidyasagar is a pleasant chap whom I rather like but have a bad conscience about. The first few weeks I worked on the *Gazette* the editor sent me round with him practically everywhere, and then sacked him. Vidya took it well. He said he guessed what was in the editor's mind when he was detailed to show me the ropes. He said, 'I don't hold it against you, Kumar, because you don't know anything.' He chips me a bit whenever we happen to meet and says that given time I might learn to be a good Indian.

"But I'm not sure I know what a good Indian *is*. Is he the fellow who joins the army (because it is a family tradition to join the army), or the fellow who is rich enough and ambitious enough to contribute money to Government War Funds, or is he the rebellious fellow who gets arrested like Moti Lal?

Or is the good Indian the Mahatma, whom everyone here calls Gandhiji, and who last month, after Hitler had shown Europe what his army was made of, praised the French for surrendering and wrote to the British cabinet asking them to adopt 'a nobler and braver way of fighting', and let the Axis powers walk into Britain. The nobler and braver way means following his prescribed method of non-violent non-co-operation. That sounds like a 'good Indian'. But then there is Nehru, who obviously thinks this attitude is crazy. He seems to want to fight Hitler. He says England's difficulties aren't India's opportunity. But then he adds that India can't, because of that, be stopped from continuing her own struggle for freedom. Perhaps then, the good Indian is that ex-Congress fellow Subhas Chandra Bose who makes freedom the first priority and is now in Berlin, toadying to Hitler, and broadcasting to us telling us to break our chains. Or is he Mr. Jinnah who has at last simplified the communal problem by demanding a separate state for Muslims if the Hindu-dominated Congress succeeds in getting rid of the British? Or is he one of the Indian princes who has a treaty with the British Crown that respects his sovereign rights and who doesn't intend to lose them simply because a lot of radical Indian politicians obtain control of British India? This is actually a bigger problem than I ever guessed, because the princes rule almost one-third of the whole of India's territory. And then again, should we forget all these sophisticated aspects of the problem of who is or is not a good Indian and see him as the simple peasant who is only interested in ridding himself of the burden of the local money lender and becoming entitled to the whole of whatever it is he grows? And where do the English stand in all this?

"The answer is that I don't really know because out here I don't rank as one. I never meet them, except superficially in my capacity as a member of the press at the kind of public social functions that would make *you* in beleaguered rationed England scream with rage or laughter. And then, if I speak to them, they stare at me in amazement because I talk like them. If one of them (one of the men – never one of the women) asks me how I learned to speak English so well, and I tell him, he looks astonished, almost hurt, as if I was pulling a fast one and expecting him to believe it.

"One of the things I gather they can't stand at the moment is the way the Americans (who aren't even in the war yet – if ever) are trying to butt in and force them to make concessions to the Indians whom of course the British look upon as their own private property. The British are cock-a-hoop that Churchill has taken over because he's the one Englishman who has always spoken out against any measure of liberal reform in the administration of the Indian Empire. His recent attempt following the defeat of the British Expeditionary Force in France to lull Indian ambitions with more vague promises of having a greater say in the running of their own country (which seems not to amount to much more than adding a few safe or acceptable Indians to the Viceroy's council) only makes the radical Indians laugh. They remember (so my editor tells me) all the promises that were made in the Great War – a war which Congress went all out to help to prosecute believing that the Crown was worth standing by because afterwards the Crown would reward them by recognising their claims to a measure of self-government. These were promises that were never fulfilled. Instead even sterner measures were taken to put down agitation and the whole sorry business of Great War promises ended in 1919 with the spectacle of the massacre in the Jallianwallah Bagh at Amritsar, when that chap General Dyer fired on a crowd of unarmed civilians who had no way of escaping and died in hundreds. The appearance of Churchill as head of the British war cabinet (greeted by the English here with such joy) has depressed the Indians. I expect they are being emotional about it. I'd no idea Churchill's name stank to this extent. They call him the arch-imperialist. Curious how what seems right for England should be the very thing that seems wrong for the part of the Empire that Disraeli once called the brightest jewel in her crown. Liberal Indians, of course, say that Churchill has always been a realist – even an opportunist – and will be astute enough to change coat once again and make liberal concessions. As proof of this they point to the fact that members of the socialist opposition have brought into the cabinet to give the British Government a look of national solidarity.

"But I wonder about the outcome. I think there's no doubt that in the last twenty years – whether intentionally or not – the English *have* succeeded in dividing and ruling, and the kind of conversation I hear at these social functions I attend – Guides recruitment, Jumble Sales, mixed cricket matches (usually rained off and ending with a bun-fight in a series of tents invisibly marked Europeans Only and Other Races) – makes me realise the extent to which the English now seem to depend upon the divisions in Indian political opinion perpetuating their own rule at least until after the war, if not for some time beyond it. They are saying openly that it is 'no good leaving the bloody country because there's no Indian party representative enough to hand it over to.' They prefer Muslims to Hindus (because of the closer affinity that exists between God and Allah than exists between God and the Brahma), are constitutionally predisposed to Indian princes, emotionally affected by the thought of untouchables, and mad keen about the peasants who look upon any Raj as God. What they dislike is a black reflection of their own white radicalism which centuries ago led to the Magna Carta. They hate to remember that within Europe they were ever in arms against the feudal *status quo*, because being in arms against it out here is so very much *bad form*. They look upon India as a place that they came to and took over when it was disorganised, and therefore think that they can't be blamed for the fact that it is disorganised now.

"But isn't two hundred years long enough to unify? They accept credit for all the improvements they've made. But can you claim credit for one without accepting blame for the other? Who, for instance, five years ago, had ever heard of the concept of Pakistan – the separate Muslim state? I can't believe that Pakistan will ever become a reality, but if it does it will be because the English prevaricated long enough to allow a favoured religious minority to seize a political opportunity.

"How this must puzzle you – that such an apparently domestic problem should take precedence in our minds over what has just happened in Europe. The English – since they are at war – call the recognition of that precedence sedition. The Americans look upon the resulting conflict as a storm in an English teacup which the English would be wise to pacify if they're to go on drinking tea at four o'clock every afternoon (which they only did after they opened up the East commercially). But of course the Americans see the closest threat to their security as coming from the Pacific side of their continent. Naturally they want a strong and unified India, so that if their potential enemies (the Japanese) ever get tough, those enemies will have to guard their back door as well as their front door.

"Working on this paper has forced me to look at the world and try and make sense out of it. But after I've looked at it I still ask myself where I stand in relation to it and that is what puzzles me to know. Can you understand that, Colin? At the moment there seems to be no one country that I owe an undivided duty to. Perhaps this is really the pattern of the future. I don't know whether that encourages me or alarms me. If there's no country, what else is left but the anthropological distinction of colour? That would be a terrible conflict because the scores that there are to settle at this level are desperate. I'm not sure, though, that the conflict isn't one that the human race deserves to undergo."

*

So there were no "sensible things" that Hari was able to tell Colin, but perhaps it was enough for each of them that over such a distance, of time as well as space, they still found it possible to make contact. There was a saying among young Indians that friendships made with white men seldom stood the strain of separation and never the acuter strain of reunion on the Indian's native soil.

"What would you do," he asked Sister Ludmila, "if you had a letter from an old friend that showed you were suddenly speaking different languages?" Perhaps it is odd that Kumar should have remembered this earlier "Journey's End" letter of Lindsey's, remembered it well enough to have it on his mind when he asked this question, as if the later one which Colin wrote after his baptism of fire asking him to tell him some sensible things was of less importance than the letter written in the nostalgic neo-patriotic mood Hari had been puzzled by. But then the unexpected side of a man's personality is more memorable than the proof he may appear to give from time to time that he is unchanged, unchangeable. The image of Lindsey as someone who spoke a new language had made its mark on Kumar, so that later he was able to say to Sister Ludmila:

"I should have challenged him then. I should have told him what it had really been like for me in Mayapore. I should have said, 'We've both changed, perhaps we no longer have anything in common. It's probably as ridiculous to believe that if I came back to Didbury now we should be at ease with each other as to believe that if you came out to Mayapore you would want even to be *seen* associating with me.' Yes, I should have said that. I didn't say it because I didn't want to think it. We continued to exchange letters whose sole purpose was to reassure ourselves that there had been a time when we'd been immune to all pressures except those of innocence.

"When Colin came to India in 1941 and wrote to me from Meerut, I felt a sort of wild exhilaration. But it only lasted a very short while. I was resigned to what I knew must happen. If he had come straight to Mayapore there might have been a chance for us. But Meerut was a long way off. It seemed unlikely that he would ever be posted to a station close enough to Mayapore to make a meeting possible. And every week that went by could only add to the width of the gulf he'd realise there was between a man of his colour and a man of mine who had no official position, who was simply an Indian who worked for his living and lived in a native town. He would feel it widen to the point where he realised there was no bridging it at all, because the wish to bridge it had also gone. I remembered my own revulsion, my horror of the dirt and squalor and stink, and knew that Colin would feel a similar revulsion. But in his case there would be somewhere to escape to. There would be places to go and things to do that would provide a refuge. He would learn to need the refuge and then to accept it as one he had a duty to maintain, to protect against attack, to see in the end as the real India – the club, the mess, the bungalow, the English flowers in the garden, the clean, uniformed servants, the facilities for recreation, priority of service in shops and post-offices and banks, and trains; all the things that stem from the need to protect your sanity and end up bolstering your ego and feeding your prejudices.

"And then even if Colin had been strong-willed enough to resist these physical and spiritual temptations and to come to Mayapore to seek me out, where could we have met and talked for longer than an hour or two? Since the war began the black town has been out of bounds even to officers unless they are on official duty of some kind. I could not go to the Gymkhana. And what would *he* have made of the other club when it's hateful even to me? If we had met at Smith's Hotel there could have been an embarrassing scene. The Anglo-Indian proprietor doesn't like it if undistinguished Indians turn up there. At the Chinese Restaurant officers are supposed to use only the upstairs dining-room, and no Indian is allowed above the ground floor unless he holds the King's commission. We could have gone to the pictures but he would have disliked sitting in the seats I would be allowed to sit in. There is the English Coffee House, but it is not called the English Coffee House for nothing. If he were stationed in Mayapore perhaps we could meet for an hour or two in his quarters. Or perhaps he could get permission to cross the bridge and visit me in the Chillianwallah Bagh. I considered all these possibilities because they had to be thought out. And of course I saw that the one constant factor was not so much the place of meeting but the determination to meet. And what friendship can survive in circumstances like that?

"From Meerut he moved to Ambala, and then to somewhere near Lahore. In his first letter he said that on the map Meerut didn't look too far away from Mayapore. In his second he said he wondered if he would ever be close enough to make a meeting possible. In his third he did not mention the possibility of a meeting at all. And then I guessed that it had happened, in just three months. He had seen what he would only be able to call *my* India. And had been horrified. Even afraid. How could he know that I had been also horrified, also afraid? How could he know that for three years I had hoped, longed to be rescued, and had confused the idea of rescue with the idea of my Englishness and with the idea of my friendship with an Englishman? How could he know any of this? In one respect I was more English than he. As an Englishman he could admit his horror if not his fear. As an Anglicised Indian, the last thing I ever dared to do in my letters to *him* was admit either, for fear of being labelled 'hysterical'. And so I saw the awful thing that had happened – that looking at what he would have to call *my* India, the suspicion that I had returned to my natural element had been confirmed.

"Well, I say I saw it, then; but did I? Didn't I still make excuses for Colin and excuses for myself? When there was no letter from Lahore, didn't I say, 'It's all right, he's not a civilian who has nothing to do but wake up, eat, go to work and come back home to see what the postman has brought.' And then when the war came close, when the Japanese bombed Pearl Harbor, invaded Siam and Malaya and Burma and even fluttered the English dovecots in Mayapore, didn't I say to myself, 'Well, poor old Colin is in the thick of it again?' And even suffer pangs of conscience that I hadn't been man enough to stand by something that was sure at least, my English upbringing, and join the army, fight for the people I had once felt kinship to, even if out here they obviously didn't feel kin to me? And didn't I see what a damned useless mess I'd made of my life since 1938, sulking as badly as those poor clerks I despised, making no new friends, repaying Aunt Shalini's kindness and affection with nothing that she would understand as love or even thanks?

"And then I saw them. English soldiers in the cantonment, with that familiar regimental name on their shoulder tabs. In the January of 1942. Familiar from the letters from Colin, first from Meerut, and then Ambala, and then from near Lahore. Captain C. Lindsey, then the name and number of the unit, followed by the address, and ending with the words India Command."

"It was," Sister Ludmila said, "the second occasion I saw him drunk that he talked so, about Colin. I told you there had been such an occasion. After he had been to the temple, with her, with the girl. This is when he told me these things. He had never told her. I said to her, that time she came to the Sanctuary to say goodbye, 'Do you know of the man Lindsey?' and she thought for a while and then said, 'No, tell me.'

"But I said, 'It's not important.' It wasn't important by then. To you perhaps it is important. So long after. 'I saw him,' young Kumar told me, 'or at least I thought I saw him, coming out of the Imperial Bank, getting into an army truck that had the same insignia on its tailboard that those British soldiers wore on their sleeves.' But he was not sure. And even then made excuses for him. Already at this time, you see, with the war suddenly brought to our doorstep by the Japanese, India had changed. There was this air of military rush and secrecy – and on the day he thought he saw Colin he went home expecting a letter saying, 'Look, I'm stationed near Mayapore and sometimes come into the cantonment. Where can we meet?' But there was never such a letter. So as the days went by he thought, 'No, the man I saw was not Colin. Colin could not come near Mayapore and send me no word at all. India could not have done that to him. Not that. How could India do that to anybody, let alone to Colin?'

"Can you imagine this? The feeling every day of Kumar's that if the post did not bring a letter then there would be a chance encounter somewhere in that area north of the river? Every day he cycled from the Chillianwallah Bagh to the office of the *Mayapore Gazette,* and on some days left the office and cycled to an event that he was required to report on. And this was another thing, another thing he told me. How even as a reporter he was invisible to white people. He would go to this event, that event. The gymkhana, the flower show, the Guides display, the Higher School Sports, the Technical College graduation, the Technical College cricket, the hospital fête. He knew nearly every important English civilian by sight and name and every distinguished Indian by sight and name, but they did not know him, for there was at these functions, you understand, what you call press officer or steward, and he, only, would be available to young Kumar, and sometimes not even him, because at an important function Mr. Laxminarayan would also be in attendance. On this occasion, I mean the second occasion of his drunkenness he said, '– oh, there was a time when I thought I would make a name for myself. People would read the *Gazette* and say, What good English! How splendid! Who is this young Kumar? But they do not even know my name. At most I am "the *Gazette* boy". My name is never printed. No one really knows that I exist. I am a vaguely familiar face. But – I had it coming. He uses me. Laxminarayan. Sometimes he keeps me chained to the desk turning *babu* English into decent English. Sometimes he sends me out. But he keeps me as an anonymous cog in his anonymous machine. Once I heard an Englishman say to him, "I say, Laxminarayan, what's happening to the *Gazette*? Apart from Topics by 'Stroller' it isn't funny any more." My editor only laughed. He did not explain why it isn't funny. He punishes me, you see, for Vidyasagar, for everything, for his own shortcomings.' "

*

"It was at such a function," Sister Ludmila said, "that he saw this Lindsey for the second time. Saw and knew, beyond a doubt, standing not far away, close enough not to mistake the features, the expression, the mannerisms, the way of holding the body – whatever it was that had impressed itself indelibly on Kumar's mind as authentic Lindsey. What occasion? I forget. But remember it was February, the end of February. And that he mentioned the *maidan*. I have even still, this recollection, not my own but Kumar's. From Kumar I have inherited it. And feel almost as if I had been there. Am there. Towards evening. In Kumar's body. A dark face in the crowd. Has it been cricket? This I would not know. Cricket I do not understand. But I understand how towards evening on the *maidan* the races came uncertainly together in a brief intermingling pattern which from above, to God you understand, looked less informal than it looked from the ground because from above you would be able to see the white current and the dark current; as from a cliff, the sea, separating itself stream from stream and drift from drift, but amounting in God's Eyes to no more than total water.

"And he sees Lindsey. Ah well, as boys, what secrets of mind and body did they share? He told me of autumn in England. This too I see and feel. And am aware of young Kumar and young Lindsey as boys, running home across chill fields to come and toast their hands at a warm grate, just as I remember the blessing of gloves in a cold winter, and the way the breath could transform a window and fill the heart with a different kind of warmth. Ah, such safety. Such microcosmic power. To translate, to reduce, to cause to vanish with the breath alone the sugary fruits in their nest of lace-edged paper. To know that they are there, and yet not there. This is a magic of the soul. But it was a magic Kumar could not conjure, on the *maidan*, that hot evening, to make Lindsey disappear. Lindsey looked at him, and then away, without recognition, not understanding that in those *babu* clothes, under the bazaar topee, there was one black face he ought to have seen as being different from the rest."

*

I am invisible, Kumar said, not only to white people because they are white and I am black but invisible to my white friend because he can no longer distinguish me in a crowd. He thinks – yes, this is what Lindsey thinks: "They all look alike." He makes me disappear. I am nothing. It is not his fault. He is right. I am nothing, nothing, nothing. I am the son of my father whose own father left home with a begging-bowl in his hand and a cloth round his loins, having blessed his children and committed their mother to their care. For a while she followed him and then sat by the roadside and returned home to live out her days in her private fantasy.

So I go from the *maidan*, in my bazaar trousers, my bazaar shirt, my Anglo-Indian topee, knowing that I am unrecognisable because I am nothing and would not be welcome if I were recognised. And meet, also coming away, Vidyasagar. He also is nothing. I do not remember the rest. There was clarity up to a point. Drinking cheap liquor in an airless room in a house in a back street on our own side of the river. And Vidyasagar laughing and telling the others that soon I would become a good Indian because the liquor was bootleg and we drank it at Government's expense. The others were young men like Vidya, dressed as Vidya was dressed, in shirts and trousers, like mine. But I remember helping them to destroy my topee because it was the badge of all government toadies. I remember too that they kept refilling my glass. They wanted me to be drunk. Partly it was malice, partly fun. In that poky little room there was desperation as well as fervour.

*

Sister Ludmila said: "He found out later that they took him back to the Chillianwallah Bagh, right to the gates of his house, so that he would not be robbed, or picked up by the police, and then left him, thinking he went inside, but he wandered out on to the road again, going back towards the river and into the waste ground. And must have stumbled and fallen down into the ditch and there become unconscious and had his wallet stolen by someone who had seen him and followed him.

" 'Who is it?' I asked Mr. de Souza. 'I don't know,' he said, and turned him over to see if there were wounds on his back, and then turned him again, shining the torch on his face. And this is what I remember, of Bibighar beginning. The eyes shut, the black hair curling over the forehead. Ah! Such darkness! Such determination to reject.

"We got him on to the stretcher then, and carried him here to the Sanctuary. 'This one is drunk, sister,' Mr. de Souza said. 'We have carried home only a drunken man.' 'To be so drunk and so young,' I said, 'he must also be unhappy. Let him lie.' And so he lay. And before I went to sleep I prayed for him."

PART SIX

Civil and Military

I

Military

Edited Extracts from the unpublished memoirs of Brigadier A. V. Reid, DSO, MC: "A Simple Life."

LATE in the March of 1942 when we were still in Rawalpindi and hard on the heels of the news that our only son Alan was missing in Burma, I received orders to go to Mayapore and assume command of the infantry brigade then still in process of formation in that area. The news of this appointment was given to me on the phone by General "Tubby" Carter. I was to leave at once and Tubby knew I should want a little time to break the news to Meg who was still unfit and would be unable to accompany me. I did not welcome the idea of leaving her on her own at a moment when we were heavy of heart hoping for further news of Alan and yet dreading what that news might be. After talking to Tubby I went straight round to the nursing home and told Meg of the task that had been entrusted to me.

She knew that in ordinary circumstances I would welcome the opportunity of getting back to a real job of soldiering. It had begun to look as if I would spend the rest of the war with my feet under a desk, and with our son also in uniform I suppose we had almost come to terms with this prospect and had accepted the fact that age and experience must eventually make way for youthful eagerness. But now, with Alan's fate uncertain, it seemed as if some understanding diety had stepped in to redress the balance and had called on me to play a part which – if the news of Alan was the worst there could be when it came – would at least give me the satisfaction of knowing I might strike an active blow at the enemy in return.

Meg reacted to the news as she had always done at times

of crisis and difficulty – with no sign of any thought for herself. Seeing how ill and pale she looked I wished that it had been in my power to call Alan into the room, fit and well, his usual cheery self, and so bring the roses back to her cheeks. I am thankful that she was spared the news that he died working on the infamous Burma–Siam railway, news which for me darkened the days of our Victory, but I am grateful that she lived long enough to share with me the hope that was revived when we first heard that he was a prisoner-of-war and not dead, as we had feared. When I said goodbye to her on the eve of my departure for Mayapore there was also the burden of realising that these were dark days for our country. There was a tough job ahead.

I arrived in Mayapore on April 3rd (1942) and immediately set about the first phase of my task, that of welding the (—th) Indian Infantry Brigade into a well-trained fighting machine which I could lead confidently into the field to play its part in a theatre of war where the Jap had temporarily proved himself master. The task was not going to be an easy one. The majority of the troops were green, and the surrounding countryside, suitable enough for run-of-the-mill training, very dissimilar from the ground we should eventually be required to contest.

I had been in Mayapore many years before. I remembered it as a delightful station with some lakes out at a place called Banyaganj where there was excellent duck-shooting to be had. The old artillery mess was a fine example of 19th Century Anglo-Indian architecture, with a lovely view on to the *maidan*. It tended to get uncomfortably warm from March onwards but one could usually get away, down to Mussoorie or up to Darjeeling. It was not too far by train from Calcutta either, so one had plenty of opportunity to relax if one's duties allowed.

I did not have any illusions about relaxation now. Obviously there was a difference between a station as it once appeared to a young subaltern who had recently met the girl he was seriously thinking of asking to marry him, and the station, the same though it was, to which he returned nearly thirty years later as a senior officer at a moment when his country's fortunes were at a low ebb, and the country to which he had dedicated his life which represented the very cornerstone of the Empire had achieved considerable measures of self-government and stood virtually on the threshold of independence, an independence that had been postponed, for the moment, in the interests of the free world as a whole.

I went to Mayapore with every confidence in the troops, and with a fervent prayer that I should not personally be found wanting. I had been glad to hear from Tubby that there was a station commander on tap who would relieve the brigade staff of the general military administration of the district, and also to hear that the collector – called in this "non-regulation" province a deputy commissioner – was a youngish fellow who was well thought of by Europeans and Indians alike. As senior military officer in the district, however, I knew I should be responsible in the last resort for the civil peace, and for the well-being of both soldiers and civilians, and the last thing I wanted was to become involved in the kind of situation that would distract me from my main job and give rise to the employment of troops on tasks that might have been avoided with a little forethought.

In view of the increasing unrest in India at this time, one of the first things I did after reaching Mayapore was to see the Deputy Commissioner, whose name was White, in order to listen to what he had to say about the state of his district and to tell him frankly that a lot of time and energy might be saved later if we agreed to show a firm hand at the first sign of trouble. I had already decided to bring the Brigade's British battalion – the (—th) Berkshires – into Mayapore and to move the 4/5 Pankot Rifles out of Mayapore, where I had found them, to the vicinity of Banyaganj where the Berkshires had been situated. My reasons were twofold. The British troops were newly out from home and I judged from my first inspection of them that they were far from happy in the rather primitive quarters which were all Banyaganj had to offer. There was an airfield in process of construction nearby (which I noted had denuded the lakes of duck), and scarcely a mile separated the far from salubrious coolie encampment from the battalion. More huts were being built but a lot of the men were under canvas and in April that was no joke. Conscious of the problem involved in appearing to make a distinction I nevertheless felt that Johnny Jawan would be less uncomfortable in Banyaganj than was Tommy Atkins. Also, in moving the Berkshires into the Mayapore barracks there was in my mind the belief that their presence in the cantonment might act as an extra deterrent to civil unrest, which at all costs I wished to avoid. I had, in any case, determined to use British soldiers in the first instance in the event of military aid being requested by the civil power.

In bringing the Berkshires into Mayapore I was also not unaware of the good effect this would have on our own people there – men and women doing difficult jobs at a time of special crisis. It was with this in mind too that I ordered an Army or War Week – complete with a military band – for the end of April, which was held on the *maidan* and was counted a great success. I feel that without immodesty (because the idea was mine but the fulfilment of it lies to the credit of those who organised or took part in it) I can claim that the excitement and "lift" which the War Week gave to Mayapore distracted attention from the fact that the Cabinet Mission which Sir Winston – then Mr. Churchill – had sent to Delhi, to seek an end to the deadlock between the British Government and those Indian politicians who claimed to represent the Indian people and were demanding even further measures of self-government, had failed to come to any kind of reasonable understanding. This was the mission known as the Cripps Mission, after its leader, Sir Stafford Cripps, the socialist minister who eventually became Chancellor of the Exchequer when, after the war, our island race paid its peculiar tribute to the architect of our victory by ousting him from office. It was after the failure of the Cripps Mission in April 1942 that Mr. Gandhi launched his famous Quit India campaign, which of course looked to us like an invitation to the Emperor of Japan to walk in and take over the reins of government!

Unfortunately I found White – the Deputy Commissioner – not wholly alive to the situation I believed might face us if Indian leaders were allowed to continue to speak out against the war effort and rouse the masses to adopt a policy of what Mr. Gandhi called non-violent non-co-operation, a policy that could bring the country to a standstill. White seemed to be convinced that when the Indian National Congress talked about non-violent non-co-operation they really meant non-violent. He obviously had more faith than I in the ability of a demonstrating crowd to resist the hysteria that can turn it in a moment into a howling mob intent on taking revenge for some imaginary act of brutality perpetrated by the police or the military. He did not, in fact, appear to anticipate demonstrations of any magnitude, unless they were organised purely for the purpose of offering *satyagraha*, in defiance of the Defence of India Rules, so that the authorities would be bound to arrest the demonstrators and have their prisons filled to overflowing. My first meeting with White took place before Mr. Gandhi had launched his Quit India campaign, but at a time when it was clear that the Cabinet Mission headed by Cripps was failing to reach agreement about the way in which Indian leaders could be identified more closely with the affairs of the nation. White still seemed to hope that at the last moment a working arrangement would be made. I had no such expectations. Right from the beginning of the war with Germany relations between ourselves and the Indians had steadily deteriorated. At the outset of that war Congress members of the central assembly had walked out to protest the sending abroad of Indian troops to the Middle East and Singapore and the Congress ministries in the provinces had resigned because the Viceroy had declared war without consulting them! Whatever our faults in the past, I as a simple soldier with only rudimentary political views could not help feeling that the sincere efforts we made in the years before the war to hand over more power to the Indians themselves had revealed nothing so clearly as the fact that they had not achieved the political maturity that would have made the task of granting them self-government easy. The act of 1935 which envisaged a federal government at the centre, representative of all walks of Indian life, and elected states governments in the provinces, seemed to a man like myself (who had everything to lose and nothing to gain by Indian independence) a statesman-like, indeed noble concept, one that Britain could have been proud of as a fitting end to a glorious chapter in her imperial history. Unfortunately it led only to a scramble for power and the central federal government scheme came to nothing. One could not help feeling that the heartrending cries for freedom sounded hollow in retrospect as one watched the scramble and listened to the squabbles that broke out between Hindus, Muslims, Sikhs, Princes and others. The Congress, for instance, openly admitted that they took provincial office in 1937 to prove that the federal scheme was unworkable at the centre and that they alone represented India. Unfortunately, this belief of theirs, that they were the democratic majority, seemed to be borne out on paper at least by their sweeping victory in the elections that were held prior to their taking provincial office. Be that as it may, one would have thought that two years of provincial power, with little or no interference from the Governors, who retained a watching brief on behalf of the central government and the Crown, would have moulded statesmen, but the resignations after the declaration of war – which left the Governors with no alternative but to assume personal control – struck most of my fellow countrymen whose thoughts now lay principally with the safety of our homeland and the fight against tyranny, as proof that nothing had been learned at all of political responsibility, and that we could therefore no longer count on "leading" Indians to take a broad view of the real things that were at stake in the free world.

I think it is true to say that we came to this realisation with reluctance, and that it was a measure of our continuing hope for Indian freedom and of our readiness to extend our patience right up to its breaking point that even in our darkest hour – the defeat of our arms in South-East Asia – we opened the bowling once again on Mr. Churchill's initiative and tried hard to find a way of giving the Indians a fair crack of the whip, which was more than Hitler would have done and more than we knew could be expected of the Jap. It was clear to us, however, that chaps like Gandhi had got on to our scent and were in full cry, heedless of the ravenous yellow pack that was on to *them*, indeed on to all of us. On April 6th a few bombs fell on Madras. Even that did not seem to bring the Indians to their senses, in fact they blamed us more than they blamed the enemy! Inspired by Mr. Gandhi they had got hold of the idea that there was no quarrel between India and Japan and that if the British absconded the Japanese wouldn't attack her. A little later, it is true, Mr. Gandhi very kindly suggested that the British army could stay in India and use it as a base from which to fight the Japanese, and that in ports like Bombay and Calcutta he could promise there wouldn't be any riots to disrupt the flow of arms and war material! – providing of course that we had otherwise left the country to be ruled by himself and his colleagues! What he thought the strategic difference was between ceasing to govern but continuing to use India as a base was not easy to tell if you looked at the situation from the point of view of the Japanese High Command! It was clear to most of us that at last his peculiar theories were being shown up for what they were: the impractical dreams of a man who believed that everyone was – or should be – as simple and innocent as himself. There were times, of course, when we found it difficult to put even this well-meaning construction on his speeches and writings.

When I looked out on to the *maidan* from the window of my room in the old artillery mess in Mayapore, or drove round the cantonment, I could not help but feel proud of the years of British rule. Even in these turbulent times the charm of the cantonment helped one to bear in mind the calm, wise and enduring things. One had only to cross the river into the native town to see that in our cantonments and civil lines we had set an example for others to follow and laid down a design for civilised life that the Indians would one day inherit. It seemed odd to think that in the battle that lay ahead to stop all this from falling into the hands of the Japanese the Indians were not on our side.

I remembered vividly the hours spent as a young man, exercising Rajah on the Mayapore *maidan*, and practising polo shots with Nigel Orme, who was ADC to General Grahame and won a posthumous VC at Passchendaele. Rajah, as readers may recall from an earlier chapter, was the first polo pony I owned, and Nigel Orme, although senior to me in rank and service, one of the best and truest friends I ever had. It looked to me as if fate had called me back to the place where I first got the "feel" of India and first realised that whatever success or failure was in store for me in the profession I had chosen, there would always be a sense of oneness with the country and a feeling of identification with our aspirations for it. I remembered Meg as she had been in my thoughts then, all those years ago, so calm, so collected, kind and generous, ever ready with a smile – to me the most beautiful girl in the world. And I thought of our son, Alan, and of our daughter Caroline – safe now from Nazi or Japanese frightfulness, thank heaven, with her Aunt Cissie in Toronto. These three were truly my hostages to fortune and our fine boy seemed already to have been taken from us in part payment. More than anything else in the world I wished for victory to our arms, health and happiness for Meg, and to be reunited with her and darling Caroline and young Alan. I do not think that any of us older serving soldiers can be blamed if, at the time, we felt bitter that the country which had benefited in so many ways from British rule appeared determined to hinder our efforts to save it from invasion at a time when we could least spare the strength. Pondering these matters on the level at which they affected me personally I couldn't help wishing that I could be left to concentrate on my main task and leave the politicians to "muddle through" in their own mysterious ways. But I knew that this could not be. The brigade was my responsibility, but so was the safety of our women and children and the peace of the district as a whole. Those of us who were in contact with "places higher up" knew that it was thought we must be prepared to face the gravest danger from within the camp as well as from outside it; from the enemy in the tent as well as from the enemy at the gate; and that it was not beyond the bounds of possibility that the Congress planned the kind of open rebellion that could snowball into a campign of terror and bloodshed and civil war such as we had not seen in India since the days of the Mutiny. As events proved later our anxieties on this score were only too well-founded. Before the summer was out the country was in the grip of rebellion and in Mayapore the commotions got off to the worst kind of start. It was in this pleasant old district that two dastardly attacks on Englishwomen were made, within a few hours of each other; the first upon an elderly mission teacher, Miss Crane, and the second on a young woman, Daphne Manners, who was criminally assaulted in a place called the Bibighar Gardens.

Although on first acquaintance Mr. Deputy Commissioner White and I did not, as they say nowadays, hit it off, I came presently to admire his tenacity. For me his physical courage was never in doubt, and I judged, correctly as it turned out, that he would never allow any personal reservations he might have about official government policy to sway him in his dutiful application of it in his own district. As a case in point, when I asked him rather bluntly what he would do if he had orders to arrest leaders of the local sub-committee of the Congress party (I knew that District Officers had been warned to keep special note of those of them whose prompt imprisonment might halt the tide of rebellion), he replied, quite simply, "Well, arrest them of course," but then added, "even though I know that that is the very worst thing we can do."

I asked him why he felt this. He said, "Because the kind of men I would have to arrest are those who honestly believe in non-violence and have the power to move the crowd to self-sacrifice rather than to attack. Put such fellows in clink and you leave the crowd to a different kind of leader altogether."

I could not agree, but recognised the sincerity of White's convictions. Of course to me, mass *satyagraha* was almost as harmful as open revolt. Naturally I asked him what he knew of or proposed to do about the kind of leader who might take the place of the Congressmen he had such faith in. He said, "Oh well, that's like looking for needles in haystacks. A few are known. You can arrest those. But the others go free, and among them probably the most efficient because they've been efficient enough not to become known. You could spend your life working up a secret file and still miss the key chaps because Congress doesn't know them and you don't know them. They're nothing to do with Congress at all. They're young or middle-aged fellows with bees in their bonnets who think Congress the lickspittle of the Raj. Well, who has a life to spend detecting that kind of needle in this kind of haystack? Isn't it better to leave the fellows who have nothing to gain by violence free to control the crowd and direct it in true *satyagraha*?"

I told him that what he said probably made sense, so long as you could trust originally in the concept of non-violence, which I personally thought a lot of eye-wash. Pressed further, White admitted that he left what he called "the needles in the haystack" to his District Superintendent of Police, a man called Merrick, whom I had met on a previous occasion and instinctively liked.

Although White's attitude left me in some uncertainty about the degree of determination to be expected from the civil power in the event of trouble in this district, I was confident that the police could be counted on to act swiftly and efficiently if need be.

White's thinking was wholly "modern", typical of the new-style administration of the Thirties that had to take into account every half-baked notion that was relevant to the workable solution of a problem. The judge was an Indian called Menen, an old-school Indian I was glad to notice, but somewhat self-contained in true judicial style. Of the triumvirate only young Merrick, the District Superintendent of Police, seemed to me to have seized happily upon the greater freedom of action that the war and the Congress provincial resignations had given to district rule.

I had a special meeting with Merrick and told him that I relied upon him to use his discretion, particularly in regard to what the Deputy Commissioner had called "the needles in the haystack". I put it to him bluntly that I had a brigade to command and train for use against the enemy at the gate and not, if I could help it, for use against the enemy in the camp. I told him I would appreciate it if he stuck his neck out occasionally. I had not mistaken my man. He was young enough still to respond to simple issues with the right mixture of probity and keenness. I could not help but admire him, too, for his outspokenness. He was a man who came from what he called "a very ordinary middle-class background". The Indian Police had been the one job he felt he could do. I knew what he meant, and liked him for his total lack of pretence. Police duties are always disagreeable, but they have to be carried out. Now that we were at war with the Axis Powers he regretted the circumstances that had led him to undertake service in a field that precluded him from wearing a different uniform. He asked me, in fact, what chance there was of strings being pulled to release him so that he could join up "even as a private". Thinking of Alan – whom physically he somewhat resembled – I appreciated his patriotic scale of values, but was unable to give him any hope of a transfer. In any case, I realised that in the present situation he was more valuable to his country as head of the local police than he would be as an untrained junior officer, let alone as a private soldier. He promised to comply with my request to keep me informed, *sub rosa*, of the temper of the district as he gauged it to be.

Having seen and talked to White and to Merrick I felt that I had done as much as could be done for the moment to buy time in which to concentrate on my job without too often casting a glance in the direction of a local threat to our security. In any case the arrival of my third battalion, the —th Ranpurs, gave me plenty to do. Originally I had been promised a battalion of Sikhs, but one from my old regiment was, needless to say, an even greater boost to my morale! Bringing one company of the Ranpurs into the Mayapore barracks (and so relieving the Berkshires of some of their station guard duties) I sent their remaining companies and the battalion headquarters into the area of Marpuri, north-west of Mayapore, an area I had already selected as the best of two likely sites chosen by my brigade staff. Now that my command was complete I could really get down to work!

*

The Berkshires were settling down well. The move from

Banyaganj into the cantonment had certainly done the trick. The old barracks near the artillery mess were spacious and cool, and the men enjoyed the unaccustomed luxury of being able to avail themselves within reason of the ministrations of the native servants attached to the barracks, many of whom were the sons of men who had looked after an earlier generation of Tommies. They were now also closer on hand to the home entertainments so readily laid on by our ladies. It was, incidentally, many years since there had actually been a gunner regiment stationed in Mayapore, but the artillery mess had been famous in its day and naturally the name had stuck. In recent years Mayapore had been the home of an NCOs' school and the cool weather station of the Pankots. Since the war began it had turned itself virtually into a brigade staging point. Unfortunately, from the point of view of my brigade staff, the colonel-commandant of the NCOs' school who had also acted as station commander was on sick leave upon my arrival – a leave that turned out to be permanent because the school was transferred to the Punjab – so I inherited on paper at least the station commander's role. The Station Staff Officer (whom I managed to retain) had to do most of the work that would normally have rested on the station commander's shoulders, but he was an old ranker and a hard and dedicated worker.

I had elected to live in the artillery mess itself rather than move into the accommodation that was available to me, not only because my poor Meg was unable to join me and establish a household, which she had done so often before, in so many different parts of India, but because I felt I wanted to be on constant call and in a position to keep my staff on its toes. The rooms I occupied in the mess in the old guest suite which overlooked the *maidan*, were spacious but simple. There in the little sitting-room that I had turned into a private office, I could find a retreat from the press of routine to think out the best solutions to the many problems that confronted me. But it was in this room, towards the end of June, when the rains had just begun, that Tubby Carter rang me with the news that Alan was reported a prisoner-of-war. Somehow one had always gone on hoping that he would reach India safely with one of the parties of our troops and civilians who had struggled back against great odds and in conditions of great privation to be restored to those who most sorely missed them. I asked Tubby if he would break the news to Meg. And here Tubby proved himself once again a good and true friend who, although my senior in rank, was always ready to use his seniority for the welfare of an old comrade-in-arms. He ordered me to Rawalpindi so that I could break the news to her myself. In less than thirty-two hours of Tubby's telephone call I was at Meg's bedside.

Neither Meg nor I had any illusions about what it meant to be a captive of the Japanese, but we found solace in the knowledge that Alan was alive and – if we knew our son – probably kicking. Speaking of him to her, I felt the relief it was to do so knowing that at least it was in order to think of him in the present rather than the past tense. That evening Tubby came to the nursing home with a bottle of champagne. In ordinary circumstances it might have seemed wrong to drink champagne at a time when our son was probably suffering hardship, but Tubby put things into perspective by raising his glass and inviting us to drink to Alan's safe return. I was proud of Meg when she raised her glass too and said simply, "To Alan," and smiled as if he were there in the room and the occasion of the toast a happy one. In the few long weeks that we had been separated she seemed to have gone down hill alarmingly. She had lost more weight and her eyes no longer sparkled. I realised suddenly that Tubby had not ordered me back to Rawalpindi only to break the news of Alan's capture to her but so that I could face up to the graver news that eventually I would have to bear.

When we had said good night to Meg, Tubby took me in to Colonel "Billy" Aitken's office and left me there. Billy said, "I'm afraid there's no doubt. Meg's got cancer." We had known Billy for years. In civilian life he could have risen to the top of his profession and become a rich man, but as he had so often said, he preferred to give his time to looking after those of his countrymen – and women – who lived ordinary lives doing often dull and unrewarding jobs abroad, than to prescribing sugar-pills for "fashionable" but hysterical women in Harley Street. I asked him, "How long?" For a moment we looked at each other. He guessed I would prefer to know the truth. He said, "Perhaps six months. Perhaps three. Perhaps less. We shall operate, but the end will be the same." He left me alone for a bit, for which I was grateful. I found it hard to believe that in just a few minutes I had to adjust myself to accept that darling Meg was to be taken from me by a fate even crueller than that which had taken Alan.

Alan at least had had the satisfaction of getting in a blow or two. I think I realised as I sat there alone in Billy Aitken's office that I should never see Alan again either.

Billy and Tubby came back together and took me to Billy's quarters. Tubby asked me whether I wanted to relinquish my command and come back to 'Pindi. He hinted that there was a job going that was mine for the asking and would carry a major-general's hat. I asked him not to press me for an answer until I had had time to think it over. A room had been reserved for me at the club. They drove me back there and I made an effort to sleep so that I could wake up and make my decision in a clearer state of mind. In the morning I asked Billy the most important thing, which I had forgotten to ask the previous evening: whether Meg knew how ill she was. He said he had not told her but he was sure she was in no doubt. I said, "Billy, *don't* tell her." He knew then what my decision was, to go back to my brigade and to go back as soon as possible, so that neither Meg nor I would have to pretend for longer than we could manage. I knew this was my duty. I knew, too, that this was what Meg would want for us both. One cannot adopt a way of life without accepting every one of its responsibilities. It was hard to accept them at this moment, but I was sustained in the belief that Meg would understand and find strength herself in my decision. In spite of this, our parting was far from easy. I thought afterwards on the 'plane to Calcutta on which Tubby had wangled me a seat that it would have been easier if she had asked me not to go back to Mayapore. There seemed to be between us a terrible burden of things we had never said to each other. Before I left, Tubby assured me that he would send for me to be with Meg at the end, but this did not prove to be possible. I shall not write her name again. Goodbye dear Meg, cherished wife and mother of my children. God willing, we shall be reunited in a happier place.

*

I had laid it down that at the commencement of the wet monsoon our training should continue so far as possible without interruption. I had managed through constant pressure in the appropriate quarters to get the last company of the Pankots in Banyaganj out of tents into huts before the rains began. The Ranpurs in Marpuri were less fortunate, but if they tended to be damp in one respect the same could not be said of their spirits!

In July our field training began to get under way and I was heartened by the keenness with which all ranks responded to the challenge of getting out on to the ground, even when the "enemy" was only imaginary. My brigade major, young Ewart Mackay, proved worth his weight in gold. A regular, his enthusiasm was infectious. It spread throughout the Brigade Headquarters staff. Cheerful, efficient and an all-round sportsman (he shone particularly at tennis) he was also a dedicated soldier and could be a stern disciplinarian. Later in the war he commanded with valour and distinction the 2nd Muzzafirabad Guides, his old regiment. His pretty wife, Christine (the elder daughter of General "Sporran" Robertson) was with him at Mayapore and fulfilled the role of hostess with charm and grace. Christine and Ewart gave me "open house" at the delightful bungalow they occupied in Fort Road, and it was Christine who organised the little dinner parties which, in other circumstances, would have been another and still dearer woman's task to arrange.

Heartened as I was on the two occasions in July when we took the brigade "out" to test its mobility and degree of cohesion, I was still unable to lose sight of the role it played as a local force for order. In taking it out the fact was not lost on me that the resulting display of military strength (more impressive to those not in the know than to those who were!) could not but make an impression on the population who were being increasingly subjected to Congress anti-war propaganda. One of the most despicable aspects of that propaganda was the tale put about that in the retreat from Burma and Malaya the authorities had shown indifference to the welfare of Indian troops and the native population. To anyone such as myself who knew the affection the English officer felt for his sepoys and native NCOs, the imaginary picture painted by Congress of Indian soldiers left behind without leaders to be captured or killed, or of groups of leaderless native troops and panicky villagers being pushed off roads, railways and ferries to give priority to "fleeing whites" was laughable.

It was in the middle of July that my divisional (and area) commander told me that local civil authorities had received secret orders from provincial governors to combat in every possible way the poison of the insidious and lying propaganda of the Indian National Congress. This was the occasion when

I sought yet a further discussion with the Deputy Commissioner.

From my point of view White was very much the unknown quantity. I was confident in the police and sure of the loyalty of our own Indian troops. Every man of the Berkshires had been trained in the drill of duties in aid of the civil power, and at the first sign of disturbances patrols and riot squads were ready to go into action. Although these young English boys (many of them civilians themselves little more than a year ago, and with only a very sketchy idea of the problems of administering Imperial possessions abroad) found the drill of "duties in aid" rather farcical, not to say puzzling when they recalled those of their countrymen who had already laid down their lives to protect India from both Nazi and Japanese tyranny, they very quickly adjusted themselves to accepting the role they might have to play as one more job to be done. When I gave this battalion of "modern" young English lads an address on the subject of military aid to the civil authorities I began by quoting those immortal lines of the soldier's poet Rudyard Kipling:

> "– it's Tommy this, an' Tommy that, an'
> 'Tommy, fall be'ind,'
> But it's 'Please to walk in front, sir,' when
> there's trouble in the wind –"

And I suppose a psychologist would say that I couldn't have chosen a better way of putting the situation to them!

One could say that the basic thinking behind the military drill for suppression of civil disturbance is as simple as this: that failing the retreat of the crowd in the face of an armed might even greater than that of the police, the life of one ringleader, forfeited, equals the saving of many other lives. There have been times in our history when this simple equation has not looked, on the ground, as simple as it looks in the textbooks. I am thinking here, of course, of the *cause célèbre* of General Dyer in Amritsar in 1919, who found himself in a position not unlike that which I myself had to anticipate in 1942.

In 1919, as in 1942, the country was seething with unrest, and all the signs indicated open rebellion on a scale equal to that of the Mutiny in 1857. Ordered to Amritsar, Dyer came to a conclusion which the historians – fortified by the hindsight historians are fortunate enough to be able to bring to their aid – have described as fatal: the conclusion that in Amritsar there was to be found the very centre of an imminent armed revolt that could well lead to the destruction of our people and our property and the end of our Imperial rule. Learning that a crowd intended to forgather at a certain hour in a large but enclosed plot of ground called the Jallianwallah Bagh, Dyer prohibited the meeting by written and verbal proclamation in accordance with the rules laid down. This proclamation was defied and his warnings ignored. He took personal command of the troops he sent to disperse it. His on-the-spot orders to disperse also having been defied, he then ordered the troops to fire. The Jallianwallah Bagh, from a military point of view, was a death-trap, and many civilians died, including women and children.

Ever since the Dyer affair, which was seized upon by "reformers" as a stick to beat us with, the army had naturally become supersensitive to the issues involved, and we were now in the unhappy position of finding ourselves in what practically amounted to a strait-jacket.

In the first place, unless the civil authority had collapsed or was otherwise non-operational – when it would be a question of proclaiming martial law – the military was powerless to intervene unless called upon, in writing, by the civil power, usually the senior civilian in the area. Such a request for aid was, in a sense, really only a call to stand by.

For example:

To: O.C. Troops

I have come to the conclusion that the Civil
Authorities are unable to control the situation
and that the assistance of the military has become
necessary. I accordingly request such assistance.

Place:
Date: Time: Signature:
Appointment.

Imagine now that having received such a request I had a platoon of infantry standing by. The civil authority might then ask me to give support at a point where trouble was imminent or had already broken out. Let us say, for instance (to choose one of the many incidents that occurred in Mayapore in August, 1942) that a threatening crowd had gathered outside the main Hindu temple in the square upon which, having crossed the river by the main Mandir Gate bridge, there debouched the road that led from the civil lines.

The platoon of the Berkshires which had hastened by truck from District Headquarters, debussed some two hundred yards from the crowd who were crossing the bridge and hastily formed up on the road in a hollow square (there being shops and buildings on either side of the road whose roof tops or windows represented a threat to the flanks and the rear). In the centre of the hollow square thus formed by the sections of the platoon were to be found the following personnel:

Platoon commander
Representative of the Police
Magistrate
Bugler
Bannermen
Medical orderly
Platoon Sergeant
Signals orderly
Diarist

The meaning of the word "aid" comes into clearer perspective when you remember that apart from the platoon commander there was also a magistrate present. In the affair of the crowd crossing the Mandir Gate bridge the magistrate in question was a Mr. Poulson, who was senior assistant to the Deputy Commissioner.

In the case we are considering, there were three distinct phases of operation. The first being what we might call the Testing phase, the second that of Decision and the third that of the Action which logically followed the decision.

Testing consisted first in the ordering by the platoon commander to the bugler to sound off, thus calling the attention of the crowd to the existence of a legally constituted force of opposition. The warning note having been given, the first of the bannermen raised the banner on which orders in English and the vernacular were inscribed. These were orders to disperse. Sometimes the raising of such a banner was enough to make a crowd obey. After the raising of the first banner a second note on the bugle was sounded and then, if the platoon commander considered that the situation warranted it, the second banner was raised. Upon this was inscribed again in English and the vernacular a clear warning that unless the crowd dispersed force would be resorted to. Since the crowd was usually making a pretty frightful din on its own account one could not rely on verbal warnings being heard: hence, the banners.

It was at the moment when the second banner giving warning of intention to fire was raised that both the platoon commander and the magistrate found themselves in the relative no-man's-land of having to make a decision which the textbooks necessarily left to the man on the spot.

Fortunately, in the case of the first Mandir Gate bridge riot, the attending magistrate, Mr. Poulson, did not hesitate to give the platoon commander the signed chit requesting him to open fire once it was seen that the crowd had no intention of falling back or dispersing. By the time all the necessary drill had been completed only a few yards separated the front of the mob from the forward file of riflemen, and brickbats were being thrown. From the town, on the other side of the river, a pall of smoke showed where an act of arson had already been perpetrated. (This was the kotwali, or police station, near the temple.) At the same time, unnoticed by the troops on the Mandir Gate Bridge road, a detachment from the crowd was making for the railway station along the tracks from the level crossing where the police had failed to hold them, and yet another platoon of the Berkshires was hastening to that area from District Headquarters to reinforce the police (commanded at that point by Mr. Merrick, their District Superintendent).

Meanwhile, to return to our platoon on the Mandir Gate Bridge road: as so often happened the mob had pushed old women to the front to inhibit the soldiers. It was the platoon commander's job to select as targets one or two of the men in the crowd, who, by their actions, he judged to be its leaders. There are occasions when only one of the soldiers, a man who has distinguished himself as a marksman, is issued with live ammunition, but the disturbances in Mayapore had gone far beyond the stage when such an insurance against a high casualty rate was considered wise. Nevertheless, in this present instance, the subaltern in charge now spoke individually to each man of the forward file, gave two of them specific targets and told the others to fire over the heads of the crowd when he gave his order to fire. It required considerable self-discipline and composure to go patiently through such motions while under attack, but badly bruised on the shoulder by a stone as he was the subaltern did so. He had to remember not to call any man by his name in case he was overheard by someone in the crowd which would lead to the man being identified! In the resulting volley both the marksmen found their targets and the crowd faltered, but only for as long as it took for new leaders to come forward and urge them in the Mahatma's current phrase "to do or die". This time the subaltern had no alternative but to order a second volley in which two civilians were killed and five wounded, including, as chance would have it, one woman. Seizing the initiative, the platoon commander ordered the detachment to advance and continue firing, but over the heads of the now retreating mob. The wounded woman was the first to be given attention by the medical orderly. The wound was found to be superficial because, no doubt, the soldier whose bullet had hit her had been sighting upon a man who had moved at the crucial moment.

Present at these proceedings there was one man, usually a member of the battalion or brigade intelligence section, whose duty was that of "diarist"; that is to say, he was required to observe and make notes for later inclusion in the war diary of the unit or formation. This was a dispassionate factual report which did not take into account the thought processes leading to particular decisions which the subaltern's own report would do. The magistrate would also be required to submit a report on the incident to the civil authority. The representative from the police (an inspector or sub-inspector) would do likewise to his superior officer. In this way a number of reports on the same incident would be available if required by any court set up to investigate charges of brutality or excessive use of force. I must emphasise, however, that it was not always possible to fulfil, to the letter, all of the drill laid down for the employment of troops in these duties. As perhaps even the least imaginative of readers may judge, there could arise situations in which any one or even several of the "required" personnel were not available, and only the need for instant action undeniably present!

*

In going into the above details I am conscious not only of digressing but of having moved my story, such as it is, forward to the point where the reader has found himself in the midst of action without knowing the stages that led to it. So I go back now to the day in July when I had a further meeting with Mr. White, the Deputy Commissioner who, I knew, had recently received orders to combat the anti-war propaganda of the Indian National Congress, and whose attitude I felt it necessary to re-assess and, if necessary, confide to my divisional commander who, as area commander also, had virtually the entire province in his military jurisdiction.

I found White somewhat changed in regard to his appreciation of the situation. I personally had little doubt but that some kind of confrontation was inevitable, and was heartened to some extent to realise that the Deputy Commissioner also now seemed to believe that the situation had probably gone beyond the point where it could be retrieved. He was, however, still convinced that the "disturbances", when they came, would be of a "non-violent" nature, unless the leaders of the Congress were put away, in which case, he said, he felt unable to answer for the civil peace. I pounced on this and asked him point-blank, "In the event of such arrests then, you would think it advisable to ask us to stand by?" He said at once that I had "taken him up too literally". He was in an uneasy frame of mind and I saw that there was no sense in pressing him, much as I should have liked to come away with a clear understanding. With regard to the Congress propaganda, he said he had talked to the editors of the various local newspapers and given warnings to those whose recent tendency had been to support the "anti-war" line. This seemed to be satisfactory. I asked him to be good enough to bear in mind as often as he could the situation from my point of view – which was that of a man who was interested in the conditions obtaining in Mayapore first of all as they did or did not affect my training programme and then as they affected our people.

It was at this meeting that White said something that has stayed in my mind ever since as an indication of the true sense of vocation our finest colonial administrators have always felt. "Brigadier," he said, "please bear one thing in mind yourself if my attitude gives you any cause to feel dissatisfied. If your assistance is asked for I know I can rely on it and upon its effectiveness. To you, afterwards, it will have been an unpleasant task effectively carried out and will therefore rank in your scale of values as one of your successes. To me, in my scale, to have called you in at all could never rank as anything but one of my personal failures." I protested that *personal* failure was putting rather too strong a point on it but he smiled and shook his head. Most of the men whom he had had to mark down for arrest if orders came from government were his personal friends.

Then he said, "But don't be alarmed, Brigadier. I am also a realist. I use the word 'failure' but I'm not a fellow to wallow in it."

With this I had to be content, and on the whole was, because as I have said before I had come to respect White for the sense of responsibility that after several meetings I could not help but get an impression of from his very demeanour, which was reserved, somewhat "intellectual", but very down-to-earth and practical in terms of action. White was fairly typical, I realise, of the new race of District Officers who reached maturity just at the moment when our Indian Empire was due to come of age and receive "the key of the door" from our government at home – perhaps prematurely, but as a token of our patience and goodwill and historical undertakings.

After the failure of the Cripps Mission and the subsequent opening of Mr. Gandhi's Quit India campaign, I recollect that the main question in the minds of most Englishmen was whether or no Mr. Gandhi would succeed in carrying the Indian National Congress (certainly the strongest political force in India) to the point where they would collectively identify themselves with his curious doctrine and so give it the force and impetus of an organised, nationwide movement. I have never been a close follower of the ups and downs of politicians, but I was aware that Mr. Gandhi had been "in" and "out" of Congress, sometimes pursuing a personal policy that the Congress endorsed and sometimes one that they did not. Mr. Nehru, who was the actual leader of the Congress, had for some time been considered by us as a more sensible middle-of-the-way fellow who knew the international language of politicians and could possibly he counted on to see sense. A lot of his life recently had been spent in jail, but as I recollect it he had been freed in order to take part in the negotiations with the cabinet mission and was still at large and very much a force to be reckoned with. It was clear to us that he found Mr. Gandhi an embarrassment and for a time our hopes rested upon his more practical and statesmanlike attitude winning the day.

Perhaps at this stage I should rehearse exactly what we knew was at stake and what we felt the opposition amounted to. In the first place we had our backs to the wall in the Far

East and had not yet been able to regain the initiative and/or end the stalemate in Europe and North Africa. At any moment we expected the Jap to commence operations against the eastern bulwark of India. A Japanese victory in India would have been disastrous. Lose India and the British land contribution to what had become a global war would virtually be confined to the islands of our homeland itself, and to the action in North Africa, and the main weight of resistance to totalitarianism thrown on to the Americas. We regarded India as a place it would be madness (as Mr. Gandhi begged us) to make "an orderly retreat from"! Apart from the strategic necessity of holding India there was of course also the question of her wealth and resources.

So much for what was at stake. As for the opposition, this amounted in the first instance to demands (inspired by Gandhi) that we leave India "to God or to anarchy" or alternatively were challenged to hold it against a massive campaign of "non-violent non-co-operation", which meant in effect that the native population would go on strike and in no way assist us to maintain the country as a going concern from which we could train, equip, supply and launch an army to chuck the Jap out of the Eastern archipelago!

Surely, we thought, men like Nehru would resist such a suicidal design?

At the beginning of August it looked like a foregone conclusion that Nehru had, as we say, sold the pass for reasons best known to himself. He had not found in himself the political strength to resist the Mahatma at this moment. Everything now depended upon the vote of the All-India Congress Committee on Mr. Gandhi's Quit India resolution. This was made on August the 8th. Historians since have attempted to prove that the passing of the resolution was no more sinister than words on paper and that Mr. Gandhi hadn't even outlined in his own mind the precise course that consolidated non-violent non-co-operation was to take. My own belief was and remains that the non-violent non-co-operation movement was planned down almost to fine detail by underground members of the Congress acting on instructions from those who wished to look publicly like that famous trio of monkeys, "hearing no evil, speaking no evil, seeing no evil".

How else can I account for the violence in my own district that erupted on the very day following the passing of the Quit India resolution and the dawn arrests of members of the

Congress party? A violence which immediately involved a European woman, Miss Crane, the mission teacher, and on the same night was directed at the defenceless person of a young English girl, the niece of a man famous in the province some years before as governor; a girl who was violently attacked and outraged by a gang of hooligans in the area known as the Bibighar Gardens? These two incidents were portents of the greatest danger to our people, and coming hard on each other's heels as they did, I could only come to one conclusion, that the safety of English people, particularly of our women, was in grave peril.

*

As it so happened I was out at Marpuri with the Ranpurs when I received a message early in the evening of August the 9th from my staff captain to the effect that there had been civil commotion in two outlying subdivisions of the district, Dibrapur and Tanpur, and that a detachment of police from Mayapore, accompanied by Mr. Poulson, the assistant commissioner, had driven out in that direction during the late afternoon and rescued a police patrol and a group of telegraph linesmen from the police post at a village called Candgarh where they had been imprisoned by rioters. Proceeding along the road towards Tanpur, Mr. Poulson had encountered first a burnt-out car and some distance farther on the English mission teacher guarding the body of a dead Indian, one of her subordinates in the mission schools, who had been battered to death by, presumably, the same roaming mob. As Mr. Poulson told me later, it was the sight of the mission teacher sitting on the roadside in the pouring rain that led him to believe that the troubles in Mayapore were to be of a greater degree than either he or Mr. White had anticipated. I had spent the night at Marpuri with the Ranpurs, and did not know either of the Congress Vote or of the arrests of Congress leaders until my staff captain telephoned me about mid-morning on the 9th. He had had a signal from Division, and had also been informed by the Deputy Commissioner that a number of local Congressmen in the district had now been detained as planned. During this first telephone call my staff captain told me everything was quiet and that the Deputy Commissioner had said there was no cause at present for alarm. I had therefore resolved to stay at Marpuri to watch the battalion exercise. But receiving the further communication from my staff captain about the incident near Tanpur, early in the evening, I resolved to return forthwith and ordered him to meet me at the Deputy Commissioner's bungalow.

I reached the Deputy Commissioner's bungalow in Mayapore at about nine o'clock. There was now further trouble in the offing. Mr. White had recently had the news that this young English girl, Miss Manners, was "missing". Merrick, the head of the police, was out looking for her. White told me that following the rumours of violence out at Tanpur and the attack on the mission teacher several of the English women who lived in the civil lines had moved into the Gymkhana club – one of the sites previously selected as a collection point in the event of serious threat to lives and property. Taking White on one side I asked him whether he didn't think it wise for us to give a combined display of strength – joint patrols of police and military – either that night or first thing in the morning. He said he did not think so because the town itself was quiet. Most of the shops in the bazaar had shut down. This was against regulations but he felt it better to allow the population to remain indoors and not to provoke them. I questioned him about the mob violence in Dibrapur and Tanpur. He said he believed it was the result of a "spontaneous reaction" to the news of the arrests, on the part of men who had the time and inclination to make a bit of trouble. Meanwhile communications with Tanpur and Dibrapur had been restored and the police there had reported that they were again in control of their subdivisions. Several men had been arrested in Tanpur, among them, it was thought, one or two of those who had attacked the mission teacher and murdered her Indian companion. The teacher herself was in the Mayapore General Hospital suffering from shock and exposure.

Later, just as I was leaving, young Poulson came in. He had toured the cantonment as far as the Mandir Gate bridge, crossed the bridge and driven down Jail road to the prison to supervise the transfer of the jailed Congressmen to the railway station where he had seen them safely stowed away in a special carriage and sent off on the journey to a destination that was to be kept secret. I had a few words with Poulson who was obviously less sanguine than his chief about the immediate future. He was pretty concerned for his wife, because she was pregnant. They already had one little girl, and she was with them in Mayapore. The Whites' two children, twin boys, had gone back to school in England the year before the war began. One knew that Mrs. White must feel the separation rather badly in the present circumstances, but she was a tireless and forthright woman – rather more commanding in "presence" than her husband who was very much the "thinker". She never showed any sign of self-pity at the prospect of not seeing her sons again until the war was won, but I knew how much this must weigh on her mind.

I had hoped, as well, to see Merrick, but he was out searching for the missing girl – Miss Manners – who lived with a Lady Chatterjee, in one of the old houses near the Bibighar Gardens. Lady Chatterjee had been a friend of Sir Henry and Lady Manners when Sir Henry was Governor of the province. Sir Henry was dead, but I had known Lady Manners slightly in Rawalpindi and recollected that I had met the Manners girl on some occasion or other both in 'Pindi and in Mayapore. She had been in 'Pindi with her aunt and since coming to Mayapore to stay with Lady Chatterjee had been doing voluntary work at the Mayapore General Hospital. She had rather shocked the ladies of the cantonment by her attachment to a young Indian. I remembered Christine Mackay, the wife of my brigade major, saying something about it. On the whole, since coming to Mayapore, I had been too occupied to pay much attention to cantonment gossip, but realising who it was who was "missing" I could not help feeling a serious premonition of trouble.

Asking White to keep me informed I then returned to my own quarters and put a call through to the Area Commander. I was heartened to hear from him that, as a whole, the province – indeed the country in general – seemed settled and quiet. The Congress committees had been banned by Government and many members of them detained under the Defence of India Rules as a precautionary measure. The General said he felt that the arrests had nipped the Congress revolt nicely in the bud and that we could now concentrate on our job of training and equipping our forces. I told him of the things that had occurred that day in my own sphere of command but he said they sounded to him like isolated incidents that had gone off at half-cock because the men who were supposed to have been behind them were now safely under lock and key. I went to bed in a relatively easy frame of mind and slept soundly, realising how tired I was as a result of my twenty-four-hour visit to the Ranpurs.

My orderly woke me at seven, as I had instructed him, and told me that the District Superintendent of Police was waiting to see me. Guessing that something was up I gave orders for him to be brought to my room at once. Arriving a few minutes later he apologised for coming so early and for intruding on my privacy. Spick and span as he was I judged from his look of fatigue and strain that he had been up all night. I said, "Well, Merrick, what's the grief this morning?"

He told me that the missing girl, Miss Manners, had been attacked in the Bibighar Gardens the previous night and raped by a gang of ruffians. Fortunately he had called at Lady Chatterjee's home for the second time that evening only a few minutes after the poor girl had herself returned after running all the way in a state of considerable distress through deserted, ill-lit roads. Merrick had at once driven to his headquarters and collected a squad and rushed to the Bibighar area. He had found five men, not far away, drinking home-distilled liquor in a hut on the other side of the Bibighar bridge. He at once arrested them (the distillation and drinking of such liquor was in any case illegal) and was then fortunate enough to find Miss Manners's bicycle, which had been stolen by one of the culprits, in a ditch outside a house in the Chillianwallah Bagh. Entering the house he discovered that there lived in it the Indian youth with whom Miss Manners had been associated. This youth, whose name as I recollect it was Kumar, had cuts and abrasions on his face. Merrick immediately arrested him and then secured all six fellows in the cells at his headquarters.

I congratulated him on his prompt action but asked him why he had come personally to see me at this early hour. He said there were several reasons. First, he wished to be sure that I had the earliest possible notification of the "incident" of which he took the most serious view. Secondly, he wanted to know whether he had my permission to transfer the detained men to the guard room of the Berkshires if he judged that it would be wise to move them to a place of greater security. Thirdly, he wished to put it to me that in his opinion the Deputy Commissioner was seriously misjudging the gravity of the situation, a situation which in a few hours had seen violent attacks on *two* English women, and the murder of an Indian attached to a Christian mission. He then reminded me that earlier in the summer I had asked him to "stick his neck out" if he thought it necessary.

I could not help but ask him in what way he felt he was sticking it out now. He said he was convinced that the men he had arrested last night were those who had assaulted Miss Manners but that it might be difficult to prove. I said, "Well, the poor girl can probably identify them," but he doubted it. He had asked if she knew any of the men responsible but she said she didn't because it had all been "done in darkness" and she had not seen them clearly enough to be able to identify them. Since one of the fellows arrested was the man she had been associating with, Merrick believed that for the moment at any rate she was not telling the truth, but he hoped she would do so when she came out of her shock and realised who her real friends were. Meanwhile he had the fellows under lock and key and had spent most of the night interrogating them. They still protested their complete innocence in the matter, but he was convinced of their guilt, particularly in the case of the man Kumar, who obviously stole her bicycle and who was caught in the act of bathing his face to reduce or remove the evidence of cuts and bruises received when the girl fought back before being overpowered.

I asked Merrick if it was known how Miss Manners had come to be at the Bibighar. He said he was afraid it looked to him as if she had gone to meet Kumar there, an aspect of the case that he hoped could be glossed over for the girl's sake. He had met her himself on several occasions and counted himself as one of her friends, enough of a friend anyway to have warned her not long ago that her association with the Indian was one she would be well advised to end. But she seemed to be completely under Kumar's spell. Kumar, Merrick said, had once been taken in for questioning by the police when they were searching the town for a prisoner who had escaped from jail. During questioning it transpired that Kumar knew the escaped man, whose name was Moti Lal, but there was no evidence at that time that their acquaintance was more than superficial. Although "westernised", Merrick considered Kumar to be a pretty unsavoury character, aware of his attraction for women and not above latching on to a white woman for the pleasure of humiliating her in subtle ways. He worked on a local newspaper, and gave no obvious trouble, but was known to have consorted with young men suspected of anarchistic or revolutionary activities – young men of the type of the other five arrested. Several of these men had been seen with Kumar on other occasions and they were all men on whose activities the police had been keeping an eye. Merrick's opinion was that Kumar and these five had plotted together to take advantage of Kumar's association with Miss Manners. Going to the Bibighar that night, expecting to find only Kumar, she found not only Kumar but five others – men who then set on her in the most cowardly and despicable way.

I was deeply shocked by this sorry tale and agreed with Merrick that the less said about her attachment to one of the suspected men the better, especially if things came to the head of a public trial. Meanwhile, I agreed, he seemed to have sufficient grounds to hold the men in custody on suspicion of this crime alone, which I thought was fortunate because once the story got round that an English girl had been outraged there wasn't a white man or woman in the country who wouldn't rejoice that the suspects were already apprehended. The effect on the Indian population of knowing that this kind of thing couldn't be got away with would also be exemplary.

Merrick said he was glad to feel that I approved of his actions. He believed that the events of the previous day were simply a prelude to a violence which, if becoming no worse, would certainly become more widespread and would take all our combined efforts to resist. He had heard of my suggestion to White that both police and military patrols should be seen to be on the alert today and regretted that this proposal had been turned down.

I invited Merrick to have breakfast with me but he declined and said he must be getting back to work. Before he went I told him that if circumstances warranted it one or all of the six prisoners could be moved into the greater security of the Berkshires' guard room, providing that the police supplied their own guards and the Berkshires were absolved of direct responsibility for them. Merrick obviously feared an attack on his own jail by a "do or die" crowd bent on releasing the men arrested for the rape. He had no doubt that by this morning the whole town knew of the incident. In India it was almost impossible to keep anything secret. Rumours began with the whispered gossip of native servants and spread quickly to the rest of the population. But a crowd attracted by the idea of rescuing their "heroes" would have to show a lot of determination to try to penetrate the Berkshires' lines because this would mean a direct attack on a military installation – and on the whole this was something Indian mobs usually avoided. Much as I sometimes found it irksome not to take immediate control of this explosive situation – which an attack on the military would have entitled me to do without signed permission of the civil authority – the last thing I wanted was to become involved at this level, which is why I qualified my permission to move the prisoners into military lines with the phrase "if circumstances warranted it". But I certainly endorsed Merrick's opinion that the six prisoners must be held under maximum security. Their forcible release to go free and boast of their attack on an Englishwoman was at all costs to be avoided.

After breakfast I rang the Deputy Commissioner and told him that I had spoken to Merrick, and that Merrick had told me about the attack on Miss Manners. I again offered to cooperate with military patrols as a precautionary propaganda measure, but he said the district was quiet and that he was trying hard to maintain an atmosphere of normality. Most District Headquarters availed themselves of the services of what I suppose we must call spies or informers. White's informers reported to him that the population was more puzzled than angry, uncertain what their arrested Congress leaders really expected of them. To provoke them now was, he was sure, the very last thing a sensible man should do. Fortunately, for the present anyway, Muslim and Hindu communities were living together on terms of amity and although in a sense this could be counted a bad sign – since it suggested an alliance against the English – in another sense it was a good thing, because there was little or no danger of a communal situation developing that would snowball into something worse.

As usual, when I spoke to the Deputy Commissioner I was impressed by his calm and balanced thinking. I asked what he felt about the attack on Miss Manners and whether he didn't see it as a prelude to attacks on Europeans in general. He said it might well have been an isolated incident, such as that at Tanpur, the work of hooligans, men who had probably come in to Mayapore from one of the outlying villages expecting to find it in the grip of civil disturbance, only to be disappointed and therefore capable of taking it out of the first defenceless person they happened to see. I said the impression I got from Merrick was that the culprits were not villagers but young anarchists who lived in Mayapore. To this he did not immediately reply, so I asked him whether he thought the men arrested were not the real culprits. He said he had to keep an open mind on the subject and that a lot depended on the girl's own evidence once she was fit enough to give it. He thought Merrick might have made a mistake, but could not criticise him for his prompt action, at least not in the light of what Merrick himself had told him of the circumstances attending the arrests.

Having spoken to the Deputy Commissioner I then called my own staff together, told them of the situation as seen (a) by Merrick and (b) by Mr. White, and finally (c) as seen by myself, that is to say one that was potentially grave but at present under the control of those whose duty it was to control it. In other words, for us, I said, it was "business as usual", and I ordered my staff car for ten o'clock so that I could pay an unexpected visit to the Pankots out at Banyaganj. Taking me on one side when the others had gone, Ewart Mackay told me that he and his wife had already heard about the attack on Miss Manners and his wife's private view was that it was something the poor girl had been heading for, although naturally Christine and he were shocked and grieved. The point was, though, that Christine Mackay felt I should know that she did not see the attack on Miss Manners as evidence that European women generally were in danger. She had asked if the man Kumar had been involved and Ewart said she would be more than glad to hear that he had actually been arrested.

In other words, from this private source, I had confirmation of the reasonableness of young Merrick's personal suspicions but also of the Deputy Commissioner's broader impersonal attitude. I therefore set off for Banyaganj fairly confident that there was at least a breathing space for us to concentrate on more important things. In Banyaganj itself work was proceeding on the construction of the airfield. My heart went out to those poor and simple labourers, men and women, who needed every anna they could earn and did not lightly drop their tools and their baskets of stones at anyone's beck and call. I could not help thinking that if every one of the women working so hard in the heat and humidity of that August morning, with her ragged saree torn and mud-spattered, had taken the Mahatma at his word, and gone home to spin cotton she would have been hard put to it to feed her children – children for whose welfare, and hers, a committee of our own women had been set up and was actually represented that morning by young Mavis Poulson and the wife of the Station Staff Officer, who were doing their best to attend single-handed to the screaming wants of Hindu and Muslim babies of both sexes and to pregnant mothers who had collapsed under the weight of the baskets. Fortunately there were some stout-looking lads from the RAF in the vicinity so I felt that Mrs. Poulson and Mrs. Brown wouldn't come to much harm, and continued my journey to the headquarters of the Pankots. I spent a pleasant day there, watching their battle drill.

This was indeed the calm before the storm! I returned to Mayapore at about 5 p.m. and gave Mrs. Poulson and Mrs. Brown a lift, to save them the discomfort of the journey back to the cantonment in the RAF bus. Mrs. Poulson also seemed to share Christine Mackay's view of the fate that had overtaken Miss Manners. Mrs. Poulson said that the whole business must be extremely distasteful to Lady Chatterjee who probably felt a special degree of responsibility for what had happened, not only because Miss Manners was her house guest but because she herself was an Indian. I asked Mrs. Poulson what she knew of the man Kumar and she said at once, hearing from me that he had been arrested, "Well, you've got the right man. A trouble-maker if ever I saw one." She thought that if poor Miss Manners had not been such an "innocent" about India this distressing business would never have arisen, and she added how extraordinary and yet how logical it was that the two Europeans who had so far suffered injury in the present troubles were both women, and both women of radical, pro-Indian views. Mrs. Brown, I noticed, was less positive on the subject, but I put this down to shyness. Her husband, as readers may remember, had risen from the ranks. I made a special point of trying to bring her into the conversation. I had a great respect for her husband's capabilities as Station Staff Officer. I am sure, however, that she felt much the same way as did Mrs. Poulson, that is to say that they both thought the girl had been unwise but of course were dismayed by her fate and determined to stand by her. I was touched by this as yet further proof of our solidarity. Armed thus, one can face any crisis.

I dropped Mrs. Brown in the cantonment bazaar where she had some shopping to do and took Mrs. Poulson back to her bungalow. Declining her kind offer to come in and have a drink I left her to her task of supervising the putting to bed of her little daughter whose name, I think, was Anne, and ordered the driver to return to brigade headquarters. The rain had let up again and the late afternoon sun had come out. The *maidan* looked peaceful and I was reminded of those far-off days when I was a young man without a care in the world. That evening after dinner I wrote some personal letters and retired early to work on a field-training scheme that my staff had drafted for my consideration. Reading it through, and finding little to criticise, I felt a glow of confidence. If only the scheme had been more than a scheme! The Japanese would not have been resting so peacefully in their beds that night!

This was, however, to be the last comfortable night's sleep I was to enjoy myself for many days.

*

In the personal diary which I kept at this time the space allotted to the following day – August 11th – is blank, but there is a brief note on August 12th headed 2 a.m. which reads, "A moment's respite after a day of widespread riots throughout the district. I received at 20.00 hours (Aug 11) a request for aid from the deputy commissioner. Cold comfort for our forces in Assam and Burma to know that those whose role is to supply and eventually reinforce them are being hindered in this way."

Looking back to that day in August which marked the beginning of disturbances throughout most of the country, and remembering – as hour by hour reports of commotions, riots, arson and sabotage began to come in – the sense that grew of what we had feared and tried to stop finally facing us I cannot but be puzzled by the opinion still held in some quarters that the uprising was indeed a spontaneous expression of the country's anger at the imprisonment of their leaders. In my opinion, final proof to the contrary, if any is needed, lies in the words spoken by the Mahatma to his followers at the time of his arrest, "Do or die." Nothing, I feel, could be plainer than that. I did not hear of those words until the 11th, on which day the crowds that collected and attacked police stations, telegraph offices, and sabotaged stretches of railway line, were crying them as their motto.

Again the immediate seat of disturbances was in Tanpur and Dibrapur, and the police in those areas were sorely pressed. During the afternoon of the 11th the police in Mayapore, directed by mounted officers, were fully occupied in dispersing and redispersing the crowds that attempted to collect. Several constables were injured. A score of men were arrested and taken to jail. In a village just south of Mayapore an Indian sub-divisional officer of the unconvenanted civil service was attacked and held prisoner in the police post and was not rescued until the following day when our own patrols scoured the area. The Congress flag was run up in the village, and also over the court house in Dibrapur – a town that was cut off for several days. The post-office in Dibrapur, which had been attacked on the 9th of August (the day of the attack on the mission school teacher) was this time destroyed by fire. Until our troops retrieved the situation on the 17th August Dibrapur – 70-odd miles away from Mayapore – was in the hands of the mob. In fact one of the mob's leaders declared himself Deputy Commissioner and district headquarters to have been transferred from Mayapore to Dibrapur! The sub-divisional officer who was legally and constitutionally in charge of that sub-division (again an Indian) was at first imprisoned but then released and installed in the court house as "District and Sessions Judge". He later claimed that he was forced to co-operate with the self-appointed Deputy Commissioner and that he had hidden most of the money from the local treasury to save it from falling into the rioters' hands. Restoration of the money and his previous good record probably saved him from paying the penalty of his apparent defection to the side of the rioters. There were, unfortunately, several cases spread throughout the country where magistrates and even senior Indian district officers complied with the orders of the mob leaders, and considerable sums of Government's money was stolen. In some areas the new self-appointed officials "fined" townsmen and villagers and put the money into their own pockets along with revenues they had collected "on behalf of free India". There was not, I think, any instance of an English civil servant being coerced in this way, and there was, thank God, virtually no loss of European life. The one instance I remember was the murder of two Air Force officers (not in our own district) by a mob who – imagining them to be the pilots of an aircraft that had recently taken part in a punitive raid on a mutinous village nearby – immediately set on them in this foul way and tore them to pieces.

But to go back to the 11th, and to Mayapore itself: the District Superintendent of Police showed, throughout that day, considerable tactical ability. It was impossible for Merrick to have men everywhere they were needed, but there were three main danger areas – the area of the Chillianwallah Bagh Extension road which led from the south of the town directly to the Bibighar bridge, the "square" opposite the Tirupati temple leading to the Mandir Gate bridge and the road leading west to the jail (the jail on the black town side of the river, not the cells at Police Headquarters in the civil lines where the six men suspected of the rape were being held). It was anticipated that there would be two main objectives of attack – the jail and the civil lines.

The day had begun normally enough until the police in the city reported that "hartal" was being observed. At 8 a.m. however (an hour that more or less coincided with the renewed uprising in Dibrapur) a crowd was found to be collecting on the Chillianwallah Bagh Extension road. This was dispersed by 9.30 a.m. but at once there was evidence that the dispersal had only led to the collection of another crowd in the vicinity of Jail road. Fortunately, Merrick had anticipated the moves that might be made in the event of any organised defiance of the agents of law and order and had already ordered his forces to deploy. There were several skirmishes. The post office on Jail road was threatened but secured. Meanwhile reports had begun to come in of "isolated" acts of violence and sabotage in the district's outlying areas. At 1200 hours the sub-inspector of police in charge of the kotwali near the Tirupati temple received an "ultimatum" to join the forces of "free India" and co-operate in the "release of the six martyrs of the Bibighar Gardens". This ultimatum was delivered to him in the form of a printed pamphlet! The attempt to identify the rebellion in Mayapore with the Bibighar Gardens affair as though it were simply a crusade to release men whom the population thought wrongfully imprisoned was, I thought, not only a cunning move but proof of the existence of underground leaders of considerable intelligence. With this Merrick agreed. At first sight of the pamphlet he had at once raided the offices of an English language newspaper called *The Mayapore Hindu* and found a press there that suggested that not only newspapers were printed on those premises but that they were also equipped to print in the vernacular. The type from which the pamphlet had been set up in English and Hindi had already been "distributed" but Merrick felt justified in arresting every member of the staff actually on the premises and in destroying the press from which pamphlets of the kind distributed could have been run off.

This operation had been completed by 1300 hours, only 60 minutes after the delivery of the pamphlet to the kotwali in the temple square, which said a lot for Merrick's capacity for prompt action, as well as for his intelligence or "spy" system. He told me that afternoon when I visited District Headquarters where the Deputy Commissioner and his staff were gathered in force, that one of the men on *The Mayapore Hindu* whom he had arrested was a close friend of the man Kumar, the principal suspect in the Manners case. He felt that it was very likely now that by interrogating this fellow (the note in my diary gives his name as Vidyasagar) Kumar's duplicity would be proved.

I confess that I felt sickened to realise the extent to which some of these so-called educated young Indians would go to defy and attack the people who had given them the opportunity to make something of themselves. I was also concerned about the capacity they had for violence in the sacred name of *satyagraha*. I said as much to Merrick who then reminded me that, in his job, he had to deal almost every day with fellows of this kind. If he sometimes "bent the rules" and paid them back in their own coin, he believed that the end justified the means. He said he was almost "off his head" at the thought that a decent girl like Daphne Manners, with every advantage civilised life had to offer, should have been taken in by a fellow like Kumar who had had the benefit of an English public school education. I was astonished to have this information about Kumar's background and felt that my own sense of values had been pretty well knocked for six.

Merrick described Gandhi on this occasion (when we drank a hasty cup of tea together) as a "crazy old man" who had completely lost touch with the people he thought he still led, and so was the dupe of his own "dreams and crazy illusions", and had no idea how much he was laughed at by the kind of young men, he, Merrick, had to keep in order.

That afternoon at district headquarters I found the Deputy Commissioner calm and decisive in his reactions to the reports that were coming in. I told him that I was prepared to order the provost in charge of the military police to assist in the transfer of the six prisoners to the Berkshires' lines. This took White by surprise because apparently Merrick had not discussed such a possibility with him. He said he had no intention of aggravating racial feeling by placing six men suspected of raping an English woman under the noses of English soldiers. I grew rather heated at what I thought to be an unwarranted criticism of my men's capacity for self-restraint. He then assured me he had not meant any such thing, but simply that the job of guarding such prisoners could only be extremely distasteful and therefore bad for the morale of the Berkshires who, if called out in aid, would need to exercise a high degree of level temper and self-discipline. It was bad enough, he said, that the news of the attack on Miss Manners had become current. He did not wish to have the Berkshires "reminded hourly by the suspects' presence in their midst of an affair that can only excite strong basic emotions".

On this subject we did not see eye to eye, and broke off conversation somewhat tartly. At eight o'clock that evening I received the expected request for aid, at once ordered what we had come to call the riot squad to report to district headquarters and the rest of the Berkshires to stand by, and drove to White's bungalow to which he had now returned and where I found him in conference with Judge Menen and members of his staff. Judge Menen looked as imperturbable as ever. I could not help wondering whether under that grave, judicial exterior lurked a heart that beat in unison with his countrymen's hopes for "freedom".

Since 4 p.m. it had apparently become clear to White that the available police were in insufficient strength to continue their task of discouraging the collection of crowds, particularly as a detachment of the city police had been sent to reinforce the police in Tanpur and attempt to re-establish contact with Dibrapur, thereby reducing their strength in Mayapore. Anticipating from the temper of the town's population that determined efforts might be made the following day to penetrate the civil lines, and getting some impression of the scale and nature of the revolt from his staff's collation of the day's reports from his own and other districts and provinces, the Deputy Commissioner decided, round about 7.30 p.m., to ask for military support. Reaching him at about 8.15 I was thanked for our prompt response. He said he still hoped that on the morrow it would not prove necessary to request the full weight of our strength. We agreed to keep the platoon of the Berkshires at District Headquarters on immediate call and to send some troops overnight to Dibrapur in the company of a magistrate and a police officer to see what was going on there and to try for pacification and reduction. Wishing to keep the Berkshires intact, I decided that the platoon going to Dibrapur should come from the Ranpurs at Marpuri. They were well placed to cross the river at a point some six miles west of Mayapore and to approach Dibrapur by a flank road from which they might catch the rebels in Dibrapur by surprise. I gave the orders at once by telephone to the duty officer at Marpuri.

I decided to be present myself at the rendezvous between the Ranpurs and the two representatives of the civil power and left with the latter in my staff car at 2200 hours. Making contact with the Ranpurs I then led the party to the bridge at a village called Tanipuram where we found the local police on their toes. The sub-inspector in charge reported that at dusk men had been seen approaching the bridge who had gone away at the sight of his men patrolling. The village had been quiet all day in spite of the rumours of Mayapore town being in a state of turmoil. Leaving the Ranpurs to proceed in the direction of Dibrapur I then drove back to the place of rendezvous – the railway halt that served the surrounding villages. I telephoned through to Mayapore and managed to get connected to District Headquarters. I left a message that the Ranpurs were safely on their way, and then – feeling I had done as much as was possible that night – was driven home. By now we were in the early hours of the morning of the 12th and a steady rain was falling which I felt would do much to dampen the ardour of any potential night-raiders!

*

In the morning, after only three hours or so sleep, my signals officer woke me with a message from the platoon of Ranpurs who had been on their way to Dibrapur that they had been held up on the road about ten miles from Dibrapur by a roadblock in the shape of a felled tree. No obstacle to the men, it was of course one to the transport. The tree had been removed with some difficulty because of the rain which was still falling and the slippery state of the road and kutcha edges. The subaltern in charge of the platoon, a young Indian, had proposed to send two sections ahead on foot to the next village one mile distant but the accompanying magistrate and the police officer had insisted on the party remaining intact while the obstruction was dealt with. If the subaltern had not been persuaded against his better judgment it is possible that the destruction of the bridge beyond the village – a bridge across a tributary of the main river flowing through Mayapore – might have been stopped. The bridge was blown some twenty minutes after they had begun work on clearing the roadblock. They heard the sound of the explosion. Reaching the village (which was deserted of all but a few old men and women) the subaltern had again got on to brigade signals and reported that the road to Dibrapur had now been rendered impassable for transport. He requested further orders.

This was the situation I was immediately faced with on the morning of the 12th. A glance at the map quickly confirmed that there was no alternative route to Dibrapur that did not involve a retracing of steps almost as far north as the bridge at Tanipuram, and the alternative route from there was little better than a good-weather track, from the point of view of mechanical transport. The bridge at Tanipuram only had to be blown now and I realised I had temporarily lost the use of two 3-ton lorries, a 15-cwt truck and valuable wireless equipment!

Fortunately my Brigade Intelligence Officer, a somewhat reserved but extremely able young man called Davidson, had already seen the danger and anticipated my orders for the police to be requested to make immediate contact with their post at the bridge at Tanipuram to check the situation there and give warning to be on the look-out for saboteurs. I rang the Deputy Commissioner and told him that I stood to lose valuable transport and equipment unless I had carte-blanche to secure the road. I told him why, and added that it seemed clear that the rebels in Dibrapur were led by pretty skilled men and that Dibrapur had obviously been chosen as the strong point for the rebellion in this district.

White gave the situation a moment or two's thought and then said that on the whole he agreed with me and gave me carte-blanche to command the road while the Ranpurs were "withdrawn". I told him that I had not necessarily been contemplating withdrawal, but instead the securing of the road during whatever period was required to re-bridge the river at the scene of demolition. We were sadly short of the necessary equipment, but even if it were several hours before the Ranpurs could proceed it was surely better late than never!

His answer amazed me. He said, "No, I request withdrawal

but agree to your commanding the road until your men are back this side of Tanipuram. I'll confirm that in writing at once."

I asked him, "And what if the bridge has gone at Tanipuram?"

He said, "That will call for another appreciation, but speaking off the cuff it would look to me as if you had lost immediate use of three trucks and a wireless." He then rang off. I dressed hurriedly and had breakfast, determined that if news came in that the bridge at Tanipuram had also gone I would order the Ranpurs to make their weight felt in that area, magistrate or no magistrate. But I was relieved, presently, to have a call from police headquarters to tell me that Tanipuram reported the bridge still standing and no sign of trouble.

I had decided not to withdraw the Ranpurs until the promised written request to that effect had come in from the Deputy Commissioner. I received this request by 0800 hours and at once told Ewart to order the transport and men to come back.

I then discussed the situation at Dibrapur with Davidson, my IO, who said he imagined that the view of the Deputy Commissioner was that if Dibrapur *were* the centre of the rebellion in the district, it could be left to stew in its own juice for a while, because the rebels had no "troops" as such, and Mayapore was of greater importance. He thought that the Deputy Commissioner had decided that the pacification of his district should spread outwards from Mayapore.

Of all my staff, I suppose Davidson had achieved the greatest degree of frankness with me (except for Ewart who was by way of being a personal friend). When I first assumed command, the IO had been a young fellow called Lindsey, whom I took an immediate shine to. He had seen action in France with the ill-fated British Expeditionary Force. His association with the Berkshires dated back to his Territorial Army days before the war. He had come out to India with the new battalion as a company commander. On reaching India he had been sent for training in Intelligence duties, on completion of which, having expressed a wish to serve in a formation which included a unit of his old regiment, he was at once put in charge of our Brigade Intelligence Section. Early in April, a week after my arrival in Mayapore, he received posting orders to a G 3 (I) appointment at Division.

I made some fuss but Ewart persuaded me not to hinder the transfer. In his opinion, since coming to Mayapore, Lindsey had shown signs of restlessness and uncertainty and Ewart suspected that he had spoken to a friend on the divisional staff about getting a move. Lindsey's successor, Davidson, did not strike me as a particularly good substitute at first and we crossed swords on several occasions. Of Jewish origin, he had a layer of sensitivity that I did not at once comprehend.

After talking to Davidson, I decided to visit White. I drove first to his bungalow, and being told by Mrs. White that he was touring the cantonment and the city, but expected to be back by ten o'clock, I decided to wait. I discussed the situation with her and found her own attitude shrewdly balanced between my own and her husband's. She said, "Robin has always tried to see at least one year ahead. He knows that the people who oppose us now are the same we are going to have to live with and feel responsible for afterwards." I said, "Yes, providing the Japanese don't take over." She said, "I know. It's what I personally feel. But then I'm thinking of the twins and of never seeing them again. Robin thinks of that too, but knows that to think it isn't what he is paid for."

I saw at once that between Mr. and Mrs. White there was the same fine sense of partnership which I had been blessed with in my own life.

When White returned, accompanied by young Jack Poulson, he at once apologised for any annoyance he might have given me earlier that morning about the Ranpurs and the bridge. I asked him whether I was right in thinking he had decided Dibrapur could be left to stew for a day or two in the hope that the successful reduction of unrest in Mayapore would leave it isolated and open to pacification. He seemed surprised, and thought for a moment, and then said, "Yes, I suppose in military terms that is a way of putting it."

I asked him what the civil terms were and he said at once, "The saving of life and protection of property." I asked him whether he therefore felt that the military were not to be trusted. He said, "Your fellows are armed. My fellows have a few delaying weapons like explosives but otherwise their bare hands and their passions."

I was surprised at his description of the rebels as "his fellows", until I realised that just as I took my share of responsibility seriously so White took his, and I was aware of the curious enmity, as well as the amity, that could grow between two men of the same background, simply because the spheres of their responsibility differed. And yet, I thought, in the end, the result we both hoped for was the same.

The news that morning on the civil side was that the employees of the British-Indian Electrical Company were out on strike and that students of the Government Higher School and the Mayapore Technical College planned mass *satyagraha* that afternoon in a march across the Bibighar bridge and along the Grand Trunk road to the airfield at Banyaganj where work had also come to a stop following acts of intimidation against the men and women who had at first resisted the Congress call to cease work.

White intensely disliked action against students, whose volatile natures were unpredictable. They might be content to march in an orderly fashion and allow a number of their fellows to be arrested and then disperse, satisfied to have embarrassed the authorities and identified themselves with Congress ideals. But the slightest "wind from another direction", as White put it, could lead them to throw themselves unarmed on the police or the military in a movement of mass hysteria that could only lead to a tragic loss of life. He asked, therefore, that his police be reinforced by troops and that the officer commanding them be asked to control the actions of the police as well as those of his own men. The police, White said, were inclined to be "tough" with students. White then put it to me that the ease with which his informants had got hold of the details of these plans only led him to see the students' demonstration as a move to tempt our forces to concentrate mainly on the Bibighar bridge and the area of the colleges. He expected another attack, across the Mandir Gate bridge, by men and women of the ordinary population and one on the Jail, and believed that these would coincide with the movement of the students.

I could not but admire his cool and, as I thought, sensible appraisal. I suggested that this morning might be a good time for a drumbeat proclamation by the civil and military authorities through the main areas of the city forbidding gatherings. He had considered this and now considered it again. Finally he said, "No, it comes under my heading of provocation and reminds me too readily of the prelude to the massacre in Amritsar. It may also remind *them*. They don't need the proclamation because they know what is allowed and what isn't."

I think that from this conversation – begun in an atmosphere of coolness almost amounting to distrust – I learned more about the workings of the civilian mind than I had ever done in a comparable time during my service in the country. I came away with a deep and abiding impression of the Deputy Commissioner's total involvement with the welfare of the people as a whole, irrespective of race or creed or colour. He must have had many doubts as to the various courses of action to be taken, but I think he had to solve them all with, in mind, what his wife had called the realisation that these were the people we were going to have to live in peace with when the troubles were over. In the aftermath of the troubles in Mayapore I believe that he was criticised for having "lost his head". If this is true, I should like to put the record straight. White "went it alone" for as long as he was able, and I, in the few days in which circumstances made his task almost impossible, tried to make the best of a bad job. I should also put on record my opinion that White would have "worked himself into the ground" before admitting he was beaten if, on the evening of August 12th, he had not received direct orders from his Commissioner (who was situated two hundred miles away from him!) and who, in turn, acted on the instructions of the provincial governor, to employ "to the utmost" the military forces available to him. I had a similar notification from my divisional and area commander. By the night of the 12th, the province, viewed as a whole, was certainly in a state of such violent unrest that without difficulty it could be called a state of rebellion – one which our immediate superiors could only view with the gravest doubts for the immediate future.

That meeting on the morning of the 12th was virtually the last between White and myself that has left any clear impression on my mind. I have already described on an earlier page – as an example of the drill of military aid to the civil power – the action that afternoon on the Mandir Gate Bridge road when, as White had anticipated, believing the authorities fully occupied in reducing the student demonstration, the mob attempted penetration of the civil lines from the temple square, set fire to the *kotwali* in the vicinity of the temple and deployed towards the railway station. Simultaneously to the action this side of the Mandir Gate bridge the police were desperately defending the jail. Two of them died and the mob in that quarter suceeded in breaking into the prison and releasing a number of prisoners before a force of the Berkshires, who were rushed to the spot, were able to regain the initiative.

As readers may recall from my earlier detailed description of the action on the Mandir Gate Bridge road, the troops "in aid" followed up the advantage they had gained in breaking up the mob in confusion with their firing, by pressing forward. In this way, the main body of the retreating rioters was pushed back across the bridge, although small groups managed to escape along some of the side roads.

Halting on the civil lines side of the bridge, the platoon commander asked the magistrate, Mr. Poulson, whether he should remain there or cross the bridge and enter the city to command the temple square where already he could see new "leaders" exhorting the fleeing crowd to stand and form up again. Poulson, intent upon keeping the force of law and order intact according to the drill book, requested the Berkshire subaltern to remain at the bridgehead. Firing could now be heard from the direction of the railway station and Poulson assumed correctly that in crossing the bridge originally the crowd had split into two, with one body advancing along the Mandir Gate Bridge road and the other infiltrating along the tracks towards the railway station. He told the subaltern that if the troops crossed over into the square they might find themselves caught between the mob that was trying to re-form in the town and the mob retreating from the firing at the railway station. As it was, when men and women fleeing from the railway station came into view they found the Berkshires holding the bridge – their one line of retreat.

Unfortunately, in spite of Mr. Poulson's prompt request and the subaltern's equally prompt response – to "open a way" across the bridge of these unarmed fleeing civilians – the civilians panicked at the sight of the troops and misinterpreted as hostile the movements of the platoon, which were actually made to give them way. Those at the front of the crowd tried to fall back and were trampled underfoot. Many scrambled down the banks of the river and attempted to swim across, and I'm afraid a number of men and women were drowned. This incident was the cause of great misunderstanding. We were accused by the Indians, later, of deliberately setting a trap and of showing no mercy towards those who were caught in it. Attempts were made to bring evidence that the troops at the bridge had fired into the mob, thereby causing many of them to throw themselves into the river. So far as I could gather this "evidence" rested entirely on the fact that several of those who were drowned were found to have bullet wounds when the bodies were recovered. These wounds can only have been incurred in the action at the railway station, when non-compliance with the orders to disperse, and attacks on the troops with stones and brickbats, had led to a volley from the troops. As I think I have mentioned, the police at the railway station were commanded by Merrick, the District Superintendent. He showed great energy and determination and recklessness for his own safety. Mounted, he continually pressed forward to scatter the crowd and stop it forming a united front. Only when he was forced to retreat did he give orders to his few armed police, and permission to the troops, to fire.

It was a bitter afternoon, the climax coming when news reached us at District Headquarters that the Jail had been attacked and forced. By now a heavy rain was falling. Between five and six o'clock a storm raged overhead as if reflecting the one which raged on the ground. It was in these inclement conditions that yet another force of Berkshires (which I myself accompanied, along with the Deputy Commissioner) were rushed across the bridge in open transports, and closed in on the jail. The rain and the alarm spread by the news of the failure of the riots in the civil lines had reduced the size of the crowds on Jail road, and no doubt the spectacle of several lorry-loads of armed troops and the speed with which I had ordered them to proceed shook the determination of the men and women still in this area. Nevertheless the area in the immediate vicinity of the jail had to be cleared by debussing the troops and firing repeated volleys over the heads of the crowd. Once we were in control of the area of access to the jail itself, the picket-gate in the huge old wooden doors of the prison had to be forced with pickaxes. The insurgents had locked themselves in. They had also broken into the armoury, but fortunately their familiarity with such weapons as they found turned out to be practically nil, otherwise our men might have found themselves forcing an entrance under serious fire. Even as it was, one of our soldiers was wounded when, led by their platoon commander, the Berkshires entered the jail courtyard.

Their failure to hold the jail was the final blow to the rebels' hopes that day, and as was usually the case when reverses of this nature were suffered, anger turned inwards. On the night of the 12th/13th when it could not clearly be said who had the upper hand in terms of civil control, factions of the mob took time off from harrying us to settle old scores between each other. There was looting and arson in the city, but it was directed this time against native shops and houses, and even against persons. A dead body found in the morning could so easily be claimed as that of a "martyr in the cause of freedom" who had been beaten to death by the police or the military! There were also a few incidents in the cantonment where small groups of men who had escaped along side roads and found places of hiding, emerged after dark and caused slight damage along the railway line. That night, too, a fire broke out in one of the depots on the railway sidings.

By now, the Deputy Commissioner had received the instructions from his superiors to contest the rebellion in his district with the full weight of the forces available to him, and I had been informed of this development by my area commander. My own "private" instructions were that if in the next few hours I deemed that the civil authority was no longer operational, I had discretion to assume full command and declare martial law. However, from what I had seen that afternoon, I believed that between us White and I could restore order so long as we agreed that the situation had deteriorated to below the point at which either of us could be held responsible for a text-book reply to every incident. I had told my area commander this, and added that my greatest concern was with the situation in Dibrapur which, after the day's experiences in Mayapore, I took an increasingly serious view of.

I had a short meeting with White late that night. This was one of the several meetings which I have no really detailed recollection of, because they were now all taking place hurriedly and in an atmosphere of urgency, but I do recall his strained face and his immediate question on seeing me, "Well, you're taking over, I suppose?" I said, "Do you request that?" He shook his head, but agreed to my sending, on the morrow, a force to Dibrapur by the direct road south from Mayapore. But the area commander phoned me again that night from his headquarters and asked me to approach Dibrapur from the north-west on foot from the demolished bridge which, meanwhile, was to be repaired as quickly as possible by the engineers so that normal communications could be re-established along the road as soon as Dibrapur was pacified.

The Ranpurs were held up constantly along that short ten-mile stretch of road beyond the bridge by road blocks and home-made "land-mines" from which they suffered several casualties. In this way, my belief that Dibrapur had been chosen as the stronghold of a planned uprising was upheld and it was not until the morning of the 17th that I was able to report to the Deputy Commissioner that the town was once again in the hands of legally constituted forces. To assist the Ranpurs I had to send a company of the Pankots along the direct route southwards through Tanpur, and by and large the operation assumed something of the nature of a full-dress military attack. I declared martial law in Dibrapur on the night of the 13th when the Ranpurs first entered the town. For three days they were engaged in restoring law and order. On the 17th an officer on the Deputy Commissioner's staff again took control on behalf of the civil authority, and those of our agents who had appeared to co-operate with the rebels (the Indian sub-divisional officer, a magistrate, and several constables) were brought back to Mayapore to be dealt with in the first instance by the Deputy Commissioner. This was the occasion when the sub-divisional officer, by restoring money he said he had hidden to stop it falling into the rebels' hand, was not proceeded against.

In the interim, throughout the district the rebellion had passed through increasingly violent stages of appearing virtually uncontrollable to a state when we could feel that the impetus that had set it in motion had been successfully counteracted. In any physical conflict the initial driving power needed to take active steps always seems to provide one with one's sharpest memories. Discipline and drill then take over and come into their own, proving their worth, but providing the individual with no especially memorable recollections. But I do recall that on the 14th of August, another serious attempt to penetrate the civil lines was made in the names of the "Martyrs of the Bibighar and the Mandir Gate Bridge".

One could not help but be moved on this occasion by the spectacle of crowds in which so many women, young and old, exposed themselves to the threat of wounds or even death. One detected in the attempts made on the 14th a closer adherence to the Mahatma's principles of non-violence. It was as if, overnight, these simple townspeople had become disenchanted with leaders who had encouraged them to grab any weapon ready to hand and to believe that the police and the soldiers could be overcome by such means. Now they came in a spirit of unarmed defiance, carrying banners which exhorted us to Quit India and deliver to them the "innocent victims" of the Bibighar Gardens. The crowd that attempted to cross the Bibighar bride was composed largely of women and children and so touching was the sight of them that our men were reluctant to fire, even although while the women were to the fore, the orders were to fire over their heads. I noticed a soldier of the Berkshires break ranks to comfort a little girl who was running up and down looking for her mother, one of the many women, no doubt, who had prostrated themselves on the road so that the soldiers would have to step over them when pressing forward to clear the bridge.

There is little doubt that the affair of the assault on Miss Manners in the Bibighar Gardens gave the population a "popular" rallying cry, but I never took seriously the arguments which were put forward to prove that it was the action taken by the police to "avenge" the rape that caused the riots in the town. The stories that the six arrested men had been brutally treated were, I am sure, quite without foundation, although once again I would add a reminder that the police, apart from the most senior officers, such as the District Superintendent, were themselves Indians, and there have been – it must be admitted – occasions in our history when white officials have been unfairly blamed for the actions of their native subordinates whom "by the book" it was their responsibility to control. I doubt that even the Indians, however, took seriously the tale that was told about one or several of the arrested men (all Hindus) being "forced to eat beef". It is true that in the police you would find a fairly high proportion of Muslims, but if the populace had really thought the beef-feeding story was true, that would have given rise at once to a rumour that Muslim members of the police were responsible and hence to the kind of communal disturbance we were fortunate to be spared at this juncture. Such tales, in relation to the Bibighar affair, were no doubt the result of gossip after the event, when peace had been restored. Certainly no tales of this kind came to my notice at the time, and when they did there seemed to me to be no point in investigating them, which in any case it would not have been my job to do.

Unfortunately, as I think it to have been, the seriousness of the uprising in Mayapore which took all of us every ounce of our energy to combat, denied the authorities the proper chance to pursue and extend the evidence against the men who had been arrested for the rape, and the inability of the girl herself to offer evidence leading to identification left the case in a judicially unsatisfactory state. There was never cause to remove the suspects to the greater security of the Berkshires' lines, but, if they were truly guilty (and my mind remained open on that score) they must have counted themselves lucky to be disposed of in the way they were. The most that could be done, relying upon the evidence of their past activities and associations, was to deal with them under the Defence of India Rules and accordingly this was done. As for the attack upon the mission teacher and the murder of her Indian subordinate, here again a failure quickly to identify any of the men arrested that day in Tanpur as those responsible, led possibly to a corresponding failure of justice, although eventually one or two men suffered the supreme penalty.

According to official statements published later, the number of occasions throughout the country on which the police and/or military had to fire upon the populace totalled over 500. Over 60,000 people were arrested, over 1,000 killed and over 3,000 severely injured. Indian authorities dispute these figures in regard to the numbers killed and put the figure even as high as 40,000! In the case of my own troops the figures were as follows: Number of incidents in which firing was resorted to: 23 (12 of these having been in Dibrapur). Number of people estimated as killed as the result of firing: 12. Number of people estimated as wounded as a result of firing: 53. I think these figures are proof of the restraint our men showed. I do not have figures relating to those arrested, because this was the task of the police. Nor do I have the figures of those in the district who were punished, for instance by whipping, a subject on which the Indians have always been tender-minded. The damage done in the towns and outlying areas of the district was severe and it was several weeks before order had been completely restored in the sense that a civil authority would minimally recognise as "order" – that is to say, an uninterrupted system of communication, full and open access by road and rail from one point to the other, and local communities wholly in the control of the police and under the jurisdiction of legally appointed magistrates. As White said, it was, finally, the people themselves who suffered from the disruption to their normal peaceful way of life. It is said, for instance, that the Bengal famine of 1943 might have been averted or, if not averted, at least alleviated had the "rebellion" never taken place. There were many cases of thoughtless destruction of shops and warehouses and food stores.

I am conscious that I have written perhaps over-lengthily of what in terms of my life as a whole was an affair neither of long duration nor of special significance from a military point of view. Perhaps the deep and lasting impression it has made on me can be related to the fact that it came at a time when I was facing the kind of personal loss it is still difficult to speak of. There were moments – as I went about these daily tasks – when I felt that my life, simple as it had been, had unkindly already distributed the whole of its rewards to me; and, seeing the strength and unity of the tide that seemed to be flowing against us, I could not help asking myself the questions: In what way are we at fault? In what way have I personally failed?

It was on the 18th of August, the day after I had been able to report to the Deputy Commissioner that Dibrapur was at last restored to his authority, and that my officers – by now scattered in many different areas of the district – believed that the worst of the insurrection was over – that a telegram reached me from Tubby Carter, ordering me to come at once to Rawalpindi. The telegram had been delayed because of the troubles, even although it originated in military channels. I knew, of course, that by "ordering" me he was simply advising me of the necessity of returning. I spoke at once on the telephone to the area commander and he gave me leave to travel immediately by any means I was able. It was already evening. I left the brigade in the capable hands of young Ewart Mackay and the CO of the Pankots, and travelled all through the night to Calcutta in my staff car, not trusting to the railway, and, I admit, wearing a loaded pistol in my holster. I was accompanied by my batman as well as the driver. My batman was a Hindu, but the driver was a Muslim. I thought how salutary a lesson it was to those who talked so readily of "differences" that in that car there could be found – travelling in perfect amity – a representative of each of the three main "powers" in India – Hindu, Muslim and Christian. The journey itself, however, seemed endless. In the dark, with all these troubles freshly behind me I pondered the immensity, the strange compelling beauty of India.

Even now, that night remains in my mind as totally unreal. I did not reach Calcutta until well into the morning of the 19th, although the driver – sensing that something was personally wrong for me – drove recklessly. Armed too, I think he would have helped to sell our lives dearly had we been attacked. I went at once, on reaching Cal, to my old friend Wing Commander "Pug" Jarvis, who had been warned by Tubby and had expected my arrival the previous morning. It was nearly midnight before the RAF plane he had got me on to took off from Dum Dum. Fortunately it was going direct to Chaklala, with only a short delay in Delhi. In the early morning of the 20th I was met by Tubby at Chaklala. He drove me direct to his bungalow and then to the resting place which she had come to just the day before, too soon for me to be present, which was an alleviation of my grief I had sorely hoped to be granted.

I returned to Mayapore in the second week of September, but about two weeks after my return I received orders to take command of a brigade which was already in the field, east of the Brahmaputra, preparing to face the real enemy. Of this brigade, and our preparations for action against the Japanese, I will write in another chapter. But in this welcome translation to a more immediately active role, I detected the understanding hand of my old friend in Rawalpindi, who knew that for me only one kind of duty was now possible.

II

The Civil

An edited transcript of written and spoken comments by Robin White, CIE (Ex-ICS)

(1) I was interested in what you sent me of the late Brigadier Reid's unpublished memoirs describing his relationship with the civil authority in Mayapore in 1942. I didn't keep a diary, as Reid appears to have done, and it is a long time since I thought much about any of the events in question, but I am sure that from a military point of view his account is a viable enough reconstruction of what happened. From the civil point of view there are of course some inaccuracies, or any-

way gaps in the narrative or alternative interpretations, that would need attention if a more general and impersonal picture were required to emerge.

I doubt, however, that there is much I myself can contribute all this time after. I have not been in India since 1948 and have long since lost touch with both old friends and old memories. I can confirm that Ronald Merrick did indeed succeed in obtaining his release from the Indian Police, but I was not concerned in any way with this and knew of no official reason why the authorities should have agreed, in his case, to let him go. He was commissioned into an Indian regiment, I think, and was wounded in Burma in either 1944 or 1945. As I recollect it he was killed during the communal riots that attended partition in 1947.

I was interested to hear of your recent visit to Mayapore and glad to learn that Lili Chatterjee is still living in the MacGregor House, a name I had quite forgotten – although I remember the house itself. I am glad, too, to hear that Srinivasan is still alive and remembers our association. I never saw him again after the morning when I had to order him and other members of the local Congress party sub-committee to be taken in custody. I knew little of the "Sanctuary" run by Sister Ludmila, which I'd also forgotten about, but I'm pleased to hear that now, as *The Manners Memorial Home for Indian Boys and Girls,* it perpetuates the name of a family which was once highly thought of in the province. You do not say in what way the Home was founded. Presumably on money left either by Miss Manners or her aunt, Lady Manners. Is it known, by the way, what happened to the child, if it survived?

I return Brigadier Reid's manuscript with many thanks. I was touched by several passages in it. Neither my wife nor I knew of the illness of Mrs. Reid until we saw a notice of her death a few days after he was summoned back to Rawalpindi. We knew that his son was a prisoner-of-war, of course. It was something I bore constantly in mind in my dealings with him. I'm sorry to realise that the son also died. There were many occasions when Reid annoyed me (obviously he felt the same about me) and others when I respected him, but on the whole he was never quite my sort of person. We rather got the impression that his posting to the command of a brigade in the field was a move on the part of the military authorities to disembarrass Mayapore of a man whose reputation, after the troubles, was thought to have become locally over-controversial. I'm glad to feel that Reid was not given this impression himself. Since you did not send me the subsequent chapters of his book, I don't know what he had to say about his eventual return to a desk job. I believe he never did attain his objective of a "confrontation with the true enemy". For a time, naturally, I followed what I could of his fortunes with some interest. But, as I say, this is all a long time ago and my own career in India came to an end not many years after.

I am sorry that I cannot be more helpful.

*

(2) I have had a letter from Lili Chatterjee, and gather it is from you that she got my address. She tells me that at the end of your stay in Mayapore this year, she delivered into your hands, as well as two letters, a journal written by Miss Manners during the time she lived with her aunt in Kashmir, awaiting the birth of the child. Lili Chatterjee tells me that for some time she kept the existence of the journal secret from you, and that she would not have handed it over unless she had finally made up her mind that your interest in what you call the Bibighar Gardens affair was genuine. I gather that she received the journal from Lady Manners several years after the events it describes, and that Lady Manners, herself then approaching death, felt that of all the people in the world whom she knew Lili Chatterjee alone should take possession of it. Lili tells me that the journal makes it clear exactly what happened.

I gather that your concern with this affair arose from a reading of Brigadier Reid's unpublished book, which came into your hands as a result of your known interest in this period of British-Indian history. Lili tells me that you have been to some trouble to trace persons who would be in a position either to describe from personal experience, or to comment on, on the basis of informed personal opinion, the events of that year in Mayapore. I gather for instance that in an attempt to "reconstruct" the story of Miss Crane, the Mission School superintendent, you visited, among other places, the headquarters of the organisation to which she had belonged, and browsed among her unclaimed relics, I met Miss Crane once or twice, and my wife knew her quite well in connexion with local committee work. I also met Miss Manners on a number of occasions, but I'm afraid I knew almost nothing of the man Kumar. I met him only casually, twice at most. Jack Poulson would have been able to tell you more about him because after the arrests I gave Poulson the job of conducting the various inquiries. Unfortunately I can't help you to trace Poulson. He emigrated to New Zealand, I believe, and I have not heard of him for many years. However, Lili tells me that you have traced and talked to a friend of Kumar's in England, a man called Lindsey – the same Lindsey, perhaps, who according to Reid's account applied for a transfer from the Brigade Intelligence staff in Mayapore? My recollection is that Kumar was originally sent to the jail in the provincial capital, but if as you say his aunt left Mayapore years ago and not even his old uncle or Srinivasan have heard of him since then, it looks as though upon his release he began an entirely new life somewhere in India or, perhaps, in Pakistan.

In view of what Lili Chatterjee has told me I am willing – subject to a prior understanding that my memory cannot be absolutely relied upon – to have a talk.

*

(3) Thank you for having given me the opportunity before we meet to read a copy of the short extract from Daphne Manners's journal in which she describes what actually happened in the Bibighar, and the letter she wrote to her aunt about Merrick's "proposal". Thank you too for letting me see what you call the deposition of the man Vidyasagar. I did not know this man at all, and at this distance his name means nothing to me. I do remember Laxminarayan and the newspaper. I was interested to hear that Laxminarayan is still living in Mayapore, and I'm glad he was able to put you in touch with Vidyasagar before you left India. Miss Manners was obviously telling the truth (I mean, writing the truth, in her journal) and if Vidyasagar's "deposition" is also true – and there seems small reason to doubt it since there could hardly be much point in his lying at this stage – then I can only express a deep sense of shock. One's own responsibility isn't shrugged off lightly. I feel perhaps that I should balance any adverse picture by explaining the ways in which I thought Merrick a responsible and hard-working officer. However, I gather from what you say that on the basis of the various documents – Reid's memoirs, Miss Manners's journal and

letters, and Sister Ludmila's recollections, not to mention Vidyasagar's deposition – you have pretty well made your mind up about the central characters in the affair and particularly about the kind of man Merrick was, and that my own contribution to your investigations should be confined to more general matters. A reading of these documents – which I now return – has certainly had much of the effect on me that you suggested it might. I find myself remembering things I have not thought of for years, and so perhaps, after all, I can be of some help.

*

(4) *Verbal Transcript*

Areas of dangerous fallibility between a policy and its pursuit? Yes, that sounds like Srinivasan. Is it this sort of dangerous area you want to try and map? Not only? I see. Very well, let's concentrate on the association between Reid and myself. But you'll have to ask the questions.

Well, I made one or two notes about inaccuracies in Reid's account, but what struck me finally was that quite apart from Reid's simple soldier attitude which antagonised me again just as much on paper as when we met face to face, he had somehow managed to make everything that happened look logical in his own terms, and I remembered more and more clearly the feeling I myself had in those days of not being able to rehearse the sequence of events that had led to a situation that seemed to be logical in itself but jolly well wasn't.

Every time Reid came into my office with that look on his face of being ready and eager to straighten us all out I felt like a man who had been playing a fish that might turn out to be either a minnow or a whale, and Reid's entrance, or even a telephone call from him, or from one of the officers on his staff, was just like someone suddenly tapping me on the elbow in midstream and telling me, quite inaccurately, what I was doing wrong. He had a genius for smothering any but your bluntest instincts, which is why I once lost my temper and told him rather rudely to leave me alone. He didn't bring that out in his book, but I'm not sure that this particular omission couldn't be traced to the fact that he had a hide like a rhinocerous and my show of temper had as much effect on him as the bite of a gnat. I know that his book gives an impression of a not insensitive man, but he was sensitive, broadly, only to major issues and *grand* emotions. In his daily contact with other human beings he did tend to bear pretty much the proportional weight of a sledgehammer to a pin.

When I first met Reid I saw him as a man it was going to take a lot of patience and energy to restrain. As so often happened when a man was taken from behind a desk, he had formed an opinion about what he was always calling his task or his role – as if it were pretty well cut and dried and took precedence over anyone else's, and I thought that having formed his opinion of his task he was also determined to carry it out *in toto*, however irrelevant some of its aspects turned out to be. I remember saying to my wife that if the Indians didn't start a rebellion Reid would be forced to invent one just so that by suppressing it he would feel he'd done his whole duty. She told me I'd better treat him gently because, as we all knew by then, his son was missing in Burma. I think I hoped as much as he did that the poor boy would turn up, and was even more concerned than he by the news that young Reid was a prisoner-of-war in the hands of the Japanese.

You could say that my association with Reid was fairly typical of the conflict between the civil and the military, so perhaps I was no less guilty of conforming to a generalised pattern of behaviour than he was.

No, you're quite right to correct me. I don't mean at all that the Civil were always progressive and the Military reactionary. I've fallen into my own trap, haven't I? Let me put it right. The drama Reid and I played out was that of the conflict between Englishmen who liked and admired Indians and believed them capable of self-government, and Englishmen who disliked or feared or despised them, or, just as bad, were indifferent to them as individuals, thought them extraneous to the business of living and working over there, except in their capacity as servants or soldiers or as dots on the landscape. On the whole civil officers were much better informed about Indian affairs than their opposite numbers in the military. In the later stages of our administration it would have been rare to find in the civil a man of Reid's political simplicity.

Put my finger on the main weakness of Reid's analysis of the political situation in India from the beginning of the 'thirties –? No, because analysis is the wrong word. He had an attitude, that was all. We all had an attitude but his struck me as pretty childish. It was emotional and non-analytical. But I was always taught that politics were people, and a lot of Englishmen thought as Reid thought and felt as he felt, which was why even when he was getting my goat most with his talk of Indians and Englishmen having to sink their differences in order to beat the Jap I recognised the *force* of his attitude. After all the Japanese were practically hammering at the door, and even though what Reid meant by Indians and English sinking differences was the Indians doing all the sinking, calling a halt to their political demands and the English maintaining the *status quo* and sinking nothing – one couldn't help admitting that the situation was very similar to the one a quarrelsome household would face if they looked out of the window and saw burglars trying to get in, or a gang of hooligans preparing to burn the house down. The head of the house would immediately feel obliged to take a lead and stand no nonsense from inside.

But straightforward as that situation might look – just a question of ceasing to squabble and presenting a united front to repel Japanese boarders – its straightforwardness depends on the nature of the squabbling in the house, doesn't it? On the whole I dislike analogies, but let's pursue this one a bit further. Let's imagine that the people in the house are a pretty mixed bunch, and that those who have the least say in how things are run are those the house belonged to originally. The present self-appointed owner has been saying for years that eventually, when he is satisfied that they've learned how to keep the roof repaired, the foundations secure and the whole in good order, he'll get out and give them the house back, because that is his job in life: to teach others how to make something of themselves and their property. He's been saying this long enough to believe it himself but ruling the household with a sufficiently confusing mixture of encouraging words and repressive measures to have created a feeling among his "family" that by and large he's kidding, and that the only language he understands is the language *he* uses – a combination of physical and moral pressure. He's also said he'll leave – but stayed put – long enough to create factions below stairs among the people who hope to inherit or rather get the house back. He hasn't necessarily intended to create these factions, but their existence does seem to suit his book. Deny people something they want, over a longish period, and they naturally start disagreeing about precisely what it is they *do* want. So he likes nothing better than to give private interviews to deputations from these separate factions and to use the arguments of minority factions as moral levers to weaken the demands put forward by the majority faction. He's got into the habit of locking up over-vociferous members of all factions in the basement and only letting them out when they go on hunger strike like Gandhi used to.

We were in India for what we could get out of it. No one any longer denies that, but I think there are two main aspects of the British–Indian affair which we prefer to forget or ignore. The first was that we were originally *able* to exploit India because the first confrontation – to use Reid's cant word – was that of an old, tired civilisation that was running down under the Moghuls and a comparatively new energetic civilisation that had been on the up-grade ever since the Tudors. English people tend to think of India as a Victorian acquisition, but it was originally really an Elizabethan one. And you only have to consider the difference between the Elizabethans and the Victorians to get an idea of the changes that took place in our attitude to our prize and therefore of the second aspect of the affair which we forget or ignore – the confusion surrounding the moral issue. The moral issue is bound to arise eventually and grow, and finally appear to take precedence in any long-standing connexion between human beings, especially if their status is unequal. The *onus* of moral leadership falls naturally on the people who rank as superior, but just as a people over-endowed with power can explain that power away as God-given and start talking about morality and the special need to uplift the poor and ignorant – the people they have power *over* – so can a people who have had too long an experience of what today is called under-privilege pass the buck to *their* god. At almost precisely the same time that the English were developing their theories of the White Man's burden to help them bear the weight of its responsibility, the Hindus and the Muslims were taking a long hard look at *their* religions, not to explain their servitude but to help them to end it. A lot of nonsense has been talked, you know, about the communal problem in India as if we waited in vain throughout the centuries of our influence for the Hindus and Muslims to settle their differences, but the communal problem never really became a problem until Hindu and Muslim revivalists and reformers got to work in the nineteenth century, in much the same way our own did, to see what comfort and support and ways forward could be found in these old philosophies. I think the English, however unconsciously and unintentionally, created the division between Muslim India and Hindu India. More recently in Kenya we shrieked accusations of barbarism at the Kikuyu for their Mau Mau rebellion, but hit a man in the face long enough and he turns for help to his racial memory and tribal gods. The Hindus turned to theirs, the Muslims to theirs. It wasn't from *social* awareness that Gandhi identified himself with the outcastes of the Hindu religion. Untouchability was foreign to original Hinduism and in this attempted return by a subject people to the source of their religious inspiration it was bound to happen that untouchability should be chosen as the intended victim of a revival, and non-violence re-emerge as a main tenet of its revitalisation. The Muslims' investigation of their religion was more dangerous, because Mohammed preached Holy War against the infidel. I think the English were perversely attracted to the idea of that danger. I always found it interesting that on the whole most English people were happier consorting with Muslims than with Hindus, but then fundamentally we've always been a bit embarrassed by the "weakness" of Christianity. We saw the same weakness in Hinduism, but a sort of Eastern version of muscular Christianity in the religion of Allah.

In those days I was intensely *puzzled* by Gandhi. On the whole I distrust great men. I think one should. I certainly distrusted Gandhi – but not in the way Reid, for instance, distrusted him. I distrusted Gandhi because I couldn't see how a man who wielded such power and influence could remain uninhibited by it, and always make the right decisions for the right reasons. And yet I always felt his appeal to my conscience behind even my severest doubts about his intentions.

There's one story about Gandhi that I didn't know at the time, and it's particularly interested me since. Perhaps you know it too?

Yes. That's it. Do you think it relevant? It strikes me as fundamental to an understanding of the man. I mean to be declared outcaste by his community merely because he expressed an intention as a young man to go to England to study law! And did you know this, that the leaders of his community declared in advance that any fellow going to see him off or wishing him good luck would be punished with a fine. Something like a rupee each. And think how long he was abroad between first departure and return. Nearly a quarter of a century altogether. I wonder what he thought of India when he eventually got back to it after all those years in England and all those years in South Africa? Do you think his heart sank? Even though he returned a hero because of what he had done for the Indians in South Africa where he first initiated *satyagraha*. I mean India is far from what Brigadier Reid called salubrious. Perhaps Gandhi took one look at it and thought, Good God, is this what I've been longing to return to? I mention this because presently we come to the important question of *doubt* in public life.

I suppose it's also relevant that he returned to India just at the time when friendly co-operation between the British and the Indians was reaching the peak of its last notable phase, early in the First World War. If I remember correctly he sailed from South Africa to England in the summer of 1914 and got there just about the time we declared war on Germany. He told Indian students in London that England's predicament was not India's opportunity – a healthy opinion which Nehru borrowed twenty-five years later – and all through the Great War, in India, he was in favour of the recruitment of young Indians to the services. By and large India really went all out to help and not hinder us in that war. There was a strong smell of freedom for them in the air, and of self-government or measures of self-government which they could earn by helping to fight Britain's enemies, which they seemed happy to do anyway. It was in 1917, wasn't it, that we actually declared specifically that the goal for India was Dominion status? I think Gandhi got back to India early in 1915, and rather crossed swords – as Reid would have said – with people like Annie Besant. But even as early as this he proved himself to be something of an enigma. In his first public speech he said he was ashamed to have to speak in English in order to be understood by a largely Indian audience. Most Indian leaders prided themselves on their English. He criticised a prince who had just referred to India's poverty, and sarcastically pointed out the splendour of the surroundings – they were laying the foundation stone of a new University. Benares? Yes, the Hindu University in Benares. Then he said there was a lot of work to be done before India could think of self-government. That was one in the eye for the politically self-satisfied! At the same time he pointed at Government detectives in the crowd and asked why Indians were so distrusted. That was a snub to the Raj. He referred to the young Indian anarchists and said he was also an anarchist, but not one who believed in violence, although without violence he admitted the anarchists wouldn't have managed to get the decision to partition Bengal reversed. What a mixture of ideas this seemed to be! Mrs. Besant tried to interrupt but the audience of students asked him to continue. The fellow in charge of the meeting told him to explain himself more clearly and he said what he wanted to do was to get rid of the awful suspicion that surrounded every move made in India. He wanted love and trust, and freedom to say what was in the heart without fear of the consequences. Most of the people on the platform left – I suppose they felt compromised or outraged or just publicly embarrassed – so he stopped speaking and afterwards the British stepped in. The police ordered him out of the city.

It must have been as it would be at a political meeting here, or in a television interview, if a well-known man actually got up or faced the camera and said exactly what was in his mind, without worrying how many times he seemed to contradict himself, and certainly without thinking of his own reputation, in a genuinely creative attempt to break through the sense of *pre-arranged* emotions and reactions that automatically accompanies any general gathering of people. In India that sense of pre-arrangement was always particularly strong because the Indians are normally the politest men and women in the world, which is probably why at a pinch they can be among the most hysterical and blood-thirsty. I suppose the widespread use of a foreign language has exaggerated their natural politeness. I've often wondered whether things wouldn't have gone infinitely better for us if all our civil servants had been compelled to acquire complete fluency both in Hindi and in the main language of their province and forced to conduct every phase of government in that language. Gandhi was right, of course, it was shameful that in talking to university students he had to speak a foreign language. The reason he had to speak it wasn't only because all the young men there had achieved their present status by learning and reading in English, but because it was probably the only language they *all* shared in common. We did nothing really to integrate communities, except by building railways between one and the other to carry their wealth more quickly into our own pockets.

Gandhi, you know, always struck me as the only man in public life anywhere in the world who had a highly developed instinct and capacity for thinking aloud – and this was an instinct and a capacity that seldom got smothered by other instincts. I'm sure it led eventually to the chap being completely misunderstood. People in public life are supposed to project what today we call an image, and ideally the image has to be constant. Gandhi's never was. The phases he went through just in the years 1939 to 1942 were inconstant enough for history to have labelled him as sufficiently politically confused to rank either as a band-wagoner or a half-baked pain in the neck. But I think what he was actually doing was trying to bring into the open the element of *doubt* about ideas and attitudes which we all undergo but prefer to keep quiet about.

And don't you think that can be partially traced back to the depression he must have felt way back in the nineteenth century at being able to leave his homeland only as an outcaste? Don't you think that the element of doubt entered very strongly at that moment as well as on his return? "Am I doing the right thing?" he must have asked himself. After all he was only nineteen or so. To go to England and study for the law was something he could only do by being publicly rejected by his caste-community. Caste probably had a truly religious significance for him in those days. Going to England was significant only in terms of his worldly ambition. No man is without ambition, but perhaps few men have been forced to doubt the power for good that ambition represents as much as Gandhi was forced to do. I felt in the end that he was working out a personal salvation in public all the time. And of course the kind of doubt a man has of himself, of his actions, of his thinking, plays a prominent but invariably secret part in the actual events of the day. It was right to bring it into the open for once. He was never afraid to say openly that he'd changed his mind or been wrong, or that he was thinking about the problem and would only express his views after he'd worked out some kind of solution.

What would have happened, I wonder, if I had publicly represented my doubts about the wisdom of imprisoning Congress leaders in August 1942? God knows. I can't have been the only district officer who felt that it was the last thing it was wise to do or the only one to write long confidential memoranda on the subject to his commissioner. But I didn't have the nerve to stand up in the open and rehearse in public the pros and cons of doing what I was instructed to do.

I sometimes wish that on August the 9th I'd gone to the

temple square beyond the Mandir Gate bridge with a megaphone, called out to the people there and said, "Look, Government tells me to imprison X Y and Z because the Indian National Congress has endorsed the Mahatma's resolution calling on us to Quit India and leave her to God, or to anarchy, in other words, so far as we are concerned, to the Japanese. But if I imprison these men, who will lead you? Will you be glad to be rid of them? Or will you feel lost? Congress talks about non-violent non-co-operation, but what does that mean? How won't you co-operate? How will you withhold co-operation without defending yourselves against us when we try to *force* you to co-operate? We'll try to force you because we believe we're fighting for our lives. When you defend yourselves how will you do so without violence? If I threw down this megaphone and struck one of your young men on the face, what would you do? What would he do? If he does nothing and I strike him again, what then? What if I then do it again and again, until his face is bloody? Until he is dead? Will you just stand by and watch? The Mahatma says so, it seems, but do *you* say so?"

But of course I never did go to the temple square with a megaphone. Doubts and all I locked up X Y and Z. And I think it was wrong. The men who ordered me to lock them up had probably had similar doubts before initiating the policy, but once it was laid on none of us was left with any official alternative but to carry it out.

I suppose true anarchy in public life is inaction arising out of the element of doubt as opposed to action following the element of decision. And of course between the doubt, the decision, the action and the consequences, I suppose you find what Srinivasan calls the areas of dangerous fallibility. Well, that's not a shattering discovery. We all know it. But Gandhi had the *courage* to operate openly on the ground of the dangerous areas, didn't he? Is that what you're getting at? Wise as we can be after the event, no one at the time pointed out that this was what he was doing. If he stepped too noticeably out of the acceptable line he was locked up, but released when it was thought his talents would be more valuable politically on a free rein.

What is clear to me beyond *any* doubt is that we turned him fundamentally into a power harmful to our policies when we resorted to the repressive measures of the Rowlatt Act, immediately after the Great War at a time when he and all

Indians had every reason to expect a major advance towards self-government as a reward for co-operating so freely in the war with Germany. Were we mad? Or plain stupid? Or merely perfidious? Or terrified? Or just common-or-garden cocky after victory, thick-skinned and determined to give away nothing? What in hell was the good of declaring Dominion status as our aim for India in 1917 and not much more than a year later instituting trial without jury for political crimes and powers of detention at provincial level under the Defence of India Rules, ostensibly to deal with so-called anarchists but in practice to make any expression of free-will and free opinion technically punishable? What kind of a "dominion" was that?

Well, you remember the result: riots, and then General Dyer at Amritsar and a return to distrust and fear and suspicion, and Gandhi emerging as the Mahatma, the one man who might provide an answer – but now it was going to be an Indian answer, not a British one. I'm sorry. I still get hot under the collar when I think about 1919. And I'm still deeply ashamed, after all these years.

No, I was too young at the time. I went out to India as a young civilian as we called ourselves in 1921. I had hardly a thought in my head. I'd done my swotting and passed the exams, and read all the myth and legend. I wanted nothing better in those days than to get out into my first sub-division under the old pipul tree, puffing at a pipe and fancying myself no end as a promising administrator who would straighten out young and old and be remembered as White Sahib, become a legend myself and still be talked about fifty years after I'd gone as the fellow who brought peace and prosperity to the villages.

But of course I had to face reality at once. I simply wasn't cut out for paternalism. My superiors were the last of that breed. I disliked my first district officer. He probably didn't deserve it. But I hated India – the real India behind the pipe-puffing myth. I hated the loneliness, and the dirt, the smell, the conscious air of superiority that one couldn't get through the day without putting on like a sort of protective purdah. I hated Indians because they were the most immediately available target and couldn't hit back except in subtle ways that made me hate them even more.

And then one day, I remember it clearly, I was touring the district with the land settlement officer, going from village to village. On horseback, old style. I was fed to the teeth with village accountants who cringed and tahsildars who presumed and cringed all in the same breath, and I was critical of the settlement officer who obviously felt and acted like God going for a casual stroll, giving with the right hand and taking with the left. Then something went wrong with the camp *bandobast*. We were bogged down in some god-forsaken village and had to spend the night in a mud-hut. I was ready to cry from frustration and from my own sense of inadequacy. The settlement officer was drinking toddy with the village elders still playing at Christ and the Apostles, and I was alone in the hut. My bowels were in a terrible state and I couldn't face anything, let alone toddy. I was lying on a charpoy, without a mosquito net, and suddenly saw this middle-aged Indian woman standing in the doorway watching me. When our eyes met she made *namaste* and then disappeared for a moment, and came back with a bowl of curds and a spoon.

I was on my dignity at once, and waved her away, but she came to the bedside and spooned up a helping of the curds and held it out and made me eat, just as if I were her nephew or son and needed building up. She said nothing and I couldn't even look at her – only at her black hands and the white curds. Afterwards I fell asleep and when I woke up I felt better and wondered whether I hadn't dreamed it all, until I saw the bowl of unfinished curds covered with a cloth, on a brass tray by the bedside and a flower on the tray next to the bowl. It was morning then, and the settlement officer was snoring in the other bed. I felt that I had been given back my humanity, by a nondescript middle-aged Indian woman. I felt that the curds and the flowers were for affection, not tribute, affection big enough to include a dash of well-meant motherly criticism, the suggestion that my indisposition could be overcome easily enough once I'd learned I had no real enemies. I remember standing in the open doorway and breathing in deeply; and getting it: the scent behind the smell. They had brass pots of hot water ready for my bathe. Before the bathe I was sat down on an old wooden chair and shaved by the *nai,* the barber, without soap, just his fingers and warm water and a cut-throat. He scraped the razor all over my face and forehead, even over the eyelids. I held my breath, waiting for the cut that would blind me. But it was all gentle and efficient, a kind of early morning *puja*, and afterwards my face felt newly made and I went to the bathing enclosure and scooped water out of the brass pots of hot water that stood waiting. Brooke had the right word for it. The benison of hot water. Later I looked among the women but couldn't tell which of them had come into the hut the night before and fed me as she would have fed her own son. There was another flower on the pommel of my saddle. It embarrassed me. But I loved it too. I looked at the settlement officer. He had no flower and hadn't noticed mine. As we rode away I looked back, and waved. The people made no move in reply, but I felt it coming from them – the good wish, the challenge to do well by them and by myself. I've never forgotten that. I expect that afterwards the bowl and spoon I'd eaten from had to be thrown away.

No. One did tend to spend the whole of one's career in the same province, but that village was not in the district where I eventually became Deputy Commissioner. Why? Did you think it lay close to Dibrapur?

*

(5) Thank you for sending me the edited transcript of the recording of our interview. I see you have ironed out a lot of the inconsistencies and repetitions but haven't been able to disguise the way that I kept leading away from the point. You were obviously right to end the interview when we got round finally to the business of Dibrapur, which probably needs more careful discussion than it would have got just then.

I don't know about Mary Tudor and Calais as you put it, but I certainly *remember* Dibrapur. There was terrible poverty there, the kind you would get in any region where an old source of wealth has retreated farther and farther. In the nineteenth century it was the headquarters of the district. I don't recall exactly when it was that they began to mine the coal, but gradually these particular veins were worked out and the adjoining district inherited the wealth and prosperity. Labour was still drawn from Dibrapur, but in decreasing quantities.

In any depressed area, anywhere in the world, you can assume that emotions and attitudes will be exaggerated. In one respect Reid was right and some kind of organised force *was* at work in Dibrapur, but how much was due to planning and how much to intelligent seizing of opportunity never was clear. Where he was wrong, I'm sure, was in attributing the force to an underground force of *Congress*, and I think Vidyasagar's deposition bears this out, and where I was right, I suspect, was in believing that *any* force of Indian national life could have been controlled by the Congress. The majority of Indians (excluding wild young men like Vidyasagar) have always respected authority – how else could we have ruled millions with a few thousand? Congress was the shadow authority. If we had not banned the Congress committees and imprisoned their leaders at the centre and in most of the provinces, I'm convinced that there would have been no rebellion of the kind that occurred. Gandhi, you know, didn't expect to be arrested this time. Politically, "Quit India" was a sort of kite he flew. Morally, it was an appeal like a cry in the dark. But even if in places like Dibrapur there had been rebellion I am equally convinced that to contain it I would only have had to appeal to a man like Srinivassan for instance to go there and talk to the people and exhort them to non-violent non-co-operative methods. Strikes, hartal, that sort of thing. I honestly believe that the Indian is emotionally predisposed against violence. That would explain the hysteria that usually marks his surrender to it. He then goes beyond all ordinary bounds, like someone gone mad because he's destroying his own faith as well. We on the other hand are emotionally disposed *towards* violence, and have to work hard at keeping ourselves in order. Which is why at the beginning of our wars we've always experienced a feeling of relief and said things like, "Now we know where we stand." The other thing to remember about Indians, Hindus anyway, is that their religion teaches them that man, as man, is an illusion. I don't say that any more of them believe that than Christians believe Christ was the son of God or was talking practical sense when he said we should turn the other cheek. But just as the Christian ideal works on our Christian conscience while we're engaged in battering each other to death, or blowing each other up, so that we know that to do so is wrong, so I think when the Indians start battering each other they feel in the backs of their minds that the battering isn't quite real. I think this partly explains why unarmed mobs were always ready to face our troops and police. They themselves weren't real, the troops weren't real, the bullets were never fired and people didn't die except in a world that was an illusion itself. I agree that this doesn't explain why in such a non-existent world it was thought worth while opposing the troops in the first place.

But of course for me the people in the Dibrapur sub-division *were* real. They were bad farmers and poor shop-keepers. It wasn't their fault. The heyday of the coal-mines was pre-Great War, but that heyday denuded part of the land permanently and led to unploughed fields, and the splitting up of families. There were several villages in that area where there were practically no young men. They'd all gone to the mining areas in the adjacent district. You know the sort of thing that happens as well as I do. We made special efforts there – I remember talking to Miss Crane about them once, because she had one of her schools near Dibrapur – but there was a lot of apathy as well as a lot of resentment. The young Indian I had out there in his own sub-divisional headquarters was an extremely intelligent and capable man. It was the toughest sub-division in the district. He had a lot of problems but also a lot of *nous*. The fellow who appointed himself deputy commissioner was one of the local tahsildars who was also a local landowner. My own man had always had a lot of trouble with him. In his account Reid leaves a slight doubt in the reader's mind about the Indian sub-divisional officer's actual behaviour during the troubles. I know at the time people were going around saying that when it was all over the chap broke down in my office and spent hours crying and asking to be let off. No such thing. We talked the situation out quite unemotionally, and I was satisfied that short of sacri-ficing his life – which I wouldn't have expected any sane man to do – the sub-divisional officer had made the best of a bad job, managed to restrain the self-appointed deputy commis-sioner quite a bit, in spite of the fact that as so-called Judge he was more or less kept prisoner. And he certainly saved a size-able sum of money for the treasury. I expect the rumour about him crying arose from the fact that when we shook hands and parted there *were* tears in his eyes, and people prob-ably noticed them as he left my bungalow. I hadn't been kind to him, just fair, I hope, but Indians have never been ashamed of responding to fairness in a way an Englishman would be ashamed to.

But that is jumping ahead. I know there was a failure in our intelligence system to pinpoint in advance the men who emerged as local leaders in Dibrapur and succeeded in cutting the town off for several days. I suppose I did use the expres-sion "needles in a haystack" when talking about such people to Reid, but I don't actually remember doing so. The police in the Dibrapur sub-division were – perhaps not unexpectedly in view of the toughness of their job – of a lower morale than elsewhere. Some ran away, and one or two constables took over and sided with the rebels. As you will have gathered, everything happened pretty quickly and our police – never numerous – were scattered very thinly in proportion to the area and the size of the population. I agreed to Reid sending troops on the night of the 11th in the hope that their prompt appearance at that particular moment would be as inhibiting as the appearance of troops usually was. Reid rather underplays the attempts made that day by the civil authority to get into Dibrapur with police and magistrates, and says nothing about the road blocks on the *main* road. There were no blown bridges on the main road, but there was a series of felled trees that denied the road to the full use of transport, and the police found that the nearer they got to Dibrapur the less helpful the villagers were in helping them to clear the road. On the night in question the message I had had from Tanpur was to the effect that one truckload of police had "disappeared". It turned out later that they were locked up in the *kotwali* in one of the villages near Dibrapur. All the wires were down, of course, between Dibrapur and Tanpur.

The news of the blown bridge on Reid's flank road was certainly a poser, but I couldn't help being rather amused because he had made the use of the flank road sound so professional and clever, and suddenly there he was in danger of losing two 3-ton lorries and a 15-cwt truck and his wireless. And he was mad as hell. I hope that my amusement didn't sway my decision. I requested the withdrawal of the troops on that road because I felt that if the rebels had the initiative and the means to blow a bridge (a fairly harmless occupation in itself, just a matter of destroying a ton or so of brick and mortar!) a meeting of the rebels and troops whose tempers had shortened might result in the very kind of bloody affair I wanted to avoid. I know that my decision is open to question, but I made it, and stand by it, and I think it was right. If there had not then been pressure from above to use troops to the full I should certainly have left Dibrapur to stew even longer than I did. That intelligence officer, Davidson, was right when he suggested to Reid that my idea was for pacification to spread outwards from Mayapore. But Reid was jumping on hot bricks. I don't offer this as an excuse, although perhaps I do offer it as a contributory factor to any decision of mine that I still have doubts about. When you have a man like Reid constantly at your elbow you do tend to lose your concentration. I think I would have withstood his nagging if the provincial civil authority hadn't begun to press too. It is difficult actually to recall the real sense of urgency that arose in a few hours when reports were coming in pointing to an uprising that was getting out of hand. Anyway there was the pressure from Reid, the pressure from provincial headquarters, and the pressure of my own doubts. So I let Reid have his way about Dibrapur. His little battle there was by no means uncontrolled. I have no complaints or accusations on that score. But I don't think it was accompanied by any *special* restraint, and I still believe, as I believed then, that the deaths of men, women and children in Dibrapur could have been avoided if the town had been allowed to "stew" until the people themselves were of the temper (and it never took long for them to regain it) to make its *realignment* (and that is the proper word) just part of the day's routine.

Perhaps it was unfair that the action of his troops in Dibrapur (of which he does not give us the benefit of any detailed description in his book) should have been the main cause of the reputation Reid had afterwards for being over-controversial in the district "during the current phase of pacification". (The official jargon for "let's all be friends again".) My commissioner asked me to comment on Reid, confidentially. Complaints against any of us, civil or military, very quickly reached a high level as you know. I gave it as my opinion that Reid had at no time exceeded his duty and had been, throughout, a constant reassurance to me in the execution of my own. I added that, left to ourselves, and not ordered to make the fullest use of the means available, the force actually used might have been less and the result the same, or even better. I didn't see why Reid should carry the can back for people who had panicked at provincial headquarters. I don't think this comment of mine pleased anyone from the commissioner upwards. For a time I expected to be moved myself, but the luck or ill-luck of the game fixed on Reid – unless it were really true that his posting could be put down to the influence of friends of his who thought that following the death of his wife he would be happier if employed in a more active role. It is so easy – particularly when looking for a chosen scapegoat of an action you have taken part in – to hit upon a particular incident as proof that a scapegoat has been found when, in fact, the authorities have simply shrugged their shoulders, and a purely personal consideration has then stepped in and established the expected pattern of offence and punishment.

*

(6) Thank you for your reply to my written comments on the transcription of our interview. Yes, I do dislike the element of "Yes, you did. No, I didn't" that all too readily rises to the surface. Reid had his attitudes and opinions and I had mine. One can't go on for ever justifying one's own and refuting someone else's with any kind of passion – but I'm sorry that the points I've been making notes of in the past few days in answer to specific statements in Reid's book don't come up now except extraneously. May I take one of them, though, and kill any idea Reid might have left that Menen, the District and Sessions Judge, was predisposed towards the rebels? Menen was predisposed towards nothing except the due process of the law which he had no special faith in, God knows, but certainly recognised his sworn duty to. I'm also slightly worried about any impression that could be left of my having either been in collusion with Merrick over – or turned a blind eye to – the treatment of the Bibighar suspects. I feel I should be allowed to say something about this if you are going to publish Vidyasagar's deposition. Vidyasagar ranks as a self-confessed lawbreaker so that's neither here nor there.

In his deposition he is noticeably unforthcoming about the names of his associates. So to what extent we can rely on his statement that Hari Kumar was not one of his fellow-conspirators, neither of us can judge accurately. The picture we get from Miss Manners's journal (or rather from that short section of it which you have allowed me to see) is not in itself *evidence* of Kumar's non-complicity in the kind of activities Vidyasagar engaged in, and it's quite possible, reading the deposition, to imagine that Vidyasagar gave Merrick cause *genuinely* to disbelieve him during his interrogation. What worries me is that people should think I at any time, then or afterwards, knew about Merrick's treatment of the men suspected of the *rape*. He admitted to me that he had "bent the rules" when dealing with the suspects – in order to frighten them and get them to tell the truth, for example threatened them with caning, and in one case had even had one boy "prepared as if for punishment" – I think his expression was. He *volunteered* this information to me on the morning following the arrests, and when Menen approached me later and said rumours were going round that the boys had been whipped I was able to say how I thought such a rumour had arisen, and that I'd already warned Merrick to "stop playing about". More serious, in my opinion, was the second rumour, that they had been forced to eat beef. Merrick said he'd look into it, and he told me later that it was quite untrue, but might have been caused by a mistake made in the cells when one of the Muslim constables who was guarding them had his own meal sent in. Reid was quite right when he said that the job of suppressing the riots distracted our full attention from the boys suspected of rape and made it finally impossible to find any concrete evidence against them in connexion with the assault. Menen did pursue the business of the rumours of caning and beef-eating. I gave him permission to have the boys themselves questioned on the matter. He told me that the lawyer whom he sent to talk to them reported that none of the boys, including Kumar, complained of having been either whipped or forced to eat beef. And none of them ever said anything about it to Jack Poulson, who had the job of examining them when we were preparing the political case against them. But all this time after I'm uncomfortably aware of having failed to investigate the rumours more fully. It seems pretty clear that they were ill-treated. However, I don't think that there was actually a miscarriage of justice. Merrick was obviously acting in the heat of the moment, believing them guilty of attacking a girl he was fond of. It didn't take long for us to realise that a charge of rape simply wouldn't stick, but the evidence available about their political activities was sufficient for us to feel justified in seeing whether they couldn't be dealt with under the Defence of India Rules. The case was referred to the Divisional Commissioner, and actually as high as the Governor. I've forgotten the details of the evidence, but it was pretty conclusive. So I still feel that the five boys first arrested were guilty of the kind of offences the rules were meant to cover. Only Kumar remains a conundrum to me. If he was treated as badly as Vidyasagar's "informant" said, why didn't he speak out when Menen's lawyer talked to him? Why didn't he complain to Jack Poulson during the official examination? One can appreciate the silence of the other boys if what Vidyasagar says about police threats is true. But Kumar had already suffered – and presumably could prove it, and he was of a different calibre from the other boys surely? Perhaps the parts of Miss Manners's journal which you haven't shown me throw some light on this problem?

I suppose it is his silence on this subject that you have in mind when you say in your note to me that "Kumar was a man who felt in the end that he had lost everything, even his Englishness, and could then only meet every situation – even the most painful – in silence, in the hope that out of it he would dredge back up some self-respect".

I quite see, from what you've told me about your "reconstruction" of Hari Kumar's life, and from what I have read in Daphne Manners's journal, that Kumar might indeed have reacted in this way, but if Vidyasagar's informant was speaking the truth when he said that on the night of his arrest Kumar was caned on Merrick's instructions "until he groaned" I should still have thought Kumar would have seized the opportunity to make charges when Menen's lawyer interviewed him and asked him point-blank whether it was true. To complain of having been unjustifiably and savagely beaten in the course of interrogation would not itself have been a betrayal of Miss Manners's request to Kumar to "say nothing". I mean, isn't there a limit to the stiffness of *any* upper lip?

But then I expect my objections to your conclusions are really based on my inner unwillingness to accept the unsupported evidence of Merrick's behaviour – or to admit my own failure to suspect it at the time. I have no comment to make on the figure you quote from "official" sources that, excluding the United Provinces, there were 958 sentences of whipping after the insurrection, except to say that this was a legal punishment for people caught taking part in riots. If Kumar had been arrested during a riot he might well have been caned. I suppose what you are getting at is that this kind of punishment was "in the air" and that Merrick seized an opportunity, bent the rules, and got away with it.

Having said all this I'll now confine myself, as you request, to the larger issue – although before finally leaving behind the question of "Yes, I did. No, you didn't", I would point out – perhaps unnecessarily – that one should not confuse the uncertainty that surrounds actions and events with the "areas of dangerous fallibility" that lie *between* doubts, decisions and actions. Taking as an example the question of the forcible feeding – it either happened or did not happen. In attempting to map the "dangerous area" we are not concerned with *facts* the truth of which, however unascertainable now, *was known to somebody at the time?*

I have thought hard about the true "dangerous area" and must admit, somewhat reluctantly, that I can't grasp the issues firmly enough to come up with anything remotely resembling a premiss from which you could work. I find myself too readily back-tracking into the old condition of statement and refutation and counter-statement. For instance, taking Reid's jejune account of the 1935 scheme for Federation – and his comment, "It led only to a scramble for power", which leaves the unknowledgeable reader with the impression that we had made a handsome offer and then had to sit back and watch in dismay while the Indians proved themselves too immature either to understand the issues or to grasp their opportunity – all I can really turn my mind to are the alternative readings that show why, as *statesmen*, the Indians rejected Federation, and how the whole federal scheme and proposal could be seen in the light of our having offered the Indians a constitution that would only have prolonged, perhaps even perpetuated, our power and influence, if only as Imperial Arbitrators.

Similarly – again taking Reid's comments as a kind of basic "norm" – one could write at length demolishing his casual inference that the Cripps Mission of 1942 failed because of Indian intransigence, or counter-state – equally casually and briefly and inaccurately – that this was a typical Churchillian move, made to dress the window and make friends and influence people abroad after the defeat in Asia, but which amounted in itself to no more than a grudging repetition of old promises and even older reservations.

And that's not what we're after, is it? Even though one is so tempted to cut away at the foundations of Brigadier Reid's apparently unshakeable foursquare little edifice of simple cause and simple effect in order to redress the balance and present the obverse, and just as inaccurate, picture of a tyrannical and imperialistic power grinding the faces of its coloured subjects in the dust.

In fact we are not at all after the blow-by-blow account of the politics that led to the action. Actually any one man would be incapable of giving such an account – if he confined himself to the blows. There were so many blows he would spend more than his lifetime recording them. To make the preparation of any account a reasonable task he would have to adopt an attitude towards the available material. The action of such an attitude is rather like that of a sieve. Only what is relevant to the attitude gets through. The rest gets thrown away. The real relevance and truth of what gets through the mesh then depends on the relevance and truth of the attitude, doesn't it? If one agrees with that one is at once back on the ground of personal preference – even prejudice – which may or may not have anything to do with "truth", so-called.

Anyway, let me imagine (as you helpfully suggested in your note) that I am about to embark on a history of the British–Indian relationship. I would have to adopt an attitude to the mass of material confronting me. What would it be?

I think it would be as simple – childlike almost – as this: I would take as my premiss that the Indians wanted to be free, and that we also wished this, but that they had wanted to be free for just that much longer than we had felt or agreed that they should be; that given this situation the conflict arose partly as a result of the lack of synchronisation of the timing of the two wishes, but also because this, in time, developed into a lack of synchronisation of the wishes themselves. Being human, the longer the Indians were denied freedom the more they wanted to be free on their own terms, and the more they wanted to be free on their own terms the more we – also being human – insisted that they must initially acquire freedom on ours. The longer this conflict continued, the more abstruse the terms of likely agreement became on either side. It was then a question of the greater morality outlasting and outweighing the lesser. Which was why, of course, in the end the Indians won.

Having put it in those simple words (and they form a mesh you could sift an enormous lot of detailed evidence through), I am reminded of what you said during our interview about "the moral drift of history", and see how perhaps the impetus behind that drift stems in the main from our consciences, and that the dangerous area is the *natural* place for our consciences to work in, with or without us, usually without. The trouble is that the word dangerous always suggests something slightly sinister, as though there were an unbreakable connexion at source between "danger" and "wrong". "Danger" does have this connotation, but I suppose it doesn't if we remember we only use the word to convey our fear of the personal consequences, the danger we'd be in ourselves if we followed our consciences all the time.

I remember that during our talk you referred to the "beat" and the "pause" and I think described these as the unrecorded moments of history. I wish I could relate this theory to a particular event in my life and see how I came out on the right side rather than the wrong, or that I could relate it to an event in Reid's. But even in attempting to relate it, I'm back again in the world of describable events. And when I attempt to relate the theory to all the events in the lives of all the people who were connected with the action – however directly or remotely – my mind simply won't take in the complex of emotions and ambitions and reactions that led, say, to any one of the single actions that was part of the general describable pattern. Perhaps though, the mind can respond to a sense of a cumulative, impersonal justice? The kind of justice whose importance lies not only in the course apparently and overwhelmingly taken, but in its exposure of the dangers that still lie ahead, threatening to divert the drift once more?

III

(*Appendix to "Civil and Military"*)

A Deposition by S. V. Vidyasagar

In my sixteenth year I was plucked in the matriculation and left the Mayapore Government Higher School with the reproaches of my parents and no prospects to a career. For nearly twelve months I was living a life of shame and wickedness, going with loose women and impairing my health. So bad did I become that my father turned me out of the house. My mother secretly gave me rupees one hundred which she had saved from the household expenses over many months. I regret that even this token of affection and motherly trust I squandered on drink and fornication. For many weeks I was at death's door in my squalid surroundings but upon recovery I was still only taking notice of girls and liquor. Many times I was praying for guidance and self-discipline, but only I had to see a pretty girl and at once I was following her and making immoral suggestions in front of everybody, so that my reputation was badly compromised and no decent person would come close to me, unless they were boys of my own kind whose parents were having nothing to do with them or not knowing that they were acting in this way until their neighbours or friends pointed it out.

In this manner I became seventeen and now, revolted by my way of life and resolving upon both moral and physical improvement, I went back to my father's house and begged forgiveness. My mother and sister wept at my return but my father was stern with me and called me to account for my past wickedness. I said that I could account for it only as a madness and that now I was trusting to recovery by God's grace and my own determination. Seeing me so sorrowful and humble of mien my father opened his arms to me once more. Beginning thus a new and upright life I took employment as a clerk with my father's assistance and recommendation and paid the whole of my monthly emolument to my mother, taking from her only a few annas for daily expenditure. At this time also I was bitterly regretting the irresponsibility and bad behaviour that had led me to well-deserved failure in the Higher School. At night I would read in my room burning the midnight oil until my mother begged me to be taking more care of my health and not running the risk of falling asleep in the office and losing my job.

So, determined not to be giving my parents any more trouble I drew up a chart which I pinned to the wall above my bed, allotting so much of my leisure hours to study, so much to sleep and so much to healthy exercise. On fine evenings I would stroll out to the Chillianwallah Bagh extension to look at the fine houses of our well-off neighbours and wander by the river bank. There I saw and caught the eyes of many girls but always I drew back before the temptation to speak to them or follow them proved too much to be difficult. I avoided those parts of the town where I might fall in with my erstwhile companions, especially the street in which many prostitutes lived and whose glances from an upper room could be the ruination of any innocent and upright young man chancing to be in the vicinity.

I was now firmly set upon a course of life both bodily healthy and spiritually uplifting and even upon these walks I would take a book with me and sit down by the river bank to study, casting but few looks at the black braids and silken sarees of the girls nearby. In this way, I happened to fall in with Mr. Francis Narayan, who was teacher at the Christian mission school in Chillianwallah Bazaar and a well-known figure in Mayapore, always riding his bicycle to and fro and speaking at random. Falling into conversation with him I found myself telling him of my earlier bad life and reformed character and my hopes for the future. Learning that I was working as a humble clerk and sadly regretting my failure in the matriculation he said he would bear me in mind for any suitable post he heard about. But expecting nothing to come of this friendly meeting I continued to apply myself daily to my tasks and programme of self-improvement and further education. Now I began to feel somewhat of impatience and to cast covetous glances upon the books in the Mayapore Book Depot in the road near the Tirupati temple which I passed daily on my way home in the evenings. My father was head clerk to a contractor and the office in which I worked was belonging to a friend of my father's employer, a merchant with two marriageable daughters. One day I stopped as usual at the Mayapore Book Depot to browse among the many volumes. Under pretext merely of examining, I was reading chapter by chapter a book about 1917 Declaration of Self-Government. I had become interested in political affairs. Dearly I wished to possess this volume but its price was beyond my means although I knew that my mother would give me the requisite money were I but to ask her. As I stood that evening reading the next chapter, I saw that I was unwatched for the moment by the owner and his assistant and without conscious thought I went out with the book under my arm. Elated and yet afraid of being followed and apprehended as a common thief I wandered without due care and found myself in my old district. A voice called out to me and looking in that direction I saw one of my old friends, a young man senior to the rest of us who had talked and mixed with us but not accompanied us on our bouts of drinking and other bad things. His name was Moti Lal. Seeing the book under my arm he took hold of it and looked at the title and said, "So you are becoming grown-up at last." He invited me to have coffee in the shop where he had been sitting and I agreed. He asked me what I had been doing all these many months, so I told him. He also was a clerk, in the warehouse of Romesh Chand Gupta Sen. I asked him whether he had seen any of our other old friends but he said they had also become respectable like me.

On this occasion suddenly I was seeing that my old life was not so disreputable as my conscience was telling me. It was wicked no doubt to drink so much bad liquor and to go with immoral women without due discrimination, but now I saw that we had been doing such things because our energies were in need of special outlet. Fortified by this discovery I walked back to the Mayapore Book Depot, restored the stolen book to its rightful owner and said that I had taken it away in a fit of absent-mindedness. After this he allowed me to sit many hours in the back of the shop studying new volumes that had come in from Calcutta and Bombay.

I was in my eighteenth year when Mr. Narayan, the mission teacher, called at my home and said that the editor of the *Mayapore Gazette* was looking for an energetic young man with good English who would act as office boy and apprentice journalist. Mr. Narayan confided in me that it was he who wrote the articles known as *Topics*, by "Stroller", for the *Gazette*, which he did in order to augment his emoluments as a teacher. My father was against the idea that I should leave my present employment. He pointed out that in due course, so long as I attended carefully to my duties, I had prospects of becoming head clerk and even of marrying one of my employer's daughters if I showed application and diligence. In the past few months my father had become in very much poor health. Every day he would walk to his office, never even one minute late, but working frequently far beyond the appointed hour of closing and returning home to face my mother's complaints that his supper was spoiled. Since adopting a more manly attitude towards my own life I had learned respect for my father where before only there had been criticism. Also I was affectionate towards him because of his no doubt love for me. I did not want to displease him but also I wished to apply for the job Mr. Narayan had already put in my way by speaking to the editor about me. Eventually my father gave his consent for me to apply to "The Gazette". I feared greatly his death – which took place six months later – and I did not want to displease him in the twilight of his life or think of him leaving this world without a son to officiate at his funeral rites. Therefore I feared my own temper and resulting quarrel and being turned out again. But I thank God who moved him to give in to my wishes. In due course I became an employee of the *Mayapore Gazette*.

After my father's death I became "head of the household"

and had to arrange the marriage of my only surviving sister, who was then sixteen. These family obligations took up a great deal of my time in 1937/8. My mother and I were now living alone together. She was also always persuading me to become married. In those days I was somewhat innocent in these respects. I feared that my experiences with immoral women would make it dangerous for me to be a husband and father, even though I had not – by God's will – suffered any lasting disease. Also I was dedicating my life, after my father's death, to politics and to my work as a "rising" journalist.

My duties now took me daily into the cantonment where the offices of the *Gazette* were situated and I was becoming familiar with the life on that side of the river. As a student also I had been going daily over the river to the Government Higher School but now as "apprentice journalist" to Mr. Laxminarayan I was learning things I was not bothering about or knowing before. For instance I became familiar with the administration of law and order, and of the social life of the English.

In this way as a young Indian of no consequence I suffered many social indignities and became bitter, remembering the care with which my father had needed to account for every penny and had feared to be absent from his profession even for one day. I became friendly with several young fellows of my age, and also again with Moti Lal, and we would talk far into the night about all this kind of thing often in my own home while my mother was sleeping. But it was not until Mr. Laxminarayan employed in my stead Hari Kumar, the nephew of the rich merchant, Romesh Chand Gupta Sen in whose employment also was Moti Lal at one time, and I took up new employment with *Mayapore Hindu,* that I became involved with groups of young men who felt as I was feeling, leaderless in a world where their fathers were afraid to lose a day's work and even Indian politicians were living on a different plane from us. We decided to be on the alert to seize any opportunity that would bring the day of our liberation nearer.

By this time the English were at war with Germany and the Congress ministries had resigned and only we could imagine that once again our country would be forced to bear a disproportionate share of the cost of a war which was not of our seeking and from which we did not expect any reward but instead only promises coming to nothing. In those days we had to be careful to avoid arrest unless of course one of us decided to seek arrest deliberately by open infringement of regulations. Also we had to be careful when choosing our friends or casual acquaintances. Many innocent-seeming fellows were police spies and one or two of my friends were arrested as a result of information given to the authorities by people of that kind who were sometimes only interested in settling old scores and would make up tales to persuade the police to arrest one of us and put us out of harm's way. Moti Lal also was arrested, for defying order under section 144 prohibiting him from speaking at a meeting of students. He was sent to prison but succeeded in escaping.

When the Japanese invaded Burma and defeated the English we felt that at last our freedom was in sight. Neither I nor my friends were afraid of Japanese. We knew that we would be able to make trouble for the Japanese also if they invaded India and treated us badly like the British. Many of our soldiers who were left behind by their British officers and captured in Burma and Malaya were given their freedom by the Japanese and formed "Indian National Army" under Subhas Chandra Bose. If the Japanese had won the war our comrades in the Indian National Army would have been recognised everywhere as heroes, but instead many of them were severely punished by the British when the war was over and our "national leaders" stood by and did nothing to save them.

In those days we were knowing that only young men who were ready to give life and take life could ever make India a "great power". We did not understand the ramblings and wanderings of our leaders. Unfortunately it was difficult for us to form anything but small groups. We told each other that if once the people rose against the oppressors we young men would be able to link up with each other and give an example of bravery and determination that would infect all.

This was the position at the time of the rebellion in 1942. With several other young men I had prepared myself for any kind of sacrifice. After my arrest I was interrogated for hours to give information about "underground system", but if there was any such system I was not knowing of it, only I knew boys like myself who were ready to take the foremost place in facing the enemy. On the very day of my arrest, August 11, I and several fellows were planning to join and exhort the crowds who would be forming up later that day to march on the civil lines. News of such plans spread quickly from one end of town to the other. A crowd had tried to form up that morning on

Chillianwallah Bagh Extension road but had been dispersed by the police who seemed to crop up everywhere at a moment's notice. I and my fellows were not among this crowd because at that hour we were engaged in printing pamphlets to distribute among the people exhorting them to help to release the boys unjustly accused of attacking an English woman. We delivered one such pamphlet to the police post near the Tirupati temple by wrapping it round a stone and throwing it through open window so that the one amongst us chosen for this dangerous task would have the chance of getting away without being seen. Having done this we then dispersed going each to our separate homes or places of employment. Only one hour later the District Superintendent of Police and many constables descended upon the offices of *Mayapore Hindu* where I was working. I and other staff-members present were immediately arrested because the police found an old hand-press in a back room that they said had been used for printing seditious literature.

This was not true and only I among those arrested was guilty of such an act to my knowledge, but I denied it. With those arrested was the editor, who told the police that I had been absent from work that morning and that his hand-press had been used only for innocent advertising purposes. I did not know about what the editor had said until later, because we were kept separately, but eventually I learned that they had all been released, although *Mayapore Hindu* was suppressed and the offices closed by order. Still I said nothing, because I hoped to keep secret the true whereabouts of the printing press and the names of my accomplices. I was removed from the kotwali to cells in police headquarters in the civil lines where the boys who had been arrested near the Bibighar two days before were being held, but I did not see any of them. I was kept in a cell secluded from others and then, after interrogation, taken to the prison in Jail road. I was in the Jail road prison when the people attacked it and overcame the guards and police at the gate and forced their way in. Several prisoners were released but unfortunately for me this act of liberation occurred in a different "block" and soon afterwards the soldiers attacked the jail and our short-lived hopes of freedom were over. In this action many innocent people lost their lives which the authorities tried to disguise giving very low figures for killed and wounded.

I had been taken from the kotwali to the cells in the civil

lines in the late afternoon of the 11th, and was interrogated there personally by the District Superintendent of Police. He was very clever with his questions but I had determined on complete silence. I knew that I would be locked up in any case, because I saw that he had a file about my suspected activities. He knew the names of many of my friends and even casual acquaintances and I wondered what spy had been in our midst. He kept asking me about Moti Lal. Also about Kumar and the other boys who had been arrested after the "attack" on the English woman. It was no good denying that I knew Moti Lal and most of these boys because the Superintendent even had a note of dates and places where some of us had been seen together, or been known to have been together, beginning with the night in February when a few of us were drinking and Hari Kumar became too drunk so that we took him home only to hear later that he had wandered out again and been arrested and questioned. Two of the other boys arrested for the "rape" were among those who were present on that occasion in February, and I could not help wondering whether after he was questioned Hari Kumar had agreed to spy on us and it was him we had to thank for our present predicament. Later I was ashamed to have had such thoughts, but I must be honest and mention that for a time I was suspicious.

None of the boys arrested for the "rape" had been my accomplices in any of my own illegal activities, but the Superintendent also had "on file" the names of three of the boys who were my accomplices and had been with me that morning at the secret press which we had taken over after Moti Lal's arrest. This press was in the house of one of the prostitutes. The police often visited this house themselves but were too alternatively engaged to notice anything of evidence that secret literature was also printed there.

When the Superintendent mentioned the names of some of the boys I had been with that morning I said (as it had been agreed between us if any of us were arrested) that we had not seen each other for two or three days. I admitted nothing to the Superintendent. I said that on that morning I had not felt well and so had gone to work late and in any case had been worried for my safety with all the troubles going on in the city.

After leaving the house where our secret printing press was, with the pamphlets which I had "run off" and which my colleagues were now going to distribute, I had taken precaution of going to my home and telling my mother to say that I had been unwell and had not left home until now. My mother was very afraid, because this was proof that I was doing things against the authorities, but she said she would tell this story if she was asked. It was the first time I had kept away from my office duties to do this kind of work, which is why I took such a precaution. When the Superintendent asked me where I had been that morning I knew that the editor or one of my fellow staff members on *Mayapore Hindu* had mentioned my absence, but I told him about not having been well, and he looked annoyed and I could see that already he had had my mother questioned. I prayed that my real accomplices had all managed to tell satisfactory stories if they had been questioned also.

I was much afraid at this interrogation because of what we had heard about the horrible treatment of the boys arrested for the attack on the English woman. It was because of what we had heard that I and my accomplices hastened to print the pamphlet and distribute it during the day. The information about the dreadful behaviour of the police towards these boys came to us from someone who had spoken to one of the orderlies in the police headquarters who said that all the boys had been beaten senseless and then revived and forced to eat beef to be made to confess. But we believed they were not guilty and suspected that the story of the attack on the English woman was much exaggerated or even a fabrication because the boy "Kumar" had been friendly with her and the English people therefore hated him. I knew nothing about Kumar's movements on the night in question but a friend of the other boys who were arrested said that except for Kumar they had merely been drinking home-distilled liquor in an old hut and knew nothing about the "attack" until the police broke in and arrested them. This friend also had been drinking but came away a few moments before the arrests which he saw from a place of hiding. He thought that the level-crossing keeper at the Bibighar bridge had given them away because the keeper knew that they used the old hut to drink home-distilled liquor in and sometimes joined them and made them give him a drink to keep quiet about this illegal activity. I know that this is true about the hut and the drinking because I also sometimes went there. It was not the same place in which we drank on the night that Hari Kumar was with us and became intoxicated. To drink such stuff we had to find different locations to put the police off the scent. If we wanted a drink we could not afford proper liquor which is why we drank this bad stuff.

During my interrogation the Superintendent said, "isn't it true that you are a close friend of Kumar and that on the night of the 9th of August you and Kumar and your other friends were drinking in the hut near the Bibighar bridge and that then you left them because they were beginning to talk badly about going into the cantonment to find a woman?"

I saw that he was offering me a chance to ingratiate myself and bear false witness, and so much fearful as I was of being beaten, I said no it was not true, only it was true that I knew Hari Kumar and some of the boys he named, but on the night of the 9th August I was working late at offices of *Mayapore Hindu* "subbing" the reports of outbreaks that had taken place during the day in Dibrapur and Tanpur, and that my editor would no doubt testify to this. I was speaking truth and the Superintendent was angry because he knew I was speaking it. He said, "You'll regret your lying before I've done with you." He then left me alone in the room. I looked round for ways of escape but there was not even a window through which I might attempt to regain my longed-for freedom. The room was lighted by one electric bulb. There was a table and a chair at which the policeman had been sitting and the stool on which I was sitting. In one corner there was an iron trestle.

When I realised that there was no escape I prayed for strength to endure my torture without giving away the names of my accomplices. I thought that in a moment they would come for me and that the Superintendent Sahib was even now ordering them to prepare things. But he came back alone and sat down at the desk again and started to ask all the same questions. I do not know how long all this went on. I was hungry and thirsty. After some time he left the room again without succeeding in hearing any different thing from me and two constables came in and took me into a truck and drove me to the jail in Jail road. On the way I hoped to be rescued by our people, but the truck drove very fast and there was no incident. I was in this jail for a week and was then taken to Court and charged with printing and publishing seditious literature. A police spy gave evidence of seeing me throw the pamphlet into the kotwali, which was not true, but I could not prove it. Also the illegal press had been found, no doubt also as result of spying, and all my accomplices apprehended. I was sentenced to two years rigorous imprisonment. To serve my sentence I was sent to the jail near Dibrapur and locked at first into a filthy cell. I believed that the Superintendent in Mayapore had given orders for me to be especially harshly treated. At first I could not eat the disgusting food they gave me, hungry though I was. One day I quite lost my reason and threw the plate on the floor. The next day I was taken out of my cell and told that for infringing prison regulations I was to receive fifteen strokes of the cane. They took me at once into a small room and there I saw the same kind of iron trestle I had seen in the room where the Superintendent had questioned me. They showed me the cane they were going to use. It was about four feet long and half an inch thick. They stripped me of all my clothes, bent me over the trestle and tied my wrists and ankles and carried out "the sentence". Towards the end I could no longer support my suffering and fainted away.

I was sent later to another prison. I was allowed no communication with anyone, not even my family. They told me one day that my mother was dead. I wept and begged of God to be forgiven for the suffering I had caused her, in this freedom-work I had felt I had to do. I did not resent any of my punishment because I was guilty of all the "crimes" I was punished for. I did not think of them as being crimes and therefore my punishment was not punishment but part of the sacrifice I was called upon to make.

It was towards the end of my imprisonment that one of the boys who had been accused of the attack on the English woman was brought also into this prison from another jail. These boys had all been kept in separate prisons because the authorities had wished to keep them apart no doubt so that two of them should not confirm the story of their unjust punishment to fellow prisoners. When I saw this boy I cried out in amazement because I had thought they were all tried and condemned long ago. In prison I had heard once that they were hanged. But this boy told me there had never been any evidence against them. He thought it had been all a "put-up job", and that there was probably no rape in the Bibighar at all. Finally the authorities had locked them all up as undesirables, all being known or suspected of indulging in subversive activities. We were not able to speak often to each other and he seemed too much afraid to talk about the rumours I had heard of torture and defilement.

When I was released from prison, my own home was no longer available. I had frequently to report to the police. My old employer Mr. Laxminarayan found lodging for me and gave me some work so that I could keep body and soul together. I was in poor health and weighed only 97 pounds and was much troubled with coughing. In time I was able to regain some of my health and strength.

Of the boys arrested after the attack in the Bibighar only one of them I ever saw again who came back to live in Mayapore. This was the boy who came to the prison where I was. Hearing he was back in his home I visited him and asked him, "Why were you afraid to speak much to me?" Even still he was reluctant to tell. He had suffered much and was afraid of the police who, he said, were always watching him. Still in those days the British were in power and had won the war and we wondered somewhat hopelessly about the future even though people kept saying that this time the British were really getting ready to quit.

This boy was speaking to me one evening in Mayapore, towards the end of 1946, and suddenly he said, "I will tell you." He spoke for a long time. He said that on the night of Bibighar when he and the other four who were still drinking in the hut were arrested they were taken at once to Police headquarters and locked in a cell. At this time only they knew that they had been caught drinking illegal liquor and were laughing and joking. Then they saw Hari Kumar brought in. His face was cut and bruised. They thought that this had been done by the police. One of them called out, "Hello, Hari", but Kumar was not taking any notice. After that, except for my informant, none of the boys saw Kumar again. My informant was telling me all this in confidence, so I prefer to respect that and not divulge his name. These days all these things are forgotten and we are living different lives. Our young men today are not taking any interest in such matters. So I will call my friend "Sharma" which is not his name nor the name of any of the other boys. Sharma was a fine, strong fellow, who like me had been "a great one for the ladies" as a youth but had also somewhat reformed. He and his companions, other than Kumar, were locked in one cell, and taken out one by one. As one by one they went and did not come back, those remaining were no longer laughing and joking. They had also headache from too much drinking and were very much thirsty. Finally only Sharma was left. When his turn came he was taken downstairs by two constables and told to strip. When he was standing there naked one of the constables knocked at a door at the far end of the room and opened it and the District Superintendent came in. "Sharma" was greatly humiliated to be forced to stand there so immodestly, especially in front of a white man. The constables now held Sharma's arms behind him and then the Superintendent – who carried a little stick – came over and held the stick out and lifted the exposed private parts and stared at them for some seconds. Sharma did not understand why this embarrassment should be done on him. He said, "Why are you doing this, Superintendent Sahib?" The policeman said nothing. After inspecting the clothing which Sharma had been made to take off – also using the little stick to turn the clothing over and look at it – the policeman left the room. Later, of course, Sharma realised that the policeman was looking for evidence of rape practised upon a lady who had bled. When the Superintendent had gone the constables told Sharma to put on his underdrawers, but they did not give him back any of his other clothes. He was now taken out of the room by another door where he found his drinking companions in a cell, also wearing nothing but their underdrawers. Kumar was not with them. They tried to joke again, asking why the Sahib was so interested in certain parts of their bodies, but they were not feeling like laughing in this instance. Then one by one they were again taken away, and did not come back. When Sharma's turn came – and he was again the last – he was taken into the room where he had been stripped, and found the Superintendent sitting behind a desk. I think this was the same room in which Superintendent Sahib questioned me two evenings later. Sharma was not given a stool to sit on, however. He was made to stand in front of the desk. Then he was questioned. He did not understand the questions because he was thinking only of being charged with drinking home-distilled toddy. But suddenly the Superintendent said, "How did you know she would be in the Bibighar Gardens?" and he began to see what might be behind all this rigmarole because of the word "she" and the humiliation recently practised on him. But still he did not know what the policeman was trying to find out, until the policeman said, "I'm inquiring into the attack and criminal assault on the English girl this evening, the girl who thought your friend Kumar was also a friend of hers." Then there were many questions, such as, "When did Kumar suggest all you fellows going together? Was she there when you arrived? How long did you wait for her? Who was the first man to assault her? You were led by Kumar, weren't you? If it hadn't been for Kumar you would never have thought of going to the Bibighar, would you? Were you just the fellow who was told to keep watch and never had the chance to enjoy her? Why should you suffer for the others if you just kept watch? How many times did you enjoy her, then? How many times did Kumar enjoy her? Why are you afraid? A fellow who has enjoyed drinking a lot of liquor starts thinking also about enjoying a woman, doesn't he? Why do you blame yourself for a perfectly natural thing? You shouldn't have drunk the liquor, but you did, and look what's happened. Why don't you be a man and admit that you drank too much and felt passionate? You're no weakling. You're a fine healthy fellow. Why be ashamed to admit your natural desires? If I drink too much liquor I also feel these things quite badly. There's no sign of blood on you or on your underclothes. She wasn't a virgin, was she? And you were the first fellow because you were the most passionate and couldn't wait. Isn't that it? Or perhaps you've been careful to wash? Or change your underclothes? Knowing what you have done was wrong? Knowing you would have to suffer if you were caught? Well, you are caught and have to suffer. Be a man and admit you deserve punishment. If you admit you deserve punishment you'll be let off lightly because I understand this kind of thing. And she wasn't a virgin, was she? She went with anyone who was able to satisfy her. And liked brown-skinned fellows. That's what young Hari Kumar told you, isn't it? Isn't it?"

This you see is what Sharma so much remembered. How the policeman finally kept saying, Isn't it? Isn't it? and banging his stick on the desk, because losing his temper at Sharma's all the time saying he knew nothing of what the Superintendent Sahib was talking about.

Then the policeman threw the stick on the desk and said, "I see there's only one way to break *you,*" and he called out to the constables who took Sharma into the next room and through a door into another room. This room was even more dimly lit but he saw Kumar, naked, fastened over one of the iron trestles. In this position also I know it is difficult to breathe. Sharma said he did not know how long Kumar had been fastened in this way, but he said he could hear the sound of Kumar trying to breathe. He did not know at first that it was Kumar. Only he could see the blood on his buttocks. But then the policeman, the Superintendent, came in and said, "Kumar, here's a friend of yours come to hear you confess. Just say 'Yes, I was the man who organised the rape' and you'll be released from this contraption and won't be beaten any more." Sharma said that Kumar only made "a sort of sound" so the Superintendent Sahib gave an order and a constable came forward with a cane and gave Kumar several strokes. Sharma shouted out to Kumar that he knew nothing and had said nothing. He also shouted, "Why are you treating this fellow so?" He said the constables then continued to beat Kumar until he groaned. Sharma could not look at this terrible punishment. After a while he was taken away and locked alone in a cell. Ten minutes or so later he was taken back into the room where Kumar had been. The trestle was now unoccupied. He was fastened to it after they had taken off his underdrawers. He said they then put what felt like a wet cloth on his buttocks and gave him nine strokes. He said the pain was so awful that he could not understand how Kumar had borne so much of it. They put the wet cloth over him so that his skin should not be cut and leave permanent marks. When they had finished he was taken back to the cell. Later he was put into another cell where his companions were. Kumar was not with them. He told them what had been done to him and to Kumar. The others had not been beaten but were afraid their turn was coming. The youngest of them began to weep. They did not at all understand what was happening. By now it was early morning. The Superintendent came down to the cell, with two constables. The constables were ordered to show the others what even nine strokes of the cane over a wet cloth could do to the buttocks. They held Sharma down and uncovered him. Then the Superintendent said that if any one of them so much as hinted at any time, to any person, during their "forthcoming interrogation, trial and punishment" that any one of them had been "hurt" or harshly treated, they would all suffer even more severely the punishment Sharma could describe to them both from personal experience and from having seen another man undergo it.

Half an hour later some food was brought in. They were hungry and tired and frightened. They began to eat. After a few mouthfuls also they vomited. The "mutton" in the curry was beef. The two Muslim jailors who were standing watching them laughed and told them that now they were outcastes and even God had turned his face from them.

PART SEVEN

The Bibighar Gardens

Daphne Manners (Journal Addressed to Lady Manners)
Kashmir, April 1943

I AM sorry, Auntie, for all the trouble and embarrassment I've caused you. I began to apologise once before, when Aunt Lili brought me back to Rawalpindi, last October, but you wouldn't listen. So I apologise now, not for my behaviour but for the effect it's had on you who did nothing to deserve our exile. But I want to thank you, too, for your loving care of me, for voluntarily taking on the responsibility of looking after me, and for never once making me feel that this was a burden, although I know it must have been, and is as bad here where you see hardly anyone as it was in Pindi where so many of your old friends made themselves scarce. I sometimes try to put myself in your shoes and work out what it must be like to be the aunt of "that Manners girl". I know that's how people speak of me and think of me, and that it rubs off on to you. And all the marvellous things you and Uncle Henry did to make things seem right in India, for English people, are forgotten. This is really what I mean when I say I'm sorry. Sorry for giving people who criticised you and Uncle Henry the last word, for seeming to prove to them that everything you and he stood for was wrong.

The awful thing is that if you ever read this I shan't be here to smile and make the apology look human and immediate. If I get through to the other side of what I have to face we shall probably continue in the state we live in at the moment, of talking about as few subjects as possible that can remind either of us of the real reason why we are here. You won't in that case read this because I only wrote it as an insurance against permanent silence. I write it because I have premonitions of not getting through and I should hate to kick the bucket knowing I'd made no attempt to set the record straight and break the silence we both seem to have agreed is okay for the living, if not for the dead. Sorry about the morbid note! I don't feel morbid, just prepared. Perhaps I've felt like that all along, ever since the doctor in London told me to take it easy and stop driving ambulances in the black-out. Possibly the suspicion that I had to cram as much of my life as I could into as short a time as possible accounts for things I've done that people settled into the comfortable groove of three score and ten would reckon hasty and ill-advised.

If I'm right, and my premonitions aren't just morbid fancies, it would be odd, wouldn't it, how someone who looks so strong and healthy could be really just a mess of physiological sums added up wrong! After Mother died I used to be afraid of getting cancer. I've since been afraid of a tumour on the brain, to account for my poor sight and occasional headaches. All these sophisticated diseases also afflict Indian peasants but *they* are just statistics in the records of the birth and death rates and life expectancy charts. I often wish that I could feel and think myself equally anonymous, stricken (if I must be stricken) by God, and not by something the doctors know all about and can account and prepare you for.

But let me say this; medically I feel there is only one thing really "wrong" with me, and that this may only be wrong for me because I'm not very efficiently put together. Like the doctor in Pindi, Dr. Krishnamurti talks about a Caesarian. I've said that I don't want that. Maybe I'm just pigheaded, but you've no idea how important it is to me to try to do this thing properly. I don't want to be cut open, to have the child torn out like that. I want to bear it. I want to give it life, not have its life or my life or both our lives saved for us by clever doctors. I want to try my best to end with a good conscience what I began with one. I think Dr. Krishnamurti almost understands this. He looks at me in such an odd way. And this is another thing I am so thankful to you for, that you've never even thought of distinguishing between an English and an Indian doctor, let alone resisted my consulting an Indian. Long ago (well, it seems long ago but can't have been much more than a year) I wrote to you from Mayapore saying how glad I was that I'd had the fortune to be with someone like you instead of like the Swinsons (whom I always remember as "my first colonials". And what a shock they were to me!) If I'd been their niece then even if they hadn't packed me off somewhere out of the way they'd never have allowed anyone but a white doctor to come near me. But perhaps if I'd been a niece of the Swinsons I'd have run a mile rather than see Dr.

Krishnamurti anyway. Or would never have got into what the Swinsons no doubt call "this mess".

Oddly enough there was a Dr. Krishnamurti in Mayapore, a colleague of Dr. Anna Klaus. I asked our Dr. Krishnamurti whether he was any relation of the one in Mayapore and he said he expected so, if you traced the family far enough back. I told him that I was glad his name was Krishnamurti, because it was a link with Mayapore. He looked embarrassed and surprised. I'm not sure that he wasn't shocked, my saying that name, Mayapore, so casually. He's got over the embarrassment of having to touch me, but not the embarrassment of what it seems I represent to Indians as well as to British. This thing – whatever it is – that I represent has now passed from the purely notional to the acutely physical phase. In Pindi I saw how even the few people who came to see us – or rather came to see you in spite of me – couldn't keep their eyes off my waist-line. Now of course the distortion caused by the unknown child (unknown, unwanted, unloved it seems by anyone but me) is the most immediately obvious thing about me. If I went down into the bazaar, and didn't confine myself to the house and garden, I'd feel it necessary to go with a little bell, like a leper, so that people could go indoors and stay clear until I'd passed! If I'd been assaulted by men of my own race I would have been an object of pity. Religiously-minded people would probably have admired me as well for refusing to abort. But they weren't men of my own race. And so even the Indians in Pindi used to avert their eyes when I went into the cantonment, as if they were afraid some awful punishment would pass from me to them.

Even you, Auntie, seem to keep your eyes level with mine these days.

*

Of course, I wasn't a virgin. Anna Klaus told me later that she had been asked and had given her answer. She wanted me to know that the question had come up and been dealt with. She didn't press me for any comment. I didn't make any. But I tell you, Auntie, to set the record straight. My first lover was a friend of my brother David. My second a man I met in London during the time I was driving the ambulances. Two lovers – but, you see, *not* lovers. We made love but weren't in love, although for a time I thought I was in love with the first man.

It is only Hari I have ever loved. Almost more than anything else in the world I long to talk about him to you, even if it were only to say, "Oh yes, Hari said something like that," or "I saw that one time when I was with Hari." Just to speak his name to another person, to bring him back into the ordinary world of my life. But I can't. I know that your face would go blank, and this is something I couldn't bear, to have him shut out like that, by you. He has been shut out enough. If I cry – and I sometimes do – it's because I know that I have shut him out as well. Is it true, I wonder, that you know where he is? I often think you know, that so many of the people I count as friends know, but won't tell me. I don't blame you, though. Your silence is for what you believe is my good, and mine has been for what I think is Hari's. God knows there have been affairs between people of Hari's colour and people of mine before, and even marriages, and children, and blessings as well as unhappiness. But this was one affair that somehow never stood a chance. I've given up hope of ever seeing him again.

This is why, especially, the child I bear is important to me. Even though I can't be positive it is his. But I think so. I believe so. If it isn't, it is still a child. Its skin may be as dark as Hari's or almost as pale as mine, or somewhere in between. But whatever colour – he, or she, is part of my flesh and blood; my own typically hamfisted offering to the future!

*

A day or two since I wrote anything in this book. I write at night, mostly, huddled in your sheepskin, close to the dying log fire. It is a land of such marvellous contrasts. Tonight, in Mayapore, the heat will be awful. One would sit under the fan, with all the windows open, but if I went to the little lattice window here and peeped through the cretonne curtains I would see the snow on the mountains. And yet in a few weeks the valley will be filled with people on leave. They will swim in the lakes and throng the river in their shikaras. Shall we move into Srinagar then, Auntie, and live on one of the houseboats and fill it with flowers and have our fortunes told?

*

Marigolds. How Bhalu hated it when I usurped his position

and went gathering them early in the morning to put in a vase for Lili's breakfast tray! I was in Bhalu's bad books for trampling one of his flower beds and cutting marigolds the day Hari first came to the MacGregor House. Since I've never talked to you about Hari I don't know how much Auntie Lili told you. But soon after I went down to Mayapore with her she was asked by someone, Anna Klaus in fact, whether she knew a Mr. Kumar, or Coomer as it was sometimes spelt, and if in any case she could ask Judge Menen what Mr. Kumar had done to deserve being hustled away by the police, hit by a sub-inspector in the presence of witnesses and taken in "for questioning". Lili didn't tell me much about any of this but I gathered that she was taking some sort of interest in a young Indian who was in trouble simply for answering back, or something like that. Her not telling me much was all part of that attitude of hers we both know so well. Like at Lahore, on our way down to Mayapore, when she sat in our compartment cool as a cucumber pretending that nothing was going on while all the time those two Englishwomen were really accusing her of having pinched a piece of their beastly luggage. As you know, Auntie, it's difficult ever to get Lili to talk about the things Indians have to put up with, but that doesn't mean she doesn't feel badly about them, or that if she can help someone who's in trouble, as Hari was, she'll just sit back and do nothing.

In fact I never heard the full story of Hari's "arrest" until Hari told me himself, long afterwards, one evening when we'd gone together to the Tirupati temple. *I didn't even know until then that the man who'd actually taken him in for questioning was Ronald Merrick*. I felt badly about that. I felt that everyone had deliberately kept it from me, Aunt Lili, Anna Klaus, Judge Menen, even Sister Ludmila – especially Sister Ludmila because it seemed it had all happened in the Sanctuary, in front of her. I felt badly because I had been out with Ronald as well as Hari, and it looked as if all the people I liked and trusted had simply sat back and watched and waited to see what might happen. Since then I've realised that it wasn't really like that. It was only like I think it always has been in India for people of either race who try to live together outside their own enclosed little circles. Inside those circles the gossip never stops and everybody knows everybody else's business. But outside them it's as if the ground is so uncertain that to stand on it is enough. Yesterday's misunderstandings or injustices are best forgotten. You learn from them but keep what has been learned to yourself, hoping others have also learned. The important thing is to keep the ground occupied, and once you start talking about anything except *today* you're adding to the danger that's always there, of people turning tail and scurrying back to the safe little place where they know they can talk their heads off because in there they all have to pretend to think alike.

But when I found out from Hari that it was Ronald Merrick who had taken him into custody and questioned him, and had stood by and watched a sub-inspector hit him, I felt I'd been made a laughing-stock. I'd always assumed that Ronald was much too high and mighty to have been involved personally in such a local little matter as the arrest and questioning of a "suspect". I was angry with Ronald for warning me about my association with Hari (as he had done only a few days before the visit to the temple) without bothering to mention that he had *personally* arrested and questioned him. I was angry with everyone, but most of all I suppose angry with myself. But what I said to Hari that night made him think I was only angry with him, and even accusing him of deceit, which is supposed to be a typically Indian failing so far as the average stolid good old no-nonsense Englishwoman is concerned. I suppose my reaction struck Hari as typical too, typical of the roughshod-riding English mem. After we parted I meant to have it out with Aunt Lili when she got back, but she was late and I went to bed. I sat up for ages, thinking of the times Ronald Merrick had been at the MacGregor House, and the times Hari had been (but never on the same occasion). I worked it out that the evening Ronald came to dinner, after I'd come to stay with Lili (I remember mentioning in my first letter to you from Mayapore that the District Superintendent of Police was coming that evening and that I had to change into my glad rags) must have been only a day or two after Lili had been rung by Anna Klaus and asked to speak to Judge Menen about "Mr. Kumar or Coomer", because I know that happened in the first few days of my stay at the MacGregor House. Perhaps if I'd been more settled I'd have asked more questions about Hari, who he was, and what had happened to him. But I didn't. On the night Lili had Ronald there to dinner, with several other guests, she must have known that *he* had been responsible for taking Hari into custody and probably knew he had stood by while

Hari was struck by the sub-inspector. But she never said anything to him about it, either then or later, so far as I could tell. Neither did she say anything to Hari on the few later occasions he came to the house, at least not in front of me.

I wondered why. And why she had never told me the whole story. But wondering this I realised that no one who knew the story had *ever* said anything to me. I only knew that after Hari's first visit Lili had become reserved about him. I sensed her lack of real liking for him. And this had made me hesitant about telling her much about what Ronald came to call "my association with Mr. Kumar". I saw the *extent* of the silence that had surrounded this association, and how I had automatically contributed to it. I'd also kept quiet – to everyone but you – about Ronald's "proposal", and this was the same *kind* of silence.

This is when I knew that I really loved Hari, and wanted him near me all the time, and also when I began to be afraid for him. There seemed to have been a conspiracy among everyone I knew at all well to say nothing, but wait, almost as if holding their breath, perhaps wanted me to like Hari, for himself, simply as a man, but scared of the consequences and also of the other thing, that I was attracted to the idea of doing something unconventional for the hell of it, which of course would have hurt him more than me. But it was a conspiracy that seemed to be rooted in love as well as fear. I felt as if they saw my affair with Hari as the logical but terrifying end of the attempt they had all made to break out of their separate little groups and learn how to live together – terrifying because even they couldn't face with equanimity the breaking of the most fundamental law of all – that although a white man could make love to a black girl, the black man and white girl association was still taboo.

And then all my determination to have things out with Lili in the morning was undermined. Partly because there was nothing really to "have out", partly because I was afraid. I couldn't see myself talking to Lili about any of this, because to talk would have been to introduce aspects of my "association" *that had nothing to do with what I felt for Hari*. But thinking of what I felt for him, and looking in the mirror as I got ready for bed, I thought, Well – but does he love me? What *am* I? Just a big-boned girl with a white skin whose mother justifiably accused her of awkwardness, and whose father and brother were kind as the men of a family are always kind to a daughter or sister who is a good sport but not much else.

Sorry, Auntie. Not making a bid for *your* kindness. Just stating the truth, and explaining the awful doubts I had, the suspicion that perhaps what people said was true, that a coloured man who goes with a white girl only does so for special reasons.

*

When I first met him I thought him horribly prickly. He was supposed to come with his Aunt Shalini, but he came alone and was ill at ease. Later Aunt Lili said she wasn't surprised he'd come alone, because his Aunt Shalini was probably one of those embarrassingly shy little Indian women who either never went anywhere or cast a blight on any place they *did*. I'd virtually forgotten whatever Lili had told me about "Mr. Kumar". It was some time in March and she'd decided to have a small cocktail party. When she made out her list she said, "And we'll ask young Mr. Kumar and see what he looks like." I said, "Which Mr. Kumar?" and she said, "Oh, you remember. The young man I was asked to speak to Judge Menen about because he got arrested by mistake." Then she said, "But don't for goodness' sake say anything to him about *that*." Well, you know me! I've always tended to put my foot in it by coming out with things baldfaced. I used to be much worse, because I was so dreadfully shy and conscious of being clumsy, and the only thing I could think to do not to look awkward was to chat at people and say the first thing that came into my head, which more often than not turned out to be the wrong thing.

I've forgotten who most of the people were who came that time for cocktails. There was Dr. Anna Klaus, I know, because that was the first time I'd met her, although I'd seen her talking to Dr. Mayhew when she came to the Mayapore General for some consultation or other. And Matron was there. And Vassi (the lawyer, Mr. Srinivasan, who was a friend of Lili's and also of Hari's aunt and "uncle"). Hari's editor on the *Mayapore Gazette*, Mr. Laxminarayan, was also supposed to be there but didn't turn up, probably because he found out Hari had been invited and he didn't feel the protocol would be right if he and a junior member of the staff were at the same function! At least that's what Hari said later. I know the Whites looked in for half an hour, and there were some teachers from the Higher School and the Technical College.

He was late turning up. He hadn't wanted to come, but had decided to face it. He was ashamed of his clothes. He didn't know any of us except Vassi and they didn't like each other much. When I say he didn't know any of us I'm wrong. He knew quite a lot of people by sight, because as a reporter on the *Gazette* it was his job to. He let slip to Aunt Lili that they had met before and that she had once answered a question he put to her when she won second prize for her roses at the flower show. I was standing next to her when he let on about that. He made it sound as if she ought to have remembered talking to him. She pretended to, but from the way she pretended I could tell that she disliked being *made* to pretend, which she only did because she thought he was hurt not to be recognised. And he saw through her pretence too. And at once became what I call prickly.

I put my foot in it too. When he spoke he sounded just like an Englishman. So I blurted out, "Wherever did you learn to speak English as well as you do?" He just looked at me and said, "England." So of course I bashed on in a panic, expressing astonishment and interest, falling over myself to be friendly, but only succeeding in being inquisitive. Then Lili took me away and made me talk to some other people and the next time I saw him he was standing more or less alone, on the edge of a group of the teachers. So I went up to him and said, "Let me show you the garden." It was getting dusk and we were already *in* the garden, so it was a frightfully stupid thing to say. But it was this time of speaking to him that I really noticed how good-looking he was. And tall. So many of the Indian men I talked to I topped by an inch or two, which was something that usually added to my hysteria at a party where I was feeling shy and awkward.

But he let me show him the garden. Which is why I remember I'd been in trouble with Bhalu that morning. I showed him the flower bed I'd trampled on getting at the marigolds. I asked him whether he'd had a nice garden when he lived in England and he said he supposed it had been all right but that he'd never taken much notice of it. Then I said, "Do you miss it all, though?" and he said at once, "Not any more," and sort of moved away and said it was time for him to go. So we walked back and re-joined the party which was breaking up. He said goodbye to Lili and thanked her rather brusquely and then just nodded goodbye to me. And I remember afterwards, when he'd gone, and one or two people stayed for dinner, all Indians, how forcibly it struck me that except for the colour of his skin he wasn't Indian at all – in the sense I understood it.

When everyone had gone and Lili and I were having a nightcap she said, "Well, what were you able to make of young Mr. Coomer?"

I said, "I think he's a terribly sad man." It was the first thing that came into my mind, and yet I didn't seem to have thought of it like that until then. And Lili said nothing except something like, "Let's have the other half and then bash off to bed."

*

I'm glad that I'm writing all this down, because even if you never read it it's helping me to understand things better. I think I've been blaming Lili for taking against Hari. No, let me be honest. I don't think I've been blaming her, I know I have. And I think I've been wrong. Reliving that first meeting with him I see how Lili, who was responsible for me to you, probably watched the way we left the party to inspect the garden, and didn't misinterpret but responded to the little warning bell that she must have learned, during her life, never to ignore. Remembering all the wonderful things about Lili, I *must* be wrong to think that she could ever really have harboured resentment of Hari for the critical attitude he adopted towards her in those few insignificant moments when they first met at her party. And Lili, after all, is a woman too. She can't have been totally unmoved by Hari's physical presence. Nor unconcerned, when she saw us going off together (only for ten minutes!), about me, and how *I* might be moved by it.

I used to think the fact that she seemed to "drop" him after that first well-meaning attempt to gather him into what was called the MacGregor House set was due to nothing more than her annoyance at his prickliness, or anyway to the stuffiness she can sometimes astonish you with if people don't behave in exactly the way she personally considers "good form". And knowing that she had put herself out to help him when he was a total stranger to her I thought she was annoyed that he hadn't shown the faintest sign of gratitude, and hadn't even said – as he was so capable of saying because the language and the idiom and the inflexions were natural to him – "Thank you for the party, *and for everything*", when he said goodbye.

Perhaps this apparent brashness contributed to her reservations about Hari, but I am sure, now, that if he and I had simply smiled distantly at each other and passed each other by, the first thing she would have said, when the party was over, would have been something like, "Poor Mr. Kumar needs bringing out. We need to knock that chip off his shoulder. After all, it's not really his fault that it's there." But she had seen that the chip on Hari's shoulder was insignificant compared with the possible danger that lay ahead for me, for him, if that clumsy but innocent walk in the garden developed into the kind of familiarity which Lili, as a woman of the world, saw at once as not unlikely.

*

Was it now that my dreams came back? Do you remember, Auntie? Those dreams I wrote to you about once? The dreams I had when I first came to India, and which I had again after I'd left Pindi and gone to Mayapore? The dreams of *faces*, the faces of strangers? Dreamed, imagined, constructed out of nothing, but with an exactness that was frightening because they were so real? The faces of strangers I had to take with me even into dreams because I felt that I was surrounded by strangers when I was awake?

The first two weeks or so in Mayapore, when everything was new to me and I was getting to know my surroundings, I didn't have those dreams. But as I told you in that letter, there was a period when the newness had worn off, when I hated everything because I was afraid of it. I think the cocktail party marked the beginning of this. I wanted to pack my bags and go back to Pindi – which interested me because when I was suffering this kind of homesickness in Pindi I wanted to pack my bags and go back to England. And just as I think you guessed something of what I was going through, so I believe did Lili. But how much of my restlessness – which I tried so hard to disguise – did she put down to my thinking about Mr. Kumar? How much, indeed, *was* due to my thinking about him?

It was at this time that I broke my vow, never to go to the club because Lili couldn't go with me. The girls I worked with at the Mayapore General were always on at me to go with them. And it was so easy to talk to them. I used to feel the relief of leaving the MacGregor House and cycling to the hospital and when I got there not caring what I said or how I said it, and being able to flop into a chair and complain about the heat – using all the little tricks of expression and gesture that you know will be understood, and which don't have to be thought about. The luxury, the ease, of being utterly natural. Giving back as good as you got if someone was edgy or bitchy. Being edgy and bitchy yourself. Letting it rip, like a safety valve.

So I started going with some of them to the club for a drink on my way home. They were usually picked up by young officers from the barracks, round about 5.30. There wasn't any serious attachment going. Just boys and girls getting together in their off-duty and maybe sleeping somewhere if it could be fixed. We used to drive to the club in tongas, or in army trucks if the boys could "swing the transport" as they called it. Then we'd congregate in the lounge-bar or the smoking-room, or on the terrace. Or there was a games room, where they had a portable and a lot of old dance records, Victor Sylvester, Henry Hall, and some new ones, Dinah Shore, Vera Lynn, and the Inkspots. Usually round about 6.30 I'd slip away and get a tonga home. I felt horribly guilty about going to the club because I'd told Lili I jolly well wouldn't. She'd always said, "Don't be silly, of course you must go." And I owned up at once, the moment I'd been, although on the way back that first time I was thinking up all kinds of excuses for being late. Once I'd owned up it made going again that much simpler, though. I felt less and less guilty and more and more at home in the club. Several times I stayed to dinner there, and only rang Aunt Lili at the last moment.

And then one day one of the boys who was a bit drunk and who'd insisted on coming with me to the phone said, "She's not really your aunt, is she?" I said, "No. Why?" And he said, "Well, you don't look as if you've got a touch of the tar brush. I've had a bet on it." And all kinds of little things fitted into place – oh, less in connexion with what the boys and girls had said, but over the sort of things some of the civilian women had said, or rather *not* said. The way they'd looked when I said "The MacGregor House" when they asked me where I was staying. The way some of the civilian men had chipped in and asked questions about you and Uncle Henry, as if (as I realised now) to test it out that I really was a niece of a one-time Governor and not some by-blow of Lili Chatterjee's family.

But there is this, too, Auntie – I think this kind of thing would have run off me like water off a duck's back if all the time, underneath the easy pleasure of being with the boys and girls, there hadn't been a sort of creeping boredom, like a paralysis. Basically I hated the way that after a few drinks everything people said was loaded with a kind of juvenile smutty innuendo. After a while I began to see that the ease of companionship wasn't really ease at all, because once you had got to know each other, and had then had to admit that none of you really had much in common except what circumstance had forced on you, the companionship seemed forced itself. We were all imprisoned in it, and probably all hated it, but daren't let go of it. I got so that I would just sit there listening to the things that were said, thinking, "No, this is wrong. And I haven't got this time to waste. I haven't this time to spare."

It was the evening I went to the club after the visit to the War Week Exhibition on the *maidan* that I first *admitted* this to myself. Was it just coincidence that I'd seen Hari again that afternoon, for the first time since the party? I suppose not. The two things were connected – the second meeting with Hari and my looking round the club and listening and saying to myself "I haven't this time to waste". And of course that other man was at the club too. Ronald Merrick I mean. Perhaps this wasn't coincidence either.

*

I went to the War Week Exhibition on the Saturday afternoon, at about four o'clock, with three or four girls from the hospital and two or three young subalterns from the Berkshires. We went to watch the parade and the military band which was the week's grand finale. There were the finals of the boxing, too, and the wrestling. The boxing was nearly all between English boys, but the wrestling was between Indians from one of the Indian regiments. One of the girls said, "Oh no, I couldn't bear to watch *that,*" so we went to the boxing and watched these young soldiers dab at each other and make each other's noses bleed. Then we went into the tea-tent.

The parade was scheduled for 5.30. I've never seen anything like that tea-tent. Flowers everywhere. Long trestle-tables covered with dazzling white cloths. Silver-plated urns. Iced cakes, cream cakes, jellies, trifles. One of the boys we were with whistled and said that "some wog contractor was putting on a show and making a packet". And of course this was probably true, and at once cancelled out the thought that only the English were having a beano, although it didn't cancel out the picture you had of people at home scuttling off to the shops with their dismal little ration books. And it didn't cancel out the thought of all the people who weren't allowed in the tent, not because they couldn't afford the price of the tea-ticket, but because this was the tent for "Officers and Guests" only. There were a few Indian women there, the wives of Indian officers. But the mass of faces was white – except behind the tables where the servants were running up and down trying to serve everyone at once. And "officers" was really only a polite way of saying "Europeans" because there were plenty of civilians and their wives there too, but only white civilians, like the Deputy Commissioner, and several men I recognised from Lili's parties as teachers or executives from the British-Indian Electrical.

The DC was standing talking to the Brigade Commander and as we passed them Mr. White said, "Hello, Miss Manners. You know Brigadier Reid, I think." Why was I so pleased? Because at once the boys I was with sort of stood to attention and the girls looked as if butter wouldn't melt in their mouths. Apparently the Brigadier was previously stationed in Pindi and had met us once or twice at parties, but we only vaguely remembered one another. He asked after you and then the DC said, "How's Lili?" and I said "Fine" and felt that somehow I was vindicated and no longer ranked in our little group as the odd girl who lived with "that Indian woman". Because even if she was "that Indian woman" the Deputy Commissioner called her Lili. And yet afterwards I was annoyed, too, because the DC hadn't said, "Where's Lili?" He knew, without even having to think about it, that she was unlikely to be in the tent and therefore probably wouldn't be on the *maidan* at all because she wouldn't go to "the other tent".

Anyway, I introduced the boys and girls, which rather made their day, but also helped to make mine later, when we were on our way across the *maidan* to the parade and I saw Hari and went up to him and talked to him for about five minutes while the others waited where I'd left them, and were prep-pared to wait because they couldn't be sure who Hari might be if I was on chatting terms with the DC and the Brig. When I got back to them one of the subalterns said, "Who was that?" so I just said, "Oh, a boy who was at Chillingborough," as if I had known him then and he had been a friend of my brother or some other male relation. Which shut them up, because none of them had been to anywhere as good. I was quite shameless. About being so snobbish, I mean. Because this was *their* weapon, not mine. I mean it was their weapon, then, in Mayapore, even if it wasn't at home. I enjoyed the brief sensation I had of turning their world momentarily up-side down.

*

Hari was at the War Week Exhibition for the *Gazette*. I didn't recognise him at first – partly because I don't see people very well without my glasses, but mainly because he looked different. It took me several meetings before I realised that since the cocktail party he'd spent money on new clothes – narrower, better fitting trousers (and not "babu" white). In spite of his awkwardness at that party, I think that after it he had expected more invitations, and spent money he couldn't afford so that he wouldn't feel so out of place. At one of our later meetings I said, "But I'm sure you used to smoke. You had a cigarette at the party." He admitted this but said he'd given it up. Even then I didn't immediately con-nect the new clothes and the money saved from giving up smoking, or see what these things meant in terms of the hopes Lili's invitation had raised for him.

He'd spent all his life in England, or anyway from the age of two when his father sold all his land in the UP and went to live there. His mother had died when he was born, and once they were in England his father cut himself off from everyone except this one sister, Hari's Aunt Shalini who had been married off at sixteen to a Gupta Sen, the brother of a rich Mayapore bania. In England Hari's father made a lot of money, but then lost it, and died and left Hari penniless and homeless. And so there he was, just in his last year at Chilling-borough, quite alone. His Aunt Shalini borrowed money from her well-off brother-in-law to pay Hari's passage back to India. He worked for a time in the uncle's office in the bazaar, but eventually got this job on the newspaper, because of his knowledge of English, Aunt Lili told me a bit of this (she got it from Vassi) but for ages I assumed that because his aunt's brother-in-law was rich money was no problem to him, and I thought his working on a newspaper was from choice, not necessity. It took some time as well for me to understand that all the plans he and his father had had for him had come to nothing, because his "Uncle" Romesh wouldn't spend a penny on further education, but set him to work, and his Aunt Shalini had virtually no money of her own. And then, of course, it took some time for the penny to drop that Hari's Englishness meant nothing in India, because he lived with his aunt in one of the houses in the Chillianwallah Bagh – which was on the wrong side of the river.

When I went up to him on the *maidan* that day I said, "It's Mr. Kumar, isn't it?" which the white people nearby obviously took note of. I misjudged the reason for his silence and the reluctant way he shook hands. I said, "I'm Daphne Manners, we met at Lili Chatterjee's," and he said, yes, he remembered, and asked how we both were. We chatted on like that for a while, with me doing most of the chatting and feeling more and more like the squire's daughter condescending to the son of one of her father's tenants, because that's how he seemed to *want* to make me feel. I wondered why. I broke off finally, saying, "Come along any evening. It's open house," for which he thanked me with that expression that meant he wouldn't dream of coming along unless specially asked and perhaps not even then because he took the invitation as a meaningless form of politeness.

So off I went and rejoined the gang and sat for an hour watching the parade and listening to the band. And in the club that evening I stayed on for dinner and we talked about the marching and the drill. All the boys were awfully proud of themselves because of the boxing and the regimental precision of the Berkshires. You could sense flags flying everywhere. When Ronald Merrick turned up he came straight over to me, which wasn't at all usual. Since the dinner party at Aunt Lili's, when we didn't particularly hit it off, we'd only exchanged a few words and had the odd drink or two for form's sake if we bumped into each other at the club. He always seemed busy and unrelaxed, and happiest in the smoking-room talking to other men and getting into arguments. He had a bit of a reputation for being on the quarrelsome side, and apart from a number of unmarried girls who chased him people didn't like him much. But this evening he came straight over to me and said, "Did you enjoy the parade? I saw you on the *maidan.*" He sat and had drinks with us, and then came out with this semi-invitation to me to come along one evening and listen to his Sousa records, which the other girls chipped me about when he'd gone, coming out with that old joke about etchings, and never trusting a policeman. One of them said, "Daphne's obviously got what it takes for Mr. Merrick. I've been trying to land *that* fish for ages." One of the boys made a joke about what she meant by "takes", so the subject was back to normal. Being a Saturday there was a dance on too, and the usual horseplay at the swimming pool. And out on the terrace you didn't only *sense* the flags waving, you could see them. Scores of little flags strung among the fairy lights. There was an atmosphere of "We'll show them". The boy I was dancing with said that War Week had given the bloody Indians something to think about. Then he began to get amorous and I had to fight him off. I left him and went into the ladies and sat on the seat and listened to the scurrilous chat going on on the other side of the door and thought, No, it's wrong, wrong. And later, back in the lounge-bar, deafened by the thumping band, I thought, "I haven't this time to waste. I haven't this time to spare."

I felt as if the club were an ocean-going liner, like the *Titanic,* with all the lights blazing and the bands playing, heading into the dark, with no one on the bridge.

*

Auntie, promise me one thing, that if the child survives but you can't bear to have it near you, you'll try to see that the money I leave is used to give it some kind of decent start in life? I look around, trying to think where the child might go if it lives and I don't. I don't presume on your affection for me to extend to what is only half my flesh and blood, and half that of someone unknown to you – perhaps someone unknown to me, someone disreputable. I have got myself used to the idea that you won't want it under your roof, in fact, please don't worry on that score. It's inevitable that a child so badly *mis*conceived should suffer a bit for *my* faults. In any case, let's be frank, you probably won't live for as long as the child would need you to if he first came to a fully conscious, recollective existence while under your roof. I think of Lili. But wonder, too. Perhaps as the child grows, some likeness to Hari will become apparent. I so much hope so. Because that will be my vindication. I have nightmares of the child growing up to resemble no one, black-skinned, beyond redemption, a creature of the dark, a tiny living mirror of that awful night. And yet, even so, it will be a child. A god-given creature, if there is a god, and even if there isn't, deserving of that portion of our blessing we can spare.

I suppose the child – if I'm not here to nurture him – will have to go into a home. Couldn't it be as well my home in a way? There is that woman whom they call Sister Ludmila. I asked her once whether she needed money. She said not, but promised to tell me if she ever did. Perhaps as she gets older (and I don't know how old she is) she will spare a thought for the new-born as well as for the dying. It's a logical progression.

By "decent start in life", I don't mean background or education, but much simpler things like warmth, comfort, enough to eat, and kindness and affection. Oh, all the things squandered on me.

If it is a boy, please name him Harry, or Hari if his skin is dark enough to *honour* that kind of spelling. If a girl – I don't know. I haven't made up my mind. I haven't thought of "it" as a girl. But if she is please *don't* call her Daphne. That's the girl who ran from Apollo, and was changed into a laurel bush! With me it's been the other way round, hasn't it? Rooted clumsily in the earth, thinking I'm running free, chasing the sun-god. When I was in my teens Mother once said, "Oh, for goodness' sake stop *gallumping*!" which puzzled and then hurt me because being tall I had an idea that I was a sort of graceful Diana type – long-legged and slender, taut as a bow, flitting through the forest! Poor Mother! She had a frightful talent for pouring cold water on people. It was David who taught me to see that she did this because she never knew from one minute to the next what it was she really wanted, so she felt that things were always going wrong around her, and had to hit out at the nearest likely culprit, usually Daddy, but often me. She adored David, though, which is probably why he saw through her more easily than Daddy and I did and was able to explain her to me. She never had her defences up for *him*. I suppose it was because even after years of living comfortably in England she still talked about India as if she had only just escaped from it a minute ago that I grew to feel sorry for it, and then to love it and want it for its own sake, as well as for Daddy's. When I was old enough to understand them he used to show me snaps and photographs and tell me what I thought were wonderful tales of the "land where I was born", so that when I first came back out here I was always looking for the India I thought I knew because I had seen it in my imagination, like a kind of mirage, shimmering on the horizon, with hot, scented breezes blowing in from far-away hills . . .

*

It's funny how in spite of what you know about the rains before you come to India you think of it as endlessly dry and scorched, one vast Moghul desert, with walled, scattered towns where all the buildings are shaped like mosques, with arches of fretted stone. Occasionally from the window of a train – the one I went up to Pindi on when I first came out – there are glimpses of the country you've imagined. I'm glad I came before and not in the middle of the rains. It's best to undergo the exhaustion of that heat, the heat of April and May that brings out the scarlet flowers of the gol mohurs, the "flames of the forest" (such a dead, dry, lifeless-looking tree before the blossoms burst) the better to know the joy of the wild storms and lashing rains of the first downpours that turn everything green. That is *my* India. The India of the rains.

*

There's another name besides Hari's that we never mention. Bibighar. So although you were in Mayapore once, and may have visited the gardens, I don't know whether you have a picture of them in your mind or not. There it is all greenness. Even in the hottest months, before the rains, there is a feeling of greenness, a bit faded and tired, but still green – wild and overgrown, a walled enclosure of trees and undergrowth, with pathways and sudden open spaces where a hundred years ago there were probably formal gardens and fountains. You can still see the foundations of the old house, the Bibighar itself. In one part of them there is a mosaic floor with steps up to it as if it was once the entrance. They've built pillars round the mosaic since and roofed it over, to make it into a sort of shelter or pavilion. Men from the Public Works come once or twice a year and cut back the shrubbery and creepers. At the back of the grounds the wall is crumbled and broken and gives on to waste ground. At the front of the garden there is an open archway on to the road but no gate. So the garden is never closed. But few people go in. Children think it is haunted. Brave boys and girls play there in the morning, and in the dry weather well-off Indians sometimes picnic. But mostly it's deserted. The house was built by a prince, so Lili told me, and destroyed by that man MacGregor, whose house is named after him, and whose wife Janet is supposed to haunt the verandah, nursing her dead baby. It was Lili who first took me into the Bibighar. Hari had heard something about it, but had never seen it, or realised that the long wall on the Bibighar Bridge road was the wall surrounding it, and had never been in it until I took him there one day. There were children playing the first time I visited it with Lili but they ran off when they saw us. I expect they thought we were day-light Bibighar ghosts. And afterwards I never saw anyone there at all.

*

Hari and I got into the habit of going to the Bibighar, and sitting there in the pavilion, because it was the one place in Mayapore where we could be together and be utterly natural with each other. And even then there was the feeling that we were having to hide ourselves away from the inquisitive, the amused, and the disapproving. Going in there, through the archway, or standing up and getting ready to go back into the cantonment – those were the moments when this feeling of being about to hide or about to come out of hiding to face things was strongest. And even while we were there, there was often a feeling of preparedness, in case someone came in and saw us together, even though we were doing nothing but sitting side by side on the edge of the mosaic "platform" with our feet dangling, like two kids sitting on a wall. But at least we could be pretty sure no white man or woman would come into the gardens. They never did. The gardens always seemed to have a purely Indian connexion, just as the *maidan* really had a purely English one.

Perhaps you say: But if you wanted to be with Hari, and he. wanted to be with you, that was no crime, surely, and there were tons of places you could have gone and been happy together? Well, but where? The MacGregor House? Yes. His house in the Chillianwallah Bagh? Yes. But where else? Auntie, where else? Where else that people wouldn't have stared and made us self-conscious, armed us in preparation to withstand an insult or a vulgar scene? The club was out. There was the other club, what they call the Indian Club, but Hari wouldn't take me there because there *I* would have been stared at by what he called the banias with their feet on the chairs. The English coffee shop was out. The Chinese Restaurant was out – after one visit when he was stopped from following me upstairs. I'd been there before with an English officer – and automatically, without thinking, began to go up. So we had to sit downstairs while I was subjected to the stage whisper comments of the people going to the room above, and the curious, uncomfortable stares of the British non-commissioned soldiers who shared the downstairs room with us. Even the poor little fleapit cinema in the cantonment was out because I wouldn't have had the nerve to try to take Hari into the sacrosanct little "balcony" and he wouldn't have made me sit on a wooden form in the pit. Neither would he take me to the Indian cinema opposite the Tirupati temple, although I asked him to. He said, "What, and sit through four hours of the *Ramayana*, holding our noses, getting fleas and sweating our guts out?"

Auntie, in Mayapore there wasn't anywhere we could be alone together in public that didn't involve some kind of special forethought or preparation. We spent a few evenings at the MacGregor House while Auntie Lili was out playing bridge, and a couple of evenings with his sweet little Aunt Shalini, but a friendship between two human beings can't be limited in this way, can it? You can't not be affected by the fact that it's a friendship you're both having to work hard at.

*

And of course it was a friendship I began in a conscious frame of mind. Naturally, as I'd known he wouldn't, he never just dropped in to open house. I told Lili I'd met him on the *maidan* and invited him to come any time. In retrospect her reaction strikes me as that of someone who was subconsciously pleased, but afraid of the consequences for me, or, if not afraid, full of reservations. She told me more about him. Perhaps she was trying to warn me, but she only succeeded in adding fuel to my reforming zeal. She must have told me about his having been to Chillingborough before I met him on the *maidan*, because I'm sure he never mentioned Chillingborough at the party. But otherwise I've forgotten exactly how and when I fitted him together in my mind. All I know, what I admit to, is this – that I was conscious at the meeting on the *maidan* of doing a good deed. The thought revolts me now. I can't bear to remember that I ever condescended, even unintentionally, to the man I fell in love with.

When a couple of weeks had gone by and he still hadn't dropped in I wrote him a note. I got his address from Aunt Lili who had it in her book. As you know I've always been hopeless at bridge, and Lili was going round to the Whites to make up a four with Judge Menen whose wife was in the Greenlawns Nursing Home. Which left me alone on the Saturday evening. After the flag-wagging of War Week I didn't want to go to the club. I didn't know what I wanted to do. I thought of Hari. I'd been thinking of him a lot. It was Saturday morning. I wrote him a note and sent it by one of the servants to the Chillianwallah Bagh. The servant came back and said that Kumar Sahib hadn't been in but that he'd left the note. So I didn't know whether Hari would come that evening or not, which made Lili's silent criticism worse, and my determination to have everything ready stronger. I told cook to prepare dinner for two, chicken pulao, with piles and piles of saffron rice and onion pickles and mounds of lovely hot chappattis, and lots of iced beer, and what I called Mango-Melba to follow. I checked the cocktail cabinet and sent the boy to the liquor store for more Carew's gin. Then I went down to the cantonment myself, to the Sports Emporium, and bought a batch of records that had just come in, and a box of needles because Lili wasn't very good about changing them and used the same ones over and over and mixed the old ones with the new. We had a Decca portable she'd bought the last time she was in Cal. And when I got back I sent Bhalu crazy the way I bashed round the garden gathering armfuls of flowers! I felt a bit like Cho Cho San getting ready for Pinkerton! Lili went off to the Whites about sixty-thirty while I was still in the bath. She came into the bedroom and called out, "Daphne, I'm bashing off now and will be back about midnight, I expect. Have a good time." I cried out, "Oh, I will. Give my love all round." And then she said, "I hope he has the good manners to turn up," so I shouted back, "Of course he will. He'd have sent a note by now if he hadn't been going to." Poor Lili. She really thought he wasn't going to. So did I. I dressed in that awful electric blue dress that turns muddy green in the artificial light, but I felt I didn't care what I looked like. I knew I could never look anything but myself. And there was joy in not caring for once, but just being myself.

And he came, bang on the dot of 7.30, in a horse tonga. To get a horse tonga he must have gone to the station, because on the other side of the river you can usually only get cycle tongas. Or perhaps he had come from the cantonment bazaar, from Darwaza Chand's shop, and had waited there while they finished making the new shirt that made him smell of fresh, unlaundered cotton.

*

I'd cheated a bit in my note by not making it really clear I'd be alone. For all I knew he was the sort of Indian boy who'd think it wrong to dine alone with a woman, or if *he* didn't mind, that his aunt would refuse to let him come if she knew Lili was going to be out. I could see he was on tenterhooks at first, waiting for Lili to appear. We were on the verandah, and Raju was serving the drinks. It must have been on this occasion that he refused a cigarette and admitted he'd given it up. Not smoking made him more on tenterhooks, and suddenly I was on them too because I saw what a trap I'd laid for myself. He'd probably think Lili had gone out to avoid him because she disapproved of the idea of his coming to a meal, or, just as bad, that I'd asked him round secretly on a night she was going out because I knew she would disapprove. So before the situation got out of hand I told him the truth, that Saturday was one of Lili's bridge nights, and I hated bridge and had wanted a quiet dinner with someone I could talk to about home, but had cheated when writing my note in case he or his aunt thought it odd for a girl to invite a boy round on an evening when she was going to be by herself.

He seemed puzzled at first. It must have been about four years since an English person had spoken to him in the way that in England he'd have been used to and thought nothing of. I hated even being conscious of this fact, but I was, so there's no use in pretending otherwise.

Even on that first evening we were having to work at a

basis for ordinary human exchange, although it was probably the only evening we met without feeling an immediate sense of pressure and disapproval from outside. Within a minute or two of realising Lili was out I could see him beginning to relax, beginning to forget himself and start looking at and considering me. We had about three gin fizzes and then went in and ate, sitting close together at one end of the table. I'd worked it out before that although it would have been nice for me if I could have just told Raju to bring the food in and leave me to serve it, it would be better for Hari's morale if we were *both* waited on hand and foot. Raju of course tried to cut Hari down to size a bit by addressing him in Hindi, but soon gave up when he realised Hari spoke it really no better than I did! And I was glad to see how he also relaxed at the table, once we'd made a joke about his inability to speak the language, and tackled the grub! Like me. We both waded in like a couple of kids. At Lili's parties I'd noticed how the Indian men sort of held back, as if it was faintly indelicate to eat hearty in mixed company. I kept sending Raju out to bring more hot chappattis which Hari ended up by scoffing without noticing how many he'd had. Later, when I had a similar dinner at his Aunt Shalini's I realised that there was a difference between our food and theirs, and understood better why Hari ate as if he'd not had a square meal for weeks. I've never been able to stand anything cooked in ghi, which affects my bileduct immediately and there was ghi in some of the dishes Mrs. Gupta Sen gave us.

But that is going on too far ahead. After we'd done right by the grub, we sort of collapsed in the drawing-room and then Raju brought in the brandy and coffee, and Hari did the honours at the gramophone. All through dinner we'd talked and talked about "home". We were almost exactly the same age, so remembered the same things in relation to the same phases of our lives, I mean like seeing the *R 101* blundering overhead. Aeroplanes and Jim Mollison and Amy Johnson, Amelia Earhart lost in the Timor Sea; films like *Rain* and *Mata Hari*. And things like cricket and Jack Hobbs, Wimbledon and Bunny Austin and Betty Nuttall, motor racing and Sir Malcolm Campbell, Arsenal and Alec James, the proms at the poor old bombed Queen's Hall – although Hari had never been there because he had no real taste for music apart from jazz and swing.

When he first started putting the records on you could

see how much pleasure they gave him, but also how they suddenly brought back his uncertainty. After he'd played two and put on a third, a Victor Sylvester, he got his courage up and said, "I've almost forgotten how and was never much good anyway, but would like to dance?" I said I was once described as an elephant with clogs on myself, but perhaps together we'd sort each other out, so we stood up and held hands and backs. At first he held me too far away for it to work properly, and we were both watching each other's feet all the time and apologising and taking it awfully seriously, and when the record ended I think he expected me to sit down or suggest going on to the verandah, not only because it hadn't worked but because he thought I might have agreed to dance with him in order not to make it look too obvious that I felt it would be distasteful to be held by an Indian. But I asked him to find a particular record "In the Mood", which, as you probably *don't* know, is quick and easy, an absolute natural, and waited for him, forced him to dance again, and this time we looked over each other's shoulders and not at our feet, and danced closer, and felt each other slipping into a sort of natural rhythm.

*

If you ever read this I shan't be around to feel diminished by your criticism. I can kid myself that I'm reliving it for no one except the one person who knows how far short of perfect re-enactment an account like this must fall. Perhaps as well as being an insurance against permanent silence it is a consolation prize to me, to give me a chance to have him with me again in a way that is more solid than unfettered recollection, but still insubstantial. But second best is better than third – the third best of random thoughts un-pinned down. Oh, I could conjure him now, just with this scratchy old pen, in a form that might satisfy you better, but do more or less than justice to what he actually was. I could do this if I ignored the uncertainty I felt, the clumsiness we both shared; do it if I pretended that from the moment we held each other we felt the uncomplicated magic of straightforward physical attraction. But it was never uncomplicated. Unless you could say that the opposing complications cancelled each other out – on his side the complication of realising that the possession of a white girl could be a way of bolstering his ego, and on mine the complication of the curious almost titillating *fear* of his colour. How else account for the fact that in dancing the second time we stared (I think fixedly) over each other's shoulders, as if afraid to look directly into each other's eyes?

We didn't dance a third time, but in sitting out now there was no sense of physical rebuff as there would have been if I'd refused to dance at all or sat down after that first awkward impersonal shuffle. Our separation, our sitting, he in his chair and I in mine, was a mutual drawing-back from dangerous ground – a drawing-back from the danger to ourselves but also from the danger to the other, because neither of us could be certain that the other fully saw the danger or understood the part that might be played by the *attraction to danger* in what we felt for each other.

And that is how Lili found us when she got back, sitting companionably at the end of an evening we had both obviously enjoyed because we were still talking easily, with our tensions so well concealed we couldn't even be certain that it was a tension the other one shared.

He stayed for no more than ten minutes after she got back; and yet during that time, while she talked to him, I could see his armour going back on layer by layer, and Lili change from faintly frosty to friendly back to frosty again – as if at one moment before he was fully re-armed she had seen the kind of vulnerable spot in him she was afraid of and so put up her own shutters, not to lock him out but to try – by putting them up – to lock me in, to keep us apart for everybody's sake.

One is not sensitive usually to the effect people have on one another unless one of them happens to be someone you love. In this case, I suppose, already I loved them both.

*

War Week was towards the end of April, so the evening Hari came to dinner at the MacGregor House must have been in the early part of May. One or two of the girls from the hospital went up that month to places like Darjeeling for a spot of leave. It was terribly hot in Mayapore. The moon was that curious lopsided shape which I think you told me is caused by dust particles in the atmosphere. There wasn't much leave going because of all the political crises that kept boiling up, simmering down and boiling up again. Matron said

I could have a couple of weeks off and I think Lili would have liked to get away into the hills for a bit, but we were pretty short-staffed at the hospital and I didn't feel I was entitled to leave so soon after starting work. I suggested to Lili that she should go by herself and leave me to cope, but she wouldn't hear of it. So we sweated it out, as practically everybody else from the Deputy Commissioner downwards was doing. It became too hot, really, to have parties – a few times out to dinner, and a few times having people in to dinner, that was about the sum total.

The day after Hari's visit he sent me a note, thanking me formally for the evening, and a few days later I got an invitation from Mrs. Gupta Sen to have dinner at her house in the Chillianwallah Bagh the following Saturday. Lili had one too, but she said it was only for form's sake, and that anyway she was playing bridge again, so couldn't go. After I'd accepted I got another note, this time from Hari, saying that as the house was difficult to find (all the numbers were haywire and the Chillianwallah Bagh was really a system of roads, not just one road) he would call for me in a tonga at about 7.15, if that was all right. He said he hoped I wouldn't find the evening too dull, there was no gramophone or anything like that. I asked Lili if she thought this was a hint that he'd like it if I took ours along, with a few records, but she said that wouldn't do at all, you couldn't take a thing like a gramophone because not only might Mrs. Gupta Sen think it wrong to have such a thing in the house (especially when the records were all European music, which probably hurt her ears) but she would more likely than not look upon it as an insult, a criticism of the kind of hospitality she had to offer. So I took Lili at her word, and I think she was right.

His Aunt Shalini was sweet, and spoke very good English. She said Hari's father taught her when she was a little girl and that she loved having Hari living with her because now she'd been able to pick it up again and improve her accent. She showed me some snaps of Hari taken in England, which her brother, Hari's father Duleep, had sent her from time to time. There were several taken in the garden, showing the house they lived in in Berkshire, which looked to me like a small mansion. Then there were later pictures of Hari, with some English friends, whose name was Lindsey.

I'd been pretty nervous, anticipating this visit to the Chillianwallah Bagh, and it didn't help when Hari was late picking me up and I was sitting alone on the verandah of the MacGregor waiting for him to arrive. Lili had already gone off to bridge. She'd warned me to have at least a couple of drinks before Hari arrived in case Mrs. Gupta Sen was teetotal, and I got a bit squiffy, drinking more than I needed because of the extra twenty minutes or so that I had to wait. He was awfully embarrassed about being late, which I think he thought I'd see as a typical Indian failing. He said he'd had difficulty getting a tonga because they had all seemed to be out ferrying people to the first house of the flicks. I was relieved when we got into the tonga and I saw the shapes of a wrapped bottle of gin and a bottle of lime or lemon in a little canvas bag on the seat. It was as good as dark by the time we got across the Bibighar bridge – actually it was as we went past the Bibighar wall that I asked Hari what he thought of the gardens. We had a bit of a laugh when it turned out he didn't even know properly what they were or that they were there. I said, "I've only been in Mayapore a few months and you've been here for four years, and I know it better than you. But then that's like living in London and never going to the Tower."

We turned off the Chillianwallah Bagh Extension road. The streets were badly lit and there was an awful smell from the river. I wondered what on earth I'd let myself in for, and I must confess my heart sank. It rose again a bit when I saw the type of house in the district we'd driven in to – cheek by jowl, but modern-looking and civilised, all squares and angles. I was amused the way Hari had to keep telling the driver things like "Dahne ki taraf aur ek dam sidhe ki rasta" just like me, muddling through in pidgin Hindi. I chipped him about it and gradually he relaxed.

But then when we had stopped at his house he became unrelaxed again because one of the servants had closed the gate. He shouted out but no one came and the tonga-wallah didn't seem prepared to get out and open it himself. So Hari climbed down and opened it. It was only a few paces between the gate and the open area in front of the porch, which was lit by an unshaded electric light bulb, and we could have walked it, which might have been better because the tonga-wallah started making trouble about the tiny space he had to turn round in, which was something I had to leave Hari to deal with. Because his Hindi was as bad as mine I understood what was going on, and how he had to bribe the fellow to come back at "gyarah baje" and refused to pay him meanwhile.

Suddenly I was fed up with the awful position Hari was being put in by a bloody-minded tonga-wallah, and was about to say "Oh, tell the stupid man I'd rather walk home than put him to any bother," but stopped myself in time, because that would have been taking charge and would have made matters worse, so instead when Hari had got his way and the man had reluctantly agreed to come back at eleven, I said, "What a fuss they make," as if I was personally used to it, which he probably knew I wasn't, and which made it look as if I was acting like a Mem, slumming. Sort of amused, at Hari's expense. Knowing what I'd done I wanted to get back into the tonga and go home, and have an enormous drink.

Instead we went indoors, encased in a sort of gloom, a sort of trembling expectancy of disaster, or if not disaster then awful boredom and discomfort, and unease. Thank heaven for Aunt Shalini, who came into the little hall like a miniature Rajput princess, beautifully and almost undetectably made up, wearing a pale lilac saree, perfectly simple and plain, just cotton, but looking marvellous and cool. She shook hands, which made my feeble self-conscious efforts at *namaste* look silly. She said. "Come in and have a drink," and led us into the living-room, small but beautifully bare and uncluttered, with a rug or two, a divan and one tiny but very comfortable wicker chair which she made me sit in while, as she said, Hari "did the honours" at the drinks table – a Bernares brass tray on a carved ebony mother-of-pearl inlaid stand, on which there were exactly three glasses and the bottles Hari had taken out of the canvas bag as surreptitiously as he could. While she was talking to me I saw the physical likeness between herself and Hari, although of course she was tiny. In front of her I felt a bit of a gawk, big, clumsy, dressed unsuitably and showing far too much bare skin. Hari was wearing a grey cotton suit, but he had to take the jacket off presently because the fans were only working at half power.

When we'd had just one drink – and by this time I felt I really needed two – she said, "Shall we go in?" and stood up and led the way next door to a small box-like dining-room. She called out to the boy to switch the fans on, and then we began to eat.

She'd taken so much trouble with the table, to make me feel at home. There was a bowl of water in the centre with frangipani blooms floating in it. And handwoven lace mats at the three places. She described every dish, but I've forgotten most of the names, and some of them I found difficult. When the main dish came on – Chicken tandoori – she said to Hari, "Haven't we any iced beer?" and he got up and went away for a while and came back with the beer in bottles, followed by a servant with glasses and a tray. She said, "Haven't we a jug, Hari?" So he sent the servant back for a jug, then went out himself again with the bottles. The boy brought the beer back decanted in a jug. The rest of the servants were watching from doorways and through the barred-window openings into the adjoining rooms. Aunt Shalini drank nothing, not even water, so Hari and I had the beer between us. My glass was an old tumbler with the Roman "key" design, and his was smaller and thicker. He was conscious, overly-conscious, of the insignificant ways in which the table fell short of what he had once been used to and thought I would consider essential – but towards the end of the meal, when I had been watching him without realising I did so, he caught my eye, and I think he saw then that whatever I noticed as "faults" had only added to my feeling of being "at home", and to my feeling for him and his aunt as people honouring me, expressing some kind of groping hope that one day our different *usages* would mean nothing, mean as little as they meant that evening to me.

After dinner was the time she showed me the snaps. I was longing for a cigarette but didn't dare open my bag. Suddenly she said, "Hari, haven't we any Virginia cigarettes for Miss Manners?" How sensitive she was to every change of mood in her guests! How tolerant of any taste she personally found *dis*tasteful – like the smoking and the drinking. And I think Hari was surprised too at the tremendous ability she had to entertain an English girl – her first English guest ever, so I discovered. What I admired Hari for was the way he didn't *press* things like drink and cigarettes, but left his aunt in control, in her own house, which an insensitive blustering boy intent on proving his Englishness probably wouldn't have done. The other nice thing he did was to have a cigarette too, so that I shouldn't feel I was the only messy person in the room, but I noticed how he just let it burn away without smoking it properly. He was afraid to get the taste for it again.

The only thing that went a bit wrong was over the business of going to the wc! When we got up from the dinner-table

Hari made himself scarce for a while. I think he'd told Aunt Shalini to be sure to give me the opportunity to go, but that she didn't quite have the nerve to say anything to me when the time came. The next time I went to the house she had got over this embarrassment, but on this particular evening I think Hari's realisation that I hadn't "been" rather cast a blight on his evening. Round about 10.30 it began to cast a blight on mine too. I began to wonder whether they even *had* a wc of the kind they felt I could be invited to use. Actually it turned out that there was a downstairs as well as whatever there might have been upstairs. No seat, but she'd thoughtfully put a chamber pot on a little stool which I didn't dare use, and there was a bowl and a jug of water, on a table that looked as if it didn't always belong there, and some soap and towels and a hand mirror. I went in there after we heard the tonga-wallah come back and Hari went out to speak to him. I stood up and said, "May I powder my nose?" So she took me into the passage near the kitchens and opened the door and switched on the light and said, "Please, anytime you come, here it is." There were a couple of cockroaches running up and down, but I didn't care. Lili shrieks blue murder if she so much as glimpses one, but although when I first got to India I was horrified to find them sharing places like bathrooms and wc's I no longer care

When I said goodbye to Aunt Shalini I wanted to stoop down and kiss her, but didn't in case that offended her. Hari insisted on coming back in the tonga with me, but wouldn't come in for a nightcap. I think he was trying to avoid doing anything that would create an atmosphere of *Well, that's all over, now we can relax*. So after he'd driven off in the tonga I sat on the verandah and had a long cool drink of nimbo and waited for Lili to come home.

*

The next day I sent one of the boys round to Aunt Shalini's with an enormous bunch of flowers I'd raided the garden for, and a note of thanks. Bhalu was very cross with me, so I gave him ten chips and asked him not to complain to Madam and get me in trouble, which made him grin, the old rascal. After that he had me wound round his little finger. Perhaps he was wound round mine too, and we were partners in crime – crime because Lili paid all the servants extra when she had anyone staying in the house and it was understood guests weren't to tip them. He never complained again to Lili about my cutting flowers, but round about the first of each month when he'd been paid his wages he used to stand about saluting and grinning, until I gave him a few chips. He bought a new pair of chappals with the first lot of money I gave him, and looked very smart, but oddly more tortoiselike than ever, with his khaki shorts and knobbly black bare legs and these enormous army-style sandals, clopping about on the gravel. You could tell he preferred bare feet, but the chappals represented status. He was once a gardener to a Colonel James in Madras, and Colonel James's household has been Bhalu's standard of pukka life ever since, even though I think he knows the garden of the MacGregor House is far superior to any other garden he's ever worked in, which may be why he has to feel the whole of it belongs to him, and that he's tending it to the honour and glory of James Sahib rather than of Lili.

*

I'm gossiping, aren't I, Auntie? Putting off the moment when I have to write about the thing you really want to know. But yet, not gossiping, because you can't isolate the good and happy things from the bad and unhappy ones. And you see for me there was a growing sense of joy, whatever there was for the people who watched and waited.

It was now that Mayapore seemed to change for me. It was no longer just the house, the road to the cantonment bazaar, the road to the hospital, the hospital, the *maidan*, the club. It extended to the other side of the river and, because of that, in all directions, across that enormous flat plain that I used to stand staring at from the balcony of my room, putting on my glasses and taking them off, doing what Lili called my eye exercises. I felt that Mayapore had got bigger, and so had made me smaller, had sort of split my life into three parts. There was my life in the hospital, which also included the club and the boys and girls and all the good-time stuff that wasn't really good-time at all, just the easiest, the least exacting, so long as you ignored the fact that it was only the easiest for the least admirable part of your nature. There was my life at the MacGregor House, where I lived with Lili and mixed with Indians and English, the kind who made an effort to work together. But this mixing was just as self-conscious as the segregation. At the club you stood on *loud*, committed ground. At the MacGregor House it was silent and determinedly neutral. With Hari I began to feel that here at last was ground wholly personal to me, where I might learn to talk in my own tone of voice. Perhaps this is why I felt Mayapore had got bigger but made me smaller, because my association with Hari – the one thing that was beginning to make me feel like a person again – was hedged about, restricted, pressed in on until only by making yourself tiny could you squeeze into it and stand, imprisoned but free, diminished by everything that loomed from outside, *but not diminished from the inside*; and that was the point, that's why I speak of joy.

Sometimes, knowing the effort it cost to squeeze into this restricted, dangerous little space, I was afraid, as I was that evening Ronald Merrick "proposed" to me and brought me back to the MacGregor House, and I wanted to run back down the stairs and call out to Ronald, and was afraid of seeing the ghost of Janet MacGregor. This occasion, the occasion of his proposal after our dinner and my coming back to the MacGregor and being afraid, was in the middle of June. The rains were late. We were all exhausted, physically and mentally. That probably also accounts for my fear that night. That, and the feeling I had that Ronald represented something I didn't fully understand, but probably ought to trust. There's an awful weight still on my mind about Ronald. I feel that just as you and the others may know where Hari is, so there are things about Ronald that no one is prepared to discuss in front of me. I think about him a lot. He is like a dark shadow, just on the edge of my life.

Auntie, did he hurt Hari in some special horrible way? I think he did. But no one would say, at least would not say to me. And I didn't dare question anyone too closely. I was equally a party to the conspiracy to keep me a prisoner in the MacGregor House after that night in the Bibighar. I only left it twice, once to visit Aunt Shalini, who wouldn't see me, and then on the day before Lili took me up to 'Pindi and I went to the Sanctuary to say goodbye to Sister Ludmila. Ronald Merrick was on Sister Ludmila's conscience too. It seems she hadn't realised that he and I knew each other more than casually, hadn't realised that I might not know that it was Ronald who took Hari in for questioning that day he found him at the Sanctuary. But by then I was afraid to probe too deeply. I trusted no one. Only to my silence. And to

Hari's. But I remembered how after the Bibighar on the one occasion we came briefly face to face Ronald would not look at me straight, the time the Assistant Commissioner came with Judge Menen and a young English sub-divisional officer and held a sort of "inquiry" at which Ronald gave evidence and I made everybody uneasy, perhaps angry, with my answers to their questions.

Before I tell you what actually happened in the Bibighar, I must say something about Ronald, and something about Sister Ludmila. I think Ronald first took real notice of me that day on the *maidan,* when I went to the War Week Exhibition; took notice of me because he saw me go up to Hari and talk to him, as a lot of English people did. If he already had his eye on Hari, as some sort of potential subversive type (nothing could have been farther from the truth, but Ronald had his job to do) he probably looked at my going up to him like that, as a policeman would, but also as an Englishman who didn't want an English girl getting mixed up with the "wrong" type of Indian. I mean that would account for the fact that when he saw me in the club that evening he came straight up to me and said, "Did you enjoy the parade? I saw you on the *maidan,*" when usually we only nodded, or occasionally had a drink if circumstances made it awkward for him not to offer me one.

He probably had an idea that it would be kind to head me off, but also – because he was a policeman – wasn't above looking at me as a possible source of information about Hari: Do you remember my saying in a letter that with Ronald I never felt there was any real candour between him and the person he was dealing with? He took his job so seriously, and I think he felt he had to prove his worth all the time, so that nothing came naturally to him, nothing came spontaneously, or easily or *happily.*

I wonder just *how* much, once he'd made the move of showing friendly to me, wanting to head me off for my own good, he was genuinely and quite unexpectedly attracted to me as a person? Certainly from then on he began to pay attention. And although I didn't appreciate it at the time I see now that he became my new contact with the sort of world the club represented, the flag-wagging little world – but through him it wore a subtler mark – the Henry Moores, the Debussy. The one constant in my life was Lili and the MacGregor House, the variants were Hari on his side and Ronald on his. Those two seemed so far apart I don't think I ever referred to one in front of the other. But they weren't far apart at all. Which was why I was so angry, felt such a fool, when I discovered the truth, that they'd been – what? enemies since that day in the Sanctuary, when Hari was struck and dragged away, and Sister Ludmila had watched it all happening.

*

She dressed like one of those sisters of mercy with huge white flyaway linen caps. I'd seen her once or twice in the cantonment bazaar, walking in front of a boy who was armed with a stick, holding a leather bag that she kept chained to the belt round her waist. I was with a girl from the hospital and I said, "Whoever's that?" She said, "That's the mad Russian woman who collects dead bodies and isn't a nun at all, but just dresses like one." I was only passingly interested, not only because India has its fair share of eccentrics of both colours but also because it was during that period of unhappiness, of dislike for everything around me. A few weeks later I saw her again and mentioned her to Lili who said, "She doesn't do any harm, and Anna Klaus helps her sometimes, and likes her, but she makes me shiver, bashing off collecting people she finds dying."

Aunt Lili hates anything grisly or sordid, doesn't she? She told me that once as a young girl, the first time she went to Bombay and saw the slums, she cried. I think well-off privileged Indians like Lili have a sort of deep-rooted guilt that they bury under layers of what looks like indifference, because there's so little they can individually do to lessen the horror and the poverty. They subscribe to charities and do voluntary work but must feel it's like trying to dam up a river with a handful of twigs. And with Lili I think there's also a horror of death. She told me about going to the morgue in Paris with a medical student and how afterwards she had nightmares of all the corpses rising up and falling back and rising up again, which is why she hated Nello to show off his cuckoo clocks in the museum room at the MacGregor House! The room where he put Uncle Henry's old briar pipe in a glass case – the one Uncle Henry gave him to improve his imitations.

I took Hari into the museum room once, round about the beginning of the time when we knew that we both liked being together and so had to face the fact that there was almost no place we could be, except at his house or at Lili's. The Bibighar came a bit later. The time I took him in to the museum room we were joking about everything, but there was this sense already of cheating, of having to cheat and hide, buy time, buy privacy – paying for them with blows to our joint pride. I thought as I looked round the room, "Well, Hari and I are exhibits too. We could stand here on a little plinth, with a card saying *Types of Opposites.* ♂ *Indo-British, circa* 1942. *Do not Touch.*" Then all the people who stared at us in the cantonment, but looked away directly we looked at them, could come and stare to their hearts' content. I think it was in Hari's mind too. We never went into the museum room again. I said, "Come on, Hari – it's mouldy and dead," and held my hand out without thinking, then realised that except for dancing, casual contact like getting in and out of a tonga, we had never touched each other, even as friends, let alone as man and woman. I nearly withdrew my hand, because the longer I held it out and he hesitated to take it, the more loaded with significance the gesture became. It hadn't been meant as significant – just natural, warm and companionable. He took it finally. And then I wanted him to kiss me. To kiss me would have been the only way of making the hand-holding right. Holding hands and not kissing seemed wrong because it was incomplete. It wouldn't have been incomplete if he'd taken my hand the moment I'd held it out. When we got out of the room he let go. I felt deserted, caught out, left alone to face something, like once at school when I admitted to some silly trivial thing several of us had done and found I was the only girl to own up, which made me look a fool, not a heroine. It was this sort of thing with Hari – these repeated experiences of finding myself emotionally out on a limb – that added up and made me feel sometimes – as I suppose I did climbing the staircase that night after Ronald Merrick's proposal – "It's probably all wrong my association with Hari Kumar" – I mean made me feel it *before* Ronald put it into so many words. And added up in that other unfinished sum that posed the question, "Well, what does he really feel for me? A big-boned white girl with not much to be said in her favour."

*

And then there were the rains. They came fresh and clean,

wild, indiscriminate. And changed the garden, Mayapore, the whole landscape. That awful foreboding colourlessness was washed out of the sky. I'd wake at night, shivering because the temperature had fallen, and listen to the lashing on the trees, the wonderful rumbling and banging of the thunder, and watch the way the whole room was lit as if from an explosion, with the furniture throwing sudden flamboyant shadows, black dancing shapes petrified in the middle of a complicated movement – a bit of secret night-time devilry that they returned to the moment the unexpected light went out, only to be caught and held still in it again a few moments later.

I was at the Chillianwallah Bagh on the last night of the dry. For two nights there had been sheet lightning and distant thunder. It was towards the end of June, about a week, perhaps less, after my dinner with Ronald Merrick when he had said, on the steps of the MacGregor House, "Some ideas take some getting used to." Sitting with Hari and Aunt Shalini this time I saw how unreal my life had become because there didn't seem to be any kind of future in front of me that I wanted and could have. *Why?* Holding one hand out, groping, and the other out backwards, linked to the security of what was known and expected. Straining like that. Pretending the ground between was occupied, when all the time it wasn't.

The tonga came at eleven and on the way home we suddenly saw her, lit by the sheet lightning – the wide white wings of the cap, a man ahead of her, and one behind carrying what looked like a pole, but was a rolled-up stretcher. I'd said – not wanting the evening to end – "Let's drive back through the bazaar and past the temple," and he'd agreed, and then I suffered pangs of conscience at the thought of the extra rupees the boy would want; because now I'd fitted Hari into place, and knew he hadn't any spare rupees to throw away. On the other hand I wouldn't have dared offer him even an anna. That time we went to the Chinese Restaurant I said quite without thinking, "Let's go Dutch on a chop suey," and his face closed down, the way Ronald Merrick's did when I rejected his proposal. The Chinese Restaurant was a far from happy experience, what with the insult it seemed I'd offered Hari suggesting Dutch and then the insult to us both when the proprietor stopped him from following me upstairs.

I said, "That's the mad Russian woman who collects dead bodies, isn't it?" She was going away from us, turning up a side street. Hari said she wasn't mad and he didn't think she was Russian. He said, "We call her Sister Ludmila." He'd once written a piece for the *Gazette* about the Sanctuary, but his editor had refused to publish it because of the implication that the British were responsible for letting people die in the streets. So he'd altered the article, because that wasn't what he'd meant. He'd altered it to show that *nobody* cared, not even the people who were dying, nobody except Sister Ludmila. But the editor still wouldn't publish it. He said Sister Ludmila was a joke. I asked Hari if I could visit the Sanctuary. He said he'd take me there if I really wanted to see it, but that I mustn't be upset if she treated me like some kind of inquisitive snooper. She kept herself very much to herself and was only really interested in people who were dying and had no bed to die in, although she also ran an evening clinic that people could go to who couldn't afford to take time off from work to go to the day-time clinics, and she doled out free rice on certain days of the week, to children and mothers mostly. I asked him how he had got to know her and he simply said, "By chance."

*

She had an image of the Siva dancing in a circle of cosmic fire, carved in wood, and a framed biblical text: "He that soweth little shall reap little, and he that soweth plenteously shall reap plenteously. Let every man do according as he is disposed in his heart, not grudging, or of necessity; for God loveth a cheerful giver." There seemed to be a connexion between the Christian text and the Hindu image, because *this* Siva was smiling. And the way the god's limbs are thrust out and jaunty-looking gives the image a feeling of happiness, doesn't it? The only immobile thing is the right foot (even the right leg is bent at the knee and springy-looking). The right foot is the one that presses down on the crouching figure of the little demon, which is why that foot has to be firm and unmoving. The left leg is kicking up, the first pair of arms are gesturing cautiously but invitingly, and the second pair are holding the circle of flame, holding it away but also keeping it burning. And of course the god is winged, which gives the whole image an airy flying feeling that makes you think you could leap into the dark with him and come to no harm.

These were the only bits of decoration in her whitewashed

"cell" – the Siva and the text. At our last meeting she gave the text to me, because she said she knew it by heart anyway. But I've always been too embarrassed to show it to you and I don't think I deserved to be given it anyway. It's in my big suitcase, the one with the straps round it.

What an extraordinary woman she was. When evening comes I think of her preparing to set out on that nightly expedition into the alleys and dark cul-de-sacs, and into the waste land between the temple and the Bibighar bridge. I got into the habit of going there about once a week straight from the hospital – to help with the evening clinic, not just because it was another place Hari and I could meet. I once asked her whether I could go with her at night on her missions. She laughed and said, "No, that is only for people who have nothing else to offer." I thought she meant I could offer money, but she said she had enough, more than enough, although promised that if ever she didn't and I still wanted to help I could.

We took to each other. Perhaps I liked her originally because she was fond of Hari and saw nothing wrong in our being there together. She used to let us sit in the office, or in her room. When it was dark he and I would cycle back to the MacGregor House, but he didn't often come in on those occasions. The days I knew I'd be going to the Sanctuary I went to the hospital on my bicycle and left early to avoid the car or van that Mr. Merrick was always sending round for me. The same in the evenings, after work. I'd leave a message for the driver that I'd either gone or was working late. Sometimes, though, I'd let myself be driven back to the MacGregor, and then go on to the Sanctuary by cycle. I didn't want the hospital to know I helped at Sister Ludmila's clinic. It wasn't often that I did, but I guessed it was against the hospital rules or something. I saw Anna Klaus there one evening and said, "Don't split on me!" She laughed and said people probably knew anyway because in a town like Mayapore it was almost impossible to keep anything a secret.

But not all the people who would have liked to know did. I mean people on our side of the river, people like Ronald Merrick. I kept it from Ronald because this was the part of my life I shared willingly with no one. Ronald was part of another life. Lili yet another. I didn't know I'd divided my life up into these watertight compartments, I mean I didn't consciously know. Subconsciously, yes, and I was aware of the subterfuge involved, but not aware of it in a way that ever allowed me in those days to use the word subterfuge – at least not until the evening when I went to the temple with Hari, and found out about Ronald's part in his arrest, and felt everyone had cheated, and then realised I'd been cheating just as badly myself, and became afraid, recognised that I'd really been afraid all along, afraid like everybody else of going out on a limb in case somebody sawed it off – which was ironic, wasn't it, because I used to kid myself that's what we all ought to do, kid myself it was what I was doing. But if I was out on a limb I had one arm securely round the tree-trunk.

I suppose I thought that everything I did was an adventure of some sort. An evening at the MacGregor House with Lili and a few "mixed" friends, an evening at the club with Ronald or the girls and boys, an hour or two at Sister Ludmila's clinic, a walk with Hari on a Sunday morning to the Bibighar. Well, they were adventures, weren't they? because each of these things was done – unintentionally but for all practical purposes – in defiance of the others. I was breaking every rule there was. The funny thing is that people couldn't be absolutely certain which rule I was breaking in what way at what time because they were so hedged about with their own particular rule they could only follow me far enough to see that I'd broken it and gone away, and become temporarily invisible, so that when I came back, when I returned to their own fold they didn't know enough about what I'd been doing and where I'd been to make real charges against me, other than the general one of being – what? Unstable? Asking for trouble? Unaligned? Bad enough of course, but people do like to be able to define other people's instability and non-alignment, and if they can't their own fear of what you might come to represent forces them to make another bid for your allegiance.

To be rejected – which I suppose is one of the easiest ways of making your mark, you have to come *right out* with something they see as directly and forcefully opposed to what they think they believe in. To be accepted you have to be seen and heard to appear to stand for what they think they believe in. To be neither one thing nor the other is probably unforgivable.

But, Auntie, it was awfully difficult for me. I did genuinely *like* several of the girls and boys I mixed with at the club. I genuinely liked Ronald, when he was the closest he could ever get to being easy and natural with me. I even liked him when he was difficult and "official" because I thought I knew why he acted like that. And I loved Lili, even at her most standoffish, when that old Rajput princess blood showed through and she sort of gathered up the hem of her cloak. Saree, I mean! I liked the *fun* of the English before it became self-conscious and vulgar and violent, and I liked the simple almost childish fun of the Indians, and their seriousness, before it became prissy and prickly and imitative of European sulks. With Hari I can't connect a word such as "like", because my liking was hopelessly encumbered with the physical effect he had on me, which turned liking into love but didn't leave me insensitive to his pigheadedness and prickliness. All of which makes me sound on paper like a paragon of virtuous broad-mindedness, until you remember the horrible mess I made of everything.

*

I hate the impression we automatically get of things and places and people that make us say, for instance, "This is Indian. This is British." When I first saw the Bibighar I thought: How Indian! Not Indian as I'd have thought of a place as Indian before I came out, but Indian as it struck me then. But when you say something like that, in circumstances like that, I think you're responding to the attraction of a place which you see as alien on the surface but underneath as proof of something general and universal. I wish I could get hold of the right words to say just what I mean. The Taj Mahal is "typically Indian", isn't it? Picture-book Moghul stuff. But what makes you give out to it emotionally is the feeling of a man's worship of his wife, which is neither Indian nor un-Indian, but a general human emotion, expressed in this case in an "Indian" way. This is what I got from the Bibighar. It was a place in which you sensed something having gone badly wrong at one time that hadn't yet been put right but could be if only you knew how. That's the sort of thing you could imagine about any place, but imagining it there, feeling that it was still alive, I said, "How Indian," because it was the first place in Mayapore that hit me in this way, and the surprise of being hit made me think I'd come across something typical when all the time it was typical of no place, but only of human acts and desires that leave their mark in the most unexpected and sometimes chilling way.

Usually it was a Sunday morning place, but one day Hari and I sheltered there from the rain, dashing in from the road in the late afternoon, on our bikes, and running up the steps that divided one level of old lawn from another, to the "pavilion", the roofed-over mosaic. We stood under it and I had a cigarette. We'd been on our way to tea at Aunt Shalini's. It was a Saturday. I had a half-day off from the hospital and after lunch I'd cycled to the cantonment bazaar to see if those awful photographs I'd had taken for your birthday were ready at Gulab Singh's where that little man Subhas Chand had a booth. I saw Hari coming out of the *Gazette* offices and called out to him. I said, "Come and help me choose my picture for Auntie Ethel, then if they're any good you can have one." So we went to Subhas Chand and looked at the proofs. I said, "Oh, Lord," but Hari said they were all pretty good and helped me choose the one to make up cabinet size for you. Afterwards I made him come to Darwaza Chand's with me while I chose that dress length. There were hardly any people shopping at that time. Those who were stared at us in the usual unpleasant manner. When I looked at my watch and saw it was already four o'clock I invited him back to the MacGregor House for tea, but he said, "No, come to see Aunt Shalini." I'd not been to his house since the night before the rains set in. I told him I'd like to but I'd better change first. He said, "Why? Unless you want to tell Lady Chatterjee where you're going." But it was her purdah hospital committee afternoon, and there wasn't any need to tell Raju, so we set off. We went the Bibighar bridge side. He hated taking me over by the Mandir Gate bridge because that way we had to go through the bazaar. And that's how we were caught, cycling past the Bibighar. Down it came, as it does, and we dashed in there, expecting it to dry up in twenty minutes or so. But it went on and on, and blew up a storm.

I told him the sort of thing I felt about the Bibighar. It was odd, sitting there on the mosaic floor, having to shout to make ourselves heard, then relapsing into silence until the noise outside got less. I asked him to have his picture taken too, but he said he made a rotten photograph. I said, "Don't be silly. What about those Aunt Shalini showed me?" He said he "was younger then"! I asked him whether he still heard from those English friends of his, the Lindseys, but he shrugged the question away. He'd always been prickly about them when Aunt Shalini mentioned them. I thought they'd given up writing to him and he felt badly about it, but from something Sister Ludmila asked me the last time I saw her I got the feeling there was more to it than that, something to do with the boy, the Lindsey son, whom Aunt Shalini always described as Hari's greatest friend "at home".

Anyway, we were marooned there in the Bibighar and it began to get dark. We'd missed having tea, and I knew I had to be back by seven to change for dinner, because Aunt Lili was having Judge Menen and his wife in, to celebrate Mrs. Menen coming out of hospital. I was shivering a bit, and I thought I'd caught a chill. I wanted him to warm me. An English boy would have snuggled up, I suppose, but there we were, with at least a foot or two between us. I got edgy. I wanted to take his hand and hold it to my face.

*

When we came away, that evening we sheltered from the rains, it felt just as if we had had a quarrel, a lovers' quarrel. But we weren't lovers and there'd been no quarrel. And again I thought: It's wrong, wrong because it doesn't *work*. He saw me home, and although the next day was Sunday neither of us mentioned any arrangement to meet. I was back at the MacGregor a few minutes before Aunt Lili and was soaking in a bath when I heard her calling to Raju on the landing. It was like hearing a homely sound after a long absence. I didn't see Hari again for over a week. I spent an evening or two at the club, once with Ronald and once with the boys and girls, and the rest of my evenings with Lili. But all the time I was thinking of Hari, wanting to see him but not doing anything about it. It was like sitting on a beach as a kid, watching the sea, wanting to go in but not having the courage. Yes – you promise yourself – when this cloud has gone by and the sun comes out then I'll go in. And the cloud goes by and the sun is warm and comforting, and the sea looks chilly.

I told myself the trouble was we'd run out of places to go where the risk of being stared at, the risk of creating a situation, could be minimised. In the club I was definitely getting the cold shoulder from the women. It was this thrashing about for ideas for new places that made me think of the Tirupati temple.

I asked Aunt Lili if English people were ever allowed in. She said she had no idea but imagined none had ever asked, because Mayapore wasn't a tourist town and the temple wasn't famous, but she'd have a word with one of the teachers at the Higher School or Technical College because if an Englishman had been in it would most likely have been a teacher or someone interested in art and culture. She wasn't sure about an English girl being allowed, though. I told her not to bother, because I would ask Hari. She said, "Yes, you could do that I suppose," and looked as if she was about to question the whole business of Hari, so I started talking about my day in the hospital to head her off. I wrote a note to Hari just saying, "I'd love to see inside the Tirupati temple. Could we go together one day? Preferably at night because it always looks more exciting after dark."

A day or two later he rang up from the *Gazette* office. They hadn't a telephone at Aunt Shalini's. He caught me a few moments before I was due to start out for the hospital and told me that if I really wanted to go he'd ask his uncle. His uncle was the kind of man who paid a lot of money to the priests in the hopes of buying the merit he didn't have time to acquire in any other way. At least that's how Hari put it. I said I really did want to go and that if he'd arrange it for the Saturday evening we could have a quiet dinner together at the MacGregor first, and then come back and play the gramophone. He sounded a bit cool. I had an idea I'd done the wrong thing asking him to take me to a *temple*. But we fixed it on a to-be-confirmed basis for the following Saturday when I knew Lili was playing bridge. Neither of us said anything about meeting meanwhile, although I thought he might turn up on the Tuesday evening at the Sanctuary. He didn't though, and I still hadn't heard from him by the Friday evening.

But I'd seen Ronald at the club, and stayed on to dinner with him. He drove me back to the MacGregor and on the way there he asked me to have dinner with him on the Saturday. I said I couldn't because I was hoping to visit the temple. When he stopped the car at the house there was no one on the porch, no sign of Raju, but he didn't get out to open the door for me. Instead he said, "Who's taking you? Mr. Kumar?" After I'd admitted it he was quiet for a bit, but then came out with what he said he'd been meaning to say for some time, that people were talking about my going out and about with an Indian, which was always tricky, but more tricky these days, especially when the man in question "hadn't got a very good reputation" and "tried to make capital out of the fact that he'd lived for a while in England", a fact which he seemed to think "made him English".

Then Ronald said, "You know what I feel for you. It's because I feel it that I haven't said anything to you before. But it's my duty to warn you against this association with Mr. Kumar."

That's when I laughed and said, "Oh, stop acting like a policeman."

He said, "Well, it's partly a police matter. He was under suspicion at one time, and still is, but of course you must know all about that."

I told him I knew nothing about it at all, and wasn't interested because I'd met Hari at a party at the MacGregor and if Lili thought him the kind of man she could invite to her house that was good enough for me. I said I'd be grateful if people would stop telling me who could be my friends and who not, and that I personally didn't care *what* colour people were, and it was obviously only Hari's colour, the fact that he was an Indian, that got people's goat.

Ronald said, "That's the oldest trick in the game, to say colour doesn't matter. It does matter. It's basic. It matters like hell."

I started getting out of the car. He tried to stop me, and took my hand. He said, "I've put it badly. But I can't help it. The whole idea revolts me."

I don't know why I was sorry for him. Perhaps because of his honesty. It was like a child's. The kind of self-centred honesty a child shows. We call it innocence. But it is ignorance and cruelty as well. I said, "It's all right, Ronald. I understand."

He let go of me as if my arm had scalded him. I shut the door and said, "Thanks for the meal and for bringing me home," but it seemed to be the wrong thing to say. There simply wasn't a right thing to say. He drove off and I went into the house.

*

On Friday evening Hari sent round a chit saying that it was fixed for us to visit the temple the following evening, between 9.30 and 10.30, so I sent the boy back with an answer asking him to come to dinner at 7.30 for 8.

Came Saturday, he arrived promptly, as if to make up for

past mistakes. He came in a cycle tonga, which explained the promptness but was probably also meant to point the difference between his life and mine. Somehow that difference became the theme of the evening. He was deliberately trying to put me off. I'm sure of that. For instance, he'd started smoking again, cheap Indian cigarettes – not bidis, but smelly and cumulatively unpleasant. I tried one but hated it, so we ended up smoking our own. He'd also brought a couple of records which he said were a present to me. I wanted to play them right away but he said, no, we'd wait until we got back from the temple, and looked at his watch. It was only 7.45 but he suggested that we ought to start eating. I said, "Don't you want the other half?" He said he didn't but would wait while I did, which meant he didn't want to, so I told Raju to tell cook we'd eat right away, and we went into the dining-room. When we got in there he complained that the fans were going too fast. I told Raju to turn them to half speed. It got very hot. When the food came in he ignored the forks and began scoffing up mouthfuls with pieces of chappatti. I followed suit. He called out to Raju, "Boy, bring water", and I began to giggle because it reminded me of the time you and I sat next to that rich Indian family in Delhi and how shocked I was at the apparently rude way the man talked to the waiter, "Boy, bring this. Boy, bring that", but you pointed out that it was an exact English translation of the pukka sahib's "Bearer, pani lao." I thought Hari was having a game, taking off rich Indians of the English-speaking middle class, and wondered if he'd been drinking before he came. Our fingers and mouths were in a bit of a mess by the time we'd finished. Raju – who noticed what was happening even if he didn't understand it – brought in napkins and bowls of warm water, and we washed. I half expected Hari to belch and ask for a toothpick. In its way it was a perfect imitation. Normally he smiled at Raju but apart from his "Boy, do so and so" he treated him as if he weren't in the room. And I began to wonder whether the Indians had got this habit from the English, or the English from the Indians, or whether the whole thing dated back to some time when servants were treated like dirt everywhere and the habit had only been kept up in the Empire by Sahibs and Memsahibs and modern Indians wanting to be smart.

The other thing Hari was doing, of course, was acting like an Indian male of that kind, very polite on the surface but underneath selfish and aggressive, ordering the arrangements to his own but not necessarily anyone else's liking – the curtailment of the pre-dinner drinks, the early start on the meal – and now the equally early start going to the temple which ended up by being a late start because at the last moment he said perhaps we'd better listen to the records he'd bought so that we could get into the mood – a curious kind of hark-back to that dance record, which made me suddenly wary, conscious that the mood Hari was in was less comic than bitter.

And even over the playing of the gramophone he made us go through a typical sort of modern Indian farce. Raju was told to bring the gramophone out, but was shoved aside when it came to winding the damn' thing up, and sent to look for the needles which were in the compartment of the gramophone where they were meant to be, all the time. Hari deliberately scratched the first record by being clumsy with it and then pretended not to notice the awful clack clack every time the needle jumped over the dent in the groove. And he had chosen Indian music, something terribly difficult, an evening raga that went on and on. What he didn't reckon with was the fact that I instinctively loved it. When he saw that I did he changed the record before it was finished, and put on one that excited and moved me even more. The odd thing was I could see it really made *him* savagely irritated and seeing that, the idea that he had been having a joke with me just wouldn't hold water any longer. I felt lost, because I realised he had been trying in his own way to put me off, as Ronald and everyone wanted, and that he was sufficiently fond of me personally to believe that what he hated – the music, and eating with your fingers – I would hate too. His discovery that I didn't hate it, but loved it or didn't mind it, was another gulf between us, one for which there was no accounting, because I was white and he was black, and my liking for what he hated or had never had the patience or inclination to learn to like, to get back to, made even his blackness look spurious; like that of someone made up to act a part.

He let the second record play to the end, and then *I* took charge and said, "We'd better go", and called out to Raju to bring my scarf. I had an idea I'd need to cover my head to go into the temple. Hari had brought an umbrella in case it rained while we weren't under cover. On the way to the temple in the cycle tonga we said almost nothing. I'd not been in a cycle tonga before. To shift the weight of two people the poor boy had to stand out of the saddle and lean his whole strength on each pedal alternately. But I liked it better than the horse tongas, because we faced the way we were going. To travel in a horse tonga, facing backwards (which I suppose one does to avoid the smell if the horse breaks wind) always gives me a feeling of trying to hang back, of not wanting things to disappear. With the cycle tonga there was the opposite feeling, of facing the road ahead, of knowing it better and not being scared when you had to get out.

*

At the temple entrance there was a man waiting for us, a temple servant who spoke a bit of English. We took our shoes off in the archway of the main gate, and Hari paid some money over that his uncle had given him. I couldn't see how much it was but guessed from the attention we got that it was probably quite a lot, more than Hari had ever been given by his uncle before.

Well, you've been in temples. Isn't it odd how even with all that noise outside, to go in is like entering somewhere quite cut off – not a place of quiet – but cut off, reserved for a human activity that doesn't need *other* human activity to make it function itself. Churches are quiet in this way, but then they are usually quiet because they are empty. The temple wasn't quiet. It wasn't empty. But it was cut off. Once through the archway you walked into the *idea* of being alone. I was glad to have Hari with me, because my *skin* was afraid, although I wasn't afraid *inside* the skin. I was astonished by the sight of men and women just squatting around, under the trees in the courtyard, squatting in that wholly Indian peasant way, self-supported on the haunches, with arms stretched out and balanced on the bent knees, and the bottom not quite touching the earth. Gossiping. At first I was critical of this, until I remembered that the shrine in the centre of the courtyard was the real temple, and outside it was like the outside of a church where our Sunday morning congregations gather and chat after the service.

Around the walls of the courtyard there were the shrines of various aspects of the Hindu gods. Some awake and lit, some asleep and dark. In those doll-like figures there's a look of what puritans call the tawdriness of Roman Catholicism, isn't there? The dolls seemed to reflect that, but knowingly, as if pointing a moral – the absurdity of the need which the poor and ignorant have for images. Hari said, "The guide wants to know if we'd like to make *puja* to the Lord Venkataswara."

The holy of holies! I was excited. I hadn't expected to be allowed in there, and I was very conscious of the uniqueness of being allowed. Every so often one was startled by the ringing of a bell at the entrance to the central shrine. There were men and women waiting. Our guide forced his way through to take us in ahead of them. I hated that. He spoke to a priest who was standing watching us. Then he came and said something long and involved to Hari. I was surprised that Hari seemed to understand. When he replied to the man's question I realised Hari had learned more of the language than he was prepared to let on and only here, in the temple, couldn't keep up the pretence. He turned to me and said, "I have to ring the bell to warn the god that we're here. When I've done so, look as if you're praying. Goodness knows what we're in for."

I put my scarf on my head. The priest was watching us all the time. The bell was hung on a chain from the roof of the shrine at the head of the steps. I could see the inside now, a narrow passage leading to a brightly lit grotto, and the idol with a black face and gilt robes and silver ornaments. Hari reached up and pulled the rope that moved the tongue of the bell, then put his hands together. I followed suit and closed my eyes and waited until I heard him say, "We go in now."

He led the way. There were ordinary tubular steel bars in the passage, forming a barricade. We took up position round them with several other people – rather as at a communion rail, except that we stood and didn't kneel, and the bars formed a rectangle, with us on the outside and a space on the inside for the priest to come down from the little grotto. He was standing by the grotto while we were sorting ourselves out, and then came with a gilt cup. We held our hands out, as for the Host, and he poured what looked like water into them. He went to the Indians first, to make sure we'd know what to do. We raised the liquid to our lips. It was sweet-sour tasting, and stung a bit. Perhaps because our lips were dry. After we'd carried our hands to our lips we had to pass them over our heads, rather like making a sign of the cross. Then the priest came back with a golden cap – a sort of basin, and held it over our heads, and intoned prayers for each of us. He also had a gilt tray and when he'd finished with the cap he put it back on the tray. Round the tray there were little mounds of coloured powder and some petals. He stuck his finger in the powder and marked our foreheads. The petals turned out to be a small string of roses, and he gave them to me, putting them round my neck. It seemed to be all over in a second or two. On the way out Hari put some more money on a tray held by another priest at the door.

I felt nothing while I was doing *puja*. But when I came out my lips were still stinging and I could smell the sweet-sourness everywhere. I had a suspicion that we'd drunk cow urine. People were staring at us. I felt protected from their hostility, if it was hostility and not just curiosity, protected by the mark on my forehead and the little string of red rose petals. I still have the petals, Auntie. They are in a white paper bag, with Sister Ludmila's text, in the suitcase. Dry and brown now. The faintest wind would blow them into fragments.

There was one other thing to do, something to see, an image of the sleeping Vishnu. Lord Venkataswara, the god of the temple, is a manifestation of Vishnu, although the black, silver and gold image looked to me far from that of a preserver. The sleeping Vishnu had a grotto to himself, behind the main shrine. The grotto was built into the outer wall. You had to go into it and then turn a corner before you found the god asleep on his stone bed. Only three or four people could get in at once. Inside it was cool. The place was lit by oil lamps and the god was quite a shock. One had expected something small, miniature like the rest: instead, this bigger than lifesize reclining figure that overpowered you with a sense of greater strength in sleep than in wakefulness. And such good dreams he was dreaming! Dreams that made him smile.

I could have stood and watched him for ages, but Hari nudged me and whispered that there were other people waiting to come in. We had to force our way through them, back into the courtyard. We went to the other gateway, the one that looked out on to the steps leading down to the river. After *puja* one should bathe, but there was only one man doing so at that moment. We could just make him out, standing in the water up to his waist. His head was shaved. Nearby there was a shed and platform where the temple barbers worked, and where devotees gave their hair to the god.

Hari said, "Shall we go and get our shoes?" He had had enough. Perhaps I had too, because I wasn't part of its outwardness at all. I felt like a trespasser. So we went back through the courtyard and collected our shoes. More money passed. I suppose it all goes into the pockets of the priests. At the gateway we were besieged by beggars. Our tonga boy was waiting for us and saw us before we saw him, and came pressing forward, ringing his bell and shouting, afraid that one of the other tonga boys would slip in and take us away. We were back in the din and the dirt. There was music from a coffee shop over the road. With my shoes back on, my feet felt gritty. Deliberately I'd not worn stockings.

*

When we got back to the MacGregor House we sat on the verandah. I asked Hari to send the tonga boy round to the back to get some food. He didn't look more than seventeen or so – a cheerful, pleasant boy who obviously felt that with this long evening hire his luck was in. Alone for a moment I went round the back and called Raju, and asked him to bring the boy to me. He appeared from nowhere, as if he'd been expecting me. I gave him ten chips. A fortune. But he deserved it. And it was part of my *puja*. I think Raju disapproved. Perhaps he extracted a percentage, or gave the boy short commons or no commons at all. In the end one can't bear it any more – the indifference of one Indian for another – and doesn't want to know what goes on.

It came on to rain, which drove us in from the verandah. Hari's earlier mood had gone. He looked exhausted, as if he had failed – not just at whatever he had set out to achieve that evening but at everything he'd set his heart on. I wanted to have it out with him, but it was difficult to know how to begin. And when we began it started off all wrong because I said, "You've been trying to put me off, haven't you?"

He pretended not to understand and said, "Put off? What do you mean, put off?" Which frustrated me so that I said, as if I were in a temper, "Oh, put off, put me off, put me off *you*, like everybody else has tried."

He asked who "everybody else" was.

I said, "Well, everybody. People like Mr. Merrick for instance. He thinks you're a bad bet."

Hari said, "Well, he should know, I suppose."

I told him that was a ridiculous thing to say because only he knew what kind of bet he was. He said, "What's all this talk about anyway? What does it mean, bet? Good bet, bad bet? What am I supposed to be, a racehorse or something? Some kind of stock or share people keep an eye on to see if it's worth investing in?"

I'd not seen him angry before. He'd not seen me angry either. We lost our tempers, which is why I don't remember just what it was we said that led me to accuse him of criticising a man he'd probably never met, and then to the realisation that we'd been talking at cross purposes because no one had ever told me it was Ronald who took him into custody and stood by and watched him hit by one of his subordinates. I remember saying something like, "You mean it was Ronald himself?" and I can still see the surprise on his face when the penny dropped at last and he knew I really hadn't known.

If only I'd contained my anger then. Well, I tried, because I wasn't angry with him but with Ronald, other people, myself as much as anybody. I said, "Where did it happen, then?" and again he looked astonished. He said, "Well, in the Sanctuary of course." That was another blow. I asked him to tell me about it.

He'd been drunk. He wouldn't say why. He'd wandered out as drunk as a coot and collapsed in a ditch in that awful waste ground near the river and been picked up by Sister Ludmila and her helpers who thought he'd been attacked or was ill, or dying, until they got him back to the Sanctuary. He slept it off there, and in the morning Ronald came to the Sanctuary with some policemen, looking for a man who'd escaped from a jail and was thought to have come back to Mayapore because that was where the escaped man used to live. He wasn't there, but Hari was. Well, you can imagine it, I expect, imagine how Hari would react to being browbeaten by a man like Ronald. The sub-inspector accompanying Ronald hit Hari in the face for not answering "smartly", and in the end he was hustled away and punched and kicked when he got into the back of the truck.

One trouble was that he knew the man the police were looking for. This came out while Ronald questioned him in front of the sub-inspector at the kotwali. But he'd only known him as a clerk in his uncle's warehouse. Another trouble was that Hari deliberately made a point of confusing the police about his name. Coomer. Kumar. He said "either would do". Finally Ronald sent the sub-inspector out of the room and talked to Hari alone, or tried to talk to him, which was probably difficult because Hari had taken a dislike to him. I don't know why Hari got drunk. Perhaps from an accumulation of blows that had finally made him feel he cared for nothing and believed in nothing. He told me he was convinced he was going to be locked up anyway, so didn't watch his tongue. I think from the way he told me all this he was trying to help find excuses for Ronald that he couldn't find himself. Ronald asked him why he'd got drunk, and where. Hari wouldn't say where because he thought – and said – that where was none of Ronald's business – but gladly explained why. He explained it by saying he'd got drunk because he hated the whole damned stinking country, the people who lived in it and the people who ran it. He even said, "And that goes for you too, Merrick." He knew Merrick's name because he'd often been in the courts as a reporter. He said Merrick only smiled when he said "and that goes for you too", and then told him he could go, and even apologised – sarcastically of course – for having "inconvenienced him". When he got back home he discovered Sister Ludmila had scared up some influential people to ask questions about his "arrest" but this only amused him, if amused is the right word to use when he was really feeling bitter. He said it had amused him when eventually Lili invited him to a party, and also amused him to see Merrick watching the way I went up to him that day on the *maidan*. I didn't know Ronald had seen that, but it fitted in. Hari thought I had always known the whole story, and was only condescending to him when I broke away from the white officers and white nurses to throw a crumb of comfort to him.

I said, "So it's amused you whenever we've been out together?"

He said, "Yes, you could put it that way. If you want to. But you've been very kind, and I'm grateful."

I said, "I didn't mean anything as kindness," and stood up. He stood up too. He would only have had to touch me, for the stupidity to have ended then, but he didn't. He was afraid to. He was too conscious of the weight that would have made touching a gesture of defiance of the rule Ronald had described a few evenings before as "basic", and he didn't have that kind of courage, and so I was deprived of my own. The defiance had to come from him first, to make it human, to make it right.

I said, "Good night, Hari." Oh, even in that good night there was a way left open to him that "goodbye" would have closed. But I mustn't blame him. He had good reasons to be afraid. I rehearsed them to myself upstairs in my room, sitting, waiting, determining to have things out with Lili. When I heard the cycle tonga go down the drive my determination began to go with it, and then I was worried, worried for him, because he was a man who would find it awfully difficult to hide, and I believed that was what he wanted to do. To hide. To disappear into a sea of brown faces.

That word Ronald Merrick used was the right one – association. Hari and I could be enemies, or strangers to each other, or lovers, but never friends because such a friendship was put to the test too often to survive. We were constantly having to ask the question, Is it worth it? Constantly having to examine our motives for wanting to be together. On my side the motive was physical attraction. I didn't have enough self-confidence to assure myself that Hari felt the same for me. But this didn't change what I felt. I was in love with him. I wanted him near me. I told myself I didn't care what people said. I didn't care what he'd done, or what people like Ronald Merrick thought he'd done or was capable of doing. I wanted to protect him from danger. If it helped him not to be seen with me any longer I was prepared to let him go, to let him hide. But because I was in love I kidded myself there was a time limit to "any longer", a magic formula that took the sting out of the decision I made to let the next move come from him.

When Lili asked me next morning about the visit to the temple I chatted away as if nothing had happened. Several times I was on the point of saying, "Did you know it was Ronald who arrested Hari?" But I didn't want to hear her say yes. I didn't want to pave the way to a discussion that might have forced Lili to confess for instance that she had since had doubts about Hari and regretted her haste in rushing to the defence of a man she didn't know but had since learned more of that made her feel Ronald had been right to suspect him and done nothing he need be ashamed of when he took Hari in for questioning.

I knew that Lili would be the first to realise something had happened between Hari and myself if the days went by without any word from him or meeting between us. I was aware of helping him by keeping quiet, aware of distracting attention from him, but not aware then of the truth of what I was actually doing – indulging my unfulfilled passion for him by weaving a protective web round him which even excluded me. I didn't feel that it excluded me. Later I did.

I went about my job, my ordinary life. No letter from him. To avoid having to answer Lili's questions, if she decided to ask them, I took to going almost every evening to the club. And people noticed it. I was glad they did. If I was at the club obviously I wasn't out with Hari. The first time I saw Ronald there he came up to me and said, "Did you enjoy the temple?" I shrugged and said, "Oh, it was all right. A bit of a racket, though. You can't say boo without it costing money." He smiled. I couldn't tell whether he was pleased or puzzled. I wondered whether he saw through my casual pretence, but then decided that even if he saw through it he wouldn't see what lay behind it. I hated him that night. Hated him and smiled at him. Played the game. And again felt how easy it was, how simple. To act at conforming. Because all the time there was nothing to conform with, except an idea, a charade played round a phrase: white superiority.

And all the time wanting Hari. Seeing him in my imagination looking over the shoulder of every pink male face and seeing in every pink male face the strain of pretending that the world was this small. Hateful. Ingrown. About to explode like powder compressed ready for firing.

I thought that the whole bloody affair of *us* in India had reached flash point. It was bound to because it was based on a violation. Perhaps at one time there was a moral as well as a physical force at work. But the moral thing had gone sour. Has gone sour. Our faces reflect the sourness. The women look worse than the men because consciousness of physical superiority is unnatural to us. A white man in India can feel physically superior without unsexing himself. But what happens to a woman if she tells herself that ninety-nine per cent of the men she sees are not men at all, but creatures of an inferior species whose colour is their main distinguishing mark? What happens when you unsex a nation, treat it like a nation of eunuchs? Because that's what we've done, isn't it?

God knows what happens. What will happen. The whole thing seems to go from bad to worse, year after year. There's dishonesty on both sides because the moral issue has gone sour on them as well as on us. We're back to basics, the basic issue of who jumps and who says jump. Call it by any fancy name you like, even "the greatest experiment of colonial government and civilising influence since pre-Christian Rome", to quote our old friend Mr. Swinson. It's become a vulgar scramble for power on their part and an equally vulgar smug hanging on on ours. And the greater their scramble the greater our smugness. You can't hide that any longer because the moral issue, if it ever really existed at all, is dead. It's our fault it's dead because it was our responsibility to widen it, but we narrowed it down and narrowed it down by never suiting actions to words. We never suited them because out here, where they *needed* to be suited and to be seen to be suited, that old primitive savage instinct to attack and destroy what we didn't understand because it looked different and was different always got the upper hand. And God knows how many centuries you have to go back to trace to its source their apparent fear of skins paler than their own. God help us if they ever lose that fear. Perhaps fear is the wrong word. In India anyway. It is such a primitive emotion and their civilisation is so old. So perhaps I should say God help us if ever they substitute fear for tiredness. But tiredness is the wrong word too. Perhaps we haven't got a word for what they feel. Perhaps it's hidden in that stone carving of Vishnu sleeping, looking as if he might wake at any minute and take them to oblivion in a crack of happy thunder.

*

Was this the difference between my own emotions and Hari's? That he could wait and I couldn't? In the end I couldn't bear the silence, the inaction, the separation, the artificiality of my position. I wrote to him. I had no talent for self-denial. It's an Anglo-Saxon failing, I suppose. Constantly we want proof, here and now, proof of our existence, of the mark we've made, the sort of mark we can wear round our necks, to label us, to make sure we're never lost in that awful dark jungle of anonymity.

But in my impatience there was Anglo-Saxon planning, forethought, an acceptance that time went through certain fixed exercises that the clock and the calendar had been invented to define. The farther away from the equator you get the more sensitive you become to the rhythm of light and dark, the way it expands and contracts and organises the seasons, so that time itself develops a specific characteristic that alerts you to its absurd but meticulous demands. If I'd been an Indian girl perhaps I'd have said in my note to Hari: Tonight, please. Instead I gave three or four days' notice. Three or four. I forget which, which shows how unimportant the actual number was, how unimportant as well the actual day suggested – although I remember that. As everybody probably does. August the ninth. In my note I said I was sorry for any misunderstanding, and that I wanted to talk to him. I said I'd go to the Sanctuary on that evening and hoped to meet him there.

I got no reply, but when the day came I felt happy, almost light-headed. At breakfast time the telephone rang. I thought it was Hari and rushed to answer before Raju could get there. It wasn't Hari. It was little Mrs. Srinivasan wanting to speak to Lili. I sent Raju up to Lili's bedroom to tell her to pick up the extension. When I went up to say goodbye to her Lili said, "They've arrested Vassi."

Well, you know all that side of things. We'd been prepared for it but it was a shock when it actually happened. When I got to the hospital the girls were acting as if they'd been personally responsible for saving the day by locking up the Mahatma and his colleagues and Congressmen all over the country. A year earlier most of them wouldn't even have known what Congress was. The atmosphere in the hospital that morning was like that in the club at the end of War Week. One of them said, "Have you noticed the orderlies? They've got their tails between their legs all right." Once this had been pointed out the girls seemed to go out of their way to find new methods of humiliating them. And there was a subtle change in their attitude to me, as if they were trying to make me feel that I'd been backing the wrong horse for months.

It wasn't until the afternoon that they began to get scared. First there was the rumour of rioting in the sub-divisions, then the confirmation that the assistant commissioner had gone out with police patrols to find out why contact couldn't be made with a place called Tanpur. It came on to rain. And about a quarter to five, when I was getting ready to go off duty, there was a flap because Mr. Poulson had brought in the mission teacher, Miss Crane. At first we thought she'd been raped, but I got the true story from Mr. Poulson. I saw him as I was going to Matron's office. Miss Crane had been attacked on her way home from Dibrapur, and had her car burnt out, and had seen one of her teachers – an Indian – murdered. She was suffering from shock and exposure. She'd sat on the roadside guarding the murdered man's body. As I'd met Miss Crane once at the Deputy Commissioner's bungalow I got permission from Matron to go in and see her. But she was already wandering and didn't recognise me. I thought she was for it. She kept saying, "I'm sorry. Sorry it's too late," mumbling about there having been too many chappattis for her to eat alone, and asking why I hadn't shared them, why had I gone hungry? I held her hand and tried to make contact with her but all she would do for a while was keep repeating, "I'm sorry it's too late." But suddenly she said, "Mine's Edwina Crane and my mother's been dead for longer than I care to remember," and then went off into a delirium about mending the roof and there being nothing she could do. "Nothing," she said, over and over. "There's nothing I can do."

*

It was raining when I left the hospital.* There was no sign of Ronald's driver or of the truck. He would have been busy that evening anyway. But I had my bicycle and my rain cape and sou'-wester. I'd told Lili that I'd be calling in at the club and I'd also promised to see the girls there, but looking in on Miss Crane had made me late and so I cycled direct to the Sanctuary, down Hospital road, Victoria road, and over the river by way of the Bibighar bridge. Perhaps the rain as well as the rumours was keeping nearly everyone indoors, because I saw few people. I got to the Sanctuary at about 5.45. The rain was letting up a bit then.

I've never described the Sanctuary to you, have I? You turn off the Chillianwallah Bagh Extension road along a track that skirts the waste ground near the river where the poorest untouchables live in horrible squalid huts. Then you come to a walled compound in which there are three old buildings that date back to the early nineteenth century. One is the office, the other the clinic and Sister Ludmila's "cell" and the third and largest the place where she tends the sick and dying. There must be nearly an acre of ground enclosed by those walls. The place looks derelict and you can smell the river most of the time. But inside the buildings everything is clean and neat, scrubbed and whitewashed.

She has one principal assistant, a middle-aged Goanese called de Souza, and several men and women whom she hires at random. I've always wondered where her money comes from.

Hari wasn't there. I went to the office first and saw Mr. de Souza. He said Sister Ludmila was in her room, and that no one had turned up so far for the evening clinic, probably because of the rumours of trouble. I went across to the clinic and knocked at her door. I'd not seen her since the week of

*** Section of Journal shown to Robin White begins here.**

the visit to the temple. She knew Hari and I had been planning to go there. She asked me to come in and tell her about it.

The rain stopped and in about ten minutes or so the sun came out, as it often does, at the end of an afternoon's wet, but of course it was already setting. She said, "Will Hari be coming?" I told her I wasn't sure. And then she asked me about the temple. She herself had never been inside it. I described our *puja* to the Lord Venkataswara and the image of the sleeping Vishnu. I wanted to ask her about the night she found Hari lying drunk in a ditch in the wasteland outside the Sanctuary, but didn't. As the minutes went by and he still did not come I thought, "It's all going, going away before I've touched any of it or understood any of it." I watched the wooden carving of the Dancing Siva. It seemed to move. There came a point when I couldn't watch it any longer because it was draining me of my own mobility. I felt I was becoming lost in it.

I turned to her. She always sat very upright, on a hard wooden chair, with her hands folded on her lap, showing her wedding ring. I never saw her without her cap so I don't know whether she'd shorn her hair. On other occasions when I'd been in her room its bareness and simplicity had always conveyed an idea to me of its safety, but this evening I thought, "No, it's her safety, not the room's." I felt this going away from me too. There was so much I wanted to know about her, but I'd only once asked her a personal question. She spoke English very well, but with a strong accent. I'd asked her where she'd learned it and she said, "From my husband. His name was Smith." One heard many different tales about her – for instance that she had run away from a convent as a young novice and wore the nunnish clothing in the hope of being forgiven. I don't think this was true. I think there was no tale about her that was true. Only her charity was true. For me it always outweighed my curiosity. When you spoke to her there wasn't any mystery. In herself she was all the explanation I felt she needed. And that is rare, isn't it? To be explained by yourself, by what you are and what you do, and not by what you've done, or were, or by what people think you might be or might become.

I stayed for an hour, until it was dusk. I told myself that Hari was probably working late, but I knew this didn't explain his silence. I wondered whether he had been arrested again but decided that was unlikely. The arrests that had been made were of prominent members of the local Congress, like Vassi. I thought of calling in at Aunt Shalini's but when I got out on the Chillianwallah Bagh Extension road I changed my mind and turned in the direction of the Bibighar bridge. It was almost dark. Thinking it might rain again I'd put my cape and sou'-wester back on instead of strapping them to the carrier, and it was warm and clammy. I crossed the bridge and the level crossing. When I got to the street lamp opposite the Bibighar I stopped and took the cape off, and put it over the handle-bars. It was stopping like this that made me wheel the bike across the road to look in through the gate of the Bibighar. When I stopped I'd had a strong impression of Hari in the Bibighar, sitting in the pavilion alone, not expecting me, but thinking of me, wondering whether I would turn up.

I went through the open gateway and along the path to the place where we always left our cycles – a place where we could lean them against the wall but keep an eye on them from the pavilion. When I got to this place there was no cycle. I looked across in the direction of the pavilion. At first there was nothing, but then I saw the glow of a cigarette being drawn on. I suppose the distance between the path by the wall and the pavilion is about a hundred yards. You can walk it straight by going up over what was once the lawn and the series of little steps. That's why we usually left our cycles against the wall, to save lugging them up the steps. The other way to the pavilion is by the path that skirts the grounds. I wasn't sure whether it was Hari in the pavilion and so I went up by the path.

When I got round to the side of the pavilion I could see the man standing on the mosaic platform. I said, "Hari, is that you?" He said, "Yes." I turned the lamp off and left the cycle against a tree and then went up to the pavilion. When I got there I found I'd brought the cape with me.

I said, "Didn't you get my note?" But it was a silly thing to ask. He didn't answer. I felt for a cigarette and realised I'd run out. I asked him for one of his. He gave it to me. It made me cough, so I threw it away. I sat down on the mosaic. The roof overhangs the edge and the mosaic is always dry. There was no need for the cape. I put it on the ground nearby. With so many trees around it sounds as if it's raining long after it has stopped. The water drips from the roof as well as from the leaves. Eventually he sat down too and lit another cigarette. I said, "Let me try one of those again." He opened the packet and held it out. I took a cigarette. Then I took hold of his hand, the one in which he held his own cigarette, and lit mine from his. I smoked without inhaling. After a while he said, "What were you trying to prove? That you don't mind our touching?"

I said, "I thought we'd got beyond that."

"No," he said, "we can never get beyond it."

I said, "But we have. *I* have. It was never an obstacle anyway. At least not for me."

He asked why I'd come to the Bibighar. I told him I'd waited for an hour at the Sanctuary, that I'd looked in on my way past because I thought he might be there.

After a while he said, "You oughtn't to be out alone tonight. I'll see you home. Throw that disgusting thing away."

He waited, then leaned towards me and held my wrist and took the cigarette and threw it into the garden. I couldn't bear it, having him so near, knowing I was about to lose him. That catching hold of my wrist was like the impatient gesture of a lover. For him it was like that too. I willed him not to let go. There was an instant when I was afraid, perhaps because he wanted me to be. But then we were kissing. His shirt had rucked up because he was wearing it loose over his waistband and my hand was touching his bare back, and then we were both lost. There was nothing gentle in the way he took me. I felt myself lifted on to the mosaic. He tore at my underclothes and pressed down on me with all his strength. But this was not me and Hari. Entering me he made me cry out. And then it was us.

*

They came when we lay half-asleep listening to the croaking of the frogs, his hand covering one breast, my own in his black hair, moving to trace the miracle of his black ear.

Five or six men. Suddenly. Climbing on to the platform. My nightmare faces. But not faces. Black shapes in white cotton clothing; stinking, ragged clothing. Converging on Hari, pulling him away. And then darkness. And a familiar smell. But hot and suffocating. Covering my head. As I began to struggle I could think of nothing but the thing that covered my head. I knew it, but did not know it because it was smothering me. And then there was a moment – the moment, I suppose, when the man holding me down and covering me with this suffocating but familiar thing, lifted his weight away – a moment when I forgot the covering and felt only my exposed nakedness. He must have lifted his weight away when the others had finished dealing with Hari and came to help. There was pressure on my knees and ankles and then my wrists – a moment of terrible openness and vulnerability and then the first experience of that awful animal thrusting, the motion of love without one saving split-second of affection.

*

I no longer dream of faces. In bad dreams now I'm usually blind. This kind of dream begins with the image of Siva. I see him only with my sense of recollection. Suddenly he leaves his circle of cosmic fire and covers me, imprisons my arms and legs in darkness. Surreptitiously, I grow an extra arm to fight him or embrace him, but he always has an arm to spare to pin me down, a new lingam growing to replace the one that's spent. This dream ends when I'm no longer blind and see the expression on his face which is one of absolution and invitation. I wake then, remembering how after they had gone I found myself holding my raincape, breathing, aware of the blessing of there being air with which to fill my lungs, and thinking, "It was mine, my own cape that I use to keep the rain off, mine all the time, part of my life." I clung to the cape. I held it to my body, covering myself. I thought I was alone. I had this idea that Hari had gone with them because he had been one of them.

But then I saw him, the shape of him, lying as I was lying, on the mosaic. They had bound his hands and mouth and ankles with strips of cloth, torn for all I knew from their own clothing, and then placed him where he would have had to close his eyes if he didn't want to see what was happening.

I crawled like a kid across the mosaic and struggled with the knots, struggled because they were tight and difficult and because I was also trying to cover myself with the cape. I untied the gag round his mouth first, in case he was finding it difficult to breathe, and then the strips of rag round his ankles, and then the one round his wrists. And as I untied him he continued to lie as they had left him, so that presently I gathered him in my arms because I couldn't bear it, I couldn't bear the sound of him crying.

*

He cried for shame, I suppose, and for what had happened

to me that he'd been powerless to stop. He said something that I was too dazed to catch but thinking back on it it always comes to me as an inarticulate begging for forgiveness.

I was suddenly very cold. He felt me shivering. Now *he* held *me*, and for a time we clung to each other like two children frightened of the dark. But I couldn't stop shivering. He moved the cape until it was round my shoulders and then covered me at the front. He got up and searched for things that belonged to me. I felt them in his hands and took them from him. He said, "Put your arms round my neck." I did so. He lifted me and carried me over to the steps and down them one at a time. I thought of all the steps between the pavilion and the gate, and then of the bicycle. I thought he was going to carry me across the garden, but he turned on to the path. When he went past the place where I'd left the bicycle I said, "No, it's here somewhere." He didn't understand. I said, "My bicycle." He put me down but continued to hold me. He said he couldn't see it, that the men must have stolen it or hidden it. He said he'd come back in the morning to look for it. I asked him about his own bicycle. He'd left it in the bazaar to be repaired. He'd not had it all day. He picked me up again and carried me down the path. I felt myself becoming a dead weight in his arms. I asked him to put me down. He did so but then lifted me again. While we were in the garden I let him do this. If I'd asked him to carry me all the way to the MacGregor House I think he'd have managed it somehow. But when we got to the gateway and he put me down again – as if to catch his breath – the world outside the garden came back into focus. On the other side of the gate there was the beginning of what another white girl would have thought of as safety. It was safety of a kind for me too. But not for him. When he moved to pick me up again I pushed him away – as you'd push away a child who was reaching out to touch something that would burn it or scald it. Seeing the gateway I imagined him carrying me through it, into the light, into the cantonment.

I said, "No. I've got to go home alone. We've not been together. I've not seen you."

He tried to take hold of my arm. I moved away from him. I said, "No. Let me go. You've not been near me. You don't know anything. You know nothing. Say nothing." He wouldn't listen. He caught me, tried to hold me close, but I struggled. I was in a panic, thinking of what they'd do to him. No one would believe me. He said, "I've got to be with you. I love you. Please let me be with you."

If he hadn't said that perhaps I'd have given in. The thought that he was right and I was wrong and that the only way to have faced it was with the truth is one of the things I have to puzzle over now and carry with me – a burden as heavy if less obvious than the child. And you may wonder why when he said he loved me my determination to resist didn't come abruptly to an end. But love isn't like that, is it? It wasn't for me. It bewildered me. It sent me from panic to worse panic, because of what they might do to him if he said to *them*, "I love her. We love each other."

I beat at him, not to escape myself but to make *him* escape. I was trying to beat sense and reason and cunning into him. I kept saying, "We've never seen each other. You've been at home. You say nothing. You know nothing. Promise me."

I was free and began to run without waiting to hear him promise. At the gate he caught me and tried to hold me back. Again I asked him to let me go, *please* to let me go, to say nothing, to know nothing, *for my sake* if that was the only way he could say nothing and know nothing for his own. For an instant I held him close – it was the last time I touched him – and then I broke free again and was out of the gateway and running; running into and out of the light of the street lamp opposite, running into the dark and grateful for the dark, going without any understanding of direction. I stopped and leaned against a wall. I wanted to turn back. I wanted to admit that I couldn't face it alone. And I wanted him to know that I thought I'd done it all wrong. He wouldn't know what I felt, what I meant. I was in pain. I was exhausted. And frightened. Too frightened to turn back.

I said, "There's nothing I can do, nothing, nothing," and wondered where I'd heard those words before, and began to run again, through those awful ill-lit deserted roads that should have been leading me home but were leading me nowhere I recognised; into safety that wasn't safety because beyond it there were the plains and the openness that made it seem that if I ran long enough I would run clear off the rim of the world.*

*

It seemed so simple at the time to say, "Hari wasn't there,"

*** End of section of Journal shown to Robin White.**

and to feel, just by saying it, that I put him out of harm's reach. It's all too easy now to think that his only real protection was the truth, however disagreeable it would have been for us to tell it, to have it told, however threatening and dangerous the truth would have been for him. Well, if he had been an Englishman – that young subaltern who began to paw me at the War Week dance, for instance – the truth would have worked and it would never have occurred to us to tell anything else, I suppose. When people realised what he and I had been doing in the Bibighar they would have stood by us while they tried to see justice done, and then when it had been done or when they'd pursued every possible line to an end short of justice because the men couldn't be caught turned round and made it clear that it was now our duty, mine in particular, to make ourselves scarce.

But it wasn't an Englishman. And of course there are people who would say that it would never have happened if it had been, and I expect they would be right because he and I would never have had to go to the Bibighar to be alone, we would never have been there after dark. He would have seduced me in the back of a truck in the car park of the Gymkhana club, or in the place behind the changing-rooms of the swimming-pool, or in a room in one of the chummeries, or even in my bedroom at the MacGregor on a night Lili was out playing bridge. And there are people who would say that even if this subaltern and I had made love in the pavilion in the Bibighar we would never have been attacked by a gang of Indian hooligans. Which is probably right too, although their reasons for saying so wouldn't be strictly correct. They'd invest the subaltern with some sort of superman quality that enabled him to make short work of a gang of bloody wogs, whereas, in fact, the gang of bloody wogs would have been made short work of by their own fear of white people. Miss Crane was hit a few times, but it was the Indian teacher with her who was murdered. They assaulted me because they had watched an Indian making love to me. The taboo was broken for them.

I think Hari understood this. I think this is what he saw and was ashamed of and asked to be forgiven for. All that I saw was the danger to him as a black man carrying me through a gateway that opened on to the world of white people.

I look for similes, for something that explains it more clearly, but find nothing, because there *is* nothing. It is itself; an Indian carrying an English girl he has made love to and been forced to watch being assaulted – carrying her back to where she would be safe. It is its own simile. It says all that needs to be said, doesn't it? If you extend it, if you think of him carrying me all the way to the MacGregor House, giving me into Aunt Lili's care, ringing for the doctor, ringing for the police, answering questions, and being treated as a man who'd rescued me, the absurdity, the implausibility become almost unbearable. Directly you get to the point where Hari, taken on one side by Ronald for instance, has to say, "Yes, we were making love," the nod of understanding that *must* come from Ronald *won't*, unless you blanch Hari's skin, blanch it until it looks not just like that of a white man but like that of a white man too shaken for another white man not to feel sorry for, however much he may reproach him.

And that is why I fought him, why I beat at him, why I said, "We've not seen each other. You know nothing."

So easy to say. "I've not seen Hari. I've not seen Hari since we visited the temple." That's what I told Lili when I was lying on the sofa in the living-room. She had understood at last what was wrong and had asked, "Was it Hari?" And out it came, perhaps too glibly, but incontrovertible. "No. No. I've not seen Hari. I've not seen him since we visited the temple."

"Who was it, then?" she asked. I couldn't look at her. I said, "I don't know. Five or six men. I didn't see. It was dark. They covered my head."

Then if you didn't see them, how can you be sure one of them wasn't Hari Kumar? That was a question that had to be answered, wasn't it? She didn't ask it. Instead she said, "Where?" and I said, "The Bibighar," and again there was a question. What was I doing in the Bibighar? It wasn't asked. Not then. Not by Lili. But the trap was beginning to close. It had been closing ever since I got back and stumbled and fell on the steps of the verandah.

I hurt my knee badly. I think I passed out for a few seconds. When I came to, and was trying to get up, Lili was there staring at me as if she didn't recognise me. I remember her saying the name Raju. I suppose she called him to help or he'd come out with her. The next thing I remember is being in the living-room and being given a glass of brandy. Raju and Bhalu must have carried me in. I remember Bhalu standing on the rug without his chappals. His bare feet. And Raju's bare feet. Black hands. And black faces. After I'd drunk the brandy Lili asked them to carry memsahib upstairs. When they came towards me I couldn't bear it and began to cry out and tell her to send them away. It was then that Lili knew what had happened. When I opened my eyes again she and I were alone and I was ashamed to look at her. She said then, "Was it Hari?" and I gave her the answer I'd rehearsed.

And I'm still ashamed of the way I cried out when Bhalu and Raju came towards me. I cried out because they were black. I'm ashamed because this proved that in spite of loving Hari I'd not exorcised that stupid primitive fear. I'd made Hari an exception. I don't mean that I loved him in spite of his blackness. His blackness was inseparable from his physical attraction. I think I mean that in loving him and in being physically attracted to him I'd invested his blackness with a special significance or purpose, taken it out of its natural context instead of identifying myself with it *in* its context. There was an element here of self-satisfaction and special pleading and extra pride in love because of the personal and social barrier I thought my love had helped me to surmount. It had not surmounted it at all. No, that is not quite true. It had partly surmounted it. Enough for me to be ashamed then, as well as now, and to ask Lili to call Raju and Bhalu back and help me upstairs. I thanked them and tried to show them that I was sorry. In the morning, on my tray, there were flowers from the garden, which Lili said Bhalu had cut for me.

*

Before they helped me upstairs Raju had rung Dr. Klaus. On our way up to my room Lili said, "Anna's coming. It's all right, Daphne. Anna's coming." Lili waited with me in my room. We heard a car or truck drive up and Lili said, "That will be her." A few moments later there was a knock on the bedroom door and Lili called out, "Come in, Anna." I didn't want to see even Anna, so I turned my head away when the door opened. I heard Lili say, "No, no, you mustn't come in." She got up and went outside and closed the door. When she came back she told me it was Ronald, that he had been at the house before, looking for me. I said, "It's very kind of him, but I'm back now, so tell him it's all right." Lili said, "But you see, my dear, it isn't, is it?" And then she began to question me again, to get the answers to questions Ronald had asked. In the Bibighar, but when? How many men? What kind of men? Did I recognise any? Would I recognise any? How did I get back?

She left me for a few minutes. I heard her talking to Ronald in the passage. When she came back she said nothing but sat on the bed and held my hand. Like that we heard Ronald drive away. He was driving very fast. Without looking at her I said, "You told him it wasn't Hari, didn't you?"

She said she had, so I knew Ronald had asked. The way they'd both jumped to the conclusion that Hari was involved only strengthened my resolve to lie my head off.

It was then just a matter of waiting for Anna. I was glad when she got there, glad to be treated like a sort of specimen, clinically, unemotionally. When she'd finished I asked her to tell Lili to get one of the boys to run a bath. I had an idea that if only I could lie in warm water for an hour I might begin to feel clean. She pretended to agree, but she'd given me a strong sedative. I remember the sound of running water, and passing into a half-sleep, imagining that the running water was pouring rain. She ran the water only to lull me. When I woke it was morning. She was still at the bedside. I said, "Have you been here all night?" She hadn't of course, but had called in first thing. I always liked Anna, but until that morning I'd also been a bit afraid of her, as one is of people whose experiences haven't been happy. One hesitates to question them. I never asked Anna about Germany. Now there was no need. We had found something in common. Which is why we were able to smile at each other, distantly, just for a moment or two, as if the connexion between us was only just discernible.

*

I've told the truth, Auntie, as well as I know how. I'm sorry I wasn't able to tell it before. I hate lies. But I think I would tell them again. Nothing that happened after the Bibighar proves to me now that I was wrong to fight for Hari by denying I'd seen him. I know in my bones that he suffered. I know that he is being punished. But I mustn't believe that he is being punished more badly because of my lies than he would have been by the truth.

When I think of the contortions people went through in an attempt to prove I was lying and in an attempt to implicate him I tremble at the thought of what could have happened to him if just once, by a slip of the tongue, I'd admitted that we were in the Bibighar together.

But this doesn't help me to bear the knowledge that those

other boys are unjustly punished. How can people be punished when they are innocent? I know that they went to prison in the end for reasons said to be unconnected with the assault. I hang on to that, in the hope that it is true. But if it hadn't been for the assault I think they'd be free today. They must have been the wrong men. I know I said I didn't see the men, and this was true. But I had an impression of them, of their clothes, their smell, a sense of them as men, not boys. They were hooligans from some village who had come into Mayapore for the hell of it. From what people said the boys who were arrested didn't sound like hooligans at all.

I didn't hear about the arrests until late the following day. Anna and Lili knew already. Ronald had come back the previous night and told them he'd got "the men responsible under lock and key". They said nothing to me at the time because I was asleep by then and nothing in the morning because one of the men was Hari. About half-past twelve Lili came in with Anna. She said, "Jack Poulson has to talk to you, but he can talk in front of Anna." I asked her to stay too, but she said it would be best for Anna and Jack to be alone with me. When Jack Poulson came in he looked like a Christian martyr who'd just refused to disown God for the last time. I was embarrassed by him and he was embarrassed by me. Anna stood by the open door on to the balcony and Jack stood close to her until I told him to sit down. He apologised for having to ask questions and explained that Mr. White had given him the job of "dealing with the evidence" since it was not merely a police matter but one that involved the station as a whole.

I had had time to think, time to worry about the questions Lili hadn't asked the previous night, but which I'd seen as ones that would have to be answered. What was I doing in the Bibighar? How did I know that Hari wasn't there if I didn't see the men who attacked me? I realised that the only way I could get through an interrogation without involving Hari was to relive the whole thing in my mind as it would have happened, as it would have had to be, if Hari hadn't been in the Bibighar with me.

My story was this: that after seeing Miss Crane I'd left the hospital and gone to the Sanctuary. I made a point of asking Jack Poulson not to say too much about the Sanctuary – if he could help it – because I went there to assist at the clinic and was sure this was a breach of hospital regulations even for a voluntary unpaid nursing officer. He smiled, as I'd intended he should. But then he stopped smiling and by his silence forced me to go on, unaided, to the difficult part of the story.

I left the Sanctuary about dusk. It had seemed clear that no one would come to the clinic because of the rumours of trouble. The whole town was unnaturally quiet. The people had imposed their own curfew. But far from frightening me it lulled me into a false sense of security. For once I felt I had Mayapore completely to myself. I cycled to the Chillianwallah Bagh Extension road and then over the Bibighar bridge and the level crossing.

At this point Jack Poulson said, "Did you see anyone near the crossing?"

I thought about that. (I still hadn't been told about the arrests.) So far we were still dealing with fact, with truth, but I had to judge the extent to which I could allow myself to tell it. I saw nothing dangerous in the truth so far, so I tried to conjure an accurate picture of crossing the bridge and the railway lines. I said, "No. There was no one about. The light showed green at the crossing – and I seem to remember lights and voices coming from the keeper's hut. When I say voices I mean a child crying. A feeling of some kind of domestic crisis that was taking up everyone's attention. Anyway, I cycled on. When I got to the street lamp opposite the Bibighar I stopped and got off."

After waiting for a moment Jack said, "Why?"

I said, "I stopped originally to take off my cape. I'd put it on when I left Sister Ludmila's because I thought it was going to rain again, but it hadn't done, and you know what it's like wearing a rain cape for no reason."

Jack nodded and then asked if I'd actually stopped *under* the streetlamp. I thought: That means somebody saw me, either that or they're trying to establish that someone could have seen me. I wasn't bothered because I was still telling the truth. But I was wary, and I was glad that the half-lie I was about to tell was closer to the truth than the story I'd first thought of and rejected – that I stopped by the Bibighar to put my cape *on* because I thought it was going to rain, or because it had come on to rain and I'd decided to shelter for a while in the Bibighar. I rejected that story because it hadn't been about to rain, and didn't rain, and anyone could have proved that it didn't.

So I said, yes, I'd stopped under the streetlamp and taken

my cape off. And my rain-hat. I'd put my hat in the pocket of the cape and put the cape over the handlebars.

Mr. Poulson said, "What do you mean when you say *originally* you stopped to take off your cape?"

This was the first real danger point. Again I was glad I'd rejected the idea of a melodramatic attack by unknown assailants who overpowered me and dragged me into the Bibighar. I said, "You'll think it awfully silly, or if not silly then foolish or careless." Now that I was actually telling the lie I congratulated myself. In an odd way the lie was so much in character. Typical of that silly blundering *gallumping* girl Daphne Manners. I looked Jack Poulson straight in the eye and came out with it. "The cantonment was so quiet and deserted I wondered whether I'd see the ghosts."

"The ghosts?" he asked. He was trying to look official but only succeeded in looking as inquisitive as I was pretending to have been, the night before. I said, "Yes, the ghosts of the Bibighar. I'd never been there in the dark" – that was dangerous, but it passed – "and I remembered having heard that the place was supposed to be haunted. So I sort of said, Up the Army, Steady the Buffs, and crossed the road and went in. You can always get in because there's no gate. I thought it was a bit of a lark and that when I got back I'd be able to say to Lili, 'Well, I've laid those Bibighar ghosts. Bring on Janet MacGregor.' I wheeled my bike up the pathway to the pavilion, then parked it, turned the lamp off, and went up on to the mosaic platform."

But Mr. Poulson had never been in the Bibighar. He went later to inspect the scene, but for the moment I had to tell him what the mosaic platform was before he was in the picture. "Anyway," I said, "I sat on the platform and had a cigarette" – (that slipped out and was also dangerous because if any cigarette ends had survived the night's rains they'd not be English ones) – "and waited for the ghosts to show up. I was saying things to myself like, Come on, ghosts, let's be having you, and then began to think about Miss Crane, and wonder whether I hadn't been an awful fool. I suppose it *was* mad of me, sitting there, last night of all nights. But I didn't take what had happened in outlying parts of the district seriously, did you? I suppose they were watching me. I didn't hear anything – except the dripping and the croaking – I mean the dripping from the leaves and the roof and the croaking of the frogs. The men came rather suddenly. Almost from nowhere."

Mr. Poulson reassumed his Christian martyr face. He said, "And you didn't see them?" Which was the other warning note. I said, "Well, for an instant perhaps. But it was all so quick. I didn't have any warning. One moment I was alone and the next surrounded."

Of course this was the part of the story Jack Poulson wanted to know about but found so acutely embarrassing he could hardly look at me while I told it. He kept glancing at Anna, for moral support, and at the time I wondered why she just stood there, obviously listening but staring at the garden, detaching herself from the interrogation, turning herself into an impersonal lump that would only spring into action and become Anna Klaus again if her patient's voice betrayed signs of distress.

Jack Poulson said, "I'm sorry to have to press these questions. But is there anything you remember about these men, or about any one of them, anything that will help you to identify them?"

I played for time. I said, "I don't think so. I mean they all look alike, don't they? Especially in the dark," and was conscious of having said something that could be thought indelicate, as well as out of character. He asked me how they were dressed. I had a pretty clear recollection of white cotton clothing – you know, dhotis and high-necked shirts, peasant dress, dirty and smelly. But the warning bells rang again. I saw *the danger to Hari if the men were ever caught*. I think that if I were taken to the Bibighar, at night, and confronted with those men, I would know them. You can recognise people again, even when you think there's been nothing to identify them by, even if there's been only a second or two to get an impression you can hardly believe is an impression, or at least not one worth describing or trying to describe. I was afraid of *being* confronted, afraid of finding myself having to say, "Yes, these are the men," because then they would plead provocation, they'd go on their knees and scream and beg for mercy and say that such a thing would never have occurred to them *if the white woman hadn't already been making love to an Indian*.

The trap was now fully sprung, Auntie, wasn't it? Once you've started lying there's no end to it. I'd lied myself into a position there was no escaping from except by way of the truth. I didn't dare tell the truth so the only thing I could do was to confuse and puzzle people and make them hate me –

that, and stretch every nerve-end to keep Hari out of it by going on and on insisting that he was never there, making it so that they would never be able to accuse or bring to trial or punish the men who assaulted me because they knew that the principal witness would spike every gun they tried to bring into action.

But of course I was forgetting or anyway reckoning without the power they had to accuse and punish on suspicion alone. There was a moment when I nearly told the truth, because I saw the way things might go. I'm glad I didn't because then I think they would have proved somehow that Hari was technically guilty of rape, because he'd been there and made love to me and incited others to follow his example. At least my lying spared him being punished for rape. It also spared those innocent boys being punished for it too. I've never asked what the punishment for rape is. Hanging? Life imprisonment? People talked about swinging them on the end of a rope. Or firing them from the mouth of a cannon, which is what we did to mutineers in the nineteenth century.

So when Jack Poulson asked me how the men were dressed I said I wasn't sure, but then decided it was safer to tell the truth and say "Like peasants" than to leave the impression of men dressed like Hari, in shirts and trousers.

Mr. Poulson said, "Are you sure?" which rather played into my hands because he said it as if my evidence was contradicting the story he'd been building up, or other people had built up for him, a picture with Hari at its centre. So I said, Yes, like peasants or labourers. And I added for good measure, "They smelt like that, too." Which was true. He said, "Did any of them smell of drink?" I thought of the time Hari was found on the waste ground by Sister Ludmila. For the moment it looked safer to tell the truth again and say I didn't remember any special smell of drink.

Mr. Poulson said, "I'm sorry to have to subject you to this." I told him it was all right, I knew it had to be done. For the first time in the interrogation we looked at each other for longer than a split second. He said, "There's the important question of the bicycle. You say you left it on the path near the pavilion. Did you leave your cape on the handlebars?"

I couldn't immediately see the significance of this question. I assumed he knew that the cape had been used to cover my head because I'd told Lili and Anna. He'd got all this kind of detail from them. He never asked a single question about the assault itself. Poor fellow! I expect he'd rather have died than do so, magistrate though he was. But it was an English girl who'd been assaulted and his magisterial detachment just wouldn't hold out. I decided to tell the truth about the cape. I said, "No, I'm pretty sure I took it with me on to the platform. In fact I did. I thought the mosaic might be damp, but it wasn't. So I didn't sit on the cape, I just kept it by me."

He seemed to be satisfied with that, and later when the whole business of the bicycle and what had happened to it blew up in my face I realised what he'd been after. He was trying to establish at what stage "they'd" found the bicycle. If I'd left the cape on the handlebars that would mean they'd known the bicycle was there before they attacked me, because they'd used the cape. If I hadn't left it on the handlebars it could mean they didn't find the bicycle until they were making off along the path. And this would suggest that they had gone along the path and not out through the broken wall at the back of the garden. There couldn't have been any footprints though, because the paths were all gravel, and anyway with the rains and the police bashing about in the dark all that kind of evidence would lead nowhere. His next question was, "You say you were suddenly surrounded. Do you mean they closed in on you from all sides of the platform?"

And again, the warning bell. If I said, Yes, from all sides, the next question wouldn't be a question at all, but a statement impossible to refute: "So you never got an impression of the man or men who came at you from behind?"

I realised it was going to be difficult to kill completely the idea of there having been at least one man I never saw, especially if he was a man who kept out of sight in case I recognised him. Hari, for instance. The pavilion is open on all sides. I could only minimise the danger. I said, "Well, no, not from all sides. Originally I was sitting on the edge of the platform, then I threw my cigarette away and turned round – as you would, to get to your feet. They were coming at me from behind. I don't know – perhaps I'd heard a sound that made me decide to get out of the place. It *was* pretty creepy. When I turned round there were these two just standing upright after climbing on to the platform and the other three or four vaulting on to it."

Did I call out? No – I was too surprised to call out. Did any of them say anything? I think one of them giggled.

Mr. Poulson questioned the margin of error there might be

in my statement about "the other three or four". Was it three, or was it four? Was the total number of men five or six? I said I couldn't remember. All I remembered was the awful sensation of being attacked swiftly by as many men as there were, five or six. Men of that kind, labourers, hooligans, stinking to high heaven. I said it was like being thrown into one of those disgusting third-class compartments on an Indian train. And that I didn't want to talk about it any more.

Anna came to life then. She turned round and said, "Yes, I think it is enough, Mr. Poulson," in that very forthright German voice of hers. He got up at once, glad enough to be out of it, if only for a while. Anna saw him to the door. She came back for a moment to make sure I was all right, then left me alone. Lili brought up some fruit and curds for my lunch and after that I dozed until late afternoon. I woke and found Lili in the room and Raju just leaving it. He'd brought up tea.

When I'd had a cup Lili said, "I think Mr. Poulson should have told you. Some boys were arrested last night. One of them was Hari."

*

My bicycle had been found in the ditch outside Hari's house in the Chillianwallah Bagh. I didn't believe it. It was such a monstrous *fatal* intervention. I said, "But he wasn't there! It wasn't Hari!" She wanted to believe me. I tried not to panic. If some men had been arrested I thought they must be the ones responsible and that they would already have talked about the Indian who'd been making love to me there. I was going to have to deny this, deny it and go on denying it, and hope that Hari would keep his promise to say nothing, to know nothing. I felt that he had *given* me that promise when he let me go. I asked Lili when he'd been arrested and why, and who by. When I took it in that he'd been in custody ever since the night before and that Ronald was responsible, that Ronald had found the bicycle outside Hari's house, I said, "He's lying, isn't he? He found the bicycle in the Bibighar and took it to Hari's house and planted it in the ditch."

Lili was shocked because she knew it *could* be true, but she refused to believe it. She couldn't accept that an English official would stoop to that. But there are only three possible explanations for the bicycle and only one is likely. I left the bicycle by the path against a tree. It was very dark on the path. You'd easily miss seeing the bicycle if you didn't know just where it was and if you had no lamp. I think when Hari carried me down the path we'd gone past the place before I said, "It's here somewhere," and he put me down. He wasn't interested in the bicycle. He was only concerned to carry me home. I suppose he had some dim idea that if the bicycle were there he could put me on it and wheel me home. But the bicycle was a bad joke, just at that moment, wasn't it? He hardly bothered to look. I think the bicycle was still where I'd left it, and that when Ronald rushed to the Bibighar with his police patrol they found it almost at once and Ronald put it into the back of a truck and drove to Hari's house and dumped it in the ditch. I think he was the sort of officer who let his men have a lot of elbow room and in return could get them to plant evidence like this for him and say nothing. Remember the incident of the sub-inspector hitting Hari and getting away with it? There was nothing to connect Hari with the assault in the Bibighar except his known association with me and Ronald's jealousy and suspicion and prejudice. What else made him go to Hari's house? And why when he got there did he spend time searching for the bicycle? If it was in a ditch outside it would have had to be *searched* for, wouldn't it?

If the bicycle *was* in the ditch before Ronald got there I suppose it's possible that one of his men found it during the course of whatever drill they go through when they go to a place to pick up a suspect. But the impression I got before the so-called inquiry was that according to Ronald they only went into the house because they found the bicycle outside it, and that it was only then that Ronald realised that the house was Hari's. If this was the impression he gave people at first he can't have been thinking very clearly because he wouldn't have to give English people any reason for going to Hari's house. Apparently he'd been there once that night already. He was probably not thinking clearly because Lili had repeated to him what I'd told her – that Hari wasn't with me, that Hari wasn't responsible. He wanted Hari to be responsible. I think he had to change the emphasis when it came to making a proper report, had to say that he'd gone to Hari's house and *then* found the bicycle, not the other way round.

I give Ronald this much benefit of the doubt, that after he left the MacGregor House, knowing what had happened to me, he went to his headquarters, collected a patrol, rushed to the Bibighar, found nothing, and then searched the area in the vicinity, arrested those boys who were drinking hooch in a hut on the other side of the river, and then headed straight for the house in the Chillianwallah Bagh, where he found Hari with cuts on his face and where his police found the bicycle. He went to the Chillianwallah Bagh because he thought I was lying, knew I was lying, and because the boys he arrested in the hut on the other side of the bridge were known to be acquaintances of Hari's. But he went mainly because he hated Hari. He wanted to prove that Hari was guilty. And this leaves only the two other explanations for the bicycle. Either Hari went back for it after I'd left him, found it, rode it home, then realised the danger and shoved it into the ditch – which would mean he lost his head because if he *saw* the danger he wouldn't leave the bicycle outside his own house. Or one of the men who attacked me knew Hari, knew where he lived, stole the bicycle and left it outside Hari's house, guessing that the police would search near there – which means that whoever it was who knew Hari also knew that Hari and I were friends. And this leads, surely, to the proposition that such a man anticipated that we'd be in the Bibighar that night. But we didn't even anticipate that ourselves. The coincidence of there being one man or several men in the Bibighar that night who recognised Hari in the dark and thought fast enough to steal the bicycle and leave it outside his house is too much to swallow, isn't it? And who could such a man be? One of Lili's servants? One of Mrs. Gupta Sen's? One who might have been able to read my note, in English, asking Hari to meet me on the night of August the 9th, *in the Sanctuary*? No, it won't wash. It won't even wash if you think – as I did for a while – of this unknown but very clever or very lucky man or boy being one of those stretcher-bearers Sister Ludmila used to hire, never for more than a few weeks because after that they got bored and "their thoughts turned to mischief". On the day I went to say goodbye to her I noticed that she had a new boy. She told me about the boys who wrote to her after they'd left, and how only one of them had ever come back to beg. And it did cross my mind that perhaps the one who came back to beg was the one who was with her and Mr. de Souza the night they brought Hari in to the Sanctuary. Such a boy might have taken an interest in Hari, followed him around, got to know his movements, even watched us on those occasions we went to the Bibighar. But why? Such a boy, back in his village, might have talked about the Indian and the white girl, and led a gang of fellow hooligans into Mayapore, attracted by rumours of trouble and the idea of loot, and come to the Bibighar from the waste-ground at the back to shelter for the night, and seen Hari there, and me, watched our love-making. The men who attacked us *had* been watching. That is certain. But the coincidence is too much to take. The men were hooligans. It was Ronald Merrick who planted the bicycle. I know it. I don't think Hari had many friends, but I don't think he had any enemies either, except for Ronald – none, anyway, who would go to the lengths that were gone to to incriminate him.

If it wasn't Ronald, then it must have been Hari himself who took the bicycle, then panicked and left it outside his house. I don't think Hari panicked.

But I did. I told Lili to leave me alone. I wanted to think. It became quite clear. Ronald searched the Bibighar, found the bicycle, put it in the truck, then drove across the bridge, towards Chillianwallah Bagh, questioned the level-crossing keeper, found the boys who were "friends" of Hari's, arrested them, drove on to Hari's house, planted the bike and then stormed into the house. And when Hari was arrested they probably searched his room. Had he destroyed my note asking him to meet me in the Sanctuary? The note was never mentioned so he must have done. This may have been the only thing he had time to do, if he hadn't thrown it away before. The photograph I gave him was mentioned. Ronald took it away, as "evidence" – a copy of the same photograph that I sent you and which Hari helped me to choose from the proofs that day at Subhas Chand's. At the informal inquiry at the MacGregor House Mr. Poulson said, "Mr. Kumar had your photograph in his bedroom. Was it one you gave him?" – you know – as if trying to establish that Hari was obsessed with me and had stolen the photograph to stare at at night, and as if giving me the opportunity to recant, to go on to their side, to get rid of my silly notions of loyalty and break down and admit that I'd been infatuated, that Hari had worked on my emotions in the most callous and calculating way, that it was a relief to tell the truth at last, that I had come to my senses and was no longer afraid of him, let alone infatuated, that he'd attacked and brutalised me and then submitted me to the base indignity of being raped by friends of his, and that then he'd tried to terrorise me with threats to my life if I gave him away, threats which he said would be all too easy to carry out because the British were about to be given the bum's rush. Oh, I know what was in their minds – perhaps against their personal judgment – but in their minds as the story they ought to believe because of what might be at stake. Of the trio who made up the board of private inquiry, or whatever it was officially called – Mr. Poulson, a startled and embarrassed young English sub-divisional officer whose name I forget, and Judge Menen – only Judge Menen, who presided, maintained an air of utter detachment. It was a detachment that struck me as that of fatigue, fatigue amounting to hopelessness. But the fact that he was there heartened me, not only because he was an Indian but because I was sure he wouldn't have been there if there was any likelihood of the accused men coming in front of him in the District Court. I suppose if the inquiry had led to what the board by now had no hope of but the English community still wanted, the case would have gone up for trial in the Provincial High Court.

But I've gone a step too far ahead. I must go back for a moment to the evening of the 10th – when I sent Lili out of the room to give myself time to think because I was panicky about what might have been found that could incriminate Hari, and about who the other arrested men were, and what they might have said. Then I was overwhelmed by the typically blunt thoughtless English way I'd assumed everything would be all right for Hari if *I* said he was innocent. I'd run away from Hari, believing that just by putting distance between us I was helping him. But I saw him now standing where I'd left him, at the gate of the Bibighar. Auntie, what did he do? Go back to look for the bicycle, and remove it, thinking he was helping *me*? Or begin his journey home on foot? There was blood on my neck and face when I got back – so Anna told me. It must have come from Hari's face when we clung to each other. In the dark I didn't see how badly or how little those men had hurt him. I never asked. I never thought. He was bathing his face, apparently, when Ronald burst into his room. Of course they tried to prove he'd been hurt by me fighting back. But all I can think of now is the callous way I left him, to face up to everything alone, to say nothing, deny everything, because I'd told him to, but having to say nothing and deny everything with those scratches or abrasions on his face that he couldn't account for. When it came out at the inquiry that his face was cut I said, "Why ask me about them? Ask Mr. Kumar. I don't know. He wasn't there." Mr. Poulson said, "He *was* asked. He wouldn't say," and then changed the subject. Ronald was giving evidence at the time. I stared at him, but he refused to look at me. I said, "Perhaps he had a scrap with the police. It wouldn't be the first time he was hit by a police officer." It did no good. It was the wrong thing to say at that time in that place. It made them sympathise with Ronald rather than me. I didn't mind, though, because in any case I was beginning to hate myself. I hated myself because I realised Hari had taken me at my word and said nothing – quite literally nothing. Nothing. Nothing. Nothing. Said nothing in spite of evidence against him, which I hadn't reckoned with when I ran off and left him.

They hurt him, didn't they? Tortured him in some way? But he said nothing, nothing. When they arrested him he must have stood there – with the cuts on his face, my photograph in his room, my bicycle in the ditch outside, and said nothing. At one time during those days of question and answer Lili told me, "He won't account for his movements. He denies having been in the Bibighar. He says he hasn't seen you since the night you both went to the temple. But he won't say where he was or what he was doing between leaving the office and getting home, some time after nine. He must have reached home about the time you did, Daphne."

And of course these were the other things I hadn't reckoned with or known about: Ronald's first visit to the house in the Chillianwallah Bagh, his visit to the MacGregor House, his visit to the Sanctuary. When I left Hari at the Bibighar I suppose I assumed that all he had to do was to pretend to have been at home all evening, to persuade Aunt Shalini to swear he had been at home, if the question ever arose, or to make up another story, whatever he thought best, whatever he thought would work. But for Hari, no story worked. *I never gave him a chance to calm me down and say – as I would have let an Englishman say* – "Look, for Pete's sake, if I haven't been here in the Bibighar, where in hell have I been? How do I account for this swollen lip, or black eye, or scratched cheek," whatever it was.

I never gave him the chance because even in my panic there was this assumption of superiority, of privilege, of believing I knew what was best for both of us, because the colour of my skin automatically put me on the side of those who never told a lie. But we've got far beyond that stage of colonial simplicity. We've created a blundering judicial robot. We can't stop it working. It works for us even when we least want it to. We created it to prove how fair, how civilised we are. But it is a white robot and it can't distinguish between love and rape. It only understands physical connexion and only understands it as a crime because it only exists to punish crime. It would have punished Hari for this, and if physical connexion between the races is a crime he's been punished justly. One day someone may come along, cross a wire by mistake, or fix in a special circuit with the object of making it impartial and colour-blind, and then it will probably explode.

*

After Lili had told me about Hari's arrest and I'd thought for a bit I rang for Raju and told him I wanted Poulson Sahib sent for. I'd got over my panic. I was angry, even angry with Lili. I felt she'd let me down by allowing them to hold Hari in custody without doing a thing to stop it. She was very patient with me, but we were shut off from each other as we'd never been before. She said that if I really wanted to see Mr. Poulson she'd ring him. I think she believed I was going to confess. She knew I'd been lying. But for her the truth would be as bad as the lies. She brought Hari in to the house, and he was an Indian. A fellow-countryman. For a day or two after the Bibighar, I felt like an interloper, one of her harpies who'd inexplicably become involved with the life of an Indian family, and had taken to sitting in her bedroom the better to keep what was left of her racial integrity intact.

Mr. Poulson came after dinner. Lili brought him up. She asked whether I wanted her to stay. I said it might be better if Mr. Poulson and I were alone. Directly she'd gone I said, "Why didn't you tell me they arrested Hari Kumar last night?" Normally I liked him. Tonight I despised him, but then I was ready to despise everybody. He looked as if he wanted to fall through the floor. He said Hari had been arrested because the evidence seemed to add up that way, in spite of my "belief" that he hadn't been involved. I said, "What evidence? What evidence that can possibly contradict *my* evidence. You must all be mad if you think you can pin anything on Hari."

He said that the evidence last night had pointed to Hari, and that it couldn't be ruled out that he was there, in spite of my belief that he wasn't.

I said it wasn't a question of belief. I asked him whether he really thought I wouldn't *know* if Hari had been among those who attacked me. That scared him. He was afraid of an intimate confession. When I realised this I thought I saw how to play the whole thing, play it by scaring them at the thought of what I might come out with, in court. I asked him about the other men. He pretended he didn't know anything about them. I smiled and said, "I see Ronald is keeping it all very much to himself. But that's no wonder, is it? After all, it's pretty obvious he planted the bicycle."

Lili had been shocked, but her shock was nothing to Jack Poulson's. He said, "What on earth makes you say a thing like that?" I told him to ask Ronald. It seemed wiser to leave it at that, to leave Mr. Poulson with something tricky to bite on. Before he went – and he went because "in his view there was nothing it would be advantageous to pursue for the moment" – I said, "Hari wasn't there. I doubt that any of the men you've arrested were there. It's the usual thing, isn't it? An English woman gets assaulted and at once everyone loses all sense of proportion. If Ronald or any of you think you're going to get away with punishing the first poor bloody Indians you've clapped hands on just to give the European community a field-day you've got another think coming. It'll never stand up in court because *I'll* stand up in court and say what I'm saying to you. Only I might be more explicit about a lot of things."

He got up and mumbled something about being sorry and that everyone appreciated what a terrible time I'd had, that he was sure no one who was innocent could possibly be punished. I said, "Then tell me this. Forget the *one* innocent man you've got locked up at the moment. Do the others fit my description of them at all?"

He said he didn't know. He hadn't seen them. But I wasn't letting him off so lightly. I was chancing my arm, but it seemed worth it. I said, "Oh, come off it, Jack. You know all right. Even if you haven't seen them you must know who they are. Are they what I said? Smelly peasants? Dirty labourers? Or boys like Hari? The kind of boy Mr. Merrick seems to have it in for?"

I'd hit the mark. But he still insisted he didn't know. He said he believed that one or two of them were known for or suspected of political activities of "the anarchist type". I pounced on that. I said, "Oh, you mean educated boys? Not smelly peasants?"

He shook his head, not denying it but closing the way to further discussion.

*

Retrospectively, I'm sorry for the bad time I gave poor Jack Poulson. But it had to be done. I'm pretty sure he went away thinking, "It won't stick. Not with those fellows Merrick's got locked up." I don't know how much more he would say when he got back to the Deputy Commissioner's bungalow, which was almost certainly where he was headed. To Mr. White probably all he needed to say was something like, "Either she's lying, or Kumar is innocent, but if she's lying or continues to lie he ranks as innocent anyway because we'll never prove him guilty. The same goes for the others. Merrick's made a gaffe."

Robin White detached himself from the affair, to the extent that he left Jack Poulson in charge of it up to the point where a final decision had to be made. If he'd been a man like his predecessor Mr. Stead (whom men like Vassi loathed) God knows what would have happened. I suppose to Robin the assault on a silly English girl wasn't very important when he compared it with the other things he had to deal with. I don't know whether Mr. Poulson ever said anything to Mr. White about the bicycle and my accusation against Ronald. It wouldn't have been an easy thing for him to pass on. At the inquiry the bicycle was never mentioned, and the only time Hari was mentioned was when Ronald was giving evidence of arrest. He answered questions which Jack Poulson seemed to have worked out carefully in advance. In fact the evidence of the arrests struck me as ridiculous. Mr. Poulson read out the names of the men arrested and simply asked Ronald where and at what time they'd been taken into custody, and what they had been doing. As I already knew from what Lili had told me, the other poor boys had been drinking hooch in a hut near the Bibighar bridge but at the inquiry the *unfairness* of it struck me all over again. According to Ronald, Hari was in his bedroom, "washing his face on which there were cuts and abrasions". I nearly interrupted and said, "What about the bicycle?" but thought better of it. The bicycle not being mentioned was a good sign. I wondered if Jack Poulson had talked to Ronald in private and decided from the answers he got that he'd better keep the bicycle business quiet, not only for Ronald's sake, but for the sake of the Service, the flag and all that. But I did come out with the remark about the cuts on Hari's face when Jack Poulson asked me whether I recalled "marking" any of the men who attacked me. I mean the remark about Hari probably having had a scrap with the police.

After the so-called evidence of arrests Ronald was dismissed and then they got down to the business of going over my statement again and asking questions, and I saw how the evidence of arrests was so thin that although it proved nothing it could also prove anything. Judge Menen had kept quiet – I mean he'd not asked me any questions so far, but towards the end he said, "I must ask you why you refused the other day to attempt to identify the men held in custody," which I had done, when the worst of the troubles in Mayapore were over and they wanted to push the case to a conclusion of some sort and get it over with. I said, "I refused to attempt identification because they must be the wrong men. I shall say so in court, if necessary."

Judge Menen said he understood why I should feel this in regard to "the man Kumar" but the refusal to attempt identification of the other men might be interpreted as wilful obstruction by the principal witness and this might lead to the prosecution being able to prove its case in spite of that witness's evidence, because the wilful obstruction might be held as a sign of general unreliability.

I thought about this. Mr. Poulson brightened up a bit. He didn't mind that Menen was an Indian and perhaps shouldn't speak to a white girl like that. It was the Law that spoke. He thought the clever old Judge had forced me into a corner by scaring me with a legal technicality, a reminder that even the principal witness couldn't obstruct the Crown in the pursuit of justice. But I thought I saw my way out. And I wasn't really convinced that Judge Menen was on particularly sure ground himself. I said, "If my evidence is thought unreliable for that reason, does it become less unreliable if I go through the farce of looking at these men, with no intention whatsoever of saying I recognise them? You prefer me to go through that farce? You'd only have my word for it that I didn't recognise them. Simply looking at them isn't a test of reliability in itself, is it?"

Menen's poker face didn't alter. He said they would assume, continue to assume, that I was telling the truth, and reminded me that the whole inquiry was based on the assumption that I was telling the truth, that it was only the refusal to comply with the request to attempt identification which could raise the question of unreliability. He went on, "In your statement you say you had a brief impression of the men who attacked you. You have described them as peasants or labourers. That being so, with such an impression in your mind, why do you refuse to co-operate in the important business of helping us, as best you can, to decide whether the men being held are held on sufficient grounds?"

Looking at him I thought: You know they're the wrong men too. You want me to go down to the jail and look at them and say, No, they aren't as I remember them at all. Either you want that, or you want me to make it *quite* plain, perhaps outrageously plain, that it's useless for anyone to expect to bring this case to court with these boys as defendants.

But I was still afraid of confronting them. I was sure they were the wrong boys, but I didn't know. I didn't want to face them. If they were the right boys there was a danger – only very slight, but still a danger – of their panicking at the sight of me and incriminating Hari. And if they were the right boys and I recognised them I didn't want to have to say, "No, these aren't the men." I wasn't sure I could trust myself to carry it off, even for Hari's sake. *I didn't want to tell that sort of lie.* There's a difference between trying to stop an injustice and obstructing justice.

I said, "No, I won't co-operate. One of these men is innocent. If one innocent man is accused I'm not interested in the guilt or innocence of the others. I refuse absolutely to go anywhere near them. The men who raped me were peasants. The boys you've got locked up aren't, so they're almost certainly all innocent too. For one thing they're all Hindus, aren't they?"

Mr. Poulson agreed that they were all Hindus.

I smiled. I'd prepared this one awfully well, I thought. I said, "Then that's another thing. One of the men was a Muslim. He was circumcised. If you want to know how I know I'm quite prepared to tell you but otherwise prefer to leave it at that. One was a Muslim. They were all hooligans. Apart from that I can't tell you a thing. I can't tell you more than I have done. The impression I had of them was strong enough for me to know that I could say, 'No, these aren't the men,' but not strong enough for me to say, 'Yes, these *are* the men.' For all I knew they could have been British soldiers with their faces blacked. I don't imagine they were, but if by saying so I can convince you I know you've got at least one wrong man, well then I say so."

Mr. Poulson and the young man whose name I don't remember both looked profoundly shocked. Judge Menen stared at me and then said, "Thank you, Miss Manners. We have no more questions. We are sorry to have had to subject you to this examination."

He got to his feet and we all stood, just as if it was a court-room and not the dining-room of the MacGregor House. But there the similarity ended. Instead of Judge Menen going out he stood still and made it clear that it was my privilege to leave first. When I got to the door Jack Poulson was ahead of me to open it. A purely automatic gesture, part of the Anglo-Indian machinery. But I could *smell* his shock. Bitter, as if he'd just eaten some aromatic quick-acting paralysing herb.

*

I went upstairs and poured myself a drink. I thought it was all over and that I'd won and Hari would be released in the next few hours, or the next day. I stood on the balcony as I'd done so often during the past two weeks. During the riots you could hear the shouting and the firing and the noise of trucks and lorries going from one part of the civil lines to the other. For a day or two there'd been policemen at the gate of the MacGregor House. They said the house might be attacked, but we'd been more worried about Anna Klaus than about ourselves. At one time she was practically a prisoner in the Purdah Hospital in the native town, and we didn't see her for a couple of days. Mrs. White wanted Lili and me to move into the Deputy Commissioner's bungalow, but Lili wouldn't go. Neither would I. That's when the police guard appeared. The sight of the police guard made me feel like a prisoner too. Ronald never came near himself. He'd washed his hands of me. I felt that with a few exceptions the whole European community was ready to do that or had already done it. I didn't care. I got to the stage of believing that everything was coming to an end for us, I mean for white people. I didn't care about that either. One evening Lili told me the rioters had broken into the jail. I thought: That's how it will resolve itself. They'll free Hari. I didn't know he wasn't in that jail. But I thought: The Indians will take over. Perhaps they won't punish me. Perhaps Hari will come to the house. But I couldn't visualise it clearly enough. Nothing like that would happen. The soldiers were out and there was the sound of firing, and everything was only a question of time for *us*, hopeless for *them*. The robot was working.

But I was worried about Anna, and Sister Ludmila. They were the only white people I knew who lived or worked on that side of the river. Sister Ludmila told me later that she defied the curfew and went out every night with Mr. de Souza and her stretcher bearer. There was plenty of work for them. The police turned them back once or twice but generally they managed to give them the slip. The "death house", as people called it, was always occupied. And every morning the police went there, and the women whose husbands or sons hadn't come home.

I was worried for you, too, until Lili told me she'd got Robin White to send you a message through official channels that I was all right. They tried to keep my name out of reports that appeared in the national newspapers. Some hopes. Thank God we'd talked on the phone before my name was given away. Even so I was afraid you'd come down to Mayapore. I bless you for not doing, for understanding. If you'd come down I couldn't have borne it. I had to work it out alone. I bless Lili for understanding that too. At first I thought her detachment was due to disapproval, then that it was due to that curious Indian indifference to pain. But of course her "indifference" was wholly "European", wholly civilised, like yours, like my own. There are pains we feel, and pains we recognise in others, that are best left alone, not from callousness but from discretion. Anna's detachmemt was rather different. Hers also was European, but Jewish, self-protective as well as sensitive, as if she didn't want to be reminded of pain because to be reminded would transfer her sensitivity from my pain to what she remembered of her own. By keeping that amount of distance she was able to establish a friendship between us, trust, regard, the kind of regard that can spring up between strangers who sense each other's mettle. One shouldn't expect more. But affection comes from a different source, doesn't it? I'm thinking of the affection there is between you and me, which is not only an affection of the blood because there is the same kind of affection between myself and Lili. It's one that overcomes, that exists, but for which there isn't necessarily any accounting because trust doesn't enter into it at all, except to the extent that you trust because of the affection. You trust after you have learned to love.

I could never feel affectionate in that way towards Anna. Neither, I'm sure, could she towards me. But we were good and trusting, understanding friends. One develops an instinct for people. I wander on about this because when I stood on the balcony, drinking my well-deserved gin and limejuice, I saw Ronald and Mr. Poulson come out of the house and get into Ronald's truck. Judge Menen wasn't with them. He stayed behind to have a drink with Lili.

And I thought: How curious. Ronald and Jack Poulson are just *people* to me. I felt no real resentment, not even of Ronald, let alone of Jack who was obviously going off somewhere to chew the rag with Ronald. But I felt they were outside the circle of those people "it was worth my while to know", as my mother put it once, probably meaning something else entirely. To me my own meaning was clear. I already *knew* them. They were predictable people, predictable because they worked for the robot. What the robot said they would also say, what the robot did they would do, and what the robot believed was what they believed because people like them had fed that belief into it. And they would always be right so long as the robot worked, because the robot was the standard of rightness.

There was no *originating passion* in them. Whatever they felt that was original would die the moment it came into conflict with what the robot was geared to feel. At the inquiry it needed Judge Menen to break through the robot's barrier – if break is the appropriate word to use to describe the actions of a man who made even getting out of a chair look like an exercise in studied and balanced movement. But he got through. At one moment he was sitting on *their* side, the robot side, and the next moment he was through. We were through together, he *brought* me through or joined me on the other side – whichever way you like to put it. So it seemed right, now, that he should have stayed behind to have a drink with Lili, and leave the robot boys to go off on their own and work out how to make it look as if the robot had brought the inquiry to some kind of logical conclusion. They had to save the robot's face, as well as their own.

It was odd to find myself thinking this about Mr. Poulson. Mr. and Mrs. White thought very highly of him. He was still pretty young, young enough to be cautious, which may sound silly, but isn't, because a young man has a living to earn, a family to support, a career to build. But it probably needs something like what came to be called the Bibighar Gardens affair to sort out the mechanical men from the men who are capable of throwing a spanner into the works. Which is another way of describing what I feel about Judge Menen. What is so interesting is that the spanner he threw into the works, the spanner that brought the inquiry to a stop was the right spanner. It must take years of experience and understanding to know which spanner to use, and the exact moment to use it. I think he knew so well, that in the end he handed the spanner to me just to give himself the additional satisfaction of letting me throw it in for him. He knew that the only way to bring the robot to a temporary halt was to go right to the heart of what had set it in motion – the little cog of judicial procedure which had been built into it in the fond hope that once it was engaged it would only stop when justice had been done. By going to the heart of the mechanism he exposed it for what it was and gave me the chance to bring it to a halt by imposing an impossible task on it – the task of *understanding* the justice of what it was doing, and of proving that its own justice was the equal or the superior of mine. But it was only a *temporary* halt.

Long before Judge Menen left I came in from the balcony and had my bath. I was finished and dressed for dinner before Lili came in and asked if I was all right, and if I would like to see Anna who had called on her way home from the Purdah Hospital. I said, "Is Judge Menen still here?" She told me he'd gone about ten minutes ago. And had sent me his love. I'd never seen Lili *moved* before. I'd only seen her amused, or wry, or disapproving, or detached. I think it was Judge Menen who had moved her with whatever it was he said to her – or rather caused her to be moved directly she set eyes on me again after talking to him. I don't know what it was he had said. I never shall. That is typical of Lili. Typical of him too. And in a terribly English way Lili and I sort of got out of each other's light – put yards of space between us, but were together again.

I went down with her and greeted Anna. Lili asked her to stay to dinner. She said she would. For me it was like a sudden treat, a picnic plan confided to a child early on a golden summer morning. When Lili went out to tell Raju to tell cook it was dinner for three I gave Anna a freshener for her drink. She said, "You look better. Please keep it up."

And I said, "I think I shall. I think we've won." I said "we" because Anna had stood by me all that time. I knew, before the inquiry, that she'd been asked that naked question: "In your opinion was Miss Manners *intacta* before the assault?"

And I knew what she had replied. When I said "I think we've won", she raised her glass.

*

This was the last evening of happiness I had. After it I was optimistic but not happy. In the end even my optimism went. I needed Hari. I needed Lili too, and Anna, and you, but most of all I needed him. I'd built my own enclosed little circle, hadn't I? The one I'd feel safe in. A circle of safety in no-man's-land. Wherever we go, whatever we do, we seem to hedge ourselves about with this illusory protection. Hours went by. Days. More than a week. I never went out. When people came I escaped to my room. The MacGregor House was gradually filled again with vibrations whose source I had never pinned down before but now did and saw as inseparable from it: trust, compromise, something fundamentally exploratory and non-committal, as if the people in it were trying to *learn*, instead of teach – and so forgive rather than accuse. There is that old, disreputable saying, isn't there? "When rape is inevitable, lie back and enjoy it." *Well, there has been more than one rape*. I can't say, Auntie, that I lay back and enjoyed mine. But Lili was trying to lie back and enjoy what we've done to her country. I don't mean done in malice. Perhaps there was love. Oh, somewhere, in the past, and now, and in the future, love as there was between me and Hari. But the spoilers are always there, aren't they? The Swinsons. The bitches who travelled as far as Lahore. The Ronald Merricks. The silly little man who summed up his own silly little island-history when he whistled and said, "some wog contractor is making a packet."

Connie White came to see me one day. She brought Mavis Poulson with her. But she realised after ten minutes or so that she'd get nowhere because bringing edgy, virtuously pregnant Mavis had been a mistake. She sent her away. As the Deputy Commissioner's wife she could do such a thing with no more than the personal courage it took to make Mavis dislike her for a day or two. When we were alone she said, "My husband doesn't know I'm here. I shan't tell him I've been. And I oughtn't to interfere, I know. But they've sent Hari Kumar away. They've put him and the other boys in prison."

It wasn't a shock. I was prepared for it. Days of silence from Lili had prepared me for it. I didn't understand it but that wasn't the same as not believing it could happen. I asked what they were putting him in prison for. She made a gesture that defined the futility of both the question and the answer. She said, "All the papers went to the Commissioner, and it's out of our hands now. But I wanted to know if there's anything you can tell *me* that you wouldn't tell Jack or Robin, or Lili."

I said, "What sort of thing, for heaven's sake?"

Again she made that gesture, whose meaning we both knew. She said probably only I could tell her what sort of thing. I thought it was a trap. I smiled at her. She said, "Well, you know what men are. They always tell themselves they can't afford the luxury of real curiosity. I mean curiosity about people. Oh, I know they solve all kinds of complex problems that prove we're made of water and gas or something, and that the universe is still exploding and travelling outwards at umpteen million light years a second which I suppose is fascinating, but of no practical use to *us* when it comes to trying to keep the servants happy and stopping them from making off just as effectively at a rate measurable in miles an hour."

I laughed. It was so absurd. Small talk. Chat. Jolly jokes. Bless her. This was her armoury. The key – the chink in the armour – was that word "curiosity". I knew what I was supposed to say. "What are you curious about?" I laughed again. I expect she thought I was bats. They say poor old Miss Crane went round the bend. Lili went to see her once while I was still at the MacGregor. Perhaps twice. I don't remember. We didn't talk about it much. Miss Crane had taken all the pictures down from her walls or something, although she wasn't going anywhere. Later she committed suttee. You saw the report of it in *The Times of India*, I think. We both saw it. Neither of us mentioned it. Perhaps Lili wrote to you and told you more about it. Of course it's wrong to say "committed" suttee. Suttee, or *sati* (is that the right way to spell it?) is a sort of state of wifely grace, isn't it? So you don't commit it. You enter into it. If you're a good Hindu widow you *become* suttee. Should I become it, Auntie? Is Hari dead? I suppose you could say we're hermits enough here to rank as *sannyasis* anyway. But no. I've not done with the world yet. I've still got at least one duty to perform.

And I knew I had a duty to perform for Connie White. After I'd stopped laughing I said, "Well then, what are you curious about?"

You can't not pay for a joke. You've got to cough up the price put on it.

She said, "Well, it all seems to begin with a man called Moti Lal."

I'd never heard of Moti Lal, but it turned out he was the man Ronald was looking for the first time he arrested Hari. Moti Lal was once employed by Hari's uncle. He was always haranguing groups of students and young men and labourers. When he started trying to organise the staff at the place where he worked old Romesh Chand sacked him. He also got served with an order under section 144 of the Criminal Procedure Code. I think Ronald instigated that. It's the one that calls on you to abstain from an act likely to cause a disturbance in the district, isn't it? Anyway, like so many other people were doing, to keep the British embarrassed, he defied it, and was prosecuted under section 188 of the Penal Code and sentenced to six months. I remember all this jabberwocky because I latched on to it while Connie talked about it, hoping it would explain what could happen to Hari. It didn't, but I looked it up afterwards in the law books in Lili's library.

Moti Lal was sent to the jail in Aligarh. He escaped. And Ronald was looking for him when he called at the Sanctuary on the morning Hari was there with a hangover. I asked Connie what all this Moti Lal business had to do with an innocent man being sent to prison for a crime he didn't commit. She said, "But that's the point. Hari Kumar isn't being sent to prison for the assault. He's being sent for political reasons. He knew Moti Lal."

Again I laughed. I said, "Hari knew Moti Lal. I know Hari. Why don't you send me to jail too? I suppose all those other boys knew Moti Lal as well?"

She said she wasn't really concerned about the other boys. There were police files on all of them. They'd all been examined by Jack Poulson. Both Jack and her husband believed that they were the kind of boys who, if they hadn't been taken into custody on the night of the Bibighar, would have been arrested within forty-eight hours for rioting or sabotage. Whatever one felt about the justice or injustice of it, they were "fair game" in present circumstances, and safer out of the way.

I said, "Fair game is the right description. You could hardly release them now, could you? They were arrested for the worst crime of all, and everybody knows it. And the same goes for Hari, doesn't it? Only it's even trickier for him. Because everybody knows we used to go out together."

She agreed that it was trickier for Hari, or rather had been trickier when it was still uncertain whether he'd taken part in the assault. But none of the boys was being charged with assault. That case was still open. The police were still working on it. But it looked unlikely that they'd ever catch the men who were responsible, unless the men began to boast – either back in their villages, or wherever they came from, or in the jails. You couldn't rule out the possibility that the men who'd assaulted me were among those arrested during the subsequent rioting. The police only hoped they weren't among those killed. Connie didn't think they would be because men of "that kind" weren't likely to have risked their lives defying the military. If they'd been arrested they'd have been with the men who got caught looting. If they were still free they could, of course, be anywhere, and probably the only thing to hope for was an informer, someone with a grudge against them who heard them boasting. The trouble was that in India you could never rely on evidence when it was come by in this way.

I don't know what Connie was trying to do. Relieve me of the anxiety that Hari might still be punished for the assault; put me on my guard, because she guessed the truth and therefore also guessed that I didn't want the men caught in case they incriminated Hari; catch me *off* my guard, hoping for a careless word that would undo all the good I'd so far done. Perhaps she was trying to do none of these things. When you've lied your head off you suspect nearly everyone of cunning and evasion and deceit. I expect she was just curious, as she said, exercising her woman's right to satisfy her curiosity now that the men had made everything irrevocable.

She said Moti Lal had never been caught. He'd gone "underground". The boys who'd been drinking hooch when they were arrested all swore they'd not seen Moti Lal since he was sent to prison. Jack Poulson thought they were lying. The trouble was that Hari Kumar had "gradually emerged" during all these investigations and interrogations as "a young man of whom the gravest suspicions had to be entertained" (which also sounded to me like something Jack Poulson must have said). The police had kept a file on him for several months. He'd been had in for questioning at the time they were looking for Moti Lal. He'd "made a mystery over his name", and had at first given the wrong one – which in itself was a punishable offence, although Ronald Merrick hadn't proceeded against him because the offence in Hari's case was only technical. But Hari had gone on record as saying, "I hate the whole stinking country, the people who live in it and the people who rule it." He'd worked in the same firm as Moti Lal. He was a one-time colleague of a young anarchist called Vidyasagar who'd been arrested for distributing seditious literature and delivering a pamphlet to the police calling on them to assist the people to "liberate the martyrs of the Bibighar Gardens". At the time of his arrest, after the assault on me, his room had been searched. The police thought it curious that there were no letters in his room; no letters, except one – a letter from someone in England who wasn't identified because he'd only signed his Christian name, but it was clear he was in the forces, and had been at Dunkirk. He described Dunkirk as a shambles. He asked Hari to bear in mind that letters might be opened. His father had opened some of them while this boy was in France and hadn't forwarded them because they were full of "hot-headed political stuff". Nobody could understand why Hari had kept just this one letter out of all the letters he must have had from time to time from different people. Of course they didn't intend to pursue the business of who this rather "bolshie" sounding English boy might be. It was enough that the letter more or less proved Hari was a bolshie himself. Without much difficulty a case had been made out to show that Hari Kumar – in spite of seeming to be such a quiet, uncommitted, well-educated young man – was a leading member of a group of dangerous fellows whose early arrest alone had deprived them of the opportunity to act openly against the war effort. The papers relating to Kumar and the other boys had been sent to the commissioner, and the commissioner had agreed with the decision Robin White had "very reluctantly" come to: the decision that these boys should be imprisoned under the Defence of India Rules.

By the time Connie got to this point in her harangue I was laughing in the way you do when the alternative is to cry. I knew who the English boy must be. I said, "But it's a farce! It's absurd! Hari can prove it's a ridiculous *monstrous* farce!"

She said, "But my dear, that's what puzzles *me*. The other boys denied everything – everything except that they all know each other, which they hardly *could* deny. They shouted and wept and insisted that they were innocent of everything except drinking hooch. And we knew they were lying. But Hari was an altogether different matter. He was examined personally by Jack Poulson. But to every question he said nothing. He neither denied nor agreed. The only thing he ever said in his own defence was 'I wasn't at the Bibighar. I haven't seen Miss Manners since the night we visited the temple.' And of course he only said that when they were accusing him of assault. To all the other questions his only answer was, 'I have nothing to say.' It's unnatural. I mean to *me* it's unnatural. The men simply took his silence as a confession of guilt. I expect if I were a man I'd have done the same. But I'm a woman, like you. I think of Hari Kumar and listen to Jack talking to Mavis about him, and to my husband talking to old Menen, and I think, 'It's wrong. A man doesn't say nothing, unless he's trying to put a noose round his own neck. He fights for his life and his freedom. He fights because he *is* a man.' "

We were sitting on the verandah. Oh, everything was there – the wicker chairs, the table with the tea tray on it, the scent of the flowers, the scent of India, the air of certainty, or *perpetuity*; but, as well, the odd sense of none of it happening at all because it had begun wrong and continued wrong, and so was already ended, and was wrong even in its ending, because its ending, for me, was unreal and remote, and yet *total* in its envelopment, as if it had already turned itself into a beginning. Such constant hope we suffer from! I think the MacGregor House was built on such foundations. The steps up to the verandah where I'd stumbled and fallen were only a few feet away. I had never seen Janet MacGregor's ghost, but I felt that she must have seen mine.

Connie said, "I expect it's frightfully silly of me, but you know if Hari Kumar had been an Englishman I could have understood his silence better, although even then it would have had to be a silence imposed on him by a woman."

I began to laugh again. I laughed because I saw that this time there really was nothing I could do – for Connie, for myself, or for Hari, for anyone. My legs – bare from the knee down – were an anachronism, an outrage. To play the scene with anything like *style* I needed a long dress of white muslin, and a little straw boater on my head. I needed to be conscious of the dignity of the occasion. I needed to be able to say, "But Harry is an Englishman," and then to rise, put up my little parasol and detach myself from Constance White's company, so that she would *know* but say nothing because this was a world where men died in the open and women wept in private, and the Queen sat like a wise old lady on her throne and succeeded in that difficult feat of proving that there was a world where corruption also died for lack of stinking air.

Oh well, it was fine, wasn't it? Me sitting there in one chair and Connie White in another, showing acres of bare ill-looking flesh, sweating under the arms, and Hari sweating in a disgusting jailhouse, beyond the reach of either of us, wondering what he'd gained by acting like a white man should when a girl made him give a promise: a promise for his sake, yes, but for her own too. She wanted him. She wanted him to be around to make love to her again. It was marvellous. Marvellous because he was black. I wanted him and he was black so his blackness was part of what I wanted. Sitting there with Connie, laughing my head off, I hoped for one bitter, selfish moment that he suffered as much as I did, for putting his bloody acquired English pride above his compulsion to enter *me*. I wished him joy of his stupid sense of values. I thought: How typical! You tell an Indian to say nothing and he takes it literally.

Afterwards, of course, I knew he hadn't taken it literally. He'd interpreted it that way deliberately. To punish himself. To give him something new about himself that he could mock. When Connie had gone, no wit the wiser for her visit, but I suppose convinced I was unbalanced, Lili found me weeping in my room, because the comic mood had gone, the melodrama had exploded, not into tragedy but just into life and all the stupid cross-currents that tossed you indiscriminately from one thought to another but managed to keep you up. You can never drown. Never, never. Until you're dead. So why be so ridiculously afraid of the truth?

But with Lili sitting on my bed, wanting to comfort me but also wanting to chastise me for my absurdity, I was a child again. I wept and cried out, "I want him, I want him. Bring him back to me, Auntie. Please help to bring him back."

She said nothing. Like Hari. For them I suppose there *is* nothing to say. Nothing, that is, if they are intent on building instead of on destroying. Behind all the chatter and violence of India – what a deep, lingering silence. Siva dances in it. Vishnu sleeps in it. Even their music is silence. It's the only music I know that sounds conscious of *breaking* silence, of going back into it when it's finished, as if to prove that every man-made sound is an illusion.

What an odd concept of the world that is! We shall never understand it. They don't really understand it themselves, I suspect. Is it to try to understand it that Sister Ludmila wanders the streets collecting the bodies of the dead and the dying? Is it just a concept that could be traced to some long-forgotten overwhelming, primitive experience of pain and suffering? I ask because it struck me, a few weeks later, when I knew I was pregnant and I asked Lili to send for Anna Klaus, that Anna stood on the same edge of reality and illusion herself, because she'd been deprived and had suffered and continued to live. She's a great believer in anaesthetising the patient, a great giver of sedatives. I remember how she stood in my bedroom frowning her little professional frown as she sorted things out in her black bag. Such a wealth of compromise there is in a doctor's bag! She seemed to be a long way away from me, and yet to be taking me with her – millions of miles away down long glazed white-tiled tunnels, subterranean passages of human degradation that were saved from filthiness because we northerners have learned how to make suffering aseptic and non-contagious. At first I had a silly idea she was preparing something for me to take to get rid of the child. I said, "What's that, what's that?" She said, "What a fuss! It is only to give you a quiet night. Expectant mothers must be contemplative. Like nuns."

So I lay there, letting her get on with it. But suddenly I said, "What am I to do, Anna? I can't live without him."

She didn't look at me. She was measuring the potion. She spoke to the medicine, not to me. After all, this was the one thing she could really trust, really believe in, really love. She said, "This you must learn to do. To live without."

She handed me the glass, and stood by, until I'd drunk every drop.

Appendix to Part 7

Letters from Lady Manners to Lady Chatterjee

Srinagar, 31 May '43

My Dear Lili,

I hope you've forgiven me for not accepting your offer to come up last month, and for the silence since then that has been broken only by my two telegrams. When I wired you a week ago I promised I would write. If you would like to, do come next month. I shall be on the houseboat.

I'm afraid there are going to be endless legal complications. Poor Daphne died intestate, so I think the money becomes subject to the statutory trusts, on the child's behalf, unless the part of it which Daphne inherited from her mother is claimed by Mrs. George's nephews and nieces. Mrs. George Manners had a married sister, someone Daphne used to refer to as Auntie Kate, who was killed in a road accident. The husband married again, but there were two or three children from the first marriage – cousins of Daphne's with whom she remembered playing as a child. I expect if Daphne had died intestate but without issue the cousins would have had some sort of claim. I'm not sure what the situation is when the child in question is illegitimate. It will all have to be gone into and dealt with by the lawyers in London – which is where all the money is held anyway. Daphne was very careful with her small inheritance. She never touched the principal but drew on the income through the banks over here. Anyway, I have asked Mr. Docherty in 'Pindi to do whatever has to be done to start sorting things out – but it will take ages before we know what properly belongs to the child and even longer before we know how use can be made of it over here.

Meanwhile the responsibility for her is mine. When you come up, Lili, perhaps you will be able to say whether you think the child is Hari Kumar's. I have a special reason for wanting to know. Not a reason connected with any legal claim or criminal charge. There is no question of attempting to establish paternity. Mr. Kumar is beyond either our incriminations or our help, *and that is how I want it left*. But in giving shelter and affection to the child for Daphne's sake – and for its own – I should be happier knowing to what extent one might do so in the belief that its parentage wasn't surrounded by doubt as well as tragedy. I know I don't need to tell you that I want your *opinion*, not your reassurance, and that if you don't feel able to give one I shouldn't want you to pretend, simply to set my mind at rest.

She is a sweet and pretty child. Her skin is going to be pale, but not nearly pale enough for her to pass as white. I'm glad. As she grows older she won't be driven by the temptation to wear a false face. At least that is one thing she'll be spared – the misery and humiliation experienced by so many Eurasian girls. I intend to bring her up as an Indian, which is one of the reasons I have called her Parvati. The other reason is that I believe this is a name Daphne would like. Parvati

Manners. Later she may decide to change that surname.

She was reluctant to come into the world but having done so seems equally determined not to let go of it. Dr. Krishnamurti has found a wet-nurse, a pretty young Kashmiri girl who has lost her own first-born and lavishes affection on Parvati. She'd make a perfect ayah but says she won't leave Srinagar. She's the wife of one of the boys who paddles the shikaras during the season and I've promised him employment as soon as I move down on to the lake. Perhaps I can persuade them both to come to 'Pindi in September. He looks a frightful rogue but they're a handsome pair and she keeps him in order. It's touching to watch them playing with Parvati as if she were their own. While she feeds the baby he stays nearby, on guard. He's partly fascinated, partly embarrassed by the process, but intensely proud of his wife's talent, and I suppose of the part he played in filling her breasts with the milk now given to someone else's child. And I suppose they both see the money she earns as a compensation for their own loss; a gift from Allah.

It would please Daphne to watch them too. She only saw the child for a second or so. She was in labour for forty-eight hours. You and I have never had children so perhaps we can be classed as almost as ignorant of the process as men are – I mean anyway men who aren't doctors. Dr. Krishnamurti was wonderful. Poor Daphne, to look at her you'd have thought her big and strong enough to have babies by the dozen, but the pelvis was wrong, and the baby was the wrong way round. He wanted her to go into hospital and have it turned, but she refused. So he did the whole thing here, bringing up a couple of nurses and an anaesthetist and loads of equipment. That was two or three weeks before she was due. He told me he'd turned the baby but that at the drop of a hat it could turn back again into a position that would lead to a breech delivery. He said he'd advised her to stand no nonsense and opt for a Caesarian so that directly it started the whole thing could just be got on with. But she refused. She had some idea that it was her duty to push the child out of her womb as nature intended. Krishnamurti and I have always been frank with one another. It's sad to think all this awful business was what was needed to make us friends. At the beginning I told him what your Doctor Klaus confided to you, that Daphne's heart was irregular. After examining her he told me it was nothing to worry about in itself, although he agreed that it was probably this irregularity that led to the doctors in London warning her off driving ambulances. It's odd that she never mentioned it. Well, no, not odd. Typical. She always pretended it was her eyesight that caused her to be what she once referred to as "dismissed the service". The point is, though, that the heart condition wasn't a complication in childbirth, only what Krishnamurti called "a slight additional debit on the balance sheet".

At one moment during that awful forty-eight hours I thought she wanted the child to die, or failing that to die herself. Since then I've changed my mind. She only wanted to "do it right". The child did turn again. I suppose because it couldn't get out. Krishnamurti had had the foresight to bring all the equipment back here. He turned the bedroom into an operating theatre. Poor Daphne wasn't compos mentis enough to know what was going on. It was I who gave permission for the Caesarian.

So I have that on my conscience. She should have been in hospital. Krishnamurti took every care. But she died of peritonitis. For a couple of days afterwards I wouldn't even look at the child. I'd seen it cut out. Krishnamurti let me watch. I was dressed up like a nurse in theatre in a white gown, with a mask over my mouth and nostrils. I needed to see this side of life. I'd never have forgiven myself for being too faint-hearted to watch. When it began I thought I'd never stand it. It seemed obscene, like opening a can – which isn't obscene but is when the can is a human abdomen. But then when the can was open and I saw what they were lifting out I felt I was being born again myself. It was a miracle and it made you realise that no miracle is beautiful because it exists on a plane of experience where words like beauty have no meaning whatsoever.

It also meant absolutely nothing to me that the curious knotted little bundle of flesh that was lifted out of Daphne – (perhaps prised is a better word because with their long rubber gloves on they seemed to have to search for and encourage it to emerge) – was obviously *not* the same skin colour as its mother. The difference in colour was subtle, so subtle that were it not for one particular recollection I'd now be persuaded that the fact that the difference between them meant nothing was due to my failing to notice one at the time. But I did notice it. The particular recollection I have is of thinking, Yes – I see – the father *was* dark-skinned. But at the time this caused no emotional response. I noted it and then forgot it. I only remembered it when Daphne was dead and they tried to show me the child to take my mind off things. But that wasn't the reason I rejected it. I rejected it because in the state of mind I was in I blamed it for killing Daphne. If anything its Indian-ness was what first made me feel pity for it and start thinking of it as "she". I thought: Poor scrap – there's not a thing she can look forward to.

I told you Daphne saw her for a second or two – between one unconsciousness and another. The nurse held the child close to her. She tried to touch it but didn't have the strength. But she did smile. Which is why I really want you to see Parvati yourself and judge if there is any resemblance at all to Hari Kumar. I'm afraid I can't see Daphne in her – but perhaps you will. Relatives are usually the last to see a family likeness.

Affectionately,

Ethel.

*

Rawalpindi, 5 Aug '47

My Dear Lili,

I have decided to leave 'Pindi. I refuse to live in a place whose people at the stroke of a pen will be turned into enemies of India – the country my husband tried to serve – and you can count on it that "enemy" isn't overstating the case. The creation of Pakistan is our crowning failure. I can't bear it. They should never have got rid of Wavell. Our only justification for two hundred years of power was unification. But we've divided one composite nation into two and everyone at home goes round saying what a swell the new Viceroy is for getting it all sorted out so quickly. Which of course is right. But he's a twentieth-century swell – and India's still living in the ninetennth century – which is where we're leaving her. In Delhi they've all been blinded by him. I mean the Indians have. What they don't realise is that he was only intended to be the glamorous dressing in the shop window – a window we've been trying to get up attractively ever since the war ended. Behind the window the shop is as nineteenth-century as ever – albeit *radical* nineteenth-century. The slogan is still insular. India's independence at any cost, not for India's sake, but for our own.

I'm going down to the Residency in Gopalakand to stay with an old friend of Henry's, Sir Robert Conway, who is adviser to the Maharajah. The maharajahs are being sacrificed too – mostly their own fault, but the people who wield the knife are really the old Fabians and crusty Trade Unionists in London, *not* the Congress. Perhaps we can meet in Gopalakand? Little Parvati sends her love to Auntie Lili – and so do I.

Affectionately,
Ethel.

*

New Delhi, June 1948

My Dear Lili,

Can you possibly join me here? I'm at HH of Gopalakand's town palace, such as it is. I've been under the weather and there are a number of things I'd like to discuss. I also want to show you – and give you if you'll take them – certain items left by Daphne, writings of hers, etc., letters and a journal.

Under the terms of my new will I've made provision for Parvati and left money for the endowment of a children's home, thereby carrying out a wish expressed by Daphne. I've named you as one of the trustees and suggested that the home should be called The Manners Memorial Home for Indian Boys and Girls – which is a way of remembering my niece but avoiding the embarrassment that a name like The Daphne Manners Memorial Home might cause people who have long memories. I've suggested that the Home should be in Mayapore. One of the things we might discuss is the use of the site known as The Sanctuary. You told me last year that that woman's eyesight was failing. If it is possible and practicable to use the Sanctuary as a base for the home, one of the provisions of the endowment should be that Sister Ludmila is entitled to continue living there in grace and favour, as it were.

When you've read poor Daphne's journal – which I've kept to myself all these years, although I think you always suspected the existence of something of the sort – you'll understand better why my thoughts have run on these lines. The other thing we must discuss is Parvati's future. I don't want to sound morbid, but the time isn't far off when my death will leave her alone in the world. I am still of the opinion that nothing should be done to try and trace the man you and I are both certain is the father. Each time you see her you say she looks more like Hari than the time before. This is a comfort to me because I know you are telling the truth and not just reassuring me; but it doesn't persuade me that the poor boy should be tracked down and made to face evidence of his responsibility. I'm sure you agree. Without any difficulty I could have arranged for this to be done while he was in prison, and if he is still alive could still arrange it, I suppose, even though he must have been released two or three years ago. I think you are right to suspect that when his Aunt Shalini left Mayapore in 1944 she returned to her old home in the UP solely in order to set up some kind of household he'd have been able to return to when he came out – even if his sojourn there was not of long duration. Obviously someone knows the truth – probably that man Romesh Chand Gupta Sen. Your lawyer friend Srinivasan's assertion – when he came out of prison himself and asked after Mrs. Gupta Sen – that Romesh Chand simply shrugged the question away and said she'd gone home to her village and that he'd broken off all connexion with the Kumar family, probably amounts to no more than an attempt on the old man's part to disguise the fact that he knew what had happened but didn't care to say. My own belief is that when Hari was released he probably went to his Aunt Shalini's but then took himself off elsewhere, perhaps even changed his name. A boy imprisoned for the reasons he was ostensibly detained for would not lack friends in the new India. My guess is he wanted none of them. He might be dead – a chance victim of that awful savagery – that Hindu-Muslin bloodbath last year that marked the end of our unifying and civilising years of power and influence.

No, my dear. Leave poor Hari Kumar to work out his own salvation, if he's still alive to work it out and if there's a salvation of any kind for a boy like him. He is the left-over, the loose-end of our reign, the kind of person we created – I suppose with the best intentions. But for all Nehru's current emergence as a potential moral force in world affairs, I see *nothing* in India that will withstand the pressure of the legacy of the division we English have allowed her to impose on herself, and are morally responsible for. In allowing it we created a precedent for partition just at the moment when the opposite was needed, allowed it – again with the best intentions – as a result of tiredness, and failing moral and physical pretensions that just wouldn't stand the strain of looking into the future to see what abdication on India's terms instead of ours was going to mean. Perhaps finally we had no terms of our own because we weren't clever enough to formulate them in twentieth-century dress, and so the world is going to divide itself into isolated little pockets of dogma and mutual resistance, and the promise that always seemed to lie behind even the worst aspects of our colonialism will just evaporate into history as imperial mystique, foolish glorification of a savagely practical and greedy policy.

Do you remember dear Nello with Henry's pipe in his mouth, pacing up and down, copying Henry, saying, in Henry's voice, "Policy? Policy? To hell with policy! What are you thinking and feeling, dear chap? That's the point! Don't let's waste bloody time on second-rate notions of what is *likely*. Let's consider the damned unlikely and see where we go from there." How I laughed at the time. Remembering it now I don't laugh any more. Such a marvellous opportunity *wasted*. I mean for us, by us. Indians feel it too, don't they? I mean, in spite of the proud chests and all the excitement of sitting down as free men at their own desks to work out a constitution. Won't that constitution be a sort of love-letter to the English – the kind an abandoned lover writes when the affair has ended in what passes at the time as civilised and dignified mutual recognition of incompatibility? In a world grown suddenly dull because the beloved, thank God, has gone, offering his killing and unpredictable and selfish affections elsewhere, you attempt to recapture, don't you, the moments of significant pleasure – which may not have been mutual at all, but anyway existed. But this recapture is always impossible. You settle for the second-rate, you settle for the lesson you appear to have learned and forgot the lesson you hoped to learn and might have learned, and so learn nothing at all, because the second-rate is the world's common factor, and any damn fool people can teach it, any damn fool people can inherit it.

What terrifies me is the thought that gradually, when the splendours of civilised divorce and protestations of continuing as good friends are worked out, the real animus will emerge, the one both our people just managed to keep in check when there was reason to suppose that it was wrong, because it could lead neither rulers nor ruled anywhere. I mean of course the dislike and fear that exists between black and white. And this is a fifth-rate passion, appropriate only to a nation of vulgar shopkeepers and a nation of fat-bellied banias. I remember that time dear Nello mimicked Henry, the look of awful shock on the face of one of Henry's aides (an awfully well-bred chap, whose grandfather made a fortune out of bottling sauce or something – not that this was against him, but he'd somehow never risen above it) and the way, while I was still laughing, this aide turned to me and seemed as if he were about to say, "Good heavens, Lady Manners! Do you allow *that* in Sir Henry's own drawing-room?" And all he meant was that Nello was brown-skinned and poor Henry was white, although actually he was grey and yellow and ill, and on his way to the grave. I suppose everything gets stripped down to *that*, in the end, because that is the last division of all, isn't it? The colour of the skin, I mean; not dying.

Well, you and I have always tried to keep open house. *You anyway, I suspect, will have to keep it open for a long time yet*. What this letter is really all about, Lili, is this: When I'm gone, will you give Parvati a roof?

My Love,
Ethel.

*

Imagine, then, a flat landscape, one that turns, upends, following in reverse the bends and twists of night flight 115, the Viscount service to Calcutta; a landscape that is dark but shows immediately below as a system of lights, clustering neatly round a central point with a few minor galaxies beyond its periphery – the flarepath of the airfield, the suburb of Banyaganj, divorced from the parent body because the link with Mayapore, the Grand Trunk Road, is unlit except by the occasional night traffic (miniature headlamps moving at what looks even from this height like excessive speed) and a relatively small and isolated constellation about midway, where the new English colony live on hand for the Technical College, the factories, and the airfield which they use as casually as a bus terminal. Apart from the stranger there is one other Englishman on flight 115 – the same man who at the club that evening occasionally looked across at Srinivasan's private party; perhaps less from curiosity than from a desire to obtain momentary relief from the business of concentrating on questions being put to him by talkative young men like Surendranath and Desai who were trying to make up for the time they think their fathers lost.

Similarly surrounded as he had been in the airport lounge, this other Englishman now sits in the almost empty airliner several seats away from the stranger. The other passengers are Indian businessmen. They, too, sit separately from each other, on their way to deals in West Bengal. When the illuminated sign on the bulkhead goes out (*Fasten seat belts. No smoking*) portfolios will be opened and papers studied. The flight is of such short duration; the respite granted as precious to a man as the time he spends in more intimate surroundings reading the morning newspapers to find out what happened yesterday and judge how it might affect what could happen today. One of them – the man who sat in the airport lounge with his feet curled up on the interior-sprung chair – wears the dhoti. There is not room on the aircraft seat for him to continue in similar comfort, for which the stranger is grateful, because who knows where those feet have been in the past twenty-four hours?

The aircraft seems to be having difficulty attaining height. From the oval shaped port the flarepath comes again into view, not much farther below than it was the last time of looking, and then the lights of Mayapore come back in focus, slightly blurred, which may be due to the condensation on the double glazing of the windows, but at least they conform to the pattern that is known and is now recognisable, because the watcher has had time to orientate himself.

One can even detect where the *maidan* lies: a dark space enclosed by evenly plotted points of illumination, Hospital road, Club road, Church road (a name unaltered in spite of Victoria having become Mahatma Gandhi), and Artillery road. The plane banks, nosing east, almost taking the course of the river that leads to Miss Crane's unimaginable coast. With this God's-eye view of the created world she never had to cope, which perhaps was a pity, because the topography she found so inhibiting from ground-level reveals itself from this height, and at this speed, as random and unplanned, with designs hacked into it by people who only worked things out as they went along.

The neon standard that lights the faithful from the Tirupati temple to the river and back again shows up relatively brightly, and plotting from this and the neon light above the keeper's hut at the level crossing at the northern head of the Bibighar bridge, the stranger (returning to Calcutta for a second inspection of mouldering missionary relics) is able to fix the approximate position of the Bibighar Gardens and the MacGregor House.

The Bibighar Gardens are dark (now, as then) – but from the MacGregor House there is the burst of light that Lili Chatterjee promised: all the lights turned on in the occupied rooms and all the floodlights in the garden; pale from here but suddenly unmistakable, so that foolishly one searches that distant area for signs of Lili herself, and imagines that she stands below the steps of the verandah with Parvati, staring up at the winking red, green and amber riding lights of the airborne commercial juggernaut.

*

This is the last image then – the MacGregor House – in which there are sounds of occupation other than those made by Lili and Parvati: of tinkling broken glass, of sensibly shod feet taking the rise from the black and white tiled hallway to the corridors above from which brass-knobbed mahogany doors lead into rooms that give their occupants the opportunity to view the reality for themselves and the dream for others, and to make up their minds about the precise meaning of what lies beyond.

These sounds are ones that the casual visitor will today attribute to Parvati's presence, not to her mother's. But Parvati steps lightly and breaks nothing (except perhaps a young man's heart). She is another story, which is why her presence here is tentative, although this suits her, because of her shyness and the impression you get of her as a girl who has not yet met the world face to face, let alone subjected it to the force of her personality. To come upon her unexpectedly, to find her standing alone in a room of the MacGregor House or sitting in the shade in the garden counting the petals of a flower – to see her expression of intense but distant pleasure (distant because in spite of its intensity the source of it is obviously far away in some private world that trembles on the brink between her youthful illusions and her maturer judgment), to hear her early in the mornings and evenings practising her singing, to listen to the grave and studious application with which she attacks a difficult phrase, admits defeat with a low cry of exasperation, then re-attacks it, this is to leave the MacGregor House with an idea of Parvati as a girl admirably suited to her surroundings where there is always the promise of a story continuing instead of finishing, and of Lady Chatterjee as the repository of a tradition established for the sake of the future rather than of the past.

"Well, I don't know about that," (Lady Chatterjee says, taking the stranger for one last look round the old place, accepting the support of his arm, shading her eyes from the late afternoon sun with her free hand – and Shafi already waiting to take him in good time to the airport). "I mean, a repository sounds like a place for storing furniture when you bash off to some other station. I suppose an Englishman could say that the whole of India is that sort of place. You all went, but left so much behind that you couldn't carry with you wherever you were going, and these days those of you who come back can more often than not hardly bother to think about it, let alone ask for the key to go in and root about among all the old dust sheets to see that everything worthwhile that you left is still there and isn't falling to pieces with dry rot." She pauses and then asks, "Has Parvati said goodbye to you properly?"

Yes, Parvati has said goodbye, and now runs down the steps from the verandah (late, because she tends to work on Mayapore time instead of Indian Standard), making her way to her evening lesson with her *guru* who has sung in London, New York and Paris, and these days receives for instruction only the most promising pupils – girls who have both the talent and the stamina for a course of training that lasts eight years. One day, perhaps, Parvati will also sing in those western capitals, and then become a *guru* herself, instructing a new generation of girls in the formal complexities of the songs her English mother once described as the only music in the world she knew that sounded conscious of breaking silence and going back into it when it was finished. Before she goes out of sight – running in a pale pink saree – she pauses and waves, and the stranger waves back, wishing her well for the evening lesson. Twice a day she runs like this, and in the intervals locks herself up for hours of rigorous practice. Sometimes a young man appears, bearing the twin drums, the *tablas*, to help her with the necessary percussion which otherwise she provides herself with sharp little flicks of her supple fingers on the onion-shaped tamboura. Her skin is the palest brown and in certain lights her long dark hair reveals a redness more familiar in the north.

> Dooliya le aō re morē babul ke kaharwa.
> Chali hoon sajan ba ke des. Sangaki sakha
> saba bichchuda gayee hai apne ri apne ghar jaun.
>
> Oh, my father's servants, bring my palanquin.
> I am going to the land of my husband. All my
> companions are scattered. They have gone to
> different homes.
>
> (A morning raga.)
> Translation by Dipali Nag.